## BOOKS BY CARLOS FUENTES

*Aura*

*Distant Relations*

*Constancia and Other Stories for Virgins*

*Terra Nostra*

*The Campaign*

*The Old Gringo*

*Where the Air Is Clear*

*The Death of Artemio Cruz*

*The Good Conscience*

*Burnt Water*

*The Hydra Head*

*A Change of Skin*

*Christopher Unborn*

*Diana: The Goddess Who Hunts Alone*

*The Orange Tree*

*Myself with Others*

*The Buried Mirror*

*A New Time for Mexico*

# THE YEARS WITH LAURA DÍAZ

# THE YEARS WITH
# Laura Díaz

Translated from the Spanish by Alfred Mac Adam

# CARLOS FUENTES

**FARRAR, STRAUS AND GIROUX**

New York

*Farrar, Straus and Giroux*
*19 Union Square West, New York 10003*

*Copyright © 1999 by Carlos Fuentes*
*Translation copyright © 2000 by Farrar, Straus and Giroux, LLC*
*All rights reserved*
*Distributed in Canada by Douglas & McIntyre Ltd.*
*Printed in the United States of America*
*Designed by Abby Kagan*
*First published in 1999 by Alfaguara, Mexico, as* Los años con Laura Díaz
*First published in the United States by Farrar, Straus and Giroux*
*First edition, 2000*

*Library of Congress Cataloging-in-Publication Data*

Fuentes, Carlos.
    [Años con Laura Díaz. English]
    The years with Laura Díaz / Carlos Fuentes ; translated from the Spanish by Alfred
Mac Adam.
        p.   cm.
    ISBN 0-374-29341-4 (alk. paper)
    1. Kahlo, Frida—Fiction.   2. Rivera, Diego, 1886–1957—Fiction.   I. Mac Adam, Alfred
J., 1941–   II. Title.

PQ7297.F793 A7613 2000
863'.64—dc21                                                                00–037648

Grateful acknowledgment is made for permission to reprint the excerpt from "Vegetation,"
from *Canto General, Fiftieth Anniversary Edition,* by Pablo Neruda, edited and translated by
Jack Schmitt, copyright © 1991 Fundacíon Pablo Neruda, Regents of the University of
California. Reprinted by permission of the University of California Press.

This edition was especially created in 2001 for Quality Paperback Book Club.

*I dedicate this book of my ancestry*

*to my descendants*

*My children*

*Cecilia*

*Carlos*

*Natasha*

# Contents

# THE YEARS WITH LAURA DÍAZ

# 1. Detroit: 1999

I KNEW THE STORY. What I didn't know was the truth. In a way, my very presence was a lie. I came to Detroit to begin a television documentary on the Mexican muralists in the United States. Secretly, I was more interested in capturing the decay of a great city— the first capital of the automobile, no less, the place where Henry Ford inaugurated mass production of the machine that governs our lives more than any government.

One proof of the city's power, we're told, is that in 1932 it invited the Mexican artist Diego Rivera to decorate the walls of the Detroit Institute of Arts. And now, in 1999, I was here—officially, of course— to make a TV series on this and other Mexican murals in the United States. I would begin with Rivera in Detroit, then move on to Orozco at Dartmouth and in California, and then to a mysterious Siqueiros in Los Angeles, which I was instructed to find, as well as lost works by Rivera himself: the mural in Rockefeller Center, obliterated because Lenin and Marx appeared in it; and other large panels which had also disappeared.

This was the job I was assigned. I insisted on beginning in Detroit for one reason. I wanted to photograph the ruin of a great industrial center as a worthy epitaph for our terrible twentieth century. I wasn't moved either by the moral in the warning or by any apocalyptic taste for misery and deformity, not even by simple humanitarianism. I'm a photographer, but I'm neither the marvelous Sebastião Salgado nor the fearsome Diane Arbus. I'd prefer, if I were a painter, the problem-free clarity of an Ingres or the interior torture of a Bacon. I tried painting. I failed. I got nothing out of it. I told myself that the camera is the paintbrush of our age, so here I am, contracted to do one thing but present—with a presentiment, maybe—to do something else very different.

I got up early to take care of my business before the film team set up in front of Diego's murals. It was 6 a.m. in the month of February. I expected darkness. I was ready for it. But its duration sapped my energy.

"If you want to do some shopping, if you want to go to a movie, the hotel limo can take you and pick you up," they told me at the reception desk.

"But the center of town is only two blocks from here," I answered, both surprised and annoyed.

"Then we can't take any responsibility." The receptionist gave me a practiced smile. His face wasn't memorable.

If the guy only knew that I was going farther, much farther, than the center of town. Though I didn't know it yet, I was going to reach the heart of this hell of desolation. Walking quickly, I left behind the cluster of skyscrapers arranged like a constellation of mirrors—a new medieval city protected against the attacks of barbarians—and it took me only ten or twelve blocks to get lost in a dark, burned-out wasteland of vacant lots pocked with scabs of garbage.

With each step I took—blindly, because it was still dark, because the only eye I had was my camera, because I was a modern Polyphemus with my right eye glued to the Leica's viewfinder and my left eye closed, blind, with my left hand extended forward like a police dog, groping, tripping sometimes, other times sinking into something I could smell but not see—I was penetrating into a night that was not only persisting but being reborn. In Detroit, night was born from night.

I let the camera drop onto my chest for an instant, I felt the dull blow over my diaphragm—two diaphragms, mine and the Leica's— and the sensation was repeated. What surrounded me was not the prolonged night of a winter dawn; it wasn't, as my imagination would have me believe, a nascent darkness, disturbed companion of the day.

It was permanent darkness, the unexpected darkness of the city, its companion, its faithful mirror. All I had to do was turn right around and see myself in the center of a flat, gray lot, adorned here and there with puddles, fugitive paths traced by fearful feet, naked trees blacker than this landscape after a battle. In the distance, I could see spectral, broken-down Victorian houses with sagging roofs, crumbling chimneys, empty windows, bare porches, dilapidated doors, and, from time to time, the tender and immodest approach of a leafless tree to a grimy skylight. A rocking chair rocked, all by itself, creaking, reminding me, vaguely, of other times barely sensed in memory . . .

*Fields of solitude, withered hill,* my schoolboy memory repeated while my hands picked up my camera and my mental hand went from snap to snap, photographing Mexico City, Buenos Aires if it weren't for the river, Río if it weren't for the sea, Caracas if it weren't a shithole, Lima the horrible, Santa Fe de Bogotá losing its faith, holy or otherwise, Santiago with no saint to cure it. I was photographing the future of our Latin American cities in the present of the most industrial city of all, capital of the automobile, cradle of mass production and the minimum wage: Detroit, Michigan. I made my way shooting all of it, old, abandoned jalopies in lots even more abandoned, sudden streets paved with broken glass, blinking lights in shops selling . . . selling what?

What could they be selling on the only illuminated corners in this immense black hole? I walked in, almost dazzled by the light, to buy a soda at one of those stands.

A couple almost as ashen as the day stared at me with a mix of mockery, resignation, and malign hospitality, asking me, What do you want? and answering me, We've got everything.

I was a little dazed, or it might have been habit, but I ordered, in Spanish, a Coke. They laughed idiotically.

"Stands like this, we only sell beer and wine," said the man. "No drugs."

"But lottery tickets we do sell," added the woman.

I got back to the hotel by instinct, changed my shoes, which were dripping all the waste of oblivion, and was just about to take my second shower of the day when I checked my watch. The crew would be waiting for me in the lobby, and my punctuality signaled not only my prestige but also my discipline. Slipping on my jacket, I looked out at the landscape from the window. A Christian city and an Islamic city coexisted in Detroit. Light illuminated the tops of skyscrapers and mosques. The rest of the world was still sunk in darkness.

We, the whole team, reached the Institute of Arts. First we crossed the same unending wasteland, block after block of vacant lots, here and there the ruin of a Victorian mansion, and at the end of the urban desert (actually right in its heart) a structure in kitschy *pompier* style from the early years of the century, clean and well preserved, spacious and accessible by means of wide stone stairways and tall doors of steel and glass. It was like a memento of happiness in a trunkful of misfortunes, an old lady, erect and bejeweled, who has outlived her descendants, a Rachel without tears. The Detroit Institute of Arts.

The enormous central courtyard, protected by a high skylight, was the setting for a flower show. It was there the crowds were gathering that morning. Where'd they get the flowers? I asked a gringo in our team; he answered by shrugging his shoulders and not even glancing at the plethora of tulips, chrysanthemums, lilies, and gladiolas displayed on the four sides of the patio—which we crossed with a speed that both the team and I imposed on ourselves. Television and movies are the kind of work you want to get away from fast, as soon as quitting time comes. Unfortunately, those who live on such work can imagine nothing else to do with their lives but to go on filming one day after another after another . . . we're here to work.

Here he was. Rivera, Diego, Diego María of Guanajuato, Diego

María Concepción Juan Nepomuceno de la Rivera y Barrientos Acosta y Rodríguez, 1886–1957.

Pardon me for laughing. It's a good kind of laugh, an irrepressible guffaw of recognition and perhaps of nostalgia. For what? I think for lost innocence; for faith in industry; for progress, happiness, and history joining hands thanks to industrial development. To all those glories Rivera had sung praise, as you'd have to in Detroit. Like the anonymous architects, painters, and sculptors of the Middle Ages who built and decorated the great cathedrals to praise God—one, everlasting, indivisible—Rivera came to Detroit as pilgrims long ago went to Canterbury and Compostela: full of faith. I also laughed because this mural was like a color postcard of the black-and-white setting for Chaplin's movie *Modern Times*. The same machines, smooth as mirrors, the perfect, implacable meshing of gears, the confidence-inspiring factories that Rivera the Marxist saw as an equally trustworthy sign of progress but that Chaplin saw as devouring jaws, swallowing machines, like iron stomachs gobbling up the worker and at the end expelling him like a piece of shit.

Not here. This was the industrial idyll, the reflection of the immensely rich city Rivera saw during the 1930s, when Detroit gave jobs and a decent life to half a million workers.

How did the Mexican painter see them?

There was something strange in this mural, with its teeming activity and spaces crowded with human figures working at shining serpentine, unending machines like the intestines of a prehistoric animal that was taking a long time to slouch back toward the present age. It also took me a long time to locate the source of my own surprise. I had a displaced and exciting sensation of creative discovery—very rare in television work. Here I am in Detroit, standing in front of a mural by Diego Rivera because I depend on my audience just as Rivera, perhaps, depended on his patrons. But he made fun of them, he planted red flags and Soviet leaders right in the very bastion of capitalism. On the other hand, I wouldn't deserve either the censure or the scandal: the audience gives me success or failure, nothing more. Click. The idiot box turns off.

7

There are no more patrons, and what's more no one gives a fuck. Who remembers the first soap opera they ever saw—or, for that matter, the last?

But that sensation of surprise in front of such a well-known mural wouldn't let me alone or let me film as I wanted. I scrutinized things. I used the pretext of wanting the best angle, the best light. Techies are patient. They respected my efforts. Until I figured it out: I'd been looking without seeing. All the American workers Diego painted have their backs to the spectator. The artist painted only working backs, except when the white workers are using goggles to protect themselves from sparks thrown by the welding torches. The American faces are anonymous. Masked. Rivera saw them the way they see us, Mexicans. With their backs turned. Anonymous. Faceless. Rivera wasn't laughing then, he wasn't Charlie Chaplin, he was only a Mexican who dared to say, None of you has a face. He was the Marxist who told them, Your work has neither the worker's name nor his face, your work is not your own.

In contrast, who is looking out at the spectator?

The blacks. They do have faces. They had faces in 1932, when Rivera came to paint and Frida checked into Henry Ford Hospital, and the great scandal was a Holy Family that Diego introduced into the mural ostensibly as a provocation, although Frida was pregnant and lost the child and instead of a child gave birth to a rag doll and the baptism of the doll was attended by parrots, monkeys, doves, a cat, and a deer . . . Was Rivera mocking the gringos or did he fear them? Was that why he didn't paint them facing the world?

The artist never knows what the spectator knows. We know the future, and in that mural of Rivera's, the black faces that do dare to look outward, who did dare to look at us, had fists and not only to build Ford's cars. Without knowing it, by pure intuition, Rivera in 1932 painted the blacks who on July 30, 1967—the date is burned into the heart of the city—set fire to Detroit, sacked it, shot it to pieces, reduced it to ashes, and delivered forty-three bodies to the morgue. Were those the only people who looked out from the mural, those forty-three future dead men painted by Diego Rivera in 1932 and killed in 1967, ten years after the death of the painter, thirty-five years after being painted?

A mural only appears to disclose itself at a glance. Actually, its secrets require a long, patient look, an examination which does not wear itself out, not even in the space of the mural, but which extends to all those who prolong it. Inevitably, the mural's context renders the gaze of the figures eternal, along with that of the spectator. Something strange happened to me. I had to direct my own gaze outside the mural's perimeter in order to return violently—the way a movie camera can move like an arrow from a full shot to a brutal close-up, to the detail—to the faces of the women workers, masculinized by their short hair and overalls but, no doubt of it, feminine figures. One of them is Frida. But her companion, not Frida but the other woman in the painting—her aquiline features, consistent with her large stature, her melancholy eyes with shadows under them, her lips thin but sensual in their very thinness, as if the fugitive lines of her mouth were proclaiming a superiority that was strict, sufficient, unadorned, sober, and inexhaustible, abounding in secrets when she spoke, ate, made love . . .

I looked at those almost golden eyes, mestizo, between European and Mexican, I looked at them as I'd looked at them so often in a forgotten passport found in a trunk as outdated as the document itself. I'd looked at them just as I had at other photos hung up, scattered around, or put away all over the house of my young father, murdered in October 1968. Those eyes my dead memory didn't recognize but my living memory retained in my soul decades later, now that I'm about to turn thirty and the twentieth century is about to die; trembling, I stared at those eyes with an almost sacred consternation which lasted so long that my team stopped, gathered around—was something wrong with me?

Was something wrong with me? Did I remember something? I was staring at the face of that strange beautiful woman dressed as a worker, and as I did, all the forms of recollection, memory of whatever you call those privileged instants of life, poured into my head like an ocean whose unleashed waves are always yet never the same: it's the face of

Laura Díaz I've just seen; the face revealed in the hurly-burly of the mural is that of one woman and one woman only, and her name is Laura Díaz.

The cameraman, Terry Hopkins, an old—even if young—friend, gave the painted wall a final illumination, filtered through blue accents, perhaps as an act of farewell (Terry is a poet), for his lighting blended in perfectly with the real sunset of the day we were living through in February 1999.

"Are you crazy?" he asked. "You're walking back to the hotel?"

I don't know what kind of look I gave him, but he didn't say another word. We separated. They packed up the annoying (and expensive) film equipment. They went off in the van.

I was left alone with Detroit, a city on its knees. I started walking slowly.

Free, with the fury of a teenage onanist, I began to take pictures in all directions, of black prostitutes and young black policewomen, of black boys wearing ragged woolen caps and thin jackets, of old people huddled around a garbage can turned into a street fireplace, of abandoned houses—I felt I was getting inside all of them—the *misérables* with no refuge, junkies who injected themselves with pleasure and scum in corners, I photographed all of them insolently, idly, provocatively, as if I were traveling down a blind alley where the invisible man wasn't any of them but me, I myself suddenly restored to the tenderness, nostalgia, affection of a woman whom I never in my life met but who had filled my life with all those kinds of memory that are both involuntary and voluntary, both a privilege and a danger: memories that are simultaneously expulsion from home and return to the maternal house, a fearsome encounter with the enemy and a longing for the original cave.

A man with a burning torch ran screaming through the halls of the abandoned house, setting fire to everything that would burn. I was hit on the back of my neck and fell, staring up at an upside-down, solitary skyscraper under a drunken sky. I touched the burning blood of a summer that still hadn't come, I drank the tears that won't wash away the darkness of someone's skin, I listened to the noise of the morning but not its desired silence, I saw children playing among the ruins, I examined the prostrate city, offering itself for examination without modesty. My entire body was oppressed by a disaster of brick and smoke, the urban holocaust, the promise of uninhabitable cities, no man's home in no man's city.

I managed to ask myself as I fell if it were possible to live the life of a dead woman exactly as she lived it, to discover the secret of her memory, to remember what she would remember.

I saw her, I will remember her.

It's Laura Díaz.

## 2. Catemaco: 1905

S OMETIMES IT'S POSSIBLE to touch memory. The family legend retold most often concerned the courage of Grandmother Cosima Kelsen when, back in the late 1860s, she journeyed to Mexico City in order to buy furniture and accessories for her house in Veracruz and, on her way back, her stagecoach was stopped by bandits who still wore the picturesque costume derived from the uniforms of nineteenth-century civil wars—wide-brimmed, round hat, short suede jacket, bell-bottom trousers, the ensemble held together by buttons of old silver, short boots, and jingling spurs.

Cosima Kelsen preferred evoking those details to recounting what happened. After all, the anecdote was better—and therefore more incredible, more extraordinary, more long-lasting, and known to more people—when many voices repeated it, when it passed (acknowledging the redundancy) from hand to hand, since the tale concerned hands. Fingers, actually.

The stagecoach was stopped at that strange spot on the Cofre de Perote where instead of ascending through the mist, the traveler descends from the diaphanous height of the mountain into a lake of fog. The gang of bandits, called *chinacos*, camouflaged by the mist, materialized with the noise of neighing horses and pistol shots. "Your money or your life" is the usual refrain of thieves, but these, more original, demanded "your life or your life," as if they understood all too well the haughty nobility, the rigid dignity the young Doña Cosima displayed as soon as they appeared.

She didn't deign to look at them.

Their leader, formerly a captain in Emperor Maximilian's defeated army, had loitered around the Chapultepec court long enough to be able to recognize social differences. He was famous in the Veracruz region for his sexual appetites—his nickname was the Hunk of Papantla—and equally famous for knowing the difference between a lady and a tart. Even though he'd been reduced to banditry after the imperial defeat, which culminated in the execution in 1867 of Maximilian along with the generals Miramón and Mejía—The three M's, *mierda*, the superstitious Mexican condottieri would exclaim—the respect this former cavalry officer showed toward ladies of rank was instinctive, and, after first seeing Doña Cosima's eyes as brilliant as copper sulphate and then her right hand clearly resting on the sill of the carriage window, he knew exactly what he should say to her:

"Please, madam, give me your rings."

The hand that Cosima had so provocatively exposed boasted a gold wedding band, a dazzling sapphire, and a pearl ring.

"These are my engagement and wedding rings. You'd have to cut them off me."

Which is exactly what the fearsome former imperial officer did without missing a beat, as if both knew the protocol of honor: one stroke of his machete and he cut off the four exposed fingers of young Grandmother Cosima Kelsen's right hand. She didn't even wince. The savage officer took off the red scarf he was wearing on his head in the old *chinaco*-bandit style and offered it to Cosima to bandage her hand. He dropped the four fingers into his hat and stood there like a haughty beggar, with the fingers of the beautiful German woman taking the place of alms. When he put his hat back on, blood ran down his face. For him, that red bath seemed as natural as diving into a lake would be for other people.

"Thank you," said the beautiful young Cosima, looking at him for the first and only time. "Will you be requiring anything else?"

The Hunk of Papantla's only answer was to lash the rump of the nearest horse, and the coach spun away down the slope toward the hot land of Veracruz, its destination beyond the mountain mists.

"No one is to touch that lady ever again," said the chief to his crew, who all understood that disobedience would cost them their lives and that their leader, for an instant and perhaps forever, had fallen in love.

"But if he fell in love with Grandmama, why didn't he give her back the rings?" asked Laura Díaz when she was old enough to think things through.

"Because he had no other souvenir of her," answered Aunt Hilda, the eldest of Cosima Kelsen's three daughters.

"But what did he do with the fingers?"

"That's something we don't talk about, child," answered the second of the trio, the young Fräulein Virginia, energetic and irritated, dropping the book she happened to be reading of the twenty she read each month.

"Watch out for die gypsie'," said the hacienda cook in her greedy coastal accent that devoured s's. "Dey cut' off die finger' for to make tamale'."

Laura Díaz stared down at her hands—little hands—and held them out and childishly twirled her fingers as if she were playing a piano. Then quickly she hid them under her blue-checkered school apron and observed with growing terror the activity of fingers in her father's house, as if all of them, at all hours of the day and night, did nothing but exercise what the Hunk of Papantla had taken away from the then young and beautiful and recently arrived Miss Cosima. Aunt Hilda, with a kind of hidden fever, played the Steinway piano brought from the port of Veracruz from New Orleans, a long voyage that seemed short because, as the passengers noted and then told Fräulein

Kelsen, seagulls accompanied the ship, or perhaps the piano, from Louisiana to Veracruz.

"Mutti would have been better off going to *la Nouvelle-Orléans* to buy her trousseau and enjoy her *nozze*," bragged and criticized Aunt Virginia in one breath. Mixing languages was as natural for her as mixing her reading matter, and it challenged, in an irreproachable way, one of her father's goals. New Orleans, in any case, was the civilized commercial point of reference closest to Veracruz, and the place where, exiled by the dictatorship of the peg-legged Santa Anna, the young liberal Benito Juárez had once worked rolling Cuban cigars. Would there be a commemorative plaque in New Orleans after Juárez—so ugly, such a little Indian—defeated the French and ordered the very Habsburg Maximilian—so blond, so handsome— shot?

"The Habsburgs governed Mexico longer than anyone, don't you forget it. Mexico is more Austrian than anything else," said the well-read and well-written Virginia to her youngest sister, Leticia, Laura Díaz's mother. For Leticia, this *news of the empire* was simply inconsequential since the only things that mattered to her were her home, her daughter, her kitchen, her diligent attention to daily life . . .

At the same time, the melancholy resonance that Hilda's agile fingers gave to Chopin's Preludes, her favorite music, augmented every particle of sadness—real, remembered, or imaginable—in the vast but simple house on the hill above the tropical lake.

"Would we be different if we'd grown up in Germany?" asked sister Hilda nostalgically.

"Yes," Virginia instantly replied. "And if we'd been born in China we'd be even more different. *Assez de chinoiseries, ma chère.*"

"Don't you feel nostalgia?" Hilda asked her youngest sister, Leticia.

"How could I? I've never been there."

"You're the only one who has," Virginia berated her, interrupting, although she was looking at Leticia, Laura's mother.

"There's a lot to do in the house," concluded Leticia.

Like all the country houses Spain left in the New World, this one, built on one level, consisted of four whitewashed sides around a central patio onto which opened dining room, living room, and bedrooms. Light entered the sitting rooms from the patio, because the external walls were windowless; defense might someday be necessary and modesty was a permanent concern.

"We live as if Indians, or English pirates, or rebel blacks were going to attack us," commented young Aunt Virginia with an amused smile. *"Aux armes!"*

Their modesty, on the other hand, was well served. Seasonal laborers brought in to harvest coffee were curious, impertinent, sometimes insolent, and thought themselves the equal of anyone. Virginia would answer them back with a mixture of Spanish insults and Latin quotations that would scatter them—as if the young woman with black eyes, white skin, and thin lips were just one more of the witches said to live on the far shore of the lake.

To reach the master's house, one had to walk through the main door, like a guest. The kitchen, to the rear, opened onto poultry yards, stables, storehouses, and fields; tanks and pipes conveyed the coffee fruits to the machines that pulped, fermented, washed, and dried them. There were few animals on the hacienda, baptized by its founder Felipe Kelsen "La Peregrina," "The Pilgrim," in honor of his wife, the brave but mutilated Cosima: five riding horses, fourteen mules, and fifty head of cattle. None of that interested little Laura, who would never set foot in those parts, which her grandfather governed with strict discipline, never complaining but noting constantly that the labor necessary to grow coffee was expensive because the product was so fragile and marketing it was so precarious. For that reason Don Felipe found himself forced into the ceaseless work of pruning trees, making sure the coffee bushes had the shade indispensable for their growth, cutting off the old stock, separating it from the new shoots, weeding the planted areas, and maintaining the drying sheds.

"Coffee is not like sugar, not like wild cane that grows anywhere. Coffee requires discipline," the master, Don Felipe, would declare, as he closely watched over the mills, wagons, stables, and famous drying sheds, dividing his day between paying minute attention to the crop in the field and paying no less careful attention to the bills.

Little Laura took not the slightest interest in any of this. She liked the fact that the hacienda extended out into the coffee hills and that behind them the forest and the lake continued in their seemingly forbidden encounter. She would scramble up to the roof terrace to catch sight, way in the distance, of the *quicksilver mirror lake*, as her reading aunt, Virginia, called it, and she didn't wonder why the prettiest thing in the place was also the thing least close to her, the farthest away from the hand the child stretched out as if to touch, giving all the power of the world to her desire. She delivered every victory of her childhood to imagination. The lake. A line of poetry.

From the salon arose the melancholy notes of a prelude, and Laura felt sad, but happy to share that feeling with her eldest aunt, so beautiful and so solitary but mistress of ten musical fingers.

The workers, under orders from her grandfather Don Felipe Kelsen, daubed the walls of the house, their hands wet with a mixture of lime and maguey sap, giving the walls the smoothness of a naked woman's back. Which is what Don Felipe said to his always upright but now very sick wife one day before Doña Cosima died: "Every time I touch the walls of the house I'm going to think I'm running my fingers over your naked back, your beautiful, delicate naked back, do you remember?"

When Grandmama died with a sigh the next morning, her husband achieved, finally, in her death, something Doña Cosima had always refused in life: to have his wife wear black gloves with cotton stuffing in the four missing fingers of the right one.

He sent her to eternity intact, he said, just as he received her when the mail-order bride arrived from Germany at the age of twenty-two, identical to her daguerreotype—hair parted in the middle and arranged in two large hemispheres that arose from a perfect part in perfect symmetry and covered her ears as if to emphasize the perfection of the mother-of-pearl earrings hanging from her hidden earlobes.

"Ears are the ugliest thing a woman has," muttered Virginia.

"All you ever do is find defects," Hilda shot back.

"I listen to you recite, Virginia, and I listen to you play, Hilda, with my horrid little ears," laughed Laura Díaz's mother. "How lucky Mutti Cosima wasn't wearing her earrings in Perote!"

At the age of twenty-two, she'd arrived from Germany with very dark hair as if to contrast the more sharply with the whiteness of her skin. In the portrait, she held a fan, opened out against her bosom, with the five fingers on her right hand.

This is why Hilda played the piano with shame and passion, as if, at the same time, she wanted to make up for her mother's deficiency and to offend her by saying, See, I can do it and you can't, with the hidden anger of the eldest child, the only Kelsen daughter who that one time had returned to Germany with her mother and with her listened, in Cologne, to a recital by the famous pianist and composer Franz Liszt. She had heard the constant sarcastic chatter of many European immigrants. Mexico was a country of Indians and brutes where nature was so abundant and rich that one could satisfy one's immediate needs without having to work. Encouraging German immigration was one way to remedy that state of affairs, introducing into Mexico another nature, the industrious nature of Europeans. But these immigrants, invited to cultivate the soil, could not endure the rural hardness and isolation, and they migrated to the cities. This is why Felipe Kelsen was faithful to his promise to work the land, to work it hard and resist two temptations: to return to Germany or to make trips to Mexico City like the one which cost his wife Cosima so dearly. As they left the concert in Cologne, Hilda asked her mother, "Mutti, why don't we stay here to live? How horrible Mexico is!"

It was then Don Felipe forbade not only any return trip to the *Vaterland* but also the speaking of German in the house, saying this with the utmost severity, fists clenched, and when he calmed down he didn't strike anything, merely insisted that from now on everyone was going to be Mexican, was going to assimilate, there would be no more visits to the Rhine, and everyone would speak only Spanish. Philip became Felipe, and Cosima, well, stayed Cosima. Only Virginia, with her mischievous tenderness, dared to call her mother Mutti and quote from

German books. Don Felipe would shrug his shoulders; the girl had turned out eccentric.

"There are those who are cross-eyed, those who are albinos, and those who are Virginias," she would say of herself, feigning a squint. *"Gesundheit!"*

No German, no involvement with anything except the house or, as modern types put it, domestic economy. The daughters became extremely hardworking, perhaps to make up for the deficiencies of their mother, who sat back in her rocking chair (another novelty brought from Louisiana) to fan herself with her left hand and stare into the distance, toward the highway to Mexico City and the mists of Perote where she had left four fingers and, some whispered, her heart.

"When a woman meets the Hunk of Papantla, she never forgets him" was the refrain the people of Veracruz repeated.

At the same time, Don Felipe did not hesitate to reproach his young bride for having made the shopping trip to Mexico City: "See? If you'd gone to New Orleans, this horrible thing wouldn't have happened to you."

Cosima had realized from the first day that it was her husband's fervent wish to assimilate into Mexico. She had been the last concession Philip Kelsen would make to the old country. Cosima simply anticipated her husband's intention to be forever from here, never more from there. And that is why she lost four fingers. "I'd rather buy my trousseau in the capital of Mexico. We're Mexicans, aren't we?"

How dangerous fingers were, little Laura imagined as she awakened from nightmares in which a severed hand scuttled across the floor, climbed the wall, and dropped onto the pillow next to the child's face. She would wake up screaming, and what she did find next to her face was a spider she didn't dare kill with a slap because it would have been the same as once again cutting off the fingers of her self-absorbed grandmother in her rocker.

"Mama, I want a white canopy over my bed."

"We keep the house very clean. Not even dust sneaks in."

"What sneaks in are my horrid, horrid dreams."

Leticia would laugh and bend down to give a hug to her little girl, who already was showing the keen wit of all the family members except beautiful Grandmother Cosima, sick with melancholy.

To the swine who attributed platonic passions to his wife, Felipe responded with three lovely daughters, one more beautiful, intelligent, and hardworking than the next. "Six fingers are enough for a woman to love a man," he bragged one night in a tavern, only to repent it immediately as he'd never repented in his life before or after. He was a hardworking man, but he had been tired and a bit drunk. He owned his own coffee plantation. He was trying to relax. He never again said what he blurted out that night. He secretly prayed that anyone who heard him utter that vulgarity would die as soon as possible or go away for good, which was much the same thing.

"To leave is to die a little," Felipe would say every so often, recalling a saying of his own French mother—when Felipe was Philip and his father Heine Kelsen and his mother Letitia Lassalle, and the Europe that Bonaparte left standing on its pedestal was being made and remade everywhere, because industry was growing and artisans were disappearing, because everyone went off to work in factories, far away from their homes and fields, home and the workplace no longer being united as they always had been; because people were talking about freedom while tyrants held power; because the breast of the nation was split open and the nation was dying from an authoritarian rifle shot; because no one knew if his foot was treading a new furrow or walking on ancient ashes, as the marvelous poet Alfred de Musset put it—a man who brought lovers together in reading, moving the men to raptures and the women to love, touching the hearts of all. Enraptured boys, fainting girls: the young Philip Kelsen, blue eyes, Greek profile, flowing beard, and dragoon cape, top hat, and ivory-handled walking stick, the visage of an eagle, wanted to understand which world he was living in, and he thought he understood it all during a great demonstration in Düsseldorf where he saw himself, recognized himself, and even loved himself, as a disquieting reflection, in the wonderful figure of the young socialist tribune Ferdinand Lassalle.

Philip Kelsen, at the age of twenty-four, felt touched by an omen as he watched and listened when that man spoke. Philip's mentor, even if almost his contemporary, had the same last name as Philip's mother, in the same way that she had the name of Napoleon's mother, Letitia: the favorable signs attracted the young German as he listened to Lassalle and evoked passages from Musset: "From the highest spheres of intelligence to the most impenetrable mysteries of matter and form, your soul and body are your brothers."

Philip silently addressed his hero as "Lassalle, my brother," happily forgetting, both voluntarily and involuntarily, the fundamental facts of his life: Heine Kelsen, his father, owed his position to a commercial and financial arrangement, subordinate but respectful, he had with old Johann Buddenbrook, a citizen of Lübeck who had made his fortune by cornering the market in wheat and selling at a high price to Prussian troops during the war against Napoleon. Heine Kelsen represented the interests of old Buddenbrook in Düsseldorf, but his assets—his money and his luck—doubled when he married Letitia Lassalle, goddaughter of the French financier Nucingen, who saw to it she received a lifetime income of a hundred thousand pounds per year as a dowry.

Philip Kelsen forgot all that when, at the age of twenty-four, he heard Ferdinand Lassalle speak for the first time.

Lassalle spoke to the Rhenish workers with the passion of a Romantic and the logic of a politician reminding them that in the new industrial and dynastic Europe, a petty Napoleon had taken the place of the great Napoleon, and the pettiness of this vile, shameless little tyrant had united the government and bourgeoisie against the workers: "The first Napoleon," Kelsen heard Lassalle exclaim at the meeting, "was a revolutionary. His nephew is a cretin and represents only the moribund, reactionary faction."

How much the fiery young Kelsen admired the fiery young Lassalle— whom even the police of Düsseldorf described as a man of "extraordinary intellectual qualities, indefatigable energy, great determination, savagely left-wing ideas, possessed of a wide circle of friendships, with great practical agility and considerable financial resources"! For all those reasons he was dangerous, the police declared; for all those reasons, his young follower Kelsen convinced himself, Lassalle was

21

admirable—because he was well dressed (while his rival, Marx, had grease stains on his vest); because he would go to receptions given by the very class he was fighting (while Marx would not leave the most miserable cafés in London); because he believed in the German nation (while Marx was a cosmopolitan enemy of nationalism); because he loved adventure (while Marx was a boring middle-class paterfamilias unable to give his wife, the aristocratic Madame von Westphalen, a ring).

For the rest of his life, Philip Kelsen would fight the Lassallian fervor of his socialist years. He lost his entire youth in that splendid illusion, which like the poet's European furrow was, perhaps, only a sinkhole of ashes. The socialist Lassalle ended up joining forces with the feudalistic Bismarck, the ultranationalist, ultrareactionary Prussian Junker, so that between them—this was the reason behind the uncomfortable alliance—they could dominate the voracious capitalists who had no country. The critique of power became power over criticism, and Philip Kelsen abandoned Germany on the same day his handcuffed hero, Ferdinand Lassalle, became his bloodied hero, killed in a duel in a forest near Geneva on August 28, 1864. The reason for the duel was as absurd and romantic as the elegant socialist himself: he fell passionately in love with Helene (von Dönniger, as the newspaper article reported it), challenged her current suitor (Yanko von Racowitz, added the article), who in due course put a bullet in Lassalle's stomach without the slightest consideration for history, socialism, the workers' movement, or the Iron Chancellor.

How much farther from the pantheon in the Jewish cemetery in Breslau where Lassalle was buried at the age of thirty-nine could the disillusioned socialist Philip Kelsen go at the age of twenty-five, than to the coasts of the New World, to Veracruz, where the Atlantic breathes its last, after a long crossing from the port of Hamburg, and then inland to Catemaco, hot, fertile, prodigal lands—*supremely fertile*, they were called in speeches—where nature and man could join forces and prosper, beyond the corrupt disillusion of Europe?

Philip retained only moving memories of Lassalle, nationalism, and the love of adventure that brought him from the Rhine to the Gulf of Mexico. But here, those attributes would be no longer German but Mexican. Old Heine in Düsseldorf applauded the decision of his rebellious son, gave him an endowment of marks, and put him on a ship for the New World. Philip Kelsen made a three-year stopover in New Orleans, working reluctantly in a cigar factory, but he was disgusted by American racism, still blazing hot amid the charred ruins of the Confederacy, so he went on to Veracruz, exploring the coast from Tuxpan in the green Huasteca to the Tuxtlas, flown over by hundreds of birds.

*Full stomach, happy heart,* said the first woman he slept with in Tuxpan, a mulatta who gave him the same sensuality in bed as she did in the kitchen, alternately placing in the voracious mouth of her young German seducer her two wine-red nipples or an enormous quantity of *bocoles, pemoles,* and the biggest tamales in all of Mexico, stuffed with pork and chile. Not yet acclimated, Philip Kelsen again found a mulatta and snacks in Santiago Tuxtla. Like her native city, her name was Santiaga, and the dishes she served up for the repose of the recently arrived, sensual little German were Caribbean: lots of sweet potatoes, garlic, and *mogo-mogo* from plantains. But what seduced Philip Kelsen more than any sexual or gastronomic dish was the beauty of Catemaco, a short distance from the Tuxtlas: a lake that could have been in Switzerland or Germany—surrounded by mountains and thick vegetation, shiny as a mirror but animated by the invisible whispers of waterfalls, birds flying overhead, and colonies of tailless macaques.

Standing on a hill overlooking the quicksilver lake, Philip Kelsen announced, in an act that reconciled all of him—his youth and his future, his romantic spirit and his financial patrimony, his idealism and his pragmatism, his sensuality and his asceticism—"I'm staying here. This is my country."

Only at a distance and through hearsay did little Laura begin to learn the story of her upright, disciplined, and handsome German grandfather, who spoke only Spanish, although who could tell if he went on thinking in German and who could know the language of his dreams? For the little girl, all dates were soon to come, never far off, and the passage of time was marked most vividly by her birthday, when, so no one would forget to pay attention to her, she would charmingly skip around the patio, starting early in the morning while she was still in her nightie and sing:

*on the twelfth of May*
*the Virgin dressed in white*
*came walking into sight*
*with her coat so gay . . .*

The entire household knew the rite by heart, and on the days leading up to Laura's birthday they would pretend to forget the celebration. If Laura knew that they knew, then she too gave no hint of it. Everyone feigned surprise, and it was prettier that way, especially this twelfth of May in the fifth year of the century, when Laura turned seven, and her grandfather gave her an extraordinary present, a Chinese doll with porcelain head, hands, and feet, its little cotton body covered by a Mandarin costume of red silk, with black edging and a dragon design embroidered in gold. For the little girl being feted, the exoticism of the costume did not detract from the joy and gladness she felt in her instantaneous love for those tiny little feet in white silk stockings and black velvet slippers, for the smiling little pug-nosed face with Asian eyes and high brows painted near the fringe of silk hair. But the diminutive hands were the doll's most delicate part. As soon as she received this most beautiful gift of her childhood, she took the doll's hand and with it shook hands with her pianist aunt, Hilda, her writer aunt, Virginia, with Mutti, the cook, Leticia, with her grandfather, the farmer Felipe, and her invalid grandmother Cosima, who involuntarily hid her mutilated right hand under her shawls and awkwardly used her left hand to greet her little granddaughter.

"Do you have a name for her yet?" asked Doña Cosima.

"Li Po," Laura answered, humming along. "We'll call her Li Po."

With a simple glance, her grandmother asked her where she'd found that name; Laura answered with a shrug that meant "just because." They all kissed her, and the child went back to bed to make Li Po comfortable among the pillows, promising her that even though she might be punished, Li Po would never be scolded, that even if things went badly for Laura, Li Po would always have her throne of cushions whence she might rule over Laura Díaz's bedroom.

"You rest, Li Po, sleep, live happily. I'll take care of you forever."

When she left Li Po behind in her room and went out of the house, her childhood instincts led her to enact, as if in a garden, the feat of returning to the natural world—so abundant, so "prodigal," but above all so detailed, close, and certain to the gaze and touch of the child who was growing up surrounded with latent forest and impatient lake and renascent coffee groves: that was the way Aunt Virginia put it in her loud, sonorous voice.

"And supremely fertile," she added, so not a word would be left out. *"Most fertile."*

But the fingers of the house held her in, like the vines in the richly detailed world of the tropical forest. Aunt Hilda was playing the piano. (I get dizzy and exalted at the same time, I'm ashamed, but it gives me a secret pleasure to use my ten fingers to abandon myself, get out of myself, to feel and say to everyone that the music they're hearing is not mine and neither am I, it's Chopin's, I play it, I'm the one who lets this marvelous sound pass through my hands, my fingers, in full knowledge that outside on her rocker, my mother listens to me, my mother who did not let me stay in Germany to study and become an important pianist, a real artist, and my father also listens to me, my father who has locked us up in this village with no future, and I reproach them both for the loss of my own destiny, Hilda Kelsen, the Hilda I might have been, the Hilda I'll never be now, no matter how I try, even if some good fortune I cannot control, to which I could say: *I made you, you're mine*, were to bring me luck; it wouldn't be my luck, it would be an accident, a gift from chance: I play Chopin's saddest Preludes and am not consoled, I only arm myself with patience and feel the intimate joy of offending my father and mother.) Aunt Virginia was writing a poem. (I live surrounded by resignation, I don't want to resign myself, I want to escape one day, and I fear that my fondness for reading and writing is merely that, an escape and not a vocation I could just as well fulfill here as in Germany or, as I quipped one day, in China, let's see if I don't end up like my little niece's doll, charming but mute, relaxing forever on a pillow.) Mutti Leticia was helping the cook prepare tamales in the coastal style. (How beautiful it is to stuff them with the smooth mix of cooked pork and chipotle chiles, then finish by wrapping each tamale tenderly in its sheet of banana leaves, like a baby in bunting, and steam them, uniting, conserving all the flavors and aromas, meat and spice, fruit and flour, what a delight for the palate, it reminds me of my husband Fernando's kisses, but I mustn't think about that, the arrangements are made, it's what's best for everyone, it's good that the girl will grow up here in the country with me, each of us has obligations, there's no reason to use up our pleasures while we're young, we should postpone them for the future, we should receive pleasure as a reward and not as a privilege, gifts are used up as quickly as whims, you think you have the right to have everything and you end with nothing; I prefer to wait, patiently, after all I'm only in my twenties, my whole life ahead of me, my whole life ahead.) Grandfather Felipe put on his glasses and went over the accounts. (I can't complain, everything has turned out fine, the plantation is prospering, the girls are growing, Hilda has her music, Virginia her books, the one who might complain most would be Leticia, living away from her husband by mutual agreement, not because of any imposition or tyranny on my part but because they want to wait for the future, not realizing that perhaps they've already lost it forever because you have to seize things at the moment, the way you catch birds on the wing, or they disappear forever, the way I threw myself into the socialist adventure until that wore itself out and then I threw myself at America, which apparently is something that never wears out, a bottomless continent, while we Europeans swallowed our history whole and now ruminate it, sometimes belching it up, bah, we defecate it, we are defecators of history, and here history has first to be made, without Europe's errors, without its dreams and disillusions, starting from scratch, what a relief, what power, to start from nothing, to own our own destiny, then one can accept falls, misfortunes, errors because they are part of our own destiny and not part of a distant historical event, Napoleon, Bismarck, Lassalle, Karl Marx . . . they all had less freedom on their thrones and behind their pulpits than I do here, going over the accounts of a coffee plantation, *Himmel und Hölle,* then.) And the silent grandmother, Cosima, rocked softly in the rocking chair brought from Louisiana instead of Mexico City. (I wanted to tell Felipe that I too was of this country, that was all; as soon as I arrived and met him, I understood that I was his last concession to his German past; why he chose me, I still don't know; why he loves me so, I hope it isn't to make up for my unfortunate adventure on the Perote highway; he's never made me feel he's sorry for me—on the contrary, he's loved me with a real man's passion, our daughters were conceived with a shameless, foulmouthed passion that no one who knows us could imagine. He treats me like a whore, and I like it, I tell him I imagine making love with the *chinaco* who mutilated me and he likes it, we're accomplices in an intense love that has no modesty or reticence, that only he and I know, and the memory of it makes all the more painful the death that's coming closer and that says to me, to us, Now one of the two of you is going to live without the other, so how are you going to go on loving? I don't know because I have no idea what comes after, but he's staying here and can remember me, imagine me, prolong me, think I didn't die, only ran off with the *chinaco* whom I never saw again—because if I were to meet up with him again, what would I do, kill him or run off with him? No, I'll only think the same thing I tell people: I did it to save the other passengers. But how could I ever forget those bestial eyes, that macho stance, that tigerlike way of walking, that unsatisfied desire, mine and his, never, never, never . . . )

Aunt Hilda was playing the piano; Aunt Virginia was still writing with a quill pen; her mother Leticia was cooking not only because she liked to but because she had a genius for the Veracruz art of uniting rice, beans, plantain, and pork, shredding the meat and adding lemon juice for the dish called *ropa vieja*, "old clothes," marinating octopus in its ink, and reserving for the end the meringues, the custards, the *jocoques* of clotted cream and the *tocino del cielo*—the sweetest sweet in the world, which had gone from Barcelona to Havana and from Cuba to Veracruz as if to stifle with sweetness all the bitterness of those lands of revolution, conquest, and tyranny.

"None of that, now. I don't want to know about Mexico's past: the New World is only future," declared the grandfather firmly whenever these topics came up. For that reason, he went out less and less to after-noon gatherings and dinners, and no longer to taverns, ever since he forgot himself that tired night . . . At first he didn't go to Mass either, under the pretext that first he was a socialist and second a Protestant. But small towns are big hells, so he ended up yielding to the customs of a Veracruz that believed in God and miracles but not in the Church and its priests. This pleased Felipe, not because he was a cynic but because it was more comfortable. But the entire town became uncomfortable when Don Elzevir Almonte appeared, a young, dark-skinned, and intol-erant parish priest sent from the very puritanical clerical city of Puebla de los Angeles. He, along with a good dozen other priests from Mexico's central plateau, had been charged by the Archbishop of Mexico with establishing discipline and good habits among the lax (if not dissolute) faithful of the Gulf coast.

Cosima Reiter, the mail-order bride, had been born and raised Protestant. Philip-Felipe, who was agnostic, had realized that he'd never find a nonbelieving wife in Mexico; here even atheists believed in God and Protestants were Catholic, Apostolic, and Roman.

To order an atheist bride from the Germany of Kaiser Wilhelm seemed not so much like an offense as a tropical joke. Philip went along with the advice of friends and relatives on both sides of the Atlantic; however, what really captivated him was that daguerreotype of the girl holding a fan in her right hand, her black hair divided into two per-fectly symmetrical curves by a strict part.

The young Lassallist did not anticipate that the moment his still very young wife reached Veracruz a conformist streak—the rule, no matter how notable the exceptions, in religious communities—would for many reasons become pronounced in her. Social pressure was the least important of those reasons. More significant was her inevitable discovery that Philip, or Felipe, had not lived a saint's life during his Veracruz bachelorhood. This foreign boy with long wavy hair, blond beard, and Greek profile would never follow a monastic rule. Rumors circulating in the small lakeside population reached Cosima's ears as soon as she'd unpacked. Twenty-three hours after the civil ceremony, the beautiful, upright German informed her stupefied husband: "Now I want a Catholic, religious wedding."

"But you and I were confirmed as Protestants. We'll have to disavow our faith."

"We're Christian. No one has any reason to know more."

"I don't see the reason for this."

"It's so your mulatta daughter can be my maid of honor and carry the train of my wedding dress."

Thus did María de la O, almost on the first day, enter the home of the newlyweds. Cosima took it upon herself to assign a bedroom to the young lady, ordering the servants to address her as "señorita." She gave her a place at the table, treated her as a daughter, and refused to acknowledge anything about her origin. No one except María de la O herself heard what Cosima Reiter said to her real mother: "Madam, choose the way in which you'd like your daughter to grow up. Go live in a place where you can make a life for yourself—Tampico or Coatza-coalcos, and you won't lack for anything."

"Except the love of my little girl," wept the black woman.

"Not even you believe that," said the brand-new Frau Kelsen, speaking to her familiarly, having quickly learned local customs and habits. One day, when she'd become an old lady, she reminded her husband of that event, not knowing that little Laura was listening from behind a potted fern.

María de la O Kelsen was the way Cosima would introduce the beautiful little mulatta, and that was how Don Felipe accepted her. The lady of the house didn't even have to beg her husband to be faithful to the humanitarian principles of his youth. Cosima took charge and began to go to Mass, first with the mulatta girl and a missal held in both hands; later, with three more daughters and the missal in one hand, proud of her four-sided maternity, indifferent to whispers, shock, or curses, even when evil tongues said that the Hunk of Papantla was the real father—with the difficulty that the bandit was Creole, Doña Cosima German, and María de la O, in that case, explicable only as a racial throwback.

Seven years older than the eldest of her sisters, Hilda, eight years older than Virginia, and ten than Leticia, María de la O was a mulatta with charming features, a quick smile, and an upright gait: Cosima had found her bent over and groveling, like a beaten, cornered little animal, her black eyes filled with even blacker visions; and not wasting a moment, the child's new mother by will and right, Cosima Reiter de Kelsen, taught María de la O to walk properly, even forcing her: "Put that dictionary on your head and walk toward me without letting it fall. Careful."

She taught her table manners, how to be neat; she dressed her in the most beautiful starched white dresses because they contrasted dramatically with her dark skin. She made her wear a white silk bow in her hair, which wasn't stiff like her mother's but relaxed like her father Philip's.

"Now you I'd bring back with me to Germany," Cosima said proudly. "You would certainly attract attention."

She went to church and told Father Morales, I'm going to have a baby and then at least two more. "I don't want any of my children to be ashamed of their sister. I want the Kelsens yet to be born to enter the world and find a Kelsen who is different but also better than they."

She rested a hand on María de la O's chignon. "Have her baptized, confirmed, rain blessings on her, and for the love of God, pray for her honesty."

He hesitated an instant and replied: "Let's hope she doesn't turn out to be a whore."

The good thing was that the priest from Veracruz, Don Jesús Morales, was a good-natured man without being servile, and everything in him—his public sermons, his private chats, the confessions he heard in secrecy—protected and exalted the Christian behavior of Doña Cosima Reiter de Kelsen, by now very much a convert to Roman Catholicism.

"Ladies, don't waste the triumphs of either faith or charity on me. All of you in good order now, dammit."

The priest Jesús Morales loved his flock. The substitute priest, Elzevir Almonte, wanted to reform it. The fingers Grandmother Cosima was missing seemed to have sprouted on the new priest, and he used them to admonish, censure, condemn . . . His sermons brought to the tropics the air of the high plateau, rarefied, suffocating, intolerable and intolerant. His parishioners began to count the prohibitions hurled at them from the pulpit by the dark young priest Almonte: no more of these loose camisoles that reveal the female form, especially when it rains and they soak through; from now on, modest undergarments and umbrellas in hand; no more of these foulmouthed Veracruz expressions and actions; though I'm not a magistrate or a justice of the peace, I declare that anyone who curses may not receive the holy body of our savior in his sacrilegious mouth—that much I can do; no more sere-nades, a pretext for nocturnal excitation that hinders Christian repose; brothels are forthwith closed, taverns are forthwith closed, and under pain of mortal sin a curfew is declared beginning at 9 p.m. whether or not the authorities approve—and if you think I'm joking, just wait and see; you will say from now on "that which I walk on," not "legs," just as you will say "that which I sit on" instead of . . .

All these things the new priest from Puebla proclaimed with an elaborate waving of hands, ridiculous and insolent, as if he wanted to give sculptural form in the air to his categorical prohibitions. The brothels migrated to Santiago Tuxtla, the taverns went to San Andrés, the harpists and guitar players marched to Boca del Río, and amid the desolation now fallen on the local merchants like a plague, Father Almonte reached the apex of authoritarianism with his techniques in the confessional.

"My child, do you look at yourself nude in the mirror?"

Felipe did not reproach Cosima for her new faith. He simply looked her straight in the eye when she came home from Mass on Sundays, and it was she who for the first time averted her haughty gaze.

"Do you touch yourself in secret, my child?"

Laura looked at herself naked and was not surprised to see what she always saw: she thought the priest might have planted something strange in her body, a flower in her navel or a spider between her legs, like the one her aunts had when they bathed on a deserted beach of the lake, where they never returned once Father Almonte began to cast suspicion everywhere.

"Would you like to see your father's sexual organ, my child?"

To see if something would happen, Laura repeated in front of the mirror the priest's strange movements and even more extraordinary words. She also imitated his voice, making it even more bombastic:

"A woman is a temple built over a sewer."

"Have you ever seen your father naked?"

Laura almost never saw her father, Fernando Díaz, dressed or naked. He was a bookkeeper in a bank, lived in Veracruz with a fifteen-year-old son, the product of an earlier marriage. After his first wife, Elisa Obregón, died in childbirth, Fernando fell in love with the young Leticia Kelsen during a visit to the festivals of Tlacotalpan. Leticia fell in love with this strange bird from the port, who always wore jacket, vest, tie, and tiepin, and whose only concession to the heat was a round straw hat—what the English called a boater, as Aunt Virginia noted, striking a resonant chord in her sister's Anglophile suitor. The Kelsens, married by mail, did not impede this "love match," as Mr. Díaz insisted on calling it; he was a man of English readings and influences, which Felipe Kelsen thought was good for helping to erase the German influence. Leticia herself accepted the arrangement of living apart, and when little Laura came into the world, Felipe, now a grandfather, roundly congratulated himself because his daughter and granddaughter lived under his protection in the country and not far away in the noisy port, which was, perhaps, as sinful—he said to Cosima—as some gossiping tongues said it was. She gave him an ironic look. Small towns, big hells.

Fernando Díaz had asked of his new family (Leticia first and then Laura, when she came exactly nine months later) one thing: "I can't give you what you deserve. Live a good life in Don Felipe's house. In Catemaco, I'd never be anything but a bookkeeper. In Veracruz, I can rise, and then I'll have you brought to join me. I don't want charity from your father or compassion from your sisters. I'm not a hanger-on."

Discomfort and being hangers-on were, in point of fact, the components of the young couple's initial situation in the Kelsen house in Catemaco, so everyone breathed a sigh of relief when Fernando Díaz made his decision.

"Why doesn't your son Santiago ever come to see us?" the maiden aunts asked.

"He's studying," Fernando would answer dryly.

Laura Díaz was dying to learn more: how had her parents met, how did they get married, who was the mysterious older half brother who had the right to live with her father at the port? When would they all get together? Was it right that her mother was so hardworking, as if taking care of two houses at the same time, that of her father present here and that of her husband absent there, as if cooking for both those who were there and those who weren't? . . . It was true. The solitude of mother and daughter spread more and more to the rest of the house, to the three spinsters, Hilda playing the piano, Virginia writing and reading, María de la O knitting wool shawls for the cold, when the north wind blew . . .

"We won't get married, Leticia, until you move in with your husband, as things should be," Hilda and Virginia would say, almost in a chorus.

"He's doing it for you and for the girl. It won't be long now, I'm sure," María de la O would add.

"Well, he should hurry up, or the three of us will die unmarried," Virginia, alone, would laugh. "I hope the gentleman, *mein Herr*, is aware of it!"

But Grandmother Doña Cosima incarnated the true solitude. "I've done everything I had to do in life, Felipe. Now respect my silence."

"And your memories? What about them?"

"Not a one is mine. I share them all with you. All."

"Don't worry. I know."

"Then take good care of them, and don't ask me for more words. I've already given you them all."

That is what Doña Cosima said in the year 1905, when everything happened.

Witty, wisecracking, and raucous: the people of Catemaco could be all that (when the spirit moved them) and devout, too, as the priest Morales knew very well and the priest Almonte knew not at all. More than the rich and the almost rich, it was the poor, the sowers and reapers, the net weavers, the fishermen, the oarsmen, the bricklayers, and their wives who gave the best offerings in church.

Don Felipe and other coffee growers would give money or sacks of food; the poorest, in secret, would bring jewelry, ancient pieces passed down in their families for centuries and offered to give thanks to the Lord Our God for their own good fortune or someone else's bad luck, both taken to be miraculous. Onyx necklaces, large silver combs, gold bracelets, unmounted emeralds: luxurious stones retrieved from who knows what hiding place, attic, or cave, from under what mat on which embankment, from what secret mine.

Everything was enthusiastically piled up, because Father Morales was scrupulous about storing away for his flock what rightly belonged to it and would sell a valuable piece in Veracruz only when he knew that the very family who'd piously offered the jewel to the Black Christ of Otatitlán needed money.

As in all the towns on the Gulf coast, the saints were celebrated in Catemaco with dances held on a wooden floor the better to hear the sound of stamping feet. The air would fill with harps, viols, fiddles, and guitars. It was then it happened—everyone remembers it from the year 1905: on the day of the feast of the Holy Child of Zongolica, Father Elzevir Almonte did not appear. People went looking for him, but neither the priest nor the treasure was to be found. The offering chest was empty and the priest from Puebla gone.

"How right he was when he'd say, 'Puebla breeding ground of saints; Veracruz fountain of crooks.' "

That was the only comment, ironic and sufficient, made by Don Felipe Kelsen. The people were harder on him, their mildest epithets being "little bastard" and "thief." The four Kelsen daughters remained impassive. Life would go back to normal without the robber priest, taverns and whorehouses would operate once again, serenades would be heard on tranquil midnights, those who had gone away would come back. Coincidentally, on that day, the self-absorbed grandmother, Cosima Reiter, began to decline, as if she'd wasted her life in a religion that didn't deserve her and wasted her love (gossips insisted) on an honorable man instead of a romantic bandit.

"Laura, sweetheart," she once said when she was already ill, as if she didn't want the secret to be lost forever, "you should have seen what a handsome man he was, what fire, how bold he was."

She didn't say, Always let yourself be tempted, sweetheart, don't be afraid, don't be intimidated, you don't get a second chance, and she didn't add temptation to the elegance and fire because she was a proper lady and an exemplary grandmother, but Laura Díaz, for the rest of her days, kept those words in her heart, that lesson imparted to her by her grandmother. Don't let it pass you by, don't let it . . .

"You don't get a second chance . . ."

The child Laura looked at herself in the mirror, not to see there the temptations enumerated by the odious priest Almonte (who, for reasons beyond her, simply made her laugh) but to discover in her own reflection a rejuvenation or at least an inheritance from her sick grandmother. My nose is too big, she said to herself, discouraged, soft features to boot, sparkling eyes devoid of seduction except that of being a seven-year-old simpleton. The Chinese doll Li Po had more personality than her pudgy-cheeked and obstreperous little mistress, who had no kissable passion, no embraceable ardor, no . . .

The day their mother was buried, the four Kelsen girls (three unmarried and one married, but for all intents and purposes . . . ) dressed in black; but Leticia, Laura's mother, saw a marvelous bird fly over the open grave, almost as if escaping from its own funeral, and exclaimed: Look! A white crow!

The others turned to look, but Laura, as if she were obeying an order from her dead grandmother, ran off after the white bird, feeling that she herself could fly, as if the albino crow were calling her, Follow me, girl, fly with me, I want to show you something.

That was the day the girl realized where she was, where she came from, as if her grandmother, in dying, had given her wings to return to the forest: playful, wise, without calling attention to herself, jumping around as she always did, provoking sighs in the family group as they watched her run off, she's just a child, what do children know about death, she didn't know Grandmother Cosima in her prime, she isn't doing it because she's bad.

She followed the white crow beyond the limits of what she knew, learning about and loving from that moment on, forever, everything she saw and touched, as if that day of death had been set aside for her to learn something unrepeatable, something only for her, and only for the age Laura Díaz had reached at that instant, having been born on May 12, 1898, when the Virgin dressed in white came walking into sight with her coat . . .

From that moment on, and forever, she learned about and loved the fig tree, the tulip tree, the Chinese lilies, whose little branchlets flowered, every single one, three times a year: she examined what she already knew but had forgotten in the forest, the red lily, the *palo rojo*, the round crown of the mango tree; she examined what she'd never known or thought but was now remembering instead of discovering, the perfect symmetry of the araucaria, which in each shoot of each branch quickly produces its immediate double, the *trueno* with its little yellow flowers, a marvelous tree that resists both hurricanes and drought.

She was going to shout in horror, but she swallowed her fear and turned it into astonishment. She'd run into a giant. Laura trembled, closed her eyes, touched the giant, it was made of stone, it was enormous, it stood out in the middle of the forest, more deeply rooted there than the breadfruit tree or even the roots of the invading laurel that devours everything—drains, fields, crops.

Covered with slime, a gigantic female figure stared into eternity, encircled with belts of shells and serpent, wearing a crown tinted green by the mimetic forest. Adorned with necklaces and rings and earrings of arms, noses, ears.

Laura ran home breathlessly—eager, at first, to tell of her discovery, the lady of the forest who gave her jewels to the poor, the lost statue who protected the property of heaven which that nasty priest Almonte had stolen—*curse him, curse him*—and she, Laura Díaz, knew the secret of the forest. But then she realized she could tell no one, not now, not to them.

She stopped running. She returned home slowly along the road of undulating hills and gentle slopes planted with coffee. In the patio, Grandfather Felipe was saying to his foremen that there was nothing to do but cut back the laurel branches, they're invading us, as if they could move, the laurels are clogging the drains, they're going to eat up the whole house, flocks of starlings gather right over here in the ceiba tree just outside the house and dirty up the entryway, this can't go on; besides, we're coming into the season when the coffee trees get covered with spiderwebs.

"We're going to have to cut down a few trees."

Aunt Virginia sighed. With complete naturalness she'd taken over her mother's rocker, even though she wasn't the firstborn.

"I just listen to them," she said to her sisters. "They don't realize no one alive is as old as a tree . . ."

Laura didn't want to tell her aunts anything. She would only talk to her grandfather. She tugged on the sleeve of his black frock coat. Grandfather, there's an enormous lady in the forest, you have to see her. Child, what are you talking about? I'll take you to her, Grandfather, if you don't come, no one will believe me, come on, if you come, I won't be afraid of her, I'll hug her.

She imagined: I'll hug her and bring her back to life, that's what the stories Grandmama used to tell me say, all you have to do is hug a statue to bring it to life.

She berated herself: how little time her decision to keep the secret of the great forest lady lasted.

Her grandfather took her by the hand and smiled, he shouldn't smile on a day of mourning, but this pretty little girl with her long, straight hair and more and more well-defined features, her baby fat disappearing—her grandfather could tell that day, before Laura saw it in any mirror or even dreamed it, how she'd look when she grew up, with very long arms and legs and a prominent nose and thinner lips than any of the other girls her age (lips like those of her writing aunt Virginia)—this child was reborn life, Cosima restored, one life continued in another and he its guardian, keeper of a soul, which required the living memory of a couple, Cosima and Felipe, to prolong itself and find new energy in the life of a girl, of this girl, the deeply moved old man said to himself—he was sixty-six! Cosima was fifty-seven when she died!—and Laura reached the clearing in the forest.

"This is the statue, Grandfather."

Don Felipe laughed.

"This is a ceiba, child. Careful now. Look at how beautiful it is but also dangerous. Do you see? It's covered over with nails, except they aren't nails but pointy spines like daggers which the ceiba produces to protect itself, don't you see? Swords come out of the ceiba's body, the tree arms itself, so no one will come near it, so no one will hug it." Her grandfather smiled. "What a naughty ceiba!"

Then bad news came. There was a miners' strike in Cananea, another strike in the textile factory at Río Blanco, right here in the state of Veracruz, the bodies of strikers killed by the federal army were carried from Orizaba to the sea in open boxcars, so everyone could see the corpses and learn a lesson.

"Do you think Don Porfirio will fall?"

"Are you serious? This shows that Porfirio Díaz has the same energy he always had, even if he's seventy-five."

"Boss, we're going to have to cut down the *chalacahuites*."

"It's a pity we have to cut down trees that shade the coffee."

"That's when coffee prices are high. Right now, prices are very low. We're better off cutting down the trees and selling them as lumber."

"It's God's will. They'll grow again."

## 3. Veracruz: 1910

H E WOULD ARRIVE LATE. He would arrive early. Always, either too late or too early. He would turn up unexpectedly for dinner. Other times, he wouldn't turn up at all.

As soon as her husband, Fernando Díaz, had her brought to Veracruz, Leticia established—as if they were the most natural things in the world, not feeling she was imposing them on anyone—the same schedules and the same order she'd had in her previous life on the Catemaco coffee plantation. It didn't matter how boisterous and disorderly the port was: the sun still rose at the same time whether she was next to the lake or the sea. Breakfast at six, midday meal at one, light supper at seven, or dinner, in special cases, at nine.

Veracruz gave Leticia Kelsen its many kinds of shellfish and fish, and Laura's mother would combine them in marvelous ways: octopus in its ink with white rice, fried plantain with beans, refried of course; white snapper from the Gulf swimming in onion, peppers, and olives; meat shredded with cilantro or congealed in dark sauces called "tablecloth stainers"; monastic desserts and worldly coffees—slowing you down, knowing all about heat and insomnia, friend to both siestas and moons.

Coffee could be had at any hour of the day in the celebrated Café de la Parroquia, where a wasp's nest of waiters with white aprons and bow ties ran through the buzz of customers carrying rolls and *huevos rancheros*, like underpaid magicians in a carnival where performances went on around the clock, poured coffee and hot milk into glasses with astonishing simultaneity from acrobatic heights. The great silver coffeemaker, imported from Germany, presided over all this, occupying the center-rear of the café like a silver queen decorated with faucets, spigots, foam, steam, and factory seals. *Lebrecht und Justus Krüger, Lübeck, 1887.*

Also from Europe came illustrated magazines and the novels for which Laura's father, Fernando Díaz, would impatiently wait every month, when the packet boats from Southampton and Le Havre dropped anchor in Veracruz for the sole purpose, or so it seemed, of satisfying his needs. There he'd be, the accountant waiting with his boater firmly in place to protect him from a sun heavy as a wet sheet. With the suit that had made people stop and stare in Catemaco when Fernando courted and won Leticia. With his walking stick with its ivory handle in one hand. His other hand in that of Laura, his twelve-year-old daughter.

"The magazines, Papa, first the magazines."

"No. First the books for your brother. Tell him they're here."

"It's better if I bring them to his room."

"As you please."

"Is it proper for a twelve-year-old girl to go into the bedroom of a boy who's almost twenty?" asked Leticia as soon as Laura, still skipping like a child, left the room.

"It's more important they love and trust each other," her husband, Fernando Díaz, would answer calmly.

Leticia would shrug her shoulders and blush, remembering the moral lessons of the cynical, fugitive priest Elzevir Almonte. But she quickly glanced around the living room of her new house proudly. It was on the upper floor above the Bank of the Republic, of which her husband, for just a month now, was the president.

He had kept his word. Through hard work, just as he'd promised, he had risen from teller to accountant to president, by sacrificing, as he said to Leticia, twelve years of conjugal life, of being close to Laura, and of domestic order, since his home, if he dared call it that, had consisted of men living alone. Fernando and his son Santiago, fruit of his first marriage to the deceased Elisa Obregón—no matter how diligent the servants might be—would leave their cigars burning here or extinguished there, a book open on a bed, their socks lost under the same bed, and, finally, the bed itself unmade for all too long.

Now Santiago could stretch out again on his bed, but now in a comfortable, almost sumptuous new home. His long nightshirt with its ruffled front looked like a nest of doves. He brought his legs together when his half sister Laura walked in carrying the books, holding them from below, her hands linked like an unstable swing, the pile forming an abbreviated Tower of Pisa that Santiago quickly caught before Anatole France and Paul Bourget spilled their words on the floor.

As soon as Santiago and Laura met, they "sympathized" with each other, as the expression of the times put it, and though of course their meeting was inevitable, both Leticia and Fernando had, each for different reasons, fears that at first they refrained from communicating to each other. The mother feared that a girl at the threshold of adolescence would suffer improper influences, even contacts, from the nearness of a young man almost eight years older than she. Her brother, yes of course, but in any case a stranger, a novelty in her life. Wasn't there novelty enough in having moved, as they always knew they would even if they'd postponed it so often, away from rural life and Don Felipe Kelsen's patriarchy, from the mutilated grandmother and the three busy aunts, to a new life, to being separated from her mother, who stopped sleeping in the same bedroom with her to move to the bed of the father, who until then had slept alone, abandoning the child, who could not sleep with her half brother (as was her first, naive desire)? Can bars be put up to keep out waves on the lake?

41

"We women mature rapidly in the tropics, Fernando. I married you when I was barely sixteen."

She didn't tell the whole truth. In the faces of my sisters and my half sister, I saw a solitary life, the three of them fated to be spinsters because they wanted other things—Virginia, to write; Hilda, to be a concert pianist—and knew they'd never have any of them yet would never, never give them up, and their silent, painful devotion would mean they'd write poems and play the piano surrounded by invisible readers and listeners except for the two people for whom "their sonnets and sonatas were a reproach": their parents, Felipe and Cosima. María de la O, on the other hand, would never marry, out of simple gratitude. Cosima had saved her from a miserable fate. María de la O would be eternally faithful to the family who took her in. Leticia—a child who quickly learned the rules of an advantageous silence in a home that divided unequally the fortune of Don Felipe and the misfortunes of Cosima and the other daughters—decided she'd get married as soon as possible and almost without conditions so as to escape the fate of the dissipated, erased, gray, and shapeless dreams of the other daughters, dreams that transformed the three Catemaco women into pantomime actresses performing in the fog. She married Fernando and saved herself from spinsterhood. She had a daughter and saved herself from being childless. She remained among her own and saved herself—this was her excuse—from ingratitude. Her husband, Fernando, understood her. He needed time to establish a career so that he could give Leticia and Laura a good life at the same time that he gave his son Santiago the attention a motherless boy required; so to both Fernando and Leticia their bizarre agreement seemed not only reasonable but bearable.

What consolidated it was the need Felipe Kelsen came to have for his son-in-law in those years—when President Porfirio Díaz grew older, the strikes were bloodily repressed, revolutionary uprisings erupted in the north of the country, anarcho-syndicalist activity started up right there in Veracruz, Don Porfirio made politically ill-timed statements to the North American reporter James Creelman ("Mexico is ripe for democracy"), and Madero and the Flores Magón brothers mounted their anti-reelection campaign: all this spread disquiet in the markets, Veracruz lost ground in its competition with the Cuban sugar industry, which had been restored after the cruel war between Spain and the United States, and not even the traditional appeal of the German business community there to the German Mining Company had any effect. War in Europe was possible. The Balkans were catching fire. France and England had concluded the Entente Cordiale, and Germany, Italy, and Austria-Hungary had signed the Triple Alliance: the only thing left to do was to dig trenches and wait for the spark that would set Europe ablaze. Capital was being set aside to finance the war and raise commodity prices, not to extend credit to German-Mexican plantations.

"I have two hundred thousand coffee trees producing fifteen hundred hundredweights of beans," added Don Felipe. "What I need is credit, what I need is money."

Not to worry, his son-in-law Fernando Díaz told him. By now he was president of the Bank of the Republic in Veracruz, and he would see to it that credit was granted to Don Fernando and the beautiful plantation "La Peregrina"—the name a reminder of the lovely German bride Doña Cosima. The bank would make up the amount by handing over the crop to the commercial houses in the port, taking a commission and crediting the rest back to the Kelsen plantation. And Leticia, together with her child Laura, could finally come to live with the paterfamilias Don Fernando Díaz and his son Santiago, all gathered together under the roof of the presidency of the Bank of the Republic in Veracruz.

How different it was for Laura to live in a house surrounded by streets instead of fields, to see people she didn't know pass under the balconies all day, to live on the second floor and have the business downstairs, to lick the railing on the balcony because it tasted of salt, and to stare at the Veracruz sea—slow, leaden, heavy, shining after the storm that had just passed and while it was getting ready for the next one, giving off hot vapors instead of the coolness of the lake . . . and the forest presided over by the statue of the jewel-covered giant woman, which she saw, which she did not dream, which was no ceiba: Grandfather Felipe must have thought she was such a fool.

"Thick walls, the sound of running water, moving air, and lots of hot coffee: that's the best defense against the heat," declared Leticia, more and more self-confident now that she was mistress of her own home, free finally of paternal tutelage and rediscovering in her husband what had delighted her when they were courting, that time they met at the Candlemas festivals in Tlacotalpan.

He was a tender man. Efficient and conscientious in his work. Determined to better himself. He read English and French, although he was more Anglophile than Francophile. But he knew that a strange void kept him from understanding the mysteries of life, secrets that are an essential part of each personality, without prejudging others to be good or evil. He read many novels to make up for the defect. Ultimately, however, for Fernando things were as they were—steady work, doing more than was expected, moderation in pleasure, and personalities (his own or others') a mystery to be respected.

For this man, now fully formed at the age of forty-five, to inquire into the souls of others was to gossip, was the prying of old busybodies. Leticia always loved him because, at the age of twenty-eight (even if she'd married when she was sixteen, she shared these virtues and, like him, was helpless when confronted by the mystery of others. Although the only time she used that formulation—"others"—Fernando dropped the Thomas Hardy novel he was reading and said, Never say "others," because it sounds as if they were superfluous, mere extras. "I suggest you always give people names."

"Even if I don't know them?"

"Make up names. Features or clothes will always tell you who a person is."

"Mr. Cross-eyed, Mr. Ugly, Mr. Street Sweeper?" laughed Leticia, her husband joining her in the silent happiness peculiar to him.

The Hunk. From the time she was a child, Laura had heard that nickname applied to the former army officer who cut off Grandmama Cosima's fingers, and now she wanted to *confide* that story (I mean tell it in secret, she thought) to her handsome half brother, dressed at twelve noon, all in white, with a high, starched collar and silk tie, linen

jacket and trousers, and high black boots which laced up in a complicated way with hooks and eyelets. His features, more than regular, were
of an attractive symmetry that reminded Laura of the araucaria leaves
in the tropical forest. In him, everything was exactly the same on both
sides, and if he had a shadow when he got out of bed, the shadow
would accompany him like an identical twin, never absent, never bent
over, always next to Santiago.

As if to give the lie to the perfection of a face that was exactly symmetrical, he wore fragile eyeglasses with scarcely visible silver frames.
They deepened his gaze whenever he used them, but that didn't make
his eyes wander when he took them off. Which is why he could play
with them—hide them for a moment in his jacket pocket, use them
like banderillas the next, toss them into the air and casually catch them
before putting them back in his pocket. Laura Díaz had never seen
such a being.

"I've finished college. My father has given me a sabbatical."

"What's that?"

"A year of freedom to decide seriously about my vocation. I'm reading. As you can see."

"Well, I really don't see much of you, Santiago. You're always out of
sight."

The boy laughed, hooked his walking stick on his forearm, and tousled the hair of his little sister, furious now at his condescension.

"I'm already twelve. Almost."

"If I were only fifteen, I'd carry you off," laughed Santiago.

Don Fernando, from the window of his office, saw his slim, elegant
son pass by, and now he feared his wife would reproach him, not so
much for the twelve years of separation and waiting, not so much for
the shared life of father and son that had excluded mother and daughter . . . they, after all, had been happy to be with each other, and the
separation had been agreed upon and understood as a bond of permanent, sure values that would give the family stability, when the time
came, in their shared life. Indeed, Don Fernando was certain that the
test to which they had subjected themselves not only was exceptional

in the era they were living in, with its endless engagements, but would give a kind of retrospective halo (let's call it, instead of test, sacrifice, anticipation, wager, or merely postponed happiness) to their marriage.

The fear was now of something else. Santiago himself.

His son was proof that all the nurturing will of a father cannot force a son to conform to the paternal mold. Fernando wondered, If I'd given him complete freedom, would he have conformed more? Did I make him different by proposing my own values to him?

The answer remained on the edge of that mystery Fernando Díaz had no idea how to pierce: the personality of others. Who was his son: what did he want, what was he doing, what was he thinking? The father had no answers. When, at the end of secondary school, Santiago asked him for a year before deciding on going on to a university, Fernando was happy to grant it to him. Everything seemed to coincide in the ordered mind of the accountant and bank president: the graduation of the son and the arrival of his second wife along with his second child, and now Santiago's absence on "sabbatical" (Fernando told himself, somewhat shamefaced), would let the new home life take shape without problems.

"Where are you going to spend your sabbatical?"

"Right here in Veracruz, Papa. Quite clever, don't you think? It's something I know little about—this port, my own city. What do you think?"

He'd been so studious, such a reader, such a fine writer throughout his adolescence. He'd published in magazines for young people: poetry, art criticism, and literary criticism. The poet Salvador Díaz Mirón, his teacher, praised him as a young man of promise. Who assured me, Fernando Díaz asked himself, that all this augured continuity? Peace, perhaps, but continuity in the end? Did it assure rebellion instead of conformity, the fatal exception? Fernando had imagined that his son, after finishing at the Preparatoria, when he asked for the year off would spend it traveling—his father had set aside the necessary money—and would return, having purged his young man's curiosity, to take up his literary career again, his university studies, and then start a family. As in the English novels, he would have done his Grand Tour.

"I'm staying here, Papa, if you don't mind."

"Not at all, my boy. This is your house. Don't be silly."

He had nothing to fear. Fernando Díaz's private life was of an exemplary spotlessness. Concerning his past, it was well known that his first wife, Elisa Obregón, a descendant of immigrants from the Canary Islands, died giving birth to Santiago; that for the first seven years of the boy's life, the now recently graduated poet lived under the protection— and thanks to the charity, almost—of a Jesuit priest from the city of Orizaba; that when Don Fernando remarried, he kept his new family far away in Catemaco but brought Santiago to live with him in Veracruz.

Asked to explain himself in one or another Veracruz gathering, this honorable if not very imaginative man of numbers said that sometimes it was necessary to defer satisfaction while doing one's duty, which, ultimately, redoubled satisfaction.

These arguments, which seemed to convince people, merely provoked the scorn of Salvador Díaz Mirón: "I never would have suspected it, Don Fernando, but you are more baroque than the poet Góngora himself."

But just as Don Fernando could not penetrate the mysteries of others, no one penetrated his—perhaps because they didn't exist. Except for the perfect bride, his second wife, Leticia, who simply was equal to him. Yet the initial arrangement between the two of them was indeed baroque. For eleven years, Leticia, accompanied by her half sister, María de la O, would visit Fernando in Veracruz once a month, and he would take a room at the Hotel Diligencias so they could be alone while María de la O would discreetly disappear. (Only the grandmother without fingers, Doña Cosima Kelsen, suspected where she went.) Every three months, in turn, Fernando would return to Catemaco, greet the German grandfather, and play with little Laura.

At the port, father and son lived in adjoining rooms in a boarding-house, Santiago in the bedroom so he could study and write, Fernando in the living room, as if in free time between business appointments.

Each one had his washbasin and his mirror for his personal grooming. The public bath was two streets away. A black woman with cloudlike hair took care of the chamber pots. They took their meals at the boardinghouse.

Now everything changed. The president's residence above the bank had all the comforts—a big living room with a view of the docks, a wicker sofa because it was cooler, tables of varnished wood with marble tops, rockers, bibelots, electric lights as well as old candelabras, commodes with vitrines that displayed all sorts of Dresden figurines—licentious courtiers, daydreaming shepherdesses—and a pair of typical genre paintings. In the first, a little rascal teases a sleeping dog with a stick; in the second the dog bites the calf of a boy who can't manage to jump over the wall and falls back bawling . . .

"*Let sleeping dogs lie,*" Mr. Díaz would invariably say in English whenever he looked, even out of the corner of his eye, at the paintings.

The dining room: with a table big enough to seat twelve and, once again, vitrines, these filled with china hand-decorated with scenes from the Napoleonic Wars, some of them edged with gold reliefs in the form of garlands.

A sort of antechamber or *pantry*, as Fernando called it, again in English: this connected the dining room and the kitchen redolent with herbs, stews, and tropical fruits that dripped with juice when cut in half, a kitchen of braziers and griddles, where the fire under the skillets and pots required untiring hands waving straw fans to keep it alive. Nothing satisfied Doña Leticia more than going from one brick-and-iron oven to the next, steadily fanning the embers to keep the broths, the rice, the sauces bubbling as she stirred them, while the Indian women from the Zongolica mountains made tortillas and the little black man Zampaya watered the flowerpots in the corridors, muttering a hymn to himself:

*Black Zampayita's dance,*
*you can see it in a glance,*
*will surely cure your every pain,*
*even help you weight to gain.*

Sometimes, little Laura, with her head in her mother's lap, would listen delightedly, for the thousandth time, to the story of how her parents met at the Candlemas festival in Tlacotalpan, a doll-house-sized village where on February 2 everyone, even the old-timers, would come at the sound of clarinets and guitars to dance on wooden floors in the plazas next to the Papaloapan River, along which passes the Virgin, from boat to boat, while all the neighbors bet on whether the Mother of God has the same hairdo as last year, hair that once belonged to Dulce María Estévez, or whether it was the hair given to her, at great sacrifice, by María Elena Muñoz. After all, every year the Virgin was supposed to have a fresh new hairdo, and it was a great honor for decent young ladies to sacrifice their hair to St. Mary.

Rows of men on horseback take off their hats when the Virgin passes, but the Veracruz widower Don Fernando Díaz, now thirty-three years old, has eyes only for the tall, slender, extremely refined Miss Leticia Kelsen (ask, and anyone will tell you), dressed in a stiff, white, parchmentlike fabric and barefoot, at the age of sixteen, not because she lacks shoes but because (as she explained to Fernando when he offered her his arm so she wouldn't slip in the mud along the riverbank) in Tlacotalpan the greatest pleasure is to walk barefoot on grassy streets. Did he know any other city with grass growing in the streets? No, laughed Fernando, and he himself, to the glee and shock of the citizens of Tlacotalpan, took off his boots with complicated hooks and eyes and his red-and-white-striped socks that sent Miss Leticia into paroxysms of laughter.

"They look like clown socks!"

He blushed and blamed himself for having done something so alien to his regular, measured habits. She fell in love with him right on the spot, because he took off his shoes and turned as red as the stripes on his socks.

"What happened next, what happened next?" asked Laura, who knew the story by heart.

"No one can describe that town, you have to see it," added her father.

"What's it like, what's it like?"

"Like a toy," Doña Leticia went on. "All the houses are one story high, all even, but each one is painted a different color."

"Blue, pink, green, red, orange, white, yellow, violet . . ." enumerated the child.

"The most beautiful walls in the world," concluded her father, lighting up a cigar.

"A little toy village . . ."

Now that they had the big house in the port of Veracruz, the Kelsen sisters came to visit, and Don Fernando would tease them: Weren't you three going to get married as soon as Leticia, Laura, and I got back together?

"And who would take care of María de la O?"

"They've always got an excuse," laughed Don Fernando.

"That's the absolute truth," María de la O agreed with him. "I'll stay and take care of my father. Hilda and Virginia can go and get married whenever they like."

"I don't need a husband," exclaimed Virginia the writer, laughing . . . "*Je suis la belle ténébreuse* . . . I don't need anyone to admire me."

Hilda the pianist interrupted the laughing banter, putting an end to the subject with words no one understood: "Everything is hidden and lies in wait for us."

Fernando glanced at Leticia, Leticia at Laura, and the girl copied the whitest aunt, moving her hands as if playing the piano, until Aunt Virginia gave her a sharp crack on the head and Laura held in her rage and her tears.

The visit of the aunts was an occasion to invite in specimens of Veracruz society. Once it happened that a group had gathered and Aunt María de la O came in late, and a lady said to her: "Girl, how good you've come. Fan me for a while, please. Don't be a lazy darky now, it's so hot . . ."

Laughter ceased instantly. María de la O didn't move. Laura rose, took her arm, and led her to an armchair.

"Sit here, Auntie, I'll be happy to fan the lady first and then you, my dear."

Laura Díaz thinks something changed forever in her life one night when she was awakened by a harsh moan in her brother Santiago's bedroom, which was next door to hers. She was frightened, but she did not run on tiptoe into the hall and to the boy's door until she heard the painful groaning again. Then she went in without knocking, and Santiago's face of pain in bed combined with an incredible, unique greeting in his eyes, gratitude for her presence, even if his words contradicted his looks: Laura, don't make any noise, go back to your room, don't wake up anyone.

The arm of his shirt was ripped open from the shoulder down, and with his right hand he was squeezing his left forearm. Could the little girl help him in any way?

"No. Yes. Go back to bed and don't say a word to anyone. Swear. I can take care of myself."

Laura made the sign of the cross. For the first time, someone needed her, even if he didn't say so, it was not she who was asking for something, she was being asked for something, with words that said "no" but meant "yes, Laura, help me."

From that night on, they went out every Saturday to stroll along the seawall. They walked hand in hand, and Laura felt Santiago's hand was rigid, tense, while the wound on his arm healed. It was their secret, and he knew he was counting on her and she felt newly proud because of this. Also, in this contact with her brother Laura felt for the first time that she belonged to Veracruz, that the sea and the sky met here in a single vibrant bay, sky and sea together, and blowing hard so that behind Veracruz the plain vibrated, too, luminous and clean-swept until it faded into the forest. To him she could tell the stories about Catemaco. He would believe that a woman of stone standing in the middle of the forest was a statue, not a tree.

"Of course. It's a figure made by the Zapotal culture. Didn't your grandfather know that?"

Laura shook her head, no, Grandfather did not know everything, she now realized, and the girl's curls shook, dark and scented with soap.

"My father was right when he said that Santiago's got the lion's share of the family's intelligence and the rest of us have leftovers."

Santiago apologized for laughing, saying that Laura knew more than he did about trees, flowers, nature. About all that he knew nothing, he knew only that he wanted to disappear one day, like that, to become forest, to be transformed into one of those trees the girl knew so well, the *palo rojo*, the araucaria, the *trueno* with its perfect yellow flowers, the laurel . . .

"No, that's a bad one."

"But it's pretty."

"It destroys everything, eats everything up."

"And the ceiba."

"No, not the ceiba either. The branches fill up with starlings and they shit on everything."

Laughing to die, Santiago went on with the fig tree, the purple iris, the tulip, and she, yes, those, yes, Santiago, laughing now not like a girl, he said to himself in surprise, laughing like a woman, like something else who was no longer the little girl Laura with dark curls and the scent of soap. With Santiago she felt that until now she'd been just like Li Po, the Chinese doll. Now everything was going to be different.

"No, you can't hug the ceiba. Daggers are born from its body."

She glanced at her brother's wounded arm, but said nothing.

He began to wait for her every Saturday at the door of the house they shared, as if he'd come from somewhere else, and brought her a present—a little bouquet of flowers, a conch to hear the sound of the sea, a starfish, a postcard, a paper boat—while Leticia, watching nervously from the roof terrace where she personally was hanging out the wash (as in Catemaco; she adored the coolness of freshly washed sheets against the body), saw the couple stroll away, not knowing that her husband, Fernando, was doing the same from the living-room balcony.

Laura received something more on those strolls than seashells, flowers, and starfish. Her half brother spoke to her as if she were older, more than the indecisive twelve she was, as if she were nineteen or twenty or even older. Did he need to blow off steam with someone, or did he really take her seriously? In any case did he think she could understand everything he was telling her? For Laura, it was marvelous enough that he took her for a walk, that he brought her things—not the little gifts but the things he carried within himself, the things he told her, what his company gave her.

One afternoon when he didn't appear for their rendezvous, she stood there, leaning against the building wall (whose lower floors were the bank offices) and feeling so unprotected in the siesta-hour city that she was on the verge of running back to her room, but that seemed like a desertion, a cowardly act (a concept she didn't fully understand although from then on she knew the feeling), and she thought it would be better to get lost in the tropical forest, where she could hide and grow up alone, in her own time, without this boy who was so handsome and intelligent who was sweeping her along all too quickly to an age that was not yet her own . . .

She started walking, and when she turned the corner she found Santiago leaning against a different wall. They laughed. They kissed. They'd made a mistake. They forgave each other.

"I was just thinking that out at the lake it would be I who would bring you to see things."

"Without you, I'd be lost in the forest, Laura. I'm from here, from the city, from the port. Nature frightens me."

She asked why without saying anything.

"It will outlast you. And me."

They walked to a certain spot by the docks, where he stopped, so immersed in thought that she became afraid for him, just as she'd become afraid when she heard him say that he sometimes wanted to go into the forest she loved so well and get lost there, never come out, never see a human face again.

"What do they expect of me, Laura?"

"Everyone says you're super-smart, that you write and talk beautifully. Father is always saying you have promise."

"He's a good man. But he's just expressing fond hopes. One day I'll show you what I write."

"I can't wait!"

"It isn't great. It's correct. It's competent."

"Isn't that enough, Santiago?"

"No, not at all. Look at it this way: if there's one thing I hate it's to be one of the herd. That's what Father is, excuse me for saying so, a good little lamb from the professional herd. What you can't be is part of an artistic herd, just one more artist or one more writer. That would kill me, Laura, I'd rather be no one than be mediocre."

"You aren't, Santiago. Don't say things like that. You're the best, I swear it."

"And you're the prettiest, I'm telling you."

"Oh, Santiago, don't always try to be the best of the first. Wouldn't you be better off as the best of the second?"

He pinched her cheek, and they laughed again, but they returned home in silence. Their parents didn't have the nerve to say anything because for Fernando it was evil to assume sin where there is none, the way the priest Elzevir did in Catemaco, who succeeded only in ruining people with imagined guilt, and because for Leticia—I know I don't really know my son, for me that boy is a mystery, but you do know everything about Laura and trust her, isn't that so?

He walked her back to that same spot on the docks the next Saturday, and told her to look at the rails, at the freight cars that came right up here loaded with bodies—the Río Blanco workers murdered by order of Don Porfirio for going on strike and sticking to it so bravely, brought right here and tossed into the sea, the dictator stays in power only by means of blood, the rebel Yaqui Indians shackled and taken out to sea near Sonora and thrown overboard, the Cananea miners shot on his orders in a place called the National Valley, hundreds of workers enslaved right here in Veracruz, the liberals locked up in the Ulúa fort, followers of Madero and the Flores Magón brothers, anarcho-syndicalists like the Spanish relatives of my mother, who came from the Canary Islands, Laura, revolutionaries. Laura, revolutionaries are people who are asking for something very simple for Mexico, democracy, elections, land, education, jobs, no reelection of the incumbent president. Don Porfirio Díaz has been in power for thirty years.

"I apologize, Laura. I can't even spare a twelve-year-old girl my speeches."

Revolutionaries. That night the word echoed in Laura Díaz's head, and again the next, and the night after that. She'd never heard it, and when she went back to the coffee plantation on a visit with her mother, she asked her grandfather what it meant and the aged face of the socialist Felipe Kelsen clouded over for an instant. What is a revolutionary?

"It's an illusion people should give up at the age of thirty."

"Hmm. Santiago is only now turning twenty."

"That's just it. Tell your brother to hurry up."

Don Felipe was playing chess in the patio of the country house with an Englishman wearing filthy white gloves. His granddaughter's question caused him to lose a bishop and be castled. The old German said nothing more on the subject, but the Englishman persevered. "Another revolution? Why? Surely they're all dead."

"As long as you're at it, Sir Richard, you might wish for no more wars, because if one should come, you're going to see more dead." Don Felipe was trying to shift Laura's attention to the Englishman in gloves and to distract him from the game.

"And besides, with you a German and me British, well, what is there to say? Fraternal enemies!"

At that, as Don Felipe protested he was no longer German but Mexican, he allowed his king to be cornered. The Englishman shouted checkmate. Just four years later, Don Felipe and Don Ricardo stopped speaking. Each, deprived of his chess partner, died of boredom and sadness. The cannons at Ypres blasted away, and the trenches witnessed the slaughter of young English and German soldiers. Only then did Grandfather Felipe reveal something to his daughters and his granddaughter.

"An incredible thing. He wore those white gloves because he had cut off the tips of his own fingers to purge himself of guilt. In India, the English cut off the fingertips of cotton weavers so as to keep them from competing with the cotton factories in Manchester. There are no people crueler than the English."

"*La pérfida Albión,*" Aunt Virginia said in Spanish, then insisting, "*Perfidious Albion.*"

"And what about the Germans, Grandfather?"

"Well, my dear. There are no people more savage than Europeans. Wait and see. All of them."

"*Über alles,*" Virginia sang under her breath, breaking her father's rule.

Laura would see nothing. Nothing more than the body of her brother Santiago Díaz, summarily executed by firing squad during November 1910 for conspiracy against the federal government and for being linked to other Veracruz plotters—liberals, syndicalists, and pro-Madero men like the brothers Carmen and Aquiles Serdán, who that same month were shot in Puebla.

It did not occur to Don Fernando Díaz, during the wake for his son, with his bullet-pierced body in the living room above the bank, that the serenity of the young man in a white suit, his face paler than usual but his features intact, and with the wounds in his chest, might be disturbed one more time by police intervention.

"This is an official building."

"But, sir, this is my house. It's the house of my dead son. I demand respect."

"Wakes for rebels are held in the cemetery. All right, then, everybody out."

"Who will help me?"

Fernando, Leticia, Zampayita the black man, the Indian maids, Laura with a flower between her incipient breasts, together they carried the coffin. But it was Laura who said, Papa, Mama, he loved the seawall, he loved the sea, he loved Veracruz, this is his grave, please, clinging to her mother's skirt, staring imploringly at her father and the servants, and they took her advice, as if each feared that if Santiago was buried, he might be exhumed someday to be shot once more.

How long it took her brother's white body to disappear into the grave of the sea, the body attached to the cushioned bed of death, the lid of the coffin deliberately open so everyone could see him disappear slowly on that night without waves, Santiago becoming more and more handsome, sadder and sadder, missed more and more, the scene more and more painful as he sank within the open casket, his head soon to be crowned by algae and devoured by sharks along with all the unwritten poems, his face protected by the condemned man's last wish: "Please don't shoot my face."

With no children other than the sea, Santiago slowly disappeared into the sea as if in a mirror that did not distort him but only sent him farther and farther away, little by little, mysteriously, from the mirror of air where he inscribed his hours on earth. Santiago slowly separated from the horizon of the sea, from the promise of youth. Suspended in the sea, he asked those who loved him, Let me disappear by becoming the sea, I could not become forest as I told you one day, Laura, I lied only about one thing, little sister, I did have things to tell, I did have things to see, I wasn't going to keep silent out of fear of being mediocre because I came to know you, Laura, and every night I fell asleep dreaming, to whom shall I tell everything if not to Laura? In a dream, I decided I would write for you, precious girl, even if you didn't find out, even if we never saw each other again, everything would be for you and you would know despite everything, you would receive my words knowing they belonged to you, you would be my only reader, for you not a single word of mine would be lost, now that I'm sinking into the eternity of the sea, I expel the little air I have left in my lungs, I make a gift to you of a few bubbles, my love, it's an intolerable pain for me to say goodbye because I don't know to whom I'll be able to speak from now on, I don't . . .

Laura remembered that her brother had wanted to lose himself forever in the forest, to become forest. She tried to make herself into sea with him, but the only thing that came to mind was to describe the lake where she grew up, how strange, Santiago, to have grown up next to a lake and never really to have seen it, it's true that it's a very big lake, almost a small sea, but I remember it in little pieces, here is the place where the aunts would swim before the priest Elzevir Almonte came, over here is where the fishermen would land, over here they'd put the oars, but the lake, Santiago, to see it the way you knew how to see the ocean, that I can't do, I'm going to have to imagine the place where I grew up, little brother, you are going to make me imagine it, the lake and everything else, right at this very minute, I'm knowing it, from now on, I'm not going to hope for things to happen, I'm not going to let them happen without paying attention to them, you are going to make me imagine the life you did not live but I swear you will live at my side, in my head, in my stories, in my fantasies, I won't let you escape from my life, Santiago, you are the most important thing that ever happened to me, I'm going to be faithful to you by always imagining you, living in your name, doing what you did not do, I don't know how, my handsome and young and dead Santiago, I'm going to be frank with you and I don't know how, but I swear I'll do it.

That was all she thought as she turned away from the remains under the waves and went home to the house next to the arcades, prepared, despite her thoughts, to be a child again, to stop being a big girl, to lose the premature maturity Santiago had momentarily given her. She asked if she could have his bullet-ridden glasses and imagined him without his spectacles, waiting for the bullets, having put them in his shirt pocket.

The next day the little black man swept the halls as if nothing had happened, singing as always:

> *You dance putting your arm*
> *around your partner's waist*
> *if she lets you, lets you,*
> *as she will surely do . . .*

## 4. San Cayetano: 1915

YOU THINK YOU KNEW Santiago well? You think your brother gave everything to you? How little you know of a man so complex, he gave you only a part of himself. He gave you what was left of his boyish soul. Another part he gave to his family, another to his poetry, another to politics. And passion, the passion of love, to whom did he give that?"

Doña Leticia, in silence, wanted to finish the hem of the ball gown.

"Stop fidgeting, child."

"It's just that I'm very nervous, Mama."

"And for no reason, a ball is nothing extraordinary."

"For me it is! It's the first time, Mutti."

"You'll get used to these things."

"What a shame." Laura smiled.

"Quiet. Let me finish. This child can't stand still!"

As soon as Laura slipped on the pale yellow dress, she ran to the mirror, but she did not see the modern ball gown her mother, as skillful in couture as in every domestic labor, had copied from the most recent issue of *La Vie Parisienne*, which, though it came late because of the war in Europe and the distance to Xalapa from Veracruz, reached them regularly. Paris had abandoned the complicated, uncomfortable styles of the nineteenth century with their Versailles remnants of crinolines, stays, and corsets. Now the fashion was *streamlined*, as Don Fernando the Anglophile would say, which is to say, as fluid as a river, simplified and linear, fitted to the real forms of the feminine body, slender and revealing from the shoulders through the bust and waist, then suddenly flaring out from the hips. Laura's Parisian dress was taken in between the hips and the calves with a lot of draping, as if a queen had picked up the train of her gown, but the train, instead of being wrapped around her forearm, had under its own power draped itself around her legs.

Laura stared at herself, not at the gown. Her seventeen years had accentuated but not yet resolved the qualities hinted at when she was twelve. She had a strong face, the forehead too wide, the nose too big and aquiline, lips too thin, though she did like her own eyes, to tell the truth; they were a light chestnut, almost golden; sometimes, at daybreak or sunset, they were truly golden. She looked as if she were dreaming while awake.

"But my nose, Mama . . ."

"You're lucky. Just look at those Italian film actresses. They've all got big beaks . . . distinct profiles. Don't tell me you'd like to be a little pie-faced pug-nose. Come, come."

"But my forehead, Mama . . ."

"If you don't like it, hide it with bangs."

"But my lips . . ."

"With lipstick you can make them whatever size you please. And just look, sweetheart, what beautiful eyes God gave you . . ."

"I'll go along with that, Mama."

"You vain little thing." Leticia smiled.

Laura didn't dare think ahead. And if the lipstick is wiped off by kisses, I'm not going to act like a jerk, he'll want to kiss me again, or should I suck in my lips like a little old lady, grab my stomach as if I were about to vomit, and run to the bathroom to put on more lipstick? How complicated it is to become a young woman.

"Don't worry about anything. You look divine. You're going to cause a sensation."

She didn't ask Leticia why she wasn't accompanying her. She would be the only girl there without a chaperon. Wouldn't that make a bad impression? Leticia had already sighed enough, but she intended to leave it at that, recalling the habit of her own mother, Cosima, sitting in the rocking chair in the Catemaco family house. She had sighed enough. As Don Fernando would put it, citing, as usual, an English proverb: *It never rains but it pours.*

The three maiden aunts were in Catemaco taking care of Grandfather Felipe Kelsen, whose ailments were slowly but surely joining forces, as he himself predicted the one time he'd been made to see a doctor in Veracruz. What did he say, Papa? asked the three sisters in one voice, a habit that was ever more deeply rooted in them and of which they were unaware.

"I have bile stones, cardiac arrhythmia, my prostate's the size of a melon, I have diverticulitis, and a touch of emphysema."

His daughters stared at him in fear, anxiety, and shock.

He merely smiled. "Don't worry. Dr. Miquis says that no one of these problems will kill me. But the day when they all join forces, I'll drop like a stone."

Leticia wasn't with her sick father because her husband needed her. After Santiago was executed, the national president of the bank summoned Fernando Díaz to Mexico City.

"This is not a stab in the back, Don Fernando, but you understand only too well that the bank lives on its good relations with the government. I know, of course, that no one is guilty of his son's actions, but the fact is they are our sons—I myself have eight, so I know what I'm talking about—and we are, if not guilty, then at least responsible for what they do, especially when they live at home with us."

"If you don't mind, sir, please get to the point. This conversation is painful for me."

"All right. Your replacement in Veracruz has already been appointed."

Fernando Díaz did not deign to comment. He stared stonily at the national president.

"But don't worry. We're transferring you to our branch in Xalapa. Look, my friend, we aren't punishing you, but we are trying to exercise prudence while at the same time not failing to recognize your merits. It's the same position but in a different city."

"Where no one will associate me with my son."

"No, our children are ours wherever we are."

"Very well, sir. This seems to be a discreet solution. My family and I thank you most sincerely."

Tearing themselves away from the house facing the sea, the rooms above the bank, was difficult for all of them—for Leticia because she was farther from Catemaco, her father, and her sisters, for Fernando because he was being penalized in a cowardly way, and for all three of them because leaving Veracruz meant leaving behind Santiago, his memory, his watery grave.

Laura spent a long time in her brother's bedroom memorizing it, evoking the night when she heard him cry out and discovered he was hurt. Should she have told her parents what had happened? Would that have saved Santiago? Why was what the boy asked her more compelling: Don't say a word. Now, saying goodbye to the room, she tried to imagine everything Santiago could have written there, everything he left blank, a long book of blind pages waiting for the irreplaceable hand, pen, ink, and handwriting of a single man.

"Look, Laura, you write alone, but you use something that belongs to everyone, language. The world lends you language, and you return it to the world. Language is like the world: it will outlive us. Do you understand what I'm saying?"

Don Fernando cautiously approached the girl. He put his hand on her shoulder and said that he too missed Santiago and constantly thought about what his son's life might have been. He'd always said, my son has promise, he's more intelligent than all the others put together, and now, here, the bedroom where the boy was going to spend his sabbatical year would remain solitary, the place where he was going to write his poems. Fernando hugged Laura; she did not want to look into his eyes. We weep for the dead once and only once, and then we try to do what they could no longer do. It isn't possible to love, write, fight, think, or work with tears clouding our eyes and mind; prolonged mourning is a betrayal of the dead person's life.

How different Xalapa was. At night, Veracruz retained—and increased—the heat of the day. Xalapa, in the mountains, had warm days and cold nights. Veracruz had swift, rackety storms, but here the rain became fine, persistent, making everything green and filling a central point in the city—the reservoir behind the El Dique dam, always about to overflow, giving an impression of sadness and security at the same time. It was from the flume that the city's light mist rose to meet the mountain's thick fog; Laura Díaz is remembering when she first came to Xalapa and noted: cold air—rain and rain—birds—women dressed in black—beautiful gardens—cast-iron benches—white statues painted green by the humidity—red tiles—steep narrow streets—market smells and bakeries, wet patios and fruit trees, the aroma of orange trees and the stench of slaughterhouses.

She entered her new home. Everything smelled of varnish. It was a one-story house, for which the family would very soon be thankful. Laura immediately told herself that in this city of intermittent fogs she would let herself be guided by her sense of smell, that that would be the measure of her tranquillity or her disquiet: humidity of parks, abundance of flowers, the many shops, the smell of tanned hides and thick tar, of saddleries and hardware shops, of cotton bales and hemp rope, the smell of shoe shops and pharmacies, of hairdressers and calico. Perfumes of boiled coffee and foamy chocolate. She pretended to be blind. She touched the walls and felt their heat, she opened her eyes and the tile roofs washed by the rain were shining, dangerously pitched, as if they longed for the sun to dry them and the rain to run down the gutters, along the streets, through the gardens, from the sky to the flume, all in motion, in this reticent city, mistress of incessant nature.

The house replicated the Hispanic model prevalent all over Latin

America. Blind, impenetrable walls faced the street, with an unadorned entry, pitched roof, and tiling in place of cornices—a typical "patio house," with public rooms and bedrooms distributed around an open quadrangle filled with large flowerpots and geraniums. Doña Leticia brought along everything she considered hers, the wicker furniture designed for the tropics that gave no protection here from the moisture, the two paintings of the rascal and the snapping dog, which she hung in the dining room.

The kitchen satisfied Leticia; it was her private domain, and in a short time the lady of the house adapted her coastal customs to the tastes of the mountains: she began to make tamales and dumplings dusted with white flour, and to the white rice of Veracruz she now added Xalapa's *chileatole*, a tasty mix of *masa*, fresh sweet corn, chicken, and cream cheese, made in the shape of little mushrooms, almost like sandwiches.

"Careful," said Don Fernando. "This food is going to fatten you—that's how people here protect themselves from the cold, with fat."

"Don't worry. We're a thin family," answered Leticia while she prepared, under the tender and always admiring eyes of her husband, the Xalapeñan *molotes*, fried turnovers filled with beans and minced meat. They made their own bread: the French military occupation a half century before had imposed the baguette as the bread of fashion, though in Mexico, where diminutives are used as a sign of tenderness for both things and people, baguette became *bolillo*, and *telera* were pieces of bread about the size of a hand. Mexico's traditional sweets were not abandoned—the sugar cookies and the *cemita*, covered with caraway seeds, as well as the wonderful sweet breads shaped like conch shells—and the tastiest gift of Spanish bakeries, *churros*, long strips of fried batter cakes covered with sugar and eaten after dipping them in hot chocolate.

Leticia did not completely give up on the octopus and the crabs of the coast, but she stopped missing them because, without thinking about it much, she adapted naturally to life, especially when life gave her, as it did in this new house, an impressive kitchen with a huge oven and a round fireplace.

The one-story house had only one attic space, way back above the rear entrance, the coach gate, which Laura wanted to claim for herself, intuitively, as an homage to Santiago. This was because, in some mute place in her head, the girl believed she was going to fulfill her life, the life of Laura Díaz, in Santiago's name; or perhaps it was Santiago who would go on fulfilling, from death, a life that Laura would incarnate in his name. In any case she associated the promise of her brother with her own space, a high, isolated place where he would have written and she, mysteriously, would find her own vocation, in homage to her dead brother.

"What are you going to be when you grow up?" asked Elizabeth García, the girl who sat next to her in the school run by the Misses Ramos. She had no idea what to say. How could she speak what was secret, incomprehensible for others: I'd like to fulfill the life of my brother Santiago by locking myself away in the attic.

"No," her mother told her. "I'm sorry, but that's where Armonía Aznar lives."

"And who is she? Why does she have any right to the attic?"

"I don't know. Ask your father. It seems she's always lived there, and one condition when we took the house was that we accept her, that no one bother her, or better still, that no one pay any attention to her."

"Is she crazy?"

"Don't be foolish, Laura."

"No," Don Fernando repeated, "Mrs. Aznar is there because in a certain sense she's the owner of the house. She's a Spaniard, or anyway the daughter of Spanish anarcho-syndicalists—many of them came to Mexico when Benito Juárez defeated the Emperor Maximilian. They thought the future of freedom was here. Then, when Porfirio Díaz came to power, they were disillusioned. A lot of them went back to Barcelona, where there was probably more freedom there in the turn-stile governments that Sagasta and Cánovas had arranged than here with Don Porfirio. Others just tossed out their ideals and became busi-nessmen, farmers, and bankers."

"And just what does all that have to do with this lady who lives in the attic?"

"The house belongs to her."

"Our house?"

"We don't own this house, child. We live where the bank tells us to live. When the bank decided to buy this house, Doña Armonía didn't want to sell because she doesn't believe in private property. Understand it as you please, and understand it if you can. The bank offered to let her stay in the attic in exchange for the use of the house."

"But how does she live, how does she eat?"

"The bank gives her everything she needs, telling her the money comes from her comrades in Barcelona."

"Is she crazy?"

"No, just stubborn. She thinks her dreams are realities."

Laura disliked Doña Armonía because, without knowing it, she became a rival for Santiago: she was depriving the young man of a place in the new house.

Armonía Aznar—no one ever saw her—disappeared from Laura's mind when she went to the Misses Ramos' school. These cultured but impoverished young women ran the best private school in Xalapa, the first, besides, to be open to both sexes. Although they weren't twins, the Misses Ramos dressed, wore their hair, spoke, and moved in exactly the same way, so everyone thought they were twins.

"Why would anyone believe that, when all you have to do is look at them to see how different they are?" Laura asked her deskmate Elizabeth García.

"Because they want us to see them that way," answered the radiant blond girl, who always wore white and who, in Laura's eyes, was either very stupid or very clever. It was impossible to know for certain if she pretended to be a fool because she was secretive or if she pretended to be intelligent to hide her stupidity. "Just figure it out. Between the two of them they know more than either one alone. But when you put them together, the one who knows music also turns out to be a mathematician, and the one who recites poetry can also describe heart murmurs. Laura, just think: poets talk about the heart this and the heart that, and it turns out the heart is nothing more than a rather unreliable muscle."

Laura decided she would devise a way to tell the Misses Ramos apart, seeing as how one was one and the other was the opposite, but when it came time to make the distinctions Laura got confused and became mute, wondering: Suppose they truly are one and the same, and both know everything, like the Encyclopaedia Britannica Papa has in his library?

Suppose they say they are the *misses* but they're actually just one *miss*? insisted Elizabeth another day, with a perverse smile. Laura said that then it was a mystery like the Holy Trinity. You simply had to believe in it without knowing anything more. Similarly the Misses Ramos were one who was two who was one, and that was that.

It was hard for Laura to resign herself to this faith, and she wondered if Santiago would have accepted the fiction of the duplicated and united teachers or if, daringly, he would have turned up at night at their house to catch them by surprise in their nightgowns and ascertain that there were two of them. Because at school they both took care never to appear together at the same time. This was the source—intentional or accidental, who knows?—of the mystery. And Santiago would also have climbed the creaking stairs to the attic over the coach house or, as people were now beginning to say, the *garage*. Yet in Xalapa, even at this late date, no one had yet seen a horseless carriage, an "auto-mobile." Besides, the colonial roads wouldn't have allowed motor traffic. The train and the horse were enough to traverse the earth, in the opinion of the writer, Doña Virginia, and if it was the sea, then a ship of war, as that song the rebels sang had it . . .

"And the stagecoach, when Grandmother's fingers were cut off."

The horses and trains of the Revolution had passed though Xalapa but almost without noticing. Those bands of men had the port as their goal, and the Veracruz customs house. It was there they could control the flow of money as well as feed and clothe the troops, not to mention the symbolic value of owning the alternate capital of the country, the place where rebel or constitutional powers established themselves to challenge the government in Mexico City: me, not you. Veracruz had been occupied by the United States Marine Corps in April 1914 in order to put pressure on the dictator, Victoriano Huerta, the murderer of the democrat Madero, for whom young Santiago had given his life.

"What fools these Yankees are," said Don Fernando the Anglophile. "Instead of bringing down Huerta, they transform him into the knight of national independence against the gringos. Who would dare fight against a Latin American dictator, no matter how sinister, when the United States is attacking him? Huerta has used the occupation of Veracruz as a pretext to intensify his conscription of troops, saying his *pelones*, his 'bald boys,' are going to Veracruz to go up against the Yankees, when in fact he's sending them north to fight Pancho Villa and south against Zapata."

The young students of the Xalapa Preparatory School mustered in their French képis and their navy blue uniforms with gold buttons and marched off with their rifles toward Veracruz to fight the gringos. They didn't get there on time. Huerta fell, and the gringos withdrew; Villa and Zapata battled Carranza, the Maximum Leader of Mexico's revolution, and occupied Mexico City; Carranza took refuge in Veracruz until the fearsome General Alvaro Obregón defeated Villa at Celaya in April 1915 and retook Mexico City.

All this passed through Xalapa, sometimes as rumor, sometimes as news; as songs sung as *corridos* and ballads when newsprint was under embargo; and only once as a cavalry charge accompanied by shouts and crackling rifle fire from some rebel group. Leticia closed the windows, threw Laura to the floor and covered her with the mattress. By 1915, it seemed that peace was returning to Mexico, but the habits of the small provincial capital hadn't been much disturbed.

Rumors reached them of a great famine in Mexico City, when the rest of the nation, convulsed and self-regarding, forgot about the luxurious and egoistic capital, stopped sending it meat, fish, corn, beans, tropical fruit, and flour, reducing it to the squalid products of milk cows in the Milpa Alta area and of the gardens scattered between Xochimilco and Ixtapalapa. As usual, there were many flowers in the Valley, but who eats carnations or calla lilies?

The rumors spread: merchants were hoarding what little food there was. Into Mexico City marched General Obregón, whose first act was to make the shopkeepers sweep the city streets, to put them to shame. He emptied their shops and reopened communications so supplies could flow into the famished capital.

This was all rumor. Just to be on the safe side, Doña Leticia slept with a dagger under her pillow.

Photographic images of the Revolution appeared in the newspapers and magazines Don Fernando consumed by the cartload: the dictator Porfirio Díaz was an ancient man with a square face, Indian cheek-bones, white mustache, and a chest covered with medals saying fare-well to the *cowntry* (as he pronounced it) from the German steamship *Ipiranga*, sailing from Veracruz; Madero was a tiny man, bald, with black beard and mustache, dreamy eyes astonished by his triumph in bringing down the tyrant; those eyes announced his own sacrifice at the hands of the sinister General Victoriano Huerta, an executioner with a head like a skull, black sunglasses, and a mouth like that of a serpent, with no lips; Venustiano Carranza was an old man with a white beard and blue sunglasses, whose vocation was to be the national *paterhe*; Obregón was a brilliant young general with blue eyes and haughty mustache, whose arm was shot off during the battle of Celaya; Emil-iano Zapata was a man of silence and mystery, as if a ghost manifesting himself for only a short time: Laura became fascinated with the enor-mous, ardent eyes of this gentleman, whom newspapers referred to as "Attila of the South," in the same way they called Pancho Villa "Cen-taur of the North." Laura had never seen a single photo of Pancho Villa in which he wasn't smiling, showing his white teeth like corn kernels and his little slits of eyes that made him look like an astute Chinese.

Above all, Laura remembered being under the mattress and the scattered shots in the streets below, now that she was staring at herself in the mirror, so straight and tall, "such a cutie pie," as her mother said, making ready to go to her first formal dance.

"Are you sure I should go, Mama?"

"Laura, for God's sake, what can you be thinking about?"

"About Papa."

"Don't worry about him. You know I'll be taking care of him."

It began with the slightest of pains in his knee, to which Don Fernando paid no special attention. Leticia rubbed on some Sloane's Liniment when the pain extended the length of his leg to his waist, but soon her husband complained that he was having difficulty walking and that his arms were numb. One morning he fell to the floor trying to get out of bed, and the doctors had no difficulty in diagnosing a diplegia that would affect his legs first and more intensely than his arms.

"Can it be cured?"

The doctors shook their heads.

"How long will it last?"

"It may last the rest of your life, Don Fernando."

"What about my brain?"

"No effect. You're fine. You'll need help moving, that's all."

This was why the family was thankful the house was on only one level, and María de la O offered to travel to Xalapa and be her brother-in-law's nurse, to take care of him, to push him to the bank in a wheelchair.

"Your grandfather's well taken care of in Catemaco by your Aunts Hilda and Virginia. We talked it over and agreed that I'd come to help your mama."

"What does Papa always say in English? *It never rains but it pours* or something like that? In other words, the thunderstorm is upon us, Auntie."

"Go on, Laura. Just one thing. Don't try to defend me if someone mistreats me. You'll just make trouble for yourself. The important thing is to take care of your father and let my sister Leticia tend to the house."

"Why are you doing this?"

"I owe your father as much as I owe your grandmother, who had me come live with all of you. One day I'll tell you about it."

The double care that fell on the house, added to their mourning for Santiago, did not terrify Doña Leticia. She simply became thinner and more active. But her hair began to turn gray and the lines of her beautiful Rhenish profile slowly but surely covered with extremely fine wrinkles, like the cobwebs that covered sickly coffee bushes.

"You have to go to the ball. Don't even think about it. Nothing is going to happen to your father or to me."

"Swear that if something happens you'll send someone for me."

"For heaven's sake, child. San Cayetano is forty minutes away from here. Besides, it isn't as if you were all alone and helpless. Elizabeth and her mama will be with you. Remember, no one can say anything about you . . . if something were to happen, I'd send Zampaya with the landau."

Elizabeth looked divine, so blond and beautifully shaped as she was at the age of sixteen, although she was shorter and plumper than Laura. And with more décolleté as well, having been shoehorned into a by now old-fashioned, though perhaps also eternal rose-colored taffeta dress with infinite layers of tulle and ruffles.

"Girls, never show your boobs," said Elizabeth's mother, Lucía Dupont, who all her life struggled to decide whether her name was as common in France as it was aristocratic in the United States, although how she could have married a García, only the masculine charms of her husband could explain, not her daughter's obstinacy in saying her name was only García and not García-Dupont, that's right, with the distinguished Anglo-American hyphen.

"Laura has no problems because she's flat, Mama, but . . ."

"Elizabeth, child, don't shame me."

"There's nothing to be done about it. God, with your help, made me this way . . ."

"All right then, forget your tits," Elizabeth's mother blurted out, with no hint of shame. "Just remember that there are more important things. Look for the most distinguished connections. Make a point of making friendly inquiries about the right families—Ollivier, Trigos, Sartorious, Fernández Landero, Estevas, Pasquel, Bouchez, Luengas."

"And the Carazas," interrupted Miss Elizabeth.

"Keep your opinions to yourself," fulminated her mother. "Hold on to the names of those in the best society. If you forget them, they will certainly forget you." She looked compassionately at the two girls. "Poor things. Just watch what everyone else is doing. Imitate them, imitate them!"

Elizabeth responded with exaggerated condescension. "Enough, Mama! You're suffocating me! I'm going to faint!"

San Cayetano was a coffee plantation, but it was the plantation house that everyone meant when they said "San Cayetano." Here Spanish traditions had been forgotten and instead a *petit château* in the French style had arisen, in the 1860s, in a beech forest near a foaming waterfall and a noisy, narrow river. Its neoclassical facade was supported by columns whose capitals were covered with carved vines.

The main house had two stories, at its entrance an enormous fig tree and a silent fountain, then fifteen steps up to reach the carved door of the ground floor, which was—Leticia warned her daughter—where the bedrooms were. An elegant, wide stone staircase led to the second floor, where the receptions were held: salons, dining rooms, and especially—this was the most notable feature of the place—a grand balustraded terrace, equal in size to half the floor space within, roofed over by an upper terrace and wrapped around three sides of the house, open to the cool night breezes and, during the afternoon, a place for sun-drenched siestas in sleepy rocking chairs.

Here, couples could rest, leaning against the balustrade of the beautiful gallery, and chat, putting their glasses down when they decided to dance right here, on any of the three sides of the second-floor terrace. All her life, this place returned again and again in Laura's memory as the site of youthful enchantment, the space where she felt the joy of knowing herself to be young.

There, awaiting her guests, was Doña Genoveva Deschamps de la Trinidad, legendary mistress of the hacienda and tutelary leader of provincial society. Laura expected to meet a tall and dominating, even haughty woman, and instead found a small, erect lady with a flashing smile, dimples in her rosy cheeks, and cordial eyes, gray, like the elegant monotone of her gown. Apparently, Mrs. Deschamps de la Trinidad also read *La Vie Parisienne*, for her gown was even more modern than Laura's: it eliminated every kind of false padding and followed, in a shine of gray silk, the lady's natural shape. Doña Genoveva's bare shoulders were wrapped in a veil of fine gauze, also gray, the entire ensemble harmonizing with her steely gaze and allowing her jewels, as transparent as water, to shine even more brightly.

Laura was thankful that her hostess was such an amiable woman, but she realized that Mrs. Deschamps, before and after cordially greeting each guest, fixed them with a strangely cold stare, even calculated, almost judicial. The stare of the rich and envied lady conveyed her seal of approbation or disapproval. People would know, at the next annual ball at the hacienda, who had received the placet and who had been damned. That cold gaze of censure or approval lasted no longer than the few seconds between one guest moving on and the next arriving, when the affable smile would glitter again.

"Tell your parents I'm very, very sorry not to see them here tonight," said Doña Genoveva, lightly touching Laura's hair, as if putting an unruly curl back in place. "Keep me abreast of Don Fernando's health."

Laura curtsied, a lesson learned from the Misses Ramos, and set about exploring the place so discussed and admired by Xalapa society. She felt rapture on seeing the pale green painted ceilings, the fleurons on the walls, the multicolored skylights, and, beyond, the heart of the party, on the terrace wrapped by balustrades adorned with urns, the orchestra whose musicians were all wearing dinner jackets, and the guests, especially the young people, the boys in white tie and tailcoats and the girls in various styles, which led Laura to conclude that a man dressed in a black uniform, white tie, and piqué shirtfront would always look elegant, would never expose anything—while every woman was obliged to exhibit, dangerously, her personal, eccentric, conformist though always arbitrary idea of elegance.

The ball had not yet begun, and each young lady received from the hands of the majordomo a dance card embossed with the initials of the hostess—DLT. They then got into position to await requests from the gallants to dance. Laura and Elizabeth had seen some of them at the much less elegant parties held at the Xalapa Casino, but the boys hadn't seen them because they were graceless girls, one flat-chested and the other bovine, frankly. Now, at the point of attaining perfect femininity, well dressed, feigning more self-confidence than they really had, Elizabeth and Laura first greeted school and family friends and allowed the boys, stiff in their frock coats, to approach.

A boy with caramel-colored eyes came up to Elizabeth and asked her for the first dance.

"Thank you, but I already have a partner."

The boy made a polite bow, and Laura kicked her friend.

"Liar. We just arrived."

"Either Eduardo Caraza dances with me first or I won't dance with anyone."

"What is it about him you like so much?"

"Everything. Money. Good looks. Look at him. Here he comes. I told you."

To Laura this Eduardo seemed neither better nor worse than anyone else.

Any outsider would have to admit it and probably be shocked: Xalapa society was whiter than it was mestizo, and as for people of color, like Aunt María de la O, there were none, although the few people with Indian features were noticeable precisely because they were presentable. Laura felt an attraction for a very dark, very thin boy who looked like one of those pirates from Malaysia in the novels of Emilio Salgari which she'd inherited from Santiago along with the rest of his books. He had perfect dark skin, without the slightest blemish, completely clean-shaven, and slow, light, elegant movements. He looked like Sandokan, Salgari's Hindu prince. He was the first to dance with her. Doña Genoveva put the waltzes first, then modern dances, and, at the end, returning to an era prior to the waltz, the polkas, lancers, and the Madrid schottische.

The Hindu prince said not a word, to the point that Laura wondered if his accent or his stupidity would destroy the illusion of his marooned Malayan elegance. Her second partner, on the other hand, was a chatterbox from a rich Córdoba family, dizzying her with inanities about breeding hens and how to mate them with roosters, all without the slightest allusive or salacious intent, merely stupid. And the third, a tall redhead she'd already seen on tennis courts showing off his strong legs, svelte and down-covered, did not hesitate to abuse Laura, squeezing her against his chest, rubbing his crotch against her, nibbling her earlobe.

"Who invited that jerk?" Laura asked Elizabeth.

"He usually behaves better than tonight. I think you got him excited. Or maybe the spiked pineapple juice has gone to his head. If you like, you can complain to Doña Genoveva."

"And how about you, Elizabeth?" asked Laura as she vigorously shook her head.

"Look at him. Isn't he a delight?"

The selfsame Eduardo Caraza waltzed by, his gaze fixed vacantly on the ceiling.

"See that? He's not even looking at his partner."

"He wants everyone to look at him."

"Same thing."

"He dances very well."

"What should I do, Laura, what should I do?" stammered Elizabeth, on the point of tears. "He'll never take any notice of me."

At which point the dancing stopped and Doña Genoveva came over, inviting Elizabeth to follow her to where Eduardo Caraza was blowing his nose.

"Young lady," the hostess pronounced in a low voice to the lachrymose blonde, "don't let on in public when you're in love. You make everyone feel you're superior to them and then they hate you. Eduardo, now the modern dances are coming, and Elizabeth wants you to show her how to dance the cakewalk better than Irene Castle."

She left them arm in arm and returned to her post, a general obliged to review her troops, looking over each guest head to foot, fingernails, ties, shoes. What wouldn't provincial society have given to look over Doña Genoveva's social notebook, where every young person was graded as if in school, passed or failed for the next year. Nevertheless, sighed the perfect hostess, there were always people you simply had to invite even if they didn't come up to standards, even if they didn't cut their nails properly, even if their shoes didn't go with their frock coats, even if they didn't know how to tie their ties, or even if they were plainly vulgar, like that tennis player.

"You can be a social arbiter, but power and money will always have more privileges than elegance and good manners."

Doña Genoveva's dinners were famous and never disappointing. A majordomo in a white wig and eighteenth-century livery announced in French: *Madame est servie.*

Laura laughed to see this dark-skinned servant, obviously from Veracruz, intone perfectly the only sentence in French that Doña Genoveva had taught him, although Elizabeth's mother, leading her two wards to the dining room, revealed another facet of the subject:

"Last year she had a little black fellow in a white wig. Everyone thought he was Haitian. But disguising an Indian as Louis XV, well . . ."

The parade of European faces that began to walk toward the dining room justified the hostess. These were the children, grandchildren, and great-grandchildren of Spaniards, French, Italians, Scots, and Germans, like Laura Díaz Kelsen or her brother Santiago, descendants of immigrants from the Rhineland and the Canary Islands, who passed through the entry port of Veracruz and remained here to make their fortunes—in the port, in Xalapa, in Córdoba, in Orizaba, in coffee, in cattle, in sugar, banking, importing, the professions, even politics.

"Look at this photograph of Don Porfirio's cabinet. He's the only Indian. All the others are white, with light eyes and English suits," pontificated a portly gentleman in his sixties, an importer of wines and exporter of sugar. "Look at the eyes of Limantour, Minister of the Treasury, they look like water; look at Landa y Escandón, the governor of Mexico City, with his bald pate like a Roman senator; look at the Minister of Justice, Justino Fernández, with his beard in Gothic-patrician style; or the Catalan bandit eyes of Casasús, Don Porfirio's favorite. And it's said about Díaz that he used rice powder to whiten himself. To think he was once a liberal *guerrillero*, a hero of the Reform."

"And what would you like, that we return to the times of the

Aztecs?" answered one of the ladies to whom the exporter-importer had uselessly directed his words.

"Don't make jokes about the only serious man in the history of Mexico," interjected another gentleman with an expression of fierce nostalgia on his face. "We're going to miss Porfirio Díaz. Just you wait and see."

"We haven't until now," answered the businessman. "Thanks to the war, we're exporting more than ever and making more money than ever."

"But thanks to the Revolution, we're going to lose everything, right down to our underwear, begging the ladies' pardon," was the answer he received.

"Oh, but those Zouaves were very handsome," Laura heard the lady who was angry with the Aztecs say. She missed the rest of the guests' conversation as they slowly advanced toward the tables piled high with galantines, pâtés, slices of ham, roast beef . . .

A very pale, almost yellow hand offered Laura an already prepared plate. She noted a gold ring with the initials OX and the starched cuff of a dress shirt, cuff links of black onyx, good-quality cloth. Something kept Laura from raising her eyes and meeting those of this person.

"Do you think you knew Santiago well?" said the naturally grave but deliberately high-pitched voice; it was obvious that his attenuated words emanated from baritone vocal cords. Why was Laura refusing to look at his face? He himself raised her chin and said to her, The terrace has three sides, on the right we can be alone.

He took her by the arm, and she, with her hands around her plate, felt at her side a svelte masculine figure, lightly perfumed with English cologne, who guided her without a pause, at a normal speed, to the farthest terrace, left of the bandstand, where the musicians had deposited their instrument cases. He helped her avoid these obstacles, but she awkwardly dropped the plate, and it smashed on the marble floor, scattering the pâté and roast beef.

"I'll get another," said the unexpected gallant in a suddenly deep voice.

"No, it doesn't matter. I'm not really hungry."

"Just as you like."

There was little light in that corner. Laura first saw a backlit profile, perfectly outlined, and a straight nose with no bridge that stopped at the edge of the upper lip, slightly withdrawn with respect to the lower lip and the prominent jaw, like those of the Habsburg monarchs who appeared in her history textbook.

The young man did not release Laura's arm. She was shocked, even fearful because of his next statement: "Orlando Ximénez. You don't know me, but I do know you. Very well. Santiago talked about you with great tenderness. I think you were his favorite virgin." Orlando burst into a silent giggle, throwing his head back.

When the moonlight fell on it, Laura discovered a head of blond curls and a strange, yellowish face with Western aspects but decidedly Asian eyes. His skin was like that of the Chinese workers on the Veracruz docks.

"You speak as if we knew each other."

"Speak familiarly please, or I'll be offended. Or perhaps you'd rather I left you in peace?"

"I don't understand, Mr. . . . . Orlando . . . I don't know what you're saying to me."

Orlando took Laura's hand and kissed her soap-perfumed knuckles.

"I'm talking to you about Santiago."

"Did you know him? I never met any of his friends."

"*Et pour cause.*" Orlando's noiseless laugh made Laura nervous. "You think your brother gave you everything, only you?"

"No, why would I believe that?" stammered the girl.

"Yes, that's what you think. Everyone who knew Santiago thinks that. He took it upon himself to convince each one of us that we were unique, irreplaceable. *C'était son charme.* He had that talent: I'm only yours."

"Yes, he was a very good man."

"Laura, Laura, 'good' *c'est pas le mot*! If someone had called him 'good,' Santiago wouldn't have slapped him, he'd have *snubbed* him. That was his cruelest weapon."

"He wasn't cruel. You're wrong. You just want to get me angry, that's all." Laura moved as if to leave.

Orlando stopped her with a strong and delicate hand whose gesture contained, surprisingly, a caress. "Don't leave."

"You're annoying me."

"It doesn't suit you. Are you going to complain?"

"No, I just want to go."

"Good, I hope at least I've upset you."

"I loved my brother. You didn't."

"Laura, I loved your brother much more than you did. But also I must admit I envy you. You knew the angelic part of Santiago. I . . . well, I must admit I envy you. How many times he said to me . . . 'What a shame Laura's a little girl! I hope she grows up soon. I confess I desire her madly.' Madly. He never said that to me. With me he was more severe . . . Think I should call him that instead of cruel? Santiago the Severe instead of Santiago the Cruel, or better, *pourquoi pas*, Santiago the Promiscuous, the man who wanted to be loved by everyone, men and women, boys and girls, poor and rich. And do you know why he wanted to be loved? So he wouldn't have to reciprocate the love. What passion, Laura, what hunger for life, in insatiable Santiago the Apostle! As if he knew he was going to die young. That he did know. That's why he gobbled down everything life offered him. Yet still, he was selective. Don't believe he was just anything for anyone. *Il savait choisir*. That's why he chose you and me, Laura."

Laura had no idea what to say to this immodest, insolent, handsome young man. But the more she listened to him, the richer her feelings for Santiago became.

She began by rejecting this guest (lounge lizard, fop, dandy: Orlando smiled again, as if he'd guessed Laura's thoughts, searching for the epithets that others repeatedly attached to him) and ended by feeling attracted to him despite herself, listening to him speak, giving her more than she knew about Santiago; her initial rejection of Orlando was going to be overwhelmed by an appetite, a need to know more about Santiago. Laura struggled between those two impulses, and Orlando guessed it, stopped speaking, and invited her to dance.

"Listen. They've gone back to Strauss. I can't stand modern dances."

He took her by the waist and by the hand, stared deeply at her with his Asian eyes, right into the depths of her eyes of shifting light, looked at her as no one had ever looked at her, and she, dancing the waltz with Orlando, had the startling sensation that beneath their evening clothes the two of them were naked, as naked as the priest Elzevir might imagine them, and that the distance between their bodies, imposed by the rhythm of the waltz, was fictitious: they were naked, and they were embracing.

Laura awoke from her trance the instant she averted her eyes from Orlando's, and she saw that all the others were observing them, standing back from them, pausing in their dance to watch Laura Díaz and Orlando Ximénez dance.

This was interrupted by a gaggle of children in nightclothes who hadn't been able to fall asleep and now burst in with a racket, carrying huge hats filled with oranges stolen from the garden.

"Well, well. You were the sensation of the ball," Elizabeth García told her schoolmate as they traveled back to Xalapa.

"That boy's got a very bad reputation," Elizabeth's mother added quickly.

"In that case, I wish he'd asked me to dance," whispered Elizabeth. "He paid me not the slightest attention."

"But you wanted to dance with Eduardo Caraza, he was your dream," said Laura, astonished.

"He didn't even talk to me. He's rude. He dances without speaking."

"You'll have other chances, sweetie."

"No, Mama, I'm disillusioned and will be for the rest of my life." And the girl dressed in rose burst into tears in her mother's arms.

Instead of consoling her directly, Mrs. García-Dupont preferred to go off on a tangent, warning Laura: "I feel I must tell your mother everything."

"There's no need for a fuss, ma'am. I'll never see that boy again."

"You're better off for it. Bad company, you know . . ."

Zampaya opened the main entrance, and the García-Duponts,

mother and daughter, took out their handkerchiefs—the mother's dry, Elizabeth's soaked with tears—to say goodbye to Laura.

"How cold it is here, miss," complained the black man. "When are we going back to Veracruz?" He did a little dance step, but Laura didn't look at him. She had eyes only for the attic occupied by the Catalan lady, Armonía Aznar.

They had to leave very early, in the landau, for Catemaco: Grandfather was going, announced Aunt María de la O. Laura stared sadly at the tropical countryside she loved so much as it was reborn under her tender gaze, already foreseeing the sadness of saying goodbye to Grandfather Felipe.

He was in his bedroom, his for so many years, first when he was a bachelor, then with his beloved wife, Cosima Reiter, and now, once again alone, with no company except for his three daughters, who used him, he knew, as a pretext for continuing to be unmarried, obliged by their widower father . . .

"Let's see if you get married now, girls," said Felipe Kelsen sarcastically from his sickbed.

The entryway to the Catemaco house seemed different to Laura, as if absence made everything smaller but at the same time longer and narrower. Returning to the past meant entering an empty, interminable corridor where one could no longer find the usual things or people one wanted to see again. As if they were playing with both our memory and our imagination, the people and things of the past challenged us to situate them in the present, not forgetting they had a past and would have a future although that future would be, precisely, only that of memory, again, in the present.

But when it is a matter of accompanying death, what is the valid time for life? That was why it took Laura so long to reach her grandfather's bedroom, as if to get there she'd had to traverse the old man's very life, from a German childhood of which she knew nothing, to a youth impassioned by the poetry of Musset and the politics of Lassalle, to political disenchantment and emigration to Mexico, to starting the work and establishing the wealth of the Catemaco coffee plantation, the love by correspondence with his bride-to-be, Cosima, the terrible incident on the highway with the bandit from Papantla, the embrace of the bastard daughter, the birth of the three daughters, the marriage of Leticia and Fernando, the birth of Laura—a passage of a time that in youth is slow and impatient and in old age our patience can't manage to slow down, which is both mocking and tragic. That is why it took Laura so long to reach her grandfather's bedroom. Reaching the dying man's bed required her to touch each and every one of the days of his existence, to remember, imagine, perhaps invent what never happened and even what wasn't imaginable, and to do so by the mere presence of a beloved being who represented everything that wasn't, that was, that could be, and that never could take place.

Now, on this exact day, near her grandfather, holding his hand with its thick veins and old freckles, caressing that skin worn transparent over time, Laura Díaz again had the sensation that she was living for others; her existence had no other meaning except that of completing unfinished destinies. How could she think that, as she caressed the hand of a dying seventy-five-year-old man, a complete man with a finished life?

Santiago had been an unfulfilled promise. Was that what Grandfather was, too, despite his age? Was there any really finished life, a single life that wasn't also a truncated promise, a latent possibility, even more . . . ? It isn't the past that dies with each of us. The future dies as well.

Laura stared as deeply as she could into her grandfather's light and dreaming eyes, still alive behind the constant deathly blinking. She asked him the same question she was asking herself. Felipe Kelsen smiled painfully.

"Didn't I tell you, child? One day all my ailments came together, and here I am . . . but before I go I want to tell you that you were right. Yes, there is a statue of a woman, covered with jewels, in the middle of the forest. I misled you on purpose. I didn't want you to fall into superstition and witchcraft. I took you to see a ceiba so that you would learn to live with reason, not with the fantasy and enthusiasms that cost me so dearly when I was young. Be careful with everything. The ceiba was covered with spines as sharp as daggers, remember?"

"Of course, Grandfather."

Abruptly, as if he had no time left for other words, not caring to whom he said them or even if no one heard them, the old man whispered: "I'm a young socialist. I live in Darmstadt, and I shall die here. I need the nearness of my river and my streets and my squares. I need the yellow smell of the chemical factories. I need to believe in something. This is my life, and I wouldn't trade it for any other. For any other . . ." His mouth filled with mustard-colored bubbles and remained open forever.

When the dance was over, Orlando had brought his lips—fleshy like those of a little girl—close to Laura's ear.

"Let's separate. We're attracting attention. I'll wait for you in the attic of your house."

Laura was left suspended amid the noise of the party, the curious scrutiny of the guests, and Orlando's astounding proposition.

"But Señora Aznar lives there."

"No more. She wanted to go to Barcelona to die. I paid her passage. Now the attic is mine."

"But my parents . . ."

"No one knows. Only you. I'll wait for you there. Come when you want." And he removed his lips from Laura's ear. "I want to give you the same thing I gave to Santiago. Don't disappoint me now. He liked it."

When she returned from her grandfather's funeral, Laura lived for several days with Orlando's words echoing like a howl in her head: You think you knew Santiago well, you think your brother gave everything to you? How little you know of a man so complex; he gave you only a part of his existence; and passion, the passion of love, to whom did he give that?

She glanced constantly toward the attic. Nothing had changed. Only she had. She did not understand very well what the change consisted of. Perhaps it was the announcement that would become fact only if she cautiously climbed the stairs to the attic, taking care that no

THE YEARS WITH LAURA DÍAZ

one saw her—her father, her mother, Aunt María de la O, Zampaya, the Indian maids. She wouldn't have to knock at the door, because Orlando would leave it ajar. Orlando was waiting for her. Orlando was handsome, strange, ambiguous in the moonlight. But perhaps Orlando was ugly, common, lying by daylight. Laura's entire body cried out to be near Orlando's body—for him, for her, for the unexpected romantic encounter at the hacienda ball, but also for Santiago, because loving Orlando was the indirect but sanctioned way of loving her brother. Could Orlando's insinuations be true? If they were lies, could she love Orlando for himself, without the specter of Santiago? Or might she come to hate both Orlando and Santiago? Hate Santiago because of Orlando? She had the chilling suspicion that it might all be a huge farce, a huge lie orchestrated by the young seducer. Laura did not need the diabolical admonitions of the priest Elzevir Almonte to shun all sexual pleasure or ease; she only needed to look at herself naked in the mirror when she was seven years old, and to see there none of the horrors the priest proclaimed, in order not to fall into the temptations that seemed, thanks to an early and radical intuition, useless if not shared with a loved one.

Love for everyone in the family, including Santiago, was happy, warm, and chaste. Now, for the first time, a man excited her in another way. Was this man real or was he a lie? Would he satisfy her, or was Laura risking sexual initiation with a man who wasn't worth her while, who wasn't for her, who was only a phantom, an extension of her brother, a deceiver, handsome, attractive, tempting, lying in ambush, diabolical, right at hand, comfortable, waiting for her in her own house, under her parents' roof?

Zampaya had supplied the key to the mystery, perhaps, without knowing it, when he drove the three of them—Laura, Elizabeth, and Mrs. García-Dupont—back to Xalapa on the night of the ball.

"Did your ladyships see the fig tree at the entrance to the cage?" asked the black man.

"What cage?" replied Mrs. García-Dupont. "It's the most elegant hacienda in the district, you ignoramus. The ball of the year."

"The best balls take place in the street, ma'am, begging your pardon."

"That's your opinion," sighed the lady.

"You didn't get cold waiting outside, now, did you, Zampaya?" asked the solicitous Laura.

"No, child. I stood there looking at the fig tree. I remembered the story of Santo Felipe de Jesús. He was a proud, spoiled boy, like some of those I saw tonight. He was living in a house with a barren fig tree. His nanny would say, The day little Felipe becomes a saint, the fig tree will flower."

"Why are you going on like this about the saints, darky?" The lady tried to cut him off. "San Felipe went to the Orient to convert the Japanese, who vilely crucified him. Now he is a saint, don't you know that?"

"It's what his nanny would say, begging your pardon, ma'am. The day Felipe was killed, the fig tree flowered."

"Well, this one is barren." Elizabeth laughed roguishly.

"Santiago's strength was that he never needed anyone," Orlando had told Laura on the San Cayetano terrace. "That's why we were always at his feet."

A month later, they say Armonía Aznar's body was found in the attic. They say it was found when the bank employee came to deliver her monthly check before Zampaya left her daily food tray at the door. She'd been dead for less than two days. There was still no stench.

"Everything is hidden and lies in wait for us." Laura repeated her Aunt Hilda's mysterious and habitual phrase. She said it to her Chinese doll, Li Po, comfortable among the pillows. And she herself, Laura Díaz, decided to save the memory of her first ball, imagining herself svelte and transparent, so transparent that her gown was her body, there was nothing under the dress, and Laura whirled, floated in a waltz of liquid elegance, until she, thankful, was covered by the veil of sleep.

## 5. Xalapa: 1920

Y OU WERE WRONG, ORLANDO. Not here. Find another way for us to meet. Use your imagination. Don't mock my family or make me hate myself."

Laura resumed family life, which had been injured by the death of her grandfather and by her father's broken health. As for the death of Mrs. Aznar and being seduced by Orlando, Laura expelled both not from memory but from recollection; she never referred to either of them again, never mentioned them to anyone, never mentioned them to herself. She was not to recollect them, no matter how hard her memory may have worked to retain them, forever, under lock and key, in the vault of the past from which nothing was to be removed. To add "Orlando Ximénez" and "Armonía Aznar" to the sorrows and difficulties of her home life would have been unendurable, and likewise the unhealthy contagion with which Orlando infected her memory of Santiago, which Laura did indeed want to preserve pure and explicit. She could not forgive him for having damaged that part of Santiago's life she still kept in her soul.

Does Santiago also live in my father's soul? wondered the girl, staring at Fernando Díaz's stricken face.

It was impossible to know. The accountant-banker's diplegia was advancing at a wicked pace, rapid and regular. First he lost the use of his legs, soon the rest of his body, and later his ability to speak. Laura had no room in her heart for anything but intense pity for him—confined, finally, to a wheelchair, wearing a bib, fed as if he were a baby by the devoted María de la O, staring at the world with indecipherable eyes that did not signal whether he was listening, thinking, or communicating, except for a desperate blinking and an equally desperate effort not to blink by keeping his eyes open, alert, inquisitive, beyond a person's normal endurance, as if one day, should he close his eyes, he would not be able to open them ever again. His gaze filled with glass and water, while his eyebrows developed remarkable movement, giving their unusual new positions an expressiveness that made Laura fearful. Like two arches supporting all that was left of his personality, her father's eyebrows did not rise in surprise but arched even more, as if both questioning and communicating.

Aunt María de la O did her best to attend to the invalid while Leticia attended to the household. But it was Leticia who learned, slowly but surely, to read her husband's eyes, to hold his hand and communicate with him.

"He wants you to put his tiepin in his tie, María de la O."

"He wants us to take him for an outing to Los Berros."

"He's in the mood for rice and beans."

Was her mother telling the truth or was she creating a simulacrum of communication and, therefore, of life? María de la O would do the painful chores for Leticia; she took charge of cleaning the invalid with warm towels and oatmeal soap, dressed him every morning in a suit, vest, starched collar, tie, dark socks, and low boots, as if the head of the household were going to the office, and undressed him at night to put him, with the help of Zampaya, in bed at nine.

The only thing Laura knew to do was to take her father's hand and read him the French and English novels he adored, learning those languages in a kind of homage to her broken father. Fernando Díaz's physical collapse was swiftly apparent on his features. He aged, but he kept control over his feelings, and Laura saw him weep only once: when she read him the emotional death scene of the boy Little Father Time, in Thomas Hardy's *Jude the Obscure*, who commits suicide when he hears his parents say they can't feed so many mouths. That weeping, nevertheless, cheered Laura. Her father understood her. Her father was listening and feeling, behind the opaque veil of his sickness.

"Go out, daughter. Live the life of people your own age. Nothing would sadden your father more than knowing you'd sacrificed yourself for him."

Why did her mother use that subjunctive mode of speech, which according to the Misses Ramos was a mode that had to be connected with another verb in order to have meaning—indicating hypothesis, the first Miss Ramos would say; or desire, the second would add; something like "If I were you . . . ," the two of them would say in one voice, although in different places. Living day to day with the invalid, without foreseeing any end, was the only health that father and daughter could share. If Fernando understood her, Laura would tell him what she was doing every day, how life was in Xalapa, what new things were going on . . . and then Laura realized there were no new things. Her schoolmates had graduated, married, gone off to live in Mexico City, far away, because their husbands took them off, because the Revolution was centralizing power even more than the Díaz dictatorship had, because new agrarian and labor laws were threatening the rich provincials, many of whom had resigned themselves to losing what they'd had, to abandoning the lands and industries that had been devastated by the fighting in order to remake their lives in the capital, safe from rural and provincial abandonment—all that carried Laura's friends far away.

Left behind were the stimulants provided by Orlando and by the Catalan anarchist; even Laura's ardent cult of Santiago cooled, yielding to a mere succession of hours, days, years. Customs in Xalapa did not change, as if the outside world couldn't penetrate its sphere of tradition, placid self-satisfaction, and, perhaps, wisdom in a city that miraculously—although by force of will, too—had not been touched physically by the national turbulence of those years. The Revolution in Veracruz meant, more than anything, for the rich a fear of losing what they had and for the poor a desire to conquer what they needed. While they were still in Veracruz, Don Fernando had spoken, vaguely, about the influence of anarcho-syndicalist ideas that came to Mexico through the port, and later the presence in his own house of the never-seen Armonía Aznar gave life to those concepts, which Laura did not know much about. The end of her school years and the disappearance of her friends—because they married and Laura didn't, because they went off to the capital and Laura stayed in Xalapa—forced her, in order to have the normalcy her mother Leticia wanted for her as a relief from the family penury, to befriend girls younger than she, juvenile compared to Laura not only in age but in experience—for she was Santiago's sister, the young object of Orlando's seduction, the daughter of a father battered by sickness and a mother unshakable in her sense of duty.

Perhaps Laura, to numb her wounded sensibility, let herself be led without much thought into a life that both was and was not her own. It was at hand, it was comfortable, it didn't matter much, she wasn't in the mood to reflect on impossibilities, not even on something simply different from daily life in Xalapa. Nothing would perturb the daily stroll through her favorite garden, Los Berros, and its tall poplars with their silvery leaves and its iron benches, its fountains of greenish water, its moss-covered railings, the little girls skipping rope, the older girls walking in one direction and boys in the other, all of them flirting, brazenly staring or averting their eyes, but all of them with the chance to look at each other for a moment, yet as often as excitement or patience might demand.

"Watch out for gentlemen with walking sticks on their shoulders in Juárez Park," mothers would warn their daughters. "Their intentions are dishonorable."

The park was the other preferred open-air meeting place. Avenues of beech trees, laurels, araucarias, and jacarandas formed a cool, perfumed vault over the minor pleasures of skating in the park, going to charity fairs in the park, and, on clear days, seeing from the park the marvel of Orizaba Peak—Citlaltépetl, mountain of the star, the highest volcano in Mexico. Citlaltépetl had a magic all its own because the great mountain seemed to move according to the quality of the daylight or season of the year: near in the diaphanous dawn, farther away in the solar heat of midday, veiled in the afternoon drizzles, given its most visible glory during sunset—the day's second birth—and at night, everyone knew that the great crest was the invisible but immobile star in the Veracruz firmament, its fairy godmother.

It rained constantly, and then Laura and her new unequal girlfriends (she couldn't even remember their names) ran to take cover outside the park, zigzagging under the eaves of houses and leaping over the gushes of water crisscrossing in the middle of the street. But it was lovely to listen to the warm showers on the roofs and the whisper of the plants. The little things decide to live. Then, as night became calm, the recently washed streets would fill with the scent of tulips and jonquils. Young people came out to stroll. From seven to eight was "the window hour," when suitors would visit their favorite girls at balconies intentionally left open and—something normal in Xalapa but strange in any other part of the world—husbands would court their own wives again at "the window hour," as if they wanted to renew their vows and rekindle their emotions.

In those years, when at almost the same time the Mexican Revolution and the European war culminated and ended, movies became the great novelty. The armed revolution was winding down: the battles after General Obregón's great victory over Pancho Villa at Celaya were only skirmishes. The once powerful Division of the North was disintegrating into bands of outlaws with each faction seeking support, arrangements, advantages, and ideals (in that order) after the triumph of Venustiano Carranza, the Constitutionalist Army, and, in 1917, the promulgation of the new Magna Carta—that was what the newspapers called it—the object of examination, debate, and constant fear among the gentlemen who gathered every evening at the Xalapa Casino.

"If the agrarian reform is put into effect exactly as written, we'll be ruined," said the father of the young man from Córdoba whom Laura had danced with and who had talked only of roosters and hens.

"They won't do that. The country has to eat. Only the big properties produce," said the father of the red-haired and abusive young tennis player, trying to be conciliatory.

"And workers' rights?" joined in the elderly husband of the lady who had waxed nostalgic about the oh-so-handsome French Zouaves. "What is there to say about 'workers' rights' stuck into the Constitution like a pair of banderillas in a bull's back?"

"Like Jesus wearing six-guns, my dear man."

"Red Battalions, House of the Workers of the World . . . I assure you, Carranza and Obregón are Communists and are going to do the same thing here that Lenin and Trotsky are doing in Russia."

"None of this is relevant here, as you gentlemen will soon see."

"A million dead, gentlemen, and all for what?"

"I assure you, most of them died not in battles but in bars."

That provoked general hilarity, but when some films of revolutionary battles made by the Abitia brothers were shown in the Victoria Salon, the cultivated public protested. No one wanted to go to the movies to see huarache-wearing men wielding rifles. Movies meant Italian movies, only Italian. Emotion and beauty were the exclusive privilege of Italy's divas and vamps of the silver screen; society suffered and exulted with the dramas of Pina Menichelli, Italia Almirante Manzini, Giovanna Terribili González—stupendous women with darkly shadowed shining eyes, disturbing brows, electric hairdos, voracious mouths, and tragic gestures. Why did the Gish sisters hide their faces when they wept, why did Mary Pickford dress up as a beggar? If you want poverty, go out on the street; if you want to avoid emotion, visit your neighbors.

The neighbors' homes went on being, in Laura's life and in the life of everyone in provincial society, the irreplaceable seats of communal life. People "received" constantly if sporadically, almost taking turns. In private homes, people played lottery and blackjack, forming large circles around the tables. It was there that culinary customs were preserved. It was there the youngest girls were taught to dance, taking little steps through the rooms, "you do it this way, lifting your skirt," preparing them for the grand soirées at the Casino; and it was the place for baptism parties, for setting up the crèche at Christmas, with the Christ Child in his manger and the Wise Men and, in the center of the room, the "French Ship" filled with sweets that was opened up after midnight Mass. And then Carnival and its masked balls, the tableaux vivants at the end of term at the Misses Ramos' school, with their representations of Father Hidalgo Proclaiming Independence or the Indian Juan Diego negotiating with the Virgin of Guadalupe. But the principal party was the Casino ball every August 19. It was there that all of local society met.

Laura would have preferred to stay at home, not only to be with her parents but because since the death of the Catalan anarchist the attic had been sealed. She began to assign a special value to every corner of her house, as if she knew that the pleasure of living and growing up there would not last forever. Her grandfather's Catemaco house, the apartment above the bank and facing the sea in Veracruz, and now the one-story home on Lerdo Street in Xalapa . . . how many more homes would she live in over the years of her life? She could foresee none of them. She could only recall yesterday's homes and memorize today's, creating sanctuaries in her uncertain life—never again foreseeable and secure as it had been during her childhood near the lake—which she would need to hold on to in the time to come. A time that young Laura could not imagine, no matter how often she said to herself, "No matter what happens, the future will be different from this present." She did not want to imagine the worst reasons why life would change. The worst of all was the death of her father. She was going to say that the saddest was staying behind, lost and forgotten, in a little town, like Aunts Hilda and Virginia in their father's house, stripped of the reason for being settled there and being unmarried. Grandfather was dead; Hilda played the piano for nothing, for no one; Virginia piled up pages, poems, that no one would ever know. The active life was preferable, a life committed to another life, which was the case of Aunt María de la O, constantly caring for Fernando Díaz.

"What would I do without you, María de la O?" the indefatigable Mutti Leticia would ask—seriously, without sighing.

Laura, as once she had memorized Santiago's bedroom in Veracruz, now, eyes closed, ran through the patios, the corridors, the floors of Marseilles brick, the palms, the ferns, the mahogany armoires, the mirrors, the four-poster beds, the clay jugs of filtered water, the dressing table, the pitcher, the closet, and, in her mother's domain, the kitchen redolent of mint and parsley.

"Don't turn in on yourself the way your Grandmother Kelsen did," Leticia would say. She could no longer endure the sadness of her own gaze. "Go out with your girlfriends. Have fun. You're only twenty-one."

"What you mean, Mutti, is that I'm *already* twenty-one. At my age, you'd been married for years, and I'd been born—and no, Mutti, don't even bother asking: I'm not fond of any boy."

"Have they stopped coming to see you? Because of everything that's happened?"

"No, Mutti, I'm the one who's been avoiding them."

As if responding to a warning of an incomprehensible change, vibrating like late-summer leaves, the girls Laura would visit, younger than she, had all decided to prolong their childhood, even if they made coquettish concessions to an adulthood they, disconcerted, did not wish. They called themselves "the chubbies" and played practical jokes inappropriate to their eighteen years. They jumped rope in the park so they'd have color in their cheeks before going on the seductive evening stroll; they would take long siestas before tennis at Los Berros; they would innocently mock their costumed boyfriends during Carnival:

"Are you a circus clown?"

"Don't insult me. Can't you see I'm a prince?"

They would skate in Juárez Park to lose the pounds they put on eating "devils," cakes filled with chocolate and covered with marzipan, the delight of sweet-tooths in this city that smelled like a bakery. They volunteered to be in the tableaux vivants at the end of the term in the Misses Ramos' academy, the only time when one could see that the teachers really were two different people, since one presided over the tableaux while the other worked behind the scenes.

"Something awful happened to me, Laura. I was playing the part of the Virgin, when I suddenly had to go. I had to make terrible faces so Miss Ramos would close the curtain. I ran to make wee-wee and came back to be the Virgin again."

"In my house, they've gotten bored with my comedies and costumes, Laura. My parents have hired only one spectator to admire me. What do you think of that?"

"You must be happy, Margarita."

"The thing is, I've decided to become an actress."

Then they all rushed madly to the balcony to see the cadets from the Preparatoria march by, rifles on their shoulders, wearing their French képis, their uniforms with gold buttons, and their very taut flies.

The bank informed them they'd have to give up the house in September, after the Casino ball. Don Fernando would get a pension, but the new bank director would, as is natural, be coming to live in the house. There would also be a ceremony up in the attic, the unveiling of a plaque in honor of Doña Armonía Aznar. The Mexican trade unions had decided to honor the valiant comrade who had donated money, had delivered mail to the Red Battalions and the House of the Workers of the World during the Revolution, and had even sheltered union men on the run right here, in the house of the bank director.

"Did you know that, Mutti?"

"No, Laura. And what about you, sister?"

"Not a clue!"

"It's better not to know everything, isn't that so?"

None of the three dared to think that a man as honorable as Don Fernando would knowingly have tolerated a conspiracy under his own roof, especially with Santiago's having been shot on November 21, 1910. When she thought about it, Laura imagined that Orlando Ximénez knew the truth, that he was the intermediary between the attic and Doña Armonía's anarcho-syndicalists. Then she discarded that suspicion; Orlando the frivolous . . . or perhaps for that very reason was he the likeliest suspect? Laura laughed heartily. She'd just read Baroness d'Orczy's *The Scarlet Pimpernel* to her father, so she was imagining poor Orlando as a Mexican Pimpernel, a dandy at night and an anarchist by day . . . saving union men from the firing squad.

No novel prepared Laura for the next episode of her life. Leticia and María de la O set about looking for a comfortable house that they could afford under Fernando's pension. The half sister thought that given the circumstances, Hilda and Virginia should sell the Catemaco coffee plantation and use the money to buy a house in Xalapa where they could all live together and save on expenses.

"And why shouldn't we all go back to Catemaco? After all, we did live there . . . and we were happy," said Leticia, without sighing like her self-absorbed mother.

Her question became superfluous as soon as the unmarried sisters Hilda and Virginia appeared at the Xalapa house, loaded with packages, boxes of books, steamer chests, seamstress dummies, cages filled with parrots, and even the Steinway piano.

People gathered in Lerdo Street to observe the arrival of such curious baggage, for the two sisters' belongings filled a mule cart to overflowing. Covered with dust, the sisters themselves looked like refugees from a battle lost many years ago, with huge straw hats tied under their chins and gauze veils that protected their faces from flies, the sun, and the highway filth.

Theirs was a brief story. The Veracruz farm workers had armed themselves and quickly occupied the Kelsen hacienda and all the other properties in the area, declared them agrarian cooperatives, and run the owners off the land.

"There was no way to warn you," said Aunt Virginia. "Here we are."

They hadn't known that the Xalapa house would no longer be theirs in September, after the Casino ball in August. Now, with her sisters added to her burden, her husband an invalid, and Laura having no marriage on the horizon, Leticia finally gave in and burst into tears. The expropriated sisters exchanged perplexed glances. Leticia begged their pardon, drying her tears on her apron, and invited them to make themselves at home. That night, Aunt María de la O came to Laura's bedroom, sat down next to her, and caressed the girl's head.

"Don't be discouraged, child. Just look at me. Sometimes you must have thought that life's been difficult for me, especially when I lived alone with my mother. But you know something? Being born is a joy even if you were conceived in sadness and misery. I mean inner sadness and misery, more than outer. You come into the world, and your origin is erased, being born is always a party, and I've done nothing but celebrate my going through life, not caring two cents where I came from, what happened at the beginning, how and where my mother gave birth to me, how my father behaved . . . Know something? Your grandmother Cosima redeemed everything, but even without her, without all I owe your grandmother and how much I adore her, I celebrate the world, I know I came to the world to celebrate life, through thick and thin, child, and I'm going to go on celebrating, damn it to hell. And excuse me for talking like someone from Alvarado, but that's where I grew up . . ."

María de la O drew her hand away from Laura's head for a moment and gave her niece a radiant smile, as if the little aunt always brought warmth and joy on her lips and in her eyes.

"And something else, Laurita, to complete the picture. Your grandfather brought me to live with you, and that saved me, I can't say it often enough. But your grandmother did not concern herself any more with my mother, as if it were enough to save me and Old Nick himself could take her. The one who did concern himself was your father, Fernando. I don't know what would have become of my mother if Fernando hadn't looked out for her, helped her, given her money, and allowed her to grow old with dignity. Pardon me for being blunt, but there's nothing sadder than an old whore. What I want to say is just this: the important thing is being alive and where you're alive. We're going to save this home and the people in it, Laura. María de la O swears it, the aunt you more than anyone else have respected. I never forget!"

She was getting fat, and it was rather hard for her to move about. Whenever she went for a walk with Fernando in his wheelchair, people would look away, not wanting to feel sorry for the two, the invalid man and the ashen mulatta with fat ankles who insisted on being out and around, ruining things for young, healthy people. María de la O's will was greater than any obstacle, and the four sisters, the day after Hilda and Virginia arrived, decided not only to find a house for the family but to turn it into a guest house, contribute to its maintenance, each one would give her part, and take care of Fernando.

"And as for you, Laura, I beg you not to worry," said Aunt Hilda.

"You will lack for nothing," added Aunt Virginia.

. . . and I wasn't worried, dear aunts, Mutti, I wasn't worried, I know I'll lack for nothing, I'm the little girl of the house, I'm not twenty-one, I'm still seven, defenseless but protected as before the first death, before the first grief, before the first passion, before the first rage, all that I've already experienced, already managed, already mastered, and by now I let myself be mastered by everything that has happened, by now I know how to live with grief, passion, rage, and death, I think I know how to live with them. But what I can't live with is with the diminution of myself, not by others but by myself, made into a child not by the silly girls or protective aunts or Mutti, who doesn't want to accept any passion so as to stay lucid and keep house because she knows that without her the house will fall apart like those sand castles children make on the Mocambo beach, and if she doesn't do the work, who will? While I'm thinking about myself, Laura Díaz, I observe myself distant from my own life, as if I were someone else, a second Laura who sees the first separated from the world around me, indifferent to the people outside my home—is it healthy to be that way?—but concerned with those living here with me, but in both cases separated and yet guilty about being a burden, like the boy in Thomas Hardy's novel, I am loved by everyone, but I weigh them down even if they don't say so, I'm the grown-up little girl about to turn twenty-two without bringing bread to the house where she gets her daily bread, the big little girl who thinks herself justified because she reads books to her paralyzed father, because she loves them all and all of them love her. I will live from the love I give and from the love I receive. It isn't enough, it isn't enough to love my mother, to weep for my brother, to feel sorry for my father, it isn't enough to adopt my own grief and my own tenderness as rights that liberate me from other responsibilities. Now I want to overflow my love for them, exceed my grief for them by freeing them from me, taking myself off their backs, giving them the gift of not worrying about me without my giving up worrying about them, Papa Fernando, Mutti Leticia, Aunts Hilda and Virginia and María de la O, Santiago my love, I'm not asking either comprehension or help from you, I'm going to do what I must to be with you without being of you but by being for you . . .

Juan Francisco López Greene was a very tall man, more than six feet, very dark, with both Indian and Negroid traces in his features—while his lips were thick, his profile was straight; while his hair was crinkly, his skin was smooth and sweet as sugar frosting, night-dark as a gypsy's. His eyes were green islands in a yellow sea. His broad, muscular shoulders spoiled the look of his neck, which was strong but longer than it seemed, just as his arms were long and his devoutly proletarian hands were large. His torso was short, his legs long, and his feet bigger than miners' shoes.

He was powerful, awkward, delicate, different.

He had come to the Casino ball with Xavier Icaza, the young labor lawyer, son of a family of aristocrats who now served the working class. It was he who brought to the dance this man so alien to the social profile of good Xalapa families: Juan Francisco López Greene.

Icaza, a brilliant but scarcely conventional man, wrote avant-garde poetry and picaresque tales; his books were illustrated with Cubist vignettes of skyscrapers and airplanes, and his poetry conveyed the sense of modern velocity that the author sought while his novels brought the tradition of Francisco de Quevedo and the *Lazarillo de Tormes* to modern Mexico City, a city that was filling up—as Icaza explained to groups of guests at the Casino ball—with immigrants from the countryside and that would only go on growing and growing. He winked at the local businessmen, now's the time to buy cheap, Colonia Hipódromo, Colonia Nápoles, Chapultepec Heights, Parque de la Lama, even Desierto de los Leones, just you wait and see how real estate is going to boom, don't be fools—he laughed with his cheery teeth—invest now.

He was called a Futurist, a Dadaist, an *Estridentista*, names that no one had ever heard before in Veracruz and that Icaza introduced with an almost insolent air by driving a yellow Isotta-Fraschini convertible, as if to establish his credentials immediately and well. He asked for the hand of Miss Ana Guido, and when her parents expressed doubts, Xavier Icaza drove his powerful automobile right up the stairs and into the cathedral one Sunday during Mass. The roar of the motor and the insane vision of the car going up the steep stairs with the young, high-spirited lawyer using all the horsepower at his disposal to do it. He dangerously stopped the car where the stairway ended and the atrium began and announced in a loud voice that he'd come to marry Ana and nothing and no one was going to stop him.

"I'm not dealing in make-believe," the young lawyer Icaza was saying to his old acquaintances at the Casino ball, "this is a matter of mutual convenience. The Revolution has set free all the country's dormant forces—the businessmen and industrialists who were thwarted while the Dictator turned over the country to foreigners, the functionaries whose careers were blocked by Porfirio's old bureaucracy, and let's not even start on the landless peasants and workers eager to organize and have a respected public voice. Listen, who were the rebels in the Río Blanco factories and the Cananea mines, the first to rise up against the dictatorship? What were they if not workers?"

"Madero didn't make any concessions to them," said the father of the young rooster expert from Córdoba.

"Because Madero didn't understand anything," Icaza claimed. "On the other hand, the executioner Huerta, the man who murdered Madero, tried to get the support of the working class and permitted the biggest May Day demonstrations ever seen. He allowed for an eight-hour workday and six-day workweek, but when the unions asked him for democracy, that's when he turned them down, he arrested the leaders and deported them. One of them is my friend here, Juan Francisco López Greene, to whom I introduce you with great pleasure. The Greene part doesn't mean he's English. Everybody in Tabasco is named

Greene because they're descendants of English pirates whose mothers were Indians or blacks, isn't that right?"

Juan Francisco smiled and nodded. "Laura, you're a cultured type. I'll leave him to you," Icaza said, charming and firm, and wandered off.

Laura suspected that this new arrival, so alien to provincial customs, who had appeared at the San Cayetano soirées like the "Jesus wearing six-guns" the Córdoba landowner had mentioned, would be personally awkward, like his huge miners' shoes, square, thick, and hobnailed. She imagined that his speaking style was like a rain of stones punctuated by silence. She was therefore surprised to hear a smooth voice, serene and even sweet, in which each word bore the weight of conviction, which is why Juan Francisco López Greene let himself seem so gentle and speak so mildly.

"Is Xavier Icaza right?" Laura asked abruptly, looking for a way to begin the conversation.

Juan Francisco insisted. "Yes. I know very well that they all try to use us."

"To use whom?" asked Laura, unaffectedly.

"The workers."

"You're a worker?" Laura again queried impulsively, speaking in the familiar mode to Juan Francisco, certain this wouldn't offend him, challenging him slightly to address her as an equal, not as "miss," uncertainly seeking common ground with this unknown man, sniffing him out, feeling herself a bit of a beast, a bit savage, as she'd never felt with Orlando, who made her think things that were perverse, refined, and so subtle that they evaporated like a poisonous perfume, strong but deleterious and short-lived.

He didn't accept the challenge. "It's a risk, miss. We just have to take the chance."

(If only he'd speak familiarly to me, begged Laura, I want him to speak familiarly to me, not call me *miss*, I'd like for once to feel different, I want a man to say things to me, do things to me I don't know or don't expect or can't ask for, I can't ask him for that, it has to come from him, and on that depends everything that may come later, from a simple *miss* or no *miss* . . . )

"What risk might that be, Mr. Greene?" Laura reverted to formality. "The risk that they'll manipulate us, Laura."

He added, without noticing (or perhaps pretending he didn't see) the change in color of the girl's face, that "we" could also extract advantages from "them." Laura became accustomed right then and there to the strange plural which, without pretensions or false modesty, embraced a community—of workers, fighters, comrades, that's right, and of the man speaking with her.

"Icaza has no illusions. But I do." He smiled for the first time, with a trace of malice but more than anything else with self-irony, thought Laura. "I do."

He said he had illusions because the Constitution made concessions to Mexican peasants and workers it did not have to make. Carranza was an old hacienda owner whose long white beard curled when he had to deal with workers and Indians; Alvaro Obregón was an intelligent but opportunistic Creole who could just as well dine with God or with the devil and make the devil believe he was actually God and convince God not to worry, because He could be a devil and had no reason to envy Lucifer; in any case, General Obregón would be the judge and would decree, *You* are the Devil . . . The Constitution consecrated the rights of the worker and of the land because without "us"—here we go again, Laura said to herself—"they" would not win the Revolution or keep themselves in power.

He asked her to dance, and she laughed through a grimace of pain and stepped-on dancing shoes, asking the labor leader if they might not better practice out on the balcony, and he also laughed and said yes, neither God nor the devil created me for ball-dancing . . . but if she was interested in what "we" were doing, he would tell her, out on the balcony, how the workers' struggle organized itself during the Revolution. People thought the Revolution involved only a Creole elite followed by peasant guerrillas. They forgot that everything began in the factories and mines, in Río Blanco and Cananea. The workers organized the Red Battalions that went out to fight Huerta's dictatorship and founded the House of the Workers of the World in the Azulejos palace in Mexico City, in the aristocracy's former Jockey Club. But because "we" were invaded by Huerta's police, who arrested us and tried to burn the palace down, "we" were forced to flee. We found ourselves in the open arms of General Obregón.

"Be careful," said Icaza, rejoining Laura and Juan Francisco. "Obregón is a fox. He wants worker support so he can undercut the followers of the peasant rebels, Zapata and Villa. He talks about a proletarian Mexico to provoke peasant and Indian Mexico. According to the Creole revolutionary leaders, who are cautious on this subject, that's still the reactionary, backward, religious Mexico, suffocated by its scapularies and fumigated by the incense of too many churches. Be careful with the fraud, Juan Francisco, very careful."

"But it's the truth," said Juan Francisco heatedly. "The peasants wear the image of the Virgin on their hats, they go to Mass on their knees, they aren't modern, but Catholic and rural, Dr. Icaza."

"Listen, Juan Francisco, stop calling me doctor or we'll end up in a fistfight. And stop acting like such a hick. When you meet a young lady from high society whom you like, you do not address her as 'miss,' you dummy. Stop behaving like a reactionary, retarded, premodern peasant." Xavier Icaza's voice pealed with laughter.

But Juan Francisco insisted, with no trace of humor, that peasants *were* reactionaries, that urban workers were *true* revolutionaries, the fifteen thousand workers who fought in the Red Battalions, the hundred and fifty thousand members of the House of the Workers of the World—when had anything like that ever been seen in Mexico?

"Want some contradictions, Juan Francisco?" Icaza interrupted him. "Think about the battalions of Yaqui Indians who joined General Obregón to defeat the oh-so-agrarian Pancho Villa at the battle of Celaya. And start getting used to it, my friend. Revolutions are contradictory, and if they take place in a country as contradictory as Mexico, well, it can drive you crazy," Icaza wailed, "as crazy as when you stare into Laura Díaz's eyes. In short, López Greene: when the Revolution came to power with Carranza and Obregón, did those leaders accept self-governance in the factories and the expulsion of foreign capitalists as the Red Battalions had been promised?"

No, said Juan Francisco, he knew "we" were going to live through a constant give-and-take with the government, but "we" are not going to give in on our fundamental principles; "we" have organized the biggest strikes in all Mexican history, we've resisted all the pressures of the revolutionary government that wanted to turn us into official labor puppets, we got salary increases, we always negotiate, we made Carranza nuts because he couldn't figure out where we were vulnerable, he jailed us, called us traitors, we cut the light in Mexico City, they captured the head of the electricians, Ernesto Velasco, and put a gun to his temple as they asked how to turn the power back on, they broke us again and again, but "we" never give up, we always return to the fight, and we always go back to the negotiating table, we win, we lose, we'll win a little and lose a lot, but it's fine, it's fine, no need to strike the colors, we know how to turn the lights on and off and they don't, they need us.

"Armonía Aznar was an exemplary fighter," said Juan Francisco López Greene when he unveiled the plaque in honor of the Catalan woman in the house where Laura and her family lived. "Like all the anarcho-syndicalists, she came to Veracruz. She arrived with the Spanish anarchist Amedeo Ferrés and secretly organized the printers and typographers during the Porfirio Díaz presidency. Then, during the Revolution, she fought in the House of the Workers of the World—with heroism and, which is more difficult, without glory, secretly delivering mail right here in Xalapa, carrying documents to and from Veracruz to Mexico City."

Juan Francisco paused and sought out, among the hundred or so at the ceremony, the eyes of Laura Díaz.

"All she did was made possible thanks to the revolutionary generosity of Don Fernando Díaz, president of the bank, who allowed Armonía Aznar to take refuge here and carry out her work in secret. Don Fernando is ill, and I will be so bold as to salute him and thank him, his wife, and his daughter in the name of the working class. This discreet and valiant man acted in this way, he told us, in memory of his son Santiago Díaz, shot by thugs in the pay of the dictatorship. Honor to all of them."

That night, Laura stared intensely into the mute eyes of her invalid father. Then she slowly repeated what Juan Francisco López Greene had said at the ceremony, and Fernando Díaz blinked. When Laura wrote on the little blackboard the family used to communicate with him, she wrote simply, THANK YOU FOR HONORING SANTIAGO. Then Fernando Díaz, as was his custom, opened his eyes very wide and made an immense effort not to blink. All of them, the women in the house, knew those two gestures well—blinking over and over again or not blinking until his eyeballs seemed ready to pop out of their sockets— though they had no idea what either meant. On this occasion, Fernando tried to raise his hands and clench his fists, but they fell on his lap, defeated. He simply arched his eyebrows like two circumflexes.

"Soon we'll find a house where we can live and have boarders right here on Bocanegra Street," Mutti Leticia announced a few days later.

"I'll read to Fernando every night," said the writing aunt, Virginia, her lips tight and her eyes feverish. "Don't worry, Laura."

Laura went in to say good night to her mute father, to read passages from *Jude the Obscure* to him for half an hour, and she could imagine her father dead, his face made beautiful by death, death that would rejuvenate him. They would all have to wait for his death with confidence, even joy, because death would erase the traces of time from Don Fernando, and Laura would always have with her the image of a tender, strong man whenever she needed it.

"Don't let this chance slip by," said her aunt the pianist, Hilda Kelsen, that same night. "Look at my hands. You know what I could have been, isn't that true, Laura? I never want you to have to say the same thing."

Laura Díaz and Juan Francisco López Greene were married in a court in Xalapa on May 12, 1920, Laura's birthday, and she who sang on the twelfth of May the Virgin dressed in white came walking into sight with her coat so gay, and the black Zampaya swept and sang *ora la cachimbá-bimbá-bimbá now my black girl dance to me now my black girl dance away,* and Laura Díaz went out with her husband on the Interoceanic to Mexico City and halfway there she burst into tears because she'd forgotten the Chinese doll Li Po in her pillows back in Xalapa and at the Tehuacán station Juan Francisco was told that President Venustiano Carranza had been assassinated at Tlaxcalantongo.

# 6. Mexico City: 1922

HERE ARE NO SEASONS in Mexico City. The dry period runs from November to March, and then comes the period of rains from April to October. There's no way to get a grip on the weather except for the water and the sun, the real heads and tails of Mexico City. And that's quite a lot. For Laura Díaz, the image of her husband, Juan Francisco López Greene, became permanently fixed one rainy night. Hatless, right in the center of the city, the Zócalo, addressing a multitude, Juan Francisco did not have to shout. His speaking voice was deep and strong, the opposite of his low, private voice. His image was the quintessence of combat, with his heavy soaked hair dripping over the nape of his neck, on his forehead and ears, water pouring off his eyebrows, out of his eyes, and into his mouth, with an oilcloth cape covering his huge body, which she, on their newlywed nights, had approached with fear, respect, suspicion, and gratitude. At the age of twenty-four, Laura Díaz had chosen.

She remembered the boys at provincial dances whom she couldn't tell one from the other. They were interchangeable, pleasant, elegant . . .

"Laura, the thing is, he's very ugly."

"But Elizabeth, he doesn't look like anyone else."

"He's dark-skinned."

"No more so than my Aunt María de la O."

"But you're not going to marry her, are you? There are so many white boys in Veracruz."

"This one's stranger or more dangerous, I don't know."

"And that's why you chose him? You're crazy! And how dangerous, Laura! I envy you, but I'm also sorry for you."

The newlyweds left Xalapa, and no sooner had Laura reached Mexico's central plateau than she missed the beauty and balance of the provincial capital, its nights so perfect that with each evening they bestowed new life on all things. She would remember her home, and her family misfortunes would seem to dissolve in the all-encompassing harmony of the life she'd lived and recalled with her parents, with Santiago, with her maiden aunts, and with her dead grandparents.

She said the word "harmony" and was upset by the memory of the heroic Catalan anarchist whom Juan Francisco referred to that rainy evening when defending the eight-hour workday, minimum wage, paid maternity leave, paid vacations, everything the Revolution had promised, he was saying in his deep, resonant voice, speaking to the crowd gathered in the plaza to defend and demand enactment of Article 123 of the Constitution that May 1, 1922, in the nocturnal rain. This was the first time in the history of humanity that the right to work and the protection of the worker had constitutional status, which was why the Mexican Revolution was a real revolution, not a military coup, not a revolt, not the kind of riot that took place elsewhere in Spanish America. What happened in Mexico was different, unique, everything created from the ground up in the name of the people, by the people, Juan Francisco was saying to the two thousand people gathered in the rain. He was saying it to the rain itself, to the night as it fell, to the new government, successors to the assassinated Venustiano Carranza, who had been eliminated, everyone thought, by the triumvirate of the Agua Prieta rebellion—Calles, Obregón, and de la Huerta—who now held power. López Greene addressed all of them in the name of the Revolution, but he was also speaking to Laura Díaz, his young wife just arrived from the provinces. A beautiful girl, tall, strange with her conspicuous, aquiline features, beautiful because of her very strangeness; he's talking to me as well, to me, I'm part of his words, I have to be part of his speech.

Now it was raining all over the central valley, and she was remembering the ascent in the train from Xalapa to the Buenavista station in Mexico City. I'm exchanging sand for stone, forest for desert, araucarias for cactus. The ascent to the central plateau passed through a landscape of mists and burned lands, then over a hard plain of quarries and workers quarrying stone who looked like stone; occasional poplars with silvery leaves. The landscape took Laura's breath away and made her thirsty.

"You fell asleep, honey."

"The landscape frightened me, Juan Francisco."

"You missed the pines in the high forests."

"Ah, that's why it smells so good."

"Don't think everything here is just bald plains. Look, I'm from Tabasco, I miss the tropics as much as you, but now I couldn't live without these highlands, without the capital."

When she asked him why, Juan Francisco changed his tone of voice, falsified it, perhaps made it a bit high-flown in order to talk about Mexico City, the very center of the country, its heart, you might say, the Aztec city, the colonial city, the modern city one on top of the other.

"Like a layer cake," laughed Laura.

Juan Francisco didn't laugh. Laura went on making comparisons. "Like one of those food trays that would be brought up to Mrs. Aznar, your heroine, my love."

Juan Francisco became even more serious.

"I'm sorry. I'm just joking."

"Laura, weren't you ever curious about seeing Armonía Aznar?"

"I was just a girl."

"You were already in your teens."

"It's probably that my childhood impression lasted, Juan Francisco.

Sometimes, no matter how old you are, you're still frightened by the ghost stories you were told when you were little."

"Forget all that stuff, Laura. You're not the little girl of the family anymore. You're at the side of a man fighting seriously."

"I know, Juan Francisco. I respect that."

"I need your support. Your logic, not your fantasy."

"I'll try not to let you down, my love. I respect you greatly. You know that."

"Begin by asking yourself why you never rebelled against your family, why you never went up to the attic to see Armonía Aznar."

"It's that I was afraid, Juan Francisco. I tell you, I was just a little girl."

"You missed the chance to meet a great woman."

"Forgive me, my love."

"You must forgive me." Juan Francisco hugged her and kissed a nervously clenched fist. "I'll take care of educating you about reality. You've lived for too long in infantile fantasies."

Orlando was no fantasy, she wanted to tell him, knowing she'd never dare mention the disturbing blond young man. Orlando, who was a seducer, wanted to meet me in the attic, and that's why I never went up there; besides, Mrs. Aznar wanted to be respected, she asked for that.

"She herself gave orders that she not be bothered. Who was I to disobey?"

"In other words, you didn't have the nerve."

"No, there are lots of things I don't have the nerve to do." Laura smiled, making a face of false repentance. "With you I would have the nerve. You'll teach me, won't you?"

He smiled and kissed her with the passion he'd been giving her since their wedding night, which they spent on the Interoceanic train. He was a big, vigorous, and loving man, with none of the mystery that had surrounded her other imminent love, Orlando Ximénez, but without his aura of evil, either. Next to the curly-haired blond of the San Cayetano ball, Juan Francisco was plainness itself, an open, almost primitive being in his direct sensual appetite. And because of that Laura was loving him more and more, as if her husband confirmed the first impression the young woman had felt in the Xalapa Casino when she met him. Juan Francisco the lover was as magnificent as Juan Francisco the orator, the politician, the labor leader.

(I don't know anything else, I don't know anything more, I can't compare, but I can enjoy and I do enjoy, the truth is I enjoy myself in bed with this huge man, this male devoid of subtleties and perfumes like Orlando, Juan Francisco, mine.)

"You're going to have to break the habit of calling me 'sweetheart' or 'darling' in public."

"Yes, darling. Sorry. Why?"

"We're in the company of comrades. We're in the struggle. You just can't do that."

"Isn't there any love among your comrades?"

"It isn't serious, Laura. Enough."

"I'm sorry. With you, next to you, for me everything is love. Even the union movement." She laughed, as she always laughed, caressing her man's long, hairy ear. She'd actually say that: You're my man and I'm your little wife, my love is macho but I mustn't call him 'darling.' "

"You always call me 'girl,' you've never called me 'darling.' and I respect you, I know it's your natural way of speaking, just as it's natural for me to call you . . ."

*"Darling . . ."*

He kissed her, but she was left with an uneasy, guilty feeling, as if, very secretly, the two of them had said something unrepeatable, fundamental, which they might one day either be happy about or deeply regret. That possibility was postponed indefinitely by the certainty that the two of them really didn't know each other. Everything was a surprise. For both of them. Each expected that little by little they would reveal themselves to each other. Was that a consolation? The immediate reason for her misgivings, the one that registered in her head, was that her husband was reproaching her for not having had the courage to climb the stairs and knock at Armonía Aznar's door. Juan Francisco's presence and his own history abolished her motive and turned it into a pretext. Mrs. Aznar herself had requested isolation and respect. Laura had that excuse, but the excuse concealed a secret: Orlando, a subject not be mentioned. Laura was left with guilt, a vague, diffuse guilt which she could not defend, transforming it, she suddenly realized, into a motive for identifying with her husband, making it a motive for solidarity with the struggle instead of an obstacle between the two of them, a distancing—she didn't know what to call it and attributed everything, in the end, to her inexperience.

"Don't call me 'darling' in public."

"Don't worry . . . darling." The young bride laughed and tossed a pillow at the tousled, hairy head of her sleepy husband, naked, dark, powerful, smiling now with his strong teeth, wide as an Indian frieze. Like kernels of white corn, said Laura in order not to deify her husband, "wow, you've got teeth like kernels of white corn," Juan Francisco was the novelty of her life, the beginning of another history, far from her family, from Veracruz, from memory.

"I hope you're not choosing him just because he's different," warned Aunt María de la O.

"Who's more different than you, Auntie, and whom do I love more than I love you?"

Niece and aunt joyfully hugged and kissed each other, and now, near Juan Francisco's face while they made love, Laura would feel his attractive darkness, his irresistible difference. Love was like satiating herself with brown sugar or getting drunk on that cinnamon perfume people from the tropics inherit, as if all of them had been conceived in a wild garden amid mangos, papayas, and vanilla. Which is what she thought about in bed with her husband, mangos, papayas, and vanilla, unable not to, thinking it again and again, understanding that in thinking these things she was paying less attention to what she was doing but also prolonging it, fearing at the same time that Juan Francisco might notice her distraction and take it for indifference and confuse the passion of their united bodies in bed with a comparison unfavorable for him, even though he'd proven that Laura was a virgin, that he was the first. Would he suspect that it wasn't being first that was disturbing him but being another, one more, the second, the third, who knows?—the fourth—in the succession of his wife's loves?

"You never tell me about your boyfriends."

111

"You never tell me about your girlfriends."

Juan Francisco's eyes, his movements, the shrugging of his shoulders meant: We machos are different. Why didn't he say so directly, openly?

"We machos are different."

Why was it unnecessary to explain that? Why was society like that, and why was it not going to change? Listening to him speak in the gigantic plaza in the heart of the city, in the rain, with his deep voice, Laura was filled from him, with him, for him, with words and arguments to which she wanted to give a meaning in order to understand him, to penetrate his mind the way he penetrated her body, so she could be his comrade, his ally. Did this revolution not include a change in what Mexican men did to their women, did it not begin a new time for women, as important as the new time for workers that Juan Francisco was defending?

She'd belonged to no other man. She chose this one. She wanted to belong completely to this one. Would Juan Francisco let himself be tempted, was he going to take her as totally as she wanted to be taken by him? Did he fear, he who never spoke of his girlfriends, he who would never say "darling" in public or private, would he fear she might penetrate him, invade his person, dispel his mystery? Did a person exist behind the personage she followed from meeting to meeting, with his serene consent, he who never told her to stay home, this is a matter for men, you'll be bored? On the contrary, he celebrated Laura's presence, Laura's giving herself over to the cause, Laura's attention to the words of her husband the leader, Juan Francisco's speech, *The Speech*, because there was only one, in defense of the workers, of the right to strike, of the eight-hour workday. It was one single speech because it was one single memory, that of the textile workers' strike in Río Blanco, the miners' strike in Cananea, the memory of the liberal and anarcho-syndicalist struggle; an evocation with no blank spaces, a river of causes and effects perfectly linked and interrupted only by calls to rebellion that could set water itself, as well as the mines' copper and silver, on fire.

Laura stopped asking herself questions. Everything was interrupted, nine months after their marriage, by the birth of their first son.

Juan Francisco was so happy about the baby's being a boy that Laura wondered, What if he'd been a girl? The simple fact that she'd borne a little boy and had noted her husband's satisfaction with this gave Laura the power to name the child.

"We'll call him Santiago, my brother's name."

"Your brother died for the Revolution. It's a good sign for the boy."

"I want him to live, Juan Francisco, not to die, not for the Revolution or for anything else."

It was one of those moments when each one held back what might have been said. The destiny of the people surpasses that of the individual, Laura, we are more than ourselves, we are the people, we are the working class. You can't be stingy with your brother and lock him up in your little heart the way you'd press a dead flower between the pages of a book. But, Juan Francisco, he's a new being, can't you accept him simply for being that, a unique creature on this earth, someone who never existed before and will never exist again? That's how I celebrate our son, that's how I kiss, rock, and feed him, singing welcome, my son, you're unique, irreplaceable, I'm going to give you all my love because you're you, I'm resisting the temptation to dream of you as a dead Santiago reborn, a second Santiago to fulfill the interrupted destiny of my adored brother.

"When I call my son Santiago, I think about your brother's heroism."

"I don't, Juan Francisco. I hope our Santiago won't become what you say. It's very painful to be a hero."

"All right. I understand you. I thought you'd like to see in the new Santiago something like the resurrection of the first one."

"Forgive me if I annoy you, but I don't agree."

He said nothing. He got up and went to the window to look out at the July rain.

How could she deny Juan Francisco the right to name their second son? Danton was born eleven months after their first, when General Alvaro Obregón had been President for two years and the country was slowly returning to peace. Laura liked this brilliant (or at least clever) President. He had an answer for everything. He'd lost an arm in the battle of Celaya that annihilated Pancho Villa and his Golden Troops, *los Dorados de Villa*, and was even able to laugh at himself: "The battlefield was like a slaughterhouse. Among all those bodies, how was I going to find the arm they'd shot off me? Gentlemen, I had a brilliant idea. I tossed a gold coin up in the air, and my arm flew up to catch it. No revolutionary general can resist a barrage of fifty thousand pesos!"

Or: "He may have only one hand, but that one is good and heavy," she heard a labor leader say when they gathered at their house to discuss politics.

She preferred to explore the city she didn't know and discover tranquil spots, far from the noise of the buses that had their stops painted on them:

ROMAMERIDACHAPULTEPECANDADDITIONALSTOPS
PENSILBUENOSAIRESPENITENCIARIASALTODELAGUA
COYOACANCALZADADELAPIEDADNIÑOPERDIDO

And the yellow trams that went even farther—CHURUBUSCO, XOCHIMILCO, MILPA ALTA—and the cars, especially the "frees," the *libres*, taxis with signs on their windshields that announced they were "free," and the *fotingos*, the Fords that confused Paseo de la Reforma with a racetrack.

Laura was a lover of parks; that's what she called herself, with a smile on her face. First one child, then two went in the pram that Laura pushed from her home on Avenida Sonora to the Bosque de Chapultepec, where it smelled of eucalyptus, pine, hay, and green lake.

When Danton was born, Aunt María de la O offered to come help Laura, and Juan Francisco raised no objections to the presence of the mulatta aunt, who was getting fatter and fatter, with ankles as thick as her arms, and thick, shaky legs. The two-story house was faced with fretted brick on the lower floor and yellowish stucco on the upper. The entrance was through a garage that Juan Francisco inaugurated the day after the birth of his second son with a Ford convertible given to him by the Regional Workers Confederation of Mexico, the CROM. The head of the central committee, Luis Napoleón Morones, gave him the car in recognition, he said, of his meritorious service on behalf of the union during the Revolution.

"Without the working class," said Morones, not just a fat man, but a thick man with thick lips, thick nose, thick neck, and thick double chins, "without the House of the Workers of the World and the Red Battalions, we would not have triumphed. The workers made the Revolution. The peasants, Villa and Zapata, were a necessary ballast, the reactionary, clerical ballast of Mexico's black colonial past."

"He told you exactly what you wanted to hear," said Laura to Juan Francisco, without a hint of a question in her voice. It was he who queried her words.

"He said nothing more than the truth. The working class is the advance guard of the Revolution."

There sat the Model T Ford, less impressive than the luxurious Isotta-Fraschini that Xavier Icaza had brought to Xalapa but very comfortable for a family of five making an excursion to the Tenayuca pyramids or the floating gardens of Xochimilco. At the back of the garage, in the place of honor, were the hot-water boilers, fed by stacks of wood and newsprint. The garage led to a small foyer with tiled mosaic floors and thence to the living room, furnished simply and comfortably. Laura had opened an account at the Palacio de Hierro department store, and Juan Francisco gave her free rein to buy a sofa and armchairs in blue velvet and lamps that imitated the Art Deco fashion much admired in the illustrated magazines.

"Don't worry, darling. There's a new arrangement called the installment plan. You don't have to pay the whole bill at once." It was a pretty living room. It rose several meters above street level and had a little balcony from which one could admire the Bosque de Chapultepec.

Glass doors led to the dining room with its square table resting on a pedestal of hollow wood, eight heavy mahogany chairs with rigid backrests, a mirror that stored up the afternoon light, and the service entrance to the kitchen with its coal stove and icebox, which required the daily visit of the wood vendor and the coal man, the milk truck and the ice truck.

Above, up a rather pretentious stairway considering the size of the house, there were four bedrooms and a bathroom with a tub, a toilet, and—something Aunt María de la O had never seen—a French bidet.

Juan Francisco wanted to have it taken out, but Laura begged him to leave it, for it was a novelty and so amusing.

"You're imagining my union friends sitting there."

"No, I imagine that potbellied Morones. Don't say anything to them. Let them figure it out for themselves."

Juan Francisco's friends sometimes came back from the bathroom with an uncomfortable air and even with wet trousers. Juan Francisco turned a blind eye to it all, with his innate, dignified seriousness, which countenanced no jokes or extinguished them with a lightning glance, at once fiery and cold.

They would gather in the dining room, and Laura would stay in the living room, reading. Reading at her invalid father's bedside in the hopes that he would understand her, as chancy as a shipwrecked sailor's tossing a bottle into the sea, became for the married woman a silent, pleasurable habit. A living literature was coming into being concerned with the recent past, and Laura read *The Underdogs* by a physician named Mariano Azuela, agreeing with the people in the novel who spoke of peasant troops as a horde of savages, albeit alive, while the urban politicians, lawyers, and intellectuals were perfidious savages, opportunists and traitors. She realized that the Revolution had passed through Veracruz almost like an omen while it roared in the north and center of Mexico.

For Laura, the gift in these readings was the discovery of a young poet from Tabasco barely twenty-three years old. His name was Carlos Pellicer, and when Laura read his first book, *Colors in the Sea*, she didn't know whether to kneel and give thanks or pray or weep, because now the tropics of her childhood came alive and were at hand between the covers of a book. And since Pellicer, like Juan Francisco, was from Tabasco, reading him drew her even closer to her husband:

*Tropics, why did you give me hands*
*Full of color?*

Besides, Laura knew that Juan Francisco liked to have her nearby to serve his friends if the meeting went on for long, but the real reason was to be a witness of what he was saying to his comrades while the aunt took care of the children. It was hard for her to put faces on the voices that reached her from the dining room because when the men came out, they were silent, distant, as if very recently emerged from dark, even invisible places. Some wore jackets and ties, but others wore collarless shirts and wool caps, and some even wore blue overalls and striped shirts with sleeves rolled up to the elbow.

One rainy afternoon the men arrived wet, some wearing raincoats, most unprotected. In Mexico City, almost no one used umbrellas, though the rain came punctually and powerfully, falling in cataracts at about two o'clock in the afternoon and continuing on and off until dawn. Then the morning sun would return. The men smelled strongly of wet clothes, muddy shoes, moist socks.

Laura watched them silently file in and silently file out. Those with caps would take them off when they saw her and then put them right back on. Those with hats would leave them at the entrance. Others didn't know what to do with their hands when they saw her. Yet they were eloquent in the dining room, and Laura, invisible to them but attentive to everything they were saying, believed she was hearing voices buried for a long time, possessors of an eloquence that had been muted for centuries. They had fought against the dictatorship of Don Porfirio Díaz—this Laura heard, that they'd fought, the oldest among them—in Light, an anarcho-syndicalist group, then in the House of the Workers of the World founded by the anarchist Professor Moncaleano, and finally in the Labor Party after Carranza dissolved the House once the Revolution triumphed, when the old ingrate forgot everything he owed his Red Battalions and the House of the Workers. But Obregón (had he ordered the death of Carranza?) offered the workers a new party, the Labor Party, and a new central workers' association, the Regional Workers Confederation of Mexico, the CROM, so they could continue their struggles for justice.

"Just tricks. You've got to realize, comrades, that governments, every single one of them, have done nothing but trick us. Madero, who was supposed to be the apostle of the Revolution, unleashed his Cossacks on us."

"What did you expect, Dionisio? That twerp wasn't a revolutionary.

He was only a democrat. But we owe him a big favor, because, look, Madero thought he was going to create democracy in Mexico without revolution, without real changes. He was naive, and it cost him his life. He was bumped off by the army, the landowners, all the people he didn't dare touch because he thought that it was enough simply to enact democratic laws. Right away."

"But look at Huerta. He murdered Madero, and he did take us into account. Did you ever see a demonstration bigger than the one on May Day in 1913? The eight-hour workday, the six-day workweek, General Huerta accepted it all."

"Just tricks. No sooner did we start talking about democracy than he ordered our offices burned, arrested us, and deported us. Don't forget that. It's a lesson. A dictatorship can give labor guarantees but not political liberty. Of course we were going to welcome General Obregón like a savior when he took Mexico City in 1915 and right away started talking about proletarian revolution, about teaching the capitalists a lesson, about—"

"You were there, Palomo, you remember how Obregón came to our meeting and embraced us one by one—he still had two arms then—and he said to each of us, You're right, pal. He told us what we wanted to hear."

"Just tricks, José Miguel. What Obregón wanted to do was to use us as allies against the peasants, against Villa and Zapata. And he got what he wanted. He convinced us the peasants were reactionaries, clerical, wore pictures of the Virgin on their hats, who knows what else, they were the past."

"Just tricks, Pánfilo. Carranza was a hacienda owner and hated the peasants. Zapata and Villa were right to distribute land without asking the old goat's permission."

"But now Obregón has won. He always defended us, even if it was to win support against Zapata and Villa. Figure it out, comrades. Obregón won out over everyone."

"You mean he killed everyone."

"If you like. That's how politics works."

"Does it have to be that way? Let's change it, Dionisio."

"Obregón won, that's reality. He won, and he's going to stick. Mexico is at peace."

"Tell it to all those restless generals. They all want a piece of the government, power has yet to be distributed, Palomo, there are miracles yet to come. Let's see how it plays out for us."

"Just tricks, that's how it'll play out for us. Tricks. Hoaxes."

"Comrades," Juan Francisco ended the discussion. "What matters to us are very concrete things—the right to strike, wages, the workday, and then further victories like paid vacations, paid maternity leave, social security. That's what's important for us to win. Don't lose sight of those goals, comrades. Don't get lost in the maze of politics."

Laura stopped knitting, closed her eyes, and tried to imagine her husband in the dining room next door, standing up, ending the argument, telling the truth, but the intelligent truth, the *possible* truth: they simply had to collaborate with Obregón, with the CROM, and its leader Luis Napoleón Morones. The rain fell harder, and Laura listened harder. Juan Francisco's comrades used the copper spittoons which were an indispensable part of every well-appointed home, of all public places, and, especially, of any room where men gathered.

"Why don't we women spit?"

Then they filed out of the dining room and wordlessly said goodbye to Laura, and she would vainly try to attribute the ideas she'd heard to the faces she watched pass—this one with sunken eyes (Pánfilo?), that one with a nose as narrow as the gates of heaven (José Miguel?), the sunny look of one (Dionisio?), the blind stumbling of another (Palomo?), the whole group and all the details about these men, the dissimulated limping, the desire to weep for some loved one, the salty saliva, the last cold, the ancient passage of hours remembered because they never took place, youth wanting to be more than youth all at once, eyes mortgaged with blood, loves postponed, the handful of dead men, the longed-for generations, hopelessness without power, life exalted without the need for happiness, a parade of promises, crumbs on shirts, a strand of white hair on a lapel, a remnant of breakfast's scrambled eggs on a lip, the haste to return to what had been abandoned, delay in order to avoid return—Laura saw all that as her husband's comrades passed by.

No one was smiling, and that alarmed her. Wasn't Juan Francisco right? Was it she who didn't understand anything? She wanted to give words to the faces leaving her house, saying farewell wordlessly. She was upset, actually came to feel guilty for wanting reasons where perhaps there were only dreams and desires.

She liked President Obregón. He was astute, intelligent, even though he didn't seem as handsome as he had in the battle photos, or as blond, young, and svelte as when he had fought with two arms; now, maimed and graying, he'd put on weight, as if he weren't getting enough exercise or the presidential sash didn't quite compensate for the lost hand. But as she strolled through the parks in the morning, before the cloudbursts, with the boys in the pram, Laura felt something new was happening. José Vasconcelos, an overexcited but brilliant philosopher, was the revolutionary government's first Minister of Education, and he had turned over the walls of public buildings to artists to paint what they pleased—attacks on the clergy, the bourgeoisie, the Holy Trinity, or, rather worse, the very government that was paying for their labor. There was freedom! Laura exclaimed to herself—taking advantage of her aunt's minding the boys to make an excursion to the National Preparatory School, where Orozco was painting, or to the National Palace, where Rivera was painting.

Like Obregón, Orozco too was one-armed, as well as nearsighted and sad. Laura admired him because he painted the walls in the Prepa as if he were someone else, with a vigorous hand and his eyes unblinkingly fixed on the sun: he painted with what he lacked. An unclouded vision, another Orozco inhabiting the body of this Orozco, guided him, illuminated him, challenged Laura Díaz to imagine what the fiery, fugitive genius must be that governed the painter's body, communicating an invisible fire to the disabled, shortsighted artist with his severe lips and bitter brow.

By contrast, Laura in her new outfit, with its bodice embroidered with precious stones and its short skirt, had barely sat down on the stairway in the National Palace to watch Diego Rivera paint when the artist became distracted, staring at her with an intensity that made her blush.

"You've got the face of a boy or a madonna. I don't know which. You choose. Who are you?" asked Rivera during a break.

"I'm a girl." Laura smiled. "And I have two sons."

"I've got two girls. Let's marry off the four of them, and when we're both free of brats I'll paint you as neither a woman nor a man but a hermaphrodite. Do you realize what the advantage is? You can love yourself both ways."

He was the opposite of Orozco. He was an immense, fat, tall frog with bulging, sleepy eyes. And when she turned up another day dressed in black with a black ribbon tied over her hair because of the death of her father, Fernando Díaz, in Xalapa, one of Rivera's assistants asked her to leave: the maestro feared the evil eye and couldn't paint while making the sign of the horns to exorcise bad luck.

"Oh, I see . . . because I'm in mourning. You must be very superstitious, red maestro, if a woman in black can frighten you."

She hadn't had time to get to Xalapa for the funeral. Her mother, Leticia, sent her a telegram. You have your own obligations, Laura, a husband and two sons. Don't make the trip. Why didn't she add anything else, your father thought of you before dying, said your name, regained his speech for the last time just to say Laura, God gave him that gift at the end, he *spoke* again?

"He was a decent man, Laura," said Juan Francisco. "You know how he helped us."

"He did it for Santiago's sake," Laura retorted, the telegram in one hand and the other pushing aside the curtain so she could peer out through the almost black rain of late afternoon, as if to see all the way to a cemetery in Xalapa. The snowy peaks of Mexico City's two volcanoes were bobbing above the storm.

When Aunt María de la O came home, she said that God knew what He was doing, Fernando Díaz wanted to die in order not to be in the way, she knew this because the two of them understood each other clearly, with just a look, direct and intelligent, how could it be otherwise with the man who had saved her mother, supported her, and given her a dignified old age.

"Is your mother still alive?"

María de la O became upset, shook her head, said I don't know, I don't know, but one morning when Laura stayed home to make the beds and the aunt took the boy and the baby in the carriage out for a stroll, she found under María de la O's mattress an old daguerreotype of a slim, good-looking black woman in a low-cut dress, with a spark on her lips, a challenge in her eyes, a wasp waist, and breasts like hard melons. She quickly put it back when she heard María de la O return, tired after only three blocks, hobbling on her swollen ankles.

"Oooh, the altitude here, Laurita."

The altitude and its airless air. The rain and its refreshing air. It was like the beat of Mexico's heart, sun and rain, rain and sun, systole and diastole, every day. Thank heaven the nights were rainy and the days clear. On weekends, Xavier Icaza would visit and teach them how to drive the Ford that the CROM had given Juan Francisco.

Laura turned out to be a better driver than her oversized, awkward husband, who almost didn't fit in the seat and had no place to put his knees. She seemed to have an instinctive talent for driving and could now take the boys on excursions to Xochimilco to see the canals, to Tenayuca to see the pyramid, and to wander around the barns at Milpa Alta and smell that unique aroma of udders and straw and moist backs and drink warm milk fresh from the cow.

One day, ducking out of the rain after she'd left the National Palace (where Rivera had readmitted her as soon as she stopped wearing mourning), Laura took the car parked on Calle de La Moneda and drove down the recently rebaptized Avenida Madero, the former Calle de Plateros, admiring as she went the colonial mansions along it, with their fiery *tezontle* tiles and matte marble, and then to Alameda and Paseo de la Reforma, where the architecture became frenchified, where beautiful villas had high mansard roofs and formal gardens.

A feeling of comfort settled over her. Her life as a married woman was comfortable, satisfactory, she had two handsome sons and an extraordinary husband—difficult at times because he was an honest man with character, a man who wouldn't give in, but an always loving man, preoccupied, burdened by his work, but who created no problems for her. As she maneuvered to the left at the Niza traffic circle to make her way to Avenida de los Insurgentes and her house on Avenida Sonora, her comfort began to discomfit her. Everything was too calm, too good, something had to happen . . .

"You believe in presentiments, omens, don't you, Auntie?"

"Well, I do believe in sentiments, and your aunts tell me theirs in letter after letter, Hilda and Virginia and your mother down there together, busy with their guests, they sit down to write letters and they feel different. I think they don't even realize what they tell me, and sometimes that offends me, they write to me as if I weren't myself, as if by writing to me they could talk to each other, dearie, I'm just the pre-text, Hilda can't play the piano anymore because of her arthritis, so she tells me how the music goes through her head, look here, read, how good God is, or how bad, I don't know, because He allows me to remember Chopin's nocturnes, note by note, in my head, absolutely exact, but He won't let me listen to the music outside my head, have you heard of that new thing, the Victrola? Chopin screeches on those records or whatever you call them, but in my head his music is crystalline and sad, as if the purity of the sound depended on the melancholy of one's soul, don't you hear it, sister, don't you hear me? If I knew that someone was hearing Chopin in their head with the same clarity I hear him in mine, I'd be happy, María de la O, I'd be sharing what I love most, I don't enjoy it all by myself, I wish I could share my musical happiness with someone, with more than one person, and I can't any longer, my fate was not the one I wanted, perhaps it's the one I imagined without wanting it, do you hear me, sister? Only a humble prayer, an impotent plea like Chopin's, who people say imagined his last nocturne when a storm forced him inside a church, do you understand my plea, sister? and Virginia doesn't talk to me but won't accept dying without having had anything published, Laura, couldn't your husband ask Minister Vasconcelos to publish your Aunt Virginia's poems? Have you seen how pretty those books are with green covers that he brought out at the university? Don't you think you could ask? Because even though out of pride Virginia never mentions these things to me, what Hilda writes to me is exactly what Virginia feels, except that the poetess has no words and the pianist does, because, as Hilda says, my music is my words and, as Virginia answers her, my words are my silence . . . Only your mother, Leticia, complains of nothing, but she isn't happy, either."

Laura felt insufficient. She decided to ask Juan Francisco to let her work with him at what he was doing, at his side, helping him at least half the day, the two of them working together, organizing the workers, and he said fine but first come with me for a few days to see if you like it.

They were together only forty-eight hours. The old city was a jumble of small shops, shoemakers, blacksmiths, carpenters, potters, disabled veterans of the revolutionary wars, old camp followers now without men who sold tamales and drinks on the corners, murmuring *corridos* and the names of lost battles, a viceregal city with a proletarian pulse, its palaces now tenements, its wide portals now cluttered with sweet shops and lottery stands, shops that sold anything and everything, saddle makers, ancient inns turned into shelters where vagrants and criminals, homeless beggars and disoriented old people slept in a repugnant collective fog older than the perfume in the streets, where prostitutes plied their trade, leaning against entryways, open to suggestions and propositions, a whorish perfume identical to the scent of funeral parlors, gardenias and penises, both erect, pulque shops reeking of vomit and stray-dog urine, battalions of loose, mangy beasts poking around in garbage dumps that grew and grew, ever grayer and more purulent, like huge, cancerous lungs that would someday suffocate the entire city. Garbage had overflowed from the few canals left from the Aztec city, the assassinated city. People said they'd be drained and filled in with asphalt.

"Where would you like to begin, Laura?"

"You tell me, Juan Francisco."

"You want me to tell you? Begin at home. Run your own house properly, girl, and you'll make more of a contribution than if you come to these neighborhoods to organize and save people—who by the way won't thank you for your trouble. Leave the work to me. This is not for you."

He was right. But that evening, back in her house, Laura Díaz was in a high state of excitement, not understanding very well why, as if the trip to a city that was both hers and not hers had aroused the passion of her childhood years with which she'd loved and explored the forest and its giant stone women covered with lianas and jewels, the trees and their gods hidden among laurels, and in Veracruz, the passion she'd shared with Santiago that had only grown in the years since his death, and in Xalapa the passion from Orlando's languid body that she'd rejected, the passion in her father's broken body that she'd tenaciously embraced. And now Juan Francisco, Mexico City, her house, the boys, and a request dashed by her husband the way you swat a fly: let me become impassioned with you and with what you're doing, Juan Francisco.

He may be right. He didn't understand me. But even so he has to give something more to what is stirring in my soul. I love everything I have and wouldn't exchange it for anything in the world. But I want something else. What is it?

He was asking for the mute obedience of an impassioned soul.

"Where's the car, Juan Francisco?"

"I gave it back. Don't give me that look. The comrades asked me for it. They don't want me to accept anything from the official union. They call it corruption."

## 7. Avenida Sonora: 1928

WHAT WAS HE THINKING about? What was she thinking about?

He was impenetrable, like a sphere of knives. She could only know what he was thinking about by knowing what she was thinking about. What did she think about when he—repeating something that irritated her more and more and discredited him—accused her of not having gone up to the attic in Xalapa to see the Catalan anarchist. Finally, she tired of it, gave up, set aside her own reasons, and began to note, in a small graph-paper notebook she used to keep household accounts, each time he, with no provocation on her part, would remind her of this omission. It was no longer a scolding but a nervous habit, like the involuntary squinting of eyes that were fixed, without their own light. What did she think when she heard yet again the same speech she'd been hearing now for nine years, so fresh, so powerful the first times, then more difficult to understand because more difficult to hear, excessively rationalist, as she waited in vain for the dream of the speech, not the speech itself but the dream of the speech, especially when she realized that, as a mother, she could speak to her sons Santiago and Danton only in dreams, in fables. Their father's speech had lost the dream. It was an insomniac speech. Juan Francisco's words did not sleep. They kept watch.

"Mama, I'm afraid, look through the window. The sun isn't there anymore. Where did the sun go? Did the sun die?"

"Juan Francisco, don't talk to me as if I were an audience of a thousand people. I'm just one person. Laura. Your wife."

"You don't admire me the way you did before. Before, you used to admire me."

She wanted to love him. What was happening to her? What was it that was happening, which she neither knew nor understood?

"Who understands women? Short ideas and long hair."

She wasn't going to waste time telling him what the boys understood each time they told a story or asked a question, that words are born from imagination and pleasure, they aren't for an audience of thousands of people or a plaza filled with flags, they are for you and for me. To whom are you speaking, Juan Francisco? She always saw him at a podium and the podium was a pedestal and that was where she'd placed him herself from the day they married. No one but she had put him there, not the Revolution, not the working class, not the unions, not the government; she was the vestal of the temple named Juan Francisco López Greene, and she'd asked her husband to be worthy of the devotion of the wife. But a temple is a place for repeated ceremonies. And what is repeated becomes boring unless faith sustains it.

It wasn't that Laura lost faith in Juan Francisco. She was simply being honest with herself, registering the irritations of connubial life, what couple doesn't get irritated over the course of time? It was normal after eight years of marriage. At first they hadn't known each other, and everything was a surprise. Now she wished she could recover the astonishment and novelty, but she realized that the second time around astonishment is habit and novelty is nostalgia. Was it her fault? She'd begun by admiring the public figure. Then she'd tried to penetrate it, only to find that behind the public figure was another public figure and another behind that one, until she realized that the dazzling orator, leader of the masses, was the real figure, there was no trick, no other personality to find, she'd have to resign herself to living with a man who treated his wife and children as a grateful audience. The problem was that the figure on the podium also slept in the conjugal bed, and one evening contact between their feet under the sheets made her, involuntarily, pull hers back, her husband's elbows began to disgust her, she would stare at that articulation of wrinkles between the upper arm and forearm and imagine all of him as an enormous elbow, a loose hide from head to foot.

"I'm sorry. I'm tired. Not tonight."

"Why didn't you say something? Should we hire a maid? I thought that between you and your aunt you managed the house very well."

"That's true, Juan Francisco. There's no need for maids. You have María de la O and me. You shouldn't have maids. You serve the working class."

"How well you understand things, Laura."

"Know something, Auntie?" she dared to say to María de la O. "Sometimes I miss life in Veracruz. It was more fun."

The aunt did not agree, simply looked attentively at Laura, and then Laura laughed as if to say the matter was of no importance.

"You stay here with the boys. I'll go to the market."

It was not a bother; she found it amusing to go to the Parián in Colonia Roma, because it broke the household routine, which in truth was no routine. Laura loved her aunt, adored her sons, and was delighted to watch them grow. The market was a miniature forest where she could find all the things that delighted her, flowers and fruits, so various and abundant in Mexico, the *azucenas* and gladiolas, the Madonna lilies, the "clouds" and pansies, the mangos, papaya, vanilla that she thought about when she made love: the mamey, the quince, the *tejocote*, the pineapple, limes and lemons, *guanábana*, oranges, the black *zapotes* and the little *zapotes*: the tastes, shapes, flavors of markets filled her with joy and with nostalgia for her childhood and youth.

"But I'm only thirty years old."

She was pensive as she returned from the Parián to Avenida Sonora and asked herself, Is there something more? Is this all there is? She answered herself with a slight shrug of her shoulders and walked faster, not even thinking about the weight of the baskets. If there was no more automobile, it was because Juan Francisco was honorable and had returned the gift to the CROM. She remembered that it had not been his idea to return it. The comrades had asked him to do it. Don't accept gifts from the official union. Don't become corrupt. It hadn't been a voluntary act on his part. They'd asked him to do it.

"Juan Francisco, would you have returned the car if your comrades hadn't asked you to?"

"I serve the working class. That's that."

"Sweetheart, why do you depend on injustice so much?"

"You already know I don't like——"

"My poor Juan Francisco, what would become of you in a just world?"

"Spare me the condescension. Sometimes I just can't figure you out. Hurry up and make breakfast, I've got an important meeting today."

"Not a day passes without an important meeting. Not a month. Not a year. Every minute there's an important meeting."

What did he think of her? Was Laura only a habit of his, a sexual rite, mute obedience, expected gratitude?

"I mean, how good it is that you have people to defend. That's your strength. It pours out of you. I love to see you come home tired."

"You're incomprehensible."

"What are you talking about? I love it when you fall asleep on my breasts, and I love the idea that I restore your strength. Your work drains you even if you don't realize it."

"You're so flighty, you make me laugh sometimes, but other times——"

"I annoy you . . . I just love the idea!"

He left without another word. What did he think of her? Did he remember the young woman he met at the Casino ball at Xalapa? The promise he made her that he would educate her, teach her to be a woman in the city and in the world? Would he remember the young mother who wanted to accompany him in his work, identify herself with him, prove that in their married life the two of them shared the life of the world, the life of work?

This idea weighed more and more on Laura Díaz. Her husband had rejected her, had not carried out the promise that they would be together in everything, united in bed, in being parents, but also in work, in that part of the whole that eats up the life of each day the way children eat the sections of an orange, transforming all the rest—bed and being parents, matrimony and dreams—into minutes to be counted and finally into empty skins to be discarded.

"The mute obedience of impassioned souls."

Laura blamed herself. She remembered the child from Catemaco, the girl from Veracruz, the young woman from Xalapa, and in each she saw the growing promise that culminated in her wedding eight years before. Ever since then I've shrunk instead of growing, I've been turning into a little dwarf, as if he didn't deserve me, as if he'd done me a favor, he didn't ask me to do it, he didn't impose it on me, I asked for it, and I imposed it on myself in order to be worthy of him. Now I know I wanted to be worthy of a mystery, I didn't know him, I was impressed by him physically, his way of speaking, of taking control of the monster of the crowd, I was impressed by that speech he gave in our Xalapa house in honor of the Catalan woman. That's what I fell in love with— to jump from my love to knowledge of the person I loved, love as a trampoline of knowing, its labyrinth, my God, I've spent eight years trying to penetrate a mystery that isn't mysterious, for my husband is what he seems to be, not more, what appears is what he is, there's nothing more to discover, I'll ask the audience whom the leader López Greene speaks to, the man is for real, what he tells them is true, there's nothing hidden behind his words, his words are his entire truth, every last bit, believe in him, there is no one more authentic, what you see is what he is, what he says is nothing more.

From Laura he demanded out of habit what had satisfied him before. Little by little, she stopped feeling satisfied with what had once satisfied both of them.

"When I met you, I thought I didn't deserve you. What do you think of that? Why don't you answer?"

"I thought I could change you."

"So what you bought in Xalapa seems pretty paltry to you now."

"You don't understand. We all progress, we all can either better ourselves or get worse."

"Are you saying you wanted to change me?"

"For the good."

"All right then, tell me something, honestly. Am I a good wife and mother? When I wanted to work with you, didn't you stop me with that little stroll through hell you set up for me? What more did you want?"

"Someone to confide in," said Juan Francisco, and first he got out of bed, but then quickly looked back at Laura with shining eyes and, with a grimace of pain, threw himself into his wife's arms.

"My love, my love."

That year, President Obregón was succeeded by Plutarco Elías Calles, another Sonora man, another one of the Agua Prieta triumvirate. The Revolution had been carried out to the chant of *FREE VOTES, NO REELECTION* because Porfirio Díaz had kept himself in office for three decades with fraudulent reelections. Now, ex-President Obregón wanted to abrogate his own ineligibility and return to the throne of the eagle and serpent. Many said it would betray one of the principles of the Revolution. But the rationale of power had its way. The Constitution was amended to allow a former president's reelection. Everyone had been certain that the three Sonora men would take turns at being President until they died of old age, just like Don Porfirio Díaz, unless another Madero, another revolution, came along.

"Morones wants us union men to back General Obregón's reelection. I'd like to discuss it with you," said Juan Francisco to the union leaders gathered once again in his house, as they did every month of every year. In the little living room, Laura put aside her book.

"Morones is an opportunist. He doesn't think the way we do. He hates the anarcho-syndicalists. He adores the corporate unionists who thicken the government's broth. If we support Obregón, our independence is over. He'll turn us into little lambs or he'll lead us to slaughter, which is pretty much the same thing."

"You're right, Palomo. What are we going to be, Juan Francisco, independent, militant unions or corporate sectors of the official labor movement? I want all of you to tell me," said another of those faceless voices that Laura struggled vainly to link, when they came in, when they left, with the faces filing through the little living room.

"Dammit, Juan Francisco—and begging the pardon of the lady in the next room—we are the heirs of Light, of the Red Tribunal, the House of the Workers of the World, the Red Battalions of the Revolution. Are we going to end up as lackeys to a government that uses us just to put on fancy revolutionary airs? Revolutionary? Hooey is what I say."

"What's in our best interest?" Laura heard her husband's voice. "To achieve what we want, a better life for the workers? Or are we going to wear ourselves out fighting the government, wasting our energy in squabbles, and letting others turn the promises of the Revolution into realities? Are we going to lose our chance?"

"We're going to lose everything, right down to our long johns."

"Does anyone here believe in the soul?"

"A revolution becomes legitimate on its own and engenders rights, comrades," Juan Francisco summed up. "Obregón has the support of those who made the Revolution. Even Zapata's and Villa's people support him. He figured out a way to win them over. Are we going to be the exception?"

"I think we should be, Juan Francisco. The workers' movement was born to be the exception. Come on, pal, don't keep us from being the ones who get to rain on the government's parade."

For her entire life as a young married woman she'd been listening to the same discussion: it was like going to church every Sunday to hear the same sermon. Habit, Laura once thought, has to have meaning, it must become ritual. She went back over the ritual moments in her own life—birth, childhood, puberty, marriage, death—she was thirty years old, and she'd known them all by now, a personal knowledge, a knowledge that intimately touched her family. It became a collective knowledge, as if the entire nation could not bring itself to divorce its bride: death; that July day when Juan Francisco returned home unexpectedly sometime around six in the afternoon, completely upset, and said, "President Obregón was assassinated at a banquet."

"Who did it?"

"A Catholic."

"Was he killed?"

"Who? Obregón? I already said he was."

"No, I mean the killer."

"No, he's in jail. His name is Toral. A fanatic."

Of all the coincidences she'd experienced in her life until that moment, none alarmed Laura so much as the one that began with the sound, one afternoon, of a hand lightly knocking at the door of the house. María de la O had taken the boys to the park; Juan Francisco was returning later and later from work. The dining-room discussions had yielded to the need to act: Obregón was dead; he and Calles had divided power between them, so now only one of the strong men was left. Had Calles murdered Obregón? Was Mexico an endless chain of sacrifices, each one engendering the next, and the last certain of its eventual destiny, to be the same as the act that created it—death to reach power, death to leave it?

"Just look, Juan Francisco, Morones and the CROM are overjoyed because Obregón is dead. Morones wants to be a presidential candidate."

"That fatso will need a double-sized chair . . ."

"No jokes, Palomo. No reelection was the sacred principle."

"Cut it out, Pánfilo. Don't use religious expressions, it really—"

"I'm telling you to be serious. The untouchable principle—is that all right?—of the Revolution. Calles betrayed Morones' presidential hopes to help out his buddy Obregón. Who comes out ahead because of the crime? Just ask yourself that simple question. Who comes out ahead?"

"Calles and Morones. And who takes all the blame? The Catholics."

"But you've always been anticlerical, Palomo. You criticize the peasants for being so Catholic."

"For that very reason, I'm telling you there's no better way to strengthen the Church than by persecuting it. That's what I'm afraid of now."

"Why is Calles persecuting the Church now? The Turk is no jackass."

"To nip the fat guy's rage in the bud, José Miguel. He had to find some way to show he's revolutionary."

"Now I don't understand anything."

"Understand this. In Mexico, even cripples are acrobats."

"Okay, but don't you forget something else. Politics is the art of swallowing toads without making a face."

She was as white as the moon, and her whiteness emphasized her thick, continuous, black eyebrows, which ran across her forehead and cast more of a shadow over the circles under her eyes, circles like the shadow of her immense eyes, as black as they say sin is black, although the eyes of this woman were swimming in a lake of omens. She was dressed in black, with long skirts and low-heeled shoes, her blouse buttoned up to her neck, and a black shawl nervously covering her back, tightly but carelessly wrapped, slipping down to her waist. Her disarray embarrassed her, as if it gave her a clownish air, and made her readjust the shawl over her shoulders, though not over her hair, which was divided strictly by a center part and gathered into a bun at the nape of her neck, where long, loose hairs had escaped as if a secret part of her were rebelling against the discipline of her costume. The loosened hairs were not as black as the tight hairdo of this pale, nervous woman, as if they were announcing something, antennas for some undesired news.

"Excuse me, but I was told a maid was needed here."

"No, miss, in this house we don't exploit anyone." Laura smiled with her ever more irrepressible irony. Was irony her only possible defense against flat and unrelieved routine, in itself neither degrading nor exalting, but stretching out as long as the horizon of her years?

"I know you need help, ma'am."

"Look, I just told you—"

She said nothing more because the white, sunken-eyed woman dressed in black thrust herself into the garage. She begged silence with her eyes and clasped Laura's hands alarmingly, then closed her eyes as if facing a physical catastrophe, while in the street a group of metallic soldiers came running, breaking the pavement with the force of their boots, sounding like steel as they marched over steel streets in a soulless city. The woman trembled in Laura's arms.

"Please, ma'am."

Laura looked into her eyes. "What's your name?"

"Carmela."

"Well, I don't see why a squad of soldiers should be hunting through the streets for a maid named Carmela."

"Ma'am, I—"

"Not a word, Carmela. At the back of the patio, there's an empty maid's room. Let's fix it up. It's filled with old newspapers. Put them next to the boiler. Can you cook?"

"I know how to make communion wafers, ma'am."

"I'll teach you. Where are you from?"

"Guadalajara."

"Say that your parents are from Veracruz."

"They're dead."

"Well then, say they were from Veracruz. I need subjects so I can protect you, Carmela. Things to talk about. Follow my lead."

"May God reward you, ma'am."

Juan Francisco reacted most docilely to Carmela's presence. Laura did not have to give him any explanations. He himself had acknowledged he was unaware of things, rarely alert to the needs of the house, to Laura's fatigue, to her interest in books and painting. The boys were growing and needed their mother to educate them. María de la O was getting old and tired out.

"Why don't you all go to Xalapa to rest? Carmela can take care of me here in the house."

Laura Díaz looked over at the attic of her old house in Xalapa, visible from the second-story terrace of the boardinghouse where her mother

135

Leticia and her Aunts Hilda and Virginia now lived and worked. Middle age was no longer creeping up on the Kelsen sisters: it had trapped them, they were leaving time itself behind.

Laura loved them, she realized in the narrow parlor where Leticia had gathered, rather inelegantly, her personal furniture, the wicker chairs from her marriage, the marble console, the paintings of the rascal and the dog. Hilda had a huge, rose-colored double chin adorned with white hairs, but her eyes were still very blue despite the thick glasses that from time to time slipped down her straight nose.

"I'm going blind, Laura. It's a blessing I can't see my hands, look at my hands, they look like the knots sailors make on the docks, like the roots of an old tree. How can I play the piano like this? At least I have Aunt Virginia, who reads to me."

Virginia kept her eyes wide open, as if in shock about something, and her hands resting on a kidskin binding, as if it were the skin of a beloved being. She tapped her fingers in time with the blinking of her very black, alert eyes. Was she waiting for the arrival of something imminent or the entrance of some unexpected but providential being? God, a mailman, a lover, a publisher? All those possibilities passed simultaneously before Aunt Virginia's all too lively eyes.

"You never spoke to Minister Vasconcelos about publishing my book of poems?"

"Aunt Virginia, Vasconcelos isn't a minister anymore. He's in opposition to Calles' government. Besides, I've never met him."

"I don't know anything about politics. Why don't the poets govern us?"

"Because they don't know how to swallow toads without making a face," laughed Laura.

"What? What are you saying? Are you insane or what? *Nett Affe!*"

Although the three sisters had decided to run the boarding house, in reality only Leticia worked at it. Weak, nervous, tall, holding her back very straight, her hair graying, a woman of few words but of eloquent punctuality in the execution of all tasks, she had the menus ready, the rooms clean, the plants watered. All with the active help of

Zampaya, who went on bringing joy to the house with his dances and songs from who knew where:

*ora la cachimbá-bimbá-bimbá*
*ora la cachimbábá*
*now my black girl dance to me*
*now my black girl dance away*

Laura was shocked to see the wiry gray hair on the black man's head. She was sure Zampaya was secretly in contact with a sect of dancing witches and an interminable chorus of invisible voices. These are the people with whom we went to give my brother Santiago's body to the sea, these are the people with whom we are witnesses. Then Laura looked toward the attic, thought about Armonía Aznar here in Xalapa, and, who knows why?, she thought about Carmela with no last name in the maid's room in Mexico City.

Leticia especially looked after old acquaintances from Veracruz passing through Xalapa. But now, with the arrival of Laura and María de la O, in addition to the presence of Aunts Hilda and Virginia, the two permanent and penniless guests, there was room for only two guests. Laura was astonished to see once more the now adult red-haired tennis player, the big fellow with strong, svelte, hairy legs who had abused the girls at the San Cayetano dances.

He greeted her with a gesture of excuse and submission as unexpected as his presence. He was a traveling salesman, he said, selling automobile tires on the Córdoba-Orizaba-Xalapa-Veracruz circuit. At least he hadn't been sent to that hell the port of Coatzacoalcos. The company gave him his own car—his face lit up, as it had when he'd frenetically danced the cakewalk in 1915—though of course it wasn't his but the company's.

The lights went out.

The other guest was, Leticia told her, an old man, he never leaves his room, I bring his meals to him.

One afternoon, Leticia was busy with something at the door and left the guest's tray of food in the kitchen, where it was getting cold. Not thinking anything of it, Laura picked up the tray and took it to the guest, who never allowed himself to be seen.

He was sitting on the edge of his bed with something in his hands that he hid as soon as he heard Laura's footsteps. She managed to detect the unmistakable sound of rosary beads. When she set the tray down, she felt a tremor run through her entire body, a chill of sudden recognition through veils and more veils of oblivion, time, and, in this case, disdain. Laura's memory had to make a gigantic leap backward to identify the young priest from Puebla, dark-skinned and intolerant, who'd disappeared one day with the church's treasure.

"Why, it's you, the priest."

"You are Laura, isn't that right? Please, don't raise your voice. Don't get your mother into trouble."

"Father Elzevir."

The priest clasped Laura's hands. "How can you remember? You were just a child."

There was no need to ask him what he was doing hidden away there. "Please, don't raise your voice. Don't get your mother into trouble." He said she didn't have to ask him anything. He would tell her he didn't get very far with what he'd stolen. He was a coward. He admitted it. When the police were about to catch him, he thought it would be better to submit to the pity of the Church, for Don Porfirio's police had none.

"I asked forgiveness, and it was granted to me. I confessed and was absolved. I repented and again entered the community of my Church. But I felt it was all too easy. It was true and profound, but easy. I had to pay for the evil I'd committed, my temptation. My illusion. God our master did me the favor of sending me this punishment, Calles' religious persecution."

He looked at Laura with the eyes of a conquered Indian. "Now I feel guiltier than ever. I have nightmares. I'm sure God punished me for my sacrilege by causing this persecution to fall on His Church. I believe I am responsible, because of my individual act, for a collective evil. I believe it profoundly."

"Father, you have no reason to confess to me."

"Oh, but I do." Elzevir squeezed Laura's hands, which he'd never stopped holding. "Oh, but I do. You were a child. But who better than a child can I ask for forgiveness for the tumult of my soul? Will you forgive me?"

"Yes, Father, I never made charges against you, but my mother—"

"Your mother and your aunts have understood. They have forgiven me. That's why I'm here. Without them, I would have been shot."

"I'm saying you did me no harm. Excuse me, but I'd forgotten all about you."

"But that was the harm. Don't you see? Being forgotten is the harm. I sowed scandal in my parish, and if my parish forgets it, the reason is that the scandal penetrated so deeply that it was forgotten and forgiven."

"My mother has forgiven you," Laura interrupted, somewhat confused by the priest's logic.

"No, she keeps me alive here, puts a roof over my head, and feeds me, all so I can know the mercy I did not bestow on my flock. Your mother is a living reproach for which I am thankful. I don't want anyone to forgive me."

"Father, my sons have not had their first communion. The fact is that my husband . . . would be outraged . . . if I even asked his permission. Wouldn't you like to—?"

"Why are you really asking me for this?"

"I want to be part of an exceptional rite, Father. Routine is killing me." Laura turned away, wailing. It was somewhere between raving and weeping.

In truth, she felt a deep satisfaction in participating in a ceremony missing from her married life, knowing she was going against her husband's implicit wishes. Juan Francisco neither went to Mass nor spoke of religion. Neither did Laura or the boys. Only María de la O kept some religious pictures stuck in her mirror, which Juan Francisco, without saying so, considered the relics of a hypocritical old woman.

"I don't oppose it, but still, I have to ask why," Leticia wondered.

"The world becomes too flat without ceremonies to mark the passage of time."

"Are you so afraid of losing track of the years?"

"Yes, Mutti. I fear time without hours. That's what death must be like."

Leticia, her three sisters, and Laura gathered together in the priest's bedroom with Santiago and Danton.

"This is my body, this is my blood," Elzevir intoned, and put pieces of bread in the mouths of the boys, now seven and six, amused because they'd been brought to a dark bedroom to eat bits of roll and hear words in Latin. They preferred running through the gardens of Xalapa, Los Berros and Juárez Park, watched over as always by their dark-skinned aunt; they felt they owned this tranquil city, a space without danger, a territory that gave them the freedom forbidden them in Mexico City, with its streets filled with trucks and wise guys and toughs from whose challenges Santiago had to protect his younger brother.

"Why are you looking so hard at the roof of that house, Mama?"

"No reason, Santiago. I lived there when I was young with your grandparents."

"I'd like to have a birdcage like that at home. I'd be the owner of the castle and defend you against the bad guys, Mama."

"Santiago, do you remember the maid I hired back in Mexico City before leaving for Xalapa? Now, when you go back, I want you to treat Carmela with respect."

"Carmela. Sure, Mama."

Laura had a premonition. She asked María de la O to stay a few more days in Xalapa with the boys while she went back to Mexico City to straighten up the house. "It must be a mess, with Juan Francisco all alone there and he so busy with politics. As soon as I have things in hand, I'll send for you."

"Laura."

"Yes, Mutti."

"Look what you forgot when you got married."

It was the Chinese doll Li Po. True. She hadn't thought of the doll since she'd gone.

"Oh, Mama, how sad it makes me that I forgot her." She hid her real sadness with a false laugh. "I think it's because I turned into my husband's Li Po."

"Do you want to take her with you?"

"No, Mutti. It's better for her to stay here in her place until I come back."

"Do you really think you'll be coming back, dear?"

Neither Carmela nor Juan Francisco was in the little house on Avenida Sonora when Laura arrived around midday from the Buenavista station after the usual delay on the trains.

She felt a difference in the house. A silence. An absence. Naturally: the boys and her cherished aunt were the noise, the joy of the place. She picked up the newspaper jammed under the garage door. She planned a solitary day. Would she go to the Cine Royal? Let's just see what's going on.

She opened *El Universal* and found the photograph of "Carmela." Gloria Soriano, a Carmelite nun, had been arrested as a conspirator in the assassination of President-elect Alvaro Obregón. She had been discovered in a home near the Bosque de Chapultepec. When she tried to escape, the police shot her in the back. The nun had died instantly.

Laura spent the remaining hours of the day in the dining room staring fixedly at this photo of the very white woman with the deep shadows under her very black eyes. Sunset came, and even though she could no longer see the photo, she did not turn on the light. She knew the face by heart. It was the face of a moral ransom. If Juan Francisco had reproached her all those years for not having visited the Catalan anarchist in the attic, how could he reproach her now for having given sanctuary to a nun being hunted down? Of course he wouldn't, they would both finally share a combative humanity, Laura told herself, repeating the word "combative."

Juan Francisco returned at 11 p.m. The house was in darkness. The big dark man tossed his hat on the sofa, sighed, and turned on the light. He was visibly startled when he saw Laura sitting there with the newspaper open in front of her.

"Oh, you're back."

Laura nodded.

"Did you see that item about the nun Soriano?" asked López Greene.

"No. I saw the item about the anarchist Aznar."

"I don't follow."

"When you came to Xalapa to unveil the plaque in the attic, you praised my father for having protected Armonía Aznar. That's when I really met you and fell in love."

"Of course. She was a heroine of the working class."

"You aren't going to praise me for giving sanctuary to a heroine of the religious persecution?"

"A nun who assassinates presidents."

"An anarchist who assassinates tsars and princes?"

"No, Armonía fought for the workers. Your Carmela fought for the priests."

"Oh, so she's *my* Carmela, not yours."

"No, she's not mine."

"She's not human, Juan Francisco, but someone from another planet?"

"Just from an outdated era, that's all."

"Unworthy of your protection."

"A criminal. Besides, if she'd just stayed put here as I asked her, the shoot-to-kill law wouldn't have been applied to her."

"I didn't know that the police of the Revolution kill people the same way the dictatorship did, shooting them in the back."

"There would have been a trial, I told her that, just as there was for the assassin Toral and his accomplice Mother Conchita—another woman, as you see."

"You must have wanted to get on someone's good side, Juan Francisco. Whose? Because you'll be on my bad side forever."

She didn't want to hear his explanations, and Juan Francisco didn't dare give any. Laura packed a suitcase, walked out to the street, hailed a cab, and gave the driver the address of her girlhood friend Elizabeth García-Dupont.

Juan Francisco rushed after her, opened the taxi door with a bang, grabbed her by the arm, tried to pull her from the car, and slapped her in the face. The cabby got out, shoved Juan Francisco to the ground, and pulled away as quickly as he could.

The friend of her adolescence received Laura with joy, hugs, courtesy, tenderness, and kisses—everything Laura hoped for. Laura moved in with Elizabeth, in her modern apartment in Colonia Hipódromo. Later, in their nightclothes, they told each other their stories. Elizabeth had just divorced the famous Eduardo Caraza, who had blithely danced with her at the balls in the San Cayetano hacienda and just as blithely brought her along when they married and moved to Mexico City because Caraza was a friend of the Treasury Minister, Alberto Pani, who was miraculously putting the nation's finances in order after the inflation during the Revolution, when every group had printed its own paper money, the famous "funny money." Eduardo Caraza thought he was irresistible, even calling himself "God's gift to women," and told Elizabeth he'd done her a great favor by marrying her.

"That's what I get for begging."

"Consider yourself fortunate, my sweet. You've got me, but I need lots of women. It's better we understand each other."

"Well, I've got you, but I also need other men."

"Elizabeth, you're talking like a whore."

"In that case, my dear Lalo, you're talking like a pimp."

"Forgive me, I didn't mean to offend you. I was just joking."

"I've never heard you speak more seriously. You did offend me, and I'd be a fool to stay around and suffer more humiliations after listening to your philosophy of life. It seems you have the right to everything and I to nothing. I'm a whore, but you're a ladies' man. I'm a disgrace, but you're what they call a gentleman, no matter what happens, correct? Bye-bye."

Fortunately, they had no children. How could they, when Lalo wore himself out in orgies and wandered in at six in the morning limp as a wet noodle?

"Juan Francisco never played that trick, he always respected me. Until tonight, when he tried to slap me."

"Tried? Take a look at your cheek."

"Well, he did slap me. But he's not that way."

"Dearest Laura, I can see that if we go on like this you'll forgive him everything and in less than a week you'll be back in the cage. Instead, let's have some fun. I'm inviting you to the Lyric Theater to see potbellied Roberto Soto in *The Fall of Napoleon*. It's a satire on that union man Morones, and they say you'll laugh your head off. It makes fun of everybody. Let's go before it's closed down."

They got a box so they'd be more protected. Roberto Soto was the very image of Luis Napoleón Morones, with double everything—chin, belly, lips, cheek, eyelids. The setting was the union leader's mansion in Tlalpam. He walked on dressed as an altar boy and singing "When I was an altar boy." Instantly, nine or ten half-naked girls in banana skirts—the kind Josephine Baker made famous in Paris in the Folies-Bergère—and little stars glued to their nipples pulled off the altar-boy robes and began singing "Long Live the Proletariat!" while a tall, dark man wearing overalls served champagne to Soto-Morones.

"Thanks, dear brother López Greene, you've helped me better than anyone. I ask only that you change your name to López Red just to be in complete harmony, understand? Because we're all red here and certainly not *green-goes*, right, girls?"

"Mutti, take care of the boys until I write again. And Auntie María de la O should stay with you too. I'll send money. I have to reorganize my life, dearest Mutti. I'll tell you everything. Meanwhile, Li Po can watch over you. You were right."

# 8. Paseo de la Reforma: 1930

S OME MEXICANS LOOK GOOD only in their coffins."

Orlando Ximénez's bon mot was applauded by everyone at the cocktail party that Carmen Cortina gave to celebrate the unveiling of the portrait of her cousin, the actress Andrea Negrete. The artist, Tizoc Ambriz, a young painter from Guadalajara, had become, overnight, the society portrait painter most sought after by those who did not want to bequeath their image to the (Communist and monstrous) posterity of Rivera, Orozco, or Siqueiros, whom they referred to contemptuously as "the daubers."

Carmen Cortina flouted conventions and invited what she herself called "the fauna of Mexico City" to her cocktail parties. The first time Elizabeth brought Laura to one, she had to tell her who the guests were, although it was impossible to distinguish them from the crashers, whom the hostess tolerated as homage to her social standing— after all, was there anyone who was someone who didn't want to be seen at Carmen Cortina's soirées? Vain and nearsighted, she herself had a hard time telling who was who, and people said she'd raised the senses of smell and touch to the level of high art, for all she had to do was bring her myopic face up to the nearest cheek to say, "Chata, what a delight you are!" or touch the finest cashmere to exclaim, "Rudy, how delighted I am to see you!"

Rudy was Rudy, but Orlando was rude. *"Watch out!"* Carmen called out in English to the star of the party, Andrea, a woman with a mother-of-pearl complexion and perfect facial symmetry accentuated by her hair, parted down the middle and, despite the sensual youth of her eternal figure, audaciously adorned with two white streaks at her temples. This was why she was disrespectfully called "Two-tone." The irrepressible Orlando, especially, would say because of her skill at two-timing. Sooner or later, Andrea would be what was called an *opulent* woman, he noted, *but not yet.* She was like a ripe, freshly picked piece of fruit, challenging the world.

"Eat me," Andrea said, smiling.

"Peel me," said Orlando very seriously.

"Vulgarian," laughed Carmen very loudly.

Tizoc Ambriz's portrait was covered by a curtain in expectation of its being unveiled at the crowning moment of the evening, when Carmen and only Carmen determined that things had reached their climax, an instant before the boiling point, when all the fauna were assembled. Carmen was making lists in her head: who's here? who's missing?

"You're a statigraphician of the high life," said Orlando into her ear, but loudly.

"Hey! I'm not deaf, you know," whimpered Carmen.

"What you are is hot." Orlando pinched her backside.

"Vulgarian! What is a statigraphician?"

"Someone who practices a new but minor science, a brand-new way to tell lies."

"What? What? I'm dying to know what that is."

"Vargas is investigating it."

"Pedro Vargas? He's the radio sensation. Have you heard him? He sings on Channel W."

"But, my dear Carmen, the Palace of Fine Arts has just been inaugurated. Don't talk to me about Channel W."

"What are you saying, that mausoleum Don Porfirio left half finished?"

"We now have a symphony orchestra. Carlos Chávez is the director."

"Which Chávez is that?"

"The one who'll give you a close chávez where you need it most."

"Get lost, you're impossible."

"I know you like a book. You're making lists in your head."

"I'm the hostess. It's my duty," Carmen declared in English.

"I'll bet I can read your mind."

"Orlando, all you have to do is look around."

"What do you see, my blind goddess?"

*"The mixture, darling, the mixture,"* Carmen went on in English.
"Social classes have been abolished: doesn't that seem significant to
you? Tell me if twenty years ago, when I was a girl—"

"Carmen, I saw you flirting—with no success—at the Centenary
Ball in 1910 . . ."

"That was my aunt. Anyway, take a look. What do you see?"

"I see a weeping willow. I see a nymph. I see an aureole. I see
melancholy. I see sickness. I see egoism. I see vanity. I see personal and
collective disorganization. I see beautiful poses. I see ugly things."

"Idiot. You're a frustrated poet. Give me names. Names, names,
names."

*"What's in a name?"*

"What, what did you say?"

"Romeo, Juliet, things like that."

"What? Who invited them?"

Laura had resisted her friend Elizabeth's importuning: you're
behaving like a widow without being one, Laura, you got rid of López
Greene at just the right time, the way I got rid of Caraza, she would say
as they walked along Avenida Madero in search of bargains. It was
Elizabeth who organized these expeditions to find sales on clothes and
accessories that were beginning to come back to post-Revolutionary
Mexico in the shops on Gante, Bolívar, and 16 de Septiembre. These
hunting parties would start with a breakfast at Sanborn's, continue
with lunch at Prendes, and finish up with a movie at the Cine Iris on

Donceles Street—where Laura liked going because it featured first-run American films from Metro-Goldwyn-Mayer with the best actors, Clark Gable, Greta Garbo, William Powell—while Elizabeth favored the Cine Palacio on Avenida Cinco de Mayo, where they showed only Mexican movies. She loved to laugh with Chato Ortín, cry with Sara García, admire Fernando Soler's histrionics.

"Remember when we went to see fatso Soto at the Follies? That's where your life changed."

"A dead marriage kills everything, Elizabeth."

"Know what happened to you? You were cleverer than your husband. Just like me."

"No, I think he loved me."

"But he didn't understand you. You walked out the day you understood you were more intelligent than he was. Don't tell me you didn't."

"No. I simply felt that Juan Francisco wasn't up to the same level as his ideals. Maybe I was more moral than he, though thinking that now annoys me a little."

"Remember fatso Soto's farce? To be considered intelligent in Mexico, you've got to be a crook. What I recommend, my love, is that you become a liberated, sensual woman, your own kind of crook. Come on, finish off that ice-cream soda, drain those straws, and let's go shopping and then to the movies."

Laura said she felt embarrassed that Elizabeth was "shooting" so many things her way. That was the way you put it in Mexico City slang, which abounded in neologisms disguised as archaisms and archaisms disguised as neologisms—all in a kind of linguistic sublimation of the armed struggle: "shooting" meant giving presents, "Carranzifying" meant stealing, "besieging" meant courting, and any serious effort was called "engaging in battle." To say "I'm doing a Wilson" meant to pass through the triumphal arch of a woman's legs like the American President who ordered General Pershing's punitive expedition against Pancho Villa and, before that, the landing at Veracruz with the Marines. Fatality was always compared to the Valentina song—if I've got to die tomorrow, why not die right now? Amorous persistence was always compared to the Adelita song—if she went off with another man, I'd follow her o'er land and sea. To compare the country to the city was like singing that only four cornfields are left or that bobbed-hair girls are finished and so is presumption, or like comparing the horribly vulgar charro Buddy-boy Beristáin—who said he was a general without having fought any battles, except against his mother-in-law—with nostalgia for the vanished refinement and grace of the Little White Cat, María Conesa, who sang "Oh, oh, oh, oh, my darling Captain" about her lover, a fearsome military man and leader of a band of thieves called the "gray car gang." To shoot someone meant to copy that person. And "to Madero" was to do what the two women were doing at that moment—to stroll down Avenida Madero, downtown Mexico City's main commercial street, once the Silversmiths Street and now rebaptized to honor the Apostle of the Revolution and Democracy.

"I read a very funny book by Julio Torri. It's called *On Executions* and he complains that the principal inconvenience in being shot by a firing squad is having to get up so early in the morning," said Laura, gazing in the shopwindows.

"Don't worry. My husband, poor Caraza, used to say that a million people died in the Revolution but not on the battlefields. Only in cantina brawls. Laura"—Elizabeth stopped outside the Chamber of Deputies on Donceles Street—"you like coming to the Iris because your husband is a deputy, right?"

They bought tickets to see *A Free Soul* with Clark Gable and Norma Shearer, and Elizabeth said the smell of candy apples at the entrance to the theater excited her.

"Fresh apples and sticky honey," sighed the young matron, who was getting blonder and blonder and plumper and plumper, when they left the theater. "Just think, Norma Shearer abandons everything—social position, an aristocratic boyfriend—how distinguished that Englishman Leslie Howard is!—for a gangster sexier than . . . Clark Gable! Divine, big ears and all! I adore him!"

"Well, I'll take the blond, Leslie Howard. Anyway, he's Hungarian, not English."

"Impossible. Hungarians are gypsies and wear earrings. Where did you read that?"

"In *Photoplay*."

"Well maybe you want a blond now—English or kidnapper or whatever he is—but you married that dark, dark Juan Francisco. Honey, you don't fool me. You like the Cine Iris because it's next door to the Chamber of Deputies. If you're lucky, you'll see him. I mean, you'll see each other. I mean. I just mean."

Laura shook her head emphatically but explained nothing to Elizabeth. Sometimes she felt her life was like the seasons of the year, except that her marriage had gone from spring to winter without any summer or fall. She loved Juan Francisco, but a man is only admirable when he admires the woman who loves him. That, in the last instance, is what Laura felt was missing. Perhaps Elizabeth was right: she had to try other waters, swim in other rivers. Even if she didn't find perfect love, she could build herself a romantic passion. Maybe it could be "platonic," a word Elizabeth didn't understand but put into practice at the parties she was always going to.

"Look but don't touch. If you touch me, you'll catch something."

She never gave herself to anyone: her friend Laura imagined that a passion could be created by force of will. This is why the two women could live together without problems and without men, avoiding the multitude of Don Juans in Mexico City liberated from hearth and home by the chaos of the Revolution and looking for lovers when what they really wanted was mothers.

The vernissage for Andrea Negrete's portrait by Tizoc Ambriz was the pretext for Laura to depart from what Elizabeth, with a certain macabre resonance, called her "stiff widowhood without a stiff," and attend an artistic "function." Enough of ruminating about the past, enough of imagining impossible loves, enough of telling stories about Veracruz or missing her sons or feeling ashamed to go to Xalapa because she felt guilty, because it was she who had abandoned her home just as she abandoned her sons, for she knew no way to justify what she'd done, didn't want to destroy Juan Francisco's image for the boys, didn't want to admit to Mutti and to her aunts that she'd made a mistake, that she would have been better off looking for a young man of her own class at the San Cayetano and Xalapa Casino dances, but above all she did not want to speak ill of Juan Francisco, wanted everyone to go on believing she'd put her faith in a fighting, valiant man, above all a leader who personified everything that had happened in Mexico in this century, didn't want to say to her family I was mistaken, my husband is corrupt or mediocre, my husband is an ambitious man unworthy of his ambition, your father, Santiago, can't live without having someone recognize his merits, your father, Danton, is defeated by his belief that other people don't give him what he deserves—my husband, Elizabeth, is incapable of recognizing that he's already lost his merit. The gold has rubbed off his medals and only the copper is left.

"Your father hasn't done anything except inform on a persecuted woman."

How could she say that to Santiago and Danton, who were going to turn, respectively, nine and eight? How could she explain herself to Mutti and her aunts? How could she tell them that all the prestige won over years of struggle had evaporated in a second because one thing had been done badly? It was better, Laura told herself in her self-imposed solitude, for Juan Francisco to go on thinking she had judged and condemned him. It didn't matter to her, so long as he believed it was only she and no one else—not the world, not his sons, not some middle-aged women hidden in a Xalapa boardinghouse and unimportant to him—who judged him. Her husband's pride would remain intact. The wife's sorrow would only be the wife's.

She did not know how to say all that to the insistent Elizabeth, just as she couldn't explain it to the family in Veracruz, to whom she wrote as if nothing had happened. The letters would arrive at Avenida Sonora, and Juan Francisco's new maid would turn them over to Laura every week. Laura would go to her old home at midday when he wasn't in. Laura was sure: if María de la O suspected something, she would keep quiet about it. Discretion was born with María de la O.

The invitation to the unveiling of Andrea Negrete's portrait was irresistible because, one day before, Elizabeth had spoken about expenses with her guest.

"Don't worry about anything, Laura. The hat, the dresses, you'll pay me back when you can."

"Juan Francisco's monthly allotment to me hasn't come yet."

"It wouldn't be enough!" laughed the rose-colored blonde tenderly. "You've got a wardrobe like Marlene's."

"I like pretty things. Perhaps because I don't have, for the moment, any compensation for such an . . . absence, I guess I'd call it."

"Something will come your way. Don't upset yourself."

The truth is that she wasn't spending very much money. She read. She went to concerts and museums alone, to the movies and to dinner with Elizabeth. The situation that separated her from her husband was for her a period of mourning. Between them was a betrayal, a death— a dead woman. But the Chanel perfume, the little Schiaparelli hat, the suit tailored by Balenciaga . . . So much had changed so quickly. Fashion: How was Laura going to appear in public wearing a flapper's short skirt like a Charleston dancer and Clara Bow hair when everyone had to dress like the new Hollywood stars? Skirts were longer, hair was wavier, busts were decked out with huge piqué lapels, those who dared wore silk evening dresses sculpted to the shape of the body, like the platinum blonde Jean Harlow, and a fashionable hat was indispensable. A woman took off her hat only to sleep or play tennis. A rubber bathing cap was called for even in the swimming pool—marcelled hair had to be protected.

"Come on now, pluck up your courage."

Before she could say hello to the hostess or admire the severe Bauhaus lines of the penthouse, decorated by Pani, or pay respects to the guest of honor, two hands covered Laura Díaz's eyes. Then came a coquettish *"Guess who!"* (in English), and before Laura's half-opened eye, the heavy gold ring with the initials OX.

For an instant, she did not want to see it. Behind Orlando Ximénez's hands was the young man she hadn't wanted to look at the first time she'd met him, in the dining room of the San Cayetano hacienda. Once again she smelled the English cologne, once again she heard the baritone voice raised intentionally as, it seemed, was the custom among the English. She imagined the tenuous light of the tropical terrace, and saw in her mind's eye the chiseled profile, the straight nose, the blond curls . . .

She opened her eyes and recognized the upper lip, slightly recessive, and the prominent chin, a bit like the Habsburg kings'. But this time there were no curls, only a receding hairline, a mature face, and quite yellowish skin, like that of the Chinese workers on the Veracruz docks.

Orlando saw the sad shock in Laura's eyes and said, "Orlando Ximénez. You don't recognize me, but I recognize you. Santiago spoke of you so tenderly. I think you were—what did I tell you . . . ?

"His favorite virgin."

"No longer?"

"Two sons."

"Husband?"

"He no longer exists."

"Did he die?"

"You figure it out."

"And here we are, you and I, still alive. Hmm. Funny how things work out."

Orlando looked around as if he were once again trying to find the San Cayetano balcony, the corner where they could be alone again and speak. A bittersweet wave of lost opportunity rolled across Laura's breast, but Carmen Cortina would not allow frivolous intimacy or shameful solitude at her parties. As if she sensed a private—that is, exclusive—situation in the making, she interrupted the couple and introduced them around: to Butt del Rosal, an old aristocrat who used a monocle and whose joke was to take the lens out of his eye and, look at this, ingest it as if it were a communion wafer—it was phony, made of gelatin; then Onomástico Galán, a fat, red-faced Spaniard who went to parties in a nightshirt and matching cap with stripes and a red tassel, carrying a candle in one hand—in case there was a power failure in this disorganized and revolutionary country, which needed a good, soft dictatorship like Primo de Rivera's in Spain; after him came a couple in sailor costumes, he with short pants and a blue cap with the words KISS ME on it and she as Mary Pickford, with a wig of big blond curls, white knee socks, patent-leather shoes, frilly panties, and a daringly short pink skirt, in addition to the requisite bow on her curly head; behind them came an art critic in an impeccable white suit and its contemptuous corollary on his lips, which he repeated constantly: "These people are all ridiculous!"

He was hand in hand with his sister, a tall, beautiful statue made of confectioner's sugar who would repeat, like some sisterly echo, "Ridiculous, we're all ridiculous," while an old painter with invisible, sharp, and powerful halitosis announced he was the teacher of this new artist, Tizoc, a position disputed by another painter of melancholic and disillusioned mien, famous for his funerary black-and-white paintings and for his pure-black lover and disciple, nicknamed "Xangó" by the painter, by Mexico City, and by the world, although to gild, I mean geld, I mean gild the lily, as Carmen Cortina would say, the powerful black had an Italian wife whom he introduced as the model for La Gioconda.

This whole circle was watched from a distance and with clinical disapproval by an English couple whom Carmen introduced as Felicity Smith, an extremely tall woman who could not observe what was going on without lowering her disdainful eyes, although, because she was courteous, she preferred to fix them on the distance; and a short, bearded, elegant man whom Carmen introduced as James Saxon and (sotto voce) as King George's bastard son, who'd taken refuge in a tropical hacienda in the Huasteca area of the state of San Luis Potosí, which said *bâtard* had transformed into a *folie* worthy, as his companion Felicity pointed out, of the king of literary eccentrics William Beckford: "When you live in James's house, you have to fight your way through orchids, cockatoos, and bamboo blinds."

"The problem," whispered Carmen to Orlando and Laura, "is that everyone here is in love with everyone else. Felicity's in love with James, who is homosexual and very interested in the critic who says 'ridiculous,' who is mad for the black Xangó, who's a false fag, who gives the melancholy painter satisfaction for reasons of state but who in fact has his fun with the Neapolitan, although she—the so-called Mona Lisa—has proposed converting the melancholy painter to heterosexuality, thus forming a ménage à trois that would be not only pleasant but economically convenient in times of crisis, my dear, when no one, absolutely no one, will buy an easel painting and the government is the only patron of the daubers, *quelle horreur!*, except that Mary Pickford is in love with the Italian woman, who secretly sleeps with the sailor, who is also something else, but she wants to prove to him that he's a real man, which is true, except that Popeye knows that by passing himself off as a fag he arouses the maternal instincts of ladies who want to protect him while he takes advantage of them by surprising them, except that La Gioconda, knowing her husband is Lothar and not Mandrake the Magician, would like to see herself playing the Narda role—are you following me, dearies, don't you read the comic strips in *El Universal?*—and try, with Xangó, to bring about the conversion to normalcy of the melancholy painter so as to integrate the trio, as I said, which threatens, as things seem to be going, to turn into a quartet, and even a quintet if we include Mary Pickford, what a mess and what a problem for a hostess who is, after all, from a proper family like my own!"

"Carmen," observed Orlando, resigned, "leave well enough alone. Imagine, if Dostoyevsky had psychoanalyzed himself he might not have written *The Idiot.*"

"Mr. Orlando," murmured Carmen Cortina, "I only invite people with high IQs, never an idiot! God forbid!" She gasped, but she still managed to introduce Pimpinela de Ovando, an aristocrat fallen on hard times, and Gloria Iturbe, suspected of being a spy for Germany's Chancellor Franz von Papen, the things people say!, but everything, my dears, is so international nowadays, that no one even bothers to mention the sins of La Malinche!

Carmen Cortina's verbal cascades multiplied into similar cataracts in the mouths of all her guests, except the cadaverous black-and-white painter ("I've eliminated everything superfluous from my paintings"), who was the one who supplied Orlando's famous dictum: "Some Mexicans look well only in their coffins," words mumbled a moment before the introduction of the Minister of Education in the current government, which gave the hostess and her protégé the painter from Veracruz the chance to unveil the painting, which they did together, raising the excitement and the scandal of the party to a fever pitch when what everyone saw was the true image of the actress who'd played in *Poppy:*

*You Won't Be Alone Anymore* in all her splendid nakedness, stretched out on a blue sofa that emphasized the whiteness of her skin and the absence of hair, the one vain, the other coy, united by the art of the painter in a sublime expression of spiritual totality, as if nudity were the habit this nun wore, inclined as she was to flagellation as a superior form of fornication, eager to sacrifice her pleasure for the sake of something more than modesty, or, as Orlando summed it up, "Look, Laura, it's like the title of that novel from the last century: *Nun, Wife, Virgin, and Martyr.*"

"It's the portrait of my soul," Andrea Negrete said to the Minister of Education.

"Well, your soul has hair on it," he retorted, his sharp eye having noticed that the painter hadn't shaved Doña Andrea's pubis but had painted her pubic hair white, just like the hair around the actress's temples.

At that, the party crested, after which the waters, as we say, became calm. Voices dropped to a whisper of shock, of damnation or admiration. It was impossible to know what people thought of Tizoc's art or Andrea's audacity. The Minister said goodbye with an impudent expression on his face and a whispered comment to Carmen, "You told me this would be a cultural event."

"It's like Goya's *Maja*, Mr. Minister. One day I'll introduce you, it's the Duchess of Alba, a great friend of mine."

"Duchess of Tarts," said the member of Ortiz Rubio's cabinet.

"Oh, how I'd love to see the members of all the members in all the cabinets," said the little sailor boy wearing the KISS ME cap.

"Goodbye." The Minister nodded his head when the sailor in short pants inflated a balloon with BLOW JOB written on it and let it float to the ceiling.

"This is over," said the merry mini-Popeye. "Where do we go from here?"

"The Leda," called out Mary Pickford.

"The Candles," suggested the painter with halitosis.

"The Crouchers," sighed the critic in white.

"How ridiculous," intoned his sister.

"The Río Rosa," chimed in the Italian woman.

"El Salón México," decreed the Englishman of *la main gauche*.

"Mexico beautiful and beloved," yawned the extremely tall English-woman.

"Mexico little Africa," growled a society columnist.

"I'm getting a highball," said Orlando to Laura.

"We have the same name." A very beautiful woman smiled at Laura as she sat down on a sofa and tried to adjust the lamp next to it. She laughed. "After a certain age, a woman depends on light."

"You are very young," said Laura with provincial courtesy.

"We must be the same age, a trifle over thirty, right?"

Laura Díaz nodded and wordlessly accepted the invitation to join the ash-blond woman on the sofa, who arranged a pillow next to her with one hand as she picked up her glass of whiskey with the other.

"Laura Rivière."

"Laura Díaz."

"Yes, Orlando told me."

"Then you know each other?"

"He's an interesting man. But with no hair. I keep telling him to shave his head completely. Then he wouldn't be merely interesting but dangerous."

"Shall I confess something? He's always made me afraid."

"Let's speak as friends, please. Me too. Know why? Let me tell you. There never was a first time."

"No."

"I wasn't asking you, my dear. I was affirming it. I wouldn't have the nerve with him."

"Me either."

"But you should. I've never seen a look like the one he aims at you. Besides, I swear it's more dangerous to close doors than to open them." Laura Rivière caressed her neck, adorned with brilliant stones. "Did you know? Ever since I separated from my husband, I've kept an antique shop. Come see me some time."

"I live with Elizabeth."

"Not forever, correct?"

"Correct."

"What are you going to do with yourself?"

"I don't know. That's my dilemma."

"I'd advise you not to postpone the impossible, dear namesake. It's better to make things over as you please, in your own time. Take a chance. Look, here comes your friend Elizabeth."

Laura looked around her: No one was left, even Carmen Cortina had gone to greener pastures with her court. Where? To listen to mariachis at the Tenampa? To hire a show with a cast of whores at the Bandit Woman? To drink rum in votive lamps under a sagging roof? To dance to the music of Luis Arcaraz's orchestra in the new Hotel Reforma? To listen to Juan Arvizu, the Tenor with the Voice of Silk, in the old Hotel Regis?

Laura Rivière fixed her hair so it covered half her face, and Elizabeth García-Dupont, ex-wife of Caraza, told Laura Díaz, ex-wife of López Greene, "I'm really, really sorry, honey, but I've got something set up for tonight at home, you know what I mean, even good girls need to let their hair down sometimes, ha-ha, just this once, but I've taken care of you, I booked you a room at the Hotel Regis, here's the key, go on over and call me in the morning."

She wasn't surprised, when she opened the hotel-room door, to find Orlando Ximénez naked, a towel wrapped around his waist. She was immediately surprised that *she* could like *another man*, not that another man could like her, that was something she took for granted, her mirror didn't simply reflect her image back to her but prolonged it through a shadow of beauty, a speaking phantom that gave her courage—as in this exact moment—to go beyond herself, to go through the mirror like Alice, only to discover that every mirror has another mirror behind it and every reflection of Laura Díaz has another image patiently waiting for her to stretch out her hand, touch it, and feel it flee to the next destiny.

She looked down at Orlando naked on the bed and would have wanted to ask him, How many destinies do we have?

He was waiting for her, and she imagined an infinite masculine variety, the same variety men imagine in women but women are forbidden to express publicly, only in the most secret intimacy: I like more than one man, I like several men, because I'm a woman, not because I'm a slut.

She began by taking off her rings. She wanted to arrive with clean, agile hands, eager for the body of Orlando, and he from the bed was trying to decipher Laura, his fist clenched and the gold ring with the initials OX daring her, that's it, reproaching her for the years lost for love, the postponed meeting, this time, yes, now, yes, and she saying yes to him as she took off her own rings, especially those from her marriage to Juan Francisco and the diamond from her grandmother Cosima Kelsen, who was left without fingers because of the amorous machete of the Hunk from Papantla, Laura dropping her rings on the rug, on the way to Orlando's bed, like Little Red Riding Hood lost in the forest dropping bread crumbs, and the birds, all without exception birds of prey, all of them beautiful predators, will eat the bread crumbs, erasing the trail, telling the lost little girl, "There's no way back, you're in the cave of the wolf."

## 9. The Interoceanic Train: 1932

ON THE SAME TRAIN that had brought her, a newlywed, from Xalapa to Mexico City, Laura was now returning. This time it was by day, not night, and she was alone. Her last companions in the capital, before she got to the Colonia station, had been a pack of dogs that both followed and preceded her, threatening mostly because meeting a pack of dogs was such a novelty. She hadn't realized two things. First, the city had dried out: one after another, the lakes and canals—Texcoco, La Viga, La Verónica, the moribund tributaries of the Aztec lake—had filled with garbage, then dirt from construction sites, and finally asphalt. The city in a lake had died forever, inexplicably in Laura's imagination, because she sometimes dreamed of a pyramid surrounded by water.

Second, Mexico City had been invaded by dogs, mixed breeds of no breeding at all, lost, disoriented, objects of simultaneous fear and compassion. Once fine collies, galloping Great Danes, or degenerated German shepherds had mixed together in a vast pack of hounds with no collars, direction, owners, identity. Families with pedigreed dogs had left the capital with the Revolution and let their pets loose to run away—or to die, of loyalty or of hunger. Behind several fancy houses in Colonia Roma and on Paseo de la Reforma one found the bodies of dogs still chained, locked in their doghouses, unable either to eat or to flee. Everyone—dogs and masters—had bet on disloyalty as long as it meant survival.

"They've grown up on their own, with no training at all. No dog knows if it has a pedigree, Laura, and if their masters return—and they're beginning to, mostly from Paris, a few from New York, by the drove from Havana—they'll never get them back."

Thus according to Orlando. On the train, she tried to erase the image of the abandoned dogs, but it was a vision that prevailed over all the images of her life with Orlando in the eighteen months that had passed since they slept together for the first time in the Hotel Regis and then stayed on, with Orlando paying for the room and the services. Together they began the social life that he called "observations for my novel," although Laura sometimes wondered whether her lover really enjoyed the facile frivolity that reigned in Mexico City at peace after twenty years of revolutionary fear, or if Orlando's tour through all the urban strata was part of a secret plan, like his intermediary relationship with the Catalan anarchist Armonía Aznar.

She never asked him. She wouldn't dare. That was the difference between him and Juan Francisco, who gave reports on everything that happened to him, turning them into speeches. Orlando never said what he was doing. Laura was likely to know what was going to happen, never what already had. Neither his relationship with the old anarchist in the attic nor that with the brother executed in Veracruz. How easy it would have been for Orlando to brag about the first and take advantage of the second. A heroic aura surrounded anyone linked to Armonía Aznar and Santiago Díaz. Why didn't Orlando profit from that splendor?

Watching him sleep, exhausted, defenseless under her wide-awake eyes, Laura imagined many things. Public modesty, for starters: he would call it elegance, reserve, though with plenty of satiric barbs aimed at himself and poisonous epigrams aimed at society. She did not hesitate to call it modesty, the modesty of a man who was intensely immodest in his sexuality: perhaps it was related to his commitment

to the secrecy required by the political cause—but which one?—
anarchism, syndicalism, no reelection, the revolution or rather the
Revolution, capitalized to show that it had turned everything in Mexico upside down, the immense mural which they all had lived in, a
mural like Diego Rivera's, with cavalry charges and murders, fights
and battles, endless heroism and equal ruination, retreats and advances,
huggings and stabbings . . . ? She remembered how as a young married
woman she'd discovered the new mural art and had seen Diego painting in the National Palace.

"He threw me out, Orlando, because I was wearing black after
Father died."

"Ever feel nostalgic for Xalapa?"

"I have you. Why would I feel nostalgia?"

"For your sons. Your mother."

"And my old aunts." Laura smiled, because Orlando was speaking to
her with unaccustomed solemnity. "To think that Diego Rivera is
superstitious."

"Yes, your old aunts, Laura . . ."

Was he a mysterious hero? Was he a discreet friend? And also, was
he a sentimental fellow? Everything that Laura might imagine each
morning about the "real" Orlando, the "real" Orlando destroyed each
night. Like a vampire, the innocent and loving angel of dawn was
transformed into an offensive devil with a poison tongue and a cynical eye as soon as the sun set. True, he never treated her badly, and
Laura could still feel the slap her husband, Juan Francisco, had given
her that evening when he tried to pull her out of the taxi. She would
never forget it. Never forgive it. A man has no idea what a slap in the
face means to a woman, an unpunished abuse, the worst offense, cowardice, an offense to the beauty that every single woman holds and
exposes in her face . . . Orlando never made her the butt of irony or
cruel jests, but he did oblige her to be present at night to the negation
of the daytime Orlando—discreet, sentimental, erotic, sober in his
treatment of the feminine body, as if it were his own, Orlando who
could be simultaneously passionate and respectful to the feminine body
united to his own.

"Get ready," he said without looking at her, grasping her arm firmly, as if they were two Christians entering the lions' ring. *"Brace yourself, my dear,"* in English. "This is the Circus Maximus, but instead of lions roaring, you hear cows mooing, lambs bleating. And yes, the howl of wolves may be detected. *Avanti, popolo romano.* Here comes our hostess. Just look at her. Just look. It's Carmen Cortina. Three verbs suffice to define her. She drinks. She smokes. She ages."

"*Darlings!* What a pleasure to see you again . . . and *still* together! Miracles, miracles . . ."

"Carmen. Stop drinking. Stop smoking. You're aging yourself."

"Orlando!" The hostess burst out laughing. "What would I do without you? You speak the same truths as my mama, may she rest in peace."

Outside the night was stormy and inside it was enervating.

"Think what you like and don't expect me to speak well of my friends," said the lugubrious painter to the critic dressed in white, who intoned his aforementioned "We are all ridiculous."

"That's not what I mean. It's that I only have indefensible friends. If they're worthy of my friendship, they can't be worthy of my defense. No one is worth that much."

"All ridiculous."

"That isn't the problem," added a young philosophy professor with a hard-earned reputation as an indiscriminate seducer. "The important thing is to have a bad reputation. That constitutes public virtue in today's Mexico. Whether your name is Plutarco Elías Calles or Andrea Negrete," said Ambrosio O'Higgins. That was the name of this tall, blond, vexed specialist in Husserl, whose personal phenomenology was a permanent grimace of displeasure and eyes which, though sleepy, were filled with obvious intentionality.

"Well, no one can beat you in that category," said the resuscitated Andrea Negrete, who after the failure of her last film, *Life Is a Vale of Tears* (subtitled *But Women Suffer More than Men*), had taken refuge in a convent in her native state, Durango, that was run by her grandmother's sister and inhabited exclusively by eleven of her cousins.

"Neither my aunt the abbess nor my cousins the nuns realized that, counting me, there were thirteen of us at the refectory table. Each one is a saint, completely without malice. The one dying of fear was me. I was afraid I would choke on the mole. Because the fact is, the best restaurant in Mexico is the convent of my aunt Sor María Auxiliadora, I swear it."

She kissed her fingers, and she made the sign of the cross, and Laura closed her eyes, imagining once again the amorous machete stroke of the Hunk of Papantla, the severed fingers of Grandmother Cosima, the mutilated nails dripping blood into the bandit's hat.

"Well, no one can beat you in that category," said the actress to the philosopher.

"Not so. You can," answered the young man with the Irish name and the paralytically arched eyebrow.

"Let's see if together we can draw even." Andrea smiled.

"To do that I'd have to get a little gray." O'Higgins took out his pipe. "Both above and below. Please note, I said get gray, not get laid."

"My boy, you're so good you don't need morality."

Andrea turned her back on them only to find the sailor with the short pants and the girl movie star covered with curls. They exchanged subtle threats.

"One day I'm going to take out my knife and leave you looking like a sieve."

"Know what your problem is, sweetheart? You've only got one ass and you want to shit in twenty pots."

"Do you see what I see, Orlando? Just look at that incredibly handsome fellow."

Orlando agreed with Laura, and they both stared at the best-looking young man at the party.

"Know what? Since we arrived, he's done nothing but look at himself in the mirror."

"But, Laura, we're all looking at ourselves in the mirror. The trouble is we don't always see the reflection. Look at Andrea Negrete. She's been posing by herself for twenty minutes as if everyone were admiring her, but no one's paying the slightest attention."

"Except you, the man who notices everything." Laura caressed her lover's chin.

"And the handsome boy looking at himself in the mirror all the time without speaking with anyone." Orlando made an abrupt gesture. "Andrea, go stand behind that kid."

"The Adonis?"

"You know him?"

"He doesn't speak to anyone. Just looks at himself in the mirror."

"Would you stand behind him? Please?"

"What are you asking me to do?"

"Appear to him. Be his reflection. That's what he's looking for. Be his ghost. I'll bet you sleep with him this very night."

"Darling, you're tempting me."

Laura Rivière came in with an arrogant, dark-skinned man "in the prime of life," as Orlando said to Laura Díaz, a millionaire and very powerful politician, Artemio Cruz, Laura's lover. Carmen Cortina went over to gossip with them. "And no one can explain why he doesn't leave his wife, a provincial vulgarian from Puebla—and, Laurita, that's no reflection on you—when he *possesses*, I underline *possesses*, one of the most distinguished women in our society."

"*C'est fou, la vie!*" Carmen blurted out, exasperated—Carmen the Blind, as Orlando called her, when tedium overcame his fading good humor.

"Laura darling." Elizabeth came over to her companion from the Xalapa balls. "Did you see who just came in? See how they whisper in each other's ear? What does Artemio Cruz want to tell Laura Rivière that he doesn't have the courage to tell her out loud? Oh, and a word of advice, darling, if you want to catch a fellow, don't talk, just breathe, that's all, panting just slightly, like this . . . I mention it because sometimes I hear you raising your voice."

"But, Elizabeth, I'm with a man . . ."

"You never know. *You never know* . . . But I didn't come to give you breathing lessons, just to tell you to go on sending me the bills for everything, the hairdresser, clothes, don't be stingy, honey, that fat-lipped Caraza left me well set up, spending is one of my pleasures, and I don't want anyone to say a friend of mine is Orlando Ximénez's kept woman."

Laura, with the hint of a bitter smile, asked Elizabeth, "Why are you offending me?"

"Offending you? Offending someone who's been my friend forever? Jesus!" Elizabeth patted dry the drops of perspiration in the cleavage between her powerful breasts.

"So, you're cutting me out of your life."

"Don't take it that way."

"I promised I'd pay you. You know my situation."

"Let's wait for the next revolution, dearie. Maybe things will go better for your husband then. Deputy from the state of Tabasco, isn't that right? Don't make me laugh. All you get out of Tabasco are priest-baiters who drink tequila, not gentlemen who pay the rent."

Laura turned her back on Elizabeth and took Orlando's hand with the urgency of someone in flight. Smiling, Orlando caressed Laura's hand.

"You don't want to run into the terrible Artemio Cruz in the elevator, do you? They say he's a shark, and around here, darling, I'm the only one who chews on you."

"Look at him. What an arrogant man. He just walked out on Laura!"

"I tell you he's a shark. And sharks never stop moving, because if they do they sink and die at the bottom of the sea."

The two Lauras spontaneously sought each other out. "The two Lauras have a look of sadness. *What*, as Rubén Darío might have said, *might be wrong with a princess who looks so sad?*" Orlando whispered and went off to get drinks for all of them.

"Why do we put up with this social whirl?" asked the blond woman point-blank.

"Out of fear, I think," answered Laura Díaz.

"Fear of speaking, fear of telling the truth, fear we'll be laughed at? You know what I mean? No one here came without being armed with jokes or funny stories or wit. Those are the swords they use to defend themselves. It's a tournament where the prize is fame, money, sex, and, most of all, feeling you're cleverer than the next person. Is that what you want, Laura Díaz?"

Laura vigorously shook her head. No.

"...?"

"Then save yourself, and quickly."

"It's too late for me. I'm a prisoner. My body's been captured by routine. But I swear that if I could escape from my own body . . . I detest it." Laura Rivière exhaled with a muffled sigh. "You know where all this leads? To a permanent moral hangover. You end up hating yourself."

"Look." Orlando returned balancing three manhattans in the bowl of his joined hands. "The Maximum Actress and the Maximum Narcissus have made contact. I was right. Famous women were invented by innocent men."

"No"—Laura Rivière took her glass—"by malicious men who condemned us to theatrics."

"Darlings," interrupted Carmen Cortina, "have I introduced you to Querubina de Landa yet?"

"No one is named Querubina de Landa," said Orlando to Carmen, to the air, to the night, to the overextended Señorita Querubina de Landa, who was hanging on the arm of the philosophic playboy. Orlando casually skewered him: "They're right to call you the Great Chicken Thief."

"In the matter of names, my dear but ignorant Orlando, no one has said it better than Plato: There are conventional names, there are intrinsic names, and there are names that harmonize nature with necessity, as, for example, Laura Rivière and Laura Díaz. Good night." O'Higgins bowed to one and all, patted the backside of the conventional, natural, harmoniously named Querubina de Landa, and said (in English), *"Let's fuck."*

"I'll bet her real name is Petra Pérez," said the cordial hostess, as she ran off to greet an unusual couple entering the living room of the penthouse overlooking Paseo de la Reforma: a very old man on the arm of a perpetually tremulous lady.

Laura Díaz's high heels sounded like hammers pounding on the sidewalk. She smiled, arm in arm with Orlando, and told him that they'd met in a Veracruz hacienda and ended up in a penthouse on Paseo de la Reforma, but with the same rules and aspirations in both places: to be admitted or disapproved by society and its empresses—Doña Genoveva Deschamps in San Cayetano, Carmen Cortina in Mexico City.

"Can't we escape? We've been together now for eighteen months, my love."

"For me, time doesn't matter if I'm with you," said the no longer very young and now balding Orlando Ximénez.

"Why is it you never wear a hat? You're the only one."

"For that very reason. To be the only one who doesn't."

They walked along the tree-lined part of the avenue that cold December night, on the earthen bridle path for early-morning riders.

"I still don't know anything about you," Laura dared to say, squeezing his hand harder.

"I'm not hiding anything from you. The only things you don't know are the things you don't want to know."

"Orlando, night after night, like this evening, we hear only clichés, predictable, expected . . ."

"Keep going. Desperate."

"You know something? I've just realized that in this world you've introduced me to it doesn't matter how we end up. Tonight was interesting for me. The people who mattered most to each other were Laura Rivière and Artemio Cruz. Do you see? He walked out, the night ended badly. That was the most important thing that happened tonight."

"Let me console you. You're right. It doesn't matter how we end up. The good thing will be that we don't notice everything is over."

"Oh, my love, I feel as if I'm falling down a collapsing staircase."

Orlando hailed a taxi and gave the driver an address unknown to Laura. The cabby stared at the couple in astonishment: "You really want to go there, boss? Sure of that?"

In 1932, Mexico City streets emptied early. Punctual evening meals brought the entire family together. And families were tight-knit, as if the prolonged civil war—twenty unbroken years—had taught the clans to live in a state of fear, clinging to one another, waiting for the worst, for unemployment, expropriation, execution, kidnapping, rape, life savings erased in an instant, useless paper money, the arrogant confusion of the rebel factions. One society had disappeared. The new one was not yet clearly defined. City dwellers had one foot in the furrow of the plow and the other in ashes, as Musset said about post-Napoleonic France. The bad thing was that sometimes blood covered both furrow and ashes, erasing the lines between soil that would be sterile forever and seed that, to produce its fruits, had first to die.

Parties like those of the celebrated, shortsighted Carmen Cortina were a relief for a worldly elite that counted among its protagonists both Seeds and Ashes, those who survived the revolutionary catastrophe, those who lived thanks to it, and those who had died in it but had yet to realize it. Carmen's parties were an exception, a rarity. Proper families would visit one another early, marry one another even earlier, and use both magnifying glass and strainer when letting in elements of the new revolutionary society . . . If a savage general from Sonora married a charming young lady from Sinaloa, relatives and family friends from Culiacán, the capital, were there immediately to approve or disapprove. General Obregón's family had no social pretensions, and the One-armed Hero of Celaya would have been better off staying on his hacienda in Huatabampo and tending turkeys instead of getting entangled in reelection and death. The Calles family, on the other hand, did want to get into high society, cut a figure in it, present its daughters at the Churubusco Country Club and then marry them all—but of course!—in religious weddings (private ceremonies, naturally). The most notable and respected case was General Joaquín Amaro, the very model of the revolutionary warlord, an unequaled horseman (he looked like a centaur), an Indian with his neckerchief and pendant earring, ebony complexion, thick, sensual, and challenging lips and eyes lost in the origin of the tribes, who married a young lady of the best northern society and as a wedding gift promised he would learn French and good manners.

There was always a goodly supply of playboys, and if there was no money anymore to send them abroad to study, they now went to the San Ildefonso Law School or the Santo Domingo School of Medicine, if they were poor; or if they were affluent, they studied architecture.

All these schools were in the old center of the city, in a quarter surrounded by bars, cabarets, and bordellos. The Mexico City of the poor
was like an invisible anthill that ran day and night, a Mexico City
crowded with men still wearing huge straw hats and huaraches or overalls and shawls: that's what my husband, Juan Francisco, showed me
when he took me to see the barrios and convinced me the problems
were so gigantic that it was better I stay home and look after my sons.

"Your husband didn't show you anything," said Orlando Ximénez
with unexpected ferocity, grabbing Laura's wrist and making her get
out in the middle of a partly built-up lot—that was the brutal shock,
the paradox: here were streets, here were houses, yet this was a wasteland within the city, a ruin built of dust, conceived as a ruin, a pyramid
of sand on whose flanks, invisible at first sight, began to appear incomplete silhouettes, forms difficult to name, a half-made world, and
Laura and Orlando made their way through this gray urban mystery,
Orlando leading Laura by the hand like Virgil with Beatrice—not
Dante; another Laura, not Petrarch's; making her look, look, now you
can see them, they're coming out of holes, emerging from the garbage,
tell me, Laura, what could you do for that woman over there called the
Frog, who hops because her torso is crushed against her thighs, look at
her, forced to hop like a frog in search of edible garbage, what could
you do for that man over there who drags himself along the street with
no nose, no arms, no legs, like a human snake? and look at them now
because it's night, because they only come out when there's no light,
because they fear the sun, because during the day they live locked in
fear, so as not to be seen, what are they, Laura? take a good look: are
they dwarfs, children? they're children, but they won't grow any more,
they're dead children with rigor mortis, on their feet but half buried in
the dust, tell me, Laura, did your husband show you this, or did he only
show you the pretty side of poverty, the workers with their cheap shirts,
the whores with their powder, the organ grinders and locksmiths, the
tamale sellers and the saddlers? is that his working class? Do you want
to rebel against your husband? hate him because he didn't give you a
chance to do something for others, treated you with contempt? well

then, I'll give you the chance, take you by the shoulders, Laura, and make you open your eyes, what, what can you do against all this? why don't you and I spend our evenings here, with the Frog and the Snake and the children who won't grow and who fear the sun, instead of with Carmen Cortina and Querubina de Landa and Fatso del Valle and the actress who dyes her pubic hair white, why not?

Laura held on tight to Orlando and released a flood of tears she'd been holding in, she said, since the day she was born, since she'd lost the first person she'd loved and asked herself, why do the people I love die, why were they born . . . ?

"What can one do? There are thousands, millions of them, perhaps Juan Francisco is right. Where would you begin? What can you do for all these people?"

"Tell me."

"Choose the very poorest. Just one, Laura. Choose one and you'll save them all."

Laura Díaz watching the calcified plateau pass by from the window of the Pullman car as she goes home, goes to the state of Veracruz, far from the pyramid of sand out of which—like caterpillars, cockroaches, crabs, along invisible rough paths sprouting in the night from holes like chancres—the frog women, snake men, and rachitic children made their way.

Until that night, she hadn't really believed in misery. We live protected lives, we're conditioned to see only what we want to see. That's what Laura said to Orlando. Now, on her way to Xalapa, she herself felt the anguished need for someone who would take pity on her: she was experiencing an urgent longing for pity, knowing that what she was asking for herself, her portion of compassion, was what was expected of her in the house on Bocanegra Street, a touch of compassion, a bit of attention for everyone forgotten—mother, aunts, two sons—all in order not to tell them the truth, to keep up the original fiction, it was better that Danton and Santiago grow up well looked after, in a provincial city, while Laura and Juan Francisco sorted out their lives, their careers, in a difficult Mexico City, in a most difficult country emerging from the furrows, the ashes, the blood of the Revolution . . . Only Auntie María de la O knew the truth, but above all she knew that discretion is the truth that hurts no one.

The four women were sitting in the old armchairs with wicker backs that the family had dragged with them all the way from the port of Veracruz. Zampaya opened the coach gate for her, and he was Laura's first shock: the jolly dancing man had white hair, and his broom was no longer for him to dance with, "putting your arm around your partner's waist if she lets you," but now a cane on which the old family retainer rested his mutilated greeting, his "Miss Laura!" instantly hushed when Laura put her finger over her lips while the black man carried Miss's valise and she let him do it to keep his self-respect, even though he could barely move it.

Laura wanted to see them first from the living-room door without their seeing her, the four sisters sitting in silence behind the worn-out curtains: Aunt Hilda nervously moving her arthritic fingers as if playing a muted piano; Aunt Virginia silently muttering a poem she was too weak to consign to paper; Auntie María de la O self-absorbed, staring at her fat ankles; and only Mutti working, Leticia knitting a thick housecoat that extended over her knees, protecting her, as she knitted, from Xalapa's December chill, when the fogs of Perote Peak combine with those of the dams, the fountains, the brooks that join together in the fertile subtropical zone between the mountains and the coast.

When she looked up to examine her work, Leticia saw Laura's eyes and exclaimed, Daughter, my daughter, as she painfully rose while Laura ran to hug her: Don't move, Mutti, don't wear yourself out, no one get up, please, and, if she had stood up, would Aunt Hilda have suffocated herself with the ribbon embedded in her double chin that narrowed her myopic eyes even more behind the glasses thick as fishbowls? Would Aunt Virginia have split open? Her face plastered with rice powder was no longer a powdered wrinkle but a wrinkled powder. Would Auntie María de la O have collapsed on the tile floor, recently mopped, her swollen ankles no longer supporting her?

But Leticia did stand up, straight as an arrow, parallel to the walls of the house, her house, hers, her posture telling Laura of her attitude, the house is mine, I keep it clean, tidy, active, modest but sufficient. Nothing is needed here.

"We need you, daughter. Your sons need you."

Laura embraced her, kissed her, remained silent. She wasn't going to remind her that they, mother and daughter, had lived for twelve years in Catemaco, separated from her father, Fernando, and her brother, Santiago, and that reasons given in the past could be invoked in the present. Even so, yesterday's present was not today's past. Carmen Cortina's parties swiftly passed through Laura's mind, at full speed, like the stray dogs near the railroad station; perhaps the dogs secretly admired the speed of the locomotives; perhaps Carmen Cortina's guests were just another pack of homeless animals.

"The boys are at school. They'll be home soon."

"How are their studies going?"

"They're with the Misses Ramos, of course."

Laura was going to exclaim, My God, the ladies haven't died yet!, but that would have been another blunder, a faux pas as Carmen Cortina would say, Carmen whose world seemed to be disappearing into the most distant and invisible unreality. Laura smiled within. That had been her world, during the year and a half of her love affair with Orlando Ximénez, the daily or rather nightly world of Laura and Orlando together.

Laura and Orlando. How different that couple sounded here in the Xalapa house, in Veracruz, in the resuscitated memory of Santiago the first. She was surprised to find herself thinking in such terms, for her brother had been shot when he was only twenty, but the new Santiago coming into the living room with his backpack was a little gentleman of eleven, as serious as a portrait and direct in his first announcement:

"Danton was kept after school. He has to copy twenty pages without a single ink blot."

The Misses Ramos would always be the same, but Santiago hadn't seen his mother in four years, though he immediately understood who she was. He did not run over to embrace her. He let her come to him, kneel down and kiss him. The child's face never changed. With a look, Laura asked for help from the four women.

"That's the way Santiago is," said Mutti Leticia. "I've never met so serious a child."

He kissed Laura's hand: who taught him that, the Misses Ramos, or was it innate courtesy, his distance? Then he scampered out. Laura rejoiced at that childish act; her son skipped in and skipped out, even though he spoke like a judge.

Dinner was slow and painful. Danton sent word with a maid that he was going to sleep at a friend's house, and Laura did not want to play the part of the active and emancipated woman from the capital or upset the ambulatory siesta that was her aunts' waking hours; nor did she want to offend her mother's admirable and nervous activity, because it was Leticia who cooked, ran about, and served while Zampaya sang his songs in the patio. In the absence of conversation, a peculiar smell, a boardinghouse smell, was taking over everywhere; it was the dead smell of many solitary nights, many hasty visits, many corners where, despite Mutti's efforts and Zampaya's broom, dust, time, and oblivion were piling up.

Because there were no guests at the moment—although one or two a week always turned up, which, along with the help Laura sent for the boys, allowed the house to be maintained modestly—the daughter listened to her mother with growing unease, longing to be alone with her, with her mother Leticia, but also with each of the women in this house without men—to shake them out of the apathy of their eternal siesta. But thinking that was not only an offense for them, but hypocrisy on Laura's part, who, after all, had lived on Elizabeth's charity for two years, dividing the monthly allowance sent by Juan Francisco, deputy of the Regional Workers Confederation of Mexico, among payments to Elizabeth, her personal expenses, and a little for her sons given refuge in Xalapa—while Laura slept until noon after staying up until three in the morning, never hearing Orlando when he rose earlier to attend to his mysterious affairs. Laura had fooled herself by reading in bed, telling herself that she wasn't wasting time, that she was educating herself, reading what she should have read as an adolescent: after discovering Carlos Pellicer, reading Pablo Neruda, Federico García Lorca, and going back to read Quevedo, Garcilaso de la Vega . . . with Orlando she would go to the Palace of Fine Arts to listen to Carlos Chávez conducting music that was all new for her, because in her memory there only floated like some perfume the Chopin Aunt Hilda played in Catemaco, and now Bach, Beethoven, and Berlioz along with Ponce, Revueltas, and Villalobos combined into a vast musical Mass; no, she hadn't wasted her time at Carmen Cortina's parties, in reading books or listening to concerts; she had simultaneously allowed her most interior and deep personal thoughts to flow, with the purpose—she said to herself—of locating herself in the world, understanding the changes in her life, proposing solid goals to herself, more certain than the easy exit—as it seemed to her now, stretched out once again on her adolescent bed, again hugging Li Po—of married life with Juan Francisco or even the very pleasant bohemian life with Orlando, something more for her sons Santiago and Danton, a more mature mother, more self-assured . . .

Now she was back at home, and this was the best thing she could have done, return to her roots and quietly sit down to a frothy soda in Don Antonio C. Báez's La Jalapeña, where a sign assured Don Antonio's customers: "This establishment does not use saccharine to sweeten its waters." She could peruse the displays in the Ollivier Brothers shop where La Opera corsets were still for sale. Browsing in Don Raúl Basáñez's bookshop La Moderna, she could leaf through the European illustrated magazines her father, Fernando Díaz, awaited with such high expectation on the docks of Veracruz. She sauntered into Wagner and Lieven, opposite Juárez Park, to buy her Aunt Hilda music by a composer she perhaps did not know, Maurice Ravel, whose works Orlando and Laura had heard conducted by Carlos Chávez in the Palace of Fine Arts.

The older women acted as if nothing had happened. That was their strength. They would forever be living on the coffee plantation owned by Don Felipe Kelsen, born in Darmstadt in the Rhineland. At dinner, they moved their hands around as if the table service were made of silver and not tin, the plates of porcelain and not pottery, the tablecloth of linen and not cotton. There was something they hadn't given up: each woman had her own starched linen napkin, carefully folded into a silver ring marked with her initials, V, H, MO, or L, elegantly and elaborately engraved. That was the first thing each one picked up when they sat down to table. It was their pride, their life preserver, the seal of rank. It was the mark of the Kelsens—before husbands, before confirmed celibacy, before death. The silver napkin ring was personality, tradition, memory, affirmation for each one of them and for them all.

A silver napkin ring holding a carefully folded napkin that was clean, crackling with starch. At table, they acted as if nothing had happened.

Laura began to chat with each of them, one at a time, alone, always with the feeling she was hunting them down. They were nervous, fleeing birds from two past seasons, Laura's and their own. Virginia and Hilda resembled each other more than even they knew. From the pianist aunt, once she'd repeated for the thousandth time her complaint against their father, Felipe Kelsen—that he hadn't allowed her to stay in Germany to study music—Laura extracted the more profound complaint, I'm a leftover old woman, Laura, a hopeless spinster, and do you know why? Because I spent my life convinced that men would prefer me if I denied them any hope. At the Candlemas party in Tlacotalpan I was besieged—it was there your parents met, remember?—and I took it upon myself, out of pure pride, to make the men who courted me understand that I was inaccessible.

"I'm sorry, Ricardo. Next Saturday, I'm returning to Germany to study the piano."

"You're very sweet, Heriberto, but I already have a boyfriend in Germany. We write to each other every day. Any day now, he'll come to me or I'll return to him."

"It isn't that I don't like you, Alberto, but you're just not in my class. You may kiss me if you like, but it will be a farewell kiss."

And when she turned up at the next Candlemas party without a boyfriend, Ricardo made fun of her, Heriberto appeared with a local girl, and Alberto was already married. Aunt Hilda's aquamarine eyes filled with tears that flowed from behind her thick glasses, clouded over like the foggy highway to Perote. She finished with the all too familiar adage: Laura, don't forget the old. Being young means not being faithful and forgetting others.

Aunt Virginia forced herself to stroll around the patio—she could no longer leave the house because of the understandable fear aging people have of falling down, breaking a leg, and not getting up until the Last Judgment. She spent hours putting on powder, and only when she felt herself to be perfectly arranged would she emerge to make the rounds of the patio, reciting in an inaudible voice her own poems or others'—it was impossible to tell which.

"Shall I come with you on your walks, Aunt Virginia?"

"No, don't come with me."

"Why?"

"You're only doing it out of charity. I forbid you."

"But no. Out of tenderness."

"Come, come, don't get me used to your compassion. I live in fear I'll be the last one left in this house and I'll die here alone. If I call you when you're in Mexico City, will you come to see me so I won't die alone?"

"Of course, I promise."

"Liar. That day you'll have a commitment you can't get out of, you'll be far away, dancing the fox-trot, and it won't matter a whit whether I'm dead or alive."

"Aunt Virginia, I swear I'll come."

"Don't swear in vain, it's sacrilegious. Why did you have children if you don't take care of them? Didn't you promise to look after them?"

"Life is difficult, Aunt Virginia. Sometimes—"

"Nonsense. The difficult thing is loving people. Your own people, understand? Not abandoning them, not forcing anyone to beg a bit of charity before dying, *sacre bleu!*"

She stopped and fixed her black-diamond eyes on Laura, eyes the more notable because of the quantity of face powder around them.

"You never got Minister Vasconcelos to publish my poems. That's how you fulfill your promises, ingrate. I'll die without anyone's having recited my poems but me."

She turned her back, with a timorous movement, on her niece.

Laura recounted the conversation with Aunt Virginia to María de la O, who could only say, "Pity, daughter, a little pity for the old left with no love or respect from others."

"You're the only one who knows the truth, Auntie. Tell me what I should do."

"Let me think it over. I don't want to make a mistake."

She looked down at her swollen ankles, and burst out laughing.

At night, Laura felt pain and fear, had trouble falling asleep, and, like Aunt Virginia, perambulated alone around the patio, barefoot so she wouldn't make noise or interrupt the sobs and memory-infused cries that escaped, unknowingly, from the bedrooms where the four sisters slept.

Which would be the first to go? Which the last? Laura swore to herself that no matter where she was, she would take care of the last sister, have the survivor live with her or come to be with her here, and not let Aunt Virginia's fear be realized: "I'm afraid of being the last and dying alone."

A nocturnal patio where the nightmares of the four women gathered together.

It was hard for Laura to include her mother, Leticia, in this chorus of fear. She reproached herself when she admitted that she hoped that if one of the four were left alone it would be either Mutti or Auntie. Aunts Hilda and Virginia had become insane and impossible; both, the niece was convinced, were virgins. María de la O was not.

"My mother made me sleep with her customers beginning when I was eleven."

Laura had felt neither horror nor compassion when Auntie confessed this; it was years earlier, in the house on Avenida Sonora. She knew that the generous, warm-hearted mulatta was telling her so Laura would understand how much Grandfather Felipe Kelsen's bastard daughter owed to the simple humanity of Grandmother Cosima Reiter—identical to her own despite differences of age, class, and race—and to the generosity of Laura's father, Fernando Díaz. The niece went to embrace and kiss her aunt, but María de la O stopped her with an outstretched arm: she didn't want compassion, and Laura only kissed the open palm of the admonitory hand.

Leticia was the last. Laura, back at home, desired with all her heart that Mutti would be the last to die, because she never complained, never gave up, kept the boardinghouse clean and in working order, and without her, Laura could imagine the other three castaways wandering through the corridors like souls in torment while dirty dishes piled up in the kitchen with its braziers, herbs grew unweeded in the garden, the larder emptied out and died of hunger, cats took over the house, and flies covered the sleeping faces of Virginia, Hilda, and María de la O with buzzing masks.

"Yes, we all face a future that has no tenderness," Leticia said unexpectedly one afternoon while Laura was helping her wash dishes, adding, after a brief pause, that she was happy Laura was back at home.

"Mutti, I've felt so much nostalgia for my childhood, for the inside spaces especially. How they stay with you, even though they fade: a bedroom, a dresser, a water pitcher, that horrible pair of pictures—the brat and the dog—I have no idea why you keep them."

"Nothing reminds me more of your father, and I don't know why, because he wasn't like them at all."

"Neither a brat nor a beauty?" Laura smiled.

"That's not it. They're just things I associate with him. I can't sit down to eat without seeing him at the head of the table with those pictures behind him."

"Did you love each other a lot?"

"We love each other a lot, Laura."

She took her daughter's hand and asked her if she thought the past condemned us to death.

"One day you'll see how much the past matters in order to go on living and, for those who loved each other, to go on loving each other."

Although she managed to reestablish intimacy with her past, Laura could not establish contact with her own sons. Santiago was a perfect little gentleman, courteous and prematurely serious. Danton was a little devil who didn't take his mother seriously or, for that matter, unseriously. It was as if she were just one more aunt in a harem with no sultan. ~~Laura didn't know how to talk to them~~, to attract them, and she felt the failure was all on her side, an emotional insufficiency that she, and not her sons, had somehow to fill.

Put another way, the younger son, at the age of ten, behaved as if he were the sultan, the prince of the house who had no need to prove anything and could act capriciously and demand (and get) the acquiescence of the four women, who looked on him rather fearfully. At the same time, they looked on the older brother with genuine tenderness. Danton seemed to take pride in the almost frightened reticence that his aunts and grandmother showed in dealing with him, although María de la O once muttered, What this brat needs is a good spanking. The next time he didn't even bother to tell them he wasn't going to be sleeping at home, Grandmother Leticia did give him a spanking, to which the child responded by saying he wouldn't forget the insult.

"I'm not insulting you, snot-nose, I'm just giving you a spanking. I reserve insults for important people, you idiot."

It was the only time Laura ever saw her mother be violent, and in that act all the lack of authority, all the lack that had begun to mark her own existence, became manifest, as if it were Laura who deserved the spanking for not being the one to discipline her unruly child.

Santiago viewed everything with a serious eye, and sometimes it seemed that the boy was restraining a sigh, resigned but disapproving, with regard to his younger brother.

Laura tried to bring them together to go on walks or play with her. They both stubbornly resisted. They didn't take offense and didn't reject her: they rejected each other and acted like rivals in opposing gangs. Laura recalled the old family discord between pro-German and pro-Allied factions during the Great War, but this was different. This was a war of character, of personality. Whom did Santiago the older resemble, whom Danton the younger? Actually, they should have been reversed, with Danton older and Santiago younger, the second Santiago. Would he be like his young uncle who'd been shot soon after his twentieth birthday? Would Danton be ambitious like his father, Juan Francisco, but would he be strong, not weak and ambitious like his father, who was happy with so little?

She had no idea how to talk to them, no idea how to attract them, and she felt that the lack was entirely hers, that it was her emotional insufficiency, not her sons', and that she would have to fill it.

"I promise you, Mutti," she said to Leticia as she bid them goodbye, "I'm going to put my life in order so the boys can come back to us."

She emphasized the plural, and Leticia raised an eyebrow with feigned surprise, reproaching her daughter for that deceitful "us." It was a wordless way of telling her that that was the difference between you two and your father and me: we put up with separation because we loved each other so much. But Laura had a sharp, undesired premonition when she repeated, "Back to us, to Juan Francisco and me."

When she took the return train to Mexico City, she knew that she'd lied, that she was going to seek a destiny for herself and her sons without Juan Francisco, that reconciliation with her husband would be the easy way out and the worst thing for the boys' future.

She lowered the window on the Pullman car, and saw herself and Juan Francisco seated in the Isotta-Fraschini that Xavier Icaza had given them as a wedding present, useless but elegant, and that they had given, also uselessly, to the four Kelsen sisters, who no longer left their house; the car was now in the hands of Zampaya, who could show off from time to time driving it around or taking the boys on a little excursion. She saw the four Kelsen sisters sitting there: they'd made the supreme effort to see her off along with the two boys. Danton didn't look at her, pretending instead to drive the car and making extravagant noises with his mouth and nose. She would never forget Santiago's gaze. He was his own ghost.

The train pulled out, and Laura felt a sudden anguish. There weren't only four women in the Xalapa house. Li Po! She'd forgotten Li Po! Where was the Chinese doll, why didn't she look for it or think about it? She tried to shout, to ask, but the train pulled out while handkerchiefs were waved.

"Can you imagine a leader in the workers' movement with a luxury car imported from Europe parked in his garage? Forget about it, Laura. Give it to your mama and your aunts."

# 10. Detroit: 1932

O RLANDO'S NOTE had been waiting for her at the desk of the Hotel Regis when she returned from Xalapa. She'd been expecting it.

Laura my love, I'm not what I say I am nor what I seem to be. And I'd rather keep my secret. You're getting too close to the mystery of your

*Orlando*

And without mystery our love would be uninteresting. I'll always love you . . .

The hotel manager had told her she needn't check out immediately, because Mrs. Cortina had taken care of everything until the following week.

"That's right, Doña Carmen Cortina. She pays for the room that you and your friend Mr. Ximénez occupy. Well, for the past three years, she's been paying for Mr. Ximénez."

Friend? Whose friend? she was stupidly going to ask. Friend in what sense?, friend of Laura, friend of Carmen, lover of which, lover of both?

Now, in Detroit, she remembered that a terrible feeling of abandonment had overwhelmed her at that moment, that she'd felt an urgent need for someone who'd feel sorry for her, "my hunger for pity." And her immediate reaction, just as sudden as the desolation, impelled her to visit Diego Rivera's house in Coyoacán and say, Here I am, remember me? I need work, I need to put a roof over my head, please accept me, maestro.

"Of course, the kid wearing black."

"Yes, that's why I dressed in mourning again. Remember me?"

"Well, mourning clothes still horrify me. They make me feel jinxed. Ask Frida to lend you something more colorful and then we'll talk. Anyway, you look very different and very pretty."

"I think so too," said a melodious voice behind her, and Frida Kahlo made her entrance with a clatter of necklaces, medallions, and rings, rings especially, one on every finger, sometimes two: Laura Díaz remembered the incident involving her grandmother Cosima Kelsen and wondered, watching this strange-looking woman enter the studio—black eyebrows, or rather one continuous black eyebrow, braided black hair tied up with wool ribbons, and a wide peasant skirt—whether the Hunk of Papantla hadn't robbed the rings from Grandmother Cosima just to give them to his lover Frida. The sight of Rivera's wife had Laura convinced that this was the goddess of transformations she and Grandfather Felipe had discovered in the Veracruz forest, the figure made by the Zapotal people which he had tried to demythologize by turning it into a mere ceiba tree, so that she wouldn't go on believing in fantasies, a marvelous feminine figure staring at eternity, crisscrossed with belts of seashells and serpents, her head adorned with a crown woven by the forest, ornamented with necklaces and rings and earrings on her arms, nose, ears. No matter what Grandfather had said, a ceiba was more dangerous than a woman. A ceiba was a tree bristling with spines. No one could touch it. No one could embrace it.

Was Frida Kahlo the temporary name of a native goddess who assumed mortal form from time to time, reappearing here and there to make love with *guerrilleros*, bandits, and artists?

"She can work with me," said Frida imperiously as she descended the studio stairs, averting her gaze neither from Rivera's bulging eyes nor from Laura's shadowy and deep-set ones. In that instant, Laura, looking at herself in Frida, looked at herself, looked at Laura Díaz looking at Laura Díaz, saw herself transformed, with a new personality about to be born in those familiar features but also about to metamorphose and, perhaps, be forgotten by Laura Díaz herself, with her sculpted, thin, powerful face, her high, strong, long nose, the bridge flanked by eyes that grew increasingly melancholy, the rings under her eyes like lakes of uncertainty restrained at the edge of her pale cheeks, happy to have found the crimson of her thin lips, now even more severe, as if Laura's entire visage had become, simply in contrast to Frida's, more gothic, more statuesque when face to face with the vegetative life of Diego Rivera's partner, a plucked flower, drained but still blooming.

"She can work with me . . . I'm going to need help in Detroit while you work and I, well . . . you know . . ."

She stumbled and slipped. Laura ran to help her, took her by the arm, and unintentionally touched her thigh—You didn't hurt yourself, did you?—and what she felt was a dry, fleshless leg, compensated for or was it confirmed—in an act of simultaneous challenge and vulnerability, a dreamy glance that the women strangely exchanged. Rivera laughed.

"Don't worry. I had no intention of touching her, Friducha. She's all yours. Just think, this kid is German like you. And one Valkyrie is enough for me, I swear."

Frida immediately liked Laura. She invited her to her bedroom, and the first thing she did was take out a mirror with an indigo-blue enameled frame. "Have you looked at yourself, woman, do you know how good-looking you are? Well, take advantage of it, you know you're strange-looking, we just don't see many great beauties, a profile that looks as if it were slashed out with a machete, the prominent nose, the eyes sunken, deep, and shadowed. Does your Orlando think he can take the mourning out of your eyes? Forget about him. I like you."

"How do you know about Orlando?"

"Wake up, sweetie. This city's like a small village. Everyone knows everything."

Frida fluffed up the pillows on her bed with its brightly painted posts and quickly said, as Laura helped her to pack, "Tomorrow we're off to Gringoland. Diego's going to paint a mural in the Detroit Institute of Arts. Commissioned by Henry Ford himself, imagine. You know where all this leads. The Communists around here are attacking him for taking capitalist money. The capitalists up there are attacking him for being a Communist. I just tell him that an artist is above all this stupid bullshit. The important thing is the work. That's what remains, no one can erase that, and that's what will speak to the people when all the politicians and critics are pushing up daisies.

"Have you got any clothes of your own? I don't want you to imitate me. You know I trick myself out as a piñata because of my own fantasies but also to cover up my sick leg and my hobble. She may limp, but she won't need pimps—that's my motto," said Frida, running her hand over the dark down covering her upper lip.

Laura came back with her valise. Would Frida like her in the Balenciaga and Schiaparelli dresses she'd bought with Elizabeth and thanks to Elizabeth's generosity, or should she revert to a simpler style? A sudden intuition told her that what would matter to this woman, so carefully turned out and decorative, and exactly because of that, would be naturalness in other people. That was her way of making others accept the naturalness of the extraordinary in her, in Frida Kahlo.

Frida kissed her hairless ixcuintle dogs goodbye, and they all took the train to Detroit.

The long journey through Mexico's northern deserts with their rows upon rows of magueys reminded Rivera of a verse by the young poet Salvador Novo: "The magueys do gymnastics in rows five hundred deep." But Frida said that Novo was no good, watch out for him, he was a backbiter, a bad fag, not like the tender, gentle queers she knew who were members of her group.

Rivera laughed. "If he's bad, then the worse he is, the better."

"Watch out for him. He's one of those Mexicans who'd sell their own mother just to bring off a cruel joke. You know what he said to me at the show of that Tizoc guy? 'Bye-bye, Pavlova.' So I answered, 'Bye-bye, Salivator.' I thought he was going to explode."

"How vindictive you can be, Friducha. If you start speaking badly of Novo, you're giving Novo permission to speak badly about us."

"Doesn't he already? The kindest insult he uses on you is to call you a cuckold. And me he calls Free-ass Kulo."

"It doesn't matter. Nothing but resentment, gossip, stories. Novo the writer stands. As does Rivera the painter. And so does life itself. The anecdotes evaporate."

"Fine. Diego, pass me the ukulele. Let's sing the Mixteca song. It's my favorite song for watching Mexico pass by."

*How far I am from the land where I was born,*
*Immense nostalgia invades my thoughts . . .*

They changed trains at the border and then again at St. Louis, Missouri. From there, they went straight to Detroit, Frida singing to her ukulele, telling dirty jokes, and then, at nightfall, while Rivera slept, staring at the passage of the infinite North American plains and talking about the pulsing of the locomotive, that steel heart which excited her with its rhythm, simultaneously spirited and destructive like that of all machines.

"When I was a girl, I would dress up as a man and raise hell in philosophy class with my pals. We called ourselves the Caps. I fit right in, liberated from the conventions of my class, with a group of boys who loved Mexico City as much as I did, and we explored it all the time, the parks, neighborhoods, studying it as if it were a book, from cantina to cantina, from stall to stall, a small, pretty city all blue and pink, a city of sweet, disorganized parks, silent lovers, wide avenues and dark alleys that took you by surprise."

All her life, she told Laura as they let the plains of Kansas and the wideness of the Mississippi run by, she'd sought out the dark city, discovering its smells and tastes, seeking above all company, friendship, any way to tell solitude to go fuck itself, to be one of the boys, to keep an eye out for the bastards, Laura, because in Mexico, all you've got to do is stick your neck out a little and a regiment of evil dwarfs cuts off your head.

"Resentment and solitude," said the woman with sweet eyes under the aggressive brows, sticking four roses into her hair instead of a crown and peering into the compartment's mirror to see the sweetness of her flower hairdo against the sunset over the great river of the plains, the Father of Waters. It smelled of charcoal, mud, dung, fertile land.

"I'd go out with the Caps and do all kinds of crazy things, like robbing trolleys and getting the cops to chase us the way they do in Buster Keaton movies, which are my favorites. Who would have known that a trolley would get even with me for stealing its chicks—because the Caps only stole single trolley cars, left at night in the Indianilla depot. We never took anything from anyone, but we did win the freedom of running around half Mexico City at night, all at whim, Laurita, following our fantasy but always on the rails, you never leave the rails, that's the secret, admit there are rails but use them to escape, to liberate yourself."

The great river, wide as a sea, origin of all the waters in the land lost by the Indians, water you can bathe in, the substance that receives you with joy, refreshes you, arranges spaces exactly the way God dreamed them: water is the divine material that welcomes you, unlike hard matter, which rejects you, wounds you, penetrates you.

"It was in September 1925, seven years ago. I was taking the bus from my parents' house in Coyoacán when a trolley smashed into us and broke my spine, my neck, my ribs, my pelvis, the entire order of my personal territory. My left shoulder was dislocated—how well my wide-sleeved blouses cover it up! Don't you think? Well, one of my feet was ruined forever. A handrail pierced my back and came out my vagina. The impact was so terrible that all my clothes flew off me, can you imagine that? My clothes just evaporated, I was left there bleeding, naked and broken. And then, Laura, the most incredible thing happened. Gold rained down on me. My naked, broken, prostrate body was covered with golden dust."

She lit an Alas cigarette and burst into a smoky guffaw.

"A worker on the bus was carrying some packages of gold dust. I was left broken but covered with gold dust, what do you think of that?"

Laura thought the trip to Detroit in the company of Frida and Diego so filled her existence that there was no room for anything else, not even for thinking about Xalapa, her mother, her sons, her aunts, her husband Juan Francisco, her lover Orlando, Carmen, her lover's lover, her "friend" Elizabeth: all of them were being left far behind like the sad, poor border at Laredo and the desert and central plateau before it, where the whole story, Frida repeated, was a matter of "defending yourself from the bastards."

Watching her sleep, Laura wondered if Frida defended herself alone or if she needed Diego's company, Diego the imperturbable master of his own truth but also of his own lie. She tried to imagine what all the men in her life would think of a man like that, those men of order and morality like Grandfather Felipe and her father, Fernando, those who were ambitious but petty like her husband, Juan Francisco, those who became broken promises like her brother, Santiago, those whose promises were as yet unspoken like her sons Danton and the second Santiago, or the perpetual enigma who was Orlando and, to close and recommence the circle, the immoral man who was also her grandfather, a man capable of abandoning his illegitimate, mulatta daughter: what would have become of the tender, adorable Auntie María de la O if the firm will of Grandmother Cosima and the equally tenacious mercy of her father hadn't saved her?

There was Rivera (seated by the dining-car window, telling fabulous lies about his physical origin—sometimes he was the son of a nun and a lovesick frog, sometimes the son of a captain in the conservative army and the insane Empress Carlota—evoking his legendary Paris life with Picasso, Modigliani, and the Russian Ilya Ehrenburg, who wrote a novel about Diego's life in Paris, *Adventures of the Mexican Julio Jurenito*, detailing his Aztec culinary taste for human flesh, Tlaxcaltecan preferably—the traitors deserved to be fried in lard—lies, all the time, sketching on huge sheets of paper spread out on the dining-car table the gigantic, detailed plan of the Detroit mural, the hymn to modern industry). For Laura, the exciting novelty was that of a creative man who was both fantastic and disciplined, hardworking as a bricklayer, dreamy as a poet, funny as a circus clown, and (finally) cruel as an artist, who insisted on being the tyrannical owner of all his time, with no thought for the needs of others, their anguish, their calls for help . . . Diego Rivera painted, and while he painted, the door to the world and to his fellow man remained shut, so that inside the cage of art its forms, colors, memories, homages could live freely, so that no matter how social or political the art might become, it was above all part of the history of art, not of politics, and it either added reality to a tradition or took it away, a tradition and reality that most mortals judge to be autonomous and flowing. The artist knows better: his art does not reflect reality; it establishes it. And to accomplish that work, generosity, concern, contact with others do not matter at all if they interrupt or weaken the work. On the other hand, cheapness, disdain, the most flagrant egoism are virtues if, thanks to them, the artist does his work.

What could a woman as fragile as Frida Kahlo hope to find in a man like that? What was his strength? Did Rivera give her the power her frailty needed, or was the important thing the sum of two strengths that would give her physical weakness its independent and painful place? And what about Diego: was he as strong as he physically appeared to be—huge and robust—or as weak as that same naked body—hairless, pink, puffy, with a tiny penis—which Laura saw one morning when she accidentally opened the compartment door? Might it not be that she, Frida the victim, gave strength to him, man of vigor and victories?

Frida was the first to take note of the changed quality of the light, before Diego did, but she mentioned it as if he had discovered it, knowing he'd be thankful for the lie at first and then make it an original truth, the property of Diego Rivera.

"Here in Gringoland there's not enough light, not enough shadow. You really hit the nail on the head, sweetheart." She shone, while he returned, trying to forget, well, for your sweetheart, your night mirror, there are only two kinds of light in the world, the afternoon light of Paris, where I became a painter, and that of the central plateau of Mexico, where I became a man. I don't understand either the light of the gringo winter or the light of the Mexican tropics, which is why my eyes are green swords in your flesh that turn into waves of light in your hands, Frida.

Thus the two of them went from the station to the hotel ready to contrast things, to fight, and not to allow anything to pass unnoticed or slip by quietly. Detroit satisfied them on all counts, nourished them from the outset, gave them opportunities—to Rivera the chance to cause a scandal, to Frida the opportunity for fun. At the hotel they got in line to check in. An old couple in front of them was turned away by the receptionist with a cutting statement: "We're very sorry, but we do not accept Jews here." The disconcerted couple stepped aside, whispering to each other, unable to find anyone even to help them with their bags. Frida asked if she could fill in the registration cards and wrote on them in huge letters: MR. AND MRS. DIEGO RIVERA, then their address in Coyoacán, their Mexican nationality, and then, in even larger letters, her religion—JEWISH. The flustered receptionist stared at them, not knowing what to say. So Frida said it for him: "Is something troubling you, sir?"

"It's that we didn't know."

"Didn't know what?"

"Excuse me, madam, your religion . . ."

"More than a religion. A race."

"It's that . . ."

"You don't allow Jews in your hotel?"

She turned on her heel without listening to the receptionist's answer. Laura held back her laughter and listened to the comments of the white hotel guests, the women wearing big straw summer hats, the men wearing those strange gringo seersucker suits and Panama hats. Could they be gypsies? And what is that woman disguised as?

"Let's go, Diego, Laura. We're getting out of here."

"Mrs. Rivera," begged the trembling hotel manager, catapulted from his office smelling of erasers, his newspaper opened to the funny pages, "we're sorry, we didn't know, it doesn't matter, you're the guest of Mr. Ford, accept our apologies."

"Go tell that old couple over there they can stay here even if they are Jews. That's right, the ones going out the door. Step on it, you shit!" ordered Frida. Later, in the suite, she collapsed in laughter, playing "Yes, We Have No Bananas" on her ukulele. "They not only let us in but let in the old fogies and lowered the price for us!"

Diego didn't waste a moment. The next day he was already in the museum, examining the spaces, preparing the fresco materials, giving instructions to his assistants, spreading out the drawings, and giving press interviews.

"I'm going to paint a new race for the age of steel."

"A people without memory is like a well-intentioned siren. It doesn't know when because it doesn't know how."

"I'm going to give an aura of humanity to a dehumanized industry."

"I'm going to teach the United States of Amnesia to remember."

"Christ chased the money changers out of the temple. I'm going to give the money changers the temple they need. Let's see if they behave better."

"Mr. Rivera, you're in the automobile capital of the world. Is it true you don't know how to drive?"

"It's true, but it's also true that I know how to break eggs. You should see how tasty my omelettes are. *Puros huevos.*"

He never stopped talking, joking, ordering, painting as he talked, as if a world of forms and colors needed a defense and a distraction external to the hubbub, the movement, and the words to gestate slowly, behind his sleepy, bulging eyes. Nevertheless, when he came back to the hotel, he was exhausted.

"I don't understand these gringo faces. I scrutinize them. I want to like them. I swear I look at them sympathetically, begging them, Say something to me, please. It's like seeing a tray of rolls in a bakery. They're all alike. They have no color. I don't know what to do. The machines are turning out great, but the men look awful. What am I going to do?"

"How do our faces become what they are, how does a body model itself?" Frida repeated to Laura when Diego went off very early in order to avoid the increasing heat of the continental summer.

"*How far I am from the soil where . . .*" Frida half sang. "Do you know why it's so hot?"

"Because we're so far from the two oceans. Sea breezes just don't get here. The only relief is the wind from the North Pole. Nice relief!"

"How do you know all that?"

"My father may have been a banker, but he read a lot. He subscribed to magazines. We'd go to the dock at Veracruz every month to pick up his European books and magazines."

"And do you also know why I feel so much heat, no matter what temperature the thermometer says it is?"

"Because you're going to have a baby."

"And how do you know that?"

Because of the way she was walking, Laura said. But I'm lame. But now the soles of your feet touch the ground. Before, you walked on tiptoe, uncertain, as if you were about to fly away. Now it's as if you were putting down roots with every step you take.

Frida hugged her and thanked her for being with her. From the first moment, she'd liked Laura. Seeing her, dealing with her, she said, she'd understood that the young woman felt useless or had been made to feel useless.

"I never saw a woman come through my door with a more desperate need to work. I think even you didn't know it."

"No, I didn't know it. I was just obsessed by a need to invent a world for myself, and I suppose that means inventing work for yourself."

"Or a child—that's a creation, too." Frida looked inquiringly at Laura.

"I have two."

"Where are they?"

Why did Laura Díaz have the feeling that her conversations with Frida Kahlo—so intimately feminine, with no tricks, no twists and turns, not a drop of malice—were, on the one hand, a recrimination that Frida directed at her irresponsible maternity, not because it wasn't conventional but because it wasn't enough of a revolt against the men—

the husband, the lover—who had distanced the mother from her children? Frida told Laura, in total frankness, that she'd been unfaithful to Rivera because he was unfaithful to her first. Between them they had only one agreement: Diego slept with women and Frida did the same, because if she slept with men, Diego would be enraged, as he wouldn't in their symmetrical, shared taste for the female sex. That wasn't the problem, the invalid woman confessed one night to Laura. Sometimes, infidelity has nothing to do with sex. It's a matter of intimacy with another person, and when the intimacy is secret, and secrets require lies to protect intimacy, the secret is sometimes called "sex."

"Whom you sleep with doesn't matter, but whom you confide in does. And whom you lie to. It looks to me as though you don't confide in anyone, Laura, and you lie to everyone."

"Do you desire me?"

"I already told you I like you. But with the situation as it is, I need you as a companion and nurse most of all. If we complicate things sentimentally, it could turn out that I'll find myself all alone, with no one to take me to the hospital when things start getting rough. Then I'll be yelling for my granny! That's on the one hand."

She laughed a lot, as usual, but Laura persisted. "And what was the other reason? You said, On the one hand, but what about the other hand?"

"I won't tell you. I might need you to give me tomorrow what I'm reproaching you for today. Let's talk about practical things."

It was July. The baby was supposed to arrive in December. If Diego finished in October, they'd have time to return safely together so the baby would be born in Mexico. But if Diego were slow, how could I have my baby here, in the cold, without friends, with no one to help me but you? And if I go back to Mexico early, don't I run the risk of losing the baby on the way, in all that confusion and jangle of trains, as my little doctors warned me?

Laura found herself looking at a very vulnerable woman, almost hunched over, shrunken, swimming in the roomy peasant costumes that hid not only her physical diminution but also her fear, her imperceptible tremor, the second fear, a fear that came from within her, that not only extended or duplicated the physical fear of the shattered woman but replaced it with another, unexpressed and shared with the being gestating within her. There was a complicity between the mother and the child who was growing in her womb. No one could enter that secret circle.

Frida guffawed and asked Laura to help her braid her hair, arrange her skirts and blouse, drape her rebozo over her shoulders, and comb her mustache. Laura lent her a hand and both sallied forth into Gringoland, to the dinners and parties in honor of the "most famous painter in the world and Mrs. Rivera," to dance with the millionaires of industry, challenging them to inquire into the invalid missteps Frida covered up by saying they were steps from Oaxaca folk dances, astonishing Indian dances, as astonishing as Henry Ford's anti-Semitic face when Frida asked him during a dinner, Mr. Ford, is it true you're Jewish? She scandalized Michigan high society with her feigned ignorance of how vulgar certain expressions were that she used in English, saying, with the most courteous smile, *Shit on you!* when she stood up after a banquet or, when she announced during a card game with society ladies, *I enjoy fucking, don't you?* Accompanied by Laura in theaters blazing hot in a city where it was already 100 degrees Fahrenheit, she saw Chaplin in *City Lights*, Laurel and Hardy—the cream pies, the houses turned upside down, the police chases, a plate of spaghetti emptied down the bodice of a stately matron—all of that killed her with laughter, she would take Laura by the hand, weep with laughter, weep, laugh, weep, shout with laughter, shout . . .

The stretcher rolled along under the lights like eyes without eyelids, and the doctors asked Laura, How has she been feeling? She feels the heat a lot, her skin gets blotchy, her uterus hurts, a handrail pierced her vagina, she was hit by a trolley. What did she eat today? Two cups of custard, salad, she threw it all up, she's the woman deflowered by a trolley. Did you know that? Her husband paints clean, shiny, steel machines, but she was raped by an old machine, rusty, indecent, toot toot and off we go, she shouted in the movie theater, she turned blue, began to bleed, they picked her up in a lake of blood, surrounded by clots of blood she'd lost from laughing, did you know? Laurel and Hardy.

She looked like a twelve-year-old girl resting in bed, her hair wet from weeping, shrunken, skinny, silent.

"I want to see my baby."

"But, Frida, it's only a fetus."

"It doesn't matter."

"The doctors won't allow it."

"Tell them it's for artistic reasons."

"Frida, it was born in shreds. It broke apart in your womb. It has no form."

"Then I'll give it a form."

She slept. She awakened. She couldn't bear the heat. She got out of bed. She tried to escape. She was put back to bed. She asked to see the child. Diego came to visit, tender, understanding, distant, pressed to return to work, his gaze fixed on the absent wall, not on the woman before him.

Then, one night, Laura heard a forgotten noise that reminded her of the days of her childhood in the Catemaco forest. She was sleeping on a cot in Frida's hospital room, and the noise awakened her. She saw Frida in her bed, completely naked with her body broken, one leg thinner than the other, her vagina eternally bleeding a flood of carnations, her back screwed in place like a sealed window, and her hair growing, visibly growing second by second, longer and longer, hair sprouting like Medusas from her cranium, trailing like spiders over her pillow, slinking like snakes along the mattress, putting down roots around the bedposts, while Frida stretched out her hands and showed her the wounded vagina, asked her to touch it, not to be afraid, we women are pink inside, take the colors out of my sex, smear them on your fingers, bring me brushes and a drawing book, Laura, don't look at me that way, how does one naked woman see another naked woman? because you're naked too, Laura, even if you don't know it, I do, I see you with your head covered with ribbons and a hundred umbilical cords tangled between your thighs: I dream your dreams, Laura Díaz, I see that you're dreaming of snails, the slowest snails that travel through your years with a fragile, slimy slowness not knowing they're in a garden that is also a cemetery and the plants in that garden weep and shriek and ask for milk, ask for the breast, the little girl plants are hungry, the little boy snails are deaf and pay no attention to their mothers, only I see them, I hear them and I understand them, only I see the real colors of the world, of the snail boys, the plant girls, the mother forest, they are blue, green, yellow, sulphur, amaranth . . . the earth is a garden, a tomb, and what you see is the truth, the hospital room is the only prodigal forest in this cement wasteland called Detroit, the hospital room fills up with yellow parrots and gray cats and white eagles and black monkeys, everyone brings me presents but you, Laura, what are you going to give me?

Diego saw her and asked Laura to bring her drawing books, pencils, and watercolors. All he needed was a look and an exchange of very few words.

"Sweetheart, you're not ugly no matter what they say, actually . . ."

"Friducha, I love you more and more."

"Who told you that you're ugly, my love?"

"Look, a newspaper clipping from Mexico. They call me the obese Huitzilopochtli."

"And what do they call me?"

"An Aztec goddess in decline."

She laughed, held Laura's hand, they all laughed a lot, and Laura?

"I baptize you Obsidian Butterfly," said Diego. "I have spoken."

With Laura at her side handing her pencils, brushes, colors, paper, Frida began to paint while talking, just like her husband, as if neither of them could create without the protective shadow of language, simultaneously alien to artists and their indispensable shadow. Frida spoke to Laura, but she was really speaking to herself speaking to Laura, she asked her to let herself be seen seeing herself in a mirror and Laura, watching the reduced woman, curled up in the bed with her hair greasy and her eyebrows in open revolt and her mustache unclipped, could do nothing, and Frida told her to consider it carefully, it was one thing to be a body and another to be beautiful, for her, knowing she was a body was enough for now, knowing she'd survived, beauty would come later, the first thing was to give form to the body that every so often and more and more threatened to disintegrate like that fetus she could only expel in a roar of laughter: she drew more and more rapidly and feverishly, like her words which Laura would never forget, ugliness is the body without shape, help me gather together everything that was scattered, Laura, give it its own shape, catch the cloud on the wing, the sun, the chalk silhouette of my dress, the red ribbon that links me to my fetus, the bloody bedsheet that is my toga, the coagulated crystal of the tears running down my cheeks, all together, please, help me gather together everything that was scattered and give it its own shape, won't you?, the theme doesn't matter, pain, love, death, birth, revolution, power, pride, vanity, dream, memory, will, it doesn't matter what animates the body so long as it gives it form and then it isn't ugly anymore, beauty only belongs to the person who understands it, not to the person who possesses it, beauty is nothing more than the truth that belongs to each one of us, that of Diego when he paints, mine I'm inventing right in this hospital bed, yours you still have to find, Laura, you understand from everything I've said to you that I'm not going to reveal it to you, it's up to you to understand it and find it, your truth, you can look at me without modesty, Laura Díaz, say that I look horrible, you wouldn't dare show me the mirror, in your eyes today I am not beautiful, on this day and in this place I am not pretty, and I won't answer you with words, I'm asking you instead for some colors and a sheet of paper and I turn the horror of my wounded body and my spilled blood into my truth and into my beauty, because you know, my true friend, my true buddy all the way, you know?, knowing ourselves makes us beautiful because it identifies our desires; when a woman desires, she's always beautiful . . .

The hospital room was filling up, first with drawing books, separate sheets of paper later, then sheets of tin when Diego brought some church retables from Guanajuato and reminded Frida how people painted in villages and out in the country, on sheets of tin and abandoned wooden planks that became, when touched by rustic hands, ex-votos giving thanks to the Holy Child of Atocha, the Virgin of

Remedies, the Lord of Chalma, for the miracle that had been granted, the daily miracle that saved the child from sickness, the father from the mine collapse, the mother from drowning in the river where she bathed, Frida from dying pierced by a handrail, Grandmother Cosima from being chopped to pieces on the road to Perote, Auntie María de la O from being abandoned in a bordello for blacks, Grandfather Felipe from dying in a trench on the Marne, brother Santiago from being shot at dawn in Veracruz, Frida again from bleeding to death in giving birth, and Laura—from what? for being saved from what should she give thanks for her salvation?

"Read this poem to Frida." Rivera handed a slim volume to Laura. "This is the best Mexican poem since Sor Juana. Read what it says on this page:

*Filled with myself, besieged in my own skin*
*by an ungraspable god who suffocates me*

And look ahead here:

*Oh intelligence, solitude in flames,*
*that conceives all without creating it!*

And then at the end:

*with Him, with me, with the three of us . . .*

See how Gorostiza understands everything? We are only three, always three. Father, mother, and child. Woman, man, and lover. Change it around any way you like, at the end you'll always be left with three, because four is immoral, five is unmanageable, two is insufferable, and one is the threshold between solitude and death."

"And why does four have to be immoral?" Frida asked in surprise. "Laura got married and had two sons."

"My husband walked out." Laura smiled timidly. "Actually, I left him."

"And there's always one child you favor, even if you have a dozen," added Frida.

"Three, always three," muttered Rivera as he walked out.

"That bastard's got something up his sleeve." Frida furrowed her bushy brows. "Hand those tin sheets to me, will you, Laura?"

When the hospital complained about the growing disorder in the room, the shreds of paper everywhere and the smell of the paints, Diego appeared like a god in a classical tragedy, Jupiter the Thunderer, and said in English, *This woman is an artist*, didn't these idiots understand that? He scolded them, but said it to her, with love and pride, This woman who is my wife puts all the truth, suffering, and cruelty of the world into the painting that pain has forced her to create: you, surrounded by the routine suffering of a hospital, have never seen so much agonizing poetry, and that's why you don't understand her.

"My little sweetheart," Frida said to him. *"Mi chiquito lindo."*

When she could be moved, they returned to the hotel and Laura sorted Frida's paintings for her. One day, the two of them finally went to see Diego painting at the Institute. Great progress had been made on the mural, but Frida saw the problem and how he had resolved it. The shining, devouring machines were woven together like great serpents of steel and proclaimed their primacy over the world of the workers who maintained them. Frida looked in vain for the faces of the American workers and understood. Diego had painted all of them with their backs turned because he didn't understand them, because they were faces of unbaked dough with no personality, flour faces. But he had introduced dark faces—blacks and Mexicans—who did, yes, face the viewers, the world.

Every day, the two women brought him a nice tasty lunch in a basket and silently sat down to watch him work while he poured out his river of words. Frida sipped teaspoonfuls of *cajeta* from Celaya, which she brought to enjoy so she could fill up on that confection of caramelized condensed milk, each day a bit more as she got her strength back. Laura was dressed very simply in a tailored suit, but Frida was decked out in green, purple, and yellow rebozos, braids of colored ribbons, and necklaces of jadeite.

Rivera had left three blank spaces in his mural of industry. He began looking more and more often at the female couple sitting at one side of the scaffolding watching him work—Frida sipping *cajeta* and clanking her necklaces, Laura carefully crossing her legs—under the scrutiny of his assistants. One day, the two came in and saw themselves transformed into men, two workers with short hair and long overalls, in work shirts and with gloved hands grasping steel tools, Frida and Laura dominating the light of the mural at the far end of the wall, Laura with her angular features accentuated, her hatchet profile, her shadowed eyes, her hair even shorter than the old hairdo she'd rejected when the woman from Veracruz decided on her bangs and pageboy, Frida too with short hair and sideburns, her eyebrows thick but her most masculine trait, the down on her upper lip, eliminated by the painter, to the stupefaction of the model: "Hey, I'd have put in the mustache."

There was another unpainted area in the center of the wall and in the upper part of the fresco, and Frida would glance nervously at those absences until one afternoon when she took Laura by the hand and said, Let's get out of here. They took a taxi back to the hotel, and Frida ripped off a sheet of paper, spread it out over the table, and began to draw again and again, insatiably, the sun and the moon, the moon and the sun, separated, together.

Laura looked out of the hotel room's high window searching for the star and its satellite, elevated by Frida to equal rank as day and night stars, sun and moon born of Venus, the first star of the day and the last of night, moon and sun equal in rank but opposite in hours, seen by the eyes of the world, not by the eyes of the universe, Laura, what will Diego put in those blank spaces in his mural?

"It scares me. He's never kept a secret like that from me."

They found out only on the day of the inauguration. A holy family of workers presided over the work of the machines and the white men with their backs to the world, the dark men facing the world, and, at the far end of the fresco, the two women dressed as men staring at the men, and above the depiction of the work and the machines a virgin wearing a humble calico dress and white beads like any Detroit shop-girl, holding a naked child, also with a halo, and seeking in vain the support of the eyes of a carpenter who had turned his back on the mother and child. The carpenter was holding the tools of his trade, hammer and nails, in one hand and two planks arranged in a cross in the other. His halo was faded and contrasted with the brilliant scarlet of a sea of flags that separated the holy family from the machines and workers.

The murmuring grew when the curtains were pulled back.

A joke, a parody, a joke on the capitalists who'd hired him, a parody of the spirit of Detroit, sacrilege, Communism. Another wall, this one of voices, began to rise opposite Diego Rivera's, the assistants began to divide up, the shouting grew louder, Edsel Ford, son of the magnate, called for calm, Rivera climbed up on a stepladder and proclaimed the birth of a new art for the society of the future and had to scramble down painted yellow and red because the pots of paint that agitators had prepared beforehand at the direction of Rivera himself were beginning to be thrown at him, while another brigade of workers, also organized by Diego, stood in front of the mural and proclaimed they would guard it forever.

The next day, Diego, Frida, and Laura took the train to New York to start work on the Rockefeller Center mural project. Rivera was euphoric, cleaning his face with kerosene, happy as a mischievous child planning his next practical joke and succeeding at them all: attacked by capitalists for being a Communist and by Communists for being a capitalist, Rivera felt he was a pure Mexican, a joking, devilish Mexican with more quills than a porcupine to defend himself from bastards on both sides of the Río Grande, devoid of the rancor that defeated both Mexicans and Americans before the game started, and delighted to be the target in the Mexican national sport of attacking Diego Rivera, which now would be seen as a national tradition as opposed to the new gringo sport of attacking Diego Rivera. Diego the fat Puck, who instead of laughing at the world from a thicket on a midsummer night could laugh from the thicket of his fresco scaffolding one moment, then fall to the floor and discover he had an ass's head but find an amorous lap where he could take refuge and be caressed by the queen of the night, who saw not an ugly donkey but an enchanted prince, the frog transformed into the prince sent by the moon to love and protect his Friducha, *mi chiquita*, my adored little girl, broken, suffering, everything is for you, you know that, don't you? And when I say, Frida, "Let me help you, poor little thing," what am I saying but help me, poor little me, help your Diego?

They asked Laura to go back to Mexico with the summer suitcases, the cardboard boxes full of papers, to put the Coyoacán house in order, to live there if she liked, they didn't have to say anything else to her because Laura saw they needed each other more than ever after the miscarriage, that Frida wasn't going to work for a while, and that in New York she wouldn't need Laura, she wouldn't be useful, because Frida had many friends there, loved going shopping with them and to the movies, there was going to be a festival of Tarzan films she didn't want to miss, she adored movies with gorillas, she'd seen *King Kong* nine times, they restored her sense of humor, made her laugh her head off.

"You know it's hard for Diego to fall asleep in winter. Now I have to spend all my nights with him so he'll get some rest and have energy for the new mural. Laura, don't forget to put a doll in my Coyoacán bed."

## 11. Avenida Sonora: 1934

ONE FINE DAY, Aunts Hilda and Virginia disappeared. Leticia got up at six in the morning, as she usually did, and prepared breakfast—mangos and quinces, mameys and peaches, *huevos rancheros*, bran bread, *café con leche*—which at seven o'clock she would arrange on the table at the places marked by the napkins rolled into silver rings.

She glanced sadly—later she realized her melancholy was a premonition—at the places set for her three sisters and the silver initials, H, V, MO. When they failed to appear by seven-fifteen, she went to María de la O's room and awakened her.

"I'm sorry. I had very annoying dreams."

"What did you dream about?"

"About a wave . . . I don't know," said the almost embarrassed Auntie. "Damn dreams, why do they leave us so quickly?"

Leticia went right to Hilda's door, where her knock was not answered. She opened it slightly and saw that the bed hadn't been slept in. She opened the armoire doors and noticed that one hanger was bare, the one that normally held the long white nightgown with the lacy bodice which Leticia had washed and ironed thousands of times. But the perfectly ordered ranks of slippers and high-top shoes were complete, like an army at ease.

She rushed in anguish to Virginia's room, certain she wouldn't find a messy bed there, either. What she did find was a note in an envelope addressed to her, leaning against the mirror:

Dear Little Sister: Hilda couldn't be what she wished, and neither could I. Yesterday, we looked in the mirror and thought the same thing. Why wait with "Christian" patience for the fatal moment, why not have the valor to walk toward death instead of giving it the satisfaction of knocking at our door one evening? Sitting here in Xalapa, taken care of by your goodness and your efforts, we were fading like two burned-down candles. Both of us wanted to do something that would be the equivalent of what we could not accomplish in life. Our sister stared at her arthritic fingers and hummed a Chopin Nocturne. I looked at the shadows under my eyes, in each wrinkle I counted a poem that was never published. We looked at each other and realized what we were both thinking—so many years living together, just imagine, we haven't separated since we were born, so we can guess each other's thoughts! Last night, you may remember, the four of us sat down to play cards in the living room. It was my turn to shuffle (Hilda can't because of the condition of her fingers), and I began to feel ill, the way someone should feel who enters their final moments without knowing it, but no matter how ill I felt, I couldn't stop shuffling, I went on aimlessly, until you and María de la O began to stare in astonishment, and then I shuffled frantically, as if my life depended on mixing the cards, and you, Leticia, said the fatal phrase, repeated that sweet, old, terrible saying: *A little old lady once died shuffling cards.*

Then I looked at Hilda and she at me, and we understood each other. You and our other sister were elsewhere, out of our world.

Looking at the cards. You led with the king of clubs.

Hilda and I looked at each other from the depths of our souls . . . don't try to find us. Last night, the two of us put on our white nightgowns, left our feet bare, woke up Zampaya and told him to drive us, in the Isotta, to the sea, to the lake where we were born. He put up no resistance. He looked at us as if we were insane for going out in our nightgowns. But he would always do what any one of us would tell him. So when you wake up and read this letter, you will not find either Hilda or me or Zampaya or the car. Zampaya will let us out where we tell him to do so, and the two of us will lose ourselves, barefoot in the forest, with no plan, no money, no bread basket, barefoot and wearing our nightgowns only out of modesty. If you love us, you will not look for us. Respect our wishes. We want to make death into art. The last. The only. Don't deprive us of that pleasure. With love from your sisters

*VIRGINIA AND HILDA*

"Your aunts were never seen again," said Leticia to Laura. "The car was found on a curve in the Acayucan road. Zampaya was found stabbed to death in, forgive me, daughter, the same bordello where María de la O grew up. Don't look at me like that. These are absolute mysteries, and I'm not going to be the one to clear them up. Enough headaches with what I already know, no need to add to them with what I don't know."

Laura had come to Xalapa the moment she found out about the disappearance of her maiden aunts, although she didn't yet know the terrible fate of the man who'd been the family's faithful servant for so many years. It was as if the evil spirit of María de la O's mother had returned, black as her skin, to take revenge on everyone who kept her from a life that, as her own daughter acknowledged, she exalted madly: "I was so happy when I was a whore. Fuck everyone who made me into a proper lady!"

Leticia went ahead and told Laura everything Laura had known for years. Mutti never bothered with gossip or with ferreting out information. She faced things as they turned up. She didn't have to ask because she understood everything and, as she'd just said, what she didn't understand she could imagine.

Back in her Veracruz home, Laura understood retrospectively, as if she were looking at a broken sun dial, that because of her aunts' fate and her mother's attitude Leticia knew everything about the failure of her marriage to Juan Francisco, about how her rebellion against her husband had dissolved in Elizabeth's protective treatment and how she'd drifted from there into her empty, prolonged, and ultimately useless relationship with Orlando; yet weren't those indispensable stages, if in themselves dispensable, in accumulating isolated instants of perception that, added together, would lead her to a new awareness, still vague, still misty, of things? The sun dial was inseparable from the shade dial.

Leticia took advantage of the flight of the old maids to look deep into Laura's eyes and silently ask her to do the thing that Laura quickly expressed: It's very hard for you and Auntie to take care of two boys who will soon be thirteen and fourteen. I'm going to take them back to Mexico City. You and Auntie too.

"No, Laura, we'll stay here. We look after each other. You'll have to remake your home on your own."

"Yes, Mutti. Juan Francisco is waiting for all of us in the house on Avenida Sonora. But I already told you, if you and your sister want to come with us, we'll get a larger house, so don't give it a second thought."

"Get used to living without us." Leticia smiled. "I don't want to leave the state of Veracruz ever again. Mexico City horrifies me."

Did one have to explain to Leticia that since Orlando had abandoned her she'd decided to rebuild her home with Juan Francisco, not out of weakness but through a strong, essential act of will that summed up for her the lessons she'd learned from her life with Orlando? She'd reproached her husband for a lack of basic sincerity, for not admitting his cowardice in not confessing a betrayal that would forever make him odious in her eyes and make her odious to herself, since the excuses she could invent when she married the labor leader now seemed insufficient to her, no matter whether youth and inexperience might justify them.

That afternoon, close to her mother in the old city of her adolescence, Laura would have wanted to say this to Mutti, but Leticia herself stopped her with a definitive conclusion: "If you want, you can leave the boys here until you settle things with your husband and you resume your married life together. But you already know that."

The two women were both about to say "Well?" but realized that without having to say a word they each knew everything, Leticia about Laura's failed marriage, and Laura about having to go back to living with Juan Francisco despite everything, to give their home and their sons a second chance. Then Laura remembered that yes, she'd been on the verge of saying that she'd wasted these last years of her life recklessly deceiving herself, that flagrant disillusion had led her to lies: she'd felt justified in abandoning her home and handing herself over to what those two worlds—the internal one of her own rage and the external one of Mexico City society—exalted as an acceptable vendetta for a humiliated woman: pleasure and independence.

Now Laura didn't know whether either enjoyment or freedom had ever really been hers. Staying with Elizabeth so long that generosity had turned into patronage, then irritation, and finally disdain. Bound over to the love of Orlando until passion revealed itself as games and trickery. Exploring a new society of artists, of old-family people or new-money arrivistes who, it's true, never fooled her, for at Carmen Cortina's parties appearance was essence and reality its mask.

Being useful, feeling herself to be useful, imagining she was good for something—that brought her under the wing of the Kahlo-Rivera clan, but all her gratitude toward the extraordinary couple who took her in at a bad moment and treated her as a friend and comrade could not disguise the truth that Laura was ancillary to the two artists' world, she was a replaceable part in a perfectly lubricated geometry like those machines of glittering steel that Diego celebrated in Detroit, but a machine on a fragile base, fragile like Frida Kahlo's wounded legs. They could take care of themselves. Laura would always love them, but she had no illusions: they loved but did not need her.

"What do I need, Mama? Who needs me?" asked Laura, after telling Leticia all these things—everything she'd sworn not to tell her and now, having blurted them out so quickly, vertiginously, clasping her mother's strong and diligent hands, not knowing if she'd actually said it all or if Leticia once again had divined her feelings and ideas without Laura's saying a word.

"Well?" asked Leticia, and Laura knew she knew.

"So the boys should stay here?"

"Only while you find your husband again."

"And what if we can't understand each other, which is very possible?"

"The fact is, the two of you will never understand each other. That's the problem. The important thing is for you to take on the burden of something real and decide to save it instead of waiting for someone to save you. Which is what you've done until now. Excuse me for saying so."

"Even if I know it will turn out badly again."

Leticia nodded. "Sometimes we have to do things knowing beforehand we're going to fail."

"What do I get from that, Mutti?"

"I'd say the opportunity to become yourself, to leave your failed efforts behind. You won't go through them again."

"I should walk into a disaster with my eyes wide open, is that what you're asking of me?"

"We have to finish things. You're leaving too much unfinished, too many loose ends. Be yourself, not someone else's toy, even if it costs you dearly to be a little more authentic."

"It wasn't authentic, everything that's happened to me since I left Orlando?"

This time, Leticia did no more than hand the Chinese doll to her daughter.

"Here. The last time you came, you forgot it. Now Miss Frida needs it."

Laura took Li Po, kissed the sleeping Danton and Santiago, and returned to what had already been finished before she came to Xalapa so alarmed at the disappearance of her aunts.

They spent the first night sleeping together side by side as if in a tomb, without warmth, without recrimination but without touching, agreeing to say some things, to arrive at certain compromises. They wouldn't rule out opportunities for sex but by the same token wouldn't define it as an obligation. Instead they would begin, once again lying side by side, with some questions and tentative affirmations, you understand, Juan Francisco, that before I met you I already knew you because of what people said, you never bragged about anything, I can't accuse you of that, on the contrary, you appeared in the Xalapa Casino with a simplicity I found very attractive, you didn't try to impress me, I was already impressed by the brave and exciting man who in my imagination took the place of the sacrificed heroism of my brother Santiago, you survived to continue the struggle in the name of my blood, it wasn't your fault that you didn't measure up to my illusions, it was my fault, I hope this time we can live together you and I with no wishful thinking. I never felt love from you, Laura, only respect, admiration, and fantasy, not passion, passion doesn't last but respect and admiration do, and if that's lost, well, what's left, Laura? Living without passion or admiration, I'd say, Juan Francisco, but with respect, respect for what we really are, without illusions and for the sake of our sons who aren't to blame for anything and whom we bring into the world without asking their permission. Is that the pact between you and me? No, something more, try to allay my fear, I'm afraid of you because you slapped me, swear you'll never hit me again no matter what happens between us, you can't imagine the terror a woman feels when a man starts beating her. That's my principal condition. Don't worry, I thought I had more strength than I really do have, forgive me.

And then time for some sad caresses on his part and she allowing him some tenderness out of gratitude, before reacting with shame and sitting up in bed. I mustn't trick you, Juan Francisco, I have to begin like this, I want to tell you everything that happened to me since you

informed on that nun Gloria Soriano and then slapped my face in the street when I walked out, I want you to know who I slept with, whom I desired, with whom I experienced pleasure; I want you to understand completely everything I've done while I was away so that you can finally answer a question for me which you haven't yet answered, why did you pass judgment on me for my will to love you but not condemn me for sleeping with someone else? I'm asking you now, Juan Francisco, before telling you everything before everything that happened happens again, are you going to judge me again this time for my will to love you, to come back to you? or are you ready right now to condemn me if I sleep with someone else again? do you have the nerve to answer me? I'm a bitch through and through, I'll admit that, but listen to what I'm asking you, will you have the courage not to judge me if I cheat on you—for the first time or the next time, that's the thing you don't know, right? You'll never know if what I confess to you is true or if I've just made it up to take revenge on you, although I can give you names and addresses, you can find out if I'm lying or telling the truth about my love life after I left you, but that doesn't change what I asked you in any way, will you not judge me ever again? I'm asking you that as retribution, in the name of the nun you turned in and the cause you betrayed, I'll forgive you that, will you forgive me? are you capable of that? . . . . . . . . . . . . . . . . . . . . . . . . . . . . . . . . . . . . . . . . . . . . . . . . . . . . .
. . . . . . . . . . . . . . . . . . . . . . . . . . . . . . . . . . . . . . . . . . . . . . . . . . .

Juan Francisco did not break the long silence that followed Laura's words until he got out of bed, buttoned up his blue-and-white-striped pajamas, took some water from the pitcher, drank it, and sat on the edge of the bed. The room was cold—it was the thunderstorm season—and hail, as thick as it was unexpected, was drumming on the roof. Through the open window flowed a newly fresh aroma of jacarandas, overcoming with its sensuality the billowing curtains and the little puddle forming under the window. Then Juan Francisco's words began, very slowly, as if he were a man without a past—where did he come from, who were his parents, why had he never revealed his origins?

"I always knew I was strong on the outside and weak on the inside. I knew it when I was just a kid. That's why I made such a huge effort to show the rest of the world I was strong. You especially. Because I knew early on the fears and weaknesses I had inside. You've heard of Demosthenes, how he overcame his timid stutter walking along the beach with pebbles in his mouth until he could overpower the noise of the waves with his voice and make himself into the most famous public orator in Greece. That's what happened to me. I made myself strong because I was weak. What you can't know, Laura, is how long you can keep winning against fear. Because fear is sickly, and when the world offers you gifts to calm you down—money, power, or sensuality, all together or one at a time, it doesn't matter—there's no way around it, you're grateful the world isn't sorry for you and you go on yielding the real strength you won when you had nothing to the false strength of the world which is starting to talk to you. Then the weakness ends up overpowering you, almost without your realizing it. If you help me, perhaps I can achieve a balance and be—not as strong as you thought when you met me but not as weak as you thought when you abandoned me."

Laura was not going to argue about who caused the break. If he went on thinking he'd been abandoned, she'd be compassionate and resign herself to seeing him play that part, and try not to lose even more respect for him. But he, in turn, would have to put up with all her truths, even the cruelest ones, not out of cruelty but so that the two of them could live from then on in the truth, disagreeable as it might be, and especially so that Danton and Santiago could live in a family without lies. Laura recalled Leticia, her mother, and wanted to be like her, to have the gift of understanding everything without using unnecessary words.

When she returned from Xalapa, she brought the Chinese doll to Frida Kahlo. The Coyoacán house was empty. Laura walked into the garden and called out, "Is there anyone at home?" And the tiny voice of a maid answered, "No, miss, there's no one here." The couple was still in New York, where Rivera was working on the Rockefeller Center frescoes, so Laura put Li Po on Frida's bed and added nothing, no note, nothing; Frida would understand, it was Laura's gift to the lost child. She tried to imagine the purity of the Oriental doll's ivory amid the tropical undergrowth that would soon invade the bedroom: monkeys, said Frida, parrots, daisies, hairless dogs, ocelots, and a jungle of lianas and orchids.

She had the boys sent from Xalapa. Punctilious, Santiago and Danton followed Leticia's precise and practical instructions and took the Interoceanic train to the Buenavista station, where Laura and Juan Francisco were waiting for them. The boys' nature, which Laura already knew, was a surprise for Juan Francisco, although it was for Laura, too, in the sense that each of them was rapidly accentuating his personal traits—Danton, clownish and bold, gave his parents two hasty kisses on the cheek and ran off to buy candy, shouting, why did Grand-mama give us money when there were no Larín chocolates or Minnie Mouse lollipops on the train, but anyway the old skinflint only gave us a few cents; then ran to a kiosk and asked for the most recent issues of his favorite magazines, *Pepín* and *Chamaco Chico*, but when he realized he didn't have enough money, resigned himself to buying the latest copy of *Los Supersabios*. Juan Francisco put his hand in his pocket to pay for the magazines, but Laura stopped him. Then Danton turned his back on them and ran down the street ahead of the rest of the family.

Santiago was different. He greeted his parents with a handshake that established an uncrossable space and kept kisses at bay. He allowed Laura to put her hand on his shoulder to guide him to the exit and wasn't too embarrassed to let Juan Francisco carry the two small valises to the black Buick parked on the street. The two boys were noticeably uncomfortable, but since they didn't want to attribute their discomfort to being with their parents, they kept on running their index fingers under their stiff collars and along the ties of the formal suits Doña Leticia had dressed them in: striped three-button jackets, knickers, knee-high argyle socks, coffee-colored square-toed shoes with hooks.

Everyone was silent during the trip from the station to Avenida Sonora, Danton absorbed in his comic book, Santiago bravely watching the majestic city pass by—the recently inaugurated monument to the Revolution, which people compared to a gigantic gasoline station, Paseo de la Reforma and all the traffic circles that seemed to do the breathing for everyone, from Caballito, the equestrian statue of Charles IV of Spain at the intersection with Juárez, Bucareli and Ejido, Christopher Columbus and his impassive circle of monks and public scribes, to the proud statue of Cuauhtémoc brandishing his spear at the intersection with Insurgentes; all along the great avenue lined with trees, footpaths, bridle paths for morning riders who at this hour were slowly plodding along, and sumptuous private mansions with Parisian facades and decorations. When they left Paseo de la Reforma, they entered the elegant streets of Colonia Roma with its two-story stone houses: garages at street level and reception rooms visible thanks to the white-framed balcony windows left open so the maids, with their complicated braids and blue uniforms, could air the interior rooms and shake out the carpets.

As they went along, Santiago read the names of the streets—Niza, Génova, Amberes, Praga—until they reached the Bosque de Chapultepec—not even there did Danton raise his eyes from his comics—and thence to their home on Avenida Sonora. To Santiago, it was like a dream—the entrance to the great park of eucalyptus and pine trees, flanked by stone lions in repose and crowned by the mythic Castle where Moctezuma had his baths, from whose parapets the Boy Heroes of the Military School threw themselves rather than surrender the Alcazar to the Yankees in 1848, where all the rulers of Mexico lived, from the Habsburg emperor Maximilian to Abelardo Rodriguez, the casino godfather, to the new President, Lázaro Cárdenas, who decided that such luxury was not for him and moved, in good republican fashion, to the modest villa at the foot of the Castle, Los Pinos.

Over the course of a second breakfast, the boys listened impassively to the new order of their lives, although the spark in Danton's eyes silently announced that he would contest each chore with some unpredictable mischief. Santiago's eyes refused to admit either strangeness or shock; he filled the void, in Laura's astute reading of her son, with nostalgia for Xalapa, for Grandmother Leticia, for Aunt María de la O. Would the young Santiago have to leave things behind in order to miss them? Laura surprised herself in thinking that—as she observed her elder son's serious face with its fine features, his chestnut hair so like that of his dead uncle, so different from Danton's swarthy appearance,

213

his cinnamon complexion, his thick dark eyebrows, his black hair held in check with brilliantine. The only curious detail was that Santiago the fair had black eyes, while the dark-skinned Danton had pale green eyes, almost yellow, like a cat's.

Laura sighed. The object of nostalgia was always the past; there was never nostalgia for the future. Even so, Santiago's gaze lit up and went out like one of those new neon signs on Avenida Juárez: I miss what is going to come . . .

They would attend the Gordon School, on Avenida Mazatlán, not far from the house. Juan Francisco would drive them in the Buick in the morning, and they would return at 5 p.m. in the orange school bus. The list of school supplies had been acquired, Eberhard pencils from Switzerland, pens with no name or national origin, meant to be dipped in desk inkwells, graph-paper notebooks for arithmetic, lined paper for essays; a national history textbook by the anticlerical Teja Zabre as if to compensate for the mathematics book by the Marist monk Anfossi; English readings, Spanish grammar, and the green books of general history by the French authors Malet and Isaac. Knapsacks. The sandwiches of beans, sardines, and chiles; the usual orange; the injunction never to buy sweets because they give you cavities . . .

Laura wanted to fill her day with her new chores. But night lay in wait for her, then dawn knocked at her door, and even in the middle of the night she could not say, The darkness belongs to us.

She reproached herself. "I can't condemn the best of myself to the grave of memory." But the silent solicitude of her husband—"How little I ask of you. Let me feel I'm needed"—could not calm Laura's recurring irritation during her time alone, when the boys were at school and Juan Francisco at the union, "How easy life would be without a husband and children." She went to Coyoacán when the Riveras came back, preceded by the black clouds of a new scandal in New York, where Diego had painted the faces of Marx and Lenin in the Rockefeller Center murals, Nelson Rockefeller asked Diego to erase the effigy of the Soviet leader, Diego refused but offered to balance Lenin's head with Lincoln's head, and it ended when twelve armed guards ordered the painter to stop work and handed him a check for $14,000 ("COMmunist Painter Gets Rich on Capitalist Dollars"). The unions tried to save the mural, but the Rockefellers ordered it chiseled out of existence and thrown into the garbage. Good, said the U.S. Communist Party: Rivera's fresco is "counterrevolutionary." Diego and Frida returned to Mexico, he depressed, she cursing "Gringolandia." They were all back, but there was no longer space for Laura: Diego wanted to get even with the gringos with another mural; Frida had painted a sorrowful self-portrait as an empty Tehuana dress hung amid soulless skyscrapers on the Mexican-U.S. border, Hi, Laura, how are you? come see us whenever you like, see you soon.

Life without a husband or children. Only one irritation, like a fly that insists on landing on one's nose again and again, chased away but tenacious: Laura knew well what life was like without Juan Francisco and the boys, and hadn't found anything greater or better in that alternative than in her renovated existence as wife and mother—but if only Juan Francisco didn't insist on combining (so obviously) the conviction that Laura was judging him with the obligation he felt to love her. Her husband was anchoring himself at an unmoving buoy. On the one hand, the excessive adoration he decided to show Laura to compensate for his mistakes of the past irritated her, because it was a way of asking forgiveness yet resolved itself in something quite different: "I don't hate him, he tires me, he loves me too much, a man shouldn't love a woman too much, there's an intelligent balance that Juan Francisco lacks, he has to learn that there's a limit between the need a woman has to be loved and her suspicion that she isn't loved as much as it might seem."

Juan Francisco, with his terms of endearment, his courtesy toward her, his diligent paternal concern for the sons he hadn't seen for six years, his new obligation to explain to Laura what he'd been doing all day without ever asking her for explanations, his insinuating heavy-handed way of asking for love, touching Laura's foot with his own under the sheets, suddenly emerging naked from the bathroom, searching like a fool for his pajamas, unaware that he was now carrying a spare tire around his waist, unaware that he'd lost his essential dark, mestizo slenderness, even making her take the initiative, speedily bringing the act to its conclusion, mechanically fulfilling his conjugal obligations . . .

She resigned herself to it all, until the day when a shadow began to manifest itself, first immaterial in the traffic on the avenue, then more visible on the sidewalk across the street, finally showing itself completely a few steps behind her, as Laura made her daily journey to the Parián market. She did not want to hire a maid. The memory of the nun Gloria Soriano pained her too much. Domestic chores filled her solitary hours. The surprising thing in this discovery is that Laura, once she realized she was being followed by one of her husband's lackeys, did not take it seriously. And that affected her more than if it had really mattered to her. Instead, for her it opened a street as narrow as the avenue where they lived was wide. She decided not to shadow him physically—as he, stupidly, was doing to her—but to use a more powerful weapon, moral shadowing.

Lázaro Cárdenas, a general from Michoacán, ex-governor of his state and head of the official party, had been elected President of Mexico. Everyone thought he would be just one more of the puppets shamelessly manipulated by the Maximum Chief of the Revolution, General Plutarco Elías Calles. The joke was so public that during a preceding presidency, some joker had hung a sign on the door of the presidential residence at Chapultepec: THE PRESIDENT LIVES HERE. THE MAN WHO GIVES THE ORDERS LIVES ACROSS THE STREET. Then President Abelardo Rodríguez, considered yet another of the Maximum Chief's servants, repressed strike after strike, first the telegraph workers, then the day laborers from New Lombardy and New Italy in Michoacán, farm workers of Italian background who were accustomed to the struggles being waged by Antonio Gramsci's Communist Party, and finally the national movement of agricultural workers in Chiapas, Veracruz, Puebla, and Nuevo León: President Rodríguez ordered that the strikers be fired and sent soldiers to take their place; the courts, dominated by the executive branch, declared all these strikes "unjustified." The army and the paramilitary thugs working for the government murdered several workers from the Italo-Mexican communities, and Abelardo

Rodríguez sent the national strike leaders, who were fighting for a minimum wage, to the desolate penal colony on the Islas Marías, among them the young writer José Revueltas.

Luis Napoleón Morones' old CROM grew weaker and weaker, incapable of defending the workers. At the same time the star of their new leader, Vicente Lombardo Toledano, rose. Lombardo—once a Thomist philosopher and now a Marxist, a thin man with an ascetic air and sad eyes, forelock dangling over them, and a pipe in his mouth—as head of the General Confederation of Mexican Workers and Peasants created an alternative for the real workers' struggle: workers struggling for land, good wages, collectively negotiated contracts, began to group themselves with the GCMW, and since Cárdenas had supported union struggles in Michoacán, everything was now expected to change: no longer Calles and Morones but Cárdenas and Lombardo.

"And union independence, Juan Francisco, where is it?" Laura heard the only old comrade who still visited her husband say one night, the now beaten-down Pánfilo, who couldn't even find a place to spit since Laura had had the hideous copper spittoons removed.

Juan Francisco repeated something that by now was his credo: "In Mexico, things change from within, not from without."

"When are you going to learn?" Pánfilo answered with a sigh.

Cárdenas was beginning to show signs of independence and Calles signs of irritation. Caught between them, Juan Francisco seemed uncertain as to which direction the workers' movement would take and what his position in it would be. Laura noted his disquiet and asked him over and over, with an air of legitimate concern: If there's a break between Calles and Cárdenas, which side will you be on? And he had no choice but to fall back on his old bad habit, political rhetoric: the Revolution is united, there will never be a break among its leaders. But the Revolution has already broken with many of your old ideals, Juan Francisco, when you were an anarcho-syndicalist (and the images of the Xalapa attic and the walled-up life of Armonía Aznar and her mysterious relationship with Orlando and Juan Francisco's funeral oration all returned to her in a wave), and he would say, like a true believer

217

repeating the credo, you have to influence things from within, try it from outside and you'll be squashed like a bug, the battles are waged within the system.

"You have to know how to adapt, isn't that so?"

"All the time. Of course. Politics is the art of compromise."

"Of compromise," she repeated in a most serious tone.

"Yes."

So as not to acknowledge what was happening, one had to keep one's heart in the dark. Juan Francisco could explain that political necessity forced him into compromises with the government.

"With all governments? With any government?"

. . . She could not ask him if his conscience was condemning him. He would have wanted to admit that he wasn't afraid of the opinions others might have but he was afraid of Laura Díaz, of being judged again by her. Then, one night, the two of them exploded again.

"I'm sick and tired of your judging me."

"And I'm sick and tired of your spying on me."

"I don't know what you're talking about."

"You've locked my soul in a basement."

"Don't feel so sorry for yourself, you make me pity you."

"Don't talk to me as if you were a saint talking to a sinner. Talk to the real me instead!"

"It's outrageous that you ask me for results that have nothing to do with reality."

"Stop imagining that I judge you."

"As long as it's only you who judges me, poor little you, it really doesn't bother me, do you think I came back so you could forgive my sins?" She bit her tongue, night tracks me, sunrise frees me, she went to the boys' bedroom to watch them sleep, to calm down.

Seeing them sleep.

It was enough to watch the two little heads sunk deep in the pillows, Santiago covered up to his chin, Danton uncovered and spread-eagled, as if even in sleep their two contrary personalities revealed themselves, and Laura Díaz asked herself, at that exact moment of her existence, did she have anything to teach her sons or at least the courage to ask them, what do you want to know, what can I tell you?

Sitting there opposite the twin beds, she could only tell them that they came into this world without being consulted and thus their parents' freedom in creating them did not save them, creatures of a heritage of rancor, needs, and ignorance that their parents, no matter how they tried, could not erase without damaging their children's freedom. It would be up to them to fight the earthly evils they'd inherited, and yet, she, the mother, could not step back, disappear, turn into the ghost of her own descendants. She had to resist in their name without ever showing it, remain invisible at the side of her sons, not to diminish the child's honor, the responsibility of the son who must believe in his own freedom, know that he is forging his own destiny. What was left to her if not to keep watch discreetly, to be tolerant, and to ask as well for a long time to live and a short time to suffer, like Aunts Hilda and Virginia?

Sometimes she would spend the entire night watching them sleep, intent on accompanying her sons wherever they might go, like a very long shoreline where sea and beach are distinct but inseparable; the voyage might last only one night, but she hoped it would never end, and over the heads of her sons floated the question: How much time, how much time will God and men allow my sons on earth?

Seeing them sleep until the sun comes up and the light touches their heads because she herself can touch the sun with her hands, asking herself how many sunrises she and her sons will be able to endure. For each allotment of light had a silhouette of shadow.

Then Laura Díaz rose, disquieted by a mild vertigo, and stepped away from the beds where her sons slept, and she told herself (and almost told them)—so they would understand their own mother and not condemn her to pity first and oblivion later—that to be a mother, hated and liberated by the hatred of her sons, hated, perhaps, but fatally unforgettable, I must be active, ardent and active, but I still don't know how, I can't return to what I've already done, I want an authentic revelation, a revelation that will be an elevation, not a renunciation.

How easy life would be without children or a husband! Again? This time for sure? Why not? Does the first effort at liberty use it up, a prior failure close the doors to possible happiness beyond the walls of home? Have I used up my destiny? Santiago, Danton: don't leave me. Let me follow you wherever you go, whatever happens. I don't want to be adored. I want to be awaited. Help me.

## 12. Parque de la Lama: 1938

IN 1938, the European democracies caved in to Hitler at the Munich Conference and the Nazis occupied Austria, then Bohemia; the Spanish Republic was in full retreat, falling back on all fronts; Walt Disney's *Snow White and the Seven Dwarfs* opened, as did Sergei Eisenstein's *Alexander Nevsky* and Leni Riefenstahl's *Olympiad*. On Kristallnacht, Jewish synagogues, businesses, homes, and schools all over Germany were burned by SS troops; in the United States, Congress established the House Un-American Activities Committee, in France Antonin Artaud proposed a "theater of cruelty," Orson Welles convinced everyone that Martians had invaded New Jersey, Lázaro Cárdenas was nationalizing the oil industry in Mexico, and two rival telephone companies—the Swedish Ericsson and Mexicana, the Mexican national company—simultaneously offered separate telephone services; as luck (bad) would have it, a person signed up with Ericsson could not call someone with Mexicana service and vice versa. This meant that a subscriber to one service had to turn to neighbors, friends, nearby offices, or phone booths to speak to someone with the other service, and vice versa.

"In Mexico, even the telephones are baroque," Orlando Ximénez declared.

The sheer size of the modern metropolis makes amorous relationships difficult; no one wants to spend an hour in a bus or car in order to enjoy ninety seconds of sex. The telephone enabled lovers to agree on intermediate rendezvous sites. In Paris, *pneumatiques*, the quick *"petits bleus,"* brought couples together; lovers opened those little blue envelopes that might contain all the promises of love with more apprehension than if they were telegrams. But in Mexico, during the year of oil expropriation, the year of the Spanish Republic's last-ditch defense of Madrid, if lovers didn't also happen to be neighbors and if one had Ericsson and the other Mexicana, they were doomed to invent bizarre, complex, or, as Orlando said, baroque communication networks.

Nonetheless, the first communication between them, the first personal message, could not have been more direct. It was, simply, a meeting of eyes. Later, she would say she was predisposed to what happened, but when she saw him, it was as if she'd never thought about him. They did not exchange glances; each anchored their eyes in those of the other. She asked herself, Why is this man different from all the rest? And he answered in silence, the two of them separated by the hundred other guests at the party, *because I'm looking only at you.*

"Because he's looking only at me."

She wanted to leave; she was frightened by this attraction, so sudden but also so complete, the novelty of the encounter alarmed her, it disturbed her to imagine the consequences of an approach, she thought about everything that might happen—passion, giving herself, guilt, remorse, her husband, her sons; it wasn't that all these issues would come afterward; involuntarily, instantaneously, they were coming first; everything entered the present moment, as in one of those living rooms where only family ghosts sat down to talk and, serenely, to judge her.

She thought of leaving. She was going to flee. He came over to her as if guessing her thoughts and said, "Stay a little longer."

They looked directly into each other's eyes; he was as tall as she, not as tall as her husband, but even before he spoke a word to her, she felt he treated her with respect, and his familiar tone was merely the way

Spaniards dealt with one another. His accent was Castilian and his physical appearance, too. He couldn't have been more than forty, but his hair was quite white, contrasting with the freshness of his skin, which had no notable wrinkles except in his brow. His eyes, his white smile, his straight profile, his courteous but impassioned eyes. His very white complexion, his very black eyes. She wanted to see herself as he saw her.

"Stay a little longer."

"You're the boss," she said impulsively.

"No." He laughed. "I'm making a suggestion."

From the first instant, she conceded three virtues to the man: reserve, discretion, and independence, together with impeccable social graces. He wasn't an upper-class Mexican like so many of those she'd met at the hacienda in San Cayetano or at Carmen Cortina's cocktail parties. He was a wellborn Spaniard, but in his eyes there was melancholy and in his body a disquiet that fascinated and disturbed her, invited her to penetrate a mystery, and she wondered if this might not be the subtlest trick of a Spanish hidalgo (as she quickly nicknamed him): to present oneself to the world as an enigma.

She tried to penetrate the man's gaze, his eyes sunk deep in his skull, near the bone, near the brain. The white hair lightened his dark eyes, the same way that here in Mexico it lightens mestizo faces. A dark young man could, with white hair, become a paper-colored old man, as if time had faded his skin.

The hidalgo made her a present of a look that combined adoration with fate. That night, together in bed in the L'Escargot Hotel facing the Parque de la Lama, the two of them caressing each other slowly, over and over, cheeks, hair, temples, he asked her to envy him because he could see her face from various perspectives and, above all, illuminated by the minutes they spent together. What does the light do to a woman's face, how does a woman's face depend on the time of day, the light of dawn, morning, midday, sunset, nighttime, what does the light that faces her, outlines her, surprises her from below or crowns her from above, attacks her brutally and without warning in broad daylight or caresses her softly in the half-light, what does it say to her face?

he asked her, but she had no answers, no wish to have answers, she felt admired and envied because in bed he asked all the questions that she always wanted a man to ask, knowing they were the questions that all women want to be asked at least once in their lives by just one man.

She no longer thought about minutes or hours, she lived with him, beginning that night, in a time without time of amorous passion, a whirlwind of time that dispensed with all the other concerns of life. All the forgotten scenes. Although at dawn on that night, she feared that the time with him, this night with him, had devoured all the previous moments of her life and had also swallowed up this one. She clung to the man's body, clasped it with the tenacity of ivy, imagining herself without him, absent but unforgettable, saw herself in that possible but totally undesired moment when he would no longer be there even if the memory of him was; the man would no longer be with her but his memory would be with her forever. That was the price she paid from that moment on, and she was pleased, thought it cheap in comparison with the plenitude of the instant. She could not keep from asking herself, in anguish, What does this face, these eyes, this voice without beginning or end mean? From the first moment, she never wanted to lose him.

"Why are you so different from the rest?"

"Because I look only at you."

She loved the silence that followed sex. She loved that silence right from the first time. It was the hoped-for promise of a shared solitude. She loved the place they'd chosen because it was at the same time a pre-destined place. The place of lovers. A hotel next to the shady, cool, and secret park within the city. That was how she wanted it. A place that might always be unknown, a mysterious sensuality in a place that everyone but lovers takes to be normal. For all time, she loved the shape of her man's body, svelte but strong, well proportioned and passionate, discreet and savage, as if the body of the man were a mirror of trans-formations, an imaginary duel between the creator god and his inevitable beast. Or the animal and the divinity that inhabit us. She'd never known such sudden metamorphoses, from passion to repose, from tranquillity to fire, from serenity to excess. A moist, fertile couple one for the other, each one endlessly divining the other. She told him she would have recognized him anywhere.

"Even feeling around in the dark?"

She nodded. Their bodies joined once again in the free obedience of passion. Outside it was growing light; the park surrounded the hotel with a guard of weeping willows, and one could get lost in the labyrinths of high hedges and even higher trees, whose whispering voices were disorienting and could make anyone lose their way with the sound of rustling leaves in lovers' ears, so far away from what would come next, so close to what was absent.

"How long has it been since you've spent a night away from home?"

"Never, since I came back."

"Are you going to give an excuse?"

"I think so."

"Are you married?"

"Yes."

"What excuse will you give?"

"That I spent the night with Frida."

"Do you have to explain?"

"I have two boys."

"Do you know the English saying 'Never complain, never explain'?"

"I think that's my problem."

"Explaining or not?"

"I'm going to feel badly about myself if I don't tell the truth. But I'll hurt everyone if I do."

"Haven't you thought that what's between you and me is part of our intimate life, and no one has to know about it?"

"Are you saying it's for the two of us? Do you have to keep quiet or talk?"

"No, I'm only asking you if you know that a married woman can conquer a man."

"The good thing is that Frida's telephone is Mexicana and ours is Ericsson. It would be hard for my husband to keep track of my movements."

He laughed at the telephone complication, but she did not want to ask him if he was married, if he had a sweetheart. She heard him say that a married woman can conquer a man who isn't her husband, a married woman can go on conquering men, and his words alone were enough to cause an exciting disturbance, almost an unstated temptation, that threw her back into his strong, slim arms, the dark hair around the sex, the hungry lips of the Spaniard, her hidalgo, her lover, her shared man, she realized immediately, he knew she was married, but she in turn imagined he had another woman, except that she could not manage to understand this intuition of another woman, to visualize her, what kind of relationship would Jorge Maura have with the woman who was and was not there?

Laura Díaz opted for cowardice. He didn't tell her who the other woman was or what she was like. She did tell him who her husband was and what he was like, but she wouldn't say a word to Juan Francisco until Jorge told her about the other woman. Her new lover (Orlando strolled down the street of her memory) was a two-story man. At the entrance to the house, he was reserved, discreet, and comported himself impeccably. Upstairs he was a man who gave of himself, an open man, holding back nothing at all for the time of love. She could not resist the combination, this complete way of being a man both serene and impassioned, open and secret, discreet while clothed, indiscreet when naked. She admitted she'd always wanted a man like that. Here he was, finally, desired forever or invented right now but revealing an eternal desire.

Looking from the hotel window toward the park that first shared dawn, Laura Díaz had the conviction that for the first time she and a man were going to see each other and know each other without having to say anything, without explanations or superfluous calculations. Each one would understand everything. Each shared instant would bring them closer together.

Jorge kissed her again, as if he'd divined her completely, mind and body. She could not tear herself away from him, from the flesh, from the body coupled to her own, she wanted to measure and retain her orgasm, she was proclaiming as hers the looks she shared during the orgasm, she wanted all the couples in the world to have as much pleasure as she and Maura had in those moments, it was her most universal, most fervent desire. No man, ever, instead of closing his eyes or turning aside his face, had ever looked into her eyes during his orgasm, wagering that by the mere act of having the two of them see each other's faces they would come at the same time. And that's how it happened each time: with their impassioned but conscious looks, they named each other man and woman, woman and man, who make love face to face, the only animals who have sex face to face, seeing each other, look at my open eyes, nothing excites me more than seeing you seeing me, the orgasm became part of the gaze, the gaze into the soul of the orgasm, any other position, any other answer remained a temptation, temptation subdued became the promise of the true, the best, and the next excitement of the lovers.

To face each other and open their eyes when they both came together.

"Let's desire this for all the lovers of the world, Jorge."

"For everyone, Laura my love."

Now he was pacing around the disorder of the hotel room like a cat. She had never seen so much paper tossed around, so many portfolios opened, so much disorder in a man so beautiful and well ordered in everything else. It was as if Jorge Maura did not like the paperwork, as if he were carrying in his briefcases something he could toss aside, something disagreeable, possibly poisonous. He didn't close up his portfolios, as if he wanted to air them or as if he were hoping that the papers would fly off or an indiscreet chambermaid would read them.

"She wouldn't understand any of it," he said with a bitter smile.

"What?"

"Nothing. I hope things work out for the best."

Laura went back to being the way she was before, but as she never was with him: languid, timid, careless, doting, strong. She went back to that because she knew what would defeat the pulse of desire, and desire could destroy pleasure itself, could become demanding, thoughtless about the woman's limits and the man's, making couples become too conscious of their happiness. That is why she was going to introduce the theme of daily life, to calm the destructive tempest which had,

227

since the first night, fatally accompanied pleasure, secretly frightening them. But she did not have to; he anticipated her. Did he really anticipate her, or was it foreseeable that one of the two would descend from passion to action?

Jorge Maura was in Mexico as a representative of the Spanish Republic, which by March 1938 had been reduced to the enclaves of Madrid and Barcelona and, in the south, the Mediterranean territory of Valencia. The Mexican government, under Lázaro Cárdenas, had given diplomatic aid to the Republicans, but this ethical action could not equal the crushing material assistance given to the rebel Francisco Franco by the Nazi and fascist regimes. Nor could it make up for the cowardly abandonment of the Republic by the European democracies: England and France. Berlin and Rome intervened with all their strength in favor of Franco, while Paris and London turned their backs on the "child Republic," as María Zambrano called it. The tiny flower of Spanish democracy was trampled by everyone, its friends, its enemies, and, at times, its supporters.

Laura Díaz told Jorge she wanted to be everything with him, share everything, know everything, that she was in love with him, madly in love.

Jorge Maura's expression did not change when he heard her declaration, and Laura did not understand if it was part of his seriousness to listen to her without a word or if the hidalgo was only pausing before beginning his story. Perhaps a bit of both. He wanted her to listen before making any decisions.

"I swear I'll die if I don't know everything about you," she ventured in turn.

Thinking about Spain locked him within himself. He said that Spain for the Spaniards is like Mexico for Mexicans, a painful obsession. Not a hymn of optimism, as their country is for Americans, not a phlegmatic joke as it is for the English, not a sentimental madness (Russians), not a reasonable irony (French), not an aggressive command, as Germans see theirs, but a conflict of halves, of opposed parts, of tugs at the soul—Spain and Mexico, countries of light and shadow.

He began by telling stories, with no commentary, while the two of them strolled among the hedges and pines of the Parque de la Lama. The first thing he told her was how shocked he was at the resemblance between Mexico and Castile. Why had the Spaniards chosen a plateau so like Castile as the site of their first and principal viceroyalty in the New World?

He was looking at the dry land, the gray-brown mountains, the snowy peaks, the cold transparent air, the desolation of the roads, the burros and bare feet, the women dressed in black and covered with shawls, the dignity of the beggars, the beauty of the children, the floral compensation and culinary abundance of two countries dying of hunger. He visited the oases, like this one, of refreshing vegetation, and he felt that he hadn't changed places, or that he was ubiquitous, and not only physically but historically because being born Spanish or Mexican transforms experience into destiny.

He loved her and wanted her to know everything about him. Everything about the war and how he lived it. He was a soldier. He obeyed orders. But he rebelled first, the better to obey later on. Because of his social origin, the government first thought to use him on diplomatic missions. He was a descendant of the first reform minister at the turn of the century, Antonio Maura y Montaner; he'd been a disciple of Ortega y Gasset; he'd graduated from the University of Freiburg in Germany: he wanted first to live the war in order to know the truth and then to defend it and negotiate for it if necessary, but first to *know* it. The truth of experience first. The truth of conclusions later. Experience and conclusion, he told Laura, those are perhaps the complete truth, until the conclusion itself is negated by other experiences.

"I don't know. I have an immense faith and an immense doubt at the same time. I think certitude is the goal of thought. And I always fear that any system we help to build will end up destroying us. It isn't easy."

He fought in the battles at the Jarama River during the winter of 1937. What did he recall of those days? Physical sensations above all. The mist that came out of your mouth. The frozen wind that emptied your eyes. Where are we? That's the most disconcerting thing in war. You don't know exactly where you are. A soldier doesn't carry a map in his head. I didn't know where I was. We were ordered to execute flanking movements, advances into nothingness, then to scatter so the bombs wouldn't kill us. That was the biggest confusion in battle. Cold and hunger were constant. The people were always different. It was hard to fix a face or a phrase beyond the day you saw or heard it. Which is why I decided to concentrate on a single person, so the war would have a face, but above all to have company. In order not to be alone in the war. So alone.

I remember I saw a pretty girl one day wearing blue overalls. She had the face of a nun, but she shouted the worst obscenities I've ever heard in my life. I'll always remember her because I never saw her again. Her hair was so black it seemed as blue as midnight. Her thick eyebrows met in a frown of rage. She had a bandage on her nose, and not even that would hide her profile—like that of a wild eagle. But her constant litany of insults camouflaged the prayer she recited silently. Of that I was so convinced that I communicated it to her with my eyes. She understood, got upset, spouted a couple of curses at me, and I answered "Amen." She was as white as a nun who's never seen the sun and had whiskers like the women of Galicia. She was pretty for all that, because of all that. Her language was a challenge, not only to the fascists but to death itself. Franco and death were a couple, two big sons of bitches. Sometimes the image of the beautiful woman with the pale blue overalls and the night-blue hair threatens to fade. He laughed. I needed someone as different from her as you are to remember her today. No, both of you were or are tall women.

But she was on her way to the Guadarramas, and I was entrenched at the Jarama. I remember the boys along the highways holding up their fists, serious and squinting into the sun, all with the face of memory. (Do you know that the orphans sent from Guernica to French and English homes scream and cry every time they hear a plane fly over?) Afterward I only remember sad, abandoned places that people passed through very quickly.

Next to a swift, yellow river.

Inside a moist cave full of stalagmites and labyrinths.

Hugging cold and hunger.

The Luftwaffe bombings began.

We knew the Germans didn't bomb military objectives.

They wanted to keep them intact for Franco.

The Stukas attacked cities and civilians, which caused more destruction and discouragement than blowing up a bridge.

That's why it was safer to rest on a bridge.

The objective was Guernica.

To teach a lesson.

Making war on the general populace.

Where are we?

Who won?

It doesn't matter: who survived?

Jorge Maura clasped Laura Díaz. "Laura, we were mistaken in our historical moment. I don't want to admit anything that would break our faith . . ."

The International Brigades began to arrive. General Mola was besieging Madrid with four columns outside the city and his "fifth column" of spies and traitors inside. What invigorated the resistance was the influx of refugees fleeing Franco. The capital was full of them. That was when people starting singing "Madrid, how well you resist" and "The women of Madrid use fascist bombs for curlers." It wasn't absolutely true. There were lots of Franco supporters in the city. Half of Madrid had voted against the Popular Front in 1936. And the "tours" made by Republican thugs who went around murdering fascists, priests, and nuns had reduced sympathy for the Republic. I think the arrival of refugees was the greatest defense of Madrid. And if it wasn't the ladies' hair curlers, it was a certain suicidal but elegant challenge that set the tone. Writers had taken refuge in a theater, and Rafael Alberti and María Teresa León organized dances in the darkness every night to help dissipate the fear sown by the Luftwaffe. I was one of them, and besides the Spaniards there were many Spanish Americans there: Pablo Neruda, César Vallejo, Octavio Paz, and the Mexican painter Siqueiros, who'd given himself the rank of "super-colonel" and who had himself followed around by a shoeshine boy so his cavalry boots could be kept polished. Neruda was slow and sleepy, like an ocean;

Vallejo carried hollow-eyed death shrouded under his eyelids. Paz had eyes bluer than the sky, and Siqueiros was a military parade all by himself. We all dressed up in theater costumes from classic Spanish plays like *Don Juan, The Leandras, The Vengeance of Don Mendo*, and *The Mayor of Zalamea*. A little bit of everything, all of us dancing on a Madrid rooftop under the bombs, unintentionally illuminated by the German Stukas, drinking champagne. What madness, what joy, what kind of party was that, Laura? Is it risible, reprehensible, or magnificent that a group of poets and painters celebrate life in the midst of death, tell the solemn cloistered enemy attacking us from above to go to hell with his infinite fascist reactionary gloom and his eternal list of prohibitions: purity of blood, purity of religion, sexual purity?

We already knew what they were like. After the Republic came to power in 1931, they opposed coeducation; when lay education was established they sent their children to school with crucifixes on their breasts, they were the false piety of long skirts and smelly armpits, they were the Goths, enemies of Arabic cleanliness and Jewish thrift; bathing was proof of the Moorish taint, usury was a Hebrew sin. They were the corruptors of language, Laura, you would have to hear them to believe it; they spoke without shame of the values they were defending—the ardent breath of God, the noble home of the nation, the chaste and worthy woman, the fertile furrow of wheat—against Republican eunuchs and Jewish Masons, Marxist sirens who introduce exotic ideas into Spain, sowing discord in the field of the robust Spanish Catholic faith; rootless cosmopolites, renegades, mobs thirsty for Spanish and Christian blood, red scum!, and for that reason Alberti's costume balls on the roof of a theater illuminated by bombs were like a challenge from the other Spain, the one that always saves itself from oppression thanks to its imagination.

It was there I met two fellows, two Americans, from the International Brigades, which the Italian Communist Palmiro Togliatti and the French Communist André Marty were put in charge of organizing. Beginning in July 1936, about ten thousand foreign volunteers crossed the Pyrenees and by early November there were about three thousand in Madrid. The phrase of the moment was *¡No pasarán!*, "They Shall

Not Pass." The fascists will not pass, but the brigade members will, received with open arms. The cafés filled with foreign soldiers and journalists. The people shouted to all of them, "Long live the Russians!" Among the others was a German Communist, an aristocrat with a fabulous name I'll never forget: Arnold Friedrich Wieth von Golsenau. He approached me as if he recognized me, saying "Maura" and all my other last names, as if to assimilate the two of us, inducting me at his side into that species of impregnable superiority that is being both an aristocrat and a Communist. He noted my reticence and smiled. "People can trust us, Maura. We have nothing to gain. There can be no doubt about our honesty. A revolution should only be carried out by rich aristocrats, people without inferiority complexes or economic needs. Then there would be no corruption. It's corruption that ruins revolutions and makes people think that if the old regime was detestable the new one is even more so because while the conservatives offered no hope, the left simply betrayed it." "Things like that happen," I answered in a conciliatory way, "because aristocrats and workers always lose revolutions while the bourgeoisie wins them." "You're right," he conceded, "they always have something to win." "And we," I reminded him, "always have something to lose." He laughed hard at that. I didn't share the cynicism of Golsenau, who was known in the Brigades by his nom de guerre, "Renn." There were two levels in this war, the level of those who talked war, theorized about it, thought about it, and invented strategies, and the level of the vast majority of the common people, who were everything but common. They were extraordinary and every day demonstrated their limitless bravery. You know, Laura, the first line of fire in all the great battles—Madrid and the Jarama, Brunete and Teruel, the defeat of Mussolini at Guadalajara—was never unmanned. The Republicans, the people, fought to be the first to die. Boys with their fists raised high, men with no shoes, women with the last family loaf of bread between their breasts, militiamen waving their rusty rifles—all fighting in the trenches, the streets, the fields. No one hesitated, no one ran. No one ever saw anything like it before. I was at the Jarama when the fighting intensified, with a thousand African troops arriving under the command of General

Orgaz, protected by tanks and by the planes of the Nazi Condor Legion. The Russian tanks on the Republican side held back the fascist advance, and the front moved back and forth between the two, filling the hospitals with wounded and also with the sick, who caught the malaria brought by the Africans. There was some black humor in the situation, up to a point. Moors expelled from Spain by Ferdinand and Isabella in the name of blood purity were fighting on the side of the German racists against a republican and democratic people supported by the tanks of another totalitarian despot, Joseph Stalin. Almost instinctively, out of liberal sympathy, and because of antipathy to Renn and Togliatti, I became friends with Americans in the Brigade. Their names were Jim and Harry. Harry was a New Yorker, a Jew, motivated by two simple things: hatred of anti-Semitism and faith in Communism. Jim was more complicated. He was the son of a famous journalist and writer from New York and had come to Spain, even though he was very young—he must have been twenty-five then—with press credentials and the support of two famous correspondents, Vincent Sheean and Ernest Hemingway. Those two were competing to see which would have the honor of dying on the Spanish front. I don't know why you're going to Spain, Hemingway said to Sheean, when the only article you'll produce is your own obituary, which won't do you any good, because I'll be the one to write it. Sheean, a brilliant and good-looking man, quickly shot back: The story of your death will be even more famous, and I'll write it. Behind them came the tall, awkward, nearsighted one, Jim, and behind him came the little Jew in a jacket and tie, Harry. Sheean and Hemingway went on to be war correspondents, but Jim and Harry stayed to fight. The Jewish boy made up for his physical weakness with the energy of a fighting cock. The tall New Yorker, as a matter of principle, immediately lost his glasses and laughed about it, saying it was better to fight without seeing the enemy you were going to kill. Both of them had that New York sense of humor: sentimental, cynical, and, above all, self-mocking. "I want to impress my friends," Jim would say. "I need to create a CV that will make up for my social complexes," Harry would say. "I want to know fear," Jim said. "I want to save my soul," said Harry. And the two of them: "So long to ties."

Bearded, in sandals, their uniforms more ragged every day, singing songs from *The Mikado* (!) at the top of their lungs, the Americans were really the wit of our company. Not only did they lose their ties and eyeglasses, they even lost their socks, but they won the goodwill of all, Spaniards and Brigade members. That a nearsighted man like Jim could ask to be allowed to lead a squad on a night scouting mission proves the heroic madness of our war. Harry was more cautious: "We've got to go on living in order to go on fighting tomorrow."

At the Jarama, notwithstanding the German planes, the Russian tanks, and the International Brigades, it was we, the Spaniards, who fought. Harry admitted it, but he pointed out, They are Spanish *Communists*. He was right. At the beginning of 1937, the Communist Party had grown from twenty thousand to two hundred thousand members, and by summer it had a million. The defense of Madrid gave them those numbers and that prestige. Stalin's policies would erase them both. Socialism never had a worse enemy than Stalin. But last year Harry could see only the victory of the proletariat and its Communist vanguard. He would argue all day, he had read the entire corpus of Marxist literature, and he'd repeat it as if it were a Bible and end his speeches saying, "We'll see tomorrow." It was his *Dominus vobiscum*. For Harry, the trial and execution of a Communist as honorable as Bukharin was an accident on the road toward a glorious future. Harry Jaffe was a small, nervous man, intellectually strong, physically weak, and morally indecisive because he would not recognize the weakness of a political conviction that had not been subjected to criticism. In every detail, he contrasted with the lanky giant Jim, for whom theory was of no importance. "A man knows when he's right," he'd say. "So you've got to fight for what's right. It's simple. Here and now, the Republic is right and the fascists wrong. You've got to be with the Republic, and that's that." They were like Don Quixote and Sancho Panza, except that their La Mancha was called Brooklyn and Queens. Well, actually they were more like Mutt and Jeff, except they were young and serious. I remember Harry and I would smoke and argue, leaning against bridge railings, on the theory that fascists never attacked communication routes. Jim, on the other hand, was always looking for the fighting, requesting the riskiest positions, always in the most advanced line, "looking for my lost glasses," he would joke. He was a tall, smiling, incredibly courteous man, very delicate in his way of speaking. ("I leave all bad words to my father. I've heard him say them so many times that they've lost their impact. In New York, there's the public language of journalism, crime, rude competition, and another, secret language of sensibility, refined regard, and happy solitude. I want to go back and write in that second language, George old boy, but in fact my father and I complement each other. He thanks me for my language, and I thank him for his: What the fuck!" laughed the clumsy, brave giant.) I climbed trees with him to get a view of the Castilian country-side. Despite the wounds that war leaves on the body of the earth, we managed to make out flocks, windmills, carnation-colored afternoons, rose dawns, the girls' solid legs, the furrows waiting for the trenches to close like scars; this is the land of Cervantes and Goya, I'd say to him, no one can kill it. It's also the new land of Homer, he'd say back, a land that is born at the same time as the rosy-fingered dawn and the fatal, ruined wrath of men. One day, Jim didn't come back. Harry and I waited for him all night, at first exchanging glances wordlessly, then joking, whiskey might kill that gringo but gunpowder never will. He never did come back. We all knew he was dead, because in a front like the Jarama anyone who didn't come back after two days was considered dead. The hospitals never took longer than forty-eight hours to report on the wounded. To keep track of the dead took longer, and at the front the daily casualties added up to hundreds of men. But in Jim's case, everybody went on asking about him as if he were only lost or absent. Harry and I realized then how all the other soldiers in the Brigade and the Republican army loved him. He'd made himself loved for a thou-sand reasons, we told each other in that retrospective act which allows us to see and say in death what we never knew how to see or say in life. We're always blind to what we see and see only what we've lost forever. Laura, I somehow convinced myself that only I knew Jim was dead, and that I was keeping him alive so as not to depress Harry and the other comrades who loved the big, well-spoken American. But then I realized we all knew he was dead, and we were all agreeing to lie and say our comrade was still alive.

"You haven't seen Jim, have you?"

"Yes, he said goodbye at dawn."

"He had orders. A mission."

"If only there was a way to tell him we're waiting for him."

"He told me he knew."

"What did he tell you?"

"I know you're all waiting for me."

"He must be sure of that. We'll wait for him here. And nobody better say he's dead."

"Look, the glasses he was waiting for came in today's mail."

Jorge Maura embraced Laura Díaz. "We were mistaken in our historical moment. I don't want to admit anything that would break our faith, how I wish we were all heroes, how I want to keep the faith."

That morning, Laura Díaz walked the length of Avenida de los Insurgentes to her house in Colonia Roma. Maura's emotional earthquake kept running through her body like an internal torrent. It didn't matter that the Spaniard hadn't told her anything about his private life. He'd told her everything about his public life: *how I wish we were all heroes*. How she herself wished she could be heroic. But after hearing Jorge Maura, she knew that heroism isn't a project that can be willed but a response to imaginable yet unforeseen circumstances. There was nothing heroic in her own life; perhaps someday, thanks to her Spanish lover, she would know how to respond to the challenge of heroism.

Juan Francisco . . . sitting on their bed, perhaps waiting for her or perhaps not waiting for her anymore, with an obvious recrimination— Santiago and Danton, our sons, I had to take care of them myself, I'm not asking you where you've been—but tied to himself, to the last post of his honor by the promise of never again spying on her, what would she say after four days of unexplained, inexplicable absence, except for what only Laura Díaz and Jorge Maura could explain: time doesn't count for lovers, passion is not subject to clocks . . . ?

"I told the boys your mother was ill and that you had to go to Xalapa."

"Thanks."

"That's it?"

"What more do you want?"

"Betrayal is harder to stand, Laura."

"You think I feel I have a right to everything?"

"Why? Because one day I turned in a woman and the next I slapped you and the next I had you followed by a detective?"

"None of that gives me the right to betray you."

"Well, then?"

"You seem to have all the answers today. Answer yourself."

Juan Francisco would turn his back on his wife to tell her, in a pained voice, that only one thing gave her all the rights in the world, the right to make her own life and betray him and humiliate him, not a kind of game in which each one scored goals on the other until they were even, no, nothing so simple, the dark, corpulent man would intolerably say, nothing except a broken promise, a deception, I'm not what you thought I was when you met me at the Casino ball, when I arrived with my fame as a valiant revolutionary.

I'm not a hero.

But one day you were, Laura wanted both to state it and to ask it, isn't that true, one day you were? He'd understand and answer as if she had actually asked, how can you maintain lost heroism when age and circumstance no longer authorize it?

"I'm not very different from the rest. We're all fighting for the Revolution and against injustice, but also against fatality, Laura, we didn't want to go on being poor, humiliated, without rights. I'm no exception. Look at all the others. Calles was a poor country schoolteacher, Morones a telegraph operator, now this Fidel Velázquez was a milkman, and the other leaders were peasants, carpenters, electricians, railroad men, how could you think they wouldn't take advantage and grab opportunity by the tail? Do you know what it is to grow up hungry, six of you sleeping in a shack, half of your brothers dead in childhood, mothers old women at the age of thirty? Tell me if you can't explain

why a man born with his roof three feet above his sleeping pallet in
Pénjamo wouldn't want a thirty-foot ceiling over his head in Polanco?
Tell me Morones wasn't right to give his mother a California-style
house, even if it was right next door to where he kept his harem of
whores? Damn, to be an honorable revolutionary, see, like that Roosevelt in the United States, you've got to be rich first, but if you grew
up sleeping on a pallet, you won't settle for just the pallet, dear, you
won't want ever to go back again to the world of fleas, you even forget
the people you left behind, you set yourself up in purgatory as long as
you don't have to go back to hell, and you let the others think whatever
they like in the heaven you betrayed, what do you think of me? The
truth, Laura, the real truth . . ."

They had no answers, just questions. What did you do, Juan Francisco? Were you a hero who tired of being one? Was your heroism a lie?
Why have you never told me of your past? Did you want to start over
from zero with me? Did you think I'd be offended that you praised
yourself? Did you expect, as actually did happen, that someone else
would do it for you? That others would fill my ears with your legend
without your having to emphasize it or correct it or deny it? Was it
enough for you that I heard what others said about you, that was my
proof, to believe what others said, and believe in you with something
more than knowledge, with pure, blind love? Because that's how you
treated me at first, like a faithful and silent little wife, knitting in the
living room next door while you planned the future of Mexico with the
other leaders in the dining room, remember? Tell me, which of your
myths am I going to transmit to our sons, the complete truth, the half-
truth, the part of your life I imagine to be good, the part I imagine to
be bad, which part of their father will touch Danton, which Santiago?

"What part of your life serves the lives of your sons best?"

"Do you know something, Laura? In catechism they tell you there's
original sin and that's why we're the way we are."

"I only believe in the original mystery. Which will yours be?"

"Don't make me laugh, stupid. If it's a mystery, there's no way to
know it."

Only time, dissipated like smoke, would reveal the truth of Juan

Francisco López Greene, the labor leader from Tabasco. Now she was wrapped in the love of a wholly different man, fervently desired. Jorge Maura is my real husband, Jorge Maura should have been my sons' real father, she imagined as she walked from the Parque de la Lama that March morning, fully intending, as soon as she reached her house, to tell her husband, I have a lover, a marvelous man, I'd give everything for him, I'd leave everything for him, I'd leave you, my sons.

She would tell him before the boys came home from school. But they had the day off: everyone was going to the Zócalo to celebrate the nationalization of the oil industry by President Cárdenas, a valiant revolutionary who had faced up to the foreign companies, ordering them to leave, recovering the wealth of the nation

the subsoil

the veins of the devil

the English companies that stole the communal lands of Tamaulipas

the Dutch companies that used paid assassins as white guards against the unions

the gringo leaders who received Mexican workers sitting down with their backs to them

gringos, Dutch, English, they all left with their white engineers and their blueprints and the wells filled with salt water

the first Mexican engineer to arrive at Poza Rica had no idea what to say to the worker who came over to ask, "Boss, should I empty the pail of water down the tube now?"

and for that reason the four of them, Juan Francisco and Laura, Danton and Santiago, were squeezed together that afternoon in the crowd in the Zócalo, between the Cathedral and the city hall, their eyes fixed on the main balcony of the Palace and on the revolutionary President, Lázaro Cárdenas, who had taught a lesson to the foreign exploiters, the eternal bloodsuckers of Mexican labor and wealth, The oil is ours! The sea of people in the square cheered Cárdenas and Mexico, the rich ladies donated their jewels and the poor women their hens to help pay the expropriation debt, London and The Hague severed diplomatic relations with Mexico, the oil belongs to the Mexicans, fine, let them drink it, let's see who'll buy it, a boycotted Cárdenas had to sell oil to Hitler and Mussolini while he was sending rifles to the Spanish Republic, and in the crowd Jorge Maura watched Laura Díaz and her family from a distance. Laura recognized him. Jorge took off his hat and said hello to all of them. Juan Francisco stared at the man with curiosity, and Laura silently communicated to him, I couldn't, my love, I couldn't, forgive me, see me again, I'll call you, you have Mexicana and I have Ericsson . . .

# 13. Café de Paris: 1939

I HAVE TO TELL you about Raquel Alemán."

He also told her about his comrades in the Republican cause who were in Mexico on missions different from his. They would meet in a very centrally located place, the Café de Paris on Avenida Cinco de Mayo. It was also the haunt of Mexican intellectuals then, led by a man of great wit and unlimited sarcasm, the poet Octavio Barreda, who was married to a sister of Lupe Marín, Diego Rivera's wife before Frida Kahlo. Carmen Barreda would sit in the Café de Paris and listen to her husband's ironies and jokes without changing expression. She never laughed, and he seemed to thank her for it; it was the best commentary on his dry, deadpan humor; it was fitting that he translated Eliot's *The Waste Land* into Spanish.

Everyone expected a great work from him, but it never came. He was a biting critic, a promoter of literary magazines, and a man of great physical distinction—tall, thin, with the features of a hero of the independence movement, light brown skin, and very green, flashing eyes. He was at a table with Xavier Villaurrutia and José Gorostiza, two marvelous poets. The prolific Villaurrutia gave the impression that his poetry, because so spare, was sparse. In point of fact, he was composing a thick volume in which Mexico City took on a nocturnal and amorous sensibility that before him no one had achieved:

> Dreaming, dreaming the night, the street, the staircase and the shout of the statue as it turns the corner. Running toward the statue and finding only the shout, wanting to touch the shout and finding only the echo, wanting to grasp the echo and finding only the wall, and running toward the wall only to touch a mirror.

Villaurrutia was small, fragile, always about to be hurt by mysterious and unnamable forces. He spent his life in his poetry. By contrast, Gorostiza—solid, sarcastic, and silent—was the author of one great, long poem, *Death Without End*, which many thought the best Mexican poem since those written by the nun Sor Juana Inés de la Cruz in the seventeenth century. Its subject was death and form, the form—a glass—postponing death, the water imposing itself, tremulously, as the very condition of life, its flow. Between form and flow stands man, contained in the profile of his vital morality "filled with myself, besieged in my own skin by an ungraspable god who suffocates me."

There were serious sympathies and antipathies among these Mexican writers, and the source of the discord seemed to be Jaime Torres Bodet, a poet-novelist who could not decide between literature and bureaucracy, who ultimately chose the latter, but who never renounced his literary ambition. Barreda sometimes posed as a Chinese laundry man and spy, Dr. Fu Chan Li, and would say to Gorostiza, affecting a Chinese pronunciation: "You watchee out fol Toles."

"What's toles?"

"Toles Bodet."

Which is to say that Jorge Maura and his friends made themselves at home in this Mexican replica of a Madrid *tertulia*—a word, Villaurrutia recalled, derived from Tertullian, the Church father who in the second century A.D. liked to gather with his friends in Socratic discussion groups—although it was hard to imagine a discussion with someone as dogmatic as Tertullian, for whom the Church, possessor of the truth, had no need to argue about anything. Barreda improvised, or recalled in Tertullian's honor, a funny verse:

*Dressed as if to go to a* tertulia,
*Judith departed for Betulia* . . .

Our discussions try to be Socratic, but sometimes they become Tertullianesque, Jorge Maura warned Laura Díaz before going to the café. The other Socratic or Tertullian discussants were Basilio Baltazar, a young man in his thirties, dark-skinned, with thick hair, dark brows, shining eyes, and a smile like sunshine; and Domingo Vidal, whose face and years on earth seemed to have been hacked out with a hatchet. He seemed to have emerged from a stone calendar. He shaved his head and let his features expand in an aggressive, mobile way, as if to compensate for the sleepy sweetness in his thick-lidded eyes.

"Well, my hidalgo, won't my presence annoy your comrades?"

"I want you to be there, Laura."

"At least you could warn them."

"They already know you're coming with me because you are me and that's that. And if they don't understand, they can get lost."

That afternoon they were going to discuss a theme: the role of the Communist Party in the war. Vidal, Jorge pointed out to Laura as they went into the café, would speak for the Communists and Baltazar for the anarchists. That was arranged.

"And you?"

"Listen to me and decide for yourself."

The two discussants greeted Laura with open hearts. She was surprised that they both talked of the war as if they were living a year or two before what was currently taking place. The Republic was not only staring defeat in the face. This *was* defeat. On the other hand, from a distance, Octavio Barreda's face expressed simple curiosity: who was with that gal Laura Díaz, who'd gone with the Riveras to Detroit when Frida lost the child? Villaurrutia and Gorostiza shrugged.

A dialogue began that Laura could instantly see was scripted or anyway predictable, as if each discussant had a role in a play. But then even this impression had already been determined by what Maura had said. Vidal began, as if following an invisible cue, arguing that the Communists had saved the Republic in 1936 and 1937, that without them Madrid would have fallen in the winter of 1937. Neither the militias nor the people's army could have withstood the street disorder in Madrid and in the factories, the lack of food and transportation, without the order imposed by the Party.

"You're forgetting all the others," Baltazar reminded him. "Those who agreed that the Republic should be saved but who did not agree with you."

Vidal furrowed his brow but burst into laughter. It wasn't a matter of disagreement but of doing what was most effective to save the Republic. We Communists imposed order on those who wanted anarchic pluralism in the midst of war, people like you, Baltazar.

"Was a series of small-scale civil wars preferable—anarchists on one side, militiamen on the other, Communists against everyone else, and everyone against us, handing victory to the enemy, who was surely united?" Vidal scratched his unshaven chin.

Basilio Baltazar was silent for a moment, and Laura thought, This man's trying to remember his lines, but his confusion is authentic and perhaps the mistake is mine, and this has to do with a pain I don't know.

"But the fact is, we've lost," said the melancholy Basilio after a time.

"We probably would have lost sooner without Communist discipline," said Vidal in an all too neutral tone, as if he respected Basilio's absent pain, anticipating the anarchist's likely question: Are you asking whether we lost because the Communist Party put its interests and the interests of the Soviet Union above those of the collective interests of the Spanish people? Well, I'll respond by saying that the interests of the Party and the Spanish people coincided, that the Soviet Union helped all of us, not only the Party, with arms and funds. All of us.

"The Communist Party helped Spain," concluded Vidal, and he stared hard at Jorge Maura, as if everyone knew that the next speech was his, except that Basilio Baltazar interrupted on a sudden impulse. Unforeseen by anyone but all the more notable because he asked his question in a hushed tone: "But what was Spain? I say it wasn't only the Communists, it was us, the anarchists, it was liberals, and parliamentary democrats, but the Party first isolated and then annihilated everyone who wasn't Communist, then strengthened itself and imposed its will by weakening the other Republicans and mocking any hope that wasn't the Party's. They preached unity but practiced division.

"That's why we lost," said Baltazar after a pause, his eyes averted, so averted that Laura guessed night away that this was something more personal than a political argument.

"You're very quiet, Maura," Vidal turned to say, respecting Baltazar's silence.

"Well"—Jorge smiled—"I see that I'm drinking coffee and Vidal has a beer, but Basilio has already grown fond of tequila."

"I don't want to disguise the fact that we disagree."

"No," said Vidal.

"Not at all," said Baltazar rather quickly.

Maura thought that Spain was more than Spain. He'd always held that opinion. Spain was the rehearsal for the fascists' general war against the entire world. If Spain fell, Europe and the rest of the world would fall . . .

("I have to tell you about Raquel Alemán.")

"Excuse me for being the devil's advocate." Vidal smiled in his peculiar way. He was the first man to enter a café in extremely formal Mexico City wearing a sweater of rough wool, as if he'd just come from a factory. "Just imagine if the revolution had triumphed in Spain. What would have happened then? Well, then Germany would have invaded us," said the devil.

"But Germany has already invaded us," Basilio Baltazar interrupted, with his quiet desperation. "Spain is already occupied by Hitler. What are you defending or fearing, comrade?"

"What I fear is a disorganized Republican triumph that only postpones the fascists' true, permanent triumph."

Vidal drank his beer like a camel who's happened on an oasis in the desert.

"You mean that would be better than Franco, so we could fight him later in a general war against the Italians, the Germans, and the Spanish fascists?" Basilio's tone suggested an even higher level of desperation.

"That's what my devil says, Basilio. The Nazis fooled the whole world. They're soaking up all of Europe, and no one puts up any resistance. The French and English are either naive or cowards, and they think that they can negotiate with Hitler. It's only here that the Nazis don't fool anyone."

"Here? In Mexico?" Laura smiled to relieve the tension.

*"Pardon, pardon mille fois,"* laughed Vidal. "Only in Spain."

"No, excuse me, please." Laura smiled again. "I understand your 'here,' Mr. Vidal. I would have said 'here in Mexico' if I were in Spain."

"What are you drinking?" Basilio asked her.

"Chocolate. It's a custom of ours. You grind it first, then add hot water. My Mutti, I mean, my mother . . ."

"Well." Vidal went back to his argument. "Let's have thick chocolate and clear conclusions, if you don't mind. If the Nazis win in Spain, perhaps Europe will wake up. They'll see the horror. We already know what it is. Perhaps in order to win the big war we have to lose the battle of Spain so as to alert the world against this evil. Spain, the battle, *la petite guerre d'Espagne.*" Vidal twisted his lips and suppressed a smile.

Jorge slept badly, talking in his sleep all night, got up to drink water, then to urinate, then to sit in an armchair with a distracted look on his face, observed by naked Laura, also nervous, satisfied after sex with Jorge but sensing with alarm that the sex was not for her, but a way of seeking relief . . .

"Talk to me. I want to know. I have a right to know, Jorge. I love you. What's happening? What happened?"

It is a beautiful but harsh nation, as if dying slowly and not wanting anyone to see its agony but at the same time wanting a witness of its mortal beauty. The marks of centuries are stamped on its face, one after another starting with the Iberians, a savage gold helmet with the same value as a clay pot. A Roman gate that endures, eaten away by time and by storms, like a marker of power and a notice of legitimacy. A great medieval city wall, the belt around the Castilian town and its defense against Islam—which nonetheless seeps in everywhere, in the Spanish words for pillow, for terrace, for the bath of cleanliness and for abominable pleasures, for the artichoke whose leaves we pull off like an edible carnation, in the semicircular arches of Christian churches, in the Moorish decoration on doors and windows near the synagogue— empty, ruined, persecuted internally by abandonment and oblivion . . .

Surrounded by its twelfth-century wall, the town of Santa Fe de Palencia has a unique center, a kind of urban navel from which flows the entire history of a community. Its main plaza is a bullring, an arena of very yellow sand waiting for the other color of the Spanish flag to be poured onto it, a plaza that instead of having seats on the sunny or shady side is surrounded by houses with huge shuttered windows, open on Sundays so that people can watch the bullfights, which give vitality and strength to the town. There is only one way into the large, enclosed plaza.

The three Republican soldiers have entered this singular town center, where the mayor, Don Alvaro Méndez, a Communist, is waiting for them. He is not uniformed, but wears a short vest over his big belly, a collarless shirt, and spurless boots. His most attractive feature is his face, with its bushy eyebrows, arched like the entrance to a mosque; his eyes have been veiled for some time by aging eyelids, one would have to search for the hard, secret shine in the depths of that invisible gaze. The faces of the three soldiers are, in contrast, open, frank, and astonished. The old man reads them and says I'm only doing my duty, you saw the Roman gate?, it's not a party question, it's a matter of law, this city is legal because it is Republican, it isn't a city in revolt on the side of fascism, it's a city governed legitimately by an elected Communist mayor, I, Alvaro Méndez, who must do his duty, no matter how terrible and painful it may be.

"It's unjust," said Basilio Baltazar through his tightly closed teeth.

"I'll tell you something, Basilio, and I'm not going to repeat it," said the mayor, standing in the center of the bullring with its yellow sand and closed windows, with curious women in black peering through the cracks. "There is fidelity in obeying just orders, but there is a higher fidelity in obeying unjust orders."

"No." Basilio held back the shout boiling in his throat. "The greater fidelity consists in disobeying unjust orders."

She betrayed us, said the mayor. She informed the enemy about Republican positions in the mountains. Look at those lights up there, look at those fires on the mountains, flying from peak to peak, fed by all of us in the name of all of us, think of those fires as instant moons, those torches of wood and hay, giving birth to others, a pelt of fire: well, those are the fiery fences of the Republic, the wall we've imposed on ourselves to protect us from the fascists. "She told them." The mayor's voice trembled with a rage more fiery than the peaks. "She told them that if they put out those lights we'd be fooled and lower our guard. She told them to put out the fires on the mountains, kill the Republican torch bearers one by one, and then you'll be able to take this seduced, defenseless town in the name of Franco, our savior."

His snakelike eyelids interrogated each of the soldiers. He wanted to be fair. He listened to the arguments. A noisily opened balcony window and a heartrending shriek interrupted them. A woman appeared with a moon-colored face and eyes the color of blackberries, dressed all in black, her head covered, her skin worn transparent by use, like a sheet of paper on which more has been erased than written. Méndez, mayor of Santa Fe de Palencia, paid no attention. He repeated: Speak up.

"Save her in the name of honor," said Jorge Maura.

"I love Pilar," Basilio Baltazar shouted, more loudly than the woman on the balcony. "Save her in the name of love."

"She must die in the name of justice." The mayor planted his boot on the immaculate sand and stared, looking for support, at the Communist Vidal.

"Save her despite politics," he said.

"Unfavorable winds." The old man tried to smile, but he remained, ultimately, hieratic. "Unfavorable."

Then the woman on the balcony shouted, Have pity! And the mayor told everyone not to confuse his obligation to justice with his wife's anger, and the woman shouted again from the balcony, You only have obligations as a mayor and a Communist? And the old man again ignored her, speaking only to Vidal, Baltazar, and Maura, I don't obey my feelings, I obey Spain and the Party.

"Have you no compassion?" shouted the woman.

"It's your fault, Clemencia, you educated her to be a Catholic against my wishes," the mayor answered finally, turning his back to the woman on the balcony.

"Don't embitter what is left of my life, Alvaro."

"Bah! Family discord doesn't take precedence over law."

"Sometimes discord is born not of hatred but of too much love," shouted Clemencia, removing the shawl covering her head and revealing her tousled white hair and her ears overflowing with prophecies. "Our daughter stands exposed, at the city gates. What are you going to do with her?"

"She's no longer your daughter. She's my wife," said Basilio Baltazar.

That night, someone let the oxen into the Santa Fe plaza. The fires on the mountain began to go out.

"The sky is full of lies," said Clemencia in an opaque voice before closing the balcony shutters.

("I must tell you about Pilar Méndez.")

There seemed to be only one theme at the next meeting in the Café de Paris: violence, its origins, its gestation, its offspring, its relationship with good and evil. Maura espoused the most difficult argument, that it is impossible to ascribe all evil to the fascists, let's not forget Republican violence, the assassination of Cardinal Soldevila in Zaragoza by the anarchists, the Socialists beating to death members of Franco's Falange as they exercised on the grounds of the Casa de Campo in 1934—they poked out their eyeballs and urinated in the sockets, that's what our side did, comrades.

"They were ours."

"And didn't the fascists later on kill the girl who urinated on *their* dead?"

"That's my argument, comrades," said Maura, taking the hand of his Mexican lover. "The escalation of Spanish violence always takes us to the war of all against all."

"How right the Catalan *escamots* were in 1934, when they cut the railroad lines to separate Catalonia from Spain forever." Basilio stared at the joined hands of Jorge and Laura—"Good for you!"—but he felt pain and envy.

Vidal roared with a laugh as woolly as his sweater. "So we all kill one another behind closed doors in a jolly regional style while the world jerks off!"

Jorge let go of Laura's hand and threw his arm over Vidal's shoulder. I'm not forgetting the mass murders perpetrated by Franco's people in Badajoz, the murder of Federico García Lorca, or Guernica. That, comrades, was my prologue.

"Friends, forget the political violence of the past. Forget Spain's supposed political fatality. This is a war, but it isn't even ours; it's been taken away from us; we're nothing but a rehearsal. Our enemies come from outside Spain; Franco is a puppet, but Hitler, unless we stop him, will conquer the world. Remember, I studied in Germany and saw how the Nazis organized. Forget our miserable Spanish violence. Just wait and see real violence. The violence of evil. Evil, that's right, with a capital E, organized like a factory in the Ruhr Valley. Our violence is going to look like flamenco dancing or bullfighting," said Jorge Maura.

("I have to tell you about Raquel Alemán.")

"And you, Laura Díaz? You haven't said a word."

She looked down for an instant and then gazed tenderly at each one. Finally, she spoke: "I really enjoy seeing that the hardest-fought discussion among men always reveals what they have in common."

The three of them blushed simultaneously. Basilio Baltazar saved the situation, which she had not fully understood. "You two are very much in love. How do you measure love in the context of all that's taking place?"

Vidal joined in. "Rephrase the question like this: Does only personal happiness count and not the disaster about to engulf millions of people?"

"I'm asking a different question, Mr. Vidal," Laura pointed out.

"Just Vidal. How formal you Mexicans are."

"Well then, Mr. Just Vidal. Can the love two people share make up for all the unhappiness in the world?"

The three men exchanged a look of modesty and compassion.

"Yes, I suppose there are ways of redeeming the world, whether we're as solitary as our friend Basilio or as affiliated as I am," Vidal responded, with mixed humility and arrogance.

("I have to tell you about Pilar Méndez.")

What the Communist said at the end, Laura, Jorge said to her as the two of them strolled alone along Avenida Cinco de Mayo, is true but troubling.

She told him he seemed reticent—eloquent, of course, but reticent almost always. He was a different Jorge Maura, another one, and she liked him, she swore she did, but she wanted to pause for a moment on the Maura in the café, understand his silence, share the reasons for his silence.

"You know that none of us dares express his true doubts," countered Maura, walking toward the Venetian-style building that was Mexico City's main post office. "The Communists were the strongest because they have the fewest doubts. But that's why it's easier for them to commit historical crimes. Don't misunderstand me. Nazis and Communists are not the same thing. The difference is that Hitler believes in evil, evil is his gospel—conquest, genocide, racism. But Stalin must say he believes in the good, in the freedom of labor, in the disappearance of the state, and in giving to each according to his needs. He recites the gospel of the civil god."

"Is that why he fools so many people?"

"Hitler recites the gospel of the devil. He commits his crimes in the name of evil: that's his horror. It's never been seen before. Those who follow him must share his malevolent will, all of them—Göring, Goebbels, Himmler, Ribbentrop, aristocrats like Papen, low-class scum like Ernst Röhm, Prussian Junkers like Keitel. Stalin commits his crimes in the name of the good, and I don't know if that isn't an even greater horror, because those who follow him act in good faith; they're not fascists but people who are usually good, and when they realize what the Stalinist horror is, Stalin himself eliminates them. Trotsky, Bukharin, Kamenev, all the comrades of the heroic period. Those who refused to follow Stalin because they preferred to follow true Communism all the way to exile or death: aren't they heroes—Bukharin, Trotsky, Kamenev? Name one Nazi who's abandoned Hitler out of fidelity to National Socialism."

"And what about you, Jorge, my little Spanish boy?"

"Me, Laura, my little Mexican girl, I'm a Spanish intellectual and, if you like, a gentleman, an *aristó*, of the kind Robespierre had guillotined."

"You have a divided soul, my little Spanish gentleman."

"No, I certainly comprehend the Nazi evil as well as the Stalinist betrayal. But I'm also conscious of the nobility of the Spanish Republic, how it is simply trying to make Spain into a normal modern country, with mutual respect, getting along with one another, and trying to solve our problems, which, damn it all, have been with us since the Goths. And to that essential nobility of the Republic, I sacrifice my doubts, Laura my love. Between the Nazi evil and the Communist betrayal, I'll choose the Republican heroism of that young gringo (as you call them), that young Jim, who came to the Jarama to die for us."

"Jorge, I'm not an idiot. Someone else suffered for the three of you. Something else links you, Baltazar, and Vidal."

("I have to tell you about Pilar Méndez.")

Standing with her back to the wall that ran around Santa Fe de Palencia, wrapped in a mantle of savage black skins, her blond hair tossed by the swirling wind from the mountain, Pilar Méndez watched the hilltop bonfires go out one by one. She did not smile to affirm her triumph—treason to her father, victory for her, strengthening her conviction that to help her side was like helping God—though her spirits sank when she heard the footsteps of the three Republican soldiers

advancing from the Roman gate to that space of restless dust and bel-
lowing oxen which she, Pilar Méndez, occupied in the name of her
God, beyond any political faith, because the Nationals and the Falange
were with God and they, the others, her father, Don Alvaro, and the
three soldiers, were victims of the devil without knowing it, thinking
they were on the good side, it was they, all of them, the reds, who
burned down churches and shot priests and raped nuns: Domingo
Vidal, Jorge Maura, and Basilio Baltazar, her love, her burning tenderness, the man in her life, her husband already without any need of
sacraments, walking through the dust and the oxen and the wind and
the dead fires toward her, the woman standing fast against the wall of
the dying city wrapped in a long mantle of dead black animals, a Spanish blonde, a Visigothic goddess with blue eyes and a mane as yellow as
the sand in the bullring.

What were these three men going to say to her?

What could they say?

Not a word. Only the sight of Basilio Baltazar like a double arrow of
life's inseparable pain and pleasure. Her lover felt like a price, the price
one paid to invert the order of life, which was love, thought Pilar Méndez as she watched the three men approach.

Basilio knelt and wrapped his arms around her knees, endlessly
repeating my love my love my cunt my tits don't take anything away
my treasure, Pilar I adore you.

"You, Domingo Vidal, Communist enemy?" asked Pilar to the other
man, to strengthen herself against Basilio Baltazar's amatory grief.

Vidal nodded his shaved head, his militia cap in his hands, as if
Pilar were the Virgin of Sorrows.

"You, Jorge Maura, aristocrat traitor, gone over to the reds?"

Jorge embraced her, and she howled like an animal, yet an animal
capable of repugnance, but Maura said, I'm not letting you go, you
must understand, you're sentenced to death, understand me?, you're to
be executed at dawn, your own father has ordered you shot, your father
the mayor your father Alvaro Méndez, he's going to kill you despite all
our begging, despite your mother . . .

Pilar Méndez's insane laugh pulled a horrified Baltazar to his feet. My mother? laughed Pilar like some wild animal, a most beautiful hyena, a Medusa without a gaze, my mother, is there anyone who desires my death more than my badly named mother Clemencia, the pig, she who made me devout until death, she who implanted the idea of sin and hell in me?, that woman doesn't want my life, she wants my martyr's death, the death of a virgin who believes, the fool, virgin, Basilio, you hear her, Basilio, what do you win by the fact that Clemencia my mother saw us the afternoon you tore out my virginity, you nibbled it bite by bite, you spit out my bloody membrane as if it were snot or a rotten host, Basilio, remember?, and you penetrated me the way a wolf penetrates a she-wolf from behind, up the ass, without seeing my face; that you remember, in the old house without furniture where you took me, my adored love, my only man, you think you have the right to save me when my own mother wants me dead, a martyr for the Movement, a saint who saves her own conscience, Clemencia the well named, the mother who hates me because I didn't marry as she wished, I gave myself to a poor boy with suspicious ideas, my handsome, adored Basilio Baltazar, why have you come here, what are you and your friends trying to do, you've gone mad, you don't know you're all my enemies, you don't know I'm against you, I'd have all of you shot in the name of Spain and Franco, I don't want thorns to grow on the old paths of Spanish death, I want to wash them away with my blood . . .

Vidal brutally covered her mouth as if he were closing a sewer, Maura made her cross her arms, Baltazar again knelt at her feet. Each of them had his own words, but they all said the same thing, we want to save you, come with us, look at the fires that have still not gone out on the hills, we'll find refuge there, your father has done his duty, he's given the order for you to be shot at dawn, we aren't going to do our duty, come with us, let us save you, Pilar, even if the price is our own death.

"Why, Jorge?" asked Laura Díaz.

In spite of the war. In spite of the Republic. In spite of her father's will. My daughter must die in the name of justice said the mayor of

Santa Fe de Palencia. She must be saved in the name of love said Basilio Baltazar. She must be saved in spite of political logic said Domingo Vidal. She must be saved in the name of honor said Jorge Maura.

"My two friends looked at me and understood. I didn't have to explain. It isn't enough that we do things in the name of love or justice. It is honor that sanctioned us. Honor in exchange for justice? That's the dilemma I saw on the face of Domingo Vidal. Betrayal or beauty? That's what Basilio Baltazar's loving eyes were asking me. I looked at the three of them, stripped of everything but the bare skin of truth, that fatal afternoon against the medieval walls and the Roman gate, surrounded by mountains that were going out, I saw the three, Pilar, Basilio, Domingo, as an emblematic group, Laura, the reason why no one but I understood then and now you too because I'm telling you. This is the reason. The need for beauty supersedes the need for justice. The interlocking trio—woman, lover, adversary—was not resolving itself in either justice or love; it was an act of necessary beauty, based on honor."

What can the duration of a sculpture be when it is incarnated not by statues but by living beings threatened with death?

Sculptural perfection—honor and beauty triumphing over betrayal and justice—dissolved when Jorge whispered to the woman, Run away with us to the mountains, save yourself, because if you don't the four of us will die here together, and she, between her clenched teeth, answered, I'm human, I haven't learned anything; even though Basilio begged, nothing is won without compassion, come with us, run away, there's time; and she, I'm like a dog for death, I smell it and I follow it until I get killed, I'm not going to give the three of you the satisfaction, I can smell death, all the graves in this country are open, there's no home left to us but the grave.

"Your father and mother at least. Save yourself for them."

Pilar stared at them with an incendiary shock on her face and began to laugh insanely. "But you understand nothing. Do you think I'm dying just out of loyalty to the Movement?"

Her laughter kept her apart for a few seconds. "I'm dying so my father and mother will hate each other forever. So they'll never forgive each other."

(I have to tell you about Pilar Méndez.)

"I think you're one of those men who are only loyal to themselves if they're loyal to their friends," said Laura, leaning her head against Jorge's shoulder.

"No." He sighed with fatigue. "I'm a man who's angry with himself because he doesn't know how to explain the truth and avoid lies."

"Perhaps you're strong because you doubt things, my Spanish boy. I think I figured that out tonight."

They crossed Aquiles Serdán and passed under the marble portico of the Palace of Fine Arts.

"I just said it now in the café, my love, we're all condemned. I confess I hate all systems, mine and the others'."

VIDAL: Now do you see? Victory will not be achieved without order. Let's win or lose now, victorious today or defeated tomorrow, we're going to need order and unity, hierarchies of command and discipline. Without them, we'll always be beaten, because they do have order, unity, command, and discipline.

BALTAZAR: Well, in that case, what's the difference between Hitler's implacable discipline and Stalin's?

VIDAL: The ends, Basilio. Hitler wants a world of slaves. Stalin wants a world of free men. Even though their means may be equally violent, their ends are totally different.

"Vidal's right," laughed Laura. "You're closer to the anarchist than to the Communist."

Jorge stopped short opposite a poster at the Palace of Fine Arts. "No one was playing a part this afternoon, Laura. Vidal really is a Communist. Basilio really is an anarchist. I didn't tell you the truth. I thought that way the two of us, you and I, could stand at a certain distance from the debate."

They stood in silence for a while, staring at the poster's black letters on yellow paper, improperly fastened to a wooden frame unworthy of the marbles and bronzes in the Palace of Fine Arts. Jorge looked at Laura.

"Forgive me. How beautiful you are."

Carlos Chávez was going to conduct his own *Indian Symphony* and Prokofiev's *Love for Three Oranges*. The pianist Nikita Magaloff would interpret Chopin's First Concerto, the one Aunt Hilda rehearsed so futilely in Catemaco.

"How I wish no one on our side had ever committed a single crime."

"That's how Armonía Aznar must have been—a woman I met, or rather never met. I had to guess how she was. Thank you for opening yourself to me without mysteries, without locked doors. Thanks, my hidalgo. You make me feel better, cleaner, clearer in my head."

"I'm sorry. It's like vaudeville. We meet and repeat the same trite lines, like one of those Madrid comedies by Muñoz Seca. You saw it today: each one knew exactly what he should say. Perhaps that's how we'll exorcise our disgust. I don't know."

He hugged her in the Fine Arts portico, the two of them surrounded by the brownish-black Mexican night, sudden and vicious. "I'm getting tired of this interminable fight. I'd like to live with no more country than my soul, with no more country . . ."

They made a half turn and went back to Cinco de Mayo, their arms around each other's waists. Their words were slowly extinguished, like the lights in the candy shops, bookstores, luggage emporia, as the streetlamps came on, opening a path of light all the way to Herrera's cathedral, where on the previous March 18 they'd celebrated the nationalization of Mexico's oil—she and Juan Francisco, Santiago and Danton, and Jorge at a distance, greeting her with his hat in his hand and, on high, a personal greeting that was also a political celebration, above the heads of the crowd, greeting and saying goodbye at the same time, saying I love you and goodbye, I've come back and I still love you.

At the Café de Paris, Barreda, who had been watching them, asked Gorostiza and Villaurrutia to guess what the Spaniards had been talking about. Politics? Art? No, wine jugs. He recited another pair of verses from the Bible turned into rhyme by a mad Spaniard, the description of Balthazar's Feast:

*Burgundy, Rhine, Pinot Blanc:*
*Sausage? All you could want.*

Villaurrutia said he didn't find Mexican jokes about Spaniards funny, and Gorostiza asked why there was this ill will against a country that gave us its culture, its language, even its mixed blood . . .

"Go ask Cuauhtémoc how it went with the Spaniards at dinnertime," laughed Barreda. "Toasted tootsies!"

"No." Gorostiza smiled. "The thing is, we don't like to admit that the winners are right. We Mexicans have been defeated too often. We like loving the defeated. They're ours. They're us."

"Are there winners in history?" asked Villaurrutia, he himself defeated by sleep or languor or death, God knows, thought the beautiful, intelligent, and taciturn Carmen Barreda.

## 14. Every Place, the Place: 1940

### 1.

H E WENT TO HAVANA, Washington, New York, Santo
Domingo, sent telegrams to her at L'Escargot, sometimes
called her house and only spoke if he heard her voice saying,
"No, it isn't Ericsson, it's Mexicana," which was their personal code
for—no problems, neither husband nor children. Sometimes Maura
threw caution to the wind and said something anyway, and she would
have to stand there in silence or babble nonsense because her husband
or her sons were nearby, no I need the plumber today, or when will that
dress be ready?, or how expensive everything is, now that there's going
to be a war, while Jorge would be saying these are the best days of our
lives, don't you think?, why don't you answer me?, and she would laugh
nervously, and he'd begin, what a good thing it was we were impatient,
my love, can you imagine if we'd restrained ourselves that first night?,
in the name of what were we supposed to be patient?, our lives are slipping away in any case, my adored wife, my "freisch and gay wyf," as he
called her, in playful medieval Spanish, and she silently staring at her

husband reading *El Nacional* or her sons doing their homework, wanting to say to Maura, silently telling him, nothing calmed my desire for life until I met you and now I consider myself satisfied. I don't ask for anything more, my hidalgo, except for you to come back safe and sound so we can be together in our little room and if you ask me to leave everything behind I would without a moment's hesitation, my sons, my husband, or my mother couldn't stop me, only you, because with you I feel I haven't used up my youth, will you allow me to speak frankly? Yesterday I turned forty-two, and I was sorry you weren't here so we could celebrate it together, Juan Francisco and Danton forgot completely, only Santiago remembered, and I told him, "It's our secret, don't tell them," and my son told me in a hug that we were accomplices, that would be my happiness, you and I my favorite son, why deny it?, why pretend we love all our children equally, it isn't so, it isn't so, there are children who have in themselves what you strongly suspect is lacking in you, children who are more than themselves, children like mirrors of the past and the future, that's how my Santiago is, the one who did not forget my birthday and who made me think you've given me a papal indulgence which a woman my age needs, and if I don't take it, my hidalgo, the life you're giving me, I will have no life to give in the times to come to my sons, to my poor husband, my mother.

## 2.

The death of Leticia, the magnificent and adored Mutti: the central feminine image in Laura Díaz's life, the column to which clung all the masculine strands of ivy—the grandfather Don Felipe, the father Don Fernando, the equally adored brother Santiago, the dolorous and doleful Orlando Ximénez, the husband Juan Francisco, the sons brought up by the grandmother while the life of Mexico became calmer after the now distant, cruel turbulence of the Revolution, while Laura and Juan Francisco uselessly sought each other out, while Laura and Orlando put on disguises so as not to see each other and not to be seen—all of them climbers to the balcony of Mother Leticia, all except Jorge Maura, the first man independent of the Veracruz tree trunk of the mother, powerful thanks to her integrity, her care, her rigorous attention to each day's chores, her discretion, her immense ability to offer confidence, to be there and say nothing.

Leticia was gone, and her death brought back Laura's childhood memories. Today's death gives presence to yesterday's life. Even so, Laura could not remember a single word her mother had spoken. It was as if Leticia's entire life had been one long sigh hidden by the cloud of activities she organized to make everything proceed properly in the houses in Veracruz and Xalapa. Her speech was her kitchen, her cleanliness, her starched clothing, her well-organized dressers scented with lavender, her four-footed bathtubs, her kettles of boiling water and her pitchers of cold water. Her dialogue was her eyes, her wise silence in understanding and in making others understand without offense or lies, without useless reproach. Her modesty was beloved because it let others imagine the presence of a love protected deep within her, with no need ever to show itself. She had had a hard school: the separation of the first years, when Don Fernando lived in Veracruz and she lived in Catemaco. But that distance was imposed by circumstance: hadn't it allowed Laura, still a little girl, to join her brother Santiago at exactly the right moment, when the two of them together could be both children and adults, playing first and crying later, with no other contact that might muddy the purity of that memory, the deepest and most beautiful in Laura Díaz's life? Not a night passes without her dreaming about the face of her young, executed brother, buried at sea, disappearing under the waves of the Gulf of Mexico.

The day of her mother's funeral, Laura lived two lives at the same time. She carried out all the rites automatically, followed all the procedures in the wake and the burial, both very solitary. No one from the old families was left in Xalapa. The loss of fortune, fear of the new anticlerical and socialist expropriating governors, the magnetic power of Mexico City, the promise of new opportunities beyond the provincial country estates, illusion and delusion—these had scattered all the old friends and acquaintances far from Xalapa. Laura visited the San Cayetano hacienda. It was a ruin. The waltzes, laughter, the hustle and bustle of servants, the clink of glass against glass, the upright figure of Doña Genoveva Deschamps existed only in Laura's memory . . .

Mutti descended into the earth, but in her daughter's second life that day, past became present, like a history without relics, the city in the mountains appeared suddenly at the seashore, old trees revealed their roots, birds passed over like lightning bolts, rivers filled with ashes emptied into the sea, the very stars were made of dust, and the forest was a hurricane-force scream.

Night and day ceased to exist.

When the world without Leticia dawned, it was decimated.

Only the perfume of Xalapa's eternal rain woke Laura Díaz from her reverie, so she could say to María de la O: "Now for certain, Auntie, now for certain you'll have to come with us to Mexico City."

But María de la O said nothing. She would never say another word. She would affirm. She would negate. With her head. Leticia's death left her wordless, and when Laura picked up her aunt's valise to leave the Xalapa house, the old mulatta stopped and slowly turned around and around, as if she and only she could convoke all the family ghosts, give them a place, confirm them as family members. Laura was deeply touched as she watched the last of the Kelsen sisters bid farewell to the Veracruz house, the one who'd arrived dispossessed and marked, to be redeemed by a good man, Fernando Díaz, for whom doing good was as natural as breathing.

Soon picks and shovels would demolish the Xalapa house on Bocanegra Street with its useless entry gate for useless horse-drawn carriages or aged gas-guzzling Isotta-Fraschinis. The eaves that protected the house from the constant drizzle that blew in from the mountains would disappear, as would the interior patio, its huge porcelain flowerpots, encrusted with bits of glass, the kitchen with its fires of diamondlike coal and its humble stone corn grinders and palm-leaf fans, the dining room and the pictures of the rascal nipped by the dog. María de la O rescued only her sisters' silver napkin rings. The picks and shovels would soon be there.

María de la O, last witness to the provincial past of her family line, put up no resistance when Laura led her to the station for the Interoceanic train. She went as gently as Leticia's cadaver had gone to the Xalapa cemetery to be laid next to the body of her husband. What was she going to do except imitate her dead sister and pretend that she could go on animating her lineage in the only manner left to her: immobile and silent as a dead woman, but discreet and respectful as her unforgettable sister, she who as a girl on her birthday dressed in white and went out on the patio of the Catemaco house to sing:

> *on the twelfth of May*
> *the Virgin dressed in white*
> *came walking into sight*
> *with her coat so gay . . .*

Because at the moment of her death, María de la O's memories of her sister Leticia and her niece Laura blended together.

## 3.

One day, a year earlier, Jorge Maura hastily returned from Washington, and Laura Díaz attributed his mood—the haste, the sadness—to the inevitable: On January 26, Franco's forces took Barcelona and advanced toward Gerona; the civilian population began its diaspora through the Pyrenees.

"Barcelona," said Laura. "That's where Armonía Aznar came from."

"The woman who lived in your house, whom you never saw?"

"Yes. My own brother Santiago was with the anarcho-syndicalists."

"You've told me very little about him."

"Two loves of that size won't fit in my mouth at the same time." She smiled. "He was a very brilliant boy, very handsome and brave. He was like the Scarlet Pimpernel"—now she laughed nervously—"posing like a glamorous fellow to cover up his political activity. He's my saint, he gave his life for his ideas, he was shot when he was twenty."

Jorge Maura kept a disturbing silence. For the first time, Laura saw him lower his head, and she realized he'd always held his Ibero-Roman head high and proud, a touch arrogantly. She assumed it was because the two of them were entering the basilica of the Virgin of Guadalupe, where Maura insisted on taking her as an homage to Doña Leticia, whom he'd never met.

"Are you a Catholic?"

"Laura, I think that in Spain and Spanish America even atheists are Catholics. Besides, I don't want to leave Mexico without understanding why the Virgin is the symbol of Mexico's national unity. Did you know that the Spanish royal troops would shoot the image of the Virgin of Guadalupe during the war of independence?"

"You're leaving Mexico?" asked Laura, keeping her tone neutral. "Then the Virgin isn't protecting me."

He shrugged his shoulders in a way that meant: I'm always leaving and returning, why are you so surprised? They were kneeling side by side in the first pew, facing the altar of the Virgin, whose image, Laura explained to Jorge, framed and protected by glass, was imprinted on the mantle of a humble Indian, Juan Diego, a *tameme* or porter to whom the Mother of God appeared one day in December 1531, when the Spanish conquest was barely over, on Tepeyac Hill, a place where an Aztec goddess had been worshipped.

"How clever the Spaniards were in the sixteenth century," said Maura, smiling. "No sooner had they carried off the military conquest than they set about the spiritual conquest. They destroy—well, we destroy—a culture and its religion, but we give the conquered people our own culture invested with Indian symbols—or perhaps we give them back their own culture with European symbols."

"That's true. Here we call her the Dark Virgin. That's the difference. She isn't white. She's the mother whom the Indian orphans needed."

"She's everything, can you imagine anything more ingenious? She's a Christian and Indian Virgin, but she's also the Virgin of Israel, the Jewish mother of the long-awaited Messiah. On top of that, she has an Arabic name, Guadalupe, river of wolves. How many cultures for the price of a single image!"

Their dialogue was interrupted by an underground hymn that was born behind them and advanced from the door of the basilica like an ancient echo that did not spring from the voices of the pilgrims but accompanied them or, perhaps, received them from earlier centuries. Jorge looked toward the choir, but there was no one, neither organist nor singing children, where they might have been. The procession was accompanied by its own cantata, low and monotonous, like all Indian music in Mexico. Even so, it could not drown out the noise of knees being painfully dragged along the stones. Everyone was moving forward on their knees, some with lighted candles in their hands, others with their arms crossed in front of them, others with their fists held tight to their faces. The women carried scapulars, the men nopal leaves over their bare, bloody chests. Some faces were veiled by gauze masks tied behind the head that transformed their features into mere outlines struggling to reveal themselves. The prayers spoken in low voices were like the trilling of birds, high and low chirping—totally unlike the even tone of the Castilian tongue, Maura realized, a language measured in neutral tones that made its angers, its orders, and its speeches all the stronger; here there wasn't a single voice that one could conceive of as growing angry, giving orders, or speaking to the others except in a tone of advice, perhaps that of destiny, but they have faith, Maura raised his voice, yes, Laura moved forward, they have faith, what's wrong, Jorge, why are you talking that way?, but she could not understand, you can't understand, Laura, then explain it to me, tell me, Maura, answered Laura, ready not to give in to the tremor of doubt, to barely controlled rage, the ironic humor of Jorge Maura in the Basilica of Guadalupe, watching a procession of devout Indians enter, people whose faith had no questions, a pure faith sustained by an imagination open to every credulous belief: It's true because it's unbelievable, repeated Jorge, suddenly carried away from the place where he was and the person who he was and the person whom he was with, the Basilica of Guadalupe, Laura Díaz, she felt it with an irrepressible force, there was nothing she could do, all that was left to her was to listen, she wasn't going to stop the torrent of passion that the entering procession of barefoot Mexican Indians unleashed in Maura, smashing his serene discourse, his rational reflection into a thousand pieces and throwing him into a whirlwind of memories, premonitions, defeats that spun around a single word, faith, faith, what is faith?, why do these Indians have faith?, why did my teacher Edmund Husserl have faith in philosophy?, why did my lover Raquel have faith in Christ?, why did Basilio, Vidal, and I have faith in Spain?, why did Pilar Méndez have faith in Franco?, why did her father the mayor have faith in Communism?, why did the Germans have faith in Nazism?, why do these destitute men and women dying of hunger, who have never received any compensation from the God they adore, have faith?, why do we believe and act in the name of our faith knowing full well we shall never be rewarded for the sacrifices faith imposes on us as a test?, toward what were these poor of the Lord advancing?, who, who, was the crucified figure Jorge Maura was now staring at, because the procession hadn't come to see Christ but His Mother, believing completely that she conceived without sin, that the Holy Spirit impregnated her, that a randy carpenter was not the true father of Jesus?, did any one of the penitents approaching the altar of Guadalupe on their knees know that Mary's conception was not immaculate?, why don't we, I, Jorge Maura and you, Laura Díaz, believe in that?, what do we believe in, you and I?, can we together believe in God because He stripped himself of the sacred impunity of Jehovah by making himself a man in Christ?, can we believe in God because Christ made God so fragile that we human beings could recognize ourselves in Him?, Laura, but in order to be worthy of Christ do we have to abase ourselves even more, so we won't be more than He?, is that our tragedy, is that our disgrace, that to have faith in Christ and be worthy of His redemption, we must be unworthy of Him, less than He is, sinners, murderers, lechers, full of pride, that the true test of faith is accepting that God asks us to do what He doesn't allow?, is there a single Indian in this temple who thinks this?, no, Jorge, none, I can't imagine it, do we have to be as good and simple and beyond temptation as these humble beings to be worthy of God, or do we have to be as rational and vain as you and I and Raquel Mendes-Alemán and Pilar Méndez and her father the mayor of Santa Fe de Palencia to be worthy of what we don't believe?, the faith of the Mexican Indian or the faith of the German philosopher or the faith of the Jewish woman who converts to Christianity or the faith of the militant fascist or the militant Communist?, which could be, for God Himself, the best, the truest faith of all?, tell me, Laura, tell me about it, Jorge . . .

"Lower your voice. What's wrong with you today?"

"Well," answered Maura intensely, "I'm looking at that poor, barefoot Indian in a cloak, and I'm seeing him at the same time wearing a striped uniform with a green triangle on his chest because he's a common criminal and a red triangle because he's a political agitator and a pink triangle because he's queer and a black triangle because he's antisocial and a Star of David because he's a Jew . . ."

Her name is Raquel Mendes-Alemán. They were both students in Freiburg. They had the privilege of studying with Edmund Husserl, not only a great teacher but a philosophic comrade, a presence who guided his students' independent thought. The sympathetic relationship between Raquel and Jorge crystallized instantly because she was a descendant of Sephardic Jews expelled from Spain in 1492 by Ferdinand and Isabella. She spoke the Spanish of the fifteenth century, and her parents read Sephardic newspapers written in the Spanish of the Archpriest of Hita and Fernando de Rojas and sang Hebrew songs in honor of the Spanish land. They had, as Sephardic Jews did, the keys of their old Castilian houses hanging from a nail in their new German houses, in expectation of the desired day—after four and a half centuries—of their return to the Iberian Peninsula.

"Spain," prayed Raquel's parents and relatives at night, "Spain, ungrateful mother, you expelled your Jewish children who loved you so much, but we don't hold that against you, you are our beloved mother and we don't want to die before returning one day to you, beloved Spain."

Raquel did not join in the prayer because she'd made a drastic decision the year she matriculated at Freiburg. She converted to Catholicism. She explained it to Jorge Maura:

"I was severely criticized. Even my own family criticized me. They thought I'd become a Catholic so as to avoid the stigma of being a Jew. The Nazis were organizing to seize power. In Weimar Germany, so impoverished and humiliated, there was no doubt who was going to prevail. Germans wanted a strong man for their weak country. I explained that I was not trying to avoid any stigma. It was entirely the opposite. It was a challenge. It was a way of saying to the world, to my family, to the Nazis: Look, we are all Semites. I'm becoming a Catholic because of a fundamental disagreement with my parents. I think the Messiah has already come. His name is Jesus Christ. They still await Him, and that wait blinds them and condemns them to be persecuted, because he who awaits the coming of the Redeemer is always a revolutionary, an element of disorder and violence. On the barricades like Trotsky, camera in hand like Eisenstein, in the classroom like Husserl, the Jew upsets and transforms, disturbs, revolutionizes . . . They can't avoid it. It is in their hope of the Redeemer. But if you admit, as I have, Jorge, that the Redeemer has *already come into the world*, you can change the world in His name without paralyzing yourself with millennial expectations, with hopes that the Second Coming will change everything the moment it happens."

"You talk as if the heirs of Jewish messianic thought were modern progressives, even Marxists," exclaimed Jorge.

"They are, don't you realize that?" said Raquel. Her voice was urgent. "And that's fine. They're the ones who await the millennial change, and in the meantime their impatience leads them to discover relativity, film, phenomenology, on the one hand, but on the other it induces them to commit all sorts of crime in the name of the promise. Without realizing it, they are executioners of the very future they desire so intensely."

"But the worst enemies of the Jews are these Nazis walking the streets in their swastikas and brown uniforms."

"It's because there can't be two chosen people. It's either the Jews or the Germans."

"But the Jews aren't killing Germans, Raquel."

"There's the difference. The Hebrew messianic spirit sublimates itself creatively in art, science, philosophy. It becomes creative because otherwise it's defenseless. The Nazis have no creative talent. They have only a genius for death, they're the geniuses of death. But fear the day when Israel decides to arm herself and loses her creative genius in the name of military success."

"Perhaps the Nazis won't allow them, as a nation, any other option. Perhaps the Jews will tire of being history's eternal victims. Sacrificial lambs."

"I pray they never become anyone's executioners. I pray the Jews will never have *their* Jews."

"I hope you realize that the Catholic Church is not innocent of crimes, Raquel. Remember, I'm a Spaniard, and you, in your way, are, too."

"I prefer the cynicism of the Catholic Church to the pharisaism of the Communist Church. We Catholics judge . . ."

"Bravo for the obsessive plural. I kiss you, my love."

"Don't be a clown, Jorge. I'm telling you, we judge the crimes of the Church because they're betraying a promise already carried out, an obligation: the imitation of Christ. The Communists can't judge the crimes of their church because they feel it would betray a promise that is to be carried out in the future. That is still not incarnate."

"Are you planning to enter a religious order? Am I going to have to become a Don Juan to seduce you in a convent?"

"Don't joke. And keep your hands to yourself, Don Juan."

"No, I'm not joking. If I'm following you correctly, this Christian purity that requires obedience to Jesus' teachings can only be put into practice if you withdraw to a convent. *Get thee to a nunnery*, Rachel!"

"No, it must be practiced in the world. Besides, how could I become a nun after knowing you?"

Together they'd taken Husserl's courses with an almost sacred devotion. They studied with the master but without realizing his power, because Husserl guided them so discreetly, keeping them independent of him, motivated by him but free thanks to the wings he gave them.

"Let's see now, George, what does Husserl mean when he talks about regional psychology?"

"I think he's referring to the way of being concrete that emotions, acts, and understanding have. What he's asking us to do is to suspend our opinion as long as we don't see all those proofs as original phenomena—in flesh and bone, as he says. First we open our eyes wide to see what's around us in our so-called region, *there*, where we really are. Philosophy comes later."

They walked a lot at night through the old university city right up to where the Black Forest begins, exploring the walls of the Gothic cathedral, getting lost in the medieval landscapes, crossing the bridges over the Dreisam as it rushes to join the Rhine.

Freiburg was like an ancient stone queen with her feet in the water and a crown of pines. The two students strolled around it, elaborating and reelaborating the lessons of the day, arm in arm at first, later hand in hand, astonished that Husserl himself was elaborating. He was nervous and noble, with a very high forehead that cleared the way for a concerned brow and menacing eyebrows, his straight nose sniffing out ideas, and his long beard and mustache covering wide lips, as wide as those of some philosophic animal, a mutant that had emerged from the nourishing water of the first creation onto an unknown land, committed to enunciating more ideas than those that fit in a speech. Husserl's words could not keep pace with his thought.

Everyone called him "the master." Naked in the eyes of his students, he proposed to them a philosophy without dogma or conclusions, open at all times to rectification and to the criticism of the professor and his students. Everyone knew that the Husserl of Freiburg was not the Husserl of Halle, where he had invented phenomenology on the basis of a simple proposal: first we accept experience, then we think. Nor was he the Husserl of Göttingen, who had focused his attention on *that which has yet to be interpreted*, because in it the mystery of things might reside. He was the Husserl of Freiburg, Jorge and Raquel's teacher, a man for whom humanity's moral freedom depended on one thing: the vindication of life in the face of everything that threatens it. He was the Husserl who'd seen Europe collapse during the Great War.

"I don't understand, George. He's asking us to reduce phenomena to pure consciousness, to a kind of cellar beneath which it cannot be reduced further. Can't we excavate more, go deeper?"

"Well, I think that nature, the body, and the mind are in that cellar, as you call it. And that's quite a lot. *E doppo?* Where does the old boy want to lead us?"

As if he were reading his students' thoughts with his hawklike eyes, which contrasted so savagely with his stiff butterfly collar, his shirtfront, his vest crossed by a watch chain, his old-fashioned black frock coat, his trousers that tended to hang over his short black boots, Husserl told them that after the Great War, Europe's spiritual world had collapsed, and that if he was preaching a reduction of thought to the very foundations of the mind and of nature, it was only the better to renovate European life, history, society, and language.

"I can't conceive of a world without Europe or Europe without Germany. A European Germany that would be part of the best Europe has promised to the world. I'm not, ladies and gentlemen, creating an abstract philosophy. I'm firmly rooted in the best we've done. That which can survive us. Our culture. That which can inspire your children and grandchildren. I won't see it. That's why I teach it."

Then Raquel and Jorge went out to celebrate in a jolly student *Keller*, which they usually avoided because of its noisy camaraderie, but that night everyone was shocked or amused at the toasts the couple made with their steins of beer on high: To intersubjectivity! To society, language, and the history that relates it all! We are not separated! We are a we, linked by language, community, and past!

They aroused laughter, sympathy, commotion, and shouts: When are you getting married? Can two philosophers get along in bed? Is it true you're going to name your first son Socrates? Oh, intersubjectivity, come to me, let me interpenetrate you!

They went to the cathedral after running their amazed, intelligent, and sensual eyes over the outside, and discovered, in that famous minster, finished at the dawn of the sixteenth century, a perfect illustration of what concerned them, as if Husserl's lessons had returned not to complement but to revive the tympanum of original sin which here, on one flank of the cathedral, preceded the Creation shown on the archivault. This told us that the Creation redeemed sin and left it behind; the Fall was not the consequence of Creation. There is no Fall, the Freiburg lovers told each other, there is Origin and then there is Creation.

On the west side of the cathedral, Satan, posing as the Prince of the World, leads a procession that walks away not only from original sin but from divine Creation. Facing this satanic procession, the main door of the cathedral opens, and it is there, not outside but inside, or rather at the very entrance to the interior, that Redemption is described and declared.

They went through that door, and almost as if at communion, kneeling next to each other, without any fear of seeming ridiculous, they prayed aloud:

*we shall return to ourselves*
*we shall think as if we'd founded the world*
*we shall be the living subjects of history*
*we shall live the world of life*

The Nazis forced Husserl out of Freiburg and out of Germany. The old exile continued teaching in Vienna and Prague, with the Wehrmacht always one step behind him. They allowed him to return to die in his beloved Freiburg, but the philosopher had said, "In the heart of every Jew there is absolutism and martyrdom." By contrast, his disciple Edith Stein, who became a Carmelite nun after renouncing Israel and converting to Christianity, would say that same year: "Disasters will rain on Germany when God avenges the atrocities committed against the Jews." It was the year of Kristallnacht, on November 9, organized by Goebbels to destroy synagogues, Jewish businesses, and Jews. Hitler announced his intention to annihilate the Jewish race in Europe once and for all.

It was the same year that Jorge Maura met Laura Díaz in Mexico and Raquel Mendes-Alemán, with the Star of David sewn to her bosom, greeted the SS in the streets with the shout "Christ be blessed!" which she repeated on the ground, bloody, kicked, and punched. "Christ be blessed!"

On March 3, 1939, the *Prinz Eugen* of the Lloyd Trieste line sailed from Hamburg with 224 Jewish passengers on board, all convinced they would be the last to leave Germany after the terror of Kristallnacht, and saved because of a series of circumstances, some attributable to the Nazis' mathematical madness—who is Jewish? only the child of Jewish parents, but what about the child with one Jewish parent? what about those with fewer than three Aryan grandparents, etc., etc., traced back through the generations to Abraham—others to the wealth of certain Jews who could buy freedom by turning over to the Nazis their money, paintings, homes, furniture (this was the case with Ludwig Wittgenstein's family, when Austria was annexed to the Reich); still others thanks to old friends who were now Nazis but who kept a warm memory of Jewish friends; others deriving from amorous favors granted to a high-ranking officer in the regime in order to save parents and siblings, as Judith did in the Bible, though this Holofernes was immortal: 卐 ; still others indebted to consular officials who, with or without their government's authorization, interceded on behalf of individual Jews.

The same day the SS beat her, Raquel began to wear the cross of Christ next to the Star of David, † ✡, with the result that she was locked into her small apartment in Hamburg, the double provocation meaning that the SS would be waiting at the door of her house with ferocious dogs, clubs, warning her, come out, if you dare, Jewish whore, rotten seed of Abraham, Slavic infestation, Levantine flea, gypsy chancre, come out, if you dare, Andalusian hetaíra, try to find food, scrape around in the corners of your pigsty, pig that you are, eat dust and cockroaches, if Jews can eat gold, they can also eat rats.

The neighbors were warned that if they gave me food, their rations would be taken away, if they did it again, they would be sent to a camp. I, Raquel Mendes-Alemán, decided to die of hunger for the sake of my Jewish race and my Catholic religion; I decided, George, to be the absolute witness of my age, and I knew I would have no salvation when the Nazis declared that "our worst enemies are the Jewish Catholics." It was then I opened my window and shouted into the street, "St. Paul said, I am a Jew! I am a Jew!" and my neighbors threw stones at me and two minutes later a burst of machine-gun fire broke my windows and I had to curl up in a corner, until the Mexican consul, Salvador Elizondo, arrived with a safe-conduct pass and told me you'd interceded so I could board the *Prinz Eugen* and escape to the freedom of the New World. I'd sworn I would stay in Germany and die in Germany as testimony to my faith in Christ and Moses. Then I gave in, my distant love, and I knew why—not out of fear of them, not out of fear that I'd be taken to one of those places whose names we all knew by then— Dachau, Oranienburg, Buchenwald—but out of shame that my own Church and my own Father, the Pope, did not raise their voices to defend us, to defend all Jews, but also Catholic Jews like me. Rome made me an orphan, Pius XII never spoke in defense of the human race, George, so it was not only that he did not speak up for the Jews but that the Holy Father never extended his hand to the human race. You did, Mexico did. There would be no better opportunity than the *Prinz Eugen*, which was going to take us to America. The Mexican President, Lázaro Cárdenas, was going to speak with Franklin Roosevelt to allow us to disembark in Florida.

During the nine-day crossing, I became friendly with the other Jewish fugitives. Some were shocked at my Catholic faith, others understood me, but all thought it was a failed trick on my part to escape the concentration camps. There are no uniform communities, but Husserl was right when he asked us, Can't we all return to a world where life can start over again, where we can find ourselves again *as fellow human beings?*

I wanted to take communion, but the Lutheran pastor on board refused to administer it. I reminded him that his legal function on a ship was to be nondenominational and to attend to all faiths. He had the effrontery to say to me, Sister, these are not legal times.

I'm a provocateur, George, I admit it. But don't accuse me of pride, of the Greek hubris we learned about in Freiburg. I'm a *humble* provocateur. Every day during our collective breakfast in the dining room, the first thing I did was take a piece of bread in one hand, make the sign of the cross with the other, and say in an even voice, "This is my body," before putting it in my mouth. I scandalize, irritate, annoy. The captain tells me, you're putting the other passengers of your race in danger. I laugh in his face. "This is the first time we've been persecuted for racial reasons, do you realize that, Herr Kapitan? We've always been persecuted for religious reasons." A lie. Ferdinand and Isabella chased us out of Spain to protect their "purity of blood." But the captain had his answer. "Frau Mendes, there are agents of the German government on board. They're watching all of us. They are fully prepared to use the slightest pretext to abort this voyage. If they permitted it, it was as a concession to Roosevelt in exchange for which the United States would maintain its limited quotas for the admission of German Jews. Each party is putting the other to the test. You must understand that. This is how the Führer always proceeds. We have a small opportunity. Control yourself. Don't throw away the chance to save yourself and your comrades. Control yourself."

George, my love, it was all in vain. The American authorities did not allow us to disembark in Miami. The captain was ordered to go to Havana and wait for the American permit. It didn't come. Roosevelt is constrained by public opinion, which is averse to allowing more foreigners in the United States. The quotas, they say, are filled. No one speaks up on our behalf. No one. I've been told that under the previous pope, Pius XI, an encyclical had been prepared about the "unity of the human race threatened by racists and anti-Semites," but he died before promulgating it. My Church is not defending us. Democracy is not defending us. George, I depend on you. George, please save me. Come to Havana before your Raquel can no longer even weep. Didn't Jesus say, "When you are persecuted, flee to another city"? Christ be praised!

## 4.

MAURA: Let me ask you something, Vidal. Doesn't the ideal you
defend become impossible whenever an individual is murdered for

the sin of thinking with us but differently from us? Because all of us defend the Republic and oppose fascists, but we're all different, I mean that Azaña is different from Prieto or Companys or Durruti, and José Díaz is different from Largo Caballero, as Enrique Lister is different from Juan Negrín. But none of them individually or taken as a group is like Franco, Mola, Serrano Súñer, or the repressor from Asturias, Doval.

VIDAL: We haven't excluded anyone. There's room for everyone in the broad front of the left-wing movements.

MAURA: As long as the left is struggling for power. But when it gets power, the Communist Party sets about eliminating all those who don't think as you do.

VIDAL: For instance?

MAURA: Bukharin.

VIDAL: Pick another man, one who isn't a traitor.

MAURA: Victor Serge. And another question: is it revolutionary to take no interest in the fate of a comrade stripped of public position, deported without trial, separated forever from friends and family, just because he's *only an individual* and a singular, solitary individual doesn't count in the grand collective epic of history? I don't see Bukharin's treason. He might have saved Russia from Stalin's terror with his project for a pluralist, human, free socialism, which would have been stronger for all those reasons.

VIDAL: Let's get this over with, and *revenons à nos moutons.* What should the Republic have done, as far as you, Maura and Baltazar, are concerned, to reconcile victory and ethics?

MAURA: Life has to be changed, Rimbaud said. The world has to be changed, Marx said. They are both wrong. We have to diversify life. We have to pluralize the world. We have to give up the romantic illusion that humanity will be happy only if it recovers its lost unity. We have to give up the illusion of totality. The word says it all: there's only a slight difference between the desire for totality and totalitarian reality.

VIDAL: You've got a perfect right to disdain unity. But without unity you can't win a war.

MAURA: But you do win a better society—isn't that what we all want?—

VIDAL: What do you mean, Maura?

MAURA: —by placing a value on difference.

VIDAL: And identity?

MAURA: Identity fortifies a culture of differences. Or do you think that a liberated humanity would be a perfectly united humanity, identical, uniform?

VIDAL: There's no logic to what you're saying.

MAURA: That's because logic is only a thing, it's a way of saying, Only *this* has meaning. You, as a Marxist, should think about dialectic, which at least offers an option, this or that.

VIDAL: And gives you unity in synthesis.

MAURA: And immediately redivides into thesis and antithesis.

VIDAL: So what do you believe in?

MAURA: In both and more. Does that seem insane to you?

VIDAL: No. But politically useless.

BALTAZAR: May I say something, my Socratic friends? I don't believe in a happy millennium. I believe in the opportunities of freedom. All the time. Every day. Unlike the poet Bécquer's swallows—let them pass, and they will not return. And if I have to choose the lesser of two evils, I'd rather choose neither. I think politics is secondary to personal integrity, because without that it isn't worthwhile living in society. And I'm very afraid that if we, the Republic that we all are, give no proof that we value morality above *means*, the people will turn their backs on us and follow the fascists, because fascism has no doubts about immorality though we may.

MAURA: And your conclusion, Basilio?

BALTAZAR: That the true revolutionary cannot talk about revolution because nothing deserves that name in today's world. The way you can identify real revolutionaries is by the fact that they never talk about revolution. And yours, Jorge?

MAURA: I find myself between two truths. One is that the world is going to save itself, the other that it's doomed. Both are true in a double sense. Corrupt society is doomed, but so is revolutionary society.

VIDAL: And you, Laura Díaz? You haven't said a word. What do you
think of all this, comrade?

Laura looked down for an instant and then gazed tenderly at each
one. Finally, she spoke: "I really enjoy seeing that the hardest-fought
polemic among men always reveals what they have in common."

"You two are very much in love," said Basilio Baltazar, looking at
Jorge and Laura. "How do you measure love in the context of everything that's going on?"

Vidal joined in. "Rephrase the question like this: Does only personal happiness count and not the disaster about to engulf millions of
people?"

"I'm asking a different question, Mr. Vidal," said Laura Díaz. "Can
the love two people share make up for all the unhappiness in the
world?"

"Yes, I suppose there are ways of redeeming the world, whether
we're as solitary as our friend Basilio or as affiliated as I am," Vidal
responded, with mixed humility and arrogance.

The look on Vidal's face did not escape Basilio or Jorge. Laura saw it
but did not know how to understand it. What her intuition told her
was that this was the *tertulia* of farewells, that there was a tension, a
sadness, a resignation, a modesty, and, encompassing them all, a love in
those exchanged glances which was the prelude to a fatal separation.
For that reason the arguments were as definitive as a tombstone. They
were farewells: visions lost forever, they were the lies in heaven that on
earth are called politics. Between the two lies, we construct a painful
truth, history. But what was there in Basilio Baltazar's brilliant, sad
eyes but a bed with the traces of love, what was there in Domingo
Vidal's frowning gaze but a parade of visions lost forever, what was
there in Jorge's melancholy and sensual face, her own Jorge Maura . . . ?
And what was there, farther back, in the eyes of the mayor of Santa
Fe de Palencia but the public secret that he'd ordered his own daughter shot to prove he loved a country, Spain, and an ideology, Communism? And in the eyes of Clemencia standing before the mirror, was

there only the repugnant vision of an ultra-pious, hypocritical old lady satisfied with suppressing the beauty and youth of her possible rival, her own daughter?

Basilio embraced Jorge and told him, "We've wept so much that we'll know the future when it comes."

"Life goes on," said Vidal in farewell, embracing both comrades at the same time.

"And fortune ebbs and flows, brother," said Maura.

"Let's grab opportunity by the tail." Vidal moved away from them, laughing. "Let's not mock fortune, and let's put aside intemperate pleasures. We'll see one another in Mexico."

But they were in Mexico. They said goodbye in the same place where they met. Were the three speaking in the name of defeat? No, thought Laura Díaz, they are speaking in the name of what is now beginning, exile, and exile has no country, it isn't named Mexico, Argentina, or England. Exile is another country.

## 5.

They covered her mouth with a bandage and ordered all the windows surrounding the Santa Fe plaza shut. Nevertheless, as if nothing could silence the scandal of her death, great shouts, barbarous shouts that perhaps only the woman condemned to death could hear, harassed her all the way from the Roman gate to the bullring. Unless, that is, the neighbors lied, because that dawn they all swore they heard shouts or songs that came from the depth of the dying night.

The windows were closed. The victim was gagged. Only Pilar Méndez's eyes were shouting—her mouth was shut, as if the execution had already taken place. "Gag her," begged Clemencia, the wife of the justice-bound mayor, "the only thing I don't want is to hear her shout, I don't want to know what she shouted." "It will be a clean execution. Don't get worked up."

I can smell death, Pilar Méndez was saying to herself, stripped now of her fur mantle, wearing only a Carmelite robe that did not hide her nipples, feet bare, feeling with her feet and her sense of smell, I can smell death, all the graves of Spain are open, what will be left of Spain but the blood the wolves will drink? We Spaniards are hounds of death, we smell it, and we follow it until we're killed.

Perhaps that was what she thought. Or perhaps the three friends, soldiers of the Republic, thought it when they stayed outside the city gates. They were all ears, attentive only to the report of the rifles that would announce the death of the woman for whom they were ready to give more than their own lives, their honor as Republican soldiers, and also their honor as men united forever by the defense of a woman loved by one of them.

They say that at the end she was dragged through the sand, raising the dust of the plaza until she was covered with dirt and disappeared in a granulated cloud. The truth is, at that dawn, fire and rain, mortal enemies, sealed a pact and fell together on the town of Santa Fe de Palencia, silencing the thunder of the rifles when Basilio, Domingo, and Jorge took root in the world as a final homage to the life of a sacrificed woman. They looked at one another and ran to the mountains to advise the outposts not to put out the fires, that the citadel of the Republic had not fallen.

"What proof do you have?"

A handful of ashes in their hands.

They did not see the autumn river clogged with leaves, struggling to be reborn from the dry summer.

They did not imagine that the ice of the coming winter would paralyze the wings of eagles in midair.

They were very far away when the crowd's shouting whipped like a scourge the plaza where Pilar Méndez was shot and where her father the mayor said to the people, I acted for the Party and for the Republic, and didn't dare glance at the shutter through which his wife, Clemencia, glared at him with satisfied hatred, secretly saying to him, Tell them, tell them the truth, you didn't order her killed, the one who hated her was her mother, I killed her even though I loved her, even though the two of us were followers of Franco, in the same party, both Catholics, but different in age and beauty: Clemencia ran to her bedroom mirror, tried to recover in her aged face the features of her dead daughter, Pilar dead would be less than an unsatisfied old woman plagued with hot flashes and the rumors that remained buried between her legs. She superimposed the features of her young daughter over her own old ones.

"Don't put out the fires. The city has not surrendered."

Laura and Jorge walked along Cinco de Mayo in the direction of the Alameda. Basilio strolled off in the opposite direction, toward the Cathedral. Vidal signaled to stop the Roma–Mérida bus and caught it on the run. But each one looked back to see the others one last time, as if they were sending a final message. "Never abandon the friend who was with you in disaster. Friends save one another or die together."

## 15. Colonia Roma: 1941

WHEN JORGE MAURA LEFT, Laura Díaz returned to her home and no longer went out at night, no longer disappeared for eternal days. She was disconcerted. She hadn't told Juan Francisco the truth, and at first she reproached herself. I did the right thing, it all turned out badly. It was a good thing I was cautious. Was I a coward? Was I very clever? Should I have told Juan Francisco everything, betting he'd accept it, risking a break and then finding myself alone again with neither of them, neither Jorge nor Juan Francisco? Didn't Maura say this was a matter of our intimate life, that it was sacred, that there was no reason, no moral imperative, obliging either of us to tell about our intimacy?

Back in the house on Avenida Sonora, she spent a great deal of time looking at herself in the mirror. Her face hadn't changed despite the storms rocking it from within. Until now. But from that moment on, she was sometimes the girl she was before and other times an unknown woman—a *changed* woman. How would her sons, her husband, see her? Santiago and Danton did not look at her, avoided her eyes, walked quickly, sometimes running the way boys run, skipping along as if they were still children, but not joyfully. They were running away from her, so they wouldn't have to admit either her presence or her absence.

So they don't have to admit I wasn't faithful. That their mother was unfaithful.

They didn't look at her, but she listened to them. The house wasn't large, and the silence amplified the echoes; the house turned into a seashell.

"Why the hell did Papa and Mama get married?"

She had no other company but the mirrors. She looked at herself and saw more than two ages. She saw two personalities. She saw the rational Laura and the impulsive Laura, a vital Laura and a spineless Laura. She saw her conscience and her desire, locked in battle on a glass surface, smooth as those frozen lakes where battles were fought in Russian movies. She would have gone off with Jorge Maura if he'd asked, gone away with him, abandoned everything . . .

One afternoon, she was sitting on the little balcony that looked out over Avenida Sonora. She took four more chairs out there and put a fifth in the middle for herself. After a while, Auntie María de la O came in, dragging her feet, and sat next to her, sighing. Then López Greene came home from the union, found them there, and sat down next to Laura. Later on, the boys came home from school, saw the unusual scene, and took the two remaining chairs, one at each end.

It isn't their mother who's convoking them, Laura herself said, the place and the time of day convoke us. Mexico City, an afternoon in 1941, when the shadows lengthen and the very white volcanoes seem to float over a burning bed of clouds, and the barrel organ plays that old song "Los Golondrinas," and posters for the recent election campaign—AVILA CAMACHO/ALMAZÁN—have begun to peel, and that first afternoon of the silent reencounter of the family contains all the afternoons to come, afternoons of dust storms and afternoons of rains that settle the unquiet dust and perfume the Valley where the city, indecisive between its past and future, is located; the barrel organ plays "Amor Chiquito," the maids hanging out the wash on the terraces sing "I'm walking along the tropical path," and teenagers in the street dance *tambora* and more *tambora* but what will be will be, cabs go by, ice trucks pass, and vendors with their jicamas sprinkled with lemon and chile powder, the candy vendor sets up, Adams Chicklets, Mimí bars, Mexican treats—*jamoncillo* and sweet potato—the kiosk closes down with its alarming headlines about the war the Allies are losing and its comics about Blondie and Dagwood and its exotic Argentine ladies' magazines, *Leoplán* and *El Hogar*, and for children, *Billiken*, neighborhood movie theaters announce Mexican films with Sara García, the Soler brothers, Sofía Alvarez, Gloria Marín, and Arturo de Córdoba, the boys, on the sly, would buy cigarettes—Alas, Faros, and Delicados—at the tobacco stand on the corner, all the kids would play hopscotch, trying to land peach pits in improvised holes, exchange bottle caps from Orange Crush, grape Chaparritas; green buses from the Roma–Piedad line race the brown-and-cream buses from the Roma–Mérida line: the Bosque de Chapultepec with an atmosphere of moss and eucalyptus rises up behind the Bauhaus-style houses, continues to ascend to the symbolic miracle of the Alcázar, where Danton and Santiago go every afternoon before coming home, as if they were really conquering an abrupt, mysterious castle reached by scaling steep paths and asphalt roads, and linked routes that hold the surprise of the grand esplanade above the city, its pigeon flights, and its mysterious rooms filled with nineteenth-century furniture.

The boys are sitting next to Laura, Juan Francisco, and the old aunt, thankful that the city offers them this repertory of movement, color, aromas, song, and the crown of Mexico, a castle that reminds all of them that there is more than we imagine in the world, there is more . . .

Jorge Maura disappeared, and something she would agree to call "reality," but very much in quotation marks, reappeared behind the romantic fog. Her husband was the first reality. He's the one who reappears first, telling the boys (Santiago is twenty, Danton nineteen), "I love her."

He accepts me, she said, cruelly and ungenerously, he accepts me even though I never told him the truth, he accepts me because he knows that his own cruelty and crudeness sanctioned my freedom, the idea that "I should have married a baker who doesn't care about the rolls he makes." Then she realized that his declaring he loved her in the presence of his sons was proof of his failure and at the same time also proof of his possible nobility. Laura Díaz embraced the idea of a regeneration for all of them, parents and sons, by means of a love she had lived with such intensity that now she had enough left over to give away to her own.

She would wake up next to her husband—they'd begun sleeping together again—and hear her husband's first words, every morning. "Something's not right."

Those words saved him and reconciled her. To make her happy, Juan Francisco, thanks to a rediscovered nobility that was perhaps innate in him, was the one who spoke to Danton and Santiago about their mother, recalling when they met, what she was like, how nervous, how independent, telling them they should try to understand her. Laura was offended when she heard him; she should have thanked her husband for interceding, but his intercession offended her, however briefly, and then in the afternoon ceremony—when they sat down in the dusk of the Valley of Mexico, opposite Chapultepec Castle and the volcanoes, which was now the way they all found to say, We're together despite everything—she said out loud one afternoon: "I fell in love with a man. That's why I didn't come home. I was with that man. I would have given my life for him. I would have abandoned all of you for him. But he left me. That's why I'm back here with you. I could have stayed by myself, but I was afraid. I came back looking for protection. I felt abandoned. I'm not asking for forgiveness. I'm asking that at your age, boys, you begin to understand that life isn't easy, that we all make mistakes and wound those we love because we love ourselves more than we love anything else, including the person who fills us with passion at a given moment. Each of you, when the time comes, will want to follow your own path and not the one your father or I would have wanted. Think about me when you do that. Forgive me."

There were no words, no emotions. Only María de la O allowed old memories to pass through her eyes, now clouded by cataracts, memories of a girl in a Veracruz brothel and a gentleman who rescued her from abandonment and integrated her into this family, overcoming the prejudices of race, of class, and of an immoral morality that in the name of convention takes life instead of giving it.

Laura and Juan Francisco invited each other to surrender, and the boys stopped running, fighting, skipping to avoid their mother's face. Santiago slept and lived with the door to his bedroom open, something entirely new to his mother, who interpreted it as an act of freedom and transparency, although it was also, perhaps, a culpable rebellion: I have nothing to hide. Danton would laugh at him: What's your next stunt going to be? Going to jerk off in the middle of the street? No, answered his older brother, I'm trying to say that we're enough on our own. Who, you and I? I'd like that, Danton. Well, I'm enough on my own, but with the door closed just in case; come and see the pictures I've cut out of *Vea* whenever you like, incredible babes, unbelievably sexy . . .

Just as Laura would look at herself in the mirror when she came home, almost always thinking that her face didn't change no matter how many vicissitudes rocked it, she discovered that Santiago looked at himself as well, especially in windows, and seemed surprised at himself and by himself, as if he were constantly discovering another person there with him. Perhaps only his mother thought those things. Santiago was no longer a boy. He was something new. Laura, in front of the mirror, confirmed that sometimes she was the unknown woman—a changeling. Would her son see her that way? She was going to be forty-three.

She didn't dare go in his room. The open door was an invitation but a jealous one, even, paradoxically, a prohibition. Look at me, but don't come in. He was drawing. With a round mirror so he could look at himself out of the corner of his eye and create—not copy, not reproduce—the face of Santiago which his mother recognized and memorized only when she saw the self-portrait her son was drawing: the sketch became Santiago's true face, revealed it, forced Laura to realize that she'd gone, returned, and hadn't really looked at her sons. How right they were not to look at her, to run, to sneak off when she didn't look at them, either; they reproached her more for not looking at them than they did for not living with them: they wanted to be seen by her, and since she didn't see them, Santiago discovered himself first in a mirror that seemed to supply the gaze he would have wanted to receive from his parents, his brother, society, always hostile to the adolescent who bursts into it with his insolent promise and ignorant self-sufficiency. A portrait and then a self-portrait.

And Danton—could there be any doubt?—discovered himself in the brightly lit store window of the city.

She returned as if they didn't exist, as if they'd never felt forgotten or hurt or eager to communicate to her what Santiago was making in that moment: a portrait she could have known during her absence, a portrait the son could have sent to his mother if Laura, as she'd wished, had gone to live with her Spaniard, her "hidalgo."

Look, Mother. This is who I am. Never come back again.

Laura imagined that she'd never have another face to give her son but the one her son was giving her now: wide forehead, amber eyes set far apart, not dark as in reality, straight nose and thin, defiant lips, straight hair, messy, of a rich, lustrous chestnut, tremulous chin; even in the self-portrait the chin that wanted to bolt from the face, brave but exposed to all the blows of the world. He was Santiago the Younger.

He had several books open and arranged around him. Van Gogh and Egon Schiele.

Where did you get them? Who gave them to you?

The German Bookstore here in Colonia Hipódromo.

Laura was about to call him a chip off the old block, your German stock's coming to the surface, but he anticipated her: Don't worry, they're German Jews in exile in Mexico.

In the nick of time.

Yes, Mama, in the nick of time.

She described Santiago's features, which the self-portrait translated and facilitated for her, but she didn't take note of the thickness of the strokes, the somber light that allowed the spectator to approach that tragic, predestined face, as if the young artist had discovered that a face revealed the tragic necessity of each life, but also its possible freedom to overcome failures. Laura stared at that portrait of her son by her son and thought about the tragedy of Raquel Mendes-Alemán and Jorge Maura's tragedy with her. Was there a difference between the dark fatality of Raquel's destiny, which she shared with the entire Jewish people, and the dramatic, honorable but ultimately superfluous response of the Spanish hidalgo Jorge Maura, who went to Havana to save Raquel just as he'd tried to save Pilar in Spain? Along with his self-portrait, Santiago gave Laura a light, an answer she wanted to make her own. We have to make time for the things that have taken place. We have to allow pain to become knowledge in some way. Why did her son's self-portrait presage these ideas?

So he and she were equals. Santiago looked at her and in a matter-of-fact way accepted her looking at him from his bedroom doorway.

She didn't separate them. They were different. Santiago assimilated everything; Danton rejected, eliminated whatever crossed his path or blocked his way: he could make a pompous teacher look ridiculous in class or, during recess, thrash a classmate he found annoying. Nevertheless, it was Santiago who better resisted the impositions the world put on him, while Danton was the one who finally accepted them after staging a violent rejection. Danton was the protagonist in the dramas about personal liberty, puberty's declarations of independence, I'm grown up now, it's my life, not yours, I'll come home when I like because I control my own time, and it was he who came home drunk, it was he who took the beatings and got gonorrhea, he who shamefacedly begged for money; he was the freer of the two brothers but also the more dependent. He made a show of himself, the more easily to give in.

While still a student, Santiago got a job working on the restoration of frescoes by José Clemente Orozco, and then Laura introduced him to Frida and Diego, so he could be Rivera's assistant on the National Palace mural project. Santiago punctually turned his salary over to his mother, as if he were a child in Dickens being exploited in a tannery. She would laugh and promise to put it aside only for him.

"It will be our little secret."

"I hope it won't be the only one," said Santiago, impulsively kissing her.

"You love him more because he forgave you," said Danton insolently. Laura couldn't stop herself from slapping him across the face.

"I won't say another word," said Danton.

Laura Díaz had hidden her passion for Jorge Maura, her passion with Jorge Maura, and she now decided not to hide her passion for and with her son Santiago, almost as an unconscious compensation for the silence that had surrounded her love of Maura. She wouldn't deny she preferred Santiago over Danton. She also knew it wasn't conventionally acceptable. "Either they're both your sons or both your stepsons." It didn't matter. Near him, watching him work at home, go out, come back on time, hand over his money, tell her his projects: this proximity wove itself into a complicity between mother and son, which was also a preference, a word that means putting ahead. Santiago began to occupy that place in Laura's life, the first place. It was almost as if with the fading of Jorge Maura's love, which revealed her to herself as Laura Díaz, a unique woman, a passionate woman, a woman who would leave everything for her lover's sake, all her passion had transferred to Santiago, not the passion of the mother for the son because that was only love and even preference, but the passion of the boy for life and for creation: that's what Laura began to make hers because Santiago was giving it to her independently of himself, free of any vanity.

Santiago, her son, the second Santiago, *was* what he did, *loved* what he did, *gave* what he did. He was swiftly progressing, assimilating what he'd only seen in reproductions, books, and magazines, or studying the Mexican murals. He's discovering the other who's inside him. His mother is discovering him at the same time. Santiago trembled with creative anticipation whenever he had a blank piece of paper before him or, later, when he stood at the easel Laura gave him for his birthday.

He transmits his tremor. He infuses excitement into the canvas he takes possession of in the same way he excites anyone watching him. He's a committed being.

Laura was beginning to live all too much from her son's artistic tremor. Watching him work and progress, she allowed herself to be infected by anticipation, as if it were a fever the boy was carrying. But he was a happy boy. He liked to eat and asked for all sorts of Mexican snacks, inviting Laura to Yucatán banquets at the Círculo del Sureste in Lucerna Street with their *papadzules* in egg and almond sauce or sweet

Neapolitan cheese, inviting her to the courtyard of the Bellinghausen restaurant on Londres Street during the season when maguey worms were served with guacamole, followed by eggnog flans, inviting her to the Danubio on Uruguay Street to enjoy scallops with a dash of lemon or with thick chipotle chile sauce—aromatic and better than all the mustards in the world.

I'll pay, Mama, let me shoot this time.

Danton's angry stare harassed them, the dragging footsteps of Juan Francisco's old slippers harassed them. Laura didn't care in the least, because life with Santiago was perfection itself for Laura Díaz this year of 1941, when she recovered her home and prolonged, sometimes with feelings of guilt, her love for Maura in her love for Santiago, knowing too that this Santiago the Second was the continuation of her love for Santiago the First, as if there were no power in heaven or on earth that could force her into a pause, a blameworthy or redemptive solitude, either. The hiatus separating brother, lover, and son was imperceptible. It lasted during a pair of afternoons on a balcony facing the vibrant park and the extinguished volcanoes.

"I'm going to Havana to rescue Raquel Mendes-Alemán. The *Prinz Eugen* was not allowed in U.S. waters, and the Cubans do what the Americans tell them to do. The ship is going to sail back to Germany. This time, no one will get out alive. Once again, Hitler set a trap for the democracies. He told them, Well now, look here, I'm sending you a boatload of Jews, give them asylum. Now he'll say, Just look, you don't want them either. Well, I want them even less, so they'll all go to their deaths and so much for that little problem. Laura, if I get there on time, I can save Raquel."

Will we ever make peace, Juan Francisco?

What more do you want from me? I let you come back to my house. I asked our sons to respect you.

Don't you realize that someone else is living in this house with us?

No. Whose ghost is that?

Two ghosts. You and I. Before.

I have no idea what to do. Calm down, will you? How's your work going?

Well. The Riveras have no idea how to manage paperwork and need someone to answer letters, save documents, review contracts.

Good. Congratulations. It doesn't take up too much time?

Three times a week. I want to put a lot of work in here in the house.

Her husband's "good" meant "it's about time," but Laura paid no attention. Sometimes she thought that marrying him was like turning the other cheek to destiny. It turned what was and perhaps always should have been an enigma, a distance, into a daily reality: the mystery of Juan Francisco López Greene's true life. She wouldn't ask him aloud what she'd asked herself so many times. What did her husband do? Where did he fail? Was he a hero who had tired of being one?

Someday you'll understand, he'd say.

Someday I'll understand, she repeated until she convinced herself the expression was her own.

Laura. I'm tired, I get a good salary from the Workers Confederation and the Union Congress. We lack for nothing here at home. If you want to take care of Diego and Frida, that's up to you. Do you also want me to be the hero of 1908, of 1917, of the House of the Workers of the World and the Red Battalions? I can make you a list of the heroes of the Revolution. It has treated all of us justly, except the dead.

I want to know. Were you really a hero?

Juan Francisco began to laugh, he laughed his head off, coughed up phlegm and roared.

No, there were no heroes, and if there were, they were killed off right away and they were honored with statues. Really ugly ones, too, so no one would go on believing in them. In this country, even the statues are phony. They're all made of copper—you just have to scrape off the gilt. What do you expect from me? Why don't you simply respect what I was and leave it at that, dammit?

I'm making an effort to understand you, Juan Francisco. Since you won't tell me where you came from, at least tell me what you are today.

A guard. A guardian of order. An administrator of stability. We won the Revolution. It's cost us a lot to achieve peace and to have a process of peaceful succession in power without military coups. We're redistributing land, we have education, roads . . . Don't you think that's something? Would you want me to oppose all that? To end up like all those dissatisfied generals—Serrano and Arnulfo Gómez, Escobar and Saturnino Cedillo—or the philosopher Vasconcelos? They didn't even get to be heroes. They just burned out. What do you want from me, Laura?

I'm just looking for a little hole in your armor, where I can love you, Juan Francisco. I'm that stupid.

A little hole? Why, I'm a sieve, my dear!

She tried to explain to Santiago, as the boy painted, that she was delighted by his artistic spirit. She told him while his father's words were still ringing in her ears.

"Diego uses the word *élan*. He lived in France for a long time."

Santiago was painting, unabashed, a man and a woman, naked but separated, standing, staring at each other, exploring each other with their eyes. Their arms were crossed. Laura told Santiago it was very difficult for a couple to love each other forever because the spirits of two people are almost never equal. There is a moment of total identification that impassions us, a balance between the two which, unfortunately, is only a revelation that one of the two will break the balance.

"I want you to understand that about your father and me."

"Well, Mama, all you did was to anticipate him. You made him understand you were not going to be the sad one. You left that role to him."

Santiago cleaned his brushes and looked at his mother.

"And the day he dies, who'll be anticipating whom?"

How could I abandon a man so weak, Laura said to herself, then responded with strength and modesty: no, what we've got to do is to change the rules of the game, rules made by men for men and for women because only they legislate for both sexes, because the rules men make are valid both for the faithful and domestic life of women and for the unfaithful and errant life of men. The woman is always guilty of submission in one case, and in the other of rebelliousness; guilty of a fidelity that lets life pass by while she's stretched out in a cold grave with a man who doesn't desire her, or guilty of the infidelity of seeking pleasure with another in the same way her husband does, a sin for her, a prize for him, he's called Don Juan and she Doña Puta, my

God, Juan Francisco, why didn't you cheat on me in style, with some great love, instead of being a camp follower for your boss Fatso Morones? Why didn't you have a love with a woman as great, as strong, as brave as Jorge Maura, my own love?

With Danton, Juan Francisco had a relationship that paralleled Laura's with Santiago: the family formed two parties. The old man—he'd turned sixty but looked seventy—forgave every one of his younger son's tricks, gave him money, and sat him down so they both could see each other's face. He did that because neither ever opened his mouth, at least not in the presence of their two rivals in the house, Laura and Santiago. Despite the silence, Laura suspected that Juan Francisco and Danton said things to each other. The old auntie, mute by act of will, confirmed this suspicion one afternoon at the healing ceremony, at the balcony, the repeated, unifying family ritual. María de la O insisted on sitting between the father and the younger brother, separating them, but she didn't take her eyes off Laura. Then, when the elderly mulatta, dressed as always in black, had Laura's attention, she rapidly moved her own eyes, like a dark eagle whose vision was split down the middle and who could see simultaneously in two directions. Several times she glanced from Juan Francisco to Danton and from the son to the father, which said to Laura something like "they understand each other," which Laura already knew, or "they're the same," which was hard to imagine: the agile, party-loving, carefree Danton seemed the complete opposite of the parsimonious, withdrawn, and anguished Juan Francisco. Where was the relationship? Yet María de la O's intuitions were rarely mistaken.

One night, when Santiago fell asleep next to his recently acquired easel—this one a gift from Diego Rivera—Laura, who was allowed to watch him paint, covered him with a blanket and cushioned his head as best she could, very softly caressing his unfurrowed brow. Leaving his room, she heard laughter and whispering in her bedroom. She walked in without knocking and found Juan Francisco and Danton on the floor, sitting with their legs crossed, studying a spread-out map of the state of Tabasco.

"Excuse me," interrupted Laura. "It's late, and you have school tomorrow, Danton."

The boy laughed. "My best school is right here with my dad."

They'd been drinking. The bottle of Potrero rum was half empty, and Juan Francisco's alcoholic heaviness kept him from raising the hand he'd stretched out over the surface of his home state.

"Off to bed now, my fine young gentleman."

"Oh, what a pain. We were having so much fun."

"But, son, tomorrow you won't be able to hold your head up if you don't get some sleep."

"Fun, son, head, dead," rhymed Danton as he marched off.

Laura stared hard at her husband and the map.

"What place is that right under your finger?" Laura smiled. "Let me see. Macuspana. Was that just an accident, or does that mean something to you?"

"It's a place hidden in the forest."

"That much I can imagine. What's it mean to you?"

"Elzevir Almonte."

Laura couldn't speak. Like an arrow, her mind flew back to the figure of the priest from Puebla who appeared one day in Catemaco to sow intolerance, impose ridiculous moral restrictions, disturb innocence in the confessional, and disappear another fine day with the offerings to the Holy Child of Zongolica.

"Elzevir Almonte," repeated Laura in a trance, remembering the priest's question that day in confession: *Would you like to see your father's sex, child?*

"He took refuge in Tabasco. He passed himself off as a layman, of course, and no one knew where he got his money. He would go to Villahermosa once a month and the next day pay off all his debts in one shot. The day my mother died there was no priest in the entire zone. I ran everywhere shouting, My mother wants to confess, wants to go to heaven, isn't there a padre to bless her? It was then Almonte revealed he was a priest and gave my mother the last rites. I'll never forget the expression of peace on my poor old mother's face. She died thanking me for sending her to heaven. Why did you hide out here? I asked Father Elzevir. He told me, and I told him, it's time you redeemed yourself. I brought him to the Río Blanco strike. He attended the workers left wounded by the rural police. The army had killed two hundred of them. Almonte blessed each and every one. They couldn't stop him even if they were in a hurry to load the corpses onto open cars and dump them into the sea at Veracruz. But Father Elzevir was indefatigable. He got together with Margarito Ramírez, a brave worker who set fire to the company store. Then he became an outlaw on two fronts. The Church was hunting him down because of his robbery in Catemaco, the government because of his rebellion at Río Blanco. I ended up asking myself, What good are these priests? Everything Father Elzevir did he could have done without the Church. My mother was going to die with or without a blessing. Porfirio Díaz's army killed the Río Blanco workers and threw them into the sea with or without a priest's blessing, and Margarita Ramírez had no need of the priest to set fire to the store. In all good faith, I asked myself what the hell the purpose of the Church was. As if to confirm my doubts, Elzevir showed what he was made of. He went to Veracruz, and declared that everything that happened at Río Blanco was an 'anarchist conspiracy' and appeared in the newspapers alongside the U.S. consul congratulating the government for its 'decisive action.' He would have done anything to get a pardon for his robbery and for running away from Catemaco. He had betrayal in his veins. He used me when he thought we were going to win, and he betrayed us as soon as we lost. He didn't know we'd win in the long run. I came to despise him and acquired a profound hatred for the Church. That explains why I approved the persecution unleashed by Calles and why I turned in the nun Soriano. They're a plague, and we've got to be implacable with them."

"You don't owe them anything?"

"I do owe Elzevir Almonte something. He told me all about your family. He described you as the most beautiful girl in Veracruz. I think he desired you. He told me how you'd make your confession with him.

He even aroused me. I decided to meet you, Laura. I went to Xalapa to meet you."

Juan Francisco carefully folded the map. He was already in his pajamas and went to bed without another word.

Laura couldn't sleep. She was thinking hard about the immense impunity a reputation based on old sentiments can give one, as if, having drunk life's hemlock, there is nothing left but to sit back and wait for death. Do we have to suffer in order to be someone? Do we receive it or seek it out? Perhaps Juan Francisco, without realizing, would have taken the story of Father Almonte—whom she'd thought of as a refugee, more a shadow than a man, in Mutti Leticia's boardinghouse in Xalapa—as more a pain than a sin. Who knows what deep religious roots each individual and each family had in Mexico? Maybe rebelling against religion was a way of being religious. And the Revolution itself, with its national ceremonies, its civil saints and its warrior martyrs: wasn't it a parallel, lay church—just as confident that it was the depository and dispenser of health as was the Apostolic and Holy Roman Church that had educated, protected, and exploited Mexicans all at the same time since the Conquest? But in the end none of that explained or justified betraying a woman who'd been granted asylum in a home, her home, the home of Laura Díaz.

Juan Francisco was unforgivable. He would die—Laura closed her eyes to fall asleep—without his wife's forgiveness. That night, she felt herself to be more the sister of Gloria Soriano than the wife of Juan Francisco López Greene. More the sister than the wife, more the sis . . .

The fact is—she went on caviling when morning came—she didn't want to attribute the change in her husband's life, from energetic and generous labor tribune in the Revolution to second-rate politico and functionary, merely and simply to the need for survival. Perhaps the game that father and son were playing with the map held the key to Juan Francisco, beyond the poor saga of Father Almonte, beyond Danton, who could be very secretive or very much a chatterbox, even a braggart, if that suited his self-esteem, reputation, and convenience.

No, she was not going to disguise sympathies and differences in this house; here people would speak the truth from now on, just as she did, giving an example for them all. She'd confessed before her family and, instead of losing respect, had won it.

That weekend she said exactly that to Danton. "I was very frank, son."

"You confess before a husband who's impotent, one son who's gay, another who's drunk, and an aunt born in a whorehouse. Wow, what bravery!"

She'd slapped him once. She'd sworn never to do it again.

"What do you want me to tell you about my father? If you slept with him, you could find out all his secrets. Be braver, Mama. I'm telling you the truth."

"You're a miserable little worm."

"No, I'm hoping to graduate and be a big worm, just you wait and see. Just as Kiko Mendive says in his song: *guachachacharachá!*" He improvised a little dance step, straightened his blue-and-yellow-striped tie, and said, "Don't worry, Mama, as far as the world is concerned, every man for himself, my brother and I can take care of ourselves. We're okay. We're not going to be a burden to you."

Laura hid her doubts. Danton was going to need all the help in the world, and since the world helps no one for free, he would have to pay. A feeling of profound revulsion toward her younger son flowed over her. She asked herself the useless questions: Where does that come from? What is there in Juan Francisco's blood? Because in mine . . .

Santiago entered a febrile stage in his life. He neglected his job with Rivera at the National Palace and transformed his bedroom into a studio reeking aggressively of oil paints and turpentine. Entering his space was like stepping into a savage forest of fir trees, pines, larches, and terebinths. The walls were smeared as if they were a concave extension of the canvases, the bed was covered by a sheet hiding the prostrate body of another Santiago, who slept while his twin the artist painted. The window was darkened by a flight of birds attracted to a rendezvous as irresistible as the call to the south during the autumn equinox, and Santiago recited aloud as he painted, himself attracted by a kind of southern gravity:

*a branch was born like an island,*
*a leaf was shaped like a sword,*
*a flower was lightning and medusa,*
*a cluster rounded off its resume,*
*a root descended into the darkness.*
*It was the twilight of the iguana.*

Then he'd say disconnected things while he painted: "All artists are tame animals; I'm a wild animal." And it was true. He was a man with a head of long hair and a boyish, scattered beard and a high, clear, fevered brow and eyes filled with a love so intense they frightened Laura, who was finding a perfectly new being in her son, on him "the initials of the earth were inscribed," because Santiago her son was the "young warrior of darkness and copper" in the *Canto General*, by the greatest poet in the Americas, Pablo Neruda, which had just been published in Mexico. Mother and son read it together, and she remembered the nights of fire in Madrid that Jorge Maura had evoked, Neruda on a roof in flames under the bombs of fascist planes, in a European world returned to the elemental ode of our America in perpetual destruction and re-creation, "a thousand years of air, months, weeks of air," "the high place of the human aurora: the tallest vessel that contained the silence of a life of stone after so many lives." Those words fed the life and work of her son.

She wanted to be just. Her two sons had already burst into extremes, both Santiago and Danton were taking shape in places of the dawn, and they were both "tall vessels" for the promising silence of two nascent lives. Until then, she'd believed in people, older than she or her contemporaries, as intelligible beings. Her sons were, prodigiously, adventurously, mysteries. She asked herself if at any moment in the years with Laura Díaz she herself had been as indecipherable for her parents as her sons seemed to her now. She vainly sought an explanation from those who could understand her—María de la O, who certainly had lived on the extreme edge of life, the frontier of abandonment that had no night or day, or her own husband, Juan Francisco, about whom she knew only a legend, first, and then a spoiled myth, and finally an old rancor, cohabiting with a resignation she'd learned to accept.

Despite everything, the alliances between parents and sons became stronger in a natural way; in every home there are gravitational fields as strong as those of the stars—which don't fall, Maura explained to her once, precisely because some attract others, lean on each other, maintain their integrity despite the tenacious, irresistible force of a universe that is permanently expanding, from beginning (if it really had a beginning) to end (if it really will have an end).

"Gravity doesn't mean falling, as is commonly thought, Laura. It's attraction. Attraction not only unites us but makes us bigger."

Laura and Santiago gave each other mutual support. The son's artistic project found an echo in the mother's moral frankness, and Laura's return to her frustrated marriage was completely justified thanks to her creative union with her son. Santiago saw in his mother a decision to be free that corresponded to his own impulse to paint. The union between Juan Francisco and Danton, on the other hand, was based first on a certain masculine pride on the father's part—this was the playboy, tough-guy son who was always in love, just like the heroes of the wildly popular Jorge Negrete movies the two went to see together in downtown theaters: the recently opened Chinese Palace on Iturbide Street, a mausoleum of papier-mâché pagodas, smiling Buddhas, and starry heavens (sine qua non for a "movie cathedral" of the time) the Alameda and the Colonial, with their viceregal, baroque references, the Lindavista and the Lido, with their Hollywood pretensions, "streamlined," as society ladies said of their outfits, their cars, and their kitchens. The father loved inviting his son out for a strong dose of all those challenges to honor, displays of horseback-riding skill, barroom brawls, and serenades to saintly girlfriends. Both of them melted, gaping at Gloria Marín's liquid eyes—she'd just prayed to the Virgin that her man might show up. Because a charro from Jalisco, even if he thought he was conquering the woman, was always the one who was conquered, thanks to the womanly arts, suffering on the gallows of an all-devouring virginity from a legion of Guadalajara maidens named Esther Fernández, María Luisa Zea, or Consuelito Frank.

Danton knew his father would enjoy his tales of bars, challenges, and serenades which, at the suburban level, reenacted the movie deeds of the Singing Cowboy. In school, he was punished for such escapades. Juan Francisco celebrated them, however, and the son gave thanks, wondering whether his father was nostalgic for the adventures of his own youth or if, thanks to the son, he was enjoying for the first time the youth he had missed. Juan Francisco never spoke of his intimate past. If Laura was betting that her husband would reveal the secrets of his origin to their younger son, she was mistaken. There was a sealed zone in López Greene's life story, the very awakening of his personality: had he always been the attractive, eloquent, brave leader she met in the Xalapa Casino when she was twenty-one, or was there something before and behind the glory, a blank space that would explain the silent, indifferent, and fearful man who now lived with her?

Juan Francisco taught the son he coddled about the glorious history of the workers movement against the dictatorship of Porfirio Díaz. After 1867, when Maximilian's empire fell, Benito Juárez found himself face to face, right here in Mexico City, with well-organized groups of anarchists who had secretly come in with the Hungarian, Austrian, Czech, and French troops who supported the Habsburg archduke. They stayed here when the French withdrew and Juárez had Maximilian shot. Those anarchists had grouped artisans into Resistance Societies. In 1870 the Grand Circle of Mexican Workers was constituted, then in 1876 a secret Bakunin group, The Social, celebrated the first general workers congress in the Mexican Republic.

"So you see, my boy, the Mexican workers movement wasn't born yesterday, even though it had to struggle against ancient colonial prejudices. There was an anarchist delegate, Soledad Soria. They tried to nullify her membership because the presence of a woman violated tradition, they said. The Congress grew to have eighty thousand members, just imagine. Something to be proud of. It was logical that President Díaz began to repress them, especially in the terrible putting down of miners in Cananea. Don Porfirio began his repression there because the American groups that dominated the copper company had sent in almost a hundred armed men from Arizona, rangers, to protect

American property. It's always the same old song from the gringos. They invade a country to protect life and property. The miners also wanted the same old thing, an eight-hour day, wages, housing, schools. They, too, wanted life and property. They were massacred. But it was there that the Díaz dictatorship cracked for good. They didn't calculate that a single crack can bring down an entire building."

Juan Francisco was delighted to have an attentive audience, his own son, for whom he could rehearse those heroic stories of the Mexican workers movement, culminating in the textile strike at Río Blanco in 1907, where Don Porfirio's Finance Minister, Yves Limantour, supported the French owners and planned to prohibit uncensored books, require passports to enter and leave the factory, as if it were a foreign country, and note in company documents the rebellious history of each worker.

"Once again it was a woman, Margarita Romero by name, who led the march to the company store and set it on fire. The army came in and shot two hundred workers. The troops set up their garrison in Veracruz, and it was then that I came to organize the resistance."

"What did you do before, Papa?"

"I think my story begins with the Revolution. Before that, I have no biography, my boy."

He brought Danton to the offices of the CTM, to a cubicle where he received telephone calls, which always ended with his saying "yes, sir," "just as you say," and "an order is an order, sir," before he went off to Congress to communicate to the labor deputies the orders of the President and Secretary of State.

That's how he spent the day. But en route from the union offices to the Chamber and then back, Danton saw a world he didn't like. It all seemed a circus of complicities, a minuet of agreements dictated from above by the real powers and repeated below mechanically in Congress and the unions, without argument or doubt but in an interminable circle of hugs, pats on the back, secrets whispered into ears, envelopes with official seals, occasional bursts of laughter, vulgar horseplay that had the obvious purpose of salvaging the leaders' and deputies' ill-treated masculinity, constant dates for grand banquets that might end at midnight in the House of the Lady Bandit, winks of "you know what I mean" in matters of sex and money, and Juan Francisco circulating among all this.

"It's orders . . ."

"It's convenient . . ."

"Of course they're communal lands, but the beachfront hotels will give jobs to the whole community . . ."

"The hospital, the school, the highway—these will all integrate your region better, Congressman, especially the highway, which will run right next to your property . . ."

"Well, yes, I do know it's his lady's whim, but let's give in. What do we have to lose? The Secretary will be grateful to us for the rest of his life . . ."

"No, there's an interest higher up that wants to stop this strike. It's over, understand? Everything can be achieved through laws and conciliation, without fights. You have to realize, Mr. Congressman, that the government's raison d'être is to ensure stability and social peace in Mexico. That, today, is what revolutionary means."

"Yes, I know President Cárdenas promised you a cooperative, comrades. And we're going to have it. The problem is that the requirements of production demand a strong leadership nationally linked to the CTM and the Party of the Mexican Revolution. If we don't have that, comrades, we'll be swallowed up by priests and landowners, as always."

"Have faith."

Wasn't he going to request a sightly more elegant office?

No, Juan Francisco told Danton, a spot like this is appropriate for me, modest, and better to work from. This way I don't offend anyone.

But I thought you made money to show off.

Then you should work as a contractor or a businessman. Those people can do what they like.

Why?

Because they create jobs. That's the formula.

And you?

We all have to play the role assigned us. That's the law of the world.

Which do you like, son: businessman, newspaperman, soldier . . . ?

None of those, Papa.

Well, what do you want to do?

Whatever I have to.

# 16. Chapultepec-Polanco: 1947

T HE INAUGURATION of President Miguel Alemán in December 1946 coincided with an astonishing event in the Avenida Sonora household. Aunt María de la O started speaking again. "He's from Veracruz, a *jarocho*," she said—of the new, young, elegant head of state, the first civilian President after a series of military men.

Everyone—Laura Díaz, Juan Francisco, Santiago, Danton—was taken aback, but Aunt María's surprises didn't stop there: for no reason at all, she started dancing *la bamba* at all hours of the day or night, her swollen ankles notwithstanding.

"No fool like an old fool," said a scornful Danton.

Then, at the beginning of the new year, María de la O made her sensational announcement: "The time of sadness is over. I'm going back to live in Veracruz. An old beau of mine from the port has asked me to marry him. He's my age, though I don't know exactly what my age is, because Mama never registered me. She wanted me to grow up quickly and follow her in the crazy life. Silly cunt, I hope she's sizzling in hell. All I know is that Matías Matadamas—that's my boyfriend—can dance the *danzón* like an angel, and he's promised to take me dancing twice a week in the city square, right along with everyone else."

"Nobody's named Matías Matadamas," said Danton the wet blanket.

"You little snot," replied Auntie. "For your information, St. Matías was the last apostle, the one who took the place of Judas the Traitor after the crucifixion so there would be an even dozen."

"Apostle and boyfriend all at the last minute!" Danton laughed. "As if Jesus Christ were a peddler who sold saints cheaper by the dozen."

"Just you wait and see if the last minute isn't sometimes the first, you disbeliever." María de la O was berating him, but truth to tell, she was not in the mood for reproofs. What she wanted was to be dancing *bulerías.* "I can just see myself, holding on to him tight," she went on with her best daydream air, "cheek to cheek, dancing on a brick, which is how you should dance the *danzón,* barely moving your body, just your feet, your feet tapping out the beat, slow, delicious, sexy. Oh boy, family, I am going to live!"

Nobody could explain Aunt María de la O's miracle; nobody could thwart her will or even take her to the train, much less to Veracruz.

"He's my boyfriend. He's my life. My time has come. I'm tired of being a parasite. From now to the grave, pure Caribbean fun and nights on the town. A little old lady died shuffling cards. To hell with that! Not me!"

With those words, a not unusual proof that the tongues of the old loosen up when there's nothing to lose, she boarded the Interoceanic train almost with relief, a renewed woman, a miracle.

Even though Auntie's chair was empty, Laura Díaz insisted on continuing the afternoon ceremony of sitting at the balcony and observing the to-and-fro of the city. It had changed little between the inauguration of General Avila Camacho and that of Mr. Alemán. During the war, Mexico had become a Latin American Lisbon (Casablanca with *nopales*, quipped Orlando), a refuge for the many men and women fleeing from the European conflict. Two hundred thousand Spanish Republicans came, and Laura told herself that Jorge Maura's labors had not been in vain. The cream of the Spanish intelligentsia arrived, a terrible bloodletting for the contemptible Franco dictatorship but a magnificent transfusion for Mexico's university life, literature, art, and science. In exchange for shelter, the Spanish Republicans renovated Mexico's culture—a wonderful example of the universalism that saves cultures from nationalist viruses.

In a small apartment on Lerma Street, the great poet Emilio Prados, with his blind man's glasses and his tangled, graying mane, lived modestly. Prados had already foreseen the "flight" and "arrival" in his beautiful poems about the "persecuted body," which Laura memorized and recited to Santiago. The poet wanted to flee, he said, "tired of hiding in the branches . . . tired of this wound. There are limits." As Laura recited, she heard the voice of Jorge Maura reaching her from far off, as if poetry were the only form of true actuality allowed by the eternal God to His poor mortal creatures. Prados, Jorge Maura, Laura Díaz, and perhaps Santiago López-Díaz as he listened to her read the poems—they all wanted to arrive "with my rigid body . . . that flows like a river without water, walking on foot through a dream with five sharp flames nailed to my chest."

Coming and going, tricked out like an Englishman taking a stroll, was Luis Cernuda with his houndstooth jackets and Duke of Windsor ties, his slicked-down hair and French movie-star mustache, scattering the most beautiful erotic poems in the Spanish language along the streets of Mexico City. Now it was Santiago who read to his mother, running feverishly from one poem to the next, never finishing one, finding the perfect line, the unforgettable words:

*What a sad noise two bodies make when they love.*
*I could knock down their body, leaving only the truth of your love . . .*
*I know no freedom but the freedom of being imprisoned in someone . . .*
*I kissed his tracks . . .*

Luis Buñuel was in Mexico City, too, expelled from New York because of the gossip and calumny there of his former friend Salvador Dalí, now anagrammed into Avida Dollars. Laura Díaz learned about him from Jorge Maura, who had shown her Buñuel's film about the Las

307

Hurdes region in Spain, a film of unbearable pain and abandonment that the Republic itself censored.

And on Amazonas Street lived Don Manuel Pedroso, former rector of the University of Seville, surrounded by first editions of Hobbes, Machiavelli, and Rousseau, with his students at his feet. Danton, brought to one of Pedroso's *tertulias* by a fellow student in the law school, remarked to his friend as they walked along Paseo de la Reforma to dine at the Bellinghausen restaurant on Londres Street, "He's a charming old man. But his ideas are utopian. That stuff's not for me."

At the next table, Max Aub was eating with other exiled writers. He looked focused: short, curly hair, immense forehead, eyes lost in the depth of a glass swimming pool, and expressions impossible to separate, like the faces on a coin, where heads was his frown and tails his smile. Aub had shared adventures with André Malraux during the war and predicted for Franco a "true death" that would be totally unrelated to any calendar date, because for the dictator it would be, more than a surprise, an *ignorance* of his own death.

"My mother knows him," said Danton to his classmate. "She's in with the intellectuals because she works with Diego Rivera and Frida Kahlo."

"And because she was the girlfriend of a Spanish Communist spy," said the friend, though that was the last thing he said, because Danton broke his nose with a punch. Chairs were turned over, tablecloths were stained, and Laura Díaz's son angrily shook off the waiters and departed the restaurant.

The torero Manolete, now living in Mexico, was bringing crowds to the bullfights. A Francoist, he was actually El Greco's last creation: thin, sad, stylized, Manuel Rodríguez "Manolete" was skillful in a priestly way. He fought standing tall, immutable, vertical as a candle. His rival was Pepe Luis Vázquez, Juan Francisco explained to Danton when father and son went to the new Plaza Monumental México along with sixty thousand fans to see Manolete, Pepe Luis being the orthodox Sevillan and Manolete the unorthodox Córdoban, who broke the classic rules by not extending the *muleta*—the short staff on which the red cape is hung—to calm and control the bull, who didn't take risks to make the bull enter the space of the fight, who stood still, calmed and ordered, never moving from his place, exposed to the bull, who was bringing the fight to him. And when the bull charged this unmoving bullfighter, the entire stadium gasped in anguish, held its breath, and exploded into an *olé* of victory when the marvelous Manolete broke the tension with an extremely slow-moving attack and sank his sword into the bull's body. Did you see that? Juan Francisco asked his son as they walked, in the crush of the crowd, out of the Plaza through the honeycomb of crisscrossing long passageways. Did you see that? He fought the whole time face to face, never bending, dominating the bull from below, our hearts all skipped a beat watching him fight! But Danton remembered only one lesson: The bull and the bullfighter saw each other's face. They were two faces of death. Only apparently did the bull die and the bullfighter survive. The truth is, the man was mortal and the animal immortal, the bull went on and on and on, charged and charged and charged, again and again, blinded by the sun, and the sand stained by the blood of a single immortal bull who saw generation after generation of mortal bullfighters pass on. When would Manolete die, in what ring would he find the death that he only apparently dealt each bull, what would be the name of the bull that would kill Manolete, where was it waiting for him?

"Manolete casts a spell on the bull," said a melancholic Juan Francisco, dining alone with Danton in El Parador after the bullfight.

The son wanted to keep to himself the lesson of that afternoon when he saw Manolete fight: triumph and glory are passing things; we have to kill one bull after another so as to put off our own final defeat, the day when our bull kills us, we have to win ear and tail and exit in triumph every day of our lives.

"They say people are selling their cars and their mattresses to buy tickets to the Plaza to see Manolete. Could that be true?" he asked.

"For the first time, there are three programs a week in the Plaza," said his father. "There must be a reason."

The dashing bullfighter strolled around the centers of Mexico City's cosmopolitan nightlife—the Casanova, the Minuit, the Sans

Souci—accompanied by Fernanda Montel, a Valkyrian woman who balanced the depth of her décolletés with the height of her hairdos, genuine towers dyed blue, green, rose. In Coyoacán, the dethroned King Carol of Romania, with his drooping mustache, oyster eyes, and receding chin, walked his poodles with his lover, Magda Lupescu, more attentive to her silver fox furs than to her exiled king. From a table at Ciro's, in the Hotel Reforma, Carmen Cortina made battle plans with her old allies—the actress Andrea Negrete, Butt del Rosal, and the English painter Felicity Smith—to recruit all the international fauna the tides of war had beached in Mexico. God bless you, Adolf Hitler! sighed the hostess to her group, seated not far from Ciro's owner, a dwarf with a tiepin named A. C. Blumenthal, front man for Bugsy Siegel, the Hollywood gangster, whose discarded lover, Virginia Hill, owner of a tremulous chin and faded hair and that sudden sadness which attacks some women from the city of Los Angeles, was drinking martini after martini, and martinis were what the novelist John Steinbeck, his Gordon's Gin eyes filled with lost battles and now in Mexico for the filming of his novella *The Pearl*, served in a bottle to his tame crocodile, thus outdoing the boastful audacity of the film's director, Emilio (the Indian) Fernández, fond of using a pistol to threaten anyone who disagreed with his plot ideas, who was in love with the actress Olivia de Havilland, in whose honor he had a street renamed "Sweet Olivia"—where he built a castle with his earnings from successes like *Flor Silvestre, María Candelaria, Enamorada.*

Laura Díaz had to go to Ciro's because Diego Rivera was painting a series of female nudes there, all inspired by Rivera's own starry love, the actress Paulette Goddard, an intelligent, ambitious woman who spoke to Laura only in order to ignore Diego and annoy him, while Laura, in turn, scrutinized Ciro's clientele with an irony as sweet as the street where "El Indio" Fernández lived: people she hadn't seen in fifteen years, Carmen Cortina's group, and the satellites coming and going from her table: the painter from Guadalajara, Tizoc Ambriz, who stubbornly dressed as a young railroad worker though he was fifty. Indelible marks of time were printed on their faces, but they were invulnerable in their pretensions, stuck in their reality like a pantheon of wax figures: two-tone Andrea, now quite plump; the once fat and jowly Spaniard Onomástico Galán, now deflated and wrinkled, like a used condom; the British painter James Saxon looking more and more like the entire House of Windsor; and her old companion from Xalapa, Elizabeth García-Dupont, ex-wife of Caraza, now thin as a mummy, one hand trembling and the other clutching a young man: dark, mustached, and imperturbably pimpish.

A hand touched Laura Díaz's shoulder. She recognized Laura Rivière, Artemio Cruz's lover, who had overcome the fifteen years that had passed thanks to the elegant opalescent beauty concentrated in her unaging melancholy eyes.

"Come see me whenever you like. Why haven't you ever visited?"

And then, homburg hat in hand, Orlando Ximénez came in. Laura could not measure time; the only face she could confer on Orlando was the same youthful one he'd had at the dances at San Cayetano more than thirty years before. She felt a mild vertigo seeing the image of the boy who made love to her on the terraces scented with nocturnal oranges and sleeping coffee trees; she excused herself and left.

Gravitating toward something is not the same as falling toward it; it's drawing closer, it's when you draw closer, Laura told Danton, who had thought, after the day with his father at the CTM and the Chamber of Deputies, This isn't for me, but my dad's right, what is for me? He too was gazing out from the balcony overlooking the Bosque de Chapultepec, and he knew that on the other side of the park was Las Lomas de Chapultepec section. That's where the rich people lived, new and old money, he didn't care, it was there that new mansions with swimming pools and lawns for garden parties and society weddings were being built, three-car garages, interior decoration by Pani and Paco el de La Granja, wardrobes by Valdés Peza, hats by Henri de Chatillon, flowers by Matsumoto, and banquets catered by Mayita.

How could a simple poor boy like himself, whose poverty was neither old nor new, get into those places? Because that's what Danton López-Díaz wanted to do. He gave due attention to his father's modest suggestions: should he be a politician, a businessman, a journalist, a military officer? Then he decided to create his own destiny—that is, his own fortune. And since in Mexico it was hard to acquire class without money, the young economics student decided he had no option but to acquire money with class. Leafing through the society magazines was enough to make him see the difference. There was the new society created by the Revolution, rich, living in Las Lomas de Chapultepec, insecure but daring, dark-skinned but cosmetically lightened, impertinently showing off its recently acquired wealth for good or ill: dark men—soldiers, politicians, impresarios—married to light women— creoles in distress, long-suffering. The revolutionaries, in their armed descent from the north, had harvested the prettiest virginal buds from Hermosillo and Culiacán, from Torreón and San Luis, from Zacatecas and El Bajío. Mothers of their children. Vestals of their homes. Resigned to the affairs of their powerful sultans.

And then there was the old, aristocratic, and impoverished society that lived on streets with the names of European cities, between Avenida Insurgentes and Paseo de la Reforma. Their houses were small but elegant, built around 1918–20, two-story buildings with stone facades, balconies, coach houses, and, overlooking the street, a *piano nobile* where one might glimpse mementos from the past—paintings and portraits, medals in velvet-lined frames, bibelots, mirrors darkened with age. Behind the public spaces, the mystery of the bedrooms, the unknown nature of the daily life of people who had once owned haciendas the size of Belgium, taken away by Zapata, Villa, and Cárdenas. Where did they bathe? How did they cook? How did they survive the catastrophe that had destroyed their world?

But oh how they prayed. That was visible. Every Sunday, just after one, the boys and girls of this "good society" met to go to Mass in La Votiva church on the corner of Génova and Reforma. Later, chatting, flirting, making plans to eat, where? At El Parador de José Luis around the corner on Niza? At Luisito Muñoz's 1–2–3 on Liverpool? At the Jockey Club at the Américas Hippodrome? At the home of one of those people with picturesquely intimate names—Gifty, Princess, Miss Chubby, Missy, Froggy, Skinny, Cheeky, Diver, Kitty? In Mexico, only aristocrats and thugs were known by their nicknames. What was the name of that highwayman who sliced off the fingers of Danton's great-grandmother with a machete? The Hunk from where?

Danton explored, calculated, and decided to begin there: one o'clock Mass in the white-and-blue La Votiva, Moorish as a repentant mosque.

The first time, no one turned around to see who he was. The second time, people looked at him with puzzled astonishment. The third time, a tall blond boy came over and asked who he was.

"I'm López."

"López?"

"Yes, López, the most well-known name in the telephone book."

That got a laugh out of the boy, who threw his head of wavy hair back, revealing a long neck where his Adam's apple bounced up and down.

"López! López! López what?"

"Díaz."

"And? What else?"

"Greene. And Kelsen."

"Listen, everybody, this guy's got more last names than all of us put together. Come have lunch at the Jockey. You look picturesque to me."

"Thanks, but I already have a date. Next Sunday perhaps."

"Perhaps? You mean the way it is in the bolero, 'perhaps-perhaps-perhaps.' You talk like a bolero, I mean like a song, not like a shoe-shine boy."

"And what's your name, blondie?"

"Blondie! He calls me blondie! People call me the Curate."

"Why?"

"I don't know. Maybe it's because Papa cures people. He's a doctor. My second last name is Landa. I'm a descendant of the last city governor in the *ancien régime*. It's my mother's name."

"And what's your father's name?"

"No jokes, now."

"But you're the one making jokes, sonny."

"Sonny! He called me sonny! Ha-ha! No, I'm called the Curate, my father's named López too, just like yours. Now that's amusing, really amusing! We're namesakes in reverse! It's fate! Anastasio López-Landa. Don't forget next Sunday. You seem like a good guy. But buy yourself a better tie. The ones you've been wearing look like a flag."

What would a "better" tie look like? Whom to ask? The next Sunday, Danton turned up in church in riding clothes, jodhpurs and boots, a coffee-colored jacket, an open shirt. And with a riding crop in his hand.

"Where do you ride? Hmm . . . What did you say your name was?"

"López, like you. Danton."

"The guillotine, ha-ha! Your parents must really be something!"

"A joke a minute. The Atayde circus hires them when things get rough."

"Ha-ha-ha, Danton! *You're a real scream, you know,*" said the other López, shifting into English.

"*Yeah, I'm the cat's pajamas,*" said Danton. A line from an American movie comedy.

"Listen, everybody, this guy knows everything. *He's the bee's knees!* He's Tarzan's mama!"

"Of course. Me Columbus. Cristobal Colón!"

"And my sons are Crystal Balls, ha-ha! Look, I live right around the corner here on Amberes. Come with me, and I'll lend you a tie, *old sport.*"

Danton turned La Votiva and the Jockey into his Sunday obligations, more sacred than taking communion—just to stay on the right side of his new acquaintances—without the benefit of confession.

At first his presence was disconcerting. He made a detailed study of the way the boys dressed. He did not let himself be put off by the girls' cool manners, though he'd never seen—he who knew only eternal mournings and the flowered silk outfits provincial women wore—so many young ladies in suits or kilts with sweaters, a cardigan over a matching sweater, and a pearl necklace on top of everything else. A Spanish girl, María Luisa Elío, attracted attention with her beauty and elegance; she was ash blond, slim as a little bullfighter, in a black beret like Michèle Morgan in the French movies they all went to see at the

Trans-Lux Prado, a checked jacket, pleated skirt, and she leaned on an umbrella.

Danton was confident in his potency, his virility, in the very fact that he stood out. He was as dark as a gypsy and hadn't lost his childhood long eyelashes, which now more than ever shaded his green eyes and olive cheeks, his short nose, and his full, feminine lips. He was about five feet ten and tended to be square, like a sportsman, but with the hands of a pianist—so he'd been told—like those of Aunt Hilda, who played Chopin in Catemaco. Danton would say, rather vulgarly, "These thoroughbred mares need a good branding," and he'd ask Juan Francisco for money, he couldn't walk in like a beggar every Sunday, he too had to shoot from time to time, I've got new friends, Dad, highclass, you don't want me to make the whole family look bad, do you? And look, I do my work all week, I never miss an eight o'clock class, I take my exams right on schedule and get A or A minus, I have a good head for economics, I swear, Papa, whatever you lend me now I'll give back with compound interest, I swear . . . When have I ever let you down?

The first rows at the Hippodrome were occupied by generals nostalgic for their own, now ancient, cavalry charges; then came big businessmen who'd arrived even more recently than the soldiers, men who'd made their fortunes, paradoxically, with the radical reforms of President Lázaro Cárdenas, thanks to which the peons, who had been locked into their social position, had left the haciendas and worked for almost nothing in new factories in Monterrey, Guadalajara, and Mexico City. Less paradoxically, the new fortunes had been made because of war, monopolies, Mexico's export of strategic materials, the rising cost of food . . .

Linking these groups was a small Italian named Bruno Pagliai, smiling and elegant, manager of the racetrack and possessor of an irresistible *furberia* that dominated, restrained, and shamed the rustic malice of even the most hard-boiled Mexican general or millionaire. Yet there persisted a clear discrimination. The world of La Votiva, of the Curate (López-Landa) and his friends, dominated the bar, the arm-

chairs, the dance floor, and it left to the merely rich the healthy out-
door life of the racetrack. The sons and daughters of generals and
tycoons were also left on the outs: they weren't taken seriously; they
were—as Miss Chatis Larrazábal put it—"not our kind, dear." But
among those who weren't "our kind," Danton one day discovered the
most beautiful girl he'd ever seen in his life, a *dream*.

The "dream" was a beauty of a kind not found in Mexico, Levantine or Oriental, from that part of the world that the Malet and Isaac
general-history textbooks called "Asia Minor." Magdalena Ayub Longoria's "Asia Minor" transformed her apparent defects—continuous
eyebrows, prominent nose, square jaw—into a counterpoint or frame
for eyes worthy of an Arabian princess, dreamy and velvety, eloquent
beneath oiled and erotic eyelids, like a hidden sex. Her smile was so
warm, sweet, and ingenuous that it would justify the veil and seraglio
concealing her from everyone but her master. She was tall, slim, but
she hinted here and there at roundnesses now scarcely imaginable: thus
did Danton describe her to himself.

His imagination was on the mark.

The first time he saw her, she was sipping a "Shirley Temple," and
from that moment on he called her "my dream." Magdalena Ayub was
the daughter of a merchant from Syria or Lebanon—Mexicans always
referred to them as "Turks"—named Simón Ayub, who'd come to
Mexico barely twenty years before and now had a colossal fortune and
the most vulgar neo-baroque mansion in Colonia Polanco. How had he
accumulated his cash? By taking over markets that had been monopolies in the days of Obregón and Calles and were enhanced during
the war by artificially elevated prices: for henequen, an essential rope-
making fiber, for the Allies, bought cheap from Yucatán communal
farms and sold dear to the gringos; vegetables exported during the winter for Yankee soldiers; pharmaceutical factories set up when gringo
medicines stopped coming and anyway could be manufactured more
cheaply in Mexico, even introducing sulfa drugs and penicillin. He was
the inventor of black thread and perhaps even of aspirin itself! Which
is why he was dubbed Aspirin Ayub, recalling, it may be, the Revolu-

tionary general who cured his soldiers' headaches with a bullet to the forehead.

And even if he was uglier than the wrong end of a mule, he'd married a pretty woman from the north, from some border town, one of those women who could tempt the Pope and make St. Joseph a bigamist. Doña Magdalena Longoria de Ayub. Danton looked her over, because everyone said that after a while your girlfriend starts looking like your mother-in-law—all girlfriends, all mothers-in-law. And big Magdalena, who really was big, passed the test. Danton told the Curate, López-Landa, that she was "ripe" or, more biblically, that her cups overfloweth.

"I swear, Dan, look over there at the mother and the daughter in their box. You tell me which you'd rather have."

"If I'm lucky, both of them," said Danton, with a manhattan in one hand and a Pall Mall in the other.

He approached the daughter and succeeded. He asked her to dance. He removed her from the isolation of the new and brought her into the community of the old. He himself was shocked it should be he, Danton López-Díaz (and Greene and Kelsen), who led the fortunate princess by the hand into the exclusive circle of the kings of ruin.

"May I introduce Magdalena Ayub? We're to be married."

Her mouth fell open with all the astonishment a nineteen-year-old can muster. The boy was joking. They'd just met.

"Listen, honey. Do you want to go back to your box with your folks to watch the mares run? Or would you like to *be* a fine mare, as they call these snooty girls over here? Would anyone but me have dared to go over to your box, say hello to your parents, and ask you to dance? What happens next? I who presented you to society, I who am not from society—so you see what the man you're going to marry is like, *my dream*—I get what I want. See? And you don't have the kind of ovaries—dreadful expression, but that's the kind of fellow I am and you might as well get used to it—to be living alone without me, abandoned in this world. What do you think of that? Do you need me or what, honeybunch?"

317

They went to dances, danced cheek to cheek, she began allowing him to take "liberties"—to caress her back, her neck, to tickle her smoothly shaved underarm, to nibble her earlobe; then came the first kiss, the second, thousands of kisses, the entreaty, just on the outside, my dream, no, Dan, I'm having my period, just between your legs, my dream, I'll use my handkerchief, don't be frightened, yes, my love, oh, my dream, I like you too much, I didn't know anything about these things, I'd never met anyone like you, how strong you are, how sure of yourself, how ambitious . . .

"I do have one weakness, Magdalena."

"What is it, my love?"

"I'll do anything that will make people admire me. Do you understand what I'm saying?"

"I'll make you feel someone's admiring you. I swear. You won't need anything else."

*Blue moon, I saw you standing alone*

Magdalena's family looked him over from head to toe. Insolently, he did the same to them.

"This house could use a good redecorating," he declared, looking with disdain at the baroque display of stucco, the false altars, and the wrought iron in the Polanco mansion. "Well, at least when you're living with me you'll be surrounded by good taste, my dream."

"Is that right?" thundered Ayub furiously. "And who's going to finance all your luxury, my fine little gentleman?"

"Why, you are, my generous father-in-law."

"My daughter doesn't require generosity. She requires comfort," blurted out the northern mother, idiotically haughty.

"What your daughter needs is a man who will respect and defend her and not make her feel inferior and isolated, which is what you two have accomplished, bad parents that you are." Danton strode out, slamming the door so hard that he almost broke the vases adorned with the image of Pope Pius XII blessing the city, the world, and the Ayub Longoria family.

He was to come back. Poor Malenita wouldn't leave her bedroom. She wouldn't eat anything. She cried all day long, well, like Mary Magdalene.

"I'm not asking for a handout, Don Simón. Let me, both of you, explain, and please, sir, don't look at me with that expression of impatience, because it makes me impatient. Control yourself. In this matter, you're not doing *me* the great favor. I'm doing *you* the favor, and I'll explain why, excuse me . . . I'm offering your daughter what she isn't and would like to be. She's already rich. What she doesn't have is acceptance. She just isn't accepted."

"Now I've heard everything. You, you poor devil, are a nobody."

"Since we're now speaking familiarly, Don Aspirin, let me tell you something: I'm what you can no longer be. Exactly. I'm what's coming. The future. For twenty years, you've had your way around here. But realize this, dearest father-in-law, you came to this country when Enrico Caruso was singing at El Toreo. Your time is over. The war's over. Now a new world is coming. We're not going to be able to monopolize anything anymore. Now there's going to be surplus production in the United States. We're not going to be indispensable allies. We're going back to being dispensable beggars. Am I getting through to you, my Aspirin?"

"Let's both be polite, Mr. Danton, please."

"As I was saying. Now either we're going to live off the internal market or we're not going to live. Now we have to create wealth right here, as well as the people to buy what we're going to produce."

"*We?* Aren't you abusing the plural, Danton?"

"We, we who love each other so much, yes, sir, Don Simón, sir. You and I, if you'll bear with me, if instead of dominating the henequen market and exploiting the poor Mayas, you invest in chains of restaurants, wholesale department stores, the things people consume—cheap soft drinks in a tropical country full of thirsty people, vacuum cleaners to reduce the workload of the lady of the house, refrigerators so food doesn't spoil instead of those inconvenient iceboxes that melt all over the place, radios to bring entertainment to the poorest of the poor . . . we're going to be a middle-class country, don't you see that? Get with the program, boss, don't settle for small potatoes."

"You're very eloquent, Danton. Go on."

"Seriously? Furniture, tinned foods, cheap clothes in good taste instead of serapes and huaraches, decent restaurants in gringo style with soda fountains and everything, no more stalls or Chinese-run cafés, cheap cars for everyone, no more buses for the poor and Cadillacs for the rich. Did you know my great-grandfather was German? Well, remember this name. Volkswagen, the people's car. Let the German factories reopen here, and you buy up the license for VW in Mexico, give half the stock to me, and we're all home free, Don Aspirin—no more headaches. I swear!"

All of them know each other, Danton explained to Laura, Juan Francisco, and Santiago. But that's all they know. Themselves, themselves, themselves. I'm going to show them today's world, those miserable mummies from the age of Don Porfirio. I've learned to imitate tones of voice, you know, ways of dressing, verbal crutches like saying *"ciao"* or *"Lord help me"* and *"voiturette."* I've dissected society the way you cut up a steak in a restaurant. Look: I found out with the López-Landa kid that a guy will admire in another guy what he isn't. That's what I found out, and what I offered the Jockey Club set was what they aren't, and that made me interesting to them. I'm offering the same thing to Magdalena, offering her what she isn't but would like to be, rich but glamorous. I let her know: you aren't what you could be, my dream, but I'll make it all come true. The Ayubs thought that they were doing me a big favor and that they could put obstacles in my path. Baloney. In this life, you've got to sign your difficulties over to other people as if they were a gift. That's the big joke."

"Your mom and dad don't like me, my dream."

"I'll make them like you, Danton."

"I don't want to make that kind of trouble for you."

"It's no trouble. That will be my gift to you, my love, my Dan . . ."

Their wealth is cruel, laughed Danton, speaking to his parents and his brother. They've been hoarding cash for a day that will never come. They've forgotten the reasons why they became rich. I'm going to revive that memory. Now those reasons are mine. Mama, Papa: I'm getting married next month, as soon as I finish my economics degree. I'm a success, why don't you congratulate me?

My brother dazzles me, said Santiago to Laura, he makes me feel inferior and stupid, he has all the answers ahead of time, while I think of them too late, when it's all over. Why should I be like that?

She said the two of them were very different. Danton was made for the outside world, but you were made for the interior world, Santiago, where answers don't have to be instantaneous or charming, because what really matter are the questions.

"And sometimes there are no answers." Santiago smiled from bed. "Only questions. You're right."

"I know, son. But I believe in you."

He got out of bed with difficulty and went over to his easel. It was hard to tell the tremor of fever from the tremor of creative anticipation. Sitting in front of the canvas, he transmitted that fever, that doubt. Laura watched him and felt him in her own skin. It's normal, that's how he's been since he discovered his artistic vocation. Every day he surprises himself, feels transformed, discovers the other who's within him.

"I discover him too, Juan Francisco, but I don't tell him. You should try to be with him a little."

Juan Francisco shook his head. He didn't want to admit it, but Santiago lived in a world he didn't understand. He didn't know what to say to his own son, they were never close. Wasn't it a deception to be near him now, because he was sick?

"It's more than that, Juan Francisco. Santiago isn't just sick."

Juan Francisco didn't understand that being an artist was synonymous with being sick. It was like imagining a double mirror which, while being itself, has two faces, each one reflecting a different reality, sickness and art, not necessarily twin realities but occasionally, yes, fraternal realities. Which came first, which nourished Santiago's uneasy days, art or sickness?

Laura watched her son as he slept. She liked to be next to the bed when Santiago awakened. What she saw was this: he awakened surprised, but it was impossible to know if it was the surprise of waking up alive or the shock of having one more day to paint.

She felt excluded from that daily choice, and she confessed she'd have liked to be part of what Santiago chose each day: Laura, my mother, Laura Díaz is part of my day. She would spend it with him, next to him, she'd given up everything to take care of him, but Santiago did not openly recognize that company, she was only in his company, or, as Laura would say, he let her in but without thanking her.

"Perhaps he's got nothing to thank me for, and I should understand and respect that."

One afternoon, he felt strong and asked Laura to help him to the balcony where the family held its afternoon gatherings. He'd lost so much weight that she could have carried him as she hadn't since he was small, before he went away with Mutti and the aunts in Xalapa. Now the mother could reproach herself for that abandonment, for her spurious reasons—Juan Francisco was beginning his political career, there was no time for the boys, and worse, Laura Díaz was going to live her independent life, her sons were excess baggage like her husband, she was a provincial girl married young to a man seventeen years older than she; it was her turn to live, take risks, learn, was the nun Gloria Soriano merely a pretext for her to leave home? The time with Orlando Ximénez and Carmen Cortina, with Diego and Frida in Detroit, was no time to be carrying around a child who himself carried so much promise, this Santiago with a brow so clear that glory, creation, and beauty could be read there. Never, she swore to herself, would she neglect to take care of this child, who always, always contained all the promise, all the beauty, all the tenderness, and all the creation in the world.

Now the lost time suddenly materialized before her with the face of guilt. Was that why Santiago did not express gratitude: had her maternal care come too late? Being a mother excluded any desire for gratitude or recognition. It should be enough in itself without argument or expectation, like the instant of sufficient tenderness.

Laura sat down with her son opposite the urban landscape. It really was undergoing a transformation: like a forest of proliferating mushrooms, skyscrapers were popping up everywhere, the old cabs were changed for taxis whose meters seemed incomprehensible and made their clients suspicious, the broken-down buses were replaced by gigantic vehicles belching black smoke like bat breath, yellow trolleys with their varnished yellow wooden benches and their route maps were replaced by threatening electric buses that looked like prehistoric beasts.

People no longer came home to eat at two in the afternoon and went back to work at five. They began living the gringo novelty of the unbroken workday. Organ grinders were disappearing, along with ragmen and knife and scissor sharpeners. Street-corner stores and tobacco stands were dying, and the rival telephone companies finally united: Laura remembered Jorge Maura (she barely ever thought of him now) and lost track of what Santiago was saying on the balcony, sitting barefoot in his robe. I love you, city, my city, I love you because you dare to show your soul in your body, I love you because you think with your skin, because you won't let me see you if I haven't dreamed you first, like the conquistadors, because even if you've been left dry, lake city, you have compassion, and you fill my hands with water when I have to put up with tears, because you let me name you only by seeing you and see you only by naming you, thank you for inventing me so I could try to reinvent you, Mexico City, thank you for letting me speak to you without guitars and colors and bullets, sing to you with promises of dust, promises of wind, promises never to forget you, promises to revive you even if I disappear, promises to name you, promises to see you in the dark, Mexico City, in exchange for a single gift from you: keep on seeing me when I'm no longer here, sitting on the balcony, with my mother next to me . . .

"To whom are you speaking, son?"

"To your beautiful hands, Mama."

. . . To the childhood that was my second mother, to the youth which happens only once, to the nights I shall no longer see, to the dreams I leave her so the city will care for them, to Mexico City which will go on waiting for me forever . . .

"I love you, city, I love you."

Laura, leading him back to bed, understood that everything her son was saying to the world he was saying to her. He didn't have to be explicit; words might betray him. Brought out into the open, a love that could live without words in the deep, moist terrain of daily company might dry out. The silence between the two of them could be eloquent.

"I don't want to be a pain, I don't want to be a bother."

Silence. Tranquillity. Solitude. That's what unites us, thought Laura, holding Santiago's burning hand in her own. There is no greater respect or tenderness than that of being together and silent, living together but living the one for the other without ever saying so. With no need to say so. Being explicit might betray that deep tenderness which was only revealed in a skein of complicities, suppositions, and acts of grace.

Laura and Santiago saw all this while he was dying, both of them knowing he was dying, but both accomplices, knowing, and thankful one for the other because the only thing they wordlessly decided to eliminate was compassion. The shining eyes of the boy, sinking deeper and deeper by the day, asked the world and the mother, the two forever identified in the son's spirit: Who has the right to take pity on me? Don't betray me with pity . . . I'll be a man to the end.

It was hard for her not to feel sorry for her son, not only not showing her sorrow but eliminating it from her spirit and from her very eyes. Not just hiding it, but not having it, because Santiago's wide-awake, electric senses could detect it instantly. It's possible to betray with compassion; those were words Laura would repeat as she fell asleep, now every night on a cot next to her feverish and emaciated son, the son of promise, the adored child.

"My son, what do you need, what can I do for you?"

"Nothing, Mama, what can I do for you?"

"You know I wish I could steal all the glories and virtues from the world and give them to you."

"Thank you. But you already did, didn't you know?"

"What else? Something else?"

What else. Something else. Sitting on the edge of Santiago's bed, Laura Díaz suddenly recalled a conversation between the two brothers she had accidentally overheard when Santiago, who always left his bed-room door open, was, extraordinarily, talking to Danton.

Papa and Mama are all confused about us, surmised Danton, they imagine too many roads for each of us . . . How good it is our ambitions don't conflict, replied Santiago, so we don't take any shortcuts . . . Even so, Danton persisted, you think your ambition is good and mine is bad, right? No, Santiago made clear, it isn't that yours is bad and mine good or vice versa; we're condemned to carry them out, or at least to try to. Condemned? Danton laughed. Condemned?

Now Danton was married to Magdalena Ayub Longoria and was living, as he'd always wished, on Avenida de Los Virreyes in Las Lomas de Chapultepec. He'd been spared the neo-baroque horrors of Polanco but not because of his in-laws' wishes. Even so, he dreamed of living in a house with straight lines and undistracting geometries. Laura saw her second son less and less. She rationalized that he too was guilty for not visiting her but acknowledged she was anxiously looking after Santiago. She didn't have to seek him out because there he was, weak-ened by recurring sicknesses, right at home. He wasn't her prisoner. Santiago was a young artist with a destiny no one could destroy because it was the destiny of art, of artworks that would ultimately outlive the artist.

Touching Santiago's fevered forehead, Laura wondered, neverthe-less, if this young artist, her son, hadn't brought together beginning and ending too quickly. The tortured and erotic figures in his paintings weren't a promise but a conclusion. They weren't a beginning but, irre-mediably, an ending. They were all finished works. Understanding that anguished her, because Laura Díaz wanted to see in her son the com-plete realization of a personality whose felicity depended on his cre-ativity. It was unfair that his body was betraying him, and that the body, calamitously, didn't depend on will—Santiago's or his mother's.

But she was in no mood to give up. She watched her abstracted, absorbed son working, painting alone and only for himself, as it should be, whatever the fate of the painting may be, my son is going to reveal his gifts, but will not have time for his conquests, he's going to work, to imagine, but will not have time to produce: his painting is an inevitability, that's the reward, my son doesn't take the place of another, and no one can take his place in what he and he alone can do, it doesn't matter for how long; there is no frustration in his work, even if his life is cut short, his progress is astonishing, dedicating oneself to art means one revelation after another, going from surprise to surprise.

"Everything good is work," the young Santiago would say as he painted. "The artist doesn't exist."

"You're an artist," Laura said boldly to him. "Your brother is a mercenary. That's the difference."

Santiago laughed, almost accusing her of being vulgarly obvious.

"No, Mama, it's good that we're different instead of being divided from within."

She repented her banality. She didn't want to make comparisons, neither critical nor reductive. She wanted to tell him it's been wonderful watching you grow, change, generate new life, I never want to ask myself, could my son have been great? Because you already are great, I watch you paint, and I see you as if you were going to live to be one hundred, my adored son, I listened to you from the first moment, ever since you asked me without saying a word, mother, father, brother, help me to get what's inside me out, let me *present myself.*

She never fully understood that request, especially when she remembered another overheard conversation between the brothers, when Danton told Santiago that the good thing about the body is that it can satisfy us at any moment, and Santiago told him it can also betray us at any moment; and that's why you've got to catch pleasure on the fly, replied Danton, and Santiago: "Other satisfactions cost dearly, you have to work for them," and then both in one voice: *"They escape from us,"* followed by a shared fraternal laugh.

Danton was afraid of nothing but sickness and death. That's true of many men. They can fight hand to hand in a trench but be unable to endure witnessing the pain of childbirth. He sought and found pretexts for not visiting his parents' house on Avenida Sonora. He preferred to telephone, ask for Santiago even though Santiago hated telephones—the most horrifying distraction ever invented to torture artists, how great it was when he was a boy and there were the two systems, Ericsson and Mexicana, when it was hard to communicate.

He looked at Laura.

That was before the sicknesses followed one after the other ever more rapidly, and the doctors could find no explanation for the boy's increasing weakness, his low resistance to infection, the incomprehensible wearing down of his immunological system, and what the doctors didn't say, what only Laura Díaz said, my son has to live out his own life, I'll see to that, nothing—not sicknesses, not useless medicines, not medical advice—matters to me, what I must give my son is everything my son should have if he were going to live for a hundred years, I'm going to give my son the love, the satisfaction, the conviction that he lacked nothing in the years of his life, nothing, nothing, nothing.

She watched over him at night as he slept, wondering, what can I save of my son the artist that will last beyond the echo of death? Surprised, she admitted that she wanted not only that her son might have what he deserved but that she, Laura Díaz, might have what her son could give her. He needed to receive. She did, too. She wanted to give. Did he?

Like all painters, Santiago the Younger, when he could still move freely, liked to step back from his paintings, to see them at a certain distance.

"I look for them as if they were lovers, but I re-create them as ghosts." He tried to laugh.

She answered those words in silence later on, when Santiago could no longer get out of bed, and she had to lie down next to him to console him, to be literally at his side, supporting him. "I don't want to be deprived of you."

She didn't want to be deprived, she meant, of that part of herself that was her son.

"Tell me your plans, your ideas."

"You speak as if I were going to live a hundred years."

"A century fits into a day of success," whispered Laura, with no fear of banality.

Santiago simply laughed. "Is being successful worthwhile?"

"No," she surmised. "Sometimes absence, silence are better."

Laura was not going to compile a list of things a boy of great talent, dying at the age of twenty-six, was not going to do, to know, to enjoy. The young painter was like a frame without a painting which she would have liked to fill with her own experiences and with their shared promises, she would have liked to bring her son to Detroit to see Diego's mural in the Arts Institute, she would have liked both of them to go to the legendary museums, the Uffizi, the Louvre, the Maurits-huis, the Prado.

She would have wanted . . .

Sleeping with you, entering your bed, extracting from nearness and dreams the forms, visions, challenges, the very strength I wish I could give you when I touch you, when I whisper in your ear, your final weakness threatens me more than it does you and I want to test your strength, tell you that your strength and mine depend on each other, that my caresses, Santiago, are your caresses, those you didn't have, will never have, accept my nearness, accept the body of your mother, do nothing, son, I bore you, I carried you inside me, I am you and you are me, what I do is what you would do, your heat is my heat, my body is your body, do nothing, I'll do it for you, say nothing, I'll say it for you, forget this night, I'll remember it always for you.

"My son, what do you need, what can I do for you?"

"Nothing, Mama, what can I do for you?"

"You know I wish I could steal all the glories and virtues from the world and give them to you."

"Thank you. But you already did, didn't you know?"

They wouldn't say it, ever. Santiago loved as if he were dreaming. Laura dreamed as if she were loving. Their bodies became again as they were at the beginning, the seed of each one in the womb of the other. She was reborn in him. He killed her in one single night. She did not want to think about anything. She allowed fugitive, whirling, lost images to pass through her mind, the perfume of the rain in Xalapa, the tree of smoke in Catemaco, the jewel-encrusted goddess in El Zapotal, the bloody hands washing themselves in the river, the green stick in the desert, the araucaria tree in Veracruz, the river flowing with a shriek into the Gulf, the five chairs on the balcony opposite Chapultepec, the six place settings and the napkins rolled up in their silver rings, the doll Li Po, Santiago her brother sinking dead into the sea, the severed fingers of Grandmother Cosima, the arthritic fingers of Aunt Hilda trying to play the piano, the ink-stained fingers of the poet aunt, Virginia, the urgent busy fingers of Mutti Leticia preparing a *huachinango* in the Catemaco, the Veracruz, the Xalapa kitchens, Auntie's swollen feet dancing *danzones* in the Plaza de Armas, Orlando's open arms inviting her to waltz at the hacienda, the love of Jorge, love, love . . .

"Thank you. Didn't you know?"

"What else? Something else."

"Don't leave the birdcages open."

"They'd come back. They are good and loving birds."

"But cats aren't like that."

She hugged him tight. She did not close her eyes, hugging her son. She looked around, the white frames, the already finished paintings leaning one against the other like sleeping infantrymen, an army of colors, a parade of possible looks that would be able or never would be able to give their momentary life to the canvas, each one the owner of a double existence, that of being looked at and not.

"I dreamed about what happens to the paintings when they lock up the museums and they're left alone all night."

That was Santiago the Younger's theme. The naked couples that look at each other and never touch, as if they knew, modestly, they were being looked at. The bodies in his paintings were not beautiful, not classical, they had a certain emaciated, even demonic aspect. They were a temptation, not that of coupling but that of being seen, surprised, in the moment of constituting themselves as a couple. That was their beauty, expressed in pale gray or very tenuous rose tones, where the flesh stood out like an intrusion unforeseen by God, as if in the artistic world of Santiago, God had not conceived of this intruder, his rival, the human being.

"Don't think I'm just resigning myself to not living. I'm not resigning myself to not working. I don't know, for days now, the sun hasn't shone on my head in the morning as it used to before. Would you open the curtains, Mama?"

After opening the curtains so the light would come in, Laura turned around to look at Santiago's bed. Her son was no longer there. All that remained was a silent lament floating in the air.

# 17. Lanzarote: 1949

## 1.

Y OU SHOULDN'T HAVE COME HERE. This island doesn't exist.
It's a mirage in the African desert. It's a stone raft detached
from Spain. It's a Mexican volcano that forgot to erupt. You're
going to believe what you see, and when you leave you'll realize there's
nothing there. By steamer, you will approach a black fortress that leaps
out of the Atlantic like a phantom far from Europe. Lanzarote is the
stone ship anchored precariously off the sands of Africa, but the stone
of the island is hotter than the desert sun.

Everything you see is false, it is our daily cataclysm, it happened last
night, it hasn't had time yet to make itself into history, and it will disappear at any moment, just as it appeared, in the twinkling of an eye.
You look at the mountains of fire that dominate the landscape and
remember that barely two centuries ago they didn't exist. The highest
and strongest peaks on the island were just born and they were born
destroying, burying the humble vineyards in molten lava, and no
sooner had the first eruption subsided a hundred years ago, than the

volcano yawned again and with its breath burned all the plants and buried all the roofs.

You shouldn't have come here. What brought you to me again? Nothing of this is real. How could a mountain range of sand and a lake of azure blue stronger than the blue of sea or sky fit within a crater under the sea? How I'd love to meet you under the waves, where you and I could again become like two ghosts of the ocean that was always separating us. Are we going to reunite now, you and I, on a tremulous island where fire is buried alive?

Look: all you have to do is plant a tree less than a meter down for its roots to burn. All you have to do is pour a pitcher of water into a hole, any hole, for it to boil. And if I could have taken refuge in the lava labyrinth that is the underground beehive of Lanzarote, I'd have done it and you'd never have found me. Why did you look for me? How did you find me? No one should know I'm here. You are here, but I don't dare look at you. This is a lie; you're here, and I don't want you to look at me. I don't want you to compare me to the man you saw for the first time in Mexico eleven years ago—though a millennium has lapsed between that meeting and this one, if it's true that hell has a history and the devil keeps track of time: the devil too is part of eternity. Now is not ten years ago, when I said,

"*Stay a little longer,*" and you've probably forgotten our discussions with Basilio Baltazar and Domingo Vidal, and you're going to laugh, Laura, because all our sense became nonsense, loss, death, inexplicable cruelty, assault on life. What's left of us, Laura? Only my eyes from ten years ago, when they anchored in yours as yours did in mine, and you asked why I was different from the others, and I answered in silence, "Because I'm only looking at you."

Does the truth you see now remain, do you see your old lover, a refugee on one of the Canary Islands, off the African coast, when the last time you saw him was in Mexico, in your arms, in a hotel hidden next to a park of pine and eucalyptus trees? Is this man the same as that one? Do you know what that man was seeking and what this one seeks? Is it the same, or are they two different things? Because this man is *seeking*, Laura—only to you would I dare say such a thing—this man who loved you is seeking something. Can you look right at me and tell me the truth: what do you see?

Separated for ten years, with the right to falsify our lives so as to explain our loves and justify what's happened to our faces. I could lie to you as I lied to myself for years. I didn't get there in time, that day we separated. The *Prinz Eugen* had already sailed for Germany when I reached Cuba. I could do nothing. The American government refused to grant asylum to the passengers, all of them Jews fleeing Germany. The Cuban government followed if not the instructions then the example of the United States. Perhaps the situation of the Jews under Hitler still hadn't penetrated the conscience of the U.S. public. Right-wing politicians were preaching isolationism, were saying that facing up to Hitler was a dangerous illusion, a left-wing trap, Hitler had restored order and prosperity to Germany, Hitler was a danger invented by perfidious Albion to draw the Yankees into another fatal European war, Roosevelt was a scoundrel capitalizing on the international crisis to make himself indispensable and win another election and then another. Let Europe commit suicide on her own. Saving Jews was not a popular idea in a country where Jews were not allowed in country clubs, expensive hotels, public swimming pools, as if they were bearers of the plague of Calvary. Roosevelt was a pragmatic President. He had no support for increasing the number of immigrants approved by Congress. He gave in. *Fuck you.*

I could lie to you. I reached Cuba that week when I abandoned you and got permission to board the ship. I had a Spanish diplomatic passport and the captain was a decent man, a sailor of the old school annoyed by the presence on his ship of Gestapo agents. They raised their arms in the fascist salute when they heard I was from Spain. They took it for granted the war was won. I returned their salute. What do symbols matter to me? I wanted to save Raquel.

My attention was drawn to the extreme youthful beauty of one of the agents, a Siegfried who couldn't have been more than twenty-five years old, blond and forthright—there was no line on his face between his closely shaven jaw and his cheeks covered with blond down—while his partner, a small man perhaps sixty years old, without his black uniform, boots, and Nazi armband could have been a bank accountant or trolley conductor or marmalade salesman. He used a pince-nez, had a tiny mustache sprouting like two fly wings on either side of the division in his lips which according to Jewish tradition the sword of the God of Israel had opened with one stroke above the mouth of the newborn so they'd forget their immense racial, prenatal memory. The little man's eyes were lost like two dead herrings in the bottom of the pot that was his shaven head. He wasn't a policeman at all; he was an executioner.

They greeted me with raised arms, the little man shouted Long live Franco! I returned the salute.

I found her crouching on the prow, next to the mast where the red banner emblazoned with the swastika was flying. She wasn't looking toward Morro Castle or the city. She was staring at the sea, returned to the sea, as if her gaze could reach all the way back to Freiburg, to our university and our youth.

I softly touched her shoulder and she had no need to see me, with her eyes closed she clasped my legs, pressing her face against my knees, and wailed with a penitent's sob, almost a shout, no longer hers, echoing in the Havana sky like a chorus not of Raquel's voices but as if she were the receptor of a hymn that flew from Europe to lodge in the voice of the woman I'd come to save.

*For the price of my love for you for . . .*
*Our love our . . .*

"Why won't anyone help us?" she asked, sobbing. "Why won't the Americans let us in, why won't the Cubans give us asylum, why won't the Pope answer the supplication of his people and mine, *Eli, Eli, lema sabachthani!* why have you abandoned us, am I not one of the four hundred million faithful the Holy Father can mobilize to save me, just me, a Jewish convert to Catholicism?"

I told her as I caressed her hair that I'd come to save her. Her hair, tousled by the cold tempestuous wind of that February morning in Cuba. I saw Raquel's windblown hair, the force of the wind, and nevertheless, the flag of the Reich on the prow was hanging, immobile, not waving, as if heavy with lead.

"You?"

Raquel raised her dark eyes, her black, unbroken eyebrows, her dark Sephardic skin, her lips half open in prayer and weeping—the similarity to fruit, her long, tremulous nose—and I could see her eyes again.

I told her I was there to take her off the ship, I'd come to marry her, it was the only way she could stay in the New World, married to me she'd be a Spanish citizen, they wouldn't be able to touch her, the Cuban authorities agreed, a Cuban judge would come on board to officiate.

"And what about the captain? Can't the captain marry us?"

"No, we're in Cuban waters."

"You're lying to me. He does have the right to. But he's afraid. We're all afraid. These animals have managed to frighten the whole world."

I took her in my arms; the ship would sail in a few hours, and no one will ever see again the Jews who were returned to the Reich, no one, Raquel, especially you and the passengers on this ship, you're guilty of having left and of not having found refuge, listen to the Führer laughing, if no one else wants them, why would I?

"Why is it that St. Peter's successor, St. Peter who was a Jewish fisherman, doesn't speak against those who persecute his descendants, the Jews?"

I wanted her not to think about that, she was going to be my wife, and then we'd fight together against this evil, because we have finally come to know the face of evil in all the suffering of that time, I said, at least we've learned that, now you know what Satan's face is like, Hitler betrayed Satan by giving him the face God took away from him when He hurled Satan into the abyss: between heaven and hell, a hurricane like this one advancing on Cuba erased Lucifer's face, left him with a face as blank as a sheet and the sheet fell in the center of the crater of hell covering the devil's body, awaiting the day of his reappearance just as St. John announced it: And I saw a Beast rising out of the sea, with ten horns and seven heads . . . Men worshipped the dragon, for he had given his authority to the Beast, saying, "Who is like the Beast, and who can fight against it?" And the Beast was given a mouth uttering haughty and blasphemous words, and that was the Beast imagined by St. John. Now we know who that Beast is. We're going to fight it. It's a shit stain on the flag of God.

"My love."

"I shall pray as a Catholic for the Jewish people, who were the bearers of the revelation until the advent of Christ."

"Christ too had a face."

"You mean Christ certainly had a face. He chose to leave the only proof of His appearance."

"Then you know the face of good but also the face of evil, the face of Jesus and the face of Hitler—"

"I don't want to know the face of good. If I could see God, I would be struck blind. God must never be seen. Faith would die. God doesn't allow Himself to be seen—so that we may believe in Him."

## 2.

He had to receive her outside the monastery because the monks did not allow the presence of women, and though they gave him a bare cell, they also arranged for him to have a hut near the town of San Bartolomé. There a hot wind blew which carried dust from the African desert and made it necessary for the peasants to protect their meager plantings with hedges.

"The whole island is fenced with stone walls to save the harvests, and they even cover the soil with moss to hold in the nighttime moisture for the vines."

She looked around the stone hut. There was only a cot, a table with a single chair, some flimsy shelves holding two plates, enough tinware for one person, and half a dozen books.

They gave him the cabin because he was not to feel himself an integral part of the monastery, but also they could say to the authorities, if asked, that he did not live there, that he was an employee, a gardener . . . When they received him, they made an exception to their rules, but on condition that he take the risk in going and coming, the risk of not feeling completely safe.

Jorge Maura understood the monks' offer. If a problem arose, they could always say he didn't live with them, he fulfilled his devotions in the chapel and did domestic work or gardening for them, yes, invisible gardening, sculpting rock, sowing volcanic rock—but he wasn't under the order's protection. The proof was that he lived outside the monastery in the town of San Bartolomé, exposed to breathing in the wandering sands from Africa, which seemed to be searching for their water clock, their hourglass for measuring a time that, with no receptacle, would become lost like the sand itself: the desert's diaspora.

They didn't put it to him like that, crudely, but they were insistent, fearful. They owed a debt to Maura's family, whose donations had made possible the construction of the monastery on Lanzarote. It was quite enough that they offered him protection: during the war he had worked with the relief agencies that brought blankets, medicines, and food to the neediest, air-raid victims, prisoners of war, internees in concentration camps, among them many Catholics opposed to Nazism. Hitler had laughed at the Catholic devotion of Franco's supporters, since for him Catholics were enemies to the same degree that Communists, Jews, and garbage were, and besides, Pope Pius XII never said a word in defense of Catholics or Jews . . . The Holy Father was a contemptible coward.

Jorge Maura had moved to Stockholm as a "displaced person" and from there had worked with aid agencies organized by the Swedish government and the Red Cross. After the war he'd gone to live in London and become a British subject. England had paid heroically for her earlier abandonment of the Spanish Republic—when Hitler could have been stopped—when during the Blitz, she had to resist the Luftwaffe's daily bombardments with help from no one. British travelers went back to Spain after the war, but Jorge Maura was not looking for sun or exoticism. He'd fought on the Republican side, and the Francoists' thirst for vengeance was still not slaked. Would they respect a subject of His Majesty George VI, or would they devise a way to arrest a "red" who'd slipped through their fingers?

The monks understood all that. Was it they who, despite all that, wanted to give him the opportunity of risk, of running into the Guardia Civil outside the monastery, of being recognized or betrayed? Or was it he, Maura, who wanted to tempt fate? If so, why? To exempt the monks from responsibility? Or to put himself at risk, to test himself, and above all to deny himself an undeserved security, he said that day of the meeting with Laura, the day she came to see him on Lanzarote? Security to which neither he nor anyone else had a right.

"Why would I lie to you, my love? I've come for you. I'm asking you to come back to Mexico with me. I want you to be safe."

She wanted to understand him. Very frankly, although who knows if wisely, she'd told him I still love you, I need you more than ever, come back with me, forgive me if I'm offering myself so openly to you like this, but I really need you. I've never loved anyone the way I still love you.

Then he looked at her in a way that she understood as sad, but that slowly but surely she began to recognize as distant.

Even so, she felt a movement of rejection in herself when he told her he wanted to be in a place where he would be in danger and at the same time need protection, so as not to feel strong. Danger didn't strip him of power, but it did give him the power to resist, never to feel comfortable.

It was an involuntary rejection. She was seated on the only chair in the cabin while he remained standing, leaning against a bare wall. Why should she be surprised? There was always something monastic and severe in Jorge Maura, even with the occasional lapses. But the practical and spiritual life of this man she loved was always enveloped, as the earth is wrapped in the atmosphere, by a skin of sensuality. She did not know him without his sex. He looked at her and read her mind.

"Don't think I'm a saint. I'm a ruined narcissist, which is rather different. This island is both my prison and my refuge."

"You're like a king who resents that the world hasn't understood him," she said, playing with the box of matches, indispensable in this abandoned space untouched by electricity.

"A wounded king, in any case."

Was he here out of conviction, because of conversion, because *she'd* become Catholic, and now *he* was seeking the way to return to the Church, to believe in God? Raquel and Jorge, the other couple.

Jorge laughed. He hadn't lost his laugh; he wasn't a martyred saint in some Zurbarán painting, but that's exactly what he looked like in this space of chiaroscuro which suggested it, which introduced her into a pictorial world where the central figure personified loss of pride as a means of redemption. Yet at the same time, one could see that redemption *was* his pride. Does God put up with the saint's pride? Can there be a heroic saint? If God is invisible, can He show himself in the saint?

She raised her eyes and met Maura's. His face had changed a great deal over the years. He'd had white hair since his twenties, but his eyes hadn't been so sunken, eyes so enamored of his brain, his face so thin; his white beard accentuated the time that had passed, that in his prolonged youth had been pure, promised time. His face had changed, yet she saw that it was the same; it hadn't changed, it wasn't another face, even if it was different.

"I can distance myself from myself but not from my body." He looked at her as if reading her thoughts.

"Remember that our bodies liked each other a great deal. I'd like to be with you again."

He told her she was the world, and she said, Tell me then, why can't you be in the world?

Jorge's silence was not eloquent, but she went on reading his thoughts, for he gave her no option but that of conjecture. Was he searching for solitude, faith, or both? Was he fleeing the world? Why?

"You're both in and not in the monastery."

"That's right."

"Are you or aren't you in the religious community?" She thought he could explain himself to her. He owed it to her after so long. "We always understood each other."

He answered very indirectly and with a distant smile. He reminded her of things she already knew. He was a privileged disciple of the Spanish and European university system that had evolved when Spain—he smiled—was emerging from the Escorial and entering

Europe, licking its wounds after losing the war with the United States and the final loss of its empire in the New World, Cuba and Puerto Rico, always the last colonies. Spain joined Europe thanks to the genius of Ortega y Gasset, and Maura was his disciple. That marked him forever. Then Husserl in Freiburg, along with Raquel . . . He was a privileged man. He had to argue to be allowed to fight against the enemies of culture, against Franco and the Falange, who with their shit-covered boots sullied the halls of universities shouting *Death to Intelligence!* He wasn't allowed: they gave him the acrid taste and swift machine-gun fire at the Jarama, but after that they told him, you're more useful as a diplomat, a man who can convince others, a loyal emissary . . . being a Republican of aristocratic origin. He was on the good side. The world was his. Even if he lost it, it would always be his. He felt closer to the people fighting in Madrid and at the Ebro and the Jarama than he did to fascism's cruel bourgeoisie and vulgar lumpen. He hated Franco, hated Millán Astray and his famous slogan *Death to Intelligence!*, hated Queipo de Llano and his radio programs broadcast from Seville and his challenge to Spanish women to have sex with Moors in Andalusia, where men were real men.

"And now you have nothing." Laura looked at him devoid of emotion. She was tired of Jorge's political history.

She wanted to tell him that he was left without the world, but she did not think, did not feel that Jorge Maura had come to Lanzarote to convince God with his sacrifice.

"Because it is a sacrifice, I see that, isn't it so?"

"You mean that when the war was over I should have gone back to my intellectual vocation, to recall my masters Ortega and Husserl and write?"

"Why not?"

He laughed. "Because it's a fucking disaster to be creative when you know you're not Mozart or Keats. Dammit, I got tired of scratching around in my past. There's nothing in me to justify the pretension of creativity. This came before anything, before you, before Raquel, this is a matter of my own emptiness, my awareness of my own limits, maybe my sterility. Does what I'm saying to you seem awful? Now you

want to come along and sell me an illusion, which I don't believe in
but which does make me believe that either you're a fool or you under-
estimate my intelligence. Why don't you just leave me alone, so I can
fill the emptiness in my own way? Let me see things for myself, learn
if something can still grow in my soul, an idea, a faith, because I swear
to you, Laura, my soul is more desolate than this rock landscape you
see here . . . why?"

She embraced him, sank to her knees and embraced his legs, leaning her head against his knees, flushing with shame for the moisture in
his cheap gray slacks—they seemed worn out by washing, as if there
hadn't been time for them to dry and they still smelled of urine, and
the shirt too, washed quickly and put right back on because it was the
only one he had, and the bad odors hadn't gone away, the smell of an
earthly body, an animal body, tired of expelling humors, shit, semen.
Jorge my love, my Jorge, I don't know how to kiss you.

"I just don't have the strength to go on scratching at my roots. The
Spanish and Spanish American malady. Who are we?"

She begged his pardon for having provoked him.

"No, it's all right. Get up. Let me get a good look at you. You look so
clean, so clean . . ."

"What are you trying to tell me?"

By now Laura can't remember how her lover is standing, with his
moist freshly washed old clothes, with a smell of defeat no soap can
purge. By now she can't remember if he is standing or sitting on the
cot, if he is looking down or staring out the door. At the ceiling. Or into
her eyes.

"What am I trying to tell you? What do you know?"

"I know your biography. From the aristocracy to the Republic to
defeat to exile and from there to pride. The pride of Lanzarote."

"The pride of Lucifer." Jorge laughed. "You leave a lot of openings,
you know?"

"I know. The pride of Lanzarote? That isn't an opening. It's right
here. It's today."

"I clean the monks' latrines and see impossible drawings on the
walls. As if a repentant painter had begun something he never finished

and, because he knew it, chose the humblest and most humiliating place in the monastery to begin an enigma. Because what I see or imagine is a mystery, and the place of the mystery is the very spot where the good brothers, whether they want to or not, shit and piss. They are body, and their bodies remind them they can never be wholly spirit, as they'd like. Wholly."

"Do you think they know? Are they that naive?"

"They have faith."

God became flesh, said Maura in a kind of controlled exaltation, God stripped Himself of His holy impunity by making Himself man in Christ. That made God as fragile as the human beings who could recognize themselves in Him.

"Is that why we killed Him?"

"Christ became a man so we would recognize ourselves in Him."

But to be worthy of Christ, we had to sink lower so we wouldn't be more than what He is.

"A monk should think that when he's shitting. Jesus did the same, but I do it with more shame. That's faith. God's in the pots and pans, St. Teresa said."

"Was He looking for it?" asked Laura. "Looking for faith?"

"Christ had to abandon an invisible holiness in order to become flesh. Why ask me to become a saint—so I can incarnate a bit of Jesus' holiness?"

"Do you know what I thought when my son Santiago died? Is this the greatest sorrow in my life?"

"Did you think it was? Or did you wonder if it was? . . . I'm sorry, Laura."

"No. I thought that if God takes something from us, it's because He gave up everything."

"His own son, Jesus?"

"Yes. I can't help thinking this ever since I lost Santiago. He was the second, did you know? My brother and my son. Both. Santiago the Elder and Santiago the Younger. Both. You're sorry? Imagine how I feel!"

"Look a bit further. God renounced everything. He had to renounce His own creation, the world, to let us be free."

God became absent in the name of our freedom, said Jorge, and since we use that freedom for evil and not only for good, God had to become flesh in Christ in order to show us that God could be a man and nonetheless avoid evil.

"That's our conflict," Maura went on. "Being free to do evil or good and to know that if I do evil I offend the freedom God gave me, but if I do good, I also offend God because I'm daring to imitate Him, to be like Him, to sin through pride like Lucifer; you yourself said so."

It was horrible to hear that: Laura took Jorge's hand.

"What am I saying that is so terrible? Tell me."

"That God asks us to do something He doesn't allow. I've never heard anything crueler."

"You haven't? Well, I've seen it."

3.

Do you know why I resist believing in God? Because I fear seeing Him one day. I fear that if I could see God, I'd be struck blind. I can approach God only to the degree that He distances Himself from me. God needs to be invisible so I can labor over a plausible faith, but at the same time I fear God's visibility because at that precise moment I'd no longer have faith but proof. Here, read St. John of the Cross's *Ascent of Mount Carmel*, come with me, Laura, into the darkest night of time, the night when I went out in disguise to seek the beloved so we could be transformed, she into me, my senses suspended, and my neck wounded by a serene hand that says: Look and don't forget . . . Who separated me from the beloved, God or the devil?

I saw the beloved fleetingly, for less than ten seconds, when our Swedish Red Cross truck passed by the barbed wire at Buchenwald, and in that instant I saw Raquel lost amid a multitude of prisoners.

It was very difficult to identify anyone in that mass of emaciated, hungry beings in their striped uniforms with the Star of David pinned to their breasts, huddled under blankets ripped by the February cold, clinging one to another. Except her.

If that was what they allowed us to see, what was there behind the visible, what were they hiding from us, didn't they realize that in showing us this they forced us to imagine the real face, the hidden face? But in offering us this terrible face, weren't they saying that the worst didn't exist—no longer existed—that it was the face of death?

I saw Raquel.

A man in uniform was holding her up, a Nazi guard was supporting her, I don't know if it was because he was ordered to show the compassion of someone helping a person in need; or so that Raquel wouldn't collapse like a pile of rags; or because between the two, Raquel and the guard, there was a relationship of reciprocal yielding, of tiny favors that to her must have seemed enormous—some extra food, a night in the enemy's bed, perhaps a simple, human portion of pity; or perhaps because it was just theater, a pantomime of humanity to impress the visitors; for perhaps a new, unforeseeable love between victim and executioner, one as hurt as the other, and both able to withstand the hurt only in the other's unexpected company, the executioner identified by the pain of his obedience and the victim by the pain of hers—two obedient beings, each one at the orders of someone stronger, Hitler had said it, Raquel repeated it to me, there are only two peoples confronting each other: Germans and Jews.

Perhaps she was saying to me: Do you see why I didn't leave the ship with you in Havana? I wanted to have happen what is now happening to me. I didn't want to avoid my destiny.

Then Raquel freed herself from the grasp of the Nazi guard and clasped the barbed wire with her bare hands; between her executioner or lover or protector or shadow and me, Jorge Maura, her university lover, with whom she had one day gone to the Freiburg cathedral and kneeled down side by side with no fear of being ridiculous and prayed out loud:

*we shall return to ourselves*
*we shall think as if we'd founded the world*
*we shall be the living subjects of history*
*we shall live the world of life*

those words we said then with profound intellectual emotion—they came back now, Laura, as a crushing reality, an intolerable fact, not because they came true but precisely because they weren't possible, the horror of the age had eliminated them yet in a mysterious and marvelous way made them possible, they were the final truth of my swift and terrible encounter with the woman I loved and who loved me . . .

Raquel stabbed her hands with the wire and then pulled them up from the steel barbs and showed them to me, bleeding like . . . I don't know like what, because I don't know and don't want to know how to compare Raquel Mendes-Alemán's beautiful hands with anything, those hands made to touch my body the way she touched the pages of a book or played a Schubert impromptu or touched my arm to warm herself when we walked together during the winter along the Freiburg streets: now her hands were bleeding like Christ's wounds, and that was what she was showing me, don't look at my face, look at my hands, don't feel sorrow for my body, feel compassion for my hands, George, have pity, friend . . . Thanks for my destiny. Thanks for Havana.

The Nazi commandant who was with us, hiding with a smile the alarm and annoyance Raquel's act had made him feel, said, fatuously: "See? That story about Buchenwald's fences being electrified is false."

"Take care of her hands. Look how they're bleeding, Herr Kommandant."

"She touched the barbed wire because she wanted to."

"Because she's free?"

"That's right. That's right. You said the right thing."

## 4.

"I'm weak. You're all I have left. That's why I came to Lanzarote."

"I'm weak."

They made their way back to the monastery at nightfall. On this night, above all others, Jorge wanted to return to the religious community and confess his carnal weakness. Laura, in her reencounter with Jorge's body, felt the man's newness, as if their bodies had never been joined before, as if this time Laura had become flesh as an exception, only to look like herself, and he only to show himself naked to her.

"What are you thinking about?"

"About God advising us to do what He will not allow. To imitate Christ!"

"It isn't that He doesn't allow it. It's that He makes it difficult."

"I imagine God saying to me all the time, 'I hate in you the same thing that you've hated in others.'"

"Which is?"

He was living here, half protected, indecisive, not knowing if he wanted complete, certain physical and spiritual salvation or risk that would give value to the security. This is why he walked every morning from the monastery to the cabin and back every afternoon, from exposure to refuge, glaring, without so much as blinking, at the Guardia Civil, who had gotten used to him, greeted him, he worked with the brothers, a servant, a minor figure of no importance.

He went from one stone house to the other in the landscape of stone. He imagined a sky of stone and a stone sea, in Lanzarote.

"All day long you've been asking me if I believe in God or not, if I've recovered the faith of my Catholic culture, my childhood faith—"

"And you haven't answered me."

"Why did I become Republican and anticlerical? Because of the hypocrisy and crimes of the Catholic Church, its support for the rich and powerful, its alliance with the pharisees and against Jesus, its disdain for the humble and defenseless, even though it preached exactly the opposite. Did you see the books I have in the cabin?"

"St. John of the Cross and that copy of Sor Juana Inés de la Cruz we bought together on Tacuba Street . . . they're like brother and sister, because he's a saint and she isn't. She was humiliated, silenced, her books and poems were taken away, even her paper, ink, and pen."

"You should take a look at a volume that's just come out in France. One of the brothers gave it to me. *Gravity and Grace*, by Simone Weil, a Jew converted to Christianity. Read it. She's an extraordinary philosopher who can actually tell us we should never think about someone we love and from whom we're separated without imagining that person dead . . . She does an incredible reading of Homer. She says the *Iliad* teaches three lessons: never admire power, never disdain those who suffer, and never hate your enemies. Nothing is exempt from fate. She died during the war. Of tuberculosis and hunger, especially hunger, because she refused to eat more than the rations given her Jewish brothers and sisters in the Nazi camps. But she did it as a Christian, in the name of Jesus."

Jorge Maura stopped for a moment before the black and furrowed earth within sight of Timanfaya. The mountain was a blazing red, like a gospel of fire.

## 5.

I pardoned all the crimes of history because they were venial sins next to this crime: doing the impossible evil. That's what the Nazis did. They showed that the unimaginable evil was not only imaginable but possible. With them around, all the centuries of crimes of political power, of churches, armies, and princes fled my memory. What they had done could be imagined. What the Nazis did could not. Until then I thought evil existed but wouldn't let itself be seen and tried to hide, or presented itself as a necessary means for attaining a good end. You remember that was how Domingo Vidal thought of Stalin's crimes, as the means to a good end, and besides, they were based on a theory of collective good, Marxism. And Basilio Baltazar sought only the freedom of human beings by any means, by abolishing power, bosses, hierarchies.

Nazism, however, was evil proclaimed out loud, announcing proudly, "I am Evil. I am perfect Evil. I am visible Evil. I am Evil and proud of it. I justify nothing but extermination in the name of Evil. The death of Evil by the hand of Evil. Death as violence and only violence and nothing more than violence, without any redemption and without the weakness of a justification."

I want to see that woman, I said to the commandant of Buchenwald.

No, you're mistaken, the woman you named is not here, never has been.

347

Raquel Mendes-Alemán. That's her name. I just saw her on the other side of the barbed wire.

No, that woman doesn't exist.

You have killed her already?

Be careful. Don't go too far.

She let herself be seen by me and for that you killed her? Because she saw me and recognized me?

No. She doesn't exist. There's no record of her. Don't complicate things. After all, you're here only because of a gracious concession by the Reich. So you can see how well treated our prisoners are. It isn't the Hotel Adlon, to be sure, but if you'd come on a Sunday, you'd have seen the prisoners' orchestra. They played the overture to *Parsifal*. A Christian opera, did you know that?

I demand to see the registry of prisoners.

The registry?

Don't play dumb. You people are very orderly. I want to see the registry.

A page in the M's had been hastily torn out, Laura. They're so precise, so well organized, they'd allowed the torn binding to show where the page was missing, with the edges rough and jagged like the cliffs on Lanzarote's mountains.

I never learned anything more about Raquel Mendes-Alemán.

When the war was over, I went back to Buchenwald, but the corpses in the common graves were no longer what they had been, and the cremated bodies became powder for the wigs of Goethe and Schiller, shaking hands in Weimar, Athens of the North, where Cranach and Bach and Franz Lizst worked. None of those men would ever have invented the motto the Nazis placed over the entrance to the concentration camp. Not the well-known *Arbeit Macht Frei*, Work Makes You Free, but something infinitely worse: *Jedem das Seine*, You Get What You Deserve. Raquel. I want to remember her on the prow of the *Prinz Eugen* anchored in Havana harbor, when I offered to marry her to save her from the holocaust. I want to remember Raquel.

No, she looked at me with her eyes deep as a night of omens, why should I be the exception, the privileged individual?

Her words sufficed, for me, to sum up my whole experience in this half century, which was going to be the paradise of progress and instead was the hell of degradation. Not only the age of fascist and Stalinist horror but of the horror that those who fought against evil could not save themselves from, no one was exempted, Laura! not the English who hid rice from the Bengalis so they wouldn't have the will to revolt and join Japan during the war, not the Islamic merchants who collaborated with them, not the English who broke the legs of rebels who wanted national independence and refused medical care, not the French who collaborated in Nazi genocide or who cried out against the German occupation but considered the French occupation of Algeria, of Indochina, of Senegal a divine right, not the Americans who kept all the Caribbean and Central American dictators in power with their jails overflowing and their beggars in the streets as long as they supported the United States. Who was saved? Those who lynched blacks, or the blacks who were executed, jailed, forbidden to drink or urinate next to a white in Mississippi, land of Faulkner?

"Starting with us, evil ceased to be a possibility and became an obligation."

"I don't want to be pitied, Jorge. I'd rather be persecuted."

Those were the last words of Raquel that I heard. I don't know if I suffer because I didn't save her or because of her suffering. But the way she looked at her executioner in the camp, more than the way she looked at me, told me that right until the last minute Raquel affirmed her humanity and left me a question I'd always live with: what is the virtue of your virtue, my love, the love of my love, the justice of my justice, the compassion of my compassion?

"I want to share your suffering, the way you share the suffering of your people. That is the love of my love."

## 6.

Laura left Jorge on the island. She boarded the little ship knowing she would never return. Jorge Maura would never again be a clearly delineated figure for her, only a haze rising from a past that was always present, whose identification would be final proof that he was there even if he no longer existed.

Go on, she said, be a saint, be a hermit, climb up and sit alone on top of your column in the desert, be a comfortable martyr without martyrdom.

He said she was very hard on him.

She answered, because I love you. "Why are you hiding on an island? It would have been better if you'd stayed in Mexico. There's no hiding place better than Mexico City."

"I don't have the strength anymore. Forgive me."

"Well, you're a Spaniard. You can be sure that death will be late in reaching you."

Was the meeting so painful for her?

"No, it's that I've learned to fear those who deform me with their love, not those who hate me. When you went to Cuba, I asked myself a thousand times, can I live without him, can I live without his support? I badly needed your support to create a world of my own that I wouldn't have to sacrifice to anyone I loved. You gave it to me, you know, you supported me so that I could return to my home and tell the truth to my family, whatever happened. Without your love supporting me, I never would have dared. Without your memory, I would have been just one more adulteress. With you, no one dared cast the first stone against me. I feel free because you are with me."

"Laura, the worst is over. Calm down. Understand that I stay here alone of my own free will."

"Alone? That word I don't understand. How are you going to be religious without the world, how are you going to reach God without leaving yourself? You see how you live halfway between the monastery and the world. Do you think the cloistered monks who forbid the presence of women have already found God, you think they can find Him without the world? How pretentious you are, pretentious bastard! Are you going to purge the sins of the twentieth century hiding away on this stone island? You are the very pride you detest. You are your own

Lucifer. How are you going to have your pride pardoned, Jorge, you bastard?"

"By imagining that God says to me: I hate in you the same thing you've hated in others."

"Imagining? Only that?"

"Listening, Laura."

"Do you know something? I leave here admiring your indifference and your serene wisdom. Which I don't have."

"Raquel is buried in an unmarked grave, mixed with hundreds of other naked bodies. Can we be more than she? I'm not better. I'm different. Just like you."

"Why do you think you're liberated?" she asked incredulously.

"Because you came to see me filled with incredulity. You're the truly incredulous person here. As I was before. I'm finding health seeing a human being with less faith than I. What insignificant things we are, Laura."

She asked him to answer the question she'd been asking since she reached Lanzarote. (You shouldn't have come here. This island doesn't exist. You're going to believe what you see, and when you leave you'll realize there's nothing there.) Do you believe or don't you?

"Which is like asking, is Christianity true or false? And I answer that your question has no importance. What I want to find out here on Lanzarote, halfway between monastic life and life as you understand it, between security and danger, is whether faith can give meaning to the madness of being here on earth."

What had he discovered?

"That the life of Christ is always possible for a Christian, but no one dares imitate it."

"No one dares, or no one can?"

"It's that they think that being like Christ is acting as Christ acted—raising the dead, multiplying loaves . . . they transform Christ into an active ideology. Laura, Christ only seeks us if we don't believe in Him. Christ finds us if we don't look for Him. It's Pascal's truth: you found me because you didn't seek me. That is my truth today. Go away, Laura. Realize I have no joy. Every afternoon on this island is very sad."

I came because your place was empty, Laura said to herself as she left the nocturnal coast of Lanzarote, sailing for Tenerife, as the night became black and the island red. I couldn't bear it anymore. It's dangerous, living in a vacant space, nostalgic for the life my son didn't have and the love you took away from me. But I lost my son, and you lost Raquel. We both gave up something precious. Perhaps God, if He exists, recognizes that loss and takes note of our sorrows, each of them. Now I no longer want to think about you. To think about you consoles me too much and keeps my imagination going. I want to renounce you completely. I never met you.

When they had separated at the monastery entrance, Laura had waited for a moment, confused. Why wouldn't they let a woman in? She saw that nothing was keeping her from entering, from looking for Jorge just once more, from feeling his hot lips for the last time, from repeating the words that would now be unspoken for all time.

I love you.

He was on all fours in the solitary refectory, licking the floor with his tongue, tenacious, disciplined, tile after tile.

# 18. Avenida Sonora: 1950

T HERE COMES A MOMENT in life when nothing but loving the
      dead has any importance. We have to do everything we can for
      the dead. You and I together, we can suffer because the dead
person is absent. Their presence is not absolute. Their absence is the
only absolute. But the desire we have for the dead person is neither
presence nor absence. There is no one left in my house, Jorge. If you
want to believe my solitude is what returned me to you, I give you permission to do so.

My husband, Juan Francisco, died.

My auntie, María de la O, died.

But the death of my adored son Santiago is the only real death for
me, it comprises all the others, gives them meaning.

My auntie's death actually gives me joy. She died as she wished, in
her beloved Veracruz, dancing *danzones* with a tiny man named Matías
Matadamas, who dressed all in powder blue to take her out in the public square twice a week dancing the *danzón* on the space of a single
brick.

The real death of Juan Francisco had occurred long before. His inanimate body merely confirmed it. He approached death dragging his feet, saying to me, "I can't think of anything," asking me, "Should we have married, you and I?" Because the day he died I asked him if we could finally stop hurting each other.

"I've lost too much time hating you."

"And I, forgetting you."

Who said what, Jorge? He or I? I don't know anymore. I don't know which of us said, "If you don't tell me I deserved your hatred, I won't tell you you deserved to be forgotten."

I want to believe I didn't love him when he died. Ever since I went back to him after you left for Cuba, I always asked myself, Why does he accept me again? Is he weak or perverse? Is he making a profession of his failure so he can get the only form of love left to him—the compassion of others? How could I abandon such a weak man?

Every day, my son Santiago makes me think that everything I love is dead.

I console myself the way we all do. Time will pass. Gradually, I'll be able to bear the absence.

Then I react violently. I don't want my pain to fade, ever. I want the absence of my son always, always, to be intolerable.

Then my pride takes control of me. I wonder if a love with no other foundation but memory won't ultimately become tolerable, I wonder if a love that always wants pain should subdue that caress of memory and demand a void, a great void in which there is no room for memory or tenderness and where absence, knowing him to be absent, will admit no consolation.

It came from where she least expected it. Pity.

It was Juan Francisco's tears over the body of Santiago. The father mourned the death of the son as if no one in the world had loved him more, more secretly, less openly. Why had he kept his distance from Santiago and drawn so close to Danton? To suffer less when Santiago died? Did he weep because he was never close to him, or did he weep because he loved him more than he loved anyone and only death allowed him to show it?

Seeing the father weep over the body of the son returned to Laura's memory one verbal slap after another, as if everything her husband and she had said to hurt each other over the years was being repeated, more venomously, at that very moment, marrying you was like turning the other cheek to destiny, don't talk to me as if you were a saint talking to a temptress, speak to me, look me in the eye, why didn't you judge me for my will to love you, Juan Francisco, instead of condemning me for the adultery? I have no idea why I thought you an exciting, brave man, that's what they said about you, you were always "they say about him," a whisper, never a reality, between the two of us there was never love, only illusion, mirages, which never last, not love based on respect and admiration, life with you has overpowered me, you've left me perplexed and sick, I don't hate you, you just tire me out, you love me too much, a real lover should never love one too much, should never cloy, Juan Francisco, our marriage is dead, either everything or nothing killed it, who knows? But let's start burying it, dearest, because it stinks to high heaven.

And now she could say thank you, thanks to your all too facile adoration I was able to achieve something better, that constant expectation which requires passion, thanks to you I reached Jorge Maura, the difference between you let me understand and love Jorge as I could never love you.

"I thought I had more strength than I do, Laura. Forgive me."

"I can't condemn the best of myself to the grave of memory. You forgive me."

And now she saw him weeping over the body of the exhausted son. She would have wanted to ask his forgiveness for having been unable, for thirty years, to penetrate beyond appearances, legends, the mystery of his origins, the myth of his past, the betrayal of his present.

It was terrible that they were finally able to speak thanks to the death of their son.

It was terrible for them to identify themselves, Laura and Juan Francisco, revealing that both, in secret, were staring with equal love at Santiago the Younger, thinking the same thoughts, he has everything, good looks, talent, generosity, everything but health, everything but life and time to live it. Only now did father and mother discover that both had refused to pity Santiago because in this house no one was permitted to pity anyone. We can betray with pity those whom we love.

"Is that why you favored Danton so openly, Juan Francisco?"

Laura had boasted of the eloquent silence between mother and son. Solitude and quietude had united them. Was that also true about the relation of Santiago to Juan Francisco? Was being explicit about what was taking place more than an offense? Was it a betrayal? Mother and son lived a skein of complicities, shared thoughts, ways of saying thank you, everything but compassion—damned, forbidden compassion . . . did the father also live and feel this, at a distance, celebrating the other son, father of both?

Every mother knows there are children who take care of themselves. Trying to protect them is an effrontery. That was how it was with Danton. To her, his father's nearness to him seemed an abuse; Juan Francisco understood nothing, gave everything to the son who needed nothing, Danton who almost from infancy played all day unaware of what might be happening in the shadows and silence of their home where his brother lived. But Laura knew instinctively that even if Danton needed no attention and Santiago did, an excessive display of it would have been more offensive and damaging to the weak boy than to the strong one. That wasn't the problem. Danton moved through the world adjusting everything to his own advantage. Santiago disregarded everything except what he considered essential to his painting, his music, his poetry, his Van Gogh and his Egon Schiele, his Baudelaire and his Rimbaud, his Schubert . . .

Now, seeing both father and son, Juan Francisco and Danton, weeping over the handsome, ascetic body of the young Santiago, Laura realized that the brothers had loved each other but were too modest to show it—brotherly love is virile; sometimes it must wait until the moment of death to show itself as love, affection, tenderness . . . Now she blamed herself. Had Laura Díaz stolen all her glories from the world just to give them solely to Santiago? All the virtue for the weak brother? Didn't the strong brother also deserve something? Had she in reality lost two sons?

"Did I ever tell you," said Juan Francisco after the funeral, "that one night I surprised them talking to each other like men? Both were saying, 'We're all we need.' They were declaring themselves independent of you and of me, Laura. How incredible to surprise your sons in the very moment when they are declaring independence. Except that Santiago really meant what he said. All he needed was himself. Danton's different. He needs success, money, society. He needs more than himself; he's fooling himself. That's why he needs us more than ever."

Would there be time to correct thirty years of errors in a shared life with two adult sons, one already dead? Santiago wrote a poem just before he died that Laura showed to Juan Francisco, especially one line: *"We are translated lives."* What did it mean? What did those everyday phrases the boy used mean? Don't leave the cage door open, those are homing pigeons in there and they won't leave, but cats are different, they go and come back to hurt . . . "The sun doesn't always hit me on the head." Perhaps they meant that Santiago knew how to detach himself from himself, transform himself, discover the other within. She discovered it, too, but didn't tell him. What about you, Juan Francisco?

"My sons are my biography, Laura. I don't have any other."

"What about me?"

"You're part of it too, darling."

Was that Juan Francisco's secret, that his life had no secret because he had no past, that his life was only external, the fame of Juan Francisco the orator, the leader, the revolutionary? And behind it, what was there that opened up behind it? Nothing?

"There was a girl in Villahermosa who suffered from mongolism. She would threaten people, hit them, and spit, all violently. Her mother had to put blinders on her, as if she were a horse, so she couldn't see the world and could calm down."

"Was she your neighbor in Tabasco?"

No, he didn't have neighbors, he said, shaking his head.

"Who are you? Where are you from? Are you ever going to tell me?"

Again, he shook his head.

"Don't you realize that separates us, Juan Francisco? Just when we're on the verge of understanding each other you deny me the story of your life once again?"

This time he nodded his head.

"What did you do, Juan Francisco? Were you a hero who simply got tired? Was your heroism a lie? Do you know that's what I've come to believe? What myth are you going to transmit to your sons, the living and the dead one, too—have you thought about that? What are you going to leave us? The whole truth? A half-truth? The good part? The bad? Which part goes to Danton, who's alive? Which to Santiago, who's dead?"

She knew that only time, which fades like smoke, would reveal her husband's jealously guarded secret. How many times had they each invited the other to give up? Could they ever say, *I'm giving everything to you, right now*?

"Later you'll understand," said the man. He was more and more beaten down.

"Do you realize what you're making me do? You're making me ask you questions. What must I give you, Juan Francisco, what do you want from me? Would you like me to call you 'sweetheart' and 'my love' again, even though you know I reserve those words for another man and for my sons, they're not your words, you're my husband, Juan Francisco, not my tenderness, my dear one, my love (my hidalgo, my adored little Spanish boy . . . )?"

She feared—or only wanted to believe—that at a certain moment Juan Francisco would shake off his lethargy and touch her with another voice, the voice, new and old at the same time, of the end. She schooled herself in patience for the end to come, visibly approaching in the physical collapse of this oversized man with wide shoulders and immense hands, short torso and long legs, like others in his caste. His caste: Laura wanted to attribute something to Juan Francisco, at least race, caste, descent, family, father, mother, lovers, first wife, illegitimate or legitimate children, what difference did it make? One day, she was on the verge of taking the Interoceanic train back to Veracruz and from there going by boat and highway to Tabasco to consult registries, but that made her feel like a contemptible busybody. So she followed her daily routine, helping Frida Kahlo, in more pain than ever, with one leg amputated, a prisoner of her bed and wheelchair, and she went to gatherings hosted by the Riveras in honor of the new wave of exiles—Americans persecuted by the House Un-American Activities Committee.

A new war had begun, the Cold War. Churchill had recognized it in a famous speech: "An iron curtain has descended over Europe . . ." Stalin proved that the democracies' suspicions of the Soviet Union were well founded. The old dictator's paranoia led him to commit delirious crimes: he jailed and ordered the execution not of his nonexistent enemies but of his friends, out of fear that one day they might become enemies. He carried out preventive assassination and imprisonment, cruel and horribly unnecessary. Yet Picasso painted the "realistic" portrait of Stalin with a dove, because devotees of that strange monster— so argued about during the evenings with Domingo Vidal, Basilio Baltazar, and Jorge Maura in the Café de Paris during the Spanish Civil War—believed he was now champion of peace, enemy of U.S. imperialism. For their part, Americans invented their own anti-Communist paranoia and saw Stalinist agents under every rug, on every New York stage, and in every Hollywood film.

The new exiles began gathering at the Riveras' house, but many stopped coming because Diego's Marxist logorrhea bored them and they were indignant about Frida's devotion to Uncle Joe, to whom she dedicated a portrait and unlimited praise despite the fact that (or perhaps because) Stalin had had her lover Leon Trotsky murdered.

Laura Díaz remembered Jorge Maura's words—there's no need to change life, no need to transform the world. We have to diversify life. We have to give up the illusion that a recovered unity is the key to a new paradise. We have to see difference as a value. Difference strengthens identity. Jorge Maura had said he found himself between two truths: that the world was going to save itself, and that the world was doomed. Both are true: capitalism's corrupt society is doomed, but the revolution's ideal society is also doomed.

"Believe in the opportunities of freedom," said a warm voice behind Laura, a voice that dominated the debates (profound) and conversations (flat) at the Riveras' house. "Remember that politics is secondary to personal integrity. Without personal integrity the social life is not worth living."

"Jorge!" exclaimed Laura in a shock of disbelief, spinning around to see the face of a still young-looking man with thick hair and brows that were no longer black as they once had been but spattered with white.

"No. I'm sorry to disappoint you. Basilio. Basilio Baltazar. Remember me?"

They hugged each other with an emotion like that attending a new birth, as if they'd both in some way been reborn in that instant and, in the emotion of their meeting, could fall in love and again be the young people they had been fifteen years earlier. But now they were both accompanied, Laura Díaz by Jorge Maura, Basilio Baltazar by Pilar Méndez. And Jorge, on his island, forever accompanied by the other Mendes—Raquel.

They looked at each other with immense tenderness, unable to speak for a few moments.

"See?" Basilio smiled behind his moist eyes. "We never escape our problems. We never stop persecuting or being persecuted."

"Yes, I do see," she said in a broken voice.

"There are some terrific people among these gringos. They're almost all film or theater directors, writers, not to mention a few veterans of our war and the Lincoln Brigade. Remember?"

"How could I forget, Basilio?"

"Most of them live in Cuernavaca. Why don't we go down one weekend and talk to them."

All Laura could do was kiss the cheek of her old friend the Spanish anarchist, as if she were once again kissing Jorge Maura, as if she were seeing for the first time the always hidden face of Armonía Aznar, as if from the bottom of the gulf arose the face of her adored brother, the first Santiago. Basilio was the catalyst of a past Laura missed terribly but considered lost forever.

"I don't think so. You make our past into a present, Basilio. Thanks."

Going to Cuernavaca to argue about politics, but this time with Americans instead of Spaniards or Mexican labor leaders betrayed by the Revolution, by Calles and Morones . . . the idea tired and depressed her as she returned that night to the family house on Avenida Sonora, now so solitary without María de la O and Santiago, both dead, Danton married and living, as he always wanted to, in Las Lomas de Chapultepec. Laura, in an aesthetic fit, had sworn she'd never set foot in his house.

"You said you were going to change your in-laws' taste, Danton."

"Just wait a while, Mama. It's a period of adjustment, an accommodation. I have to make my father-in-law happy so I can dominate him. Don Aspirin's half senile. Don't worry, at least we got rid of the fountains on the terrace."

"What about your wife?"

"Mama, I swear poor Magda was so completely ignorant I had to finish her toilet training."

"You're as vulgar as they come." But Laura couldn't keep from laughing.

"I've actually got her convinced that the stork will be bringing the baby."

"What baby?" said Laura, hugging her son.

I'm fifty-two and I'm going to be a grandmother, she kept saying to herself on the way home from the Coyoacán party and Basilio Baltazar. She'd been forty when she met Jorge Maura. Now I live alone with Juan Francisco, but I am going to be a grandmother.

The mere sight of Juan Francisco in bathrobe and slippers opening the door reminded her that she was, like it or not, a wife. She instantly rejected a repugnant but all too noble idea that had flashed through her mind. We only survive at home. Only those who stay at home survive. Out in the world, chasing the light, the fireflies burn up and die. That had to be what her grandfather must have thought, the old German Don Felipe Kelsen, who crossed the ocean to lock himself away in the Catemaco coffee plantation never to leave again. Was he happier than his descendants? Children shouldn't be judged by their parents, much less the grandchildren. The idea that the generation gap has never been greater is false. The world has always been made up of generations standing on opposite sides of an abyss. It's also made up of couples divided at times by clamorous silences, like the one that separated Grandfather Felipe from his beautiful and mutilated Doña Cosima, whose self-absorbed gaze was never distracted—Laura knew from the time she was a child—from the dangerous and dashing bandit of Papantla. Seeing Juan Francisco in his robe and slippers open the door—old slippers with a hole for the big toe on his right foot to air, the chenille robe with gaudy stripes like a serape turned into a towel—she was seized with laughter thinking that her husband might be the secret child of that highwayman from the era of Benito Juárez.

"What the devil are you laughing at?"

"At the idea that we're going to be grandparents, old boy," she said, giggling hysterically.

In some unconscious way, the news of his daughter-in-law's pregnancy buried Juan Francisco for good. It was as if the announcement of an imminent birth demanded the sacrifice of a hasty death, so that the child could take the space now uselessly occupied by the old man; he was now sixty-nine. Well, that was an educated guess, said Laura, smiling, because no one had ever seen his birth certificate. She saw him as dead beginning the night when he opened the door of their solitary home. Which is to say, she took away the time left to him.

Now there would be no time for a few sad caresses.

She saw him close the door, double-lock it and slide the bolt, as if there were something worthy of being stolen in that sad, poor place.

Now there would be no time to say that after all he'd had a happy life.

He shuffled off to the kitchen to make the coffee that both put him to sleep and gave him the sensation of doing something useful, something he could do on his own without Laura's help.

Now there would be no time to change that winter smile.

He sipped his coffee slowly, moistening the remnants of a roll in it.

Now there would be no time to rejuvenate a soul that had become old. Not even believing in the immortality of the soul would make it conceivable that Juan Francisco's might survive.

He cleaned his teeth with a toothpick.

Now there would be no time for a new and first look of love, neither sought nor foreseen yet astonishing.

He left the kitchen and glanced at the old newspapers saved for the hot-water heater.

Now there would be no time for the pity the old deserve even when they've lost love and respect.

He crossed the room filled with the velvet-covered furniture where years ago Laura had whiled away long hours while her husband argued labor politics in the dining room.

Now there would be no time to become indignant when results and not words were demanded of him.

He made a half turn back to the dining room, as if he'd left something behind, a memory, a promise.

Now there would be no time to justify himself, saying he'd joined the official party to convince those in power of the error of their ways.

Stumbling, he grabbed the banister on the stairway.

Now there would be no time to try to change things from within the government and the party.

Each stair took a century.

Now there would be no time to feel himself judged by her.

Each stair had turned to stone.

Now there would be no time to feel himself condemned or satisfied that it was only she who judged him, no one else.

He managed to reach the second floor.

Now there would be no time for his own conscience to condemn him.

He felt disoriented. Where was the bedroom? Which door led to the bathroom?

Now there would be no time to recover the prestige he'd accumulated over years and lost in an instant, as if nothing counted but that instant when the world turns its back on you.

Ah yes, this was the bathroom.

Now there would be no time to hear her say, What did you do today? and to answer the usual thing, You know.

He knocked modestly at the door.

Now there would be no time to keep an eye on her every moment during the day, to have her followed by detectives, to humiliate her a bit because he loved her too much.

He went into the bathroom.

Now there would be no time for her to pass from tedium and disdain to love and tenderness. No more time.

He looked at himself in the mirror.

Now there would be no time for the workers to love him, for him to feel loved by the workers.

He took down his razor, the shaving soap, and brush.

Now there would be no time to relive the historic days of the Río Blanco strikes.

Slowly he worked up a lather with the moistened brush and the soap.

Now there would be no time to form the Red Battalions of the Revolution again.

He spread the lather on his cheeks, upper lip, and neck.

Now there would be no time to revive the House of the Workers of the World.

Slowly he shaved.

Now there would be no time for his revolutionary deeds to be recognized, because now no one remembered anymore.

He was in the habit of shaving at night before going to bed, so as to save time in the morning before going to work.

Now there would be no time for them to give him his rightful place, fucking bastards, he was someone, he did things, he deserved a place.

He finished shaving.

Now there would be no time to admit failure.

He dried his face with a towel.

Now there would be no time to ask, Where did I go wrong?

He laughed into the mirror for a long time.

Now there would be no time to open a door to love.

He looked at an old man he didn't recognize, another man who was himself emerging from the depth of the mirror to meet him now.

Now there would be no time to say I love you.

He looked at the wrinkled cheeks, defeated chin, curiously elongated ears, the sacks under his eyes, the gray hair everywhere—on his ears, his head, his lips, like frozen hay, a weather-beaten old pine tree.

He felt a huge desire, painful and pleasurable at the same time, to sit down and shit.

Now there would be no time to fulfill the promise of an admirable, glorious destiny he could bequeath.

He lowered the trousers of the striped pajamas that Danton had given him for his birthday and sat down on the toilet.

Now there would be no time . . .

He pushed hard and fell forward, his bowels emptied and his heart stopped.

Damned weather-beaten old pine tree.

At Juan Francisco's wake, Laura set about forgetting her husband, erasing all the memories that weighed on her like an early tombstone on the grave of her marriage, but instead of grieving for Juan Francisco, she closed her eyes, standing next to the coffin, and thought about the pain of giving birth, thought about how her sons were born—so much pain and such an eternity between contraction and contraction for the elder son, smooth as swallowing caramel cream for the second, liquid and smooth like melted butter . . . but with her hand on her husband's coffin, she decided to live the pain of childbirth, not that of death, realizing that someone else's pain, the death of others, ends up being just that in our minds, someone else's, neither Danton nor Santiago felt his mother's birth pangs, for them entering the world was a cry of neither happiness nor sadness, the victory cry of the newborn, his *Here I am!*, while the mother was the one who suffered, and perhaps like her in the terrible traumas when Santiago was on the way, she shouted without caring whether the doctor and nurses heard her, "Damn it all! Why did I have a child? this is horrible!, why didn't anyone tell me? I can't bear this, I can't bear this, just kill me, I want to die, damn brat, I hope he dies too . . ."

And now Juan Francisco was dead and didn't know it. He felt no pain at all.

Nor did she. Which is why she preferred remembering the pain of giving birth, so that those who came to the wake—old comrades, union men, minor government functionaries, the odd deputy, and, in brutal contrast, Danton's family and rich friends—could see in her face the traces of a shared pain, but this was false since the pain, the real pain, can be felt only by the one who feels it, the woman giving birth, not the doctor who helps her or the child being born, only the man being shot feels the bullets penetrate him, not the firing squad or the officer giving the order, only the sick person feels it, not the nurses . . .

Who knows why, Laura recalled the image of the Spanish woman Pilar Méndez at the gates to Santa Fe de Palencia, shouting in the middle of the night so that her father would show her no mercy, only justice as political fanaticism conceived it, shot at sunrise for betraying the Republic and aiding the Cause. Like her, Laura wished she could shout, but not for her husband, not for her sons, for herself, remembering her own pains, banal and terrible, in giving birth, indescribable and impossible to share. They say pain destroys language. It can only be a shout, a whimper, a disembodied voice. Those who speak of pain don't feel it. Those who possess the language of pain describe the pain of others. True pain has no words, but Laura Díaz, the night of her husband's wake, did not want to shout.

Her eyes still shut, she remembered other cadavers, those of the two Santiagos, Santiago Díaz Obregón, her half brother, shot in Veracruz at the age of twenty, and Santiago López-Díaz, her son, dead at the age of twenty-six in Mexico City. Two handsome dead men, equally beautiful. She dedicated her mourning to them. That night, her two Santiagos, the Elder and the Younger, gathered together the dispersion of the world spilled out in no order over the years so as to give it proper form, the form of two young, handsome bodies. But it's one thing to be a body and another to be beautiful.

The comrade workers wanted to lay the red flag with the hammer and sickle over Juan Francisco's coffin. Laura refused. Symbols were superfluous. There was no need to identify her husband with a red rag that could be put to better use in a bull ring.

The comrades walked out, offended but silent.

The priest officiating at the wake offered to say the rosary.

"My husband wasn't a believer."

"God receives all of us in His mercy."

Laura Díaz pulled off the crucifix adorning the lid of the coffin and handed it to the priest.

"My husband was anticlerical."

"Madam, don't offend us. The cross is sacred."

"Take it. The cross is a rack of torture. Why don't you put a little gallows on the coffin, or a guillotine. In France, Jesus Christ would have been guillotined, right?"

The murmur of horror and disapproval that arose from the pews where Danton's family and friends were seated satisfied Laura. She knew she'd done something unnecessary, provocative. It was a natural reaction. She couldn't have repressed it. It gave her pleasure. It seemed, suddenly, like an act of emancipation, the beginning of something new. After all, who was she now if not a solitary woman, a widow, companionless, with no family but a distant son now captive in a world Laura Díaz found detestable?

People began to leave, humiliated or offended. Laura exchanged glances with the only person looking at her fondly. It was Basilio Baltazar. But before they could speak to each other, a decrepit small man, shrunken like a badly washed sweater, wrapped in a cape too big for him, a tiny man with features both well defined and faded by time, with little clumps of matted hair above his ears, like frozen grass, handed Laura a letter, telling her in a voice from the depths of time, Read it, Laura, it's about your husband . . .

There was no date, but the handwriting was old-fashioned, ecclesiastical, more appropriate for noting baptisms and funerals, life's alphas and omegas, than for communicating with another person. She read the letter that night.

Dear Laura, may I address you that way? After all, I've known you since you were a child, and even though the difference in our ages is a thousand years, my memory of you remains fresh. I know that your husband, Juan Francisco, died keeping the secret of his origin as if it were something shameful or disgraceful. But do you realize he died the same way, anonymously, making no noise? Could you yourself, if I were to ask you today, give an account of your husband's life over the past twenty years? You'd find yourself in the same situation as he did. There'd be nothing to tell. Do you think the vast majority of those who come into this world have something extraordinary to tell about their lives? Are they, therefore, less important, less worthy of respect and, sometimes, of love? I write you, my dear friend, whom I've known since you were a girl, to ask you to stop torturing yourself thinking about what Juan Francisco López Greene was before he met and married you. Before making a name for himself as a fighter for justice in the Veracruz strikes and when the Red Battalions were created during the Revolution. That was your husband's life. Those twenty years of glory, eloquence, fearlessness, they were his life. He had no life before or after his moment of glory, if you'll permit me to call it that. With you, he sought the safe harbor for a tired hero. Did you give him the peace he silently begged of you? Or did you demand of him what he could no longer give? A tired hero who'd lived something no one lives twice, his moment of glory. He came from far away and from the depths of society, Laura. When I met him, he was a little boy in Macuspana, wandering around like an animal with no master, no family, stealing food here and there when bananas, which Tabasco gives freely to the hungriest of the poor, weren't enough for him. I took him in. I dressed him. I taught him to read and write. You know well that this is common practice in Mexico. The young priest teaches a poor boy to read and write the language the boy will use against our Holy Mother Church as a man. That was the case with Benito Juárez, and that was the case with López Greene. That last name. Where did he get it, when he had neither father nor mother nor sister nor brother? "I heard it, Father . . ." López is a very common name in Hispanic genealogy, and Greene is a name found frequently among families in Tabasco that descend from English pirates of colonial times, when Sir Henry Morgan himself attacked the coast of the Gulf of Campeche and sacked the ports whence Mexico's gold and silver were shipped to Spain. And *Juan*? Again, the commonest name in the Spanish language. But *Francisco* because I taught him the virtues of the most admirable saint in Christendom, the man from Assisi . . . Ah, my dear girl Laura, St. Francis abandoned a life of luxury and pleasure to become God's jester. I took the opposite route, as you know. Sometimes faith falters. There would be no faith without doubt. I was young when I came to Catemaco to take the place of a beloved parish priest, you remember him, Father Jesús Morales. I'll confess several things. I was annoyed by the aura of sanctity surrounding Father Morales. I was very young, imaginative, even perverse. If St. Francis went from sin to sanctity, I would do the same, perhaps in reverse, I'd be a perverse, sinful priest, what horrors did I not pour into your ear, Laura, defying the greatest commandment of Our Lord Jesus Christ, not to scandalize children? What greater crime than running off with the treasure of the poorest, offerings to the Holy Child of Zongolica? Believe me, Laura, I sinned to be holy. That was my project, my perverted Franciscanism, if you prefer. I was defrocked, and that's how you found me, surviving on my stolen money as your mother's guest, may God have her in His glory, in Xalapa. You must have said something to your husband. He remembered me. He came looking for me. He thanked me for my teaching. He knew about my sin. He confessed his own. He betrayed the nun who called herself Carmela, Sister Gloria Soriano, implicated in the assassination of President-elect Alvaro Obregón. He did it out of revolutionary conviction, he said. The policy then was to extinguish the clericalism that in Mexico had exploited the poor and supported the exploiters. He didn't hesitate to turn her in: it was his obligation. He never thought that you, Laura—you weren't even a believer—would take it so seriously. How strange, but how wrong. We never measure the moral consequences of our acts. We think we're obeying the mandates of ideology, whether we're revolutionaries, clericalists, liberals, conservatives, Cristeros, and what slips through our fingers is the precious liquid we call, for lack of a better word, "the soul." Your brutal reaction to his betrayal of Gloria Soriano at first disconcerted Juan Francisco and then depressed him. It was like the tombstone over his career. He was finished. He did ridiculous things, like hiring a detective to spy on you. He repented of his silliness, I assure you. But once a priest always a priest, you know that not even if they cut off my fingertips I could never give up hearing confessions and absolving people of their sins. Laura: Juan Francisco asked me to forgive his betrayal of Gloria Soriano. It was his way of thanking me for having taken in a barefoot, ignorant boy and educated him sixty-five years ago, just imagine. But he did something else. He returned the treasure of the Holy Child of Zongolica. One afternoon, as they came into the church for vespers, the townspeople found the jewelry, the offerings, everything they'd given and saved, back in its proper place. You never knew, because Catemaco news never leaves Catemaco. But the bedazzled town attributed it to a miracle wrought by the Holy Child, capable of re-creating His own treasure and returning it to where it belonged. It was as if He'd said, If I made you wait it was so you would feel the absence of my offerings and rejoice even more when you recovered them. How did you pay for all that? I asked Juan Francisco. With contributions from the workers, he confessed. Did they know? No, I told them it was for victims of an epidemic after the Usumacinta River flooded. No one ever kept any accounts. Laura, I hope you'll return to your hometown to see how beautiful the altar is thanks to Juan Francisco. Laura, forgive men who have nothing more to give than what they carry within them. Sometimes the well runs dry. As with me, I'm running out of communions. I don't think we'll ever see each other again. I don't want us to see each other again. It was very hard for me to appear today before you at the funeral parlor. How good it was you didn't recognize me. Damn, I don't even recognize myself!

Remember, with a drop of tenderness,

*ELZEVIR ALMONTE*

That weekend, Basilio Baltazar rented a car, and the two of them drove to Cuernavaca, Laura and her old friend the Spanish anarchist.

## 19. Cuernavaca: 1952

LAURA DOVE into the pool, framed in bougainvillea, and didn't surface until she reached the far end. On the side, a large group of foreign men and women were chatting, the majority Americans, a few in bathing suits but most of them dressed, the women in full skirts and "Mexican-style" short-sleeved blouses with flower-embroidered bodices, the men in short-sleeved shirts and summer slacks, most of them getting their feet used to huaraches, all of them, every single one of them, holding a drink, all of them guests of the splendid English Communist Fredric Bell, whose house in Cuernavaca had become a sanctuary for the victims of McCarthyite persecution in the United States.

Bell's wife, Ruth, was an American who balanced the high, dry irony of her British husband with an earthy coarseness, close to the soil, as if she were dragging along her roots in the Chicago slums where she was born. She was a woman from the Great Lakes and immense prairies who by chance had been born on the asphalt of the "big-shouldered city," in Carl Sandburg's words. Ruth's shoulders easily carried her husband, Fredric, and her husband's friends, she was Sancho Panza to

Fredric, the tall, slim Englishman with blue eyes, clear brow, and thin, completely white hair surrounding his freckled skull.

"A Quixote of lost causes," Basilio Baltazar told Laura.

Ruth had the strength of a steel die, from the tips of her bare toes on the grass to her curly, short gray hair.

"Almost all of them are directors and screenwriters," Basilio went on as he drove along the recently opened highway between Mexico City and Cuernavaca, which reduced the trip to only forty-five minutes, "a few professors, but mostly movie people."

"You're safe, then, you're in the minority." Laura smiled. She had a kerchief tied over her head against the wind blowing over the MG convertible that García Ascot, a Republican poet exiled in Mexico, had lent to his friend Basilio.

"Can you see me as a professor, teaching Spanish literature to proper young ladies at Vassar?" asked Basilio maliciously, as he steered smoothly around the highway curves.

"Is that where you met this gang of reds?"

"No. On the side, I moonlight on weekends—extra, unpaid work at the New School for Social Research in New York. The students there are workers, older people who had no time to get an education. That's where I met a lot of the people you're going to meet today."

She wanted to ask a favor of Basilio, that he not treat her with pity, that he simply relegate the past that both knew to a tranquil, silent memory, the past whose pains and joys leave their marks on our bodies.

"You're still a beautiful woman."

"I'm over fifty. A bit."

"Well, there are women twenty years younger than you who wouldn't be seen in a one-piece bathing suit."

"I love swimming. I was born next to a lake and grew up on the seacoast."

Good manners did not let the group take overt notice of her when she dove into the pool, but when she came out, Laura noticed the curious, approving, smiling glances of the gringos gathered for dinner that Saturday in Cuernavaca at the house of the Communist Fredric Bell, and she also saw, as if in a Diego Rivera mural or a King Vidor film, the "crowd," the simultaneously collective and singular combination of people, appreciated it, knowing that this group of people was united by one thing, persecution, but that each had managed to save his or her individuality. They weren't a "mass," no matter how much they believed in such a thing; there was pride in their eyes, in the way they stood, held a glass, or raised their chins, a way of being themselves, which impressed Laura, the visible awareness of wounded dignity and the time needed to regain it. This was an asylum for political convalescents.

She knew something about their stories. Basilio had told her more on the trip, that they had to believe in their own individuality because to transform them into enemies the persecutors had tried first to turn them into a herd, a red flock, lambs of Communism, and then to strip away their singularity.

"Did you go to the tribute to Dimitri Shostakovich at the Waldorf-Astoria?"

"Yes."

"Did you know that he is a prominent figure in Soviet propaganda?"

"All I know is that he's a great composer."

"We're not talking about music here but about subversion."

"Senator, are you saying that Shostakovich's music turns the people who listen to it into Communists?"

"Exactly. That's my conviction as an American patriot. It's obvious to this committee that you don't share this conviction."

"I'm as American as you are."

"But your heart's in Moscow."

(We're very sorry. You cannot work for us anymore. Our company cannot get involved in controversies.)

"Is it true that you scheduled a festival of Charlie Chaplin movies on your television station?"

"Certainly. Chaplin is a great comic artist."

"A poor, tragic artist, you mean. He's a Communist."

"Possibly. But that has nothing to do with his films."

"Don't play dumb with us. The red message gets through without anyone's realizing it."

"But, Senator, Chaplin made those silent films before 1917."

"What happened in 1917?"

"The Soviet Revolution."

"Well, Charlie Chaplin isn't only a Communist, he paved the way for the Russian Revolution, that's what you want to show, a manual for insurrection disguised as comedy. . ."

(We're very sorry. The company cannot approve your programming. Our sponsors have threatened to withdraw their support if you go on showing subversive films.)

"Are you now or have you ever been a member of the Communist Party?"

"Yes. So are or have been the fourteen veterans who are with me here before this committee. They were all maimed in the war."

"The red brigade, ha-ha."

"We fought in the Pacific for the United States."

"You fought for the Russians."

"They were our allies, Senator. But we only killed Japanese."

"Well, the war's over. You can go live in Moscow and be happy."

"We're loyal Americans, Senator."

"Prove it. Give the committee the names of other Communists."

( . . . in the armed forces, in the State Department, but especially in the movies, in radio, in the new medium of television: the congressional inquisitors loved above all else to investigate movie people, rub elbows with them, appear in photos with Robert Taylor, Gary Cooper, Adolphe Menjou, Ronald Reagan, who all named names, or with Lauren Bacall, Humphrey Bogart, Fredric March, Lillian Hellman, Arthur Miller, who had the courage to denounce the inquisitors . . . )

"That was the tactic: strip away our individuality and turn us into either enemies or collaborators, scapegoats or squealers. That was the crime of McCarthyism."

Laura's head emerged from the water, and she saw the group around the pool and thought her own thoughts, and for that reason was surprised that she noticed a small man with narrow shoulders, a sad expression, thin hair, and a face so carefully shaven that it looked erased, as if every morning the blade took away his features, which would spend the rest of the day struggling to be reborn and recognized. A loose-fitting, sleeveless khaki shirt and loose trousers of the same color held up by a snakeskin belt of the kind sold in tropical markets where everything is put to use. He was barefoot. His naked feet caressed the grass.

She got out of the pool without taking her eyes off him, although he wasn't looking at her—or anyone else . . . Now Laura was out of the water. No one paid attention to her matronly nakedness, more than fifty years old but still attractive. Tall and right-angled, Laura since childhood had had that impulsive and defiant profile, not a little rosebud nose; from childhood had had those almost golden eyes submerged in a veil of shadows, as if age itself were a veil some people are born with, though it's almost always acquired; had had the thin lips of a Memling madonna, as if she'd never been visited by the angel with the sword that divides the upper lip and banishes oblivion at birth.

"That's an old Jewish legend," said Ruth, mixing a new pitcher of martinis. "When we're born, an angel comes down from heaven with his sword, strikes us between the tips of our noses and our upper lips, and makes this split, which is otherwise inexplicable." Here Ruth scratched an imaginary mustache, like that of the proto-Communist Chaplin, with an unpolished fingernail. "But according to the legend, he also makes us forget everything we knew before we were born, all the deep memory within the womb, including our parents' secrets and our grandparents' triumphs." *"Salud!"* said the matriarch of the Cuernavaca tribe in Spanish—a title Laura bestowed on her then and there, as she laughingly told Basilio. Basilio agreed completely. Ruth couldn't not be like that, and the others wouldn't admit they needed her. But who doesn't need a mama? Basilio smiled. Especially if every weekend she prepares a bottomless bowl of spaghetti.

"The witch-hunters publish a rag called *Red Channels*. They justify themselves by invoking their equally vigilant patriotism and anti-Communism. But neither they nor their publication would prosper if there weren't denunciations. They began a feverish search for people who could be implicated, sometimes for reasons as far-fetched as listening to Shostakovich or seeing a Chaplin film. Being denounced by *Red*

*Channels* was the beginning, and the persecution would continue with letters to the suspect's employers, threatening publicity against the guilty company, intimidating telephone calls to the victim—all culminating in a summons to appear before Congress from the House Un-American Activities Committee."

"You were going to say something about a mother, Basilio."

"Ask anyone here about Mady Christians."

"Mady Christians was an Austrian actress who had the lead in a very famous play, *I Remember Mama*," said a man with heavy tortoise-shell glasses. "She taught drama at New York University, but her obsession was protecting political refugees and people displaced by the war."

"She offered to protect us Spanish exiles," recalled Basilio. "That's how I met her. A very beautiful woman, about forty, very blond, with the profile of a Nordic goddess and a look in her eye that said, I won't give up."

"She also protected us German writers expelled by the Nazis," added a man with a square jaw and lifeless eyes. "She created a Committee for the Protection of Those Born Abroad. These were crimes that justified *Red Channels'* denouncing her as a Soviet agent."

"Mady Christians." Basilio Baltazar smiled fondly. "I saw her before she died. She would be visited by detectives who wouldn't identify themselves. She got anonymous calls. Hardly anyone offered her parts. One television company did telephone her, but the investigators did their work, and the company withdrew their offer, though they did agree to pay her a fee. How can anyone live with that fear, that uncertainty? So the defender of exiles became an internal exile. 'This is incredible,' she managed to say before dying of a cerebral hemorrhage at the age of fifty. The playwright Elmer Rice said at her funeral that she represented America's generosity, that in return she received calumny, persecution, unemployment, and illness. 'It's no use appealing to the McCarthyites' conscience, because they have none.' "

Many pasts were reunited in Fredric Bell's house, and as she made visit after visit, at first with Basilio but later alone when the anarchist professor had gone back to the virginal order of Vassar College, Laura began to sort out the stories she heard, trying to separate real experience from the wounded justifications, unnecessary or urgent. All of that.

To say there were many different pasts was also to say there were many different personal origins, and among the weekend guests, many of whom were living in Cuernavaca, the Central European Jews were notable—they were the oldest, and they'd gather in circles, husbands and wives together, to tell each other stories about a past that seemed historical but that was barely more than a half century of life. (That's how quickly U.S. history goes, said Basilio.) They would laugh sometimes as they noted they'd been born in neighboring villages in Poland or just a few miles from the border between Hungary and Bessarabia.

A little old man with trembling hands and jolly eyes explained it to Laura: We were tailors, peddlers, shopkeepers, discriminated against because we were Jews; we emigrated to America, but in New York we were still foreigners, excluded, so we went to California, where there was nothing but sun, sea, and desert, California, where the continent ends, Miss Laura, we all went to that city with the angelic name, many angels, the union with wings that seemed to be waiting for us, Jews from Central Europe, to make our fortunes, Los Angeles, where, as our hostess Ruth tells, a winged being descends from heaven and uses his memory sword to take away what we were and no longer wanted to be. It's true, we Jews not only invented Hollywood but invented the United States as we wished it to be, dreamed the American Dream better than anyone, Miss Laura, and stocked it with immediately identifiable good guys and bad guys. We always had the good guy win; we linked being good with innocence, gave the hero an innocent girlfriend, created a nonexistent America, rural, small-town, free, where justice always triumphs; and it turns out that's what Americans wanted to see, or it was how they wanted to see themselves, in a mirror of innocence and goodness where love and justice always triumph, that's what we gave the Americans, we persecuted Jews of Mitteleuropa. So why are they persecuting us now? Are we Communists? We the idealists?

"Out of order," McCarthy shouted back.

"You, Senator, you're the red," said the small, bald man.

"The witness is about to be in contempt of Congress."

"You, Senator, are paid by Moscow."

"Take this witness away."

"You're the best propaganda the Kremlin ever invented, Senator McCarthy."

"Get him out of here! Take him away!"

"Do you think that by acting like Stalin you're defending American democracy? Do you think you can defend democracy by imitating your enemy?" shouted Harry Jaffe. That was the name Basilio Baltazar mentioned. The two of them had been comrades on the Jarama front, along with Vidal, Maura, and Jim. Comrades.

"Order, order. The witness is in contempt," shouted McCarthy with his whining kidnapper's voice, his mouth twisted into an eternal smile of disdain, his beard showing dark only hours after he shaved, his eyes those of an animal chased by itself: Joe McCarthy was like an animal aware of being a man and nostalgic for his earlier freedom as a beast in the jungle.

Another old man interrupted. The people to blame for the whole thing are the Warner Brothers, who started putting politics into movies, social themes, delinquency, unemployment, abandoned children who slide into a life of crime, the cruelty of prisons, movies that said to America, you're not innocent anymore, you're not rural anymore, you live in cities plagued by poverty, exploitation, organized crime, and criminals of all kinds from gangsters to bankers.

"Just as Brecht said: which is worse, robbing a bank or founding a bank?"

"I'll tell you what's what," answered the first old man, Laura's confidant. "A movie is a collective effort. No matter how clever he is, a writer can't pull the wool over the eyes of Louis B. Mayer or Jack Warner and make him see white by putting red in front of him. The man has yet to be born who could trick Mayer by saying to him, Look, this film about noble Russian peasants is really camouflaged praise of Communism. Mayer won't be conned, because he's the greatest con man of all. That's why he was the first to denounce his own workers. The wolf was tricked by the lambs. The wolf got a pardon because he turned over the lambs to the slaughterhouse so he'd be spared the knife.

Mayer must have been furious about McCarthy drinking the blood of all the actors and writers he'd hired instead of letting him do it!"

"Vengeance is sweet, Theodore . . ."

"On the contrary. It's a skimpy diet if you're not the one drinking the blood of the person who got crucified because you squealed. It's bitter for the squealer to have to keep his mouth shut, to not be able to brag in private, to have to live with shame."

Harry Jaffe got up, lit a cigarette, and walked through the garden. Laura Díaz followed the trail of his firefly, a Camel burning in a dark garden.

"We're all responsible for a picture," the old producer named Theodore continued. "Paul Muni isn't responsible for Al Capone because he starred in *Scarface*, or Edward Arnold for plutocratic fascism because he personified it in *Meet John Doe*. From the producer to the distributor, we're all responsible for our pictures."

"*Fuenteovejuna*, one for all, all for one," said Basilio Baltazar. He didn't care that none of the gringos would recognize this great line from Lope de Vega's play about a town that stands up and acknowledges its collective guilt.

Elsa, the old producer's wife, said innocently, "Well, who knows if they aren't right when they say it was one thing to go into social themes during the New Deal and another to exalt Russia during the war."

"They were our allies!" Bell exclaimed. "We were supposed to be nice to the Russians!"

"We were told to promote pro-Soviet sentiment," Ruth interrupted. "Roosevelt and Churchill asked us to."

"And one fine day, someone knocks at your door and you get a summons to appear before the House Un-American Activities Committee because you portrayed Stalin as good old Uncle Joe with his pipe and peasant wisdom defending us against Hitler," said the tall man who looked like an owl because of his heavy tortoiseshell glasses.

"And wasn't that the truth?" answered a small man with frizzy, tangled hair that rose to a high, natural topknot. "Didn't the Russians save us from the Nazis? Remember Stalingrad? Have we already forgotten Stalingrad?"

"Albert," countered the tall, myopic man, "I'll never argue with you. I'll always agree with a man who walked with me, next to me, both of us in handcuffs because we refused to denounce our comrades to the McCarthy committee. You and I."

There was more, Harry told Laura one night when the cicadas were raising a racket in the Bells' garden. It was an entire era. It was the misery of an era, but also its glory.

"Before I went to Spain, I was active in the Black Theater Project with Roosevelt's WPA, which set off riots in Harlem in 1935. Then Orson Welles put on a black *Macbeth* that caused a furor and was savagely attacked by the theater critic of *The New York Times*. The guy died of pneumonia a week after the review appeared. It was voodoo, Laura." Harry laughed and asked her if it was all right to call her by her first name.

"Of course. Laura," she said.

"Harry. Harry Jaffe."

"Yes, Basilio told me about . . . you."

"About Jim. About Jorge."

"Jorge Maura told me the story."

"No one ever gets the whole story, you know," said Harry. His tone expressed challenge, sadness, and shame all at once, Laura thought.

"Do you have the whole story, Harry?"

"No, of course not." The man tried to recover his normal expression. "A writer should never know the whole story. He imagines one part and asks the reader to finish it. A book should never close. The reader should continue it."

"Not finish it, just continue it?"

Harry agreed, with his balding head and immobile but expressive hands. Jorge had described him on the Jarama front in 1937, compensating for his physical weakness with the energy of a fighting cock. "I need to create a CV that will make up for my social complexes," Harry said at that time. His faith in Communism expiated his inferiority complexes. He argued a lot, Jorge Maura had recalled, he'd read all the Marxist literature, and he'd repeat it as if it were a Bible and end his speeches saying, "We'll see tomorrow." Stalin's mistakes were mere misdirections. The future was glorious, but Harry Jaffe in Spain was small, nervous, intellectually strong, physically weak, and morally indecisive—Maura had thought—because he didn't know just how weak an uncritical political conviction really is.

"I want to save my soul," Harry would say at the front.

"I want to know fear," his inseparable friend Jim would say. Jim, the tall, gawky New Yorker, with Harry—Maura would smile—the classic twosome of Don Quixote and Sancho Panza, or Mutt and Jeff, Basilio said now, adding his smile to that of his absent friend.

"So long to neckties," said Jim and Harry in one voice when Vincent Sheean and Ernest Hemingway went off to report on the war, arguing about which of the two would have the honor of writing the other's obituary.

The little Jew in jacket and tie.

If the description of the Harry Jaffe of fifteen years earlier was accurate, then that decade and a half had been a century and a half for this man who could not hide his sadness, who perhaps wanted to hide it; but the sadness managed to show itself in his infinitely distant gaze, his tremulously sad mouth, his nervous chin and supernaturally inert hands, controlled with great effort to reveal no genuine enthusiasm or interest. He would sit on his hands. He would clench his fists. He would clasp them desperately under his jaw. Harry's hands were witness, offended and humiliated, to the vicious cruelty of McCarthyism. Joe McCarthy had paralyzed Harry Jaffe's hands.

"We never win, it's just not true that at any given moment we triumphed," said Harry, in a voice as neutral as dust. "There was excitement, oh yes. Plenty of excitement. We Americans like to believe in what we're doing, and we get excited doing it. How could a moment like the first night of *The Cradle Will Rock*, Marc Blitzstein's musical drama, not be one of pleasure, faith, excitement? With its daring, direct reference to events of the day—the automobile strike, riots, police brutality, workers shot in the back and killed? How could we not be excited—indignant!—about our production causing a cutoff in the official subsidy for the workers' theater? They confiscated the sets. The stagehands were fired. And then? We had no theater. So we had the brilliant idea of bringing the play to the scene of the action, to the steel factory. We'd put on a workers' theater in the workers' factory."

How hard for me that look of defeat is turning out to be whenever he opens his eyes, that look of reproach whenever he closes them, thought Laura as she watched him intently, as she always did, the little needy man sitting on a leather armchair in the garden with its view of Cuernavaca, city of refuge, where Hernán Cortés had commanded a stone palace be built, protected by watchtowers and artillery, to escape the heights of the conquered Aztec city, which he destroyed and rebuilt as a Renaissance city laid out on a right-angled grid.

"What do you think Cortés would feel if he came back to his palace and found himself in Rivera's murals painted as a merciless conquistador with reptilian eyes?" Harry asked Laura.

"Diego makes up for it by painting heroic white horses that shine like armor. He can't help feeling a certain admiration for the epic. It's true for all Mexicans," said Laura, bringing her fingers close to Harry's.

"I got a little scholarship after the war. Went to Italy. That's how Ucello painted medieval battles. Where will you take me tomorrow so I can learn more about Cuernavaca?"

Together they went to the Borda gardens, where Maximilian of Austria came to take refuge with his pleasures in the hidden, moist, lecherous gardens, far from the imperial court at Chapultepec and the insomniac ambition of his wife, Carlota.

"Whom he wouldn't touch because he didn't want to give her syphilis," they both said, laughing, at the same time, wiping the beer foam from their lips in Cuernavaca's main square, Cuauhnáhuac, the place by the trees where Laura Díaz listened to Harry Jaffe and tried to penetrate the mystery hidden in the depths of his story, lightened occasionally with irony.

"The culture of my youth was a radio culture, blind theater, which is how Orson Welles managed to scare everyone into thinking that a simple adaptation of a work by the other Wells, H. G., was really happening in New Jersey."

Laura laughed a lot and asked Harry to listen to the latest chachachá on the tavern's jukebox:

*The Martians have landed, ha-ha-ha!*
*They came down dancing the chachachá!*

*"You know?"*
So they took Blitzstein's drama to the scene of the crime, the steel factory. Which is why the plant managers decided to give the workers a picnic that day, and the workers chose a day in the country over a session of political theater.

*"You know?* When they finally put on the play again, the director scattered the actors in the audience. The spotlights would focus on us, and we'd suddenly be revealed. The spot came on me, the light hit me in the face, blinding me, but then I had to speak: *'Justice. We want justice.'* That was my only line, from the audience. Then the lights went down, and we went home to hear the invisible truth of radio. Hitler used the radio. So did Roosevelt and Churchill. How could I refuse to speak on the radio, when the very government of the United States, the American army, asked me: This is the Voice of America, we have to defeat fascism, Russia is our ally, we have to praise the Soviet Union? What was I going to do? Anti-Soviet propaganda? Just imagine, Laura, me doing anti-Communist propaganda in the middle of a war. They would have shot me as a traitor. But today, the fact that I did it condemns me as an anti-American subversive. *Damned if you do, damned if you don't."*

He didn't laugh when he said that. Later, at dinner, the group, about a dozen guests, listened carefully to the old producer Theodore tell the story of Jewish migration to Hollywood, the Jewish creation of Hollywood. But a younger screenwriter, who never took off his bow tie, rudely told him to shut up, every generation has its problems and suffers them in its way, he wasn't going to feel nostalgia for the Depression, unemployment, lines of freezing men waiting for a cup of watery hot soup, there was no security, no hope, there was only Communism, the Communist Party, why not join the Party?, how could he ever renounce his Communism, when the Party gave him the only security, the only hope of his youth?

"To deny I was a Communist would be to deny I was young."

"Too bad we denied ourselves," said another guest, a man with distinguished features (he looked like the Arrow shirt man, Harry noted slyly).

"What do you mean?" asked Theodore.

"That we weren't made for success."

"Well, *we* were," grumbled the old man and his wife in unison. "Elsa and I were. We certainly were."

"We weren't," retorted the good-looking man, wearing his gray hair well, proud of it. "The Communists weren't. Being successful was a sin, a kind of sin anyway. And sin demands retribution."

"You did all right." The old man laughed.

"That was the problem. The retribution. First there was commercial work, done halfheartedly. Scripts for whores and trained dogs. Then compensatory dissipation—whores in bed, whiskey not as well trained as Rin Tin Tin. Finally came panic, Theodore. The realization that we weren't made for Communism. We were made for pleasure and dissipation. That was the punishment in the end, of course. Denounced and out of work for having been Communists, Theodore. McCarthy as our exterminating angel—it was inevitable. We deserved it, *fuck the dirty weasel.*"

"And what about the people who weren't Communists, who were wrongly accused, smeared?"

Everyone turned to see who'd asked that. But the questions seemed to come from nowhere. They seemed to have been said by a ghost. It was the voice of absence. Only Laura, sitting opposite Harry, realized that the Spanish Civil War veteran had thought and perhaps said them, but no one else noticed, because the lady of the house, Ruth, had already changed the tone of the conversation as she served her endless bowl of pasta and sang under her breath:

*You're going to get me into trouble*
*If you keep looking at me like that.*

Harry had said that radio was invisible theater, a call to imagination . . . and actual theater, what was that?

"Something that disappears with the applause."

"And movies?"

"The ghost that outlives us all, the speaking, moving portrait we leave behind so we can go on living."

"Is that why you went to Hollywood, to write movies?"

He nodded without looking at her, it was hard for him to look at anyone and everyone avoided looking at him. Little by little Laura realized this fact—so flagrant as to be a mystery, invisible, like a radio program.

Laura felt she could be the object in Harry's line of sight because she was new, different, innocent, because she didn't know the things the others did. But the courtesy all the exiles showed to Harry was impeccable. He turned up every weekend at the Bells' house. He sat down to dinner with them every Sunday. Only no one looked at him. And when he spoke it was in silence, Laura realized with alarm, no one listened to him, that was why he gave the impression that he never spoke, because no one listened to him but her, only her only I, Laura Díaz, I pay attention to him, and that's why only she listened to what the solitary man said without his having to open his mouth.

Before, whom would he talk to? Nature in Cuernavaca was so prodigal, though so different, rather like the Veracruz of Laura Díaz's childhood.

It was a perturbed nature, redolent of bougainvillea and verbena, of freshly cut pine and bleeding watermelon, scents of saffron but also of shit and garbage piled in the deep gullies around every orchard, every neighborhood, every house . . . Would Harry Jaffe speak to that nature—the little New York Jew who'd made his pilgrimage from Manhattan to Spain and from Spain to Hollywood and from Hollywood to Mexico?

This time Laura was the foreigner in her own homeland, the other to whom this strangely taciturn and solitary man might perhaps speak, not aloud but in the whisper she learned to read on his lips as they became friends and drifted away from the Bells' red stronghold into the silence of the Borda gardens or the buzz of Cuernavaca's main square, or the light and careless inebriation at the Hotel Marik's open-air café, or the cathedral's peaceful solitude.

There, Harry pointed out to her that the nineteenth-century murals, in their pious St. Sulpice style, were hiding another fresco that had been painted over, bad taste and clerical hypocrisy having deemed it primitive, cruel, and not especially devout.

"You know what it is, do you?" asked Laura, not hiding her curiosity and surprise.

"I do. An angry—very angry—priest told me. What do you see here?"

"The Sacred Heart, the Virgin Mary, the Wise Men," said Laura—though she was thinking about Father Elzevir Almonte and the jewels of the Holy Child of Zongolica.

"You really don't know what's underneath?"

"No."

"The missionary expedition of Mexico's only saint, St. Felipe de Jesús. Felipe went to convert the Japanese in the seventeenth century. Painted here, but painted over now, are the scenes of danger and terror—rough seas, shipwrecks. The saint's heroic and solitary sermons. Finally, his crucifixion by the infidels. His slow death agony. A great movie."

"His nursemaid said, The day the fig tree blooms, our little Felipe will be a saint. A servant we once had, a man I loved a lot, Zampaya, told me that story."

"All that was covered up. By piety. By lies."

"A pentimento, Harry?"

"No, not a repentant painting, but one that pride superimposed on truth. A triumph of simulation. I'm telling you, it's a movie."

He invited her, for the first time, to the little house he was renting, surrounded by mangroves. It wasn't far from the square, but in Cuernavaca one had only to walk a few yards beyond the main streets to find houses almost like lairs, hidden behind high walls painted indigo blue, genuine silent oases—with green lawns, red roof tiles, ocher facades, and thickets running toward black gullies one after the other. It smelled of moisture and decaying trees. Harry's house had a garden, a brick terrace that was hot all day and freezing at night, a roof of broken tiles, a kitchen where a silent old woman sat immobile with a palm fan in her hands, and a bed-sitting room with its spaces divided by curtains, which transformed the carefully made bed—as if someone would punish Harry if he left his bed unmade—into a secret.

Three open suitcases, full of clothes, papers, and books, clashed with the scrupulous order of the bed.

"Why haven't you unpacked?"

He hesitated before answering.

"Why?"

"I might leave any time."

"Where would you go?"

*"Home."*

"Home? But you don't have a home anymore, Harry. This is your home, haven't you figured that out yet? You've lost everything else!" Laura was suspicious and exasperated.

"No, Laura, no, you don't know when—"

"Why don't you sit down and get to work?"

"I don't know what to do, Laura. I'm waiting."

"Work," she said, meaning "stay."

"I'm waiting. In a while. Any time now."

Laura gave herself to Harry for many reasons: because of his age, because she hadn't made love since the night Basilio said goodbye before returning to Vassar and she hadn't had to ask, nor did Basilio, because it was an act of humility and memory, homage to Jorge Maura and Pilar Méndez, only she and he, Laura and Basilio together, could represent their absent lovers tenderly and respectfully, but that act of love between them for love of others had aroused in Laura Díaz an appetite that began to grow, an erotic desire she'd believed was, if not lost, then certainly overshadowed by age, modesty, memory of the dead, a superstitious sense she had of being watched from some dark land by the two Santiagos, by Jorge Maura, by Juan Francisco—the dead or disappeared who lived in a territory where the only business was to spy on her, still in this world, Laura Díaz.

"I don't want to do anything that would violate my respect for myself."

"*Self-respect*, Laura?"

"*Self-respect*, Harry."

Now the nearness of Harry in Cuernavaca aroused a new tenderness in her which at first she could not identify. Perhaps it was born from the play of glances in the weekend parties: no one looked at him, he looked at no one, until Laura came, and they looked at each other. Hadn't her love for Jorge Maura begun that way, with exchanged glances during a party at the house of Diego Rivera and Frida Kahlo? How different the power of her Spanish lover's glance from the weakness, not only in the glance but in the entire body of this sad American, disoriented, wounded, humiliated, and in need of affection.

First, Laura embraced him, the two of them sitting on the bed in the little house in the gully. She hugged him as if he were a child, putting her arms around him, holding his hand, almost cuddling him, asking him to raise his head, to look at her, she wanted to see Harry Jaffe's true face, not the mask of exile, defeat, and self-pity.

"Let me put your things away for you."

*"Don't mother me! Fuck you!"*

He was right. She was treating him as if he were a weak cowardly child. She had to make him feel, You're a man, I want to stir up the fire still within you, Harry, even though you no longer feel any passion for success, work, politics, or the rest of humanity—waiting, perhaps, crouched, mocking, like a genie, your sex unable always to say no, the only part of your life, Harry, that maybe goes on saying yes, out of pure animal spirit perhaps, or perhaps because your soul, my soul, has only the stronghold of sex but doesn't know it.

"Sometimes I imagine sexes like two little dwarfs poking their noses out from between our legs, making fun of us, challenging us to yank them from their tragicomic niche and toss them in the garbage, since they know that no matter how much they torture us we'll always live with them, the little dwarfs."

She didn't want to compare him to anything. He defied comparison. There he was. What she imagined. What he'd forgotten. An impassioned surrender, deferred, noisy, unexpectedly *spoken* and *shouted* by both of them, as if they both were being released from a jail that had held them for too long, and right there, at the prison door, on the other side of the bars, was Laura waiting for Harry and Harry waiting for Laura.

"*My baby, my baby.*"

"*We'll see tomorrow.*"

"I'm a rich old Jewish producer who's got no reason to be here except I want to share the fate of the young Jews this McCarthyite persecution is directed against."

"Do you know what it means to begin each day saying to yourself, This is the last day I'm going to live in peace?"

"When you hear someone knocking at the door, and you don't know if it's thieves, beggars, police, wolves, or just termites . . ."

"How can you tell if the person who's come to see you, who's supposed to be a lifelong friend, hasn't become an informer, how can you know?"

"I'm exiled in Cuernavaca because I couldn't stand the idea of being grilled a second time."

"There is something harder than putting up with persecution against yourself, and that's looking at betrayal practiced by someone else."

"Laura, how are we going to reconcile our pain and our shame?"

"*My baby, my baby.*"

## 20. Tepoztlán: 1954

### 1.

I SHOULD keep my mouth shut forever."

She wanted to bring him to Mexico City, to a hospital. He wanted to stay in Cuernavaca. They compromised, agreeing to spend some time in Tepoztlán. Laura imagined that the beauty and solitude of the place—a large subtropical valley enclosed by impressive, pyramidal mountains, sheer vertical masses with no slopes or hills leading up to them, erect and challenging like great stone walls raised to protect the fields of sugarcane and heather, rice and oranges—would be a refuge for both of them. Perhaps Harry would decide to start writing again; she'd take care of him, that was her role; she took it on without a second thought. The bond that had formed between them during the past two years was unbreakable; they needed each other.

Tepoztlán would restore the health of her tender, beloved Harry, far away from the constant repetition of tragic events in Cuernavaca. They rented a little house protected but overshadowed by two huge masses: the mountain and an immense church, a fortress monastery built by the Dominicans in competition with nature, as so often happens in Mexico. Harry pointed that out to her, the Mexican tendency to create architectural rivals to nature, imitations of mountains, precipices, deserts. Their little house competed with nothing, which is why Laura Díaz chose it, because of the simplicity of its naked adobes facing a dirt road traveled more by stray dogs than by human beings. The interior showed that other Mexican ability—to pass from a poor, neglected town to an oasis of green, serene patios with red and green plants, watermelon colors, shining fountains, and cool corridors that seemed to come from far away and never end.

There was only one bedroom with a rough old bed, a minimal bathroom decorated with fragile tiles, and a kitchen like those of Laura's childhood—no electrical appliances, charcoal-burning braziers that one had to fan to keep blazing, and an icebox that required the iceman's daily visit for chilling the bottles of Dos Equis that were Harry's joy. House life centered on the patio and its rattan chairs with leather seats and rattan, leather-topped table. It was hard to write on that table, which was soft and stained by too many circles made by moist beer bottles. The notebooks and pens remained in a bedroom drawer. When Harry did begin to write again, Laura secretly read the pages in the cheap notebooks whose paper absorbed the ink from Harry's Esterbrook pen. He knew she was reading them; she knew he knew. Neither spoke of it.

Jacob Julius Garfinkle, that was his real name. We grew up together in New York. If you're a Jewish boy from the Lower East Side of Manhattan, you're born with eyes, nose, mouth, ears, feet, and hands—the whole body—but something else only we have: a chip on your shoulder. You use it to challenge strangers (and who isn't a stranger if you're born in a neighborhood like ours?) to knock it off, with either a hard slap or a disdainful finger flick. We all carry that chip, and we all know no one put it there, we were born with it, it's part of our humiliated poor Italian, Irish, or Jewish (Polish, Russian, Hungarian, but anyway Jewish) immigrant flesh. You see it even more when we strip to take a shower or to make love or to sleep poorly, but even when we're dressed the chip cuts through the shirt or jacket, shows itself, tells the world, Just try to bother me, just try to insult me, hit me, humiliate me, just go ahead and try. Jacob Julius Garfinkle: I knew him from boyhood. He had the biggest chip of all. He was small, dark, a dark-skinned Jew with a snub nose and smiling cruel lips, mocking and dangerous, like his eyes, like his fighting bantam-rooster posture, his machine-gun way of talking, his always being on the alert—because the challenge was just around the corner, every corner, in every doorway, bad luck could fall off a fire escape, walk out of a bar, find you on a termite-eaten dock by the river . . . Julie Garfinkle brought the damned streets and dark gutters of New York to the screen. He showed himself naked and vulnerable, but he was armed with courage to fight injustice and come out in defense of all those who'd been born like him, in the immense, eternal ghettos of "Western civilization." I met him in the Group Theatre. He was the "golden boy" in Clifford Odets' play of that name, the young violinist who exchanges his talent for success in the ring and is left at the end without hands, fingers, or fists, nothing to attack even Joe Louis (who was also Jewish) or Felix Mendelssohn (who was also black). He'd sign anything. If someone said, Look, Julie, look at the injustices being committed against Jews, blacks, Mexicans, Communists, Russia, homeland of the proletariat, against poor children, against people with onchocerciasis in New Guinea, Julie would sign, he signed everything and his signature was strong, broken, round, like a caress, like a punch, it was sweat like a tear, that's how my friend Julie Garfinkle was. When they brought him to Hollywood after his success in the Group Theatre, he didn't stop being the street Quixote he always was. He played himself and he fascinated audiences. He wasn't handsome, elegant, courteous, or ironic, wasn't Cary Grant or Gary Cooper. He was John Garfield, the scrappy kid from the mean streets of New York, reborn in Beverly Hills, walking into mansions surrounded by rosebushes with his mud-covered shoes and washing them clean in crystalline swimming pools. Which is why his best role was with Joan Crawford in *Humoresque*. Again he played the part, like the one at the beginning of his career, of the poor boy with a talent for the violin. But she was equal to him. She looked like a rich aristocrat, the patron of the young genius who springs from the invisible city, but in reality she too is poor, she too has fled from the fringes of society by pretending to be rich, cultured, and elegant to disguise the fact that she too is a kid from the street, an arriviste with hard nails and a smooth ass. Which is why they were so explosive as a couple: they were the same but different. Joan Crawford and John Garfield, she pretended, he didn't. When the McCarthyite flood poured out of the sewers of America, Julie Garfinkle looked like the perfect character for a congressional investigation. He had an anti-American look, suspicious, dark, different, Semitic. And he wasn't guilty of anything. That was essential for McCarthy: to terrorize the innocent. Julie wasn't guilty of anything. But they accused him of everything, of signing petitions in favor of Stalin during the Moscow purges, demanding a second front during the war, being a crypto-Communist, financing the Party with the patriotic American money Hollywood paid him, showing himself to favor the poor and dispossessed (that alone was enough to make him suspicious; it would have been better to ask for justice for the rich and powerful). The last time I saw him, his Manhattan apartment was a mess—open drawers, papers scattered everywhere, his wife in despair staring at him as if he were insane, and Julie Garfield looking through checkbooks, portfolios, file cabinets, old books, and worn-out wallets for proof of the checks they alleged he'd signed, shouting, "Why don't they leave me alone?" He was brave, accepting the invitation from the House Un-American Activities Committee, but he made the mistake that people who believed they were falsely accused made. Merely appearing before the committee was proof enough for its members that the person was guilty. Immediately, all the

ultrareactionaries in Hollywood—Ronald Reagan, Adolphe
Menjou, Ginger Rogers' mother—corroborated their suspicion,
and then the congressmen would pass on the information to
Hollywood gossip columnists. Hedda Hopper, Walter Winchell,
George Sokolsky all lived on the blood of the sacrificed stars,
like ink-and-paper Draculas. Then the American Legion would
mobilize its forces to picket the movies in which the suspects
appeared—John Garfield, for example—not allowing people in.
Then the studio producer could say what was said to Garfield:
You're a risk. You put the security of the studio at risk. And fire
him. "Ask forgiveness, Julie, confess, and live in peace." "Name
names, Julie, or your career's over." Then the tough kid from the
streets of New York was reborn, naked and snub-nosed, his fists
clenched and voice hoarse. "Only a fool would defend himself
against fools like McCarthy. Do you think I'm going to be a prisoner of what a poor devil like Ronald Reagan says? Let me go on
believing in my humanity, Harry, let me go on believing I have
a soul." We can't protect you, Hollywood said at first; then: We
can't employ you anymore; finally: We're going to give evidence
against you. The company, the studio, was more important. "You
have to understand, Julie, you're just one person. We employ
thousands of people. Do you want them to die of hunger?" Julie
Garfinkle died of a heart attack at the age of thirty-nine. It may
be true—he had a bad heart, on the point of bursting—but the
fact is he was found dead in bed with one of his many lovers. I
believe John Garfield died fornicating, a death to be envied. At
his funeral, the rabbi said that Julie arrived like a meteor and
left like a meteor. Abraham Polonsky, who directed one of
Julie's last and perhaps greatest films, *Force of Evil*, said, "He
defended his street-boy honor, and they killed him for it." He
was killed. He died. Ten thousand people passed by his coffin to
bid him farewell. Communists? Agents sent by Stalin? Standing
there weeping was Clifford Odets, author of *Golden Boy*, glory
of the literary left, transformed into an informer by the committee; first he informed on the dead because he thought it

couldn't hurt them, then on the living in order to save himself, then on himself when he, like so many others, said, "I didn't name anyone who hadn't already been named." When Odets walked out of John Garfield's funeral in tears, a fistfight broke out. Right to the end, Jacob Julius Garfinkle lived by slugging it out in the streets of New York.

When the summer rains soaked the garden and seeped through the house walls, leaving obscure medallion-shaped stains on the skin of the adobe, Harry Jaffe felt he was suffocating and asked Laura Díaz, please, read the pages about John Garfield.

"But there were accused people who didn't name names and didn't let themselves become anguished or depressed, isn't that true, Harry?"

"You met them in Cuernavaca. Some of them were among the Hollywood Ten. And yes, it's true they had the courage not to talk or let themselves be scared, but most of all they had the courage not to fall into despair, not to commit suicide, not to die. Are they better people for that? Another pal from the Group Theatre, the actor J. Edward Bromberg, asked to be excused from appearing before the committee because of his recent heart attacks. Congressman Francis E. Walker, one of the worst inquisitors, told him that Communists were very skillful at presenting excuses signed by doctors—who no doubt were at the very least red sympathizers. Eddie Bromberg died in London three years ago, Laura. Sometimes, after he was blacklisted, he'd call me to say, Harry, there are always guys standing outside my house, day and night. They take turns, but there're always two of them in plain sight next to the streetlight, while I spy on them spying on me. I'm constantly waiting for the phone to ring; I never leave the telephone, Harry, they might call me to the committee again, they might call to tell me the role they promised has gone to someone else, or the other way around, they might call me to tempt me with a part on condition that I cooperate, that is, squeal, Harry, this happens five or six times a day, I'm always next to the telephone, tempted, tearing myself to pieces, should I talk or not, should I think about my career or not, I won't talk, Harry, no, I didn't want to hurt anyone, Harry, but most of all, Harry, I didn't want to hurt myself, my loyalty to my comrades was loyalty to myself. I didn't save them or myself."

"And you, Harry, are you going to write about yourself?"

"I really feel sick, Laura, give me a beer. Be a good girl . . ."

Another morning—the parrots were screeching in the sunlight, showing off their crests and wings as if they were announcing a bulletin, good or bad news—as he ate his breakfast Harry answered Laura.

"You only told me about the people who were destroyed for not talking. But you said that others saved themselves, came out stronger for keeping their mouths shut," Laura persisted.

*How can there be innocence when no one's guilty?* quoted Harry. "Dalton Trumbo said that at the beginning of the witch-hunt. During the witch-hunt, he outsmarted the inquisitors, wrote scripts under pseudonyms, won an Oscar under a pseudonym, and the Academy almost shit in its pants it was so angry when Trumbo revealed he was the author. And when it's all over, I suspect it'll be Trumbo who will say there were neither heroes nor villains, saints nor devils, only victims, Laura. The day will come when all the accused will be rehabilitated and celebrated as cultural heroes, and the accusers will be accused and degraded as they justly deserve. But Trumbo was right. We'll all have been victims."

"Even the inquisitors, Harry?"

"Yes. Even their children change their names. They don't want to admit they're the children of the mediocrities who drove hundreds of innocent people to sickness and suicide."

"Even the informers, Harry?"

"They're the worst victims. They have the mark of Cain branded on their foreheads."

Harry took a knife from the fruit bowl and cut his forehead.

And Laura watched with horror but didn't stop him.

"They have to cut off a hand and cut out their tongues."

And Harry put the knife in his mouth, and Laura screamed and stopped him, snatched the knife out of his hand and embraced him sobbing.

"And they're sentenced to exile and death," murmured Harry, almost inaudible, into Laura's ear.

Early on, Laura had learned to read Harry's thoughts just as he'd learned to read hers. They were helped by the punctual round of tropical sounds. She'd known it since she was a girl in Veracruz, but had forgotten it when she lived in Mexico City, where noises are accidental, unforeseen, intrusive, shrieking like evil fingernails scratching a school blackboard. But in the tropics the chirping of birds announces the dawn and their symmetrical flight the dusk, nature fraternizes with the church bells ringing matins and vespers, vanilla trees perfume the ambient air when we give it our intermittent attention, and the clusters of harvested beans give an air at once newborn and refined to the cupboards where they're stored. When Harry sprinkled pepper on his *huevos rancheros* at breakfast, Laura would glance at the flowering peppers in the garden, yellow jewels set in a fragile airy crown the color of afternoon. There were no delays in the tropics. They went from the garden to the table killing scorpions, first in the house, then hunting preventively in the garden, later under stones. They were white, and Harry laughed as he stepped on them.

"My wife used to tell me to take some sun once in a while. Your stomach is as white as a fish fillet before it's fried. That's how these scorpions are."

"Fish belly," Laura said, laughing.

"Get out of this fix, she'd tell me, you're not part of it, you don't believe in it, your friends aren't worth all that. And then she'd go back to her usual theme. Your problem isn't that you're a Communist, Harry, it's that you've lost your talent."

And despite everything, he finally did sit down to write, for when all was said and done, he needed to write, and in Tepoztlán he began to do so more regularly, beginning with his mini-biographies of victims like Garfield and Bromberg, who'd been his friends. Why didn't he write about his enemies, the inquisitors? Why did he write only about the wounded and destroyed people like Garfield and Bromberg, but not about the solid individuals who overcame the drama, didn't cry, fought, resisted, and, above all, made fun of the monstrous stupidity of the whole trial? Dalton Trumbo, Albert Maltz, Herbert Biberman . . . those who came to Mexico, passed through Cuernavaca or stayed there. Why was it that Harry Jaffe said almost nothing about them? Why didn't he include them in the biographies he was writing in Tepoztlán? Above all, why did he never mention the worst of the lot, the ones who did squeal, who did name names—Edward Dmytryk, Elia Kazan, Lee J. Cobb, Clifford Odets, Larry Parks?

Harry used his shoe to smash a scorpion.

"Evil insects make their nests in the most hostile places and live where there seems to be no life. That's how Tom Paine described prejudice."

Laura tried to imagine what Harry was thinking, all the things he didn't say to her that were passing through his feverish eyes. She didn't know that Harry was doing the same thing, thinking he could read Laura's thoughts. He'd watch her from the bed as she brushed her hair in front of the mirror every morning. He could compare the still-young woman he'd met two years before, emerging from the swimming pool framed in bougainvillea, with the fifty-five-year-old lady whose hair, getting grayer and grayer, she arranged simply, in a bun at the nape of her neck, emphasizing her clear forehead and her angular features, her fine, large nose mounted on an easel, her lips as thin as those of a Gothic statue. And all saved by the intelligence and fire of her amber eyes glittering in their shadowy depths.

He also watched her doing the household chores, taking care of the kitchen, making the bed, washing the dishes, preparing the meals, taking long showers, sitting on the toilet, discontinuing the use of sanitary napkins, suffering hot flashes, cuddling up to sleep in a fetal position, while he, Harry, rested straight as a board, until one day they simply exchanged positions, and he slept like a fetus and she stretched out, rigid, like a governess and a child . . .

He told himself he thought what she thought when she looked at herself in the mirror, when she separated from their tender, nocturnal lovers' embrace: it's one thing to be a body, another to be beautiful . . .

How warm and tender it was to embrace and love each other, but above all how healthful, the salvation of love meant forgetting one's own body and fusing with the body of the other and letting the other absorb my body so as not to think about beauty, not to contemplate oneself *apart* from the other but blind, united, pure touch, pure pleasure, with no sanctions of ugliness or beauty, which no longer matter in the dark, in the intimate embrace, when each body fuses with the other and they cease contemplating each other outside each other, cease judging themselves outside the couple that couples until it makes one from two and loses all notions of ugliness or beauty, youth or age . . . Harry said this to himself thinking that Laura was saying it to him, I only contemplate internal beauty in you.

It was easy in his case: more and more emaciated, white as a fish belly, said Laura, he wasn't even a distinguished bald man but a sparsely hairy man with abrupt little tufts that resisted dignified, complete baldness, hair like outcroppings of dry grass on the crown of his head, above his ears, on the back of his scruffy neck. It was more difficult in her case: Laura Díaz's beauty was intelligible, Harry tried to tell her, it resembled classical beauty which was nothing more than the idea of beauty imposed since the time of the Greeks but which could have been another norm of beauty, that of an Aztec goddess, for example, Coatlicue instead of the Venus de Milo.

"Socrates was an ugly man, Laura. He prayed every night to see his own internal beauty. It was the gift of the gods. Thought, imagination. That was Socrates' beauty."

"Didn't he want others to see it as well?"

"I think his way of speaking was that of a vain man. So vain that he preferred to drink the hemlock rather than admit he was wrong. He wasn't. He held his ground."

They always ended up talking about the same thing but they couldn't get to the bottom of what "the same thing" was. Like the victims of McCarthyism. The opposite of McCarthy's informers. And now Harry was looking at her looking at herself in the mirror, and he wondered if she saw the same thing he saw, an external body in the process of losing its beauty, or an internal body that was becoming more beautiful. Only making love, only in sexual union did the question cease to have meaning. The body disappeared in order to be only pleasure, and pleasure overwhelmed any possible beauty.

She, on the other hand, did not seem to judge him. She accepted him just as he was, and he felt tempted to be disagreeable, to ask her, Why don't you color your hair, why don't you do your hair more stylishly, why has she abandoned all coquetry; he's looking at me as if I were his nurse or his nanny, he'd like me to turn into a siren, but my poor Odysseus is scuttled, immobile, dissolving in a sea of ashes, drowned by smoke, disappearing little by little in the mist of his four packs of Camels a day whenever Fredric Bell gives him a carton or his five packs of unfiltered Raleighs which taste like soap, he says, whenever he had to put up with the best the corner tobacco stand had to offer.

"The best is sometimes all there is. Here all there is is almost always the worst."

They went to the Saturday market, and he decided to buy a tree of life. She had no reason to oppose the purchase, but she did. I don't know why I objected, she thought later on, when they'd stopped speaking to each other for an entire week, in reality those candelabras painted a thousand different colors aren't ugly and don't offend anyone even if they aren't the marvels of folkloric audacity and sensibility he says they are, I don't know why I told him they're vulgar kitschy things that only foreigners buy, why don't you buy some puppets with pink socks or a multicolor mat, or, why not?, a serape for you and a shawl for me? We'll sit down in the afternoon protected from the sudden cold that rolls down the mountain, wrapped in Mexican folklore, do you want to lower me to that? Isn't it enough you watch me so insistently while I fix myself up in front of the mirror, letting me think what he thinks, she's getting old, doesn't take care of herself, is going on fifty-six, no longer needs Kotex? On top of that, you want to fill up the house with tourist crap, trees of life, mats, market marionettes? Why don't you just buy a machete, Harry, the ones with cute inscriptions on the handle, like "I'm like a green chile, hot but tasty," so the next time you try to cut off your fingers and cut out your tongue you succeed, succeed in feeling sorry for yourself, for what you were and for what you weren't, for what you are and for what you could have been.

Harry was too weak to slap her. It was she who felt compassion for him when he raised his hand and she smashed the tree of life on the brick floor and the next day swept up the scattered pieces and threw them into the garbage. Only a week later, she returned alone from the market and put the new tree of life on the shelf opposite the table and chairs where they ate.

Then she tried to make up for her inexplicable hatred for the multi-colored structure of angels, fruits, leaves, and tree by deeply inhaling the scent of the plants in the garden, the shine of the rain on the leaves of the banana tree, and, beyond, in her memory, the trees that shaded the coffee bushes, the symmetrical lemon and orange orchards, the fig trees, the red lily, the round crown of the mango tree, the *trueno* with its tiny yellow flowers that could withstand both hurricane and drought—all the flora of Catemaco. And, at the end of the forest, the ceiba. Covered with spikes. The pointy spines the ceiba produces to pro-tect itself. A trunk covered with swords defending itself so no one gets too close. The ceiba at the end of the road. The ceiba covered with fin-gers cut off in a single machete stroke by a bandit on the Veracruz highway.

At dusk, they always sat side by side in the garden. They would talk about everyday things, the price of food in the market, what they'd eat the next day, how long it took for American magazines to reach Tepoztlán (if they ever got there), how kind it was of the Cuernavaca group to send them articles, always articles, never whole newspapers or magazines, what a blessing shortwave radio was, should they go to Cuernavaca to the Ocampo Cinema to see such and such a cowboy movie or the Mexican melodramas that made Laura laugh and Harry cry—but they never visited the Bells' house, Aristotle's Academy as Harry called it, he was bored by the eternal discussion, always the same discussion, a three-act tragicomedy.

"The first act is reason. The conviction that brought us to Commu-nism, to sympathize with the left, the cause of the workers, faith in Marx's arguments and in the Soviet Union as the first workers' revolutionary state. With that faith, we answered the reality of the Depression, unemployment, the ruin of American capitalism."

There were fireflies in the garden, but not as many as the intermittent lights given off by the cigarettes Harry chain-smoked, lighting the next with the butt of the last.

"The second act is heroism. First the fight against the economic depression in America, then the war against fascism."

A brutal fit of coughing interrupted him, a cough so deep and strong that it seemed alien to his body, which was growing thinner and paler by the day. That body could not contain such a deep hurricane in Harry's chest.

"The third act is the victimization of men and women of good faith, Communists or simply humanitarians. McCarthy is the same human type as Beria, Stalin's policeman, or Himmler, Hitler's policeman. He's driven by political ambition, because the easy way to get ahead is by joining the anti-Communist chorus that materialized when the hot war ended and the Cold War began. A cold calculation that one could gain power on the basis of ruined reputations. Squealing, anguish, death . . . and the epilogue . . ." Harry spread his hands, showing his open palms, his yellow fingers, then shrugged his shoulders and coughed lightly.

It was she who said to him, said to herself, without knowing in what order or how it would be best to communicate it to Harry: the epilogue has to be reflection, the effort of intelligence to understand what happened, why it happened.

"Why do we in America behave the same way they behave in Russia? Why did we become the same thing we said we were fighting? Why are there Berias and McCarthys, all those modern Torquemadas?"

Laura listened, she wanted to tell Harry that the three acts and epilogue in political dramas never appear that way, well ordered and Aristotelian, as Harry would say, mocking the "Academy" in Cuernavaca. They come tangled together, both of them knew that, sense mixed with nonsense, hope with despair, justification with criticism, compassion with disdain.

"If I could only go back to my time in Spain and stay there," Harry would sometimes say. And, feverishly, turning brutally to Laura, he would go on in a softer and softer but also hoarser voice: "Why don't you leave me, why are you staying with me?"

It was the moment of temptation. The moment when she experienced doubt. She could pack up and leave. It was possible. She could stay and put up with everything. That too was possible. But she could do neither: neither walk out just like that nor stay passively. She listened to Harry and again and again made the same decision: I'll stay, but I'll do something, I won't just take care of him, I won't just try to encourage him, I'll try to understand him, to find out what happened to him, why he knows all the stories of that infamous time and yet doesn't know his own story, why he won't tell me, the one who loves him, his story, why . . .

It was as if he read her mind. It happens with couples linked more by passion than by custom, we read each other's mind, Harry, a look is enough, a wave of a hand, a feigned distraction, a dream penetrated the same way a body is penetrated sexually, to know what the other is thinking, you're thinking about Spain, about Jim, about how he saved himself by dying young, how he didn't have time to become a victim of history, he was a victim of the war, that's noble, that's heroic; but being a victim of history, not foreseeing, not dodging history's blow in time, or not taking its full force when it does hit us, that's sad, Harry, that's terrible.

"It's all been a farce, an error."

"I love you, Harry, that's neither a farce nor an error."

"Why should I believe you?"

"I'm not tricking you."

"Everybody's tricked me."

"I don't know what you mean."

"Everybody."

"Why don't you tell me about it?"

"Why don't you find out on your own?"

"No, I'd never do anything behind your back."

"Don't be a fool. I'm giving you permission. Go ahead, go back to

Cuernavaca, ask them about me, tell them I gave you permission, they should tell you the truth."

"The truth, Harry?"

(The truth is that I love you, Harry, I love you in a different way from the way I once loved my husband, different from the way I loved Orlando Ximénez or even Jorge Maura, I love you the way I loved them, as a woman who lives and sleeps with a man, but with you it's different, Harry, besides loving you as I loved those men, I love you as I loved my brother Santiago the First and my son Santiago the Second, I love you as if I'd already seen you die, Harry, as I saw my brother, dead and buried with his unfulfilled promise, my son, resigned and handsome, that's how I love you, Harry, as a son, a brother, and a lover, but with one difference, my love: I loved them as a woman, as a mother, as a lover, and I love you as a bitch, I know neither you nor anyone else will understand me, but I love you as a bitch, I wish I could give birth to you and then bleed to death, that's the image that makes you different from my husband, my lover, or my sons, my love for you is the love of an animal that would love to put itself in your place and die instead of you, but only at the price of becoming your bitch, I've never felt this before and I'd like to explain it to myself and can't, but that's how it is and that's the way it is, Harry, because only now, at your side, I ask myself questions I never asked before, I ask myself if we deserve this love, I ask myself if it's love that exists, not you and I, and for that reason I'd like to be your animal, your bleeding, dying bitch, to say that love does exist the way a dog and a bitch exist, I want to take your love and mine away from any romantic idealism, Harry, I want to give your body and mine a last chance by rooting them in the lowest ground but also the most concrete and certain ground, where a dog and a bitch sniff, eat, entangle sexually, separate, forget each other, because I'm going to have to live with your memory when you die, Harry, and my memory of you will never be complete because I don't know what you did during the terror, you won't tell me, maybe you were a hero and your humility disguises itself in pugnacious honor, like John Garfield, so you won't tell me your exploits and make your heart sentimental, you who weep when Libertad Lamarque sings in those movies of hers, but maybe you were a traitor, Harry, a squealer, and that shames you and that's why you'd like to go back to Spain, be young, die at the side of your young friend Jim in the war and have war and death instead of history and dishonor: which is the truth? I think it's the first, because if it weren't you wouldn't have been accepted in that circle of victims over in Cuernavaca, but it may be the second because they never look at you, never address you, they invite you over and let you sit there, not talking to you but not attacking you, until your chair is like the dock where the accused sits, and you know me and you're not alone anymore and we should leave Cuernavaca, leave your comrades behind, not hear those arguments repeated ad nauseam anymore.)

"We should have denounced Stalin's crimes before the war."

"Don't kid yourself. You'd have been expelled from the Party. Besides, when you're up against the enemy you simply have to forget certain things."

"Still, that doesn't mean we wouldn't have talked about the errors of the Soviet Union among ourselves. We'd have been more human, we'd have defended ourselves better against the McCarthyite assault."

"How could we imagine what was going to happen?" Harry said one night, drinking beer at nightfall in the little garden backed by the mountain and redolent of the aromas of the blooming flowers and dying trees. "We American Communists fought first in Spain, then in the war against the Axis. It was the French Communists who really organized the Resistance, the Russian Communists who saved everyone at Stalingrad, who'd have thought that when the war was over being a Communist would be a sin and that all of us Communists would end up on the bonfire? Who?"

Another cigarette. Another Dos Equis.

"Being faithful to the impossible. That was our sin."

Laura had asked him if he was married, and Harry said he was but he preferred not to talk about it. "It's all over." He tried to end the conversation.

"You know it isn't. You have to tell me everything. We have to live it together. If we are going to go on living together, Harry."

"The rages, the fights, the sermons, the nervousness about the secret meetings, the suspicion that the accusers were right? *I married a Communist.* Sounds like the title of one of those bad movies they make to justify McCarthyism as patriotism. That's how the studio magnates expiate their pinko guilt. *Fuck them. We'll see tomorrow.*"

"Were you honest with your wife?"

"I was weak. I spilled my guts to her. Everything. I told her my doubts. Was what I wrote for the movies valid, or did they make me believe it was good because it served a cause—the cause, the only good cause? Are we paying a very high price for something that wasn't worth it? And she said to me, Harry, what you write is shit. But not because you're a Communist, my love. It's that your little flame went out. See things as they really are. You had talent. Hollywood stole it from you. It was a small talent, but it was a talent. You lost what little you had. That's what she told me, Laura."

"Things will be different with me."

"I can't, I can't. No more."

"I want to live with you." (In the name of my brother Santiago and my son Santiago, and take care of you now, as I either didn't know how to or couldn't take care of them, you understand, you get mad, you ask me not to treat you like a child, and I show you I'm not your mother, Harry, I'm your bitch, you don't use your mother like an animal, you don't use your lover that way, your romantic Hollywood sensibility wouldn't let you, Harry, but in my case, I'm asking you for it, let me be your bitch, even if I bark at you sometimes, I'm not your mother, your wife, or your sister.)

"Be my bitch."

He smoked and drank, attacking his lungs and his blood each time he opened his mouth. She pretended to drink with him, but she drank cider, saying it was whiskey, feeling like a cabaret whore who drinks colored water that her customer takes to be French cognac. She was ashamed of the trick, but she didn't want to get sick, because if that happened, who would take care of Harry? One day, she'd woken up in Cuernavaca in 1952 and seen the weak, sick man at her side. She'd right away decided that from then on her life would have meaning only if she devoted it to caring for him, taking charge of him, because Laura Díaz's life was now reduced to that conviction: my life has meaning only if I dedicate it to the life of someone who needs me, if I care for a needy person, giving my love to my love, totally, no conditions, no *arrière-pensées*, as Orlando would say. This is now the meaning of my life, even if there are arguments, failures to understand, irritations on his or on my part—broken dishes, whole days when we don't speak to each other, better that way, without those rough spots we'd turn into soft taffy, I'm going to unleash my irritation with him, I'm not going to control it, I'm going to give him his last chance for love, I'm going to love Harry in the name of what can't wait any longer, I am going to incarnate that moment in my life and it's already here: I know he's thinking the same thing, Laura, *this is the last chance*, what's between you and me can't wait any longer, and it's what was announced, it's what already happened and yet is happening now, we're living in anticipation of death because right before our eyes, Laura, the future is unfolding as if it had already taken place.

"That's something only the dead know."

"I'm going to ask you all a question," Fredric Bell addressed the usual dinner guests on Cuernavaca weekend. "We all know that during the war and thanks to the war, industry made enormous fortunes. I ask you, should we have gone on strike against the exploiters of labor? We didn't. We were patriots, nationalists, but we weren't revolutionaries."

"And what if the Nazis had won the war because American workers struck against American capitalists?" asked the epicurean who never took off his bow tie despite the heat.

"Are you asking me to choose between committing suicide tonight and being shot at dawn tomorrow? Like Rommel?" interjected the man with the square jaw and faded eyes.

"I'm saying we're at war, the war isn't over now and will never be over, the alliances change, one day they win, the next we win, the important thing is not to lose sight of the goal, and the funny thing is that the goal is the origin, do all of you realize that? The goal is the original freedom of mankind," concluded the Arrow shirt man.

No, Harry said to Laura, the origin wasn't freedom, the origin was terror, a struggle against beasts, distrust among brothers, fighting for wife, mother, the patriarchy, keeping the fire going, don't let it go out, sacrificing the child to keep death away, plague, hurricanes, that was the origin. There never was a Golden Age. There never will be. The thing is you can't be a good revolutionary if you don't believe that.

"And what about McCarthy? And Beria?"

"They were cynics. They never believed in anything."

"I respect your drama, Harry. I swear I respect you a great deal."

"Don't waste your time, Laura. Come here and give me a kiss."

When Harry died, Laura Díaz went back to Cuernavaca to tell the exiles. They were all together, as they were every Saturday night, and Ruth was dishing out huge servings of pasta. Laura saw that while the cast had changed, the parts were the same, and the absences were made up for with new recruits. McCarthy never tired of looking for victims, the stain of persecution was spreading like an oil spill on the sea, like pus from a penis. The old producer Theodore died, and his wife, Elsa, wouldn't last long without him; the tall, nearsighted man with tortoiseshell glasses had a chance to make a movie in France, and the small man with the curly hair and pompadour could write Hollywood screenplays under a pseudonym, using a "front."

Others went on living in Mexico, keeping company with Fredric Bell, protected by people on the Mexican left like the Riveras or the photographer Gabriel Figueroa, and always faithful to the arguments that would let them live, remember, argue, deaden the pain of the growing list of those who were persecuted, excluded, jailed, exiled, those who committed suicide, those who disappeared. They became deaf to the footfalls of old age, pretended to be blind to the certain if minute changes in the mirror. Now Laura Díaz was a mirror for the Cuernavaca exiles. She told them, Harry is dead, and they all suddenly became older. Yet at the same time Laura felt with visible emotion that each and every one of them shone like sparks from the same fire. For a second, when she gave them the simple message, Harry is dead, the fear that pursued them all, even the bravest—the fear that was Joe McCarthy's best-trained bloodhound nipping at the heels of the "reds"—dissipated in a kind of sigh of final relief. Without a word, they were all telling Laura that Harry would not be tormenting himself anymore. Nor would he torment them.

The looks of the American refugees in Cuernavaca were enough to precipitate in her heart an intolerable memory of everything Harry Jaffe had been—his tenderness and his anger, his bravery and his cowardice, his political pain translated into physical pain. His affliction, Harry her lover as an afflicted being, nothing more.

The English Bell remarked that those who were summoned before the House Un-American Activities Committee could do one of four things.

They could invoke the First Amendment to the Constitution, which guarantees freedom of expression and association. The risk in this was of being charged with contempt of Congress and going to jail. Which is what happened to the Hollywood Ten.

The second option was to invoke the Constitution's Fifth Amendment, which allows all citizens the right of not incriminating themselves. Those who opted to "take the Fifth" risked losing their jobs and appearing on blacklists. Which is what had happened to most of the Cuernavaca exiles.

The third possibility was to inform, to name names and hope the studios would give you work.

Then something extraordinary happened. All of the seventeen guests, along with Bell, his wife, and Laura, went down the highway to the little Tepoztlán cemetery where Harry Jaffe was buried. There was moonlight, and the modest graves decorated with flowers stretched out at the foot of Tepozteco's impressive height; its three-story pyramid descended to the blue, rose, white, and green crosses as if they weren't graves but just another kind of flower in the Mexican tropics. An always premature cold fell over Tepoztlán in the evening, and the gringos had brought jackets, shawls, and even parkas.

They were right to do so. Despite the bright moonlight, the mountains cast an immense shadow over the valley, and they themselves, these persecuted exiles, moved as if they were reflections, like the dark wings of a distant eagle, a bird that one day looks at itself in the mirror and no longer recognizes what it sees, because it imagined itself one way and the mirror shows it wasn't that at all.

Then, in the Tepoztec night, under the light of the moon, as if in a final Group Theatre presentation (the last curtain before closing on an empty house), each one of the exiles said something over the grave of Harry Jaffe, the man admitted to the group but whom no one had looked at except Laura Díaz, who arrived one day, dove into the bougainvillea-framed pool, and surfaced opposite her poor, disgraced, sick love.

"You only named those who'd already been named."

"Everyone you named was already on the blacklist."

"Between betraying your friends and betraying your country, you chose your country."

"You said to yourself that if you stayed in the Party, the fountains of your inspiration would dry up."

"The Party told you how to write, how to think, and you rebelled."

"First you rebelled against the Party."

"It horrified you to think that Stalinism could govern in the U.S.A. as it governed in the U.S.S.R."

"You went to speak before the committee, and you trembled with fear. Here in America, now, was the very thing you feared. Stalinism was interrogating you, but here it was called McCarthyism."

"You gave not one name."

"You faced up to McCarthy."

"Why did you do it when you knew they already knew? To inform on the informers, Harry, to cast infamy on the infamous, Harry."

"To go back to work, Harry. Until you realized that there was no difference between squealing and not squealing. The studios didn't give work to reds, but they also didn't give work to people who admitted being reds and informed on their comrades."

"It didn't work, Harry."

"You knew that anti-Communism had become the refuge of the scum of America."

"You didn't name the living. But you also didn't name the dead."

"You didn't name those who'd never been named. You also didn't name only those who'd already been named."

"You didn't even name those who named you, Harry."

"The Party demanded obedience of you. You said that even though you detested the Party, you weren't going to submit to the committee. The Party in its best moment was always better than the committee at any moment."

"My worst moment was not being able to tell my wife what was going on. Suspicion ruined our marriage."

"My worst moment was living in hiding, in a house where we never turned on the lights so we wouldn't be summoned by the agents of the committee."

"My worst moment was knowing that my children were ostracized in school."

"My worst moment was not telling my children what was happening, even though they already knew it all."

"My worst moment was having to decide between my socialist ideal and Soviet reality."

"My worst moment was having to choose between the literary quality of my writing and the dogmatic demands of the Party."

"My worst moment was choosing between writing well and writing commercially, as the studio wanted."

"My worst moment was looking into McCarthy's face and knowing that American democracy was lost."

"My worst moment was when Congressman John Rankin said to me, Your name isn't Melvin Ross. Your real name is Emmanuel Rosenberg, and that proves that you're a fake, a liar, a traitor, a shameful Jew."

"My worst moment was running into the person who informed on me and seeing him cover his face with his hands in pure shame."

"My worst moment was when my informer came crying to me to ask forgiveness."

"My worst moment was being mentioned by those disgusting society columnists, Sokolsky, Winchell, and Hedda Hopper. Their mentioning me was worse than McCarthy. Their ink smelled of shit."

"My worst moment came when I had to disguise my voice on the telephone to speak to my family and friends without getting them into trouble."

"They said to my daughter, Your father is a traitor. Don't have anything to do with him."

"They said to friends of my son, Do you know who his father is?"

"They said to my neighbors, Stop talking to that family of reds."

"What did you tell them, Harry Jaffe?"

"Harry Jaffe, rest in peace."

They all went back to Cuernavaca. Laura Díaz—in consternation, agitated, perplexed—went to get her belongings from the little house in Tepoztlán. She also gathered up her own pain, and Harry's. She gathered them up and gathered herself up. Alone with Harry's spirit, she wondered if the pain she was feeling was appropriate, her intelligence told her it wasn't, that one can only feel one's own pain, that pain is not transferable. Even though I saw your pain, Harry, I couldn't feel it as you felt it. Your pain had meaning only through mine. It's my pain, Laura Díaz's pain, that's the only pain I feel. But I can speak in the name of your pain, that I can do. The imagined pain of a man named Harry Jaffe who died of emphysema, drowned in himself, mutilated by air, with fallen wings.

Aside from the three possible ways of responding to the committee—Fredric Bell came to tell her one afternoon, the same day she returned to Mexico City—there was the fourth. It was called Executive Testimony. Witnesses who made public denunciations went through a private rehearsal, and in that case the public event was merely a matter of protocol. What the committee wanted was names. Its thirst for names was insatiable, *sed non satiata*. Generally, the witness was summoned to a hotel room and there he or she informed in secret. So the committee already had the names, but that wasn't enough. The witness had to repeat them in public for the glory of the committee but also in order to defame the informer. There were confusions. The committee would have the informer believe the secret confession was enough. The atmosphere of fear and persecution was such that the witness would delude himself and seize that life preserver, thinking, I'll be the exception, they'll keep my testimony secret. And sometimes there were exceptions, Laura. It's inexplicable why certain persons who talked in executive session were immediately summoned to public sessions and others weren't.

"But Harry was brave facing the Senate committee. He told McCarthy, You're the real Communist, Senator."

"Yes, he was brave facing the committee."

"But he wasn't brave in executive testimony? Did he inform first and recant later? Did he inform on friends first and then denounce the committee in public?"

"Laura, the victims of informers do not inform. All I can tell you is that there are men of good faith who thought, If I mention someone no one suspects, a person against whom they can't prove anything, I'll win the committee's favor and save my own skin. And I won't be hurting my friends."

Bell stood up and shook hands with Laura Díaz.

"My friend, if you can take flowers to the graves of Mady Christians and John Garfield, please do it."

The last thing Laura Díaz said to Harry Jaffe was: I'd rather touch your dead hand than the hand of any man living.

She doesn't know if Harry heard her. She didn't even know if Harry was dead or alive.

## 2.

She'd always been tempted to say to him, I don't know who your victims were, let me be one of them. She always knew he would have answered, I don't want life preservers. But I'm your bitch.

Harry said that if there was blame, then he would take it, completely.

"Do I want to save myself?" he would ask with a distant air. "Do I want to save myself with you? We'll have to find that out together."

She admitted it was very hard to live reading his mind, without his ever telling her exactly what had happened. But she quickly repented of her own frankness. She'd understood for years now that Harry Jaffe's truth would always be a fully endorsed check, undated and with no figure written on it. She loved an oblique man, chained to a double perception, the view of Harry held by the exile group and the view of the group held by Harry.

Laura Díaz went on wondering about the reason for the distance the exiles had kept from Harry, and why, at the same time, they had accepted him as part of the group. Laura wished he would tell her the truth, refusing to accept third-party versions, but he told her without smiling that if it was true that defeat is an orphan and victory has a hundred fathers, it was also the case that lies have many children but truth lacks progeny. Truth is solitary and celibate, which is why people prefer lies. Lies put us in touch with one another, make us happy, make us participants and accomplices. Truth isolates us and transforms us into islands surrounded by a sea of suspicion and envy. That's why we play so many lying games. Then we won't have to suffer the solitude of truth.

"Well, then, Harry, what do we know, you and I, about one another?"

"I respect you. You respect me. Together we're enough."

"But we're not enough for the world."

"That's true."

It was true that Harry was exiled in Mexico, like the Hollywood Ten and the others. Communists or not, it didn't matter. There were some unique cases, like the old Jewish producer Theodore and his wife, Elsa, who hadn't been accused of anything and who exiled themselves in solidarity; movies—they said—were made in collaboration, eyes wide open, and if someone was guilty of something or the victim of someone else, then all of them, without exception, had to be guilty.

"*Fuenteovejuna*, one for all and all for one." Laura Díaz smiled, remembering Basilio Baltazar.

There were recalcitrant ones who were faithful to Stalin and the U.S.S.R. but disillusioned with Stalinism, who didn't want to behave like Stalinists in their own land. "If we Communists were to take over in the United States, we too would slander, exile, and kill dissident writers," said the man with the pompadour.

"Then we wouldn't be real Communists. We'd be Russian Stalinists. They are products of a religious authoritarian culture that has nothing to do with Marx's humanitarianism or Jefferson's democracy," answered his tall, nearsighted companion.

"Stalin has corrupted the Communist idea forever, don't kid yourself."

"I'm going to go on hoping for democratic socialism."

Laura, who gave neither face nor name to these voices, blamed herself for not doing so. But she was right: similar arguments were repeated by different voices of different men and women who came and went, were there and then disappeared for good, leaving only their voices floating in the bougainvillea of the Bells' Cuernavaca garden.

There were also ex-Communists who feared ending up like Ethel and Julius Rosenberg, executed in the electric chair for imagined crimes. Or for crimes committed by others. Or for crimes that were alleged in an escalation of suspicion. There were Americans on the left, sincere socialists or "liberals," deeply concerned by the climate of persecution and betrayal that had been created by a legion of disgusting opportunists. There were friends and relatives of McCarthy's victims who left the United States to express their solidarity.

What there wasn't in Cuernavaca was a single informer.

Which of all these categories was the right one for the small, bald, thin, badly dressed man sick with emphysema, plagued by contradictions, whom she had come to love with a love so different from the love she had felt for other men, for Orlando, for Juan Francisco, and especially for Jorge Maura?

Contradictions: Harry was dying of emphysema but didn't stop smoking four packs of cigarettes a day because he said he needed them to write, it was a habit he couldn't break. The problem was, he didn't write anything but went on smoking. He was watching, with a kind of resigned passion, the great sunsets in the Valley of Morelos when the perfume of laurels overwhelmed his dying breaths.

He breathed with difficulty, and the valley air invaded his lungs and destroyed them: there was no room for oxygen in his blood. One day his own breath, the breath of a man named Harry Jaffe, escaped from his lungs as water pours from a broken water main, and it invaded his throat until it suffocated him with the very thing his body needed: air.

"If you listen carefully"—the ghost of a grin appeared on the sick man's face—"you can hear the sound of my lungs, like the snap, crackle, and pop in that cereal. Right, I'm a bowl of Rice Krispies." He laughed with difficulty. "But I should be Wheaties, breakfast of champions."

Contradictions: Does he think they don't know and they do know but don't say so? Does he know they know and they think he doesn't know that?

"How would you write about yourself, Harry?"

"I'd have to write history, words I detest."

"History, or your history?"

"Personal histories have to be forgotten for real history to emerge."

"But isn't real history a totality of personal histories?"

"I can't answer you. Ask me again some other day."

She thought about the totality of her carnal loves, Orlando, Juan Francisco, Jorge, and Harry; about her family loves, her father Fernando and her Mutti Leticia, her Aunts María de la O, Virginia, and Hilda; her spiritual passions, the two Santiagos. She stopped, upset and cold at the same time. Her other son, Danton, did not appear on any of those personal altars.

Other times she would say to Harry, I don't know who your victims were, or if there were victims, Harry, maybe you had no victims, but if you did, let me be one more.

He looked at her incredulously and forced her to see herself in the same way. Laura Díaz had never sacrificed herself for anyone. Laura Díaz was no one's victim. Which is why she could be Harry's victim, cleanly, gratuitously.

"Why don't you write?"

"Maybe it would be better if you'd ask me what it means to write."

"All right, what does it mean?"

417

"It means descending into yourself, as if you were a mine, so you can emerge again, Laura, emerge into pure air, with my hands full of myself."

"What do you bring out of the mine—gold, silver, lead?"

"Memory? The mud of memory?"

"Our daily memory."

"Give us this day our daily memory. It's pure shit."

He would have wanted to die in Spain.

"Why?"

"For symmetry. My life and history would have coincided."

"I know lots of people who think as you do. History should have stopped in Spain when you were all young and all heroes."

"Spain was salvation. I don't want to be saved anymore. I told you that already."

"Then you should get a grip on what followed Spain. Did the guilt continue then?"

"There were lots of innocents, there and here. I can't save the martyrs. My friend Jim died at the Jarama. I would have died for him. He was innocent. No one was innocent after that."

"Why, Harry?"

"Because I wasn't, and I wouldn't let anyone else be innocent again."

"Don't you want to save yourself?"

"Yes."

"With me?"

"Yes."

But Harry was destroyed; he didn't save himself, and wasn't going to die again on the Jarama front. He was going to die of emphysema, not from a Falangist or Nazi bullet, a bullet with a political purpose, he was going to die of an implosion from the physical or moral bullet he carried within himself. Laura wanted to give a name to the destruction that in the last analysis linked her inexorably to a man who no longer had any other company—even to go on destroying himself, with a cigarette or with repentance—but Laura Díaz.

They had left Cuernavaca because the facts remained, and Harry said he hated things that remained. Why do they accept me at the same time they reject me? asked Laura in Harry's voice. Because they don't want to accord me the discriminatory treatment they themselves suffered? Because if I informed secretly they won't accuse me publicly? Because if I acted in secret, they can't treat me as an enemy, yet I can't tell the truth.

"And live in peace?"

"I don't know who your victims were, Harry. Let me be one."

If he took refuge in Mexico was it because they went on persecuting him in the United States? Because he went on accusing—if that were the case—the witch-hunters? Because he informed on no one? Or—that's it—because he did inform? But what kind of squealing did he do, which lets me live among my victims? Should he have denounced himself to the others as an informer? What would he gain by doing that? What? Penitence and credibility? He'd be penitent and then they'd believe in him, look at him, speak to him? Had they all made a mistake, he and they?

(Laura, the informer is impregnable; to attack the credibility of the informer is to undermine the very foundations of the system of informing.

(Did you inform?

(Suppose I did. But also suppose no one knows I did, people think I'm a hero. Isn't that better for the cause?)

"I assure all of you. He could return, and no one would bother him."

"No. Inquisitors always find new reasons to persecute."

"Jews, converted Jews, Muslims, fags, impure races, lack of faith, heresy," Basilio reminded her during one of his sporadic visits. "The inquisitor never lacks motives. And if one motive fails or grows old, Torquemada pulls a new, unexpected one out of his sleeve. It's a story with no ending."

In an embrace at night, making love with the lights out, Harry stifling his cough, Laura in a nightgown to hide a body she no longer liked, they could say things to each other, they could speak with caresses, he could tell her this is the last chance for love, and she could say to him what's happening now has already been announced, and he, what already happened, what is happening, you and me is what already happened between you and me, Laura Díaz, Harry Jaffe, she had to suppose, she had to imagine. At breakfast, at the crepuscular cocktail hour, when only a diaphanous martini defended her from the night, and during the night itself, at the time of love, she could imagine answers to his questions.

"But you didn't talk, did you?"

"No, but they treat me as if I did."

"True. They insult you. They treat you as if you didn't matter. Let's go away from here, just the two of us."

"Why do you say that?"

"Because if you do have a secret and they respect it, it's because you don't seem important to them."

"You whore, you bitch, you think you can get me to talk with your traps."

"Men tell whores their problems. Let me be your whore, Harry, talk."

Harry laughed sarcastically. "Old bitch, old whore."

She no longer had the capacity for being insulted. She herself had begged him, let me be your bitch.

"Okay, bitch, imagine I talked in secret testimony. But imagine I mentioned only innocent people—Mady, Julie. You follow my logic? I imagined that because they were innocent, the committee wouldn't touch them. They did touch them. They killed them. I imagined they'd only go after Communists, and for that reason I didn't name Communists. They swore they'd only go after reds. They didn't keep their promise. They didn't imagine the same way I did. That's why I went from executive session to public session and attacked McCarthy."

(Are you now or have you ever been a member of the Communist Party?

(You're the Communist, Senator, you're the red agent, Moscow pays you, Senator McCarthy, you're the best propaganda for Communism, Senator.

(Point of order! Contempt! The witness is guilty of contempt of Congress.)

"Is that why I spent a year in jail? Is that why they have no choice but to respect me and accept me as one of their own? Is that why I'm a hero? But am I also an informer? Do they imagine I informed because I believed no one could prove the unprovable, that Mady Christians or John Garfield was a Communist? Do they think I didn't understand the logic of the persecution, which was to turn the innocent into victims? Do they imagine I named only innocents because I myself was guilty of innocence? Was it easier to terrorize the innocent rather than the culpable? Could someone say, I was or am a Communist and take the consequences honorably? Is that the logic of terror? Yes, terror is like an invisible vise that crushes you the way emphysema is suffocating me. You can't do anything, and you end up exhausted, dead, sick, or a suicide. Terror kills the innocent with fear. It's the inquisitor's most powerful weapon. Tell me I was an idiot, that I wasn't able to foresee that."

"Why didn't the inquisitors denounce you, why didn't they reveal that you'd talked in secret session?"

"Because if they revealed my double game, they would also reveal their own. They would have lost an ace from their deck. They kept their mouths shut about my betrayal, they ultimately made martyrs of the people I named, which was no problem for them, because they had their list of victims prepared beforehand. An informer only confirmed publicly what they wanted to hear. Many more witnesses denounced Mady Christians and John Garfield publicly. That's why they said nothing about my informing. They jailed me for rebelliousness, sent me to jail, and when I got out, I had to go into exile. Either way, they defeated me, made me impossible for myself."

"Do your friends in Cuernavaca know all that?"

"I don't know, Laura. But I suppose they do. They're divided. For them it's good to have me among them as a martyr, better than expelling me as an informer. But they don't talk to me or look me in the eye."

She begged him to leave Cuernavaca with her; both of them, alone, elsewhere, could give each other what two solitary beings can give each other, two losers, together we can be what we are what we aren't. Let's go before an immense void swallows us up, my love, let's die in secret, with all our secrets, let's go, my love.

"I swear I'll keep my mouth shut forever."

## 21. Colonia Roma: 1957

### 1.

WHEN AN EARTHQUAKE SHOOK Mexico City in July 1957, Laura Díaz was staring out at the night from the roof terrace of her old house on Avenida Sonora. Breaking her own rule, she was smoking a cigarette. In honor of Harry. He'd died three years before, but her devout love had left her full of unanswered questions, had burdened her with blocked mental horizons. Her heart was still alive, but she had no man and had lost the one she loved. Also, she'd just turned fifty-nine.

The memory filled her days and sometimes, as now, her nights. Ever since Harry's death and her return to Mexico City, she was sleeping less than she once had. The fate of her American lover obsessed her. She did not want to classify Harry Jaffe as a failure, because she didn't want to blame his failure either on McCarthyite persecution or on his own internal collapse. She didn't want to admit that persecution or no persecution Harry had stopped writing because he had had nothing to say. He'd taken refuge in the witch-hunt.

Her doubts persisted. Did the persecution begin just when Harry's abilities failed him, or had he already lost them? Then was the persecution a mere pretext to turn sterility into heroism? It wasn't his fault. He wanted to die in Spain, at the Jarama with his buddy Jim, when ideas and life were identical for him, when nothing separated them, when, Laura, I didn't suffer this damned alienation . . .

From the terrace, as she thought about her poor Harry, Laura Díaz could contemplate, on her left, the dark tide of the sleeping forest, its treetops undulating like the breathing in and out of an ancient sleeping monarch on his throne of trees and crowned by his stone castle.

To the right, far away, the gilded Angel of Independence added to its own painted gleam the glow of spotlights outlining its air-borne silhouette, golden damsel of the Porfirio Díaz era disguised as a Greek goddess but representing, like a celestial transvestite, the virile angel of a feminine saga, Independence . . . The he/she Angel held up a laurel branch in his/her right hand, stretched his/her wings, and began a flight—but not the one intended, a flight that instead was catastrophic, brutal, and abrupt, from the top of the airy column into the very air, then crashing into shattered pieces at the base of its own pedestal, a fall like Lucifer's, the ruined he/she Angel vanquished by the shaking earth.

Laura Díaz saw the Angel fall and—who knows why?—thought that it wasn't the Angel but Antonieta Rivas Mercado, who had posed mythically for the sculptor Enrique Alciati, never imagining that one day her beautiful effigy, her entire body, would fall to pieces at the foot of the slender commemorative column. She watched the treetops ebb and flow and she watched the Angel fall but, more than anything else, she felt her own house creaking, snapping apart like the Angel's wings, breaking into pieces like a fried tortilla between the teeth of the monstrous city—where she'd toured with Orlando Ximénez one night to see the face of its true misery, the invisible misery, the most horrible of all, the misery that didn't dare show itself because it could beg for nothing, and because no one would give it anything anyway.

She waited for the earthquake to wear itself out.

The best thing to do was to stay where she was. There was no other way to fight that underground force, one had to resign oneself to it and then overcome it with its mirror opposite: immobility.

She'd only once before experienced a serious tremor, in 1943, when the city quavered because of an extraordinary event: as a peasant in Michoacán was plowing his field, smoke began to pour out of a hole, and out of the hole emerged, in just a few hours, as if the earth had really borne it, a baby volcano, Paricutín, vomiting stone, lava, sparks. Every night its glow was visible from farther and farther away. The Paricutín phenomenon was amusing, astonishing, but comprehensible precisely because so bizarre (the name of the place was unpronounceably Tarascan: Paranguaritécuaro, abbreviated to Paricutín). A country where a volcano can appear overnight, out of nowhere, is a country where anything can happen . . .

The 1957 earthquake was crueler, faster, dry, and it slashed the sleeping body of Mexico City like a machete. When calm returned, Laura carefully walked down the cast-iron circular stairs to the bedroom floor and found things scattered every which way: armoires and drawers, toothbrushes, glasses and soaps, pumice stones and sponges, and on the ground floor pictures hung at crazy angles, not a single light burning, plates broken, parsley knocked over, bottles of Electropura water smashed in pieces.

It was worse outside. When she stepped out onto the street, Laura could see the full and savage damage the house had suffered. The facade looked not so much smashed as if it had been slashed with a knife, peeled like an orange, uninhabitable . . .

The earthquake woke up the ghosts. The telephone worked. While Laura was eating a bean-and-sardine snack and having some grape juice, she had calls from Danton and Orlando.

She hadn't seen her younger son since Juan Francisco's wake, when she'd scandalized her daughter-in-law's family and especially her daughter-in-law, Magdalena Ayub Longoria.

"I couldn't care less what that bunch of snobs think," Laura told her son.

"It doesn't matter," answered Danton. "Water and oil, you know . . . but don't worry. I'll take care of you."

"Thank you. I wish we could see each other."

"So do I."

In the eyes of her in-laws the scandal grew when Laura went off to Cuernavaca with a gringo Communist, but Danton's money was always there, punctually and abundantly. It was their agreement, and there was nothing more to say. Until the day of the earthquake.

"Are you all right, Mama?"

"I'm all right. The house is a ruin."

"I'll send builders around to look it over. Move into a hotel and then call me so I can take care of things."

"Thanks. I'll go to Diego Rivera's."

There was an uncomfortable silence, and then Danton, in a cheery voice, said, "The things that happen. The roof collapsed on top of Doña Carmen Cortina. While she was sleeping. Did you know her? Just imagine. Buried in her own bed, as flat as a pancake. *Mexico, beautiful and adored!* as the song goes. They say she was the life of the party back in the 1930s."

A little while later, the telephone rang again, and Laura flinched. She remembered the two different telephone companies, Ericsson and Mexicana, with different lines and numbers, complicating everyone's life, when she had Mexicana and Jorge Maura had Ericsson. Now there was only one telephone company, so today's lovers, Laura thought nostalgically, were missing the excitement of the game, the telephone as disguise.

As if to put off the insistent caller, Laura tried to think about everything that had come into the world since her grandfather Philip Kelsen had left Germany in 1864: moving pictures, radio, cars, planes, telephones, telegraphs, television, penicillin, mimeograph machines, plastic, Coca-Cola, long-playing records, nylon stockings . . .

Perhaps the sense of being in a catastrophe reminded her of Jorge Maura, and she began to associate the ringing phone with her own heartbeats and hesitated for a few moments. She was afraid to pick up the receiver. "Laura?" She tried to recognize the baritone voice, deliberately high-pitched to sound more English, who greeted her saying, "It's Orlando Ximénez speaking. You've heard about Carmen Cortina's tragedy. She was crushed to death. While she was asleep. The roof fell in on her. We're holding a wake for her in Gayosso's, over on Sullivan Street. I thought, well, for old times' sake . . ."

The man who stepped out of the taxi at seven that evening said hello from the edge of the sidewalk and then came toward her with an uncertain gait and a mobile smile, as if his mouth were a radio dial searching for the right station.

"Laura. It's me, Orlando. Don't you recognize me? Look." He laughed as he showed her his hand and his gold ring with the initials OX. There was no other way she would have recognized him. He was totally bald and made no effort to hide it. The strange thing—the serious thing, Laura said to herself—was that the extreme smoothness of his skull, bare as a baby's backside, contrasted brutally with his infinitely wrinkled face, crisscrossed by tiny lines running in all directions. A face that was an insane compass rose, its cardinal points not at north, east, south, and west but scattered in every direction, a cobweb with no symmetry.

Orlando Ximénez's white skin and blond looks had put up a poor defense against the passage of the years; the wrinkles on his face were as uncountable as furrows in a field plowed for centuries and yielding poorer and poorer crops. Even so, he maintained the distinction of a slim, well-dressed body, with a double-breasted glen plaid suit and a black tie appropriate for the occasion, and—the coquettish touch, inveterate in him—a Liberty handkerchief peeking *sans façon* from his breast pocket. "Only vulgarians and men from Toluca wear matching ties and handkerchiefs," he'd once said to her years before in San Cayetano and in the Hotel Regis.

"Laura dear," he said, speaking first, seeing that she hadn't recognized him right away, and after planting two fugitive little kisses on her cheeks, stepping back to observe her, keeping hold of her hands. "Let me get a look at you."

He was the same old Orlando: he'd never let her have an advantage he could take for himself. Without a word from her, he went on, "How you've changed, Laura," before she could blurt out, "How you've changed, Orlando."

On the way to Sullivan Street (who the devil was Sullivan? An English composer of operettas? But he was always linked like a Siamese twin to Gilbert, the way Ortega was joined to Gasset, joked irrepressible Orlando), Laura's old sweetheart spoke of Carmen Cortina's horrible death and the mystery that had always surrounded her. The famous hostess of the 1930s, the woman whose energy had saved Mexican society from a drowsy convulsion (if you could say such a thing; I agree, it's an oxymoron, Orlando said, smiling), had been bedridden for years with phlebitis, which immobilized her. The question was, could Carmen Cortina have gotten out of bed to save herself from the collapse, or did her physical prison condemn her to watch while the ceiling fell on her and crushed her? Well, well, why worry about the fine points? Like the *cucaracha* in the song, she just couldn't walk . . .

"*But I am a chatterbox,*" he said in English, "forgive me." Orlando laughed, caressing Laura Díaz's bare fingers with his gloved hand.

Only when they stepped out of the taxi on Sullivan Street did he take her by the arm and whisper in her ear, don't be frightened, Laura dear, you're going to find all our old friends from twenty-five years ago, but you won't recognize them. If you're in doubt, just squeeze my arm— don't let go of me, *je t'en prie*—and I'll whisper in your ear who's who.

"Have you read Proust's *The Past Recaptured*? No? Well, it's the same situation. The narrator returns to a Parisian salon thirty years later and no longer recognizes the intimate friends of his youth. Face to face with the old marionettes, says Proust's narrator, he has to use not only his eyes but his memory. Old age is like death, he adds. Some face it with indifference, not because they're braver than the rest but because they have less imagination."

Orlando made a show of looking for the name Carmen Cortina on the chapel directory.

"Of course, the difference between us and Proust is that he finds old age and the passage of time in an elegant salon in French high society, while you and I, proudly Mexican, find them in a funeral parlor."

There was no intrusive smell of flowers to nauseate the guests at the wake. So the perfumes on the women asserted themselves all the more offensively. They were like the last clouds in a sky about to fade forever into night, as one by one they passed before Carmen Cortina's open coffin, where she lay as reconstructed by the mortician, put back together piece by minute piece, looking neither like herself nor like any living being seen before. She was a window-display dummy, as if her turbulent career as a social hostess had prepared her for this final moment, this last act in what had been in life a permanent stage show: a mannequin reposing on white silk cushions under clear plastic, hair carefully tinted mahogany, cheeks smooth and pink, mouth obscenely swollen and half open in a smile that seemed to lick death as if it were a lollipop, nose stuffed with cotton balls, to keep what remained of Carmen's vital juices from leaking out, eyes closed—but without the glasses that as hostess she had wielded with the wisdom of the elegantly blind—as if they were darts, or a replacement finger, or an exhausted pennant, or a menacing stiletto, but always as the baton with which Carmen Cortina conducted her brilliant social operetta.

Without those glasses Laura Díaz did not recognize Carmen. She was on the verge of suggesting to Orlando—caught up in her first boyfriend's unshakably festive tone—that some charitable soul should put glasses on the cadaver. Carmen was quite capable of opening her eyes. Of coming back to life. Now Laura failed to recognize a woman with a mother-of-pearl complexion and overflowing corpulence who was being pushed along in a wheelchair by the painter Tizoc Ambriz, recognizable because his picture appeared so frequently on the culture and society pages, though he was transformed, given the color, tautness, and texture of his skin, into a scaly black-and-silver sardine. Thin and small, he was dressed, as always, in blue denim—trousers, shirt, and jacket—as if to stand out while at the same time, in contradiction, imposing a fashion.

He devoutly pushed the wheelchair of the woman with drowsy eyes, invisible eyebrows, but—Oh! exclaimed Orlando—no longer a face of perfect symmetry with that eternal maturity which presumes eternal youth, as she had been thirty years earlier, at the very edge of an opulence that Laura's companion had once compared to a piece of fruit at the peak of ripeness, freshly cut from the branch.

"It's Andrea Negrete. Don't you remember the vernissage of her portrait by Tizoc in Carmen's little flat? She was nude—in the painting of course—with two white streaks at her temples and her pubis also painted white, bragging about having gone gray in the groin—*can you imagine*. Dear, dear, now she doesn't have any use for dye."

"Eat me," Andrea whispered to Orlando as they entered the room where a priest was leading the prayer for the dead in front of a dozen of Carmen Cortina's friends.

"Eat me."

"Peel me."

"You vulgarian," laughed the actress, while the whisper of *Lux perpetua luceat eis* vaguely drowned out the comments and gossip.

The painter Tizoc Ambriz, on the other hand, had lost all facial expression. He was an idol, a diminutive Tezcatlipoca, Puck of the Aztecs, condemned to wander like a ghost through the bewitched nights of México-Tenochtitlán.

Tizoc looked toward the entrance, where a tall, dark young man with curly hair was coming in with a woman on his arm, a woman swollen in every roll of her obesity and reworked in every centimeter of her epidermis. She made her way forward proudly, even impertinently, on the arm of her ephebe, showing off how light her step was despite the immensity of her weight. She sailed like a galleon in Spain's Invincible Armada over the tempestuous seas of life. Her tiny feet supported a solid fleshly sphere crowned by a minuscule head with blond curls framing a sculpted, surgically enhanced, restored, composed, replaced, and displaced face—stretched like a balloon about to burst yet lacking expression, a pure mask fixed by invisible pins around her ears and stitched under a chin that had eliminated the double chin visibly struggling to be reborn.

"Laura, Laura dearest!" exclaimed this nightmare apparition wrapped in black veils and dripping with jewelry. My God, who can it be? Laura asked herself. I don't remember her! Then she realized that the scarred blimp wasn't greeting her but was lightly making her way to someone behind her, and Laura turned to follow this living advertisement for face-lifts and saw her kiss on both cheeks a woman who was her opposite, a thin, small lady in a black suit, with pearls and a tiny pillbox hat from which hung a black veil so close to her skin that it seemed an integral part of her face.

"Laura Rivière, how happy I am to see you," exclaimed the scar-faced fatty.

"What a pleasure, Elizabeth," answered Laura Rivière, discreetly drawing away from the exuberant Elizabeth García-Dupont, formerly Caraza. Laura Díaz was astonished: it was her adolescent pal in Xalapa, whose mother, Doña Lucía Dupont, had said, Girls, never show your boobs, as she stuffed Elizabeth into her old-fashioned ball gown, rose-colored with layer upon layer of infinitely floating tulle . . .

(Laura has no problems because she's flat, Mama, but I . . .

(Elizabeth, child, don't shame me.

(There's nothing to be done about it. God, with your help, made me this way.)

She hadn't recognized Laura just as Laura hadn't recognized her, either because Laura—glancing at herself in the mortuary mirror—had changed just as much, or perhaps Elizabeth actually had recognized her but didn't want to say hello because resentment, however old, was still alive. Or perhaps to avoid comparisons, lies, you haven't changed a bit! How do you do it? Made a pact with the devil? The last time, in Ciro's in the Hotel Reforma, Elizabeth had looked like an anorexic mummy.

Laura Díaz waited for Elizabeth García to separate from Laura Rivière before approaching her namesake, offering her hand, receiving one that was dry, fine, and then she tried to recognize her in the depth of the black veil, in the very well-cared-for white skin below the cylindrical, low hat crowning her head instead of the languid ash-blond hair-cut of her youth.

"I'm Laura Díaz."

"I've been waiting for you. You promised to call me."

"I'm sorry. You told me to save myself."

"Did you think I couldn't help you?"

"You told me yourself, remember? *It's too late for me. I'm a prisoner. My body's been captured by routine.*"

"But if I could escape from my own body . . ." Laura Rivière smiled. "I detest it. That's what I told you, you probably remember . . ."

"I'm sorry I didn't call you."

"So am I."

"You know? We might have been friends."

"*Hélas.*" Laura Rivière sighed. Then she turned away from Laura Díaz with a melancholy smile.

"She really loved Artemio Cruz," Orlando Ximénez confided to Laura as he took her back to Avenida Sonora, threading their way through the rubble of the city. "She was a woman obsessed by light, lamps, light in interiors, yes, the proper arrangement of lamps, the exact wattage, how to illuminate faces. She's her own self-portrait."

(I can't go on, my love. You have to choose.

(Be patient, Laura. Just realize . . . Don't force me . . .

(To do what? Are you afraid of me?

(Aren't we fine just as we are? Is something missing?

(Who knows? Artemio. It may well be that nothing's missing.

(I didn't deceive you. I didn't force you.

(I didn't transform you, which is different. You're not ready. I'm getting tired.

(I love you. As I did the first day.

(It's no longer the first day. No longer. Make the music louder.)

As she was getting out of the taxi, Orlando tried to kiss her. Laura felt the touch of those wrinkled lips, the nearness of that skin which looked like graph paper, like a weak, pink piece of meat on the grill. And she felt it repellent. She pushed him away, disgusted and shocked.

"I love you, Laura. As I did the first day."

"It's not the first day anymore. Now we know each other. Far too well. Goodbye, Orlando."

And the mystery? Will they both die without Orlando's ever revealing his secrets? Orlando, intimate friend of the first Santiago in Veracruz; Orlando, seducer of Laura because of that; mysterious mailman between the invisible anarchist Armonía Aznar and the world; Orlando, her lover and her Virgil in the infernal circles of Mexico City.

It was impossible to attribute any mystery whatsoever to this out-of-fashion lounge lizard, mummified and banal, who had gone with her to Carmen Cortina's wake, to the burial of an entire era in the history of Mexico City. She preferred to hold on to the mystery. The homage to "old times" nevertheless left Laura with a bitter taste in her mouth.

The electricity had been restored. She began to pick up fallen objects, pots and pans in the kitchen; she straightened up the dining room, then especially the living room, and the balcony where, when the family reconciled after Laura Díaz's passion for Jorge Maura, she and her husband Juan Francisco, her sons Santiago and Danton, and the ancient auntie from Veracruz, María de la O, had watched the afternoons fade in the Bosque de Cohapultepec. She replaced the books knocked off their shelves. Out from between the pages of Bertram D. Wolfe's biography of Diego Rivera had fallen the photograph Laura Díaz took of Frida Kahlo the day she died, July 13, 1954. The day Laura left Harry Jaffe alone in Tepoztlán and raced to the Riveras' house in Coyoacán.

"Here," Harry said, handing her a Leica. "I used it to take stills in Hollywood. Don't come back without bringing me Frida Kahlo dead."

She had restrained the rage Harry sometimes aroused in her. Frida was dying, amputated and ill, but even on her deathbed she'd gone on painting—right to the last moment. Harry was dying in a tropical valley, but he was too cowardly to pick up pen and paper. The main reason why Laura took the photo of Frida's body was to show it to Harry and tell him, "She never stopped creating, not even on the day she died."

But now Harry, too, was dead. So was Carmen Cortina, and the rage Laura felt toward Harry, like the sense of absurdity she felt seeing Carmen Cortina's embalmed body, was turning, as she stared at the photo of Frida dead, into something more than love or admiration.

In her coffin, Frida Kahlo showed off her black hair braided with colored ribbons. Her ring-covered fingers and her arms laden with bracelets rested on a bosom decked out for the final journey in sumptuous necklaces of thin gold and silver from Morelia. Her pendant earrings of green turquoise no longer hung from her earlobes but lay at rest like her, mysteriously retaining the dead woman's final warmth.

Frida Kahlo's face did not change in death. Her eyes were closed but seemed alert, thanks to the inquisitive vivacity of her thick unbroken eyebrows, her trademark, that dangerous and fascinating whip. The thickness of her brows did not succeed in masking Frida's mustache, the notorious and notable down on her upper lip that made you think that a penis, the twin of Diego's, might be trying to spring up between her legs to confirm the probability, not just the illusion, that she was a hermaphrodite, and parthenogenic to boot, able to fertilize herself and generate with her own semen the new being that her feminine half would bear thanks to the vigor of her masculine half.

That's how Laura Díaz photographed her, for Laura thought she was taking the picture of an inert body, not realizing that Frida Kahlo had already set out on the journey to Mictlan, the Mexican Indian underworld you can reach only if you are guided by three hundred ixcuintles, those hairless dogs Frida collected which now, motherless, were howling disconsolately on the patios and in the kitchens and on the roof terraces of the funeral home.

Frida Kahlo's recumbent position was a deception. She was heading for Mictlan, an inferno that resembled a painting by Frida Kahlo but without the blood, the spines, and the martyrdom, without the operating rooms, the scalpels, the steel corsets, the amputations, without the fetuses—a hell only of flowers, of warm rains and hairless dogs, a hell piled high with pineapples, strawberries, oranges, mangos, *guanábanas*, mameys, lemons, papayas, *zapotes*, where she would arrive on foot, humble and haughty at the same time, with a sound body, cured, prior to hospitals, virgin of all accidents, greeting Señor Xolotl, ambassador of the Universal Republic of Mictlan, Chancellor and Plenipotentiary Minister of Death, that is, of THIS PLACE. *How do you do, Señor Xolotl*: that's what Frida would be saying as she entered hell.

She entered hell. From her house in Coyoacán they took her, dead, to the National Palace of Fine Arts. There she was draped with the Communist flag, an act that led to the dismissal of the Institute director. Then she was brought to the crematorium: she was put into the oven—all decked out, dressed, bejeweled, with beribboned hair, the better to burn. And when the flames sprang up, Frida Kahlo's body sat up, sat up as if she were going to chat with her oldest friends, the Caps group whose practical jokes had scandalized the National Preparatory School in the 1920s; as if she were getting ready to talk once again with Diego; that's how Frida's body sat up, animated by the crematorium flames. Her hair flamed like a halo. She smiled one last time at her friends, and dissolved.

All that remained to Laura Díaz was the photo she had taken of Frida Kahlo's cadaver. It showed that death for Kahlo was a way to distance herself from everything ugly in this world, not to avoid it but to see it better; to discover the affinity of Frida, woman and artist, not with beauty but with truth.

She was dead, but through her closed eyes passed all the pain of her paintings, the horror more than the pain, according to some observers. No, in Laura Díaz's photo, Frida Kahlo was the conduit of the pain and ugliness of hospitals, miscarriages, gangrene, amputations, drugs, immobile nightmares, the company of the devil, the wounded passage to a truth that becomes beautiful because it identifies our being with our essence, not with our appearance.

Frida gives form to the body: Laura photographed it.

Frida gathers together what is scattered: Laura photographed that integration.

Frida, like an all too infrequent phoenix, rises when touched by fire.

She was reborn to go off with the hairless dogs to the other neighborhood, to the land of Madam Baldy, La Pelona, Miss Toothy, La Dientona, Lady Toasty, La Tostada, Mistress Fancy, La Catrina, Charley's Aunt.

She went dressed up for a party in Paradise.

## 2.

With the photo of dead Frida in one hand and the camera Harry had given her in the other, Laura looked at herself in the mirror of her new apartment on Plaza Río de Janeiro, where she moved after the earthquake had made the old house on Avenida Sonora uninhabitable.

Danton, who owned it, decided to demolish it and build in its place a twelve-story condominium.

"I thought your father and I were the owners of our home," said Laura in surprise but under no illusions, the day Danton visited her to explain the new order of things.

"The property's been mine for a long time," answered Laura's younger son.

The mother's shock was an act; the real surprise was the physical change that had taken place in the thirty-five-year-old man she hadn't seen since Juan Francisco's funeral, when Laura's in-laws ostracized her.

It wasn't the few gray hairs at his temples or his slightly larger potbelly that had changed Danton but his insolent mien, a display of power he couldn't hide, not even in the presence of his mother, although, perhaps—precisely—he exaggerated it because she was there. Everything, from his hair, which he wore in the same cut Marlon Brando had in *Julius Caesar*, to the charcoal-gray suit, the narrow English regimental tie, right down to his black Gucci loafers, affirmed power, self-confidence, the habit of being obeyed.

With nervous self-assurance, Danton stretched out his arms to show his ruby-colored cuff links.

"I've got my eye on a sweet apartment for you in Polanco, Mother."

No, she insisted, I want to stay in Colonia Roma.

"It's getting polluted very fast. The traffic congestion will be terrible. Besides, it's out of fashion. And it's where the earthquakes hit hardest."

And for all those reasons I want to live here.

"Do you know what a condominium is? The one I'm building is the first in Mexico. It's going to be the fashion. Vertical property is the future of this city, guaranteed. You should get in on it before it's too late. Besides, those apartments you like in the Plaza aren't for sale. They're rentals."

Precisely. She wanted to pay her own rent from now on, without his help.

"What are you going to live on?"

"How old do you think I am?"

"Don't be so stubborn, Mother."

"I thought my house belonged to me. Do you have to buy everything to be happy? Let me be happy in my own way."

"Dying of hunger?"

"Independent."

"Okay, but call if you need me."

"Likewise."

With the Leica in her hands, Laura Díaz reacted in the same way to the dissimilar deaths of first Frida Kahlo and then Carmen Cortina in the year of the earthquake. Orlando made her remember the invisible, lost city of an asphyxiating misery and degradation that he had taken her to see that night after the penthouse party on Paseo de la Reforma. Now, camera in hand, Laura walked the streets in the heart of Mexico City and found them simultaneously crowded and abandoned. Not only did she fail to find that lost city, the true beggars' paradise, where Orlando had taken her to convince her that *there was no hope*, but she discovered that the visible city of the 1930s was now the real invisible or, at the least, abandoned, city, left behind by the incessant outward expansion of the capital. The first block around the Zócalo, great center of the city's celebrations since the time of the Aztecs, wasn't empty—there were no open spaces in Mexico City—but it had ceased to be the center and was just another neighborhood, the oldest and in a certain way the most prestigious because of its history and architecture. Now a new center was springing up around the fallen Angel of Independence, on both sides of Paseo de la Reforma, neighborhoods named either for rivers or for foreign cities: urban Colonia Juárez and fluvial Colonia Cuauhtémoc.

Two thousand new people a day were moving into Mexico City, sixty thousand new inhabitants a month fleeing hunger, arid farmland, injustice, unpunished crime, brutal political bosses, and indifference; the capital, meanwhile, was alluring, with its promises of well-being, even beauty. Didn't the beer ads promise top-caliber blondes, and weren't all the characters in the ever more popular television soap operas also blond, rich, well-dressed upper-class types?

For Laura, none of this answered her questions about the unstoppable migratory flow: Where did these people come from? What was their final destination? How did they live? Who were they?

That was Laura Díaz's first great photo-essay. It summed up the experience of a lifetime—her provincial origins, her life as a young married woman, her two experiences of motherhood, her loves and what her loves brought her: the Spanish world of Maura, the terrible memory of Raquel's martyrdom in Buchenwald, the merciless execution of Pilar at the walls of Santa Fe de Palencia, McCarthy's persecution of Harry, the double death of Frida Kahlo, first immobile death and then resuscitation by fire—she poured it all into a single image taken in one of the nameless cities springing up like loose threads and patches on the great embroidered sackcloth that was Mexico City.

Lost cities, anonymous cities built on the outskirts of the dry valley, amid rocky fields and mesquite trees, with houses nailed together any which way, caves made of cardboard and flattened tin cans, dirt floors, poisoned water, and dying candles (until the people's ingenuity discovered a technique for stealing electricity from streetlights and the pylons supporting high-tension power cables).

Which is why the first photograph Laura Díaz took, after Frida Kahlo's body, was of the fallen Angel, the statue smashed to pieces at the foot of its slender column, the bodiless wings, the split, blinded face of the model who, according to legend, posed for it, Antonieta Rivas Mercado, who years after went to Notre Dame in Paris to commit suicide in front of an altar because of her love for the philosopher José Vasconcelos, Mexico's first Minister of Education. Vasconcelos' memoir, *Ulises Criollo*, had caused a sensation in 1935 because of its frankness, and Orlando, in one of his most felicitous remarks, said, "It's a book you have to read standing up."

When she photographed the broken figure of the Angel who was the philosopher's lover, Laura Díaz had to measure the seasons—in a city of "perpetual spring" that seemed never to have one. She realized she hadn't really taken notice of how the years had passed. The city has no seasons. January is cold. Dust storms in February. March blazes. It rains in summer. In October, the storms remind us that appearances are deceiving. December is transparent. January is cold.

She thought about the years she'd lived in Mexico City and began to superimpose Vasconcelos' various faces on them—from the young, romantic student to the dashing intellectual *guerrillero* of the Revolution, to the noble educator with the interminable forehead who commissioned Diego Rivera to paint murals, to the Bergsonian philosopher of *élan vital*, to the Americanist of the "cosmic race," to the presidential candidate who opposed the Maximum Chief Calles and his court jester Luis Napoleón Morones, the man who'd corrupted Juan Francisco, to the resentful exile who ended up, old and choleric, praising Franco and fascism and ordering his own books expurgated.

Vasconcelos was the mutable and dramatic image of revolutionary Mexico, and his fallen lover, Antonieta Rivas Mercado, Angel of Independence, was the fixed, symbolic supernatural image of the nation in whose name the heroes who venerated her had fought, the same ones who'd fucked her. Today, both the philosopher and his angel were in ruins, in a city that neither would recognize and that Laura went out to photograph.

Laura was sleeping differently. Before, she had dreamed without reflecting but with concern. Now there was neither reflection nor concern. She slept as if everything had already happened. She slept like an old lady.

She reacted. She wanted to sleep again as if nothing had happened, as if her life would only begin when she woke up, as if love were still a pain unknown to her. She wanted to wake up with a desire to see anew each morning and to file what she was seeing in the most precise place in her feelings, where heart and head joined forces. Before, she'd seen without seeing. She didn't know what to do with her everyday images, the daily coins that each day put in her empty hands.

Laura Díaz began to ask herself, What will I do next year? Before, when she was young, everything was unforeseen, natural, necessary, and, despite everything, pleasant. But Frida's death especially made her remember her own past as if it were a blurry photo. The earthquake, seeing Orlando again, and the death of Carmen made her think, Can I give the past its lost focus, its absent clarity?

The city and death woke her up. Mexico surrounded her like a great, sleeping serpent. Laura woke next to the heavy breathing of the serpent that wrapped around her but did not suffocate her. She woke up and photographed the serpent.

She had photographed Frida dead. Now she photographed the family house on Avenida Sonora before it was demolished as her son had ordered. She photographed the splintered facade and the condemned interiors, too, the garage where Juan Francisco parked the car the CROM labor union had given him, the dining room where her husband had met with labor leaders, the living room where she would wait, patient as a Creole Penelope, for the moment of grace and solitude when her husband returned home, the threshold where the persecuted nun Gloria Soriano sought refuge, and the kitchen where Auntie María de la O maintained the traditions of Veracruz cuisine—the aromas of chile chipotle, purslane, and cumin still permeated the walls. Then there was the hot-water tank fueled by yellowed newspapers where all the figures of power, crime, and entertainment were gradually consumed, where the flames devoured Calles and Morones, Lombardo and Avila Camacho, Trotsky and Ramón Mercader, the murderer Chinta Aznar and the insane rapist and murderer Sobera de la Flor, the pudgy Roberto Soto and Cantinflas, Meche Barba the rumba dancer and Jorge Negrete the singing *charro*, the bargains at Puerto de Liverpool and the ads that told you *Betterall's Better at Making You Better* (Mejor Mejora Mejoral) and Twenty Million Mexicans Can't Be Wrong, the great bullfighters Manolete and Arruza, the city-planning accomplishments of the regent Ernesto Uruchurtu, and the swimmer Joaquín Capilla's Olympic medal: fire consumed them all, just as death devoured the bedroom her son Santiago transformed into sacred space, a fountain of images, a cavern where shadows were reality, and paintings and drawings piled up; and Danton's secret room, which no one could enter, an imagined room which could just as easily be decked out with pictures of naked women torn out of the magazine *Vea* as be kept with bare walls as a penitence, until he found his own fortune, as he did; and the matrimonial bedroom where Laura was overwhelmed by the images of the men she'd loved, why she'd loved them, how she'd loved them.

She went out to photograph the lost villages in the great city's misery, and there she found herself, in the very act of photographing something totally alien to her own life. She found herself because she did not deny her fear, all alone with her Leica, of penetrating a world that lived in poverty but revealed itself in crime, first a man stabbed to death on a street of unquiet dust; fear of the ambulances with the howling, deafening noise of their sirens at the very edge of the territory of crime; women stomped to death by drunken husbands; newborn babies tossed on garbage dumps; old people abandoned and found dead on mats that later were used as their shrouds, stuck in a hole in the ground a week later, their bodies so dry that they didn't even smell. Laura Díaz photographed all that and thanked Juan Francisco, despite everything, for having saved her from such a fate, the fate of the violence and misery around her.

She would go into a tavern in a lost city and find all the men shot to death, all having inexplicably killed each other as if in a caroming series of crimes, all anonymous—but now saved from oblivion by Laura's photographs. She thanked Jorge Maura for having saved her from the violence of ideologies, from the fear a woman might have of the world of thought he had introduced her to. In her memory she had an impossible photo—of Jorge licking the monastery floor in Lanzarote, cleansing his own spirit of ideologies and of the bloody twentieth century.

Jorge Maura was the antidote to the violence the abandoned children lived in; she photographed them in sewers and tunnels, surprising their inexpungible beauty of childhood, as if her camera cleansed them the way Jorge had cleansed the monastery floor, children cleansed of snot, rheum, greasy hair, rachitic arms, heads hairless from mange, hands discolored by pinta, the tropical skin disease, bare feet with crusts of mud as their only shoes. And when she photographed them she also thanked Harry for the weakness of loyalties and for nostalgia for the unique, unrepeatable moment of heroism. She thought about the great photograph of the fallen Republican soldier taken by Robert Capa during the Spanish Civil War.

She'd turn up at local police stations and at hospitals. No one took any notice of an old, gray-haired lady with full skirts and worn-out sandals (it was she). They let her photograph a woman, not breathing, with an empty Coca-Cola bottle jammed between her thighs, a drug addict in his cell twisted with pain, scratching the walls and stuffing saltpeter into his nose, men and women beaten in their houses or in some alley, it was all the same, bloody, blinded by disorientation more than because their eyes were swollen from punches, clubbings, the arrival of the Black Marias, the entrance into the police station of whores and fags, transvestites and drug dealers, the nightly harvest of pimps . . .

Lives tossed through bar doors, house windows, thrown under the wheels of a bus. Disemboweled lives, with no possible gaze on them but that of Laura Díaz's camera, Laura herself, Laura burdened with all her memories, her loves and loyalties, but no longer solitary Laura, now instead Laura on her own, dependent on no one, returning his filial checks to Danton, punctually paying the rent for her apartment on Plaza Río de Janeiro, first selling her individual photographs and her articles to newspapers and magazines and individual buyers, then having her first show in Juan Martín's gallery on Génova Street, finally under contract as one more star for the Magnum agency, which also represented Cartier-Bresson, Inge Morath, Robert Capa.

The artist of Mexico City's grief but also its joy, Laura and a new-born boy dressed by his mother's eyes as if he were the baby Jesus himself, Jesus reborn; Laura and a man with a scarred face and restrained violence piously kissing the image of the Virgin of Guadalupe; Laura on the little pleasures and tragic premonitions of a debutante ball, a wedding, a baptism; Laura's camera, depicting the instant, managed to depict the future of the instant: that was the strength of her art, an instantaneity with descendants, a plastic eye that restored tenderness and respect to vulgarity, and amorous vulnerability to the harshest violence. It wasn't only the critics who said it: her admirers felt it, Laura Díaz, almost sixty years of age, is a great Mexican photographer, the best after Alvarez Bravo, high priestess of the invisible, she was called, the poet writing with light, the woman who learned to photograph what Posada could engrave.

When she achieved independence and fame, Laura Díaz kept the photo of the dead Frida for herself, that one she would never give out for publication, that photo was part of her rich, rich memory, the emotional archive of a life that had suddenly, in maturity, flourished like a plant that flowers late but perennially. The photograph of Frida was testimony to all the photographs Laura hadn't taken in the years she'd lived with others; it was a talisman. Alongside Diego and Frida, without noticing it, as if in a dream, she had gained the artistic sensibility that flourished much later on, when many of the years with Laura Díaz had gone by.

She didn't complain about that time or condemn it as a calendar of subjection to the world of men, how could she if in her pages lived the two Santiagos, her lovers Jorge Maura, Orlando Ximénez, and Harry Jaffe, her parents, her aunts, the jolly black sweeper Zampayita, and her poor but sympathetic, and (to her) compassionate, husband Juan Francisco? How could she forget them, but how could she not feel sorry that she had not photographed them. She imagined her own eye as a camera able to capture everything it saw and felt over the six decades of her life, and felt a chill of horror. Art was selection. Art meant losing almost everything in exchange for the salvation of very little.

It was impossible to have art and life at the same time, and in the end Laura Díaz was thankful that life had preceded art—for art, premature or even prodigal, might have killed life.

It was when she discovered something that should have been obvious, when she recovered her son Santiago's paintings and drawings from the rubble of the family house on Avenida Sonora and brought them to her new apartment on Plaza Río de Janeiro, when in among the mass of pencil and pastel drawings, sketches, and two dozen oil paintings, she discovered the canvas with the naked man and woman staring at each other without touching, desiring only each other but satisfied with the desire.

In her haste to abandon the fallen family home, to set herself up in her new apartment on Plaza Río de Janeiro, to start her new, independent life, and go out to photograph Mexico City and the lives in it, following, she said to herself, the inspiration of Diego Rivera and Frida Kahlo, Laura had not stopped to take a close look at her own son's paintings. Perhaps she felt so much love for Santiago the Younger that she preferred to distance herself from the physical proof of her son's existence in order to keep him alive, if only in his mother's soul. Perhaps she had to discover her own vocation to rediscover her son's. Busy arranging her own photos, she went on to arrange Santiago's paintings and drawings, and among the two dozen oils, this one, the naked couple staring at each other without touching, held her attention.

At first she was critical of the piece. The angular, prominent, twisted, and cruel outline of the figures derived from Santiago's admiration for Egon Schiele and from his long study of the Viennese albums that had miraculously turned up at the German Bookstore in Colonia Hipódromo. The difference, Laura quickly noticed when she compared the books with the painting, was that Schiele's figures were almost always unique, solitary, or, rarely, intertwined diabolically and innocently in a frozen physical union that was merely physiological and always—whether together or apart—airless, having no reference to any landscape, or room, or other space, as if in an ironic return by the most modern artist to the most ancient art, Schiele the blasé Expressionist returned to Byzantine painting, where the figure of God the Pancreator is fixed before the creation of anything in the absolute void of solitary majesty.

This painting by the young Santiago took from Schiele's tortured figures, no doubt of it, but also gave back to them, as in a renaissance of the Renaissance, the way that Giotto and Masaccio gave air, landscape, and location to the ancient iconography of Byzantium. The naked man in Santiago's canvas—emaciated, pierced by invisible thorns, young, beardless, but with the face of an unconquerable malady, a corrosive sickness running through his unwounded body that was conquered from within for having been created without being consulted first— fixed his gaze on the belly of the naked woman, pregnant, blond (Laura quickly checked for resemblances in the books Santiago had collected), just like the Eves by Holbein and Cranach, resigned to passive conquest of the man with one less rib, even though this time they were deformed by desire. The earlier Eves were impassive, fatal, but this, the new Eve of Santiago the Younger, participated in the anguish of the convulsed, young, condemned Adam who stared intensely at her belly while she, Eve, stared intensely into his eyes, and neither—only now did Laura notice this obvious detail—had their feet on the ground.

They didn't levitate. They ascended. Laura felt a deep emotion when she understood her son Santiago's painting. This Adam and Eve did not fall. They ascended. At their feet, the skin of the apple and the skin of the serpent fused in a single mass. Adam and Eve left the garden of delights, but they did not fall into the inferno of pain and toil. Their sin was of another kind. They ascended. They rebelled against the divine decree—thou shall not eat this fruit—and instead of falling, they rose. Thanks to sex, rebellion, and love, Adam and Eve were the protagonists of the Ascent of Humanity, not its Fall. The evil of the world was believing that the first man and the first woman fell and condemned us to a heritage of vice. For Santiago the Younger, on the other hand, Adam and Eve's guilt was not hereditary, wasn't even guilt, and the drama of the Earthly Paradise was a triumph of human freedom over God's tyranny. It wasn't drama. It was history.

In the deepest part of the landscape in her son's painting, Laura saw painted, very small, like Brueghel's Icarus, a barque with black sails leaving the coasts of Eden behind with a single passenger, a tiny figure divided in a singular way: half of his face was angelic, the other half diabolical; one half blond, the other half red; but the body itself, wrapped in a cape as long as the sails, was shared by angel and demon, and both, Laura guessed, were God, with a cross in one hand and a pitchfork in the other: two instruments of torture and death. The lovers ascended. The one who fell was God, and the fall of God was what Santiago had painted: a departure, a distance, shock on the face of the Creator, who abandons Eden perplexed because His creatures have rebelled, because they have decided to ascend instead of fall, because they have mocked the perverse divine plan to create the world only in order to condemn it to sin, transmitted from generation to generation, so that men and women for all time will feel inferior to God, dependent on God, condemned by Him, and absolved—before falling again— only by God's capricious grace.

On the back of the canvas, Santiago had written: "Art isn't modern. Art is eternal. Egon Schiele."

Line dominated color. Which is why the colors were so strong. The black ship. The red half of the Creator. The greenish red of the apple peel that was the mutable skin of the serpent. But Eve's skin was as translucent as that of a Memling Virgin, while Adam's was spotty, green, yellow, and sick, like an adolescent painted by Schiele.

The man stared at the woman. The woman stared at the sky. But neither of them was falling. Because both desired each other. There was that equivalence in the difference which Laura made her own, comparing her own emotions to those of her son, the young, dead artist.

She hung Santiago the Younger's painting in her living room and understood for all time that the son was father of the mother, that, unwittingly, Laura Díaz the photographer owed more to her own son than to any other artist. At first she did not understand this, and the secret, unknown identification was for that reason all the stronger.

Now nothing mattered but the equivalence of the emotion.

## 3.

Show after show of photographs followed, sales first to newspapers and magazines and then in books.

Blessings of animals and birds.

Old men with huge mustaches gathered around singing *corridos* from the Revolution.

Flower vendors.

The crowded pools on St. John's Day.

The life of a metalworker.

The life of a hospital nurse.

Her celebrated photograph of a dead gypsy woman with no lines on her hand, open under her breasts, a gypsy with an erased destiny.

And now something she owed Jorge Maura: a report on the exiled Spanish Republicans in Mexico.

Laura now realized that for years the Spanish Civil War had been the epicenter of her historical life, not the Mexican Revolution, which had passed through the state of Veracruz so mildly and tangentially, as if dying in the Gulf were a unique, moving, and untouchable privilege reserved for Laura's older brother, Santiago Díaz, sole protagonist, as far as she was concerned, of the 1910 insurrection.

In Spain, on the other hand, Jorge Maura, Basilio Baltazar, and Domingo Vidal had fought, the young gringo, Jim, had died, and the sad gringo, Harry, had survived. In Spain, the beautiful and young Pilar Méndez was shot at the Roman gate of Santa Fe de Palencia by order of her own father, the Communist mayor Alvaro Méndez.

Bearing that heavy emotional weight, Laura began to photograph the faces of Spanish exile in Mexico. President Cárdenas had given sanctuary to a quarter million Republicans. Each time she photographed one of them, Laura remembered with emotion Jorge's trip to Havana to rescue Raquel from the *Prinz Eugen*, anchored opposite Morro Castle.

Each one of her models could have suffered that fate: jail, torture, execution. She understood that.

She photographed the miracles of survival. She knew that's who they were.

The philosopher José Gaos, disciple of Husserl like Jorge Maura and Raquel Mendes-Alemán, leaning on the iron railing above the patio of the Escuela de Mascarones, the philosopher with a patrician Roman head, bald and strong, as strong as his jaw, as strong as his pencil-thin lips, as skeptical as his myopic eyes behind their small, round glasses, suitable for a Franz Schubert of philosophy. Gaos leaning on the railing, and from the beautiful colonial patio the young men and women of the School of Philosophy raise their faces to look at the master with smiles of admiration and gratitude.

Luis Buñuel arranged to meet her in the bar of the Parador, where the director ordered perfect martinis from his favorite bartender, Córdoba, while he replayed the film of a cultural cycle through his memory, which went from the Student Residence in Madrid to the filming of *Un Chien Andalou*, in which Buñuel and Dalí used the eye of a dead fish surrounded by eyelashes to simulate the heroine's eye sliced open with a straight razor, to *L'Age d'Or* and its image of the ecclesiastical hierarchy transformed into petrified bone on the coast of Mallorca, to his participation in Parisian Surrealism in its New York exile, to Dalí's denunciation ("Buñuel is a Communist, an atheist, a blasphemer, and an anarchist. How can you let him work in the Museum of Modern Art?"), to his arrival in Mexico with forty dollars in his pocket.

Humor, anger, and daydreams passed ceaselessly and simultaneously across Buñuel's green eyes: his gaze stopped on a fixed point in his past, and Laura photographed a boy in the Aragonese village of Calanda playing drums on Good Friday until his hands bled, this to free himself from the sensual charm of the image of the Virgin of Pilar, inhabitant of his onanistic childhood bed.

Thanks to the intervention of the Basque writer Carlos Blanco Aguinaga, Laura photographed the marvelous poet from Málaga, Emilo Prados, in his modest apartment on Lerma Street. She'd met him before with Jorge Maura. Prados was hidden in a couple of rooms behind mountains of books and papers, sickness and exile etched in every line on his face, but able to transform suffering into two expressions Laura was able to photograph. The infinite sweetness of his face was that of an unredeemed Andalusian saint now veiled by a cascade of white locks and thick, aquarium-style glasses, as if the poet, embarrassed by his own innocence, wanted to conceal it. And you could see the lyric strength behind his suffering, poverty, disillusion, old age, and exile:

> *If I could give you*
> *all the light of dawn . . .*
> *Like the sun, I would*
> *slowly pierce your breast,*
> *until I emerged without blood*
> *or pain into the night . . .*

Manuel Pedroso, the wise old Andalusian who had been rector of the University of Seville, was adored by the small group of his young disciples who every day went with him as he walked from the Law School near the Zócalo to his small apartment on Amazonas Street.

Laura left graphic testimony of that daily journey, as well as of gatherings in the master's library, packed with ancient books that smelled of tropical tobacco. Francisco Franco's troops had burned his library in Seville, but Pedroso recovered jewel after jewel in the secondhand bookstalls in La Lagunilla, Mexico City's thieves' market.

The books were stolen from him, other thieves stole from other people, but the books always returned, like nostalgic and unremitting lovers, to Pedroso's long, thin hands, a gentleman painted by El Greco, hands always on the verge of tensing, warning, as if convoking a ceremony of thought. Laura captured Pedroso in the instant when he held out his hands with their long, beautiful fingers to beg for some light from the world, to bank the fires of intolerance, and to affirm his faith in his Mexican students.

Laura photographed a noisy, cheery, argumentative, and affectionate group of young exiles who adapted to Mexico but who never abandoned Spain, who always spoke with the Castilian lisp and let their eyes express the tenderness they felt for everything they had explicitly renounced: chocolate with the parish priest, the novels of Pérez Galdós, café discussion groups, old women in black, tasty treats like hot *churros*, *cante hondo*, and bullfights, the punctuality of church bells and funerals, the madness of families who took to their beds to avoid forever the temptations of the world, the flesh, and the devil. Laura photographed them in their perpetual, eternal arguments, as if they were Irishmen and didn't know each other because they came from Madrid, Navarra, Galicia, and Barcelona and because their names were Oteyza, Serra Puig, Muñoz de Baena, García Ascot, Xirau, Durán, Segovia, and Blanco Aguinaga.

But Laura Díaz's favorite exile was a young woman whom Danton mentioned as having been the most interesting feminine presence in the Jockey Club in the 1940s. She lived with her husband, the poet and filmmaker García Ascot, in a strange building at right angles to Villalongín Street, and her beauty was so perfect that Laura despaired either of finding her bad side or of being able to capture in one or a thousand photographs the charms of this fragile, svelte, and elegant woman, who walked around her house barefoot like a cat, followed by another cat that posed as her mistress's double, both desired and envied by the entire feline race because of her aggressive profile and weak chin, her melancholy eyes and irrepressible, all-inclusive laugh.

María Luisa Elío had a secret. Her father had been in hiding since 1939, living in an attic in a village in Navarre, under sentence of death from Franco's Falange. She could not speak of it, but her father dwelled in his daughter's gaze, in her fabulously clear eyes, thanks to the pain, the secret, the wait for the phantom who might finally, one day, escape from Spain and show up in Mexico and for his daughter as what he was: a ghost incarnate and an oblivion remembered from an empty balcony.

Another ghost—carnal, this one, all too carnal, but in the end steadfast in the sensuous specter of his words—was Luis Cernuda, an elegant homosexual gentleman who would appear in Mexico City from time to time, who was always received by his colleague Octavio Paz, with whom he fought, his arrogance being outrageous while Paz's was deceptive, but with whom he always in the end reconciled because of their shared poetic fervor. A consensus gradually formed: Luis Cernuda was the greatest Spanish poet of his generation. Laura Díaz tried to keep her distance from him, the better to see him stripped of the appearance (or disguise) he affected of a Madrid dandy. She asked him to read:

*I want to live when love dies . . .*
*Just as your death awakens my desire for death*
*Just as your life awakened my desire for life*

She missed Basilio Baltazar, but they kept missing each other—the dates of Laura's shows didn't coincide with Basilio's university vacations, so Laura would hang an empty frame in the center of the exhibit with the name of her old friend next to it.

His absence was also homage to the absence of Jorge Maura, whose distance and anonymity Laura decided to respect, it being the wish of the man she'd loved most. Perhaps Basilio couldn't appear among the portraits of Spanish exile without his comrade Jorge.

And Vidal? He wasn't the only one who'd disappeared.

Malú Block, the gallery director, told Laura that something strange was going on. Every afternoon at around six o'clock, a woman in black would come to the gallery and stay for an entire hour—not a minute more, not a minute less, even though she never looked at her watch—opposite the empty frame for Basilio Baltazar's missing portrait. Almost immobile, she would sometimes shift her weight from one foot to the other or she would step back a centimeter or turn her head, as if to formulate a better appreciation of what wasn't there: Basilio's effigy.

Laura hesitated between giving in to natural curiosity and being discreet. One afternoon, she went to the gallery and saw the woman in black standing opposite the empty frame. She didn't dare approach her, but the woman herself, the mysterious visitor, half turned, as if attracted by the magnet in Laura's eyes, and allowed herself to be seen: a woman about forty years old with blue eyes and long sandy-yellow hair.

She looked at Laura but didn't smile, and Laura was grateful for the woman's imperturbable seriousness because she feared what she might see if the enigmatic visitor opened her mouth. Such was the cold and nervous style of this visitor: she tried to hide the emotion of her gaze but did not quite succeed. She knew it and transferred the enigma to her mouth, closed in sorrow, sealed with manifest difficulty in order not to show . . . Her teeth? Laura wondered. Does this woman want to hide her teeth from me? If she could only be identified by her eyes, Laura Díaz, accustomed to discovering eyes and making them into metaphors, saw in them instantaneous moons, torches of straw and wood, lights on the mountain—and she stopped, biting her lower lip, as if to restrain her own memory, so as not to remember those words as spoken by Maura, Jorge Maura, in the Café de Paris almost twenty years before, with Domingo Vidal and Basilio Baltazar, the three of them safe in that bohemian setting on Avenida Cinco de Mayo yet at the same time exposed to the most brutal storms, like the hyenas and oxen and wind and lights on the mountain, whenever they opened their mouths.

"I am Laura Díaz. I took these photographs. May I assist you?"

The woman dressed in black turned to look at the empty frame where Basilio's portrait should have been and told Laura, If you know this man, tell him I've returned.

She smiled then and showed her savagely ruined teeth.

## 22. Plaza Río de Janeiro: 1966

Laura Díaz's grandson, Santiago López-Ayub, and his girlfriend, Lourdes Alfaro, came to live with her at Christmas in 1966. The apartment was old but spacious, the building itself a relic from the previous century that had survived the implacable transformation of Mexico City, from the town of pastel colors and two-story buildings which Laura first saw when she arrived as a new bride in 1922, to what it was now, a blind giant, growing and destroying everything in its path, demolishing the nineteenth-century French architecture, the eighteenth-century neoclassical architecture, and the seventeenth-century baroque architecture. In some sort of grand regressive reckoning, the past was being burned away until there appeared, pulsing like a forgotten, awful, painful wound, the very sediment of the Aztec city.

Laura was not merely ignoring the impudence of her generous, though hardly disinterested, son Danton when she rejected his help and set herself up in the old building on Plaza Río de Janeiro, adapting the flat to her work needs—with living space but also a darkroom, an archive, space for her illustrated reference works. She had, for the first time in her life, the famous "room of one's own" that Virginia Woolf had said women deserved so they could have their sacred zone, their minimal redoubt of independence: a sovereign island of their own.

After she'd left the family house on Avenida Sonora and grown accustomed to living alone and free as she went from being fifty-nine to being sixty-seven with a profession and a livelihood, gratified by fame and success, Laura did not feel threatened by the renewed youth Santiago and Lourdes offered her, and she was pleased by how easy it was for the three of them to share household chores, by the understandable but unexpected richness which their after-dinner conversations developed, by the sharing of their experiences, desires, and similar tastes that living together afforded them right from the first moment the third Santiago appeared at Laura's door and said, Grandmother, I can't live with my father anymore and I don't have enough money to live alone and take care of my girlfriend.

"Hello. Let me introduce myself. I'm your grandson Santiago, and this is my girlfriend, Lourdes, and we've come to ask you to put us up." Santiago smiled with Danton's strong, white teeth but with his uncle's sweet, melancholy eyes. He had an elegant, even excessive way of moving, too, that reminded Laura of the dissimulating affectation of the Scarlet Pimpernel of the Revolution in Veracruz, Santiago the Elder.

Lourdes Alfaro by comparison was modestly beautiful and dressed the way all young people dressed nowadays, in pants and a T-shirt—one day with the face of Che Guevara, Mick Jagger the next—a long mane of black hair and no makeup whatsoever. She was small and shapely, a "tiny mistress full of virtues," an epithet which, Laura recalled, Jorge Maura used to quote from the medieval Archpriest of Hita's *Book of Good Love* when he teased her about her own Teutonic stature.

The presence of the young lovers in her house was enough to gladden Laura Díaz's heart, and she opened her arms to the couple—they had a right to happiness now and not after twenty years of violence and unhappiness, as had been the case with Laura and Jorge, or with Basilio Baltazar and Pilar Méndez (now reunited as Jorge and Laura could never have dreamed of being, since destiny can't succeed twice in turning a tragedy into a happy ending).

The third Santiago and Lourdes for all these reasons had all the rights in the world, in the eyes of Laura Díaz. The boy, whom she'd never met before, given Danton's stubborn rancor and his wife's arrogance, now told her about himself, told her he knew and admired her, because, he said, he was going into his first year of law school and didn't have the artistic talent of either his grandmother or his uncle Santiago, who'd died so young . . .

"That painting of the couple looking at each other, is it his?"

"Yes."

"What a great talent, Grandmother."

"Yes."

He didn't sing his own virtues, but Lourdes told Laura one night while she was preparing dinner—saffron rice and drumsticks—Santiago is a tough guy, a real man, considering how young he is, Doña Laura, nothing fazes him . . . at one point I thought I'd just be a burden to him, given his career, and especially given his relations with his parents, but you should have seen, Doña Laura, how firmly Santiago faced up to them and made me feel that he needed me, that instead of a burden I was someone he could lean on, that he respected me.

They'd met at the school dances Santiago liked more than the parties organized by his parents and his parents' friends, where everything was about exclusivity and only children of "well-known families" were invited. But at the school dances, social barriers fell and buddies studying the same subjects could meet regardless of their wealth or their family connections. Along with the boys came girlfriends, sisters, and the odd maiden aunt—the tradition of "chaperons" wouldn't die . . .

Danton approved of those gatherings. Lasting friendships were made in school, and even though your mother'd prefer that you went to parties only with people of our class, if you notice, son, the people who govern us never come from the upper classes, they develop at the bottom or in the middle class, and it's important for you to know them when you can help them, because one day, I assure you, they'll help you. In Danton's eyes, poor friends could be a good investment.

"Mexico is a country open to talent, Santiago. Don't forget that."

In his first year at law school, Santiago met Lourdes. She was in nursing school and came from Puerto Escondido, a beach town on the Oaxaca coast where her parents had a modest hotel with the best *temazcal* in the region, she said.

"What's that?"

"A steam bath with fragrant herbs that cleanses you of all toxins."

"I think that's just what I need. When are you going to invite me?"

"Whenever you like."

"Sounds good."

Together they went to Puerto Escondido and they fell in love there, facing the Pacific, which meets the steep bluffs along a treacherously sandy, sweet beach, but in fact it's an abyss where anyone can quickly lose his footing, with no support to withstand the swift currents, which caught Santiago and dragged him, more in anguish than in danger, until Lourdes dove into the water, hooked an arm around the boy's neck, swam with her free arm, helping him to get to shore, and there, exhausted but excited, they exchanged their first kiss.

"You tell me that with your voice trembling," said Laura.

"It's that I'm afraid, Doña Laura."

"Forget the doña. You make me older than I am."

*"Okay, Laura."*

"Afraid of what?"

"Santiago's papa is a very hard man, Laura, he won't put up with anything he himself hasn't ordered, he becomes like a panther, and it's something terrifying."

"He's not as fierce as you think, that little cat. He roars and scares you until you roar back and put him in his place."

"I don't know how."

"I do, my dear. I do. Don't you worry."

The creep actually went down to Puerto Escondido, Grandmother, usually he sends one of his thugs to scare people, but this time he went himself in his private plane to see Lourdes' family and tell them not to get any big ideas, this thing with his son was nothing but a rebellious, spoiled brat's adventure, he asked them to explain that to their daughter, that Santiago shouldn't fool her, she should be careful, he might make her pregnant and then walk out on her, but pregnant or not he was going to walk out on her.

"Your son has never said anything like that to us," said Lourdes' father.

"Well, I'm saying it, and I'm the one who gives the orders."

"I would like to hear it from your son."

"He can't speak for himself. He's just a confused kid."

"That doesn't matter."

"Don't be stubborn, Mr. Alfaro. Don't be stubborn. I'm not playing around. How much do you want?"

Face to face with Santiago, Danton did not treat him as a "confused kid." He simply presented "reality" to him. He was an only child since unfortunately his mother couldn't have a second child, which would have killed her, Santiago was her dream, her cherished filial love, but he, Danton, as a father, had to be more severe and objective, couldn't afford the luxury of sentimentality.

"You're going to inherit my fortune. It's wonderful you're studying law, though I'd suggest some postgraduate work in economics and business administration in the United States. It's only natural that a father would like to have his son carry on in his place, and I'm sure you won't fail me. Neither me nor your mother, who adores you."

She was a woman whose beauty had evaporated—"like the dew," she herself was in the habit of saying. Magdalena Ayub de López-Díaz, until the high noon of her life, kept the attractions that so seduced Danton during those Sundays at the Jockey Club: her obvious defects— unbroken eyebrows, prominent nose, square jaw—in counterpoint to her Arab princess eyes, dreamy, velvety, with their olive eloquence under their glossy lids, provocative, like a hidden sex. By contrast, most of the marriageable young ladies of that period, pretty but all too "decent," left the nuns' school as if someone had stamped a *nihil obstat* on a secret part of their body and elevated it to the public category of "face." A knee, an elbow, or an ankle could serve as models for the sweet, acceptable, insipid faces of the Sacred Heart schoolgirls whom their beaux called "chicks" (a corruption of "chic"). Their features, joked the young Danton, were useful but faded.

Magdalena Ayub—"my dream," Danton called her when he courted her—was different. She was, besides, the mother of the third Santiago, whose birth instantly erased forever the remains of the youthful charms of Don Danton's lady wife. She was weighed down by the sentence of the doctors: one more child would kill you, ma'am. She kept her unbroken eyebrows and her hips widened.

Santiago grew up with that stigma: I almost killed my mother when I was born, and I have destroyed any chance of life for possible sisters or brothers. But Danton turned guilt into obligation. Santiago, being an only child, having almost torn away his mother's life to have his own, now had to do the right thing. Danton asked nothing special from his son: he had to study, graduate, marry a girl of his own class, add to the family fortune, ensure the survival of the species.

"And give me a calm and satisfied old age. I think I deserve one, after all my years of work."

He spoke with one hand in the side pocket of his blue pin-striped double-breasted suit, the other caressing his lapel. His face was like his suit: buttoned up, double-breasted, striped, with his bluish beard and brows and still-black hair. He was, altogether, a midnight-blue man. He never looked at his shoes. They glistened. No need to look.

The third Santiago did not dispute the chart drawn for him by his father until he fell in love with Lourdes, when Danton reacted with a brutality and lack of elegance that the son, from that moment, began to see as attributes of a father he'd loved and whom he'd thanked for so much—the allowance, the four-door Renault, the novelty of the American Express card (with a spending limit), the freedom to wear Macazaga suits (though Santiago preferred leather jackets and jeans)— without judging the motives, acts, justifications or errors in the "that's the way things are" mode of his father's words; his father was a man anchored in the security of his economic position and his personal morals, with the nerve to say to his son, "You will follow my path," and to his son's girlfriend, "You're nothing but a stone in the road, get out of the way or I'll kick you out of the way."

His father's attitude riled the young Santiago, enraged him at first, but then encouraged him to do things that had never occurred to him before. He became aware of his own moral nature, and aware that Lourdes too was aware of it: they wouldn't sleep together until the situation was quite clear; they wouldn't cheat each other, either with a baby "by mistake" or with sex as mere defiance. Santiago began to ponder, Who is my father, what has my father got that he should have this absolute power over people and this self-confidence?

He told Lourdes, Let's outsmart him, mi amor, let's stop seeing each other every day, only in secret on Friday evenings, so the old boy doesn't get suspicious.

Santiago told Danton, fine, he'd study law, but he also wanted to learn practical things, and to do that he should work in his father's office. Danton's satisfaction with his son's attitude blinded him. He couldn't imagine any danger in letting his own son into the offices of Cooperative Resource Allotment Partnership (CRAP), a building of glittering glass and stainless steel on Paseo de la Reforma, a few yards from the statue of Christopher Columbus and the Monument to the Revolution. It had once been the site of the Paris-style house with the mansard roof where Butt del Rosal had awaited snow in Mexico—that old aristocrat of the Don Porfirio days whose trick was to eat his gelatin monocle at Carmen Cortina's soirées. But Paseo de la Reforma—the avenue that the Empress Carlota had created to connect her residence in Chapultepec Castle as Maximilian's consort with the center of the city (she conceived it as a reproduction of the Avenue Louise in her native Brussels)—was coming to resemble a street in Houston or Dallas, lined with more and more skyscrapers, parking lots, and fast-food outlets.

There, Santiago would learn the business, let him explore every floor, get to know everything, he's the boss's son . . .

He became friends with the file clerk who was mad about bullfighting by giving him season tickets—that year Joselito Huerta and Manuel Capetillo were the stars. He became friends with the telephone operators by getting them passes to the Churubusco Studios so they could watch Libertad Lamarque make her movies: the same Argentine tango singer who'd brought tears to the eyes of Harry Jaffe in Cuernavaca.

Who was this Miss Artemisa who called Don Danton every day? Why did they treat her so deferentially when Santiago wasn't there and so secretively when he was around? Who was the man his father treated with respect bordering on servility, yes, sir, we're here to serve you, sir, whatever you say, sir, so strikingly different from those who received only his usual rapid, implacable, and unadorned commands: I need it this minute, Gutierritos, don't fall asleep on me now, there's no room for lazy fuckers here and you look like the laziest fucker I've ever seen, what's wrong with you, Fonseca, did the sheets stick to your skin or what, I expect you in a half minute or you'd better start thinking about another job; which differed in turn from those who got the more serious threats, If you have any consideration for your wife and children, I'd recommend you do what I tell you, no, I'm not giving you some orders, I'm commanding you, that's the way I deal with errand boys, and you, Reynoso, just remember the papers are in my possession and all I have to do is give them to *Excelsior* to publish and you'll be up shit's creek.

"As you say, sir."

"Get that report up to me on the double."

"Don't stick your nose in someone else's business, you bastard, or you're going to wake up someday with your balls in your mouth and your tongue up your ass."

As he penetrated the metal-and-glass labyrinth his father dominated, Santiago searched with equal tenderness and voracity—two names of need but also of love—for Lourdes' affection. They held hands at the movies, they stared deep into each other's eyes in cafeterias, they kissed in Santiago's car, they petted in the darkness, but they waited until they could live together to join completely. They agreed on that, no matter how strange and at times even ridiculous it might seem, sometimes to one, sometimes to the other, sometimes to both. They had something in common. Postponing the act excited them. Imagining each other.

Who was Miss Artemisa?

She had a deep sugary voice, and the finishing touch was when she'd say on the telephone to Danton, "I wuve wou, Tonton, I wuve wou, my widdle sugar pwum." Santiago almost died laughing when he listened illicitly to this saccharine dialogue, and his laughter redoubled when the severe Don Danton said to his widdle sugar pwum, "What are my little titties up to, how's my little lazy balls, what does my little Tricky eat to make her kisses taste so pricky?" "I suck bananas every Thursday," answered the hoarse, professionally tender voice. Lourdes, said Santiago, this is really getting good, let's find out who this Artemisa or Tricky is and what she really tastes like. My old man takes the cake, I swear!

Santiago wasn't thinking about the fact that the forgotten Doña Magdalena was being cheated on, he wasn't a puritan, but I'm curious, Lourdes, and so am I, laughed the fresh and nubile girl from Oaxaca as the two of them waited for Danton to leave the office one Thursday night, when dear old Papa took the inconspicuous Chevrolet out alone, with no chauffeur, and drove to Darwin Street in the Nueva Anzures neighborhood, followed by Santiago and Lourdes in a rented Ford so no one would notice.

Danton parked and went into a house with plaster statues of Apollo and Venus in the entryway. The door closed, and mystery reigned. After a while, music and laughter could be heard. The lights went on and off capriciously.

They came back one morning when a gardener was clipping hedges around the entrance and a maid was dusting the erotic statues. The front door was ajar. Lourdes and Santiago caught a glimpse of a normal bourgeois living room with brocade armchairs and vases filled with calla lilies, marble floors, and a staircase right out of a Mexican movie.

Suddenly at the top of the stairs appeared an arrogant young man with closely cropped hair wearing a silk dressing gown, a cravat at the neck, and—an extravagant detail—putting on white gloves.

"What do you want?" he asked, his brow highly arched and very well plucked, in contrast to his hoarse voice. "Who are you?"

"So sorry, we're at the wrong house," said Lourdes.

"Jerks," muttered the man with the gloves.

I guess it's all right, said CRAP's file clerk to Santiago, if you're the boss's son, go right ahead.

Every afternoon, while his father prolonged his lunches at the Focolare, the Rivoli, or the Ambassadeurs, Santiago went very carefully, yet despite everything painfully, through the company's papers, passing them, as it were, through a strainer of mixed repugnance and love, because, as the young student ceaselessly repeated to himself, He's my father, I've lived on this money, this money educated me, these deals are the roof and floors of my house, I drive a brand-new Renault thanks to my father's business . . .

"Let's act as if we're secret lovers," Santiago said to Lourdes. "Imagine we don't want to be seen."

"By whom? By each other?"

"No! Come on, honey, I mean this seriously. Where would we go if we didn't want to be seen?"

"Santiago, don't be silly. Just follow your father's car!" She laughed.

Chez Soi was a spacious dark place on Avenida de los Insurgentes, with lots of room between tables, only intimate lighting with a small, low lamp at each table: it was perpetual twilight. Red-and-white-checked tablecloths gave the French touch.

Lourdes and Santiago followed Danton and watched him go to Chez Soi three weeks in a row, punctually at nine every Tuesday evening. But he entered and left alone.

One night, Santiago and Lourdes went at eight-thirty, sat down, and ordered rum and Cokes. The French waiter looked down at them scornfully. There were couples at every table but one. A woman with an outrageous décolleté, proudly showing off half her bosom, raised an arm to arrange her abundant reddish hair, revealing a perfectly shaved armpit, took out a compact and touched up her abundantly whitened face around her plucked eyebrows, her arrogant eyes, and her exaggeratedly wide mouth, like a Joan Crawford in decline. The curious thing was that she did all this without taking off her white gloves.

When Danton made his entrance, he kissed her on the lips and sat down next to her. Lourdes and Santiago were off in a dark corner and had already paid their check. That night, they drove the Renault to the Oaxaca coast. Santiago drove all night without saying a word, wide awake, negotiating the endless serpent of curves linking Mexico City, Oaxaca, and Puerto Escondido. Lourdes slept with her head on his shoulder, but Santiago had eyes only for the dark forms of the landscape, the great backbones of the mountain range, the wild, abundant body of the country in all its contrasts: pine forests and clay deserts, basalt walls and crowns of snow, immense organ cactuses, sudden spurts of jacaranda. A desolate geography, without villages or inhabitants. The country yet to be created busy destroying itself first.

The sea appeared at eight in the morning. No one was on the beach; Lourdes awakened with a cry of joy, this is the best beach on the coast, she said, stripping to go in, then Santiago took off his clothes and together they went naked into the sea, the Pacific was their sheet, their kisses deeper than the green, placid waters, they felt their bodies supported over the sandy bottom and excited by the saline vigor, and Lourdes raised her legs when she felt the tip of Santiago's penis rubbing her clitoris, wrapped her legs around him as he embraced and entered her in the sea, thrusting hard against her mons as women like it while he felt himself within her as men like it, and they came and they washed and they frightened off the seagulls.

As soon as you can, learn the rules of the game, Danton had said to Santiago when he began working at CRAP. Those who want to rise by going into the PRI have to be content with whatever comes their way. It's true. They're seasoning for any sauce. Whatever's offered them, they take. One day you can be a high official, the next Secretary of State, and the day after that a mere bridge and road inspector. It doesn't matter. They have to swallow everything. Discipline pays off. Or not. But they don't have an alternative. That's where the common code begins for everyone, those who are rising and those who already have it made. Never make an enemy of someone who has power or who might have it, son. If you're going to get into a fight, it should be over something serious, not just a joke. Don't make waves, son. This country can only navigate in a Sargasso Sea. The calmer it is, the more we believe we're making progress. It's kept secret and it's a paradox, I agree. Never say anything in public that might make for controversy. We don't have problems here, Mexico progresses in peace. There's national unity, and anyone who acts up and disturbs the peace pays dearly for it. We're living the Mexican miracle. We want something more than a chicken in every pot, as the gringos say. We want a fully stocked refrigerator in every home and, if possible, stocked with products purchased in the supermarkets of your grandfather, Don Aspirin, God bless him. I convinced him that business has to be big business. Dear Don Aspirin, he was a small-time player.

He poured two fingers of Chivas Regal into a heavy cut-crystal tumbler, took a sip, and went on.

"I'm going to make sure you're well connected, Santiago, don't you worry. We all have to begin young, but the hard thing is to last it out. Look, the politicians also begin young, but most of them don't last. We businessmen begin young and last a lifetime. No one chooses us, and as long as we don't say anything in public, we're neither seen nor criticized. You don't have to make a splash. Publicity and self-promotion are forms of rebellion in our system. Forget that stuff. Don't ever risk yourself by saying something you'll be sorry for the next day. Your thoughts, keep them for yourself. And no witnesses."

Santiago accepted the glass his father handed him and emptied it in one swallow.

"That's what I like to see," laughed Danton. "You have everything. Be discreet. Don't take chances. Put money on all the horses, but stay close to the winner when the big race comes around, the presidential succession. Loyalty means nothing, being attentive and courteous does. Take advantage of the first three years of the six-year term to make deals. Then come the falling-off, the craziness, the dreams of being reelected or winning the Nobel Prize. And Presidents go nuts. You have to accommodate yourself to the successor, who, even if the incumbent chose him, will tear his predecessor apart, along with his family and friends, the moment he sits on the presidential throne. Sail in silence, Santiago. We're the secret continuity. They're the noisy divisiveness—and sometimes ruinous, of course."

He should take this girl out dancing, and that one out to dinner. This Perengana's papa is one of Don Danton's partners and has a modest fortune of fifty million dollars, but Loli Parada's papa has around two hundred million, and even though he's less manipulable than the partner, he adores his daughter and would give her everything . . .

Everything? Santiago asked his father. What do you call everything, Father? Shit, you don't even follow your own advice, Papa asshole, you leave too many papers around, even if you do hide them well, your files are full of evidence you've been storing up to blackmail the people you did favors for and refresh the memories of those you owe favors to; both ways you were corrupt, you old bastard, don't look at me like that, I'm not going to be cautious, fucker, I have photocopies of all your stinking maneuvers, I know by heart every bribe you got from a Secretary of State to take care of a public matter as if it were private, every commission you got for being an intermediary and straw man in an illegal real estate deal in Acapulco, every check you received for being a front for gringos investing in activities from which foreigners are barred, every peso you banked for taking over community lands of Indians who were evicted while peasants were murdered so that a President and his partners could develop tourism there; I know about the murder of independent union leaders and of stubborn agrarian leaders, you were paid for it all and you paid everybody, my father, you son of a bitch, you haven't committed a legal act in your fucking life, you live off the system and the system lives off you, you're proven guilty by the evidence you needed to condemn everyone who either served you or was served by you, but the secret's out now, old bastard, I have copies of everything, don't worry, I'm not going to give anything to the newspapers, what would I get from that? I'm not going to say a word, unless you go crazier than you already have, asshole, and have me killed, and in that case everything's set to see the light of day, and not here, where you pay off the press, shitty corrupter that you are, but in the United States, where it will really hurt you, where you'll be ruined, son of a bitch, because you launder money for Yankee and Mexican criminals, because you break the sacred laws of the sacred American democracy, you bribe their bankers, you send little presents to their congressmen, motherfucker,

you even have your own personal lobby in Washington, I swear I actually admire you, Papa, you're better than Willie Mays, you touch all the
bases, I also swear I have even more contempt for the fucking system
you've helped to build than I do for you, you and those like you are rotten to the core, from the President to the last policeman you're rottener
than a piece of dry shit that you've divided up among yourselves for
forty years and you've been feeding us all, go fuck yourself Don Danton
López-Díaz! I don't want to eat shit, I don't want a cent from you, I don't
want to see your fucking face ever again in my life, I don't want to see a
single one of your partners, or any leaders of the CTM, or redeemers of
the CNC, or bankers saved from ruin by the government, not a single
one . . . I swear, I'm going to fight against all of you, and if something
happens to me, something worse is going to happen to you, Papa dear.

Santiago threw the copies of the papers into his father's face, Danton mute, trembling, his cramped fingers reflexively poised over the
alarm buttons though he couldn't move, reduced to the brutal impotence his son wanted for him.

"Remember. There're copies of every single document. In Mexico.
In the United States. In a safe place. You'd better protect me, Papa,
because you have no other protection than your disobedient son. Fuck
you!"

And Santiago embraced his father, embraced him and whispered
into his ear, I love you, Papa, you know that despite everything I love
you, you old bastard.

Laura Díaz presided over the table that Christmas night of 1966. She
sat at the head of the table, the two couples on either side. She felt
secure, perfected in some way by the symmetry of love between her
grandchildren on one side and her friends on the other. She was no
longer alone. On her right, her grandson Santiago and his girlfriend
Lourdes announced they would be getting married on New Year's Eve,
he would look for a job, and meanwhile . . .

"No," Laura interrupted him. "This is your house, Santiago. You
and your wife should stay here and bring joy to the life of an old
woman . . ."

Because having the third Santiago with her was like having the other two, the elder and the younger, brother and son. They should have their child, Santiago should finish his studies. For her it was a party, filling the house with love, noise . . .

"Your Uncle Santiago never shut his bedroom door."

To fill the house with happy love. Right from the start, Laura wanted to protect the young, handsome couple, perhaps because on her left was sitting the couple who had waited thirty years to reunite and be happy.

Basilio Baltazar had gone gray, but he still had the dark, precisely outlined gypsy profile of his youth. Pilar Méndez, on the other hand, showed the ravages of a life of bad luck and deprivation. Not physical deprivation, she hadn't gone hungry, but an internal desolation: her face was etched with the doubts, the divided loyalties, the constant obligation to choose and then to bind up with love the wounds caused by family cruelty, so factious and also fantastic. The woman with the ash-blond hair and bad teeth, beautiful still with her Iberian profile, with all the mixed encounters—Islamic and Goth, Jew and Roman—carried on her face like a map of her homeland, also still bore the signs of those hard words, declaimed as if in an ancient tragedy staged opposite the classical background of the Roman gate to Santa Fe.

"The greater fidelity consists in disobeying unjust orders."

"Save her in the name of honor."

"Have mercy."

"Heaven is full of lies."

"I'm dying so that my father and mother will hate each other forever."

"She must die in the name of justice."

"What part of pain doesn't come from God?"

Laura said to Pilar that the grandchildren, Santiago and Lourdes, had a right to hear about the drama that had taken place in Santa Fe in 1937.

"It's a very old story," said Pilar.

"There's no story of the past that's not repeated in our time." Laura caressed the Spanish woman's hand. "I really mean that."

Pilar said she hadn't complained when facing death back then, and she wouldn't do so now. Complaint only augments pain. Enough is enough.

"We thought she'd been shot at dawn outside the city walls," said Basilio. "We thought so for thirty years."

"Why did you believe it?" asked Pilar.

"Because that's what your father told us. He was one of us, the Communist mayor of Santa Fe, so of course we believed him."

"There's no better fate than to die unknown," said Pilar, looking at the young Santiago.

"Why is that, ma'am?"

"Because if you're identified, Santiago, you have to apologize for some people and condemn others and you end up betraying them all."

Basilio wanted to tell the young people what he'd already told Laura, about how he'd asked for emergency leave and had rushed back to Mexico to see his wife, his Pilar. Don Alvaro Méndez, Pilar's father, had faked his daughter's execution that morning and had hidden her in a ruined house out in the Sierra de Gredos, where she'd lack for nothing for the duration of the war; the owners of the neighboring farm were impartial, friends of both Don Alvaro and his wife, Doña Clemencia. They wouldn't betray anyone. Even so, Pilar's father said nothing to his wife, who remained convinced that her daughter was a Martyr to the Movement. That's how she described it when Franco triumphed. Don Alvaro was executed on the very spot where his daughter was supposed to have died. The mother cultivated a devotion to her martyred daughter, dedicating the place where Pilar had supposedly fallen, though the body was never found because the reds must have taken it away, most likely tossing it into a common grave . . .

The heroine Pilar Méndez, the martyr executed by the reds, was put on the Falange's list of saints, and the real Pilar, hidden in the mountains, could not reveal herself, lived invisibly, torn at first between revealing herself and telling the truth or hiding out and maintaining the myth, but in the end convinced, when she learned of her father's death, that in Spain history is tragic and always ends badly, therefore it was better to go on being invisible, because that protected both the faithful memory of her father and the holy hypocrisy of her mother. She became accustomed to it, first in the refuge given her by her father's friends' kindness and then, much later, when they feared they were in danger because of Franco's avenging siege, protected by the charity of a convent of Discalced Carmelites, the order founded by St. Teresa of Avila and under her regulations, in which Pilar Méndez— protected by Christian charity though longing to join the rules of the sisters—found a discipline that, as she accustomed herself to it, was a salvation: poverty, the woolen Carmelite habit, rough sandals, abstinence from meat; sweeping, sewing, praying, and reading, because St. Teresa said that nothing seemed more detestable than "a stupid nun."

The nuns soon discovered Pilar's gifts. She was a girl who could read and write, so they gave her the Saint's books and with the passing years so ingrained the customs of the convent in her (her personal austerity reminded the sisters of their Holy Founder, that "errant woman," as King Philip II had called her) that the authorities raised no objections when the Mother Superior asked for a pass for this humble, intelligent convent worker, Ursula Sánchez, who wanted to visit some relatives in France and had no documents because the Communists had burned all the papers in her hometown.

"I left blinded, but with such an intense memory of my past that it wasn't hard for me to remember it when I got to Paris, to recover what might have been my fate if I hadn't spent my life in towns with bad water where the rivers flow down the mountains white with lime. The sisters had recommended me to the Carmelites in Paris, where I began to stroll the boulevards, regain my feminine tastes, covet elegant clothes—I was thirty-four and wanted to look pretty and well dressed—and I made friends in the diplomatic corps, managed to get a job in the Mexican House at the Cité Universitaire and I met a rich Mexican whose son was studying there, we had an affair, he brought me to Mexico, he was jealous, so now I was living in a tropical cage in Acapulco filled with parrots, and he gave me jewels, but I felt I'd been living in cages all my life, village cages, convent cages, and now a gilded cage, but always a prisoner, incarcerated mostly by myself, first so I wouldn't betray my father, then so I wouldn't rob my mother of her satisfied rancor, or of the holiness she ascribed to me thinking I was dead, which let her feel saintly, and I was used to living in secret, to being someone else, to never breaking the silence imposed on me by my parents, the war, Spain, the peasants who protected me, the nuns who gave me refuge, the Mexican who brought me to America."

She paused a moment, surrounded by the others' attentive silence. The world had thought her sacrificed. She had to sacrifice herself for the world. What part of pain comes to us from others, and what part comes from ourselves?

She looked at Basilio. She took his hand.

"I always loved you. I thought my death would preserve our love. My pride was to believe there was no better fate than to die unknown. How was I going to scorn what I was most thankful for in my life— your love, the friendship of Jorge Maura and Domingo Vidal, ready to die with me if necessary?"

"Remember," interrupted Basilio, "we Spaniards are hounds of death. We sniff it out and follow it until we ourselves get killed."

"I'd give anything to undo the past," said Pilar sadly. "I chose my stupid political militancy over the affection of three marvelous men. I hope they forgive me."

"Violence breeds violence." Laura smiled. "Luckily, love breeds love. We come out even, in general." She took Lourdes' hand on her right and Pilar's on her left.

"That's why, when I saw the announcement for an exhibit of portraits of exiled Spaniards, I flew from Acapulco and found Basilio's empty frame."

She looked at Laura. "But if you hadn't been there, we'd never have gotten together again."

"When did you tell your Mexican lover you weren't going back to him?" asked Santiago.

"As soon as I saw the empty frame."

"That was brave of you. Basilio might have been dead."

Pilar blushed. "No, all the photos had birth and death dates when called for. Basilio's had no death date, so I knew. Excuse me."

The young people hadn't spoken much. They were giving all their attention to the story of Pilar and Basilio. Santiago once exchanged a loving look with his grandmother and found something marvelous in Laura Díaz's eyes, something he wanted to tell Lourdes about later, something that shouldn't be forgotten, he didn't say so, the eyes, the entire attitude of Laura Díaz said so that Christmas of 1965, and those eyes took in the people at the table but also opened to them, gave them a voice, invited them to see and read each other, lovingly to disclose themselves.

But she was the world's fulcrum.

Laura Díaz had learned to love without asking for explanations because she had learned to see others, with her camera and with her eyes, as they themselves might never see themselves.

She read after dinner a brief note of congratulations from Jorge Maura, written in Lanzarote. Laura could not resist: she'd told him about the marvelous and unexpected reunion of Pilar Méndez and Basilio Baltazar.

Jorge's note simply asked, "What part of happiness doesn't come from God?"

On New Year's Eve, Lourdes Alfaro and Santiago López-Ayub were married. The witnesses were Laura Díaz, Pilar Méndez, and Basilio Baltazar.

Laura thought of a fourth witness. Jorge Maura. They would not see each other again.

## 23. Tlatelolco: 1968

N O ONE HAS THE RIGHT to identify a body. No one has the right to remove a body. We will not tolerate five hundred funeral processions in this city tomorrow. Throw them all in a common grave. Allow no one to identify them."

Make them disappear.

Laura Díaz photographed her grandson Santiago the night of October 2, 1968. She made her way on foot from the Calzada de la Estrella to watch the marchers enter the Plaza of the Three Cultures. She'd been photographing all the events in the student movement beginning with the first demonstrations—the growing presence of police squads, the bazooka fired against the door of the National Preparatory School, the occupation of University City by the army, the arbitrary destruction of laboratories and libraries by paid thugs, the university protest march headed by the rector, Javier Barros Sierra, and followed by the entire university community, the gathering in the Zócalo, where the crowd shouted to President Gustavo Díaz Ordaz: SHOW YOUR FACE—SHOW YOUR FACE—YOU'RE A DISGRACE—TO THE HUMAN RACE!, the silent march of a hundred thousand gagged citizens.

Laura recorded the nights of discussion with Santiago, Lourdes, and a dozen or more young men and women whose passions had been aroused by the events. They met in a room Laura had cleared for them in the Plaza Río de Janeiro apartment, moving old files and throwing out useless trash that actually represented precious memories, but Laura told Lourdes that if at the age of seventy she hadn't stored up in her memory what was worth remembering, she'd be crushed by the weight of the miscellaneous past. The past had many forms. For Laura, it was an ocean of paper.

What was a photograph, after all, but an instant transformed into eternity? The flow of time was unstoppable, so trying to save it in its totality would be a kind of madness—time that went on, under the sun and stars, with or without us, in an uninhabited, lunar world. Human time meant sacrificing the totality to give privilege to the instant and the prestige of eternity to the instant. The painting by Santiago the Younger in the apartment dining room said it all: we aren't falling, we're rising.

Laura had shuffled the contact sheets nostalgically, thrown the ones that seemed pointless to her into the trash, and cleared out the room for her great-grandchild to come. Shall we paint it blue or pink? Lourdes asked, laughing, and Laura laughed with her. Male or female, the baby would sleep in a cradle surrounded by photography smells, the walls were impregnated with the unmistakable perfume of wet photographs, of developer, of prints hung up with clothespins to dry like freshly washed clothes.

She observed her grandson's growing enthusiasm and would have wanted to warn him, Don't let yourself be swept along by enthusiasm, for in Mexico disillusion quickly punishes anyone with faith and tosses that faith out the door. We were taught this in school, Santiago would say to his comrades, kids between seventeen and twenty-five, dark-haired and blond, the way Mexico is, a rainbow country, said a pretty girl with hair down to her waist, very dark skin and very green eyes, a country on its knees that has to be stood on its feet, said a dark boy, tall with very small eyes, a democratic country, said a boy who was pale and short, muscular and calm, with glasses that were always sliding down his nose, a country united with the great revolts in Berkeley, Tokyo, and Paris, a country that won't ever say *"Interdit d'interdire"* and where imagination can seize power, said a blond boy, very Spanish, with a full beard and intense eyes, a country where we don't forget the others, said another boy who looked Indian, very serious and hidden behind thick glasses, a country where we can all love one another, said Lourdes, a country without exploiters, said Santiago, we're doing nothing more than bringing to the street what we were taught in school, we were educated with ideas called democracy, justice, freedom, revolution; they asked us to believe in all that, Doña Laura, can you imagine, Grandmama, a student or teacher defending dictatorship, oppression, injustice, reactionary thinking, but they showed themselves and we saw their faces, said the tall dark boy, and we cited demands, said the Indian boy with thick glasses, listen here, where are the things you taught us in school?, listen here, the dark girl with green eyes added her voice to the chorus, who do you think you're fooling?, look here, said the boy with the full beard and intense eyes, just dare to look at us, there are millions of us, thirty million Mexicans under the age of twenty-five, do you think you can fool us forever?, the tall boy with small eyes leaped to his feet, where is democracy in the farcical elections that the PRI organizes with stuffed ballot boxes?, where is the justice—Santiago went on—in a country where seventy people have more money than seventy million citizens?, where is the freedom in unions handcuffed by corrupt leaders? asked the girl with hair to her waist, in newspapers paid off by the government, added Lourdes, in television that hides the truth?, where is the revolution? concluded the boy who was pale and short, muscular and calm, in the names of Villa and Zapata inscribed in gold on the Chamber of Deputies, concluded Santiago, on the statues the night birds shit on and the morning goldfinches shit on again when they write the PRI's speeches?

It would have been useless to warn him. He'd broken with his parents, he identified himself with his grandmother, she and he, Laura and Santiago, had knelt down together one night right in the Zócalo and together had put their ears to the ground and together heard the same thing, the blind tumult of the city and the nation about to explode.

"The hell that is Mexico," said Santiago. "Are we predestined for crime, violence, corruption, poverty?"

"Don't talk, son. Listen. Before I photograph, I always listen . . ."

She wanted to bequeath to her descendants a luminous liberty. The two of them raised their faces from the icy stone and looked at each other with a questioning look filled with tenderness. Laura understood then that Santiago was going to act as he acted, she was not going to say to him, You've got a wife, you're going to have a baby, don't get involved. She wasn't Danton, she wasn't Juan Francisco, she was Jorge Maura, she was the gringo Jim at the Jarama front, she was the young Santiago the Elder shot in Veracruz. She was those who doubted every-thing but never hesitated to act.

Her grandson Santiago, in every march, in every speech, at every university gathering, incarnated change, and his grandmother followed him, photographed him, he paying no attention to being pho-tographed, and Laura watched him with the tenderness of a comrade: with her camera, she recorded all the moments of change, sometimes change brought on by uncertainty, sometimes change brought on by certainty, but the final certitude—of acts, of words—was less certain than doubt. The most uncertain thing was certainty.

Laura felt during those days of the student revolt, in sunlight or torchlight, that change was certain because it was uncertain. Through her memory passed the dogmas she'd listened to all her life—the almost prehistoric antagonisms between the Franco-British allies and the Central Powers in the 1914 war, Vidal's Communist faith and Basilio's anarchist faith, Maura's Republican faith and Pilar's Falangist faith, Raquel's Judeo-Christian faith and also Harry's confusion, Juan Francisco's opportunism, Danton's greedy cynicism, and his brother Santiago's generosity.

Through his grandmother, this new Santiago was heir to them all, whether he knew it or not. The years with Laura Díaz had formed the days of Santiago the New, which is how she thought of him, like the new apostle in the long line of namesakes of the son of Zebedee who had been a witness at Gethsemane of Christ's transfiguration. The Santiagos, "sons of lightning," all violently killed. St. James pierced by the swords of Herod. St. James the Less garroted by the Sanhedrin. Santiago saints: history recorded two; she, Laura, had four of them, and a name, said the grandmother, is a manifestation of our most intimate nature. Laura, Lourdes, Santiago.

Now the faith of the friends and lovers of all the years with Laura Díaz was the faith of Laura Díaz's grandson, who, along with hundreds of young Mexicans, men and women, went to the Plaza of the Three Cultures, the ancient Aztec ceremonial center Tlatelolco, with no more illumination than that which came from the dying afternoon in the old valley of Anáhuac. Everything was old here, thought Laura Díaz, the Indian pyramid, the church of Santiago, the Franciscan convent and college, but also the modern buildings, the Foreign Ministry, the apartment buildings. Perhaps the most recent things were the oldest because they'd stood the test of time least, being already cracked, with peeling paint, smashed windows, sagging clotheslines, the lamentation of too many sobbing, penitential rains coming from the walls: the streetlights in the square were beginning to come on, the spotlights on prestigious buildings, lamps in kitchens, terraces, living rooms, and bedrooms; hundreds of young people were coming in on one side, dozens of soldiers surrounding them were coming from other sides; nervous shadows appeared on the roof terraces, fists covered with white gloves were raised, and Laura photographed the figure of her grandson Santiago, with his white shirt, his stupid white shirt, as if he were asking to be a target, and his voice saying to her, Grandmother, we don't fit into the future, we want a future that will give room to young people, I don't fit into the future my father invented, and Laura said to him, yes, that with her grandson she too had come to understand that all her life Mexicans had dreamed of a different country, a better country, her grandfather Felipe who emigrated from Germany to Catemaco and her grandfather Díaz who left Tenerife for Veracruz, both dreamed of a country of work and honor, as the first Santiago had dreamed of a country of justice and the second Santiago of a country of creative

475

serenity and the third Santiago, this one entering Tlatelolco Plaza with all those students on the night of October 2, 1968, continued the dream of those whose name he bore, his namesakes, and seeing him enter the plaza, photographing him, Laura said, Today the man I love is my grandson.

She fired her camera, the camera was her weapon, and she fired only at her grandson, realizing the injustice of her attitude, since hundreds of young men and women were coming to Tlatelolco Plaza to demand a new country, a better country, a country faithful to itself, and she, Laura Díaz had eyes only for the flesh of her flesh, for the protagonist of her descendance, a boy with his hair tousled, his white shirt and dark skin and honey-green eyes and bright teeth and sturdy muscles.

I am your comrade, Laura said to Santiago from afar, I'm no longer the woman I was, now I'm yours, tonight I understand you, I understand my love Jorge Maura and the God he adores and for whom he licks the floor of a monastery in Lanzarote, I say to you, my God, take away everything I've been, give me sickness, give me death, give me fever, chancres, cancer, tuberculosis, give me blindness and deafness, cut out my tongue and my ears, my God, if that's what's necessary to save my grandson and my country, kill me with evils so my nation and my children may have health, thank you, Santiago, for teaching all of us that there are still things to fight for in this sleeping and self-satisfied and tricky and tricked Mexico of 1968, Year of the Olympic Games, thanks, my son, for teaching me the difference between the living and the dead—then the commotion in the plaza was like the earthquake that toppled the Angel of Independence, Laura's camera looked up to the stars and saw nothing, then, trembling, it looked down and found the eye of a soldier staring at her like a scar, the camera firing and the rifles firing, extinguishing the songs, slogans, voices of the young people, and then came a horrifying silence, and one heard only the moans of the wounded and dying young people, Laura looking for the figure of Santiago and finding only white gloves against the sky, closing into insolent fists, "mission accomplished," and the impotence of the stars to tell the story of what had happened.

Rifle butts beat Laura out of the plaza, chased out not for being Laura the photographer, grandmother of Santiago, but because all witnesses are being chased away, they want no witnesses, yet under her full skirt Laura hides her roll of film, in her panties, next to her sex, but she cannot photograph the smell of death that rises from the plaza soaked in young blood, she can no longer capture the blinded sky of the night of Tlatelolco, she cannot print the widespread fear of the great urban cemetery, the groans, the screams, the echoes of death . . . The city grows dark.

Not even Danton López-Díaz, the powerful Don Danton, has the right to remove his son's body? No, not even he.

To what do the young widow and the grandmother of Santiago, young rebel leader, have a right? If they wish, they may go to the morgue and identify the body. As a concession to Don Danton, personal friend of President Gustavo Díaz Ordaz. They may see him, but they may not remove or bury him. No exceptions. There will not be five hundred funeral processions on October 3, 1968, in Mexico City. It would make traffic impossible. It would break the rules and regulations.

Laura and Lourdes entered the ice shed, where a strange pearly light illuminated naked bodies laid on wooden pallets mounted on sawhorses.

Laura feared that death would strip away the personalities of these stripped victims, victims of the sedition of a President gone mad with vanity, overweening power, fear, and cruelty. That would be his final victory.

"I haven't killed anyone. Where are the dead? Come on, let them speak out. Let them talk. Me kill anyone?"

They weren't the dead for the President. They were agitators, subversives, Communists, ideologues of destruction, enemies of the nation, the nation incarnated in the presidential Sash. Except the eagle, that night at Tlatelolco, flew off the Sash and away, flew far away, and the serpent, ashamed, thought it better to shed its skin, and the cactus grew wormy, and the water of the lake once again caught fire. Lake of Tlatelolco, throne of sacrifices, where the Tlatilca king was thrown from the top of the pyramid in 1473 to consolidate Aztec power, from the top of the pyramid the idols were cast down to consolidate Spanish power, from all four sides Tlatelolco was besieged by death, the *tzom-pantli*, the wall of skulls cemented together in an immense funeral necklace, thousands of skulls forming a defense and warning about power in Mexico, raised up, time and again, over death.

But the dead here in the morgue were singular, there wasn't one face like another, not one body identical to another, not even uniform postures. Each bullet had left a different rosette on a murdered man's chest, head, thigh; each man's sex was in different repose, each woman's sex a singular wound, that difference was the triumph of the young people sacrificed in their defeat of a violence that went unpunished, a violence that knew itself to be absolved beforehand. The proof was that two weeks later, President Gustavo Díaz Ordaz inaugurated the Olympic Games with the release of a flock of peace doves and with a smile of satisfaction as wide as his bloody snout. In the presidential box, covered with smiles of national pride, were Santiago's parents, Don Danton and Doña Magdalena. The nation had returned to order, thanks to the President's disciplined energy.

When they recognized Santiago's body in the improvised morgue, Lourdes, in tears, threw herself on the naked body of her young husband, but Laura caressed her grandson's feet and hung a tag on his right foot:

## SANTIAGO THE THIRD
### 1950–1968
## A WORLD TO BE MADE

Clasping each other, the old woman and the young woman looked at Santiago for the last time and walked away, sharing a diffused, unplaceable fear. Santiago had died with a grimace of pain. Laura lived wishing that the dead boy's smile could restore peace to his body and to her.

"It is a sin to forget, a sin," she repeated to herself over and over, telling Lourdes, don't be afraid, but the young widow did feel fear, every time there was a knock at the door, she wondered, could it be he, a ghost, a murderer, a mouse, a cockroach?

"Laura, if you had the chance to put someone in a cage like a scorpion and leave him hanging there without bread or water—"

"Don't think such thoughts, daughter. He doesn't deserve it."

"What do you think about, then, Laura, aside from him?"

"I think there are those who suffer and because of their suffering they cannot be replaced."

"But who takes on the pain of the rest, who is exempt from that obligation?"

"No one, daughter, no one."

The city had been turned over to death.

The city was an encampment of barbarians.

Someone was knocking at the door.

# 24. Zona Rosa: 1970

## 1.

LAURA, WHO HAD SEEN EVERYTHING with her camera, stopped one August day opposite the mirror in her bathroom and asked herself, How do people see me?

She kept, perhaps, that memory of a memory which is our past face, not the simple accumulation of years on our skin, not even the layers of years, but a kind of transparency: this is how I am, as I see myself right now, how I always was. The moment can change but it's always just one moment, even if in my head I keep everything that belongs in my head; I always sensed, but now I know, that what belongs to the mind never leaves it, never says goodbye; everything dies except what lives forever in my mind.

I'm the girl from Catemaco, the San Cayetano debutante, the young wife in Mexico City, the loving mother and unfaithful wife, Harry Jaffe's tenacious companion, refuge for my grandson Santiago, but most of all I am Jorge Maura's lover; among all the faces in my existence, his is the one I keep in my imagination as the face of my faces, the face that contains all faces, the image of my happy passion, the face that supports the masks of my life, the final bones of my features, the one that will remain when the flesh has been devoured by death . . .

But the mirror did not reflect the face of Laura Díaz during the 1930s, which she, knowing it had been transitory, imagined was eternal. She read a lot about the ancient history and anthropology of Mexico the better to understand the present she was photographing. Ancient Mexicans had the right to choose a death mask, to put on an ideal face for the journey to Mictlan, that other world of the Indians, both inferno and paradise. If she were an Indian, Laura would choose the mask of her days of love with Jorge and superimpose it on all the others, those of her childhood, her adolescence, her maturity, and her old age. Only the mask of her son Santiago's death agony could compete with that of Jorge Maura's amorous passion, which yielded the desire of happiness. This was her mental photograph of herself. That's what she wanted to see in the mirror on that August morning in 1970. But that morning the mirror was more faithful to the woman than the woman herself.

She'd taken great care with her appearance. Very early in life, observing Elizabeth García-Dupont's ridiculous changes in hairstyle, she decided she'd choose a hairstyle for good and never give it up. Orlando's circle confirmed this: you change your hair, and right away you feel pleased and renovated, but then people notice that your face has changed, look at those crow's-feet, look at those creases in her forehead, my my my, she's made the leap into old age, she's worn out. So Laura Díaz—after toying with the idea of keeping the bangs she'd worn as a girl to cover her forehead that was too high and too wide and to shorten a face that was too long—decided, after meeting Jorge Maura, to reject the hairstyles *à la garçon* of Mexico's Clara Bows, or the platinum-blond ones of the silky Jean Harlow, or the undulating marcelled tresses of the local Irene Dunnes; she pulled her hair back, revealing her clear forehead and her "Italian" nose, as Orlando called it, prominent and aristocratic, fine and nervous, as if it never stopped inquiring about things. And she rejected the bee-stung lips of Mae Murray, Erich von Stroheim's merry widow, and Joan Crawford's immensely wide mouth, painted like a fearsome entryway into the hell of sex, and kept to her thin lips, with no lipstick, which accentuated the sculptured Gothic look of Laura Díaz's head, she was descended after all from people of the Rhine and the Canary Islands, from Murcia and Santander. She bet everything on the beauty of her eyes, which were of a chestnut, almost golden color, greenish in the evening, silvery during the open-eyed orgasm Jorge Maura asked of her, I come when I see your eyes, my love, let me see your open eyes when I come, your eyes excite me, and it was true, sexes aren't beautiful, they're even grotesque, Laura Díaz says to her mirror this morning in August 1970, what excites us are eyes, skin, the reflection of the sex in the hot eyes and sweet skin that draws us closer to the inevitable thicket of sex, the lair of the great spider that is pleasure and death.

She no longer looked at her body while bathing. It no longer concerned her. And Frida Kahlo, of course. Frida helped her friend Laura give thanks for her old but intact body. Before Jorge Maura, there was Frida Kahlo, the best example of an invariable style, imposed once and for all, impossible to imitate, imperial and unique. That was not the style of her friend and occasional secretary Laura Díaz, who once had followed the changes in fashion—even now she went through yesterday's outfits in the closet—the short flapper dresses of the 1920s, the long satin whiteness of the 1930s, the tailored suits of the 1940s, Christian Dior's "New Look," when full skirts made a comeback after the scarcity of textiles during the war years. But after her trip to Lanzarote, Laura too adopted a comfortable uniform, as it were, a kind of tunic, with no buttons, zippers, or belt, nothing to hamper her, a long monastic shift she could put on or take off without fuss and which turned out to be ideal, first in the tropical valley of Morelos and then—so she could fly, as if the simple cotton cloth gave her wings—on all the stairways in that Rome of the Americas, Mexico City, city of four, five, seven levels superimposed on each other, as high as the sleeping volcanoes, as deep as the reflection in a smoking mirror.

But that August day in 1970, while it rained outside and the fat drops beat against the opaque glass of the bathroom, the mirror reflected back to me, merciless, true, cruel, without dissimulation, no longer the preferred face of my thirties but my face of today, that of my seventy-two years, my high forehead furrowed, my dark-honey eyes lost between the bags beneath them and the lids like used curtains, my nose grown beyond anything she remembered, lips with no lipstick, cracked, all the corners of her mouth and planes of her cheeks worn like tissue paper used too many times to wrap too many useless gifts, and the revelation that nothing can disguise, the neck that proclaims her age.

"Damned turkey wattle!" Laura decided to laugh into the mirror and go on loving herself, loving her body and combing her graying hair.

Then she joined her hands over her breasts and felt them frozen. She saw the reflection of her hands, pecked by time, and remembered her young woman's body, so desired, so well exhibited or hidden according to the decision of that great prompter of vanity which is pleasure, beauty, and seduction.

She went on loving herself.

"Rembrandt painted himself at every stage, from adolescence to old age," said Orlando Ximénez when he invited her, for the umpteenth time, to the Scotch Bar at the Hotel Presidente in the Zona Rosa, and she, "for old times' sake," as Orlando himself insisted, agreed just once to see him for a bit at six o'clock, when the bar was empty. "There is no pictorial document more moving than that of a great artist who can see himself without any idealism as he was all through his life, culminating in a self-portrait in old age that has in the eyes all the earlier stages, all of them without exception, as if only old age can reveal not just the totality of a life but each one of the multiple lives we have lived."

"You're still nothing but an aesthete." Laura laughed.

"No, listen to me. Rembrandt's eyes are almost closed under his old eyelids. His eyes are tearing, not out of emotion but because age liquefies them. Look at my eyes, Laura, I have to wipe them all the time! I look as if I have a perpetual cold!" Orlando laughed in turn, as he picked up his scotch and soda with a tremulous hand.

"You look very well, very snappy," offered Laura in genuine admiration of the dry trimness of her old beau, stiff and dressed with outmoded elegance, as if one could still buy clothes in the Duke of Windsor style—glen plaid jackets, ties with wide knots, wide-cuffed trousers, Church shoes with thick soles.

Orlando had turned into a well-dressed broom crowned with a bare skull; a fringe of thin gray hair, well oiled at the temples, was scrupulously combed to the nape of his neck.

"No, let me tell you, the prodigious thing about that last portrait of the old Rembrandt is that the artist doesn't blink at the sight of the ravages of time, but lets us remember not only all his earlier years but our own, so we keep the most profound image those little eyes possess. He was resigned—but astute."

"What image?"

"The image of eternal youth, Laura, because it's the image of the artistic power that created all his work, that of his youth, his maturity, and his old age. That's the true image Rembrandt's last self-portrait gives us: I'm eternally young because I'm eternally creative."

"How little everything costs you." Laura laughed again, this time defensively. "Being frivolous, cruel, charming, innocent, perverse. And sometimes even intelligent."

"Laura, I'm a firefly, I light up and go dark without wanting to." Orlando returned her laugh. "It's my nature. You don't approve?"

"I know you're like that," Laura answered quickly.

"Do you remember the first time I asked you, Does your body approve of me, do I get an A?"

"I'm astonished by your question."

"Why?"

"You talk about the past as if it could be repeated. You talk about the past so that you can proposition me now, in the present." Laura stretched out her hand and patted Orlando's; she noted that his old gold ring with the engraved OX was now too big on his thin finger.

"For me," said the eternal suitor, "you and I are always on the terrace of the San Cayetano hacienda in 1915 . . ."

Laura drank her favorite dry martini more quickly than she should have. "No, we're in a bar in the Zona Rosa in 1970, and it seems ridiculous for you to evoke—what shall I call it?—the romantic lyricism of our first meeting, my poor Orlando."

"Don't you understand?" The old man furrowed his brow. "I didn't want our relationship to cool off out of habit."

"My poor Orlando, age cools everything off."

Orlando peered into the bottom of his glass of whiskey. "I didn't want poetry to turn into prose."

Laura fell silent for a few moments. She wanted to tell the truth without hurting her old friend. She didn't want to take advantage of her age to judge others from an unjust height. That was a temptation of age, to make judgments with impunity. But Orlando spoke first.

"Laura, would you like to be my wife?"

Rather than answer, Laura told herself three truths in a row, repeated them several times: absence simplifies things, prolongation corrupts them, profundity kills them. With Orlando, the temptation was to simplify: just to leave. But Laura felt that to walk out on a man and a situation that were already close to absurd was a kind of betrayal, which she wanted to avoid at all costs, I'm not betraying myself or my past if I don't run off, I'm not simplifying, not laughing, if I prolong this instant even if it ends in disaster, and deepen it even if it ends in death.

"Orlando." Laura leaned closer. "We met in San Cayetano. We became lovers in Mexico City. You abandoned me, leaving a note in which you said that you weren't what you said you were or what you seemed to be. *You're getting too close to my mystery*. You reproached me."

"Not reproached, warned."

"You threw it in my face, Orlando. *I'd rather keep my secret*, you wrote me then. And without mystery, you added, our love would be uninteresting."

"I also said, I'll always love you."

"Orlando, Orlando, my poor Orlando. Now you're telling me the time has come for us to unite. Does this mean there's no more mystery?"

She caressed his cold, emaciated hand with genuine tenderness.

"Orlando, be faithful to yourself to the end. Be Orlando Ximénez, leave everything in the air, everything open, everything unfinished. That's your nature, don't you realize? Actually, that's what I most admire in you, my poor Orlando."

Orlando's glass of whiskey turned into a crystal ball for a while. The old man wanted to see into the future.

"I should have asked you to marry me, Laura."

"When?" She felt she was wearing out.

"Do you mean I'm the victim of my own perversity? Have I lost you forever?"

He had no idea that "forever" had happened half a century before, at the ball in the tropical hacienda, he didn't realize that then and there, when they met, Orlando had said "never" to Laura Díaz when he meant "forever," confusing postponement with what he'd just said: I didn't want our relationship to cool off out of habit, I didn't want you to get too close to my mystery.

Laura shivered with cold. Orlando was proposing a marriage for death. An acceptance that now there were no more games to be played, no more ironies to show off, no more paradoxes to explore. Did Orlando realize that when he talked like that he was negating his own life, the mysterious and unfinished vocation of his entire existence?

"Do you know"—Laura Díaz smiled—"I remember our entire relationship as a fiction? Do you want to write a happy ending for it now?"

"No," muttered Orlando. "I don't want it to end. I want to start over." He raised the glass to his mouth until she couldn't see his eyes. "I don't want to die alone."

"Careful. You don't want to die without knowing what might have been."

"That's right. What might have been."

Laura found it very hard to get the register of her voice right. Did she hammer at him, pronounce, summarize, or start over? Whatever she chose she did it with all the tenderness she could muster. "What might have been already was, Orlando. Everything happened exactly as it should have happened."

"Should we resign ourselves, then?"

"No, maybe not. We should carry some mysteries to the grave."

"Of course. But where do you bury your demons?" Orlando automatically bit his emaciated finger where the heavy gold ring was slipping around. "We all carry a little devil around inside us who won't abandon us even in the hour of our death. We will never be satisfied."

After she left the bar, Laura took a long walk through the Zona Rosa, the fashionable new neighborhood where the young generation gathered en masse, the young people who'd survived the Tlatelolco massacre and ended up in jail or at a café, both prisons, both enclosed. They'd invented, in the space bounded by Chapultepec, Paseo de la Reforma, and Insurgentes, an oasis of cafeterias, restaurants, malls, mirrors, where they could stop, look at themselves, be admired, show off the new styles—miniskirts, wide belts, black patent-leather boots, bell-bottom trousers, and Beatles haircuts. Half of Mexico City's ten million inhabitants were under twenty years of age, and in the Zona Rosa they could have a drink, show off, pick someone up, see and be seen, believe again that the world was livable, conquerable, without spilled blood, without an insomniac past.

Here in these same streets—Génova, Londres, Hamburgo, and Amberes—the impoverished aristocrats of the Porfirio Díaz era had lived; here the first elegant nightclubs—the Casanova, the Minuit, the Sans Souci—had opened during the Second World War, which transformed the city; here, in the La Votiva church, Danton had daringly begun his climb to success; here too, along Paseo de la Reforma, the young people of Tlatelolco had marched to their death, and here appeared the cafés which were like guild halls for the young literary set, the Kineret, the Tirol, and the Perro Andaluz; here were restaurants frequented by the rich, the Focolare, the Rivoli, and the Estoril, along with the restaurant that was everyone's favorite, the Bellinghausen, with its maguey worms, its noodle soups, its *escamoles* and *chemita* steaks, its delicious flans flavored with *rompope* eggnog and its steins of beer, colder than anywhere else. And right here, when the subway system was built, there began to appear, vomited out by the trains, the *gandallas, onderos, chaviza*—the fuckers, the new-wavers, the bucks—all the names invented for the hordes of the new poor from the lost neighborhoods, dispatched from the urban deserts to the oasis where camels drink and caravans repose: the Zona Rosa, as the artist José Luis Cuevas called it.

Laura, who'd photographed it all, felt powerless to depict this new phenomenon: the city was escaping her eyes. The capital's epicenter had shifted too many times during her life—from the Zócalo, Madero, and Avenida Juárez to Las Lomas and Polanco, to Reforma (now converted from a residential street like one in Paris to a commercial avenue like one in Dallas), and now the Zona Rosa. But its days, too, were numbered. Laura Díaz could smell it in the air, see it in the faces, feel it on her skin—it was a time of crime, of insecurity and hunger, asphyxiating air, invisible mountains, only the fleeting presence of stars, an opaque sun, a mortal fog over a city transformed into a bottomless, treasureless mine, lifeless canyons replete with death . . .

How can one separate passion from violence?

Mexico's question, Mexico City's question, was Laura's answer: yes, after all is said and done, as she walked away from her final meeting with Orlando Ximénez, Laura Díaz could declare, "Yes, I think I've managed to separate passion from violence."

What I haven't achieved, she said to herself as she strolled quietly from Niza Street to Plaza Río de Janeiro along Orizaba Street, the familiar, almost totemic, places of her daily life—the church of the Holy Family, the Chiandoni ice-cream parlor, the department store, the stationery store, the pharmacy, the newspaper stand at the corner of Puebla Street—what I didn't do was solve those many mysteries, except Orlando's, which I finally figured out this afternoon. He was waiting for something that never came; to wait for something that would never come was his fate, which he tried to change this afternoon by proposing to me, but fate—experience transformed into fatality—took control again. That was fatal, murmured Laura, sheltered by the sudden splendor of a long, agonic afternoon enamored of its own beauty, a narcissistic afternoon in the Valley of Mexico. She recited one of Jorge Maura's favorite poems:

*Fortunate the tree, which is barely sensitive,*
*more fortunate still the hard stone, because it feels nothing.*

*There is no greater pain than the pain of being alive,*
*nor any greater sorrow than conscious life . . .*

This "song of life and hope" by the marvelous Nicaraguan poet Rubén Darío shrouded Laura in its words that August afternoon, clean and clear because of recent rain, when Mexico City recovered for a few seconds the lost promise of its diaphanous beauty.

The thunderstorm had carried out its punctual chore, and, as Mexico City denizens say, "it cleared up." On her way home, Laura amused herself reviewing the unsolved mysteries, one by one. Did Armonía Aznar really exist? Had that invisible woman really lived in the attic of the Xalapa house, or was she merely a cover story for the conspiracies of the anarcho-syndicalists from Catalonia and Veracruz? Was she a figment of the young, mischievous, irrepressible imagination of Orlando Ximénez? I never saw Armonía Aznar's body, Laura Díaz was surprised to hear herself saying, now that I think about it. I was only told that "it didn't stink." Was her grandmother Cosima Reiter really in love with the handsome, brutal outlaw, the Hunk of Papantla, who cut off her fingers and left her self-absorbed for the rest of her days? Did her grandfather Felipe Kelsen ever miss his lost rebel youth in Germany? Did he ever resign himself completely to the fate of being a prosperous coffee grower in Catemaco? Would Aunts Hilda and Virginia have been more than they were? If they'd been educated in Germany and if they hadn't had the pretext of isolation in a dark corner of the Mexican forest, would they have been in Düsseldorf a recognized concert pianist and a famous writer? It was no mystery what would have been Auntie María de la O's life if Grandmother Cosima had not energetically separated her from her mother, the black prostitute, and integrated her into the Kelsen household. The goodness and rectitude of her own father, Don Fernando Díaz, was also no mystery; nor was the pain he bore for the death of the promising young man, the first Santiago, shot by Porfirio Díaz's soldiers at the Gulf. But Santiago himself was a mystery, the politics he chose by necessity and the private life he chose by act of will. Perhaps the latter was just another myth invented by Orlando Ximénez to seduce Laura Díaz by exciting her. And what happened at the outset of her husband Juan Francisco's life, a man who shone with such glory in the public eye for twenty years only to fade away and die defecating? Nothing, nothing before and nothing after the interlude of glory? Born from shit and dying in shit? Was the interlude the entire performance of his life, or something that had happened between the acts? Nothing? Infinitely painful mysteries: if her son Santiago had lived, if the promises of his talent were there, present and fulfilled, if Danton hadn't had the ambitious genius that led him to wealth and corruption. And if the third Santiago, dead at Tlatelolco, had submitted to the destiny planned by his father, would he be alive today? And his mother, Magdalena Ayub Longoria, what did she think of all this, of these lives which were hers and which she shared with Laura Díaz?

Had Harry informed on his left-wing comrades to McCarthy?

And finally, above all, what had become of Jorge Maura? Was he alive, was he dying, had he already died? Did he find God? Had God found him? Had Jorge Maura sought for spiritual well-being so strenuously only because he'd already found it?

Arriving at that final mystery, the fate of Jorge Maura, Laura Díaz stopped, granting her lover a privilege she would soon grant to all the other protagonists of the years with Laura Díaz: the right to carry a secret to the grave.

## 2.

When the third Santiago was murdered in the Plaza of the Three Cultures, Laura presumed that the young, pregnant widow, Lourdes Alfaro, would continue to live with her. Lourdes transformed her grief into a decision to honor—twice over—the memory of Santiago. In April 1969 she gave birth to a boy, who was of course named Santiago, the fourth to be named after the Greater Apostle, witness of the agony and transfiguration of the victims: the Santiagos, "sons of the lightning," descendants of Christ's first disciple, executed by the power of Herod and saved for love, home, and the memory of Laura Díaz.

Lourdes did her duty as a mother and—with the infant Santiago in a rebozo on her back—she organized demonstrations to seek the release of political prisoners from 1968, helped other young Tlatelolco widows like herself who had small children who needed nursemaids, medicine, care, and also, Lourdes said to Laura, the living memory of their fathers' sacrifice. Of course, there were times when the situation was reversed and the fathers were widowers whose young student wives had fallen in Tlatelolco.

Thus a union of survivors of October 2 came into being. Lourdes met, came to know, and fell in love with a young man who was twenty-six years old. Jesús Aníbal Pliego, who was starting out as a filmmaker and had managed to shoot bits and pieces—shadowy fields, blood-red filters, echoes of machine-gun fire—of the night at Tlatelolco. That same night, Jesús Aníbal's young wife had also died, and the widower, a tall, dark, curly-headed young man with a radiant smile and eyes, was left with a little girl just a few months old, Enedina, who was in the same day-care center Lourdes used for her son, the fourth Santiago in the line of Laura Díaz.

"I have something to tell you, Laura," Lourdes blurted out after pussyfooting around for several weeks. Laura, of course, had already guessed everything.

"You don't have to tell me anything, dear girl. You're like my daughter, and I understand everything. I couldn't think of a better match for you than Jesús Aníbal. You've got so much in common. If I were old-fashioned, I'd give you my blessing."

They had something more than love in common: work. Lourdes, who had learned a great deal at Laura's side, could now work more and more with Jesús Aníbal as his photographic assistant. But what Lourdes had to tell Laura was that she, her husband, and the two children—Enedina and Santiago the Fourth—were going to live in Los Angeles. Jesús Aníbal had gotten an excellent offer from an American movie company: in Mexico he had few chances to work because the Díaz Ordaz government had confiscated his Tlatelolco films.

"You don't have to explain anything, mi amor. I know how things are."

The apartment on Plaza Río de Janeiro was empty.

The fourth Santiago barely left a trace in the memory of his great-grandmother. Just saying that word fills me with pride, satisfaction, consolation, and disconsolation, makes me afraid and makes me sad, convinces me in a happy way that I've finally managed to kill vanity— I'm a great-grandmother!—but also that I've managed to revive death, my own death forever accompanying that of each Santiago—the one shot in Veracruz, the one who died in Mexico City, the one murdered in Tlatelolco, and now the one who's going to Los Angeles, my little *bracero*—now I'm going to laugh—my little wetback whom I'll never get to dry with the towels my mother Leticia gave me when I married. How certain things last! . . .

Living alone was no problem for Laura Díaz. She kept herself agile, busy, deriving pleasure from little things, like making the bed, washing and hanging out clothes, keeping herself "snappy," as she said to Orlando, shopping at the new Aurrerá supermarket, just as she'd once gone, a young bride, to the old Parián market on Avenida Alvaro Obregón. Late in the day, she'd inherited from her mother Leticia a taste for cooking. She rescued old Veracruz recipes—rice and beans, the wonderful shredded beef of *ropa vieja*, tamales in the coastal style, stuffed crabs, squid in its own ink, snapper swimming in a sea of onions, olives, and tomatoes, strong, hot coffee the way they used to serve it in the Café de la Parroquia, hot coffee to keep out the heat, as Doña Leticia Kelsen de Díaz recommended. And as if it had just arrived from another celebrated café, the one in Almendares Park in Havana, the cloyingly sweet *tocinillo del cielo* along with the full gamut of Mexican sweets which Laura would buy at the Celaya candy store on Avenida Cinco de Mayo—the bicolored *jamoncillos*, the marzipans and glazed sweet potatoes; the peaches, pineapples, figs, cherries, and crystallized quince—and for her breakfasts, *chilaquiles* in green sauce, *huevos rancheros*, fried tortillas with chicken, lettuce, and fresh cheese, "divorced" eggs (red and green), and, again, all the different kinds of Mexican breads: rolls, biscuits, white bread, the sugar cookies, the conch shells, and *chilindrinas*.

She classified her negatives, attended to requests to buy prints of her classic photographs, prepared books, and dared to request prefaces from new writers—Salvador Elizondo, Elena Poniatowska, Margo Glantz, and the youngsters of the Onda movement, José Agustín and Gustavo Saínz. Diego Rivera had died in 1957; Rodríguez Lozano, María Izquierdo, and Alfonso Michel had died, artists she'd known and who had inspired her (the pure, brutal blacks, whites, and grays of the first, the false naiveté of the second, the wise shock of each color in the third), and the only two who'd survived, antagonistic but huge, Siqueiros the Big Colonel with fists raised against the celebratory velocity of the world in motion, and Tamayo, handsome, shrewd, and silent, his head just like the volcano Popocatépetl. There wasn't much to cling to. Unless it was disappearing memory and will. One after another, the guardians of shared memories were disappearing.

One dry, no longer rainy afternoon during the beautiful Mexican autumn, someone knocked at Laura's door. When she opened it, she had a hard time identifying the woman in black, the first thing Laura noticed being the dark suit in expensive good taste, as if to call attention to a figure that was attractive without needing attention, such was the faded aspect of the face with no memorable features, not even a trace of lost beauty. The beauty innate in all young women. Even in ugly ones. Here, instead, was an evident pride, concentrated, painful, submitted—that word emanated from the lady's eyes, uncomfortable eyes, uncertain and troubled beneath thick brows as the unknown visitor emitted an "Oh!" as submissive as the rest of her person and shifted her eyes to the floor in alarm.

"My contact lens fell out," said the stranger.

"Well, let's find it." Laura Díaz laughed.

The two of them, on all fours, felt around on the entryway floor until Laura touched the tiny piece of moist lost plastic with the tip of her index finger. But with her other hand she touched a distant but familiar flesh as she presented the saved lens to Magdalena Ayub Longoria. I'm Danton's wife, your daughter-in-law, the woman explained, standing up but not daring to put the lens back in its place while Laura invited her in.

"Oh, with all this pollution these lenses go coffee-colored right away," said Magdalena as she put the lens in her Chanel bag.

"Is something wrong with Danton?" asked Laura, trying to anticipate her.

A smile fleetingly sketched itself on Magdalena's face, followed by a strange giggle, almost an involuntary flourish. "There's nothing wrong . . . with your son . . . I mean my husband . . . there's never anything wrong with him, Señora, in the sense of anything serious. But you know that. He was born to win."

Laura said nothing, but inquired with her eyes, What do you want?, Come on, tell me.

"I'm afraid, Señora."

"Just call me Laura, don't be formal."

Everything in her guest was approximation, doubt, unnecessary expense but perfectly planned to cover appearances, from her hairdo to her shoes. One would have to anticipate her, ask her fear about what, about her husband, about Laura herself, about memory, the memory of her rebellious son, her dead son, her grandson now emigrated, far away from the country where violence held sway over reason and, worse, over passion itself.

"Afraid of what?" asked Laura.

They sat down on the blue velvet sofa Laura had been dragging with her since Avenida Sonora, but Magdalena looked around the disordered room, with the piles of magazines, books, papers, newspaper articles, and the photos tacked to cork panels. Laura understood the woman was seeing for the first time the place her son had gone to die. She stared for a long time at the picture of Adam and Eve painted by Santiago the Younger.

"You must know, Señora."

"Just call me Laura, for heaven's sake." Laura feigned exasperation.

"All right. You must understand that I'm not what I seem. I'm not what you think I am. I admire you."

"It might have been better if you'd loved and admired your son a bit more," said Laura with great tranquillity.

"That's what you have to understand."

"Understand?"

"You're right to doubt me. It doesn't matter. If I can't share my truth with you, then there's no one left I can share it with."

Laura said nothing but looked at her daughter-in-law attentively and respectfully.

"Can you imagine how I felt when Santiago was killed?" asked Magda.

Laura felt a bolt of lightning crossing her face. "I saw you and Danton sitting in the presidential box at the Olympics, when your son's body was not yet cold."

Magdalena's expression was one of supplication. "Imagine my pain, please, Laura, my shame, my fury, how I had to hold everything in, how the habit of serving my husband won out over my pain, my rage, how I ended up as I always do, submitting to my husband . . ." She looked into Laura's eyes. "You must understand."

"I've always tried to imagine what happened between you and Danton when Santiago died," Laura said, trying to read her mind.

"That's the bad part. Nothing happened. He went on with his life as if nothing had happened."

"Your son was dead. You were alive."

"I was dead long before my son died. For Danton, nothing changed. At least when Santiago rebelled, he lost his illusions. When our son died, well, it was as if he were saying he brought it on himself."

Danton's wife fluttered her hands as if she were tearing away a veil. "Laura, I've come to you because I have to unburden myself. I don't have anyone else. I can't bear it anymore. I need to open myself up to you. You're all I have left. Only you can understand everything, the hurt I feel, all the disappointment and pain rotting inside me for so many years."

"You've stood up pretty well."

"Don't think I don't have my pride, no matter how submissive you think I am, believe me I never lost the pride I had in myself, I'm a woman, I'm a wife, I'm a mother, I feel pride in being those things, even though Danton hasn't shared my bed in years, Laura, accept that for just this reason I am furious and I have some pride, despite my submission to the intimidations I've endured."

She stopped for an instant.

"I'm not what I seem," she went on. "I thought only you could understand me."

"Why, daughter?" Laura caressed Magda's hand.

"Because you've lived your life freely. That's why you can understand me. It's very simple."

Laura was on the verge of saying to her, saying to you, what can I do for you now that the final curtain's about to fall, just as it did with Orlando, why does everyone expect me to write the last scene in the play?

Instead, she lifted Magdalena's chin and asked, "Do you think there ever was a single minute in your life when you took charge of yourself, alone and completely?"

"Not me," Magdalena blurted out. "You did, Laura. We all know that."

Laura Díaz smiled. "I'm not saying it about you, Magda. I'm saying it about myself. I'm begging you now to ask me a question. Ask me, Magdalena: were you always equal to your own demands?"

"No, not me," stuttered Magdalena. "Obviously not."

"No, you don't understand me," Laura replied. "Ask *me* that question. Please."

Magdalena pronounced some confused words, you yourself, Laura Díaz, were always equal to your own demands . . .

"And those of others," Laura went on.

"And those of others." Magda's eyes shone, as she began to take flight on her own.

"Did you ever feel temptation? Did you want to be seen only as a proper lady? Did it ever strike you that the two things could coexist— being a proper lady and, for that very reason, being a corrupt woman?" Laura went on.

She paused. "Your husband, my son, represents the triumph of fraud." Laura wanted to be implacable. Magda's face registered disgust. "He's always believed that other people's lives depend on him. I swear to you, I detest him and despise him. Excuse me." Laura hugged

Magda's head against her bosom. "Did it ever occur to you that the sacrifice of your son redeems Danton from all his sins?"

Now Magdalena freed herself from Laura's arm, disconcerted.

"You have to understand that, child. If you don't, your son has died in vain."

Santiago the son redeemed Danton the father. Magda raised her eyes and joined them to Laura's in a look that mixed horror, weakness, and rejection, but the seventy-two-year-old woman—not the widow, not the mother, not the grandmother, just the woman named Laura Díaz—looked out her window and watched her daughter-in-law Magdalena Ayub walk down the street, hail a taxi, and look back to the window where Laura waved goodbye with infinite tenderness, begging her to understand what I've said, I'm not asking you to accept things but to be outraged, brave, to have the unexpected triumph over a man who expects everything from his submissive wife except the generosity of forgiveness.

Laura saw Magda's smiling eyes as she entered the taxi. Perhaps the next time she would come in her own car, with her own chauffeur, without hiding herself from her husband.

## 25. Catemaco: 1972

S HE BOARDED THE INTEROCEANIC TRAIN that had taken her
back to Veracruz so many times. Like so many things from the
past, the luxurious train of yesteryear linking Mexico City to
Xalapa and the port had shrunk and, obviously, aged. Worn-out seat
covers, sunken seats, exposed springs, opaque windows, stained head-
rests, blocked sinks. Laura decided to take a private compartment in the
Pullman, separated from the rest of the sleeping car, which during the
day was an ordinary car and at night miraculously dropped down beds
already made up with white pillows and freshly washed sheets covered
by green blankets. Similarly, the regular seats turned into beds hidden,
during sleeping hours, by thick canvas curtains with copper buttons.

The compartment Laura took, on the other hand, clung to an elegance Orlando Ximénez would call *fané*, with its patinated mirrors, a
sink with gold-plated faucets, a certain *trompe-l'oeil* (Orlando), and, as
the supreme anachronism, a silver cuspidor, like the ones in the first
home of her married life, where Juan Francisco would meet with the
labor leaders. The soap was Palmolive. The towels mere veils of their
ancient newness. Nevertheless, the private space was permeated by a

nostalgia of past glory. This was the train that connected Mexico's capital with its principal port and that night would connect Laura with the feeling of proving that you can go home again. The price of return, that was the problem, and the ticket from the National Railroads of Mexico did not indicate what it was.

She slept through the night. Xalapa passed without making itself felt; the road to the San Cayetano hacienda was overgrown. But the morning port received her with its mix of early coolness already sheltering the heat of the day—that was its delight. The sun would be splendid. Even so, she did not want to linger in nostalgia for a place that revived intense memories of her puberty, of her strolls along the seawall hand in hand with the first Santiago, and of the death of the brother buried under the waves.

Instead, ensconced in the high dovecote that was the Hotel Imperial, she enjoyed the latent challenge of the Gulf's horizon, where the most brilliant day hides the surprise of a storm, a "norther," rain, wind . . . and at night when she went down to the square, she sat down alone at a little table in the arcade, feeling herself more than ever in company—such was the pleasure that nights in Veracruz always arouse in us—amid the noise, the crowd, the coming and going of waiters carrying trays of beer, rum and Coca-Cola, *mojitos*, and the Veracruz mint julep, with its toupee of mint soaking in rum.

Bands representing all the music played in Mexico—*tamboras* from the north, mariachis from the west, trios from the capital performing boleros, *jaranas* from Yucatán, marimbas from Chiapas, and Veracruz *sones* played on harp and *vihuela*—competed in an exalted cacophony that could be jolted into respect and repose only by the *danzón* in front of the town hall, where the most respectable couples danced with that slight movement which compromises only the feet and imposes incomparable erotic seriousness on the rest of the body, as if the slightest movement from the knee down will unleash the sensual attractions from the knee up.

It was here that Auntie María de la O had come to dance away her final days, married to the famous Matías Matadamas, most certainly a tiny man, as puny, cold, and bluish, all of him—hair and skin, suit and tie, shoes and socks—as this one who, seeing her alone, invited Laura to join in the rhythm of the *danzón* hymn, the one called "Nereids." He asked her to dance without saying a word, said nothing while he danced, but she, during the *danzón*, asked herself secretly: What did I lose? What did I win? Do I have nothing left to lose? How do I measure the distance of my life? Only by the voices that rise up out of the past and speak to me as if they were here? Should I give thanks because there's no one left to weep over me? Should I suffer because I have no one else to lose? Is the mere fact that I'm thinking all this enough to certify it: Laura Díaz, you're an old woman? What did I lose? What did I gain?

The powder-blue little old man respectfully escorted her to her table. One eye oozed tears and he never smiled, but when he danced, he knew a way of caressing the woman's body with his look, with his rhythm, and with the intense contact of one hand in hers and the other on her waist. Man and woman. The *danzón* was still the most sensual dance because it was the one that transformed distance into nearness yet didn't lose the distance.

Would Laura ever hear the *danzón* "Nereids" again, ever dance to it again after this night before her road trip to Catemaco? She took a Hotel Imperial taxi, and when she reached the lake, she got out and told the driver to go back to Veracruz.

"Don't you want me to wait?"

"No, thanks. It isn't necessary."

"And your bags, ma'am? What should I tell them?"

"Tell them to hold the bags for me."

From a distance, the Catemaco house again seemed different to her, as if absence made everything smaller but at the same time longer and narrower. Once again, returning to the past meant entering an empty, interminable corridor where one could no longer find the usual things or people one wanted to see again. As if they were playing both with our memory and with our imagination, the people and things of the past challenged us to situate them in the present without forgetting they had a past and would have a future, although that future would be, precisely, only that of memory, again, in the present.

But when it is a matter of accompanying death, what is the valid time for life? Ah, sighed Laura Díaz, she would certainly have to revisit each and every one of the years of her existence, remember, imagine, perhaps invent what never happened, even the unimaginable, with the mere presence of a being who could represent everything that wasn't, what was, or what could have been, and what could never happen.

Today that being was she herself, Laura Díaz.

From the moment Dr. Teodoro Césarman confirmed that her cancer would allow her, with the best care, no more than a year of life, Laura Díaz decided to travel as soon as possible to the place where she was born. For that reason, on this radiant May morning in 1972, she climbed the little hill leading to the Kelsens' old family house. It had stood abandoned now for forty years: after Don Felipe the grandfather died, the three spinster sisters had been able to survive on the rent from the estate and the building; then, when Fernando Díaz fell ill, his family in Xalapa was helped by money earned by Laura Díaz's diligent mother, Doña Leticia Kelsen; then when the property of the hacienda "La Peregrina" was expropriated, Mutti decided to overrule the family's modesty and rent out rooms to guests "on condition that they be people we know."

Laura smiled as she remembered her parents' longing for decency and prepared herself, with her smile, to look directly at the ruin of the old single-story coffee-plantation house, with its four whitewashed sides around the central patio where Laura had played as a child, with the patio doors that opened to and closed away the living places in the house—bedrooms, living room, dining room. From the outside, she could see from a distance, the outer walls were still unbroken by windows. An inexplicable reserve came over Laura as she walked toward her ancestral home, as if, before entering the ruined house, her spirit needed renewed contact with the opulent nature surrounding the house, the fig tree, the tulip tree, the red lily, the *palo rojo*, and the round crown of the mango tree.

Cautiously she opened the gate at the entrance and closed her eyes, blindly walking along an imaginary corridor, expecting the groan of air through the hallways, the whine of sagging doors, the screech of sick hinges, the repose of forgotten dust . . . Why look right at the ruin of her family home? It was like looking right at the abandonment of her own childhood, however hard, with her eyes closed, Laura Díaz, at the age of seventy-four, could hear the broom of the little black man Zampaya sweeping the patio and singing "Mr. Zampayita's dance / you can see it in a glance, / will surely cure your every pain, / even help you weight to gain," recalling herself on her birthday, when she hopped around the patio very early in the morning, still in her nightgown, singing "on the twelfth of May / the Virgin dressed in white / came walking into sight / with her coat so gay," hearing the melancholy notes of a Chopin nocturne which right at this moment reached her from the room where Aunt Hilda had dreamed of being a great concert pianist in Germany, listening to the voice of Aunt Virginia reciting Rubén Darío's verses and dreaming in turn of being a great poet published in Mexico City, smelling the tasty stews whose aromas reached her from the kitchen supervised so matter-of-factly by her mother Leticia, awaiting the return of Don Felipe from his farm chores, a hardworking and disciplined man, his dreams as an impassioned young German socialist long forgotten.

In just this way, blindly, Laura Díaz made her way through the family house, certain that her sense of direction would not fail her, that she would reach her own childhood bedroom, open the door from the patio, approach the bed, touch it, sit down, and stretch out her hand to find the doll on its pillows, happy in her Oriental princess repose, Li Po, her adored little doll, the doll with head, hands, and feet made of porcelain, with a little cotton body covered by a mandarin costume of red silk and her eyebrows painted near the silk bangs, which Laura, when she opened her eyes, found there, really, reclining on pillows, waiting for Laura to pick her up in her arms, rock her, allow her, as before, as always, to move her porcelain head, open and shut her eyes, without moving those very thin eyebrows painted over her expectant, serene eyelids. Li Po hadn't aged.

Laura Díaz held back a cry of emotion when she picked up Li Po, looked around her childhood bedroom only to find it perfectly clean, with the washbasin that had always been there, the dresser she'd used as a little girl, the door with gauze curtains hanging from copper rods. But Li Po had gone to Frida Kahlo's house. Who had brought her back to Catemaco?

She opened the bedroom door, went out onto the perfectly clean patio, overflowing with geraniums, ran to the living room, and found her grandparents' wicker furniture, the mahogany tables with marble tops, the lamps brought from New Orleans, the vitrines with the little porcelain shepherdesses, and the twin pictures, the little rascal in the first teasing a sleeping dog with a stick, and in the second bitten on the calf by the same dog, now awake, while the mischievous little boy weeps in pain . . .

She walked quickly to the dining room, now expecting what she found there, the table set, the big white tablecloth starched, the chairs in place, three on each flank of the armchair at the head of the table where old Don Felipe always sat, but each place set with Dresden china, knives, forks, spoons in order, and to the right of each plate a stiff napkin rolled up in a silver ring inscribed with the initial of the person who would sit there, Felipe, Cosima, Hilda, Virginia, Leticia, María de la O, Laura . . .

And on Grandmother Cosima's plate, four jewels, a gold wedding band, a sapphire ring, and a pearl ring . . .

I'm dreaming, Laura Díaz said to herself. I'm dreaming this. Or perhaps I'm already dead and don't know it.

She was interrupted when the dining-room door opened brusquely and a rough figure burst in, a dark, bearded man in boots, drill trousers, and a perspiration-soaked shirt. He had a shotgun in one hand and a red handkerchief was tied around his head as a sweatband.

"Excuse me, ma'am," he said. His voice was sweet, with a heavy Veracruz accent, no *s*'s. "The house is private. You have to get permission."

"Excuse *me*," answered Laura Díaz. "It's that I grew up here. I wanted to see the house before—"

"The master doesn't want anyone entering without his permission, you'll excuse me, ma'am."

"The master?"

"Of course. You should see, ma'am, how carefully he's restored the house. It was a ruin, after being the most important hacienda in Catemaco, according to what people say. Then the master came and made it just like new. It took him about five years to get everything together, he said he wanted to see the house exactly the way it was a hundred years ago, or something like that."

"The master?" Laura insisted.

"Sure, my boss. Don Danton. He owns this house and all the land around here right down to the lake."

Laura had a moment of doubt as to whether she should take Li Po with her or leave her resting comfortably in her bed, surrounded by pillows. She saw her so happy, so pleased in her old bed . . . She went back over her memories again, the living room, the dining room, the silver rings . . .

"Rest, Li Po, sleep, live happily ever after. I'll take care of you forever."

In the patio, Laura took a long look at the young caretaker, as if she'd known him forever. Then she went out onto the estate, told herself that no matter how big it might be it would always be the poor patch of earth we all finally have forever, after our season on earth. But this May afternoon, she was ever more thankful for the symmetry of the araucaria, which in the flowering of each branch immediately engendered its double, am I going to reproduce myself that way, will I be another Laura Díaz, a second Laura Díaz, not in myself but in my ancestors and descendants, in the people I come from and the people I leave in the world, the people toward whom I'm going and the people I leave behind, the whole world will be like an araucaria that grows a double in each of its flowers, that is not destroyed by storms, that is protected from the lightning by the lightning of its yellow flowers, the marvelous tree that can withstand both hurricanes and droughts?

She walked into the forest. Her thoughts thickened as the forest opened up. She was charged with life, her own and that of the people who went with her to live it, well or badly; that's why her life wasn't ending, the life of Laura Díaz, because I'm not only my life, there are many lines, many generations, the true history, which is the life lived but above all imagined; am I only the weeping woman, the suffering woman, the mourning woman? No, I refuse that, I always walked with my head held high, I never begged, I walk and try to measure the distance of my life, measure it by the voices that arise from the past and speak to me as if they were here, the names on the seven silver napkin rings, the names of the four Santiagos and the four men in my life, Orlando and Juan Francisco, Jorge and Harry, I wouldn't be the suffering woman, I wouldn't be the weeping woman, I would walk with my head held high, even though I'd humbly accept that I can never own nature because nature survives us and asks us not to own her but to be part of her, to return to her, to leave behind history, time, and the pain of time, no longer to delude ourselves that we have owned anything or anyone, not even our children, not even our loves, Laura Díaz owner only of our art, of what we could give to others from our own body, the body of Laura Díaz, transitory and limited . . .

She remembered the desire of her brother, the first Santiago, to lose himself in the forest as, eventually, he lost himself in the sea.

She would carry out the desire of Santiago the Elder. She would become forest as he became sea.

She would enter the forest as one enters a void from which no message will return.

With her were the unfulfilled lives of a brother, a son, and a grandson.

With her were the eyes and words of her grandfather Felipe Kelsen, was there ever a single truly finished life, a single life that wasn't cutoff promise, latent possibility . . . ?

She remembered the day her grandfather died, when Laura held his hand with its thick veins and old freckles, caressed the skin faded to transparency, and had the sensation that each one of us lives for others: our existence has no other meaning but to complete unfinished destinies . . .

"Didn't I tell you, child? One day all my ailments came together and here I am . . . but before I go I want to tell you that you were right. Yes, there is a statue of a woman, covered with jewels, in the middle of the forest. I lied to you on purpose. I didn't want you to get caught up in superstition and witchcraft, Laurita. I took you to see a ceiba so that you would learn to live with reason, not with the fantasy and enthusiasms that cost me so dearly when I was young. Be careful with everything. The ceiba is covered with spines as sharp as daggers, remember?"

"Of course, Grandfather."

The forest arises like its own deep breathing, its own profound heartbeat.

The forest roads divide.

On one side can be seen the woman of stone, the Indian statue decked out with belts of conch shells and serpents, wearing a crown tinted green by nature imitating art, adorned with necklaces and rings and earrings on ears, nose, and arms . . .

On the other side is the way to the ceiba, queen of the virgin forest, whose crown is made up of the spines that are also spattered all over its brown body like wounding daggers, ageless, immobile but longing, its branches open like arms awaiting a mortal caress, which the great body of wounding daggers can give and wants to give.

Laura Díaz embraced the mother ceiba with all the strength remaining to her, the protecting ceiba, queen of a void from which no message will return.

# 26. Los Angeles: 2000

O NE YEAR AFTER being attacked in Detroit, Santiago López-Alfaro was given a commission that allowed him to continue his television work on Mexican muralists. This time too his vocation and his profession could miraculously join forces: he was assigned to cover the unveiling of the restoration of the mural that David Alfaro Siqueiros had painted in 1930 on Olvera Street in Los Angeles.

This "typical" street was invented by Anglo Americans to pay homage to the Spanish American past of La Puebla de Nuestra Señora de Los Angeles de Porciúncula, founded in 1769 by a Spanish expedition looking for sites for Christian missions and to give themselves—as Enedina Pliego said to me as we rolled along the Pomona Freeway at about seven miles an hour—a romantic past and a good conscience in the present with respect to Mexicans, who did not live on picturesque Olvera Street but, with or without documentation and numbering over a million, lived in the slums of East Los Angeles, whence they were transported in buses or Chevys to West Los Angeles and its Mexican-manicured lawns and rosebushes.

"My grandfather galloped with Zapata in Morelos," said the old gardener to whom Enedina and I gave a ride from Pomona. "Now I gallop by bus from Whittier to Wilshire."

The old man laughed, and added that Los Angeles, California, was now where he worked and that Ocotepec, Morelos, was where he spent his vacations, where he sent his dollars, and where he returned to rest and see his people.

Enedina and I exchanged glances and joined the old man's laughter. The three of us, Angelenos, talked like foreigners in the city, immigrants as recent as those who at that very moment were slipping past the border patrol at the wall between San Diego and Tijuana, between the two Californias. I'd been out of Los Angeles for a year, enough time for everyone, including my girlfriend Enedina, to think I'd left forever, because that was the rule here: you've just arrived and you're already on your way, or you'd just left, you're always passing through, and it wasn't true, we agreed, Indians, Spaniards, and Mexicans—all of us were here before anyone else, and instead of disappearing there are more and more of us, wave after wave of Mexican migrations have poured into Los Angeles as if they were returning to Los Angeles. In just the past century, the Mexicans fleeing from Porfirio Díaz's dictatorship came first, then those fleeing the Revolution, then the Cristeros, enemies of the Maximum Leader Calles, then Calles himself expelled by Cárdenas, then *braceros* to aid in the war effort, then the *pachucos* who shouted, *Here we are!*, and always the poor, the poor who made Los Angeles' wealth and art, the poor Mexicans who worked here and started small businesses and then made money, the illiterates who went to school here and could translate what they had within them—dance, poetry, music, novels. They passed by a gigantic mural of graffiti and of broken, irreplaceable symbols: the Virgin of Guadalupe, Emiliano Zapata, La Calavera Catrina, Comandante Marcos, the masked man of today, and Zorro, the masked man of yesterday, Joaquín Murrieta the bandit, and Fray Junípero Serra the missionary.

"They didn't manage to erase Siqueiros," I said cheerfully. I drove slowly, thinking that driving in Los Angeles was the equivalent of "reading the city in the original."

"Can you imagine his patroness's rage if she were to see what you and I are going to see?" wondered Enedina, who had come to Los Angeles as an infant with her father, the cameraman Jesús Aníbal Pliego, married to my mother, Lourdes Alfaro de López, both of whom had lost their spouses in Tlatelolco and were parents of children who'd lost a parent—pals, friends, and now lovers, Enedina and I.

Los Angeles was transformed into a gigantic Mexican mural, raised like a multi-colored dike so that all California—as we three could see it, two young lovers and an old gardener from the hills of Puente—wouldn't pour down the mountains into the sea in a final earthquake . . . Leaving. Returning. Or arriving for the first time. From the hills one could see the Pacific through a veil of pollution, and from the foot of the mountains the city spread without a center, a mestiza city, a polyglot city, a Babel of immigrants, a Constantinople of the Pacific, zone of the great continental drift to nothingness . . .

There was nothing beyond this. Here the continent ended. It began in New York, the first city, and ended in Los Angeles, the second, perhaps last city. There was no more space to conquer space. Now people would have to go to the moon or to Nicaragua, to Mars or Vietnam. The land conquered by pioneers had run out, the epic of expansion was consummated, the voracity, manifest destiny, philanthropy, urgent need to save the world, to deny others their own destiny, and to impose instead, for their own good, an American future.

I was thinking all this, moving forward at a tortoise pace along highways designed for modern hares. I saw asphalt and concrete, but also development, construction, lots for sale, gas stations, fast-food stands, multiplex cinemas, the baroque-and-roll variety of the great city of Los Angeles. Still, in the mind of a young photographer, great-grandson of Laura Díaz, images alien to my vision of the city were superimposed on it: a tropical river entering the sea in a hurricane shout, thunderbirds crossing the Mexican forests, dust stars disintegrating in instantaneous centuries, a poor careless world, and death cleansing its bloody hands in a deep *temazcal* in Puerto Escondido, where my father, the third Santiago, and my mother, still alive, Lourdes Alfaro . . .

A ceiba in the forest.

I shook my head to banish all those images and concentrate on my own projects, which are what brought me back to Los Angeles; they gave intelligible continuity to the impressionist waterfall of the California Byzantium. I wanted to put together a book of photographs about Mexican muralists in the United States. I'd already photographed Orozco's murals at Dartmouth and Pomona; I'd found on the docks of New York the condemned murals that Diego Rivera had painted for Rockefeller Center; and now I was back in Los Angeles, the city where I'd grown up when my mother and her new husband, Jesús Aníbal, with his daughter, Enedina, left Mexico in 1970, after another wound named Tlatelolco, to photograph, seventy years after it was painted, Siqueiros' mural on Olvera Street.

"Olvera Street," exclaimed Enedina portentously. "The Disneyland of Totonacan tropical tourism."

What caught my attention was the consistency with which the Mexican murals in the United States had been objects of censure, controversy, and obliteration. Were the artists merely provocateurs, the patrons simply cowards, how could they be so naive as to think that Rivera, Orozco, or Siqueiros would paint conventional, decorative works in the taste of those who were paying for them? The gringo Medici of New York, Detroit, and Los Angeles—blind, generous, and vile all at once—thought, perhaps (this was Enedina's idea) that ordering and paying for a work of art was enough to nullify its critical intention, to make it innocuous, and to incorporate it, castrated, into the patrimony of a kind of tax-free puritan beneficence.

The old gardener thanked us for the ride and got off at Wilshire in search of a second ride to Brentwood. Enedina and I wished him luck.

"And if you know of a garden that needs attention"—the old citizen of Ocotepec smiled at us—"just let me know, and I'll take care of it. Don't you two have a garden?"

Enedina and I went on to Olvera Street.

There we found Siqueiros' mural, painted on the high exterior wall of a three-story building. The work had been restored after seventy years of blindness and silence. In 1930, a rich California lady who had heard of the "Mexican Renaissance" had commissioned it. And since Rivera was committed to Detroit and Orozco was at Dartmouth, she hired Siqueiros and asked him what the theme of his work would be.

"Tropical America," answered the muralist with frizzy, tangled hair, flashing green eyes, immense nostrils, and, curiously, a way of speaking in which he constantly interrupted his words with hesitations and little crutches, with "well"s and "hmm"s and "don't you agree"s.

The patron had a marvelous vision of palm trees and sunsets, according to Siqueiros, quivering rumba dancers and gallant *charros*, red-tiled roofs and decorative nopals. She signed the check and told him to get started.

On the day of the opening, with the old square crowded with officials and society people, the curtain fell revealing "Tropical America," and there appeared the mural of a Latin America represented by a dark-skinned Christ, enslaved and crucified. A Latin America crucified, naked, in agony, hanging from a cross above which flew, with fierce intent, the emblematic U.S. eagle.

The patron fainted, the officials hit the roof, Siqueiros had placed Los Angeles in hell, and the next morning the mural was completely whitewashed over, made invisible to the world, as if it had never existed. Nothing. *Nada*.

Seeing it restored, in place, that afternoon during the first year of the new millennium moved Enedina more than me. The girl with green eyes and olive skin raised her arms and tossed her long hair away from her neck, rolling it into a tight knot that grounded her emotion like a lightning rod. The restored work restored herself, Enedina told me later; it was the diploma proving that the Chicana personality belonged as much to Mexico as to the United States. There was nothing to hide, nothing to cover up, this land belonged to all, all races, all languages, all histories. That was its destiny because that was its origin.

On the other hand, I was too busy photographing the mural, happy that for once a job coincided with one of my own projects, which had been interrupted in Detroit when I was mugged after leaving the Institute of Arts, after I'd discovered the face of a woman that was mine, of my blood, of my memory, Laura Díaz, grandmother of my father, murdered in Tlatelolco, mother of another Santiago who couldn't fulfill his artistic promise but who perhaps transmitted to his grandnephew the continuity of the artistic image, sister of a first Santiago shot in Veracruz and delivered to the waves in the Gulf of Mexico.

Now, here, in Los Angeles, the American Babel, Byzantium of the Pacific, the utopia of the new century, I was finishing a chapter in my artistic and family inheritance, the chronicle that Enedina and I had decided to call *The Years with Laura Díaz.*

"Is there anything more to say?" Enedina asked me that night, as we embraced, naked, in our Santa Monica apartment near the murmuring of the sea.

Yes, no doubt there was always something more, but between the two of us, almost brother and sister from childhood, but absolute lovers, each one belonging to the other, no explanations asked, from the time we arrived in California as infants and then grew up together, went to school together, studied together at UCLA and became impassioned by our courses in philosophy and history, on the Mexican Revolution, the history of socialism and anarcho-syndicalism, the workers' movement in Latin America, the Spanish Civil War, the Holocaust, McCarthyism in the United States, studying the writings of Ortega y Gasset, Husserl, Marx, and Ferdinand Lassalle, seeing Eisenstein's Mexican films and Leni Riefenstahl's on Hitler's glory and Alain Resnais on Auschwitz, *Night and Fog*, reviewing the photographs of Robert Capa, Cartier-Bresson, Weegee, André Kertèsz, Rodchenko, and Alvarez Bravo: the totality of these apprenticeships, curiosities, and shared disciplines cemented our love. She flew to Detroit as soon as she found out that I'd been attacked and spent hours by my side in the hospital.

Speaking.

I'd had a concussion, dreamed wild dreams, had to stay in bed before getting back the use of my broken leg, but I didn't forget my dreams, even when it took forever to regain the use of my leg.

Speaking.

Speaking with Enedina, recalling everything possible, inventing the impossible, freely mixing memory and imagination, what we knew, what we'd been told, what the generations of Laura Díaz knew and dreamed, the factual but also the possible, about their lives, the genealogy of Felipe Kelsen and Cosima Reiter, the sisters Hilda, Virginia, and María de la O, Leticia (Mutti), and her husband, Fernando Díaz, the first Santiago, son of Fernando, Laura's first ball at the San Cayetano hacienda, her marriage to Juan Francisco, the birth of the second Santiago and Danton, her love for Orlando Ximénez and for Jorge Maura, her devotion to Harry Jaffe, the death of the third Santiago at Tlatelolco, the liberation, the pain, the glory of Laura Díaz, daughter, wife, lover, mother, artist, old woman, young woman: Enedina and I remembered it all, and what we didn't remember we imagined and what we didn't imagine we discarded as unworthy of a life lived for the inseparable possibility of being and not being, of carrying through one part of existence by sacrificing another part and always knowing that nothing is totally possessed, neither truth nor error, neither wisdom nor memory, for we descend from incomplete but intense loves, from intense but incomplete memories, and we can only inherit what our ancestors bequeathed us, the community of the past and the will of the future, united in the present by memory, by desire, and by the knowledge that every act of love today carries out, in the end, the act of love begun yesterday. Today's memory consecrated, as it deformed, the memory of yesterday. Today's imagination was the truth of yesterday and tomorrow.

From our bed, Enedina and I stared for a long time at the painting of Adam and Eve ascending from Paradise instead of falling from Paradise, the painting of the first naked lovers, possessors of their own sensuality, created by the second Santiago, Santiago the Younger, before he died. Laura Díaz, in her will, had bequeathed the painting to us.

"I love you, Santiago."

"And I love you, Enedina."

"I love Laura Díaz a lot."

"How wonderful that between the two of us we could recreate her life."

"Her years. The years with Laura Díaz."

# Acknowledgments

T HE BEST NOVELISTS in the world are our grandmothers, and it
is to them I owe the first memory on which this novel is based.
My maternal grandmother was Emilia Rivas Gil de Macías,
widow of Manuel Macías Gutiérrez; she born in Alamos, Sonora, he in
Guadalajara, Jalisco; she the descendant of Spanish immigrants from
Santander and, according to rumors I've heard, Yaqui Indians from
Sonora. My grandfather Macías died tragically in 1919, leaving my
grandmother with four young daughters—María Emilia, Sélika, Carmen, and my mother, Berta Macías de Fuentes.

My paternal grandmother, Emilia Boettiger de Fuentes, was born
in Catemaco, Veracruz, daughter of Philip Boettiger Keller, a German
immigrant from Darmstadt, married to a young lady of Spanish origin,
Ana María Murcia de Boettiger, with whom he had three daughters:
Luisa (Boettiger de Salgado), María (Boettiger de Alvarez), and Emilia
(Boettiger de Fuentes). Emilia married Rafael Fuentes Vélez, president
of the National Bank of Mexico in Veracruz and son of Carlos Fuentes
Benítez and Clotilde Vélez, who was attacked and mutilated on the
stagecoach between Mexico City and Veracruz. A fourth Boettiger sis-

ter, Anita, was a mulatta, the issue of a never-acknowledged love affair of my great-grandfather. She was always a confident and loving member of the Boettiger family.

My paternal grandparents had three sons, Carlos Fuentes Boettiger, my young uncle, a promising poet, disciple of Salvador Díaz Mirón, and editor of the Xalapa magazine *Bohemian Muse*. He died in Mexico City, where he'd gone to study, at the age of twenty-one, of typhoid fever. My aunt, Emilia Fuentes Boettiger, remained unmarried for many years, taking care of my grandfather Don Rafael, who'd been afflicted with a progressive paralysis. My parents, Rafael Fuentes Boettiger and Berta Macías Rivas, married in January 1928. I was born in November of that year and inherited the constellation of stories my family transmitted to me.

But many other stories were told to me by two magnificent survivors of "the years with Laura Díaz," Doña Julieta Olivier de Fernández Landero, widow of the Orizaba industrialist Manuel Fernández Landero, and Doña Ana Guido de Icaza, widow of the lawyer and writer Xavier Icaza López-Negrete, who appears as a character in this novel. I have emotional and grateful memories of them both.

Finally, I began *The Years with Laura Díaz* during a detailed, informative, and most of all affecting trip with my friend Federico Reyes Heroles to places that are part of our shared background: Xalapa, Coatepec, Catemaco, Tlacotalpan, and the Tuxtlas, Santiago and San Andrés. My very special thanks to Federico and his wife, Beatriz Scharrer, herself deeply schooled in agrarian life and the German migration to the state of Veracruz.

London
August 1998